AWARDS

In the Net of Dreams, 1990 Recommended Reading List, "First Novels" (Feb 1991)
In the Net of Dreams, The 1991 *Locus* Poll and Survey, #7, "Best First Novel" (July 1991)

REVIEWS

IN THE NET OF DREAMS

"Its execution is peppy rather than sophisticated, and author Wm. Mark Simmons sometimes shows more daring than skill in his world-building. None-the-less, *In the Net of Dreams* comes about as close as possible to translating the sheer experience of fantasy gaming into novel form.

The concept isn't totally new: We've seen other giant computer game-computers into which players can plug their consciousnesses and play out their fantasies. But the Cephtronics Dreamworld is a better-realized game construct than most; Simmons knows his game mechanics and populates his realm with all the familiar denizens of dungeon, tavern, and wilderness.

Simmons' fantasy quest is rambling but fast-paced, and his treatment of the computer-intelligence aspects of the plot is spirited as well. There's a fair dose of humor and pun-craft, but it serves as an effective background rather than the tale's centerpiece. If anything, there's more here than will fit comfortably in a single novel (and despite a solid ending, Simmons leaves a tag line that virtually demands a sequel).

In the Net of Dreams is what gamers may have hoped for, but didn't get, from Kevin Anderson's Gamearth books."—John C. Bunnell, *Dragon*, January 1991

"*In the Net of Dreams* by Wm. Mark Simmons is not the first fantasy novel to mix cyberspace and role-playing games, but is one of the best, and a highly impressive first novel. Hundreds of players are trapped in a game run by a program with a mind of its own—and a sorry taste for puns bequeathed it by the original programmer. It's funny, yes, but also has some serious things to say about the conventions of fantasy and about creator's rights."—Carolyn Cushman, "Recommended Reading",—*LOCUS*, February 1991

"How many times have you seen someone staring into an arcade game so intently that they seemed almost a part of the game? So will it be any surprise when the intrepid game designers come up with a way to let the player become a living part of the game?

"That is exactly the premise that Wm. Mark Simmons has used as the jump-off point for his first novel *In the Net of Dreams.*

"The tendency in humorous fantasy fiction is to shovel in as many bad puns as there are adjectives, which gets very tiring after awhile. Thankfully that is something that Simmons manages to avoid. He injects just the right amount of subtle humor into the story. Often the jokes and puns are cleverly concealed and only register on you if you are very alert (check out Ripley's fencing students and the inn that the characters Boris and Natasha find).

"Simmons is a good storyteller who takes his work seriously, but isn't afraid to have fun and to give his readers a good time. Check it out!!!"—Bradley H. Sinor, Ledger Book Reviewer

"Dreamland is a complex world of computer-generated dream games. Nothing is real and the Gamer can be, and do, anything he chooses. But when computer skullduggery strikes Dreamworld and the Gamers are trapped in that world and may die, game whiz and former programmer Robert Ripley is sent in to rescue the Gamers and discover what has infected the computer. His only problems are the computer, his ex-wife, and an old friend. A high-tech heroic fantasy full of adventure, puns, and damn good reading. Well thought out."—*Pulsar* 256

"This is one of those combinations of sf and fantasy which make categorizing impossible. The basic concept is that by building a huge biostruct computer it is possible to program in enough detail to allow it to particpate in an interactive roleplaying game as not only opponent, but a reality character, able to create sensory stimuli indistinguishable from the outside world. But what happens if the computer decides to *truly* take a hand in the game?

Told in the terms of an amusing fantasy, this book deals with some very old but still unanswered questions: what is human and what *is* real? Recommended to those who enjoy gaming, computer programmers, and those who just like amusing fantasy."—M. R. Hildebrand

WHEN DREAMS COLLIDE

"As usual, Simmons rarely lets the pace drop below a brisk gallop."—John C. Bunnell, *Dragon* #232

"Dreamworld, a cross between a life-size computer game and a deluxe theme park, has been closed ever since one of its complexes "locked up," trapping Dreamwalkers inside. Simmons (*In the Net of Dreams*) doesn't throw in a rule book for his computer game, so readers have to pick things up on the fly. The off-the-wall result is something frenetic...but frequently fun. Just watch out for groaningly bad puns."—*Publisher's Weekly,* 1992

"After the events that took place in Dreamland before, Robert Ripley thought he had things wrapped up. But during a trip to Russia Ripley learns that things aren't going so well. The psychotic Artificial Ego and the Superego of Dreamland have escaped and plan to kill six billion innocents. But as Ripley enters the system something goes wrong and Ripley gets more than one identity. Enough to fight zombies, cyberpunks, goblins, and bad puns. A roller-coaster of a ride that combines fantasy gaming and computers to bring about a stimulating read. A remarkable combination of fantasy and science fiction. **Do read this one!**"—*Pulsar* #314

"*When Dreams Collide* manages to combine enough wacky hilarity to satisfy a Terry Pratchett fan, and a plethora of puns guaranteed to make a Piers Anthony buff groan, with a serious consideration of Artificial Intelligence and the consequences of creating it, Mark might have even created himself a new genre—CyberLaff."—Mercedes Lackey

"In *In the Net of Dreams*, which came out in 1990, the story is a science fiction premise—virtual reality, with improvements—given a fantasy twist, in that the "reality" into which the customers of this commercialized enterprise slip is a fantasy world, complete with gorgons, pegasi, warlocks, wood nymphs, and even the ex-wife of Robert Ripley, the master programmer who created it.

This book, by the way, is a *LOCUS* recommended book, so you don't have to take just my word for it that it's worth reading—in part for the outrageous puns that crop up from time to time.

When Dreams Collide is out recently. Once again Ripley has to go into the Matrix to extract somebody. Only this time it's somebody he thought he got the first time, and certainly somebody who's out and about—running for President of the U.S., as a matter of fact—at the same time he's still in the Matrix. This one also involves several Ripleys, as it turns out.

I think the second book is even more outrageous, and fun, than the first. I'm really glad I went to Neocon"—Algis Budrys, 1992

"Mark has come up with a second book in his Dreamland series (at least I hope this is a series) that is every bit as entertaining as his first: *In the Net of Dreams*. Chock full of puns, twisted clichés, sly references to movie personalities, mythical characters, fans, writers (can you find Misty Lackey and hubby Larry Dixon?), it is more than a fantasy book involving gaming and technology. It is a challenge to see how many goodies you can find (it's also a good way to drive the spouse nuts with your intermittent laughter!).

"The book is a fun read, no doubt about it. There are a few confusing moments, when Ripley once again awakens (didn't he just…?). And now I'm going to need a list of characters and their avatars to keep it all straight, 'cause my mind's all a-swirl (but then I had that problem with *Lord of the Rings*). However, I'm rally looking forward to the next book."—Fran Mullen

Dreamland Chronicles

"Wm. Mark Simmons"s ability to mingle side-splitting humor with layers of depth makes him one of the most exciting new sf/f novelists to appear in years."—Elizabeth Ann Scarborough

"Forget criticspeak. Wm. Mark Simmon"s *Dreamland Chronicle*s is flat-out superb. A solid, satisfying and full-contact romp of a read that hits all the right marks and pushes all the right buttons. Epic fantasy without the stiff neck, science fiction without the technobabble, and enough trademark Simmons punnage to warrant drawing and quartering the man. A gem of a collection."—Lee Martindale, Author of *To Stand As Witness* and Editor of *Such A Pretty Face.*

"In *The Dreamland Chronicles*, Wm. Mark Simmons sets up a fantasy within a science fiction framework and fills a medieval landscape with a cast of fascinating characters and improbable problems. The master computer has broken down, the master programmer has become a program, there's a bunch of diplomats and government officials trapped in the Dreamland, and the hero, Ripley, doesn't know whether he's real or Memorex. Oh, and did I mention the trademark Simmons puns? Lively, fun, and in the best sense, entertaining. Don't miss this one."—Dennis E. Smirl, co-author of "Dream in a Bottle", *Writers of the Future Vol. II* and DAW"s *1987 Annual World"s Best SF*

"Science fiction and humor is always a potentially dangerous mixture for any writer, but for William Mark Simmons it's not just dangerous, it's explosive—explosively funny. If 'laughter is medicine for gods and men,' then *The Dreamland Chronicles* ia *the* physicians' desk reference."—Robin Wayne Bailey

"A nonstop romp through a complex and captivating world! Highly recommended!"—K. D. Wentworth

"An inventive, well-thought-out series that keeps the reader constantly on the move! From start to finish, Simmons has molded together a landscape unique and exciting as he enters our dreams and nightmares and turns them upside down!"—Richard A. Knaak

"I read a lot. Three monthly SF magazines and a bimonthly fantasy zine, plus a books and such. For me to remember any given piece, it has to be, at the least, unusual. So for me to remember *The Dreamland Chronicles* after all these years tells you that it's an unusual series. I can further add that's full of irreverent wit and almost amounts to a roadmap of our popular culture. What more do you want?"—Rob Chilson

By Wm. Mark Simmons

Dreamland Chronicles:
In The Net Of Dreams
When Dreams Collide
The Woman Of His Dreams

One Foot In The Grave
Dead On My Feet

DREAMLAND CHRONICLES

BY

WILLIAM MARK SIMMONS

Meisha Merlin Publishing, Inc
Atlanta, GA

DREAMLAND CHRONICLES

An MM Publishing Book
Published by Meisha Merlin Publishing, Inc.
PO Box 7
Decatur, GA 30031

Editing & interior layout by Stephen Pagel
Copyediting & proofreading by Josh Mitchel
Cover art by Keith Birdsong
Cover design by Kevin Murphy

ISBN: Hard cover 1-892065-59-2
Soft cover 1-892065-60-6

http//www.MeishaMerlin.com

First MM Publishing edition: July 2002

Printed in the United States of America
0 9 8 7 6 5 4 3 2 1

Table of Contents

Dedication

For my mother, Lorna, who taught me to dream
&
My wife, Janice, the woman of my dreams

Author's Foreword[1]

There are old knights and there are bold knights...

But there are no old, bold knights.

That old dictum was similar to my perception of the Fantasy industry in the late Seventies/early Eighties. There were epic Fantasies and there were silly fantasies, usually in the form of outright "spoofs." But fortunately—or unfortunately—I was blissfully unaware that there might be anything in-between[2]. If I had, *In the Net of Dreams* might never have come to be written.[3]

As a matter of fact, I was blissfully unaware of a number of things when I first set pencil to paper back in 1980. Computer fantasy games were text-based affairs, RPGs utilized the same graphite and wood pulp technology[4] that I was using to create my first draft, and "Virtual Reality" wasn't even a technological term yet, much less the buzz-word of the nineties. In cinema the stark, primitive arcade stylings of *Tron* were a couple of years in the future and *Dreamscape's* interactive dream intervention plot even two years further away. The holodeck on the Enterprise-D wouldn't debut until 1987 and it would be another decade or more before short-lived series like *VR-5*, *Sleepwalkers,* and *Harsh Realm,* would attempt to bring virtual worlds or dream programming to the small screen. *In The Net*

---

[1] With footnotes

[2] In other words, a "serious silly fantasy"

[3] Which some might think not such a bad thing—especially since the publication of this paper brick has resulted in the deforestation of southern Ecuador.

[4] That's pencil and paper for all you mouth-breathers.

The Net Of Dreams was "The Matrix goes Medieval" nearly a decade before Neo had his own encounter with a character named Morpheus.

I'm not suggesting that the Dreamlands books broke new ground—certainly not in literary hindsight[5]. If there are any truly new ideas in genre literature, somebody trot out the list. But it is worth noting how much has changed in a relatively short amount of time. Virtual reality is no longer confined to the provenance of science fiction. The flip side of VR, Augmented Reality[6] is about to make its debut in some cities. Human/computer interfaces are developing rapidly. The complexity of computer games and the connectivity of the Internet continue to increase exponentially. What seemed terribly futuristic when I first fiddled with the Dreamland concept some twenty-odd years ago now seems rather pedestrian in some respects. Perhaps it will be anachronistic in another ten-to-twenty.

That's okay. The Dreamland stories look back as well as ahead in matters of the human experience. Like Ripley and his future contemporaries, some of us yearn to return to "simpler" times. How else to explain our fondness for fantasies of yore even as we revel in the latest technologies that enhance our everyday lives? There is something that resonates deep within our souls when the right tale-teller[7] comes along and breathes life into the ancient archetypes and tells stories of sweep and grandeur with monsters as metaphors and quests

---

[5] The term "hindsight" seriously begs for a footnote and extended commentary. However, after serious soul-searching I've decided that I really don't want to go there.

[6] Augmented reality will enable a person wearing special glasses, receiving and processing gear to view informational overlays on the landmarks in their field of vision—i.e. flight information on a plane passing overhead, "special of the day" at a nearby restaurant, routes and schedules for the corner bus stop.

[7] Since the right tale-teller doesn't come along all that often, the rest of us figure—hey, the pool's unlocked, the lifeguard's on break, *caannonnbbaallll!*

that serve as parables filled with allegories and symbols and truths great and small.

This brings me to the culpability of John Ronald Reuel Tolkien in all of this.

It seems unfair to "blame" *The Lord of the Rings* for weighty doorstop you now hold in your hands but much of modern mythic fantasy has come about as a result of the influence Tolkien's works, influencing readers and writers from the mid 20th century on. In the case of *The Dreamland Chronicles,* however, there's a more twisted connection to the realm of Middle Earth…

I was toddling off to college in the '70s and I began hearing rumors of a literary masterpiece that was a cultural metaphor for our generation[8]—and a whopping good yarn, as well. (Living in the Midwest, we got our cultural updates a little behind the folk on either coast.) One day, while doing a quick browse through a local bookstore, I spied a paperback edition in the racks and grabbed it forthwith. Later that evening I opened my latest acquisition and began the "Tale of the Quest."

And began to laugh my *** off[9].

Obviously my experience with this much-touted literary classic was at odds with that of my contemporaries. What was wrong? A more studious perusal of the cover and Author's Foreword[10] revealed my error born out of haste. Instead of purchasing J.R.R. Tolkien's *The Lord of the Rings,* I had grabbed a copy of The Harvard Lampoon's outrageous parody, *Bored of the Rings.*

---

[8] Hell, it's a cultural metaphor for any generation, even though it resonates most strongly when one considers the parallels to the historical period in which it was written—Saruman and the original Axis of Evil, indeed.

[9] If you don't know what "***" stands for, go ask your mother. Then again, on second thought, maybe it's best you don't. And don't try hiding this book under your mattress, either: it's a dead giveaway and the chiropractic bills will just upset her all the more.

[10] Who really reads those, anyway?

Well, there was nothing for it but to plunge on ahead, reading a book that was clearly meant for those who had already charted the course of the original trilogy. It was remarkably silly and skewered every cliché of fantasy literature—many of which had yet to achieve their full, formulaic shagginess until the last quarter of the last century. Well then, of course, I had to go out and get all three books of the Tolkien trilogy and experience the originals. And, again, I laughed throughout much of the story—even the gloomy middle stretch—as I finally "got" the remaining jokes—that is to say, those more subtly set up in the Lampoon version.

Clearly, this was not an auspicious introduction to the oeuvre of J.R.R.Tolkien much less epic fantasy in general.[11]

Still, there is something that resonates in mythic fantasy, even the silly or badly written attempts. There was a time when our hunger for far away places with strange sounding names, populated by elves, dwarves, and fantastical creatures, drove the publishing industry to supply readers with a glut of fantasy stories with quests, magic rings, wizards, and swords that were the enchanted equivalent of a Swiss army knife. Sturgeon's Law applied. With the glut came a number of…shall we say, "less than memorable" works of literary art?

Fortunately, I know my limitations[12]. When the urge struck, I knew I couldn't emulate the masters. But I was sure I could have some fun with the clichés. And, as I said at the beginning, I was lured by the illusion of unplowed ground between the serious and the silly. The result was *In the Net of Dreams,* which achieved some cult status in spite of the

---

[11] My court-appointed psychiatrist suggests that this not only explains my seeming inability to write a serious novel but also my inexplicable compulsion to stand up in a crowded fire station and yell: "Movie!"

[12] When I'm not sure, my wife makes sure she reminds[13] me.

---

[13] Occasionally utilizing graphs, visual aids, and anatomically-correct models.

fact[14] that it was "out of print"[15] about a month after its publication date. *When Dreams Collide* followed a year-and-a-half later and enjoyed greater longevity while (judging from hundreds of letters, emails, and internet postings) driving readers nuts in trying to hunt down the prequel.

Meisha-Merlin has finally made it possible to enjoy[17] the complete[18] adventures of Robert Remington Ripley III and, when not actually reading, utilize this volume for a healthy regimen of weight training or step aerobics.[19]

When discussing literary humor some distinctions should be recognized. Some comedies are based on the joke, itself: the characters often no more than cardboard cutouts maneuvered to serve the punch line. Some are spoofs, a direct or indirect parody of a parent work or genre form. There are farces, burlesques, satires, ironies—and elements of all can be found scattered throughout the three books included here[20]. But, at their core, the Dreamland Chronicles uses a hard SF premise, wrapped in a soft Fantasy setting—replete with Elves baking cookies in hollow trees and Werebears who hate forest fires—to ask some serious questions about the nature of reality, what makes us human, and the issues of personal responsibility.

---

[14] Or, perhaps, because of...

[15] A publishing euphemism for "remaindered"[16]

[17] If "enjoy" is the correct term here...

[18] As of this date. It remains to be seen whether a streak of masochism runs sufficiently deep in both the reading public and the author to ever inflict a Ripley 4.0 version or beyond. My editor expressed the opinion that sometimes it's best to let sleeping dogs lie.

[19] Always consult your physician before exercising with a volume of this size and weight.

[20] Don't ask your mother about this, either. Just watch old reruns of "Three's Company" on *Nick At Nite* and you'll figure it out sooner or later.

---

[16] A publishing euphemism for taken out of the warehouse and used to stoke the boilers of Panamanian freighters.

And while some scenarios are reminiscent of Saturday morning cartoon fare, sputtering bombs and dropped anvils do maim and kill in the Fantasyworld program.

Still, as the old adage goes: "Dying is easy, comedy is hard[21]." If I've learned one thing from years of cards and letters and emails and personal conversations with my readers it's that there is no anatomically standard location for each person's funny bone. Different people laugh at different things. And while it's patently impossible to please everyone all of the time, one strives to include something for everyone—just not the same thing[22].

So, hopefully you, gentle reader[24] will find sufficient amusement from what is contained within, without minding the rest. If not, you may still get your money's worth by utilizing this tome to prop up the sofa, heat your home during the first three weeks of November, or practice curling for the next Winter Olympics. For those of you who have enjoyed the past predicaments of Bob Ripley, I hope *The Woman of His Dreams* brings you a sense of closure. Your therapist should go out

---

[21] Not that there's a great deal of difference when you boil things down. Comics talk about "dying out there" when jokes fall flat and "killing the audience" when successful. And, when you think about it, humor is almost always about some form of pain or humiliation.

[22] I like to explain that many of the humorous bits are structured for a particular reader demographic, subtly hidden so that, for example, the gamers or the computer programmers or the devotees of popular cinema are the only ones who get the joke and no one else notices the "speed bump" of an obscure joke or reference.[23]

[24] Many readers have reported a predilection for throwing their paperback editions of *In the Net* or *Dreams Collide* across the room at certain points of the narrative. It is hoped that this practice will cease with the current edition as serious harm and/or destruction would be the result. The author and Meisha-Merlin are not responsible for irrational responses or unsafe booking practices on the part of the reader.

---

[23] It's a more comforting premise than the idea that a particular bit just isn't funny.

and get some new patients and not expect you to keep up the payments on his Swiss chalet.

In addition to thanking Stephen Pagel[25] and Meisha-Merlin for the opportunity to inflict my first two novels on the reading public again, I am also grateful for the opportunity to fix some continuity problems between the first and second books. *In the Net of Dreams* was already in print[27] and *When Dreams Collide* nearly finished when the Soviet Union[28] suddenly ceased to exist as a geopolitical entity. Obviously there was a back-story problem for Borys and Natasha and, at the time, I reworked material in the second book as best I could. This edition enables me to fix the first book[29] as well. The other primary continuity problem was small and totally due to the author's inattention but I still blame the Russians for the Soviet collapse: it was most inconsiderate of them. Alas, this and a little light editing was all that time and encroaching projects allowed.[30]

It was also nice to bring this particular story-arc to a semblance of a conclusion.

---

[25] If his name is still in the Foreword when this goes to press, it proves that he actually didn't do the copyediting, himself. (He still claims he was drunk and under the impression that I was Robert Heinlein[26] when he signed the contract.)

[27] And out again. See footnotes 15 and 16.

[28] If you're too young to remember this you actually can go and ask your mother.

[29] If you are the proud possessor of an original copy of In the Net of Dreams, just tell yourself there's an extra layer of "Alternate History" involved—that's another sub-genre of speculative fiction but, hey, I've thrown everything else in but the kitchen sink.

[30] In other words, I was too lazy and the publisher too cheap to finance the serious rewriting these dogs demand.

---

[26] I'd have to say seriously drunk…

Finally, I'm always happy to answer readers' questions.[31] There's just not enough space here to address a fraction of them and I'm already wracked with guilt over how many trees have died to make this trilogy possible. But you can email your questions to *wm.mark.simmons@sff.net* or I can post responses on my website. If http://www.sff.net/people/wm.mark.simmons doesn't find me some years hence, you can always plug "Wm. Mark Simmons" into Google or some search engine and sift the results.

Again, thanks to the loyalty and perseverance of my readers[32] and Meisha-Merlin Publishing's need for a quick tax write-off, a new generation of readers is being given the chance to see why Terry Pratchett is rich and famous[33] and I'm not.

Read long and prosper.[34]

Wm. Mark Simmons

---

[31] Example: No, the character in the first chapter is not named for the John Carter on the television show ER; he's named for the character in the Edgar Rice Burroughs' Mars stories…but nice of you to notice since most people don't connect his first and last name at all.

[32] Not to mention the negatives from a SFWA party locked away in an anonymous safety deposit box…

[33] Not to whine but he does have the advantage in being British.

[34] Sorry, no more footnotes.

IN THE NET OF DREAMS

"We are such stuff
As dreams are made of, and our little life
Is rounded with a sleep."
—*The Tempest*; Act IV, Scene 1—

"What dreams may come,
When we have shuffled off this mortal coil?"
—*Hamlet*; Act III, Scene 1—

"And now for something completely different..."
—Monty Python's Flying Circus—

PROLOGUE

DREAMLAND FILES / MEMORY EXTRACT
Subfile: FANTASYWORLD
Cephalic Index: P2A <Michael Kelson Straeker>
Cellular Unit:
927664[Om]793^216.557[Sub]4 | | | 2 | 20 | 53 | | |

The Ghost in the Machine.

That's what I am, Straeker mused as he stood before the highest window in his wizard's tower. He shook his head, then inhaled deeply, savoring the scent of freshly cut wheat. It smelled real, but the olfactory stimuli were as much a computerized contrivance as everything else.

Down below, a line of peasants were scything their way through the field adjacent to the old stone tower like a wave undulating in slow motion. "Serfs up," he murmured, wishing Ripley was here; the rest of the programming staff never seemed to appreciate his obscure puns.

He gazed at the fields and forests, spreading out before him like a patchwork quilt of green, gold, and brown, stitched with fifteenth century stone and wattle huts. Again (as so many times before) he tried to dispel their apparent reality to his senses.

He couldn't. Even though he knew better.

He knew that the world he now inhabited was not reality—unless, of course, you included "Virtual" as a qualifier. The fields and forests were nothing more than Program-generated conceptualizations—hypnogenous projections of a master computer known as "The Machine."

It was supposed to be a game: the ultimate evolutionary step in VR and interactive computer programs. At the Dreamland Complex you could choose between several dozen Programworlds, enter sensory deprivation/life-support tanks dubbed "Cradles," and have your consciousness—or *psyche*—projected into a dreambody or "avatar" in the Computer-fabricated milieu of your choice.

The Programworlds were not actualities within the physical universe. They were computerized counter-realities that only existed in that infinitesimal void between the synapses of the human brain and the interface circuitry of Dreamland's supercomputer.

The Ghost in the Machine…

In a sense, every visitor to the Fantasyworld Program was a ghost in The Machine. The significant difference was that their psyches all had real bodies, back in the real world, to return to when they exited the program.

Mike Straeker, alias Daggoth the Dark, did not.

His "real" body was surely dead by now. And that neat little paradox made his present circumstances very unique: more than anyone else, he truly was the Ghost in The Machine.

As he contemplated the view, he experienced another wave of dizziness. He staggered and clutched at the window's mossy sill as vertigo was followed by a burst of blinding pain that ricocheted around the inside of his skull. It was always the same—no worse than the previous attacks. And no better. And unlikely to get any worse or any better but almost certain to stay the same and plague his existence for all of the days and months and years to come.

Perhaps for all eternity.

Cursing roundly, he turned and stumbled across the flagstoned chamber toward the bookshelves. There was no doubt in his mind, now; he had waited too long before making the final download.

Oh, he had been *so* clever: cheating death by escaping into the Program Matrix, trading the real world for a virtual reality so that he could exchange his failing body for a healthy dreambody—an avatar with the promise of a long life free of pain and infirmity.

But he had waited too long in making the final commitment: the disease had been left behind, but not before the tumor had taken a sizable chunk of his brain. Which meant a sizable chunk of his current Cephalic Index file. The tumor was gone, but so was the brain tissue where the malignancy had made its inroads. Since the template was damaged, his last psyche-pattern update had been corrupted, as well. He had escaped his own mortality. But not soon enough to enter the Fantasyworld Program whole.

Regrets and recriminations were useless, though. By now his body had been discovered, disconnected from the cerebral links and bio-sensors, removed from the womblike environment of his Cradle, and buried somewhere. Or cremated. In the outside world Michael Kelson Straeker was officially dead. There he had been beyond help.

But here he still might have a chance.

In Fantasyworld his wizard's avatar wielded powers beyond anything imaginable in the mundane world of so-called reality. And, even though his consciousness, his very existence, was now reduced to piezoelectric patterns in an extensive computer program, it still seemed a far better alternative to that final, unknown void that waited on the other side of death.

The question of his soul (mortal or immortal?) bothered him less than these damnable migraines! He had to believe that his programming skills might achieve the healing here that medical science had failed to provide outside of The Machine.

The room was half-filled with dusty stacks of tomes and illuminated scrolls. He had hoped that one of this world's arcane sciences might provide the cure for his malady. But hundreds of hours of research had yielded nothing in the way of relief, and puzzling out the thaumaturgic texts had often made his headaches worse.

Another spasm of pain caused his anger to flare. He kicked the stack nearest his foot and the mystical books flew across the chamber. A couple of them flapped around the room a bit before deciding to roost on a high shelf.

There was a hissing sound and he whirled around, tripping on his sorcerer's robe in the process. A black cat, perched on a footstool in the corner, was watching him with wide golden eyes. "Shut up!" the mage snapped in annoyance.

"But I didn't say anything," the cat protested in a wounded voice.

"You were going to!"

The ebony feline gestured with one paw. "Am I that predictable now?"

"Yes." Daggoth the Dark tugged at his robe and adjusted his conical headgear, recovering a little of his lost dignity in the process. "That's part of what makes you—"

"A familiar!" groaned the cat. It jumped down from the stool. "You want I should go see the apothecary this afternoon?"

"I'm not out of aspirin yet!" he roared, swinging his foot at another stack of books. They prudently scattered in all directions before his foot could make contact.

"But it's your head again?" the cat asked in a way that held no question at all. "How about an anti-pain spell?"

"I need something permanent, dammit!" He flung himself down on an anachronistic sofa and moaned. "It's not just the pain—

it's the gaps in my memory, in my thinking. If I have a train of thought, it gets derailed." He shook his head. "Blank spots…mental fuzziness…not to mention occasional double-vision."

"Sounds more like the end result of a three-day bender to me."

"Out!" bellowed the magician. "Out, out, damned cat!"

"I'm only trying to help," it protested peevishly, backing toward the door.

"No one can help me," Daggoth the Dark said softly. "The answer I seek can't be found in the books and tomes of lesser sorcerers. I'm the greatest mage left to this world, and not even I have the power to conjure myself to health!" He smiled ruefully. "Magician, heal thyself."

His black-furred famulus paused halfway out the door. "Well, if magic itself is not powerful enough, perhaps the powers of the gods are. That is, if you want a cure badly enough to get religion."

"The gods?" Daggoth snorted disdainfully. "Bob Ripley and I created those so-called gods. We programmed most of them out of textbooks on mythology. This world has only one true god and that is The Machine! And, before I fled from the world beyond, I was its High Priest: I *am* the Programmer!" He started to rise but suddenly fell back and covered his eyes with a shaking hand. "Was," he corrected in a small voice. "I *was* the Programmer. The Chief of Programming, to be precise. They must have someone new, by now."

"Then you are out of favor with your god?"

"Out of favor?" The man considered. "Nooo. More like out of touch. No console, no access protocol, no means of interfacing with even the peripheral data banks. In other words, out of luck!"

Straeker thought upon the reality beyond the boundaries of the Program, of the Access and Monitoring Ports in Dreamland's Control Central. "If I were on the outside, again, I could pull my original psyche-patterns out of the Cephalic Index Files: I could impress those healthy engrams over the damaged brain-patterns I'm stuck with now." He sat up, a flicker of hope striking sparks in his eyes. "That might just do it! That might restore the neural paths and memory clusters lost to the tumor since that last psychescan!" Then he clutched his head, his eyes going dark. "But it's no use! I don't have that kind of access from *inside* the Program!" Slowly, he lay back down.

His familiar did not understand the meaning of most of the words, but it had caught the tone behind them. "Then your god will not help you?"

"My 'god' can go to hell!"

There was a long and thoughtful pause. "He can?"

"Yes," snapped the mage, turning his face to the wall; "*it* can!"

"Oh! I did not comprehend before. This one you call 'The Machine'—it is a Demon?"

"As appropriate a term as any I could devise under the present circumstances," muttered Daggoth.

"Does that mean yes?"

"Yes, yes…" His voice was muffled and distant.

"They why do you not conjure this Demon and demand its services? Adjure its cooperation with bell, book, and candle?"

It took a moment to sink in. "What?" he roared, coming up off the couch like a volcanic eruption.

"You know the process better than I." The cat was backing away again, trying to keep one eye on the apoplectic wizard and the other on its own escape route. "Draw a pentagram, conjure the Demon, and command it to do your bidding."

"Conjure the—" The wizard nearly choked on his laughter. "How do you conjure a Computer and force it—a thing of hardware and logic—by magic, to alter the Program of its own internal reality? You're talking about summoning The Machine to appear inside of one of its own master programs! The Program would be running the Computer instead of vice versa! That's…" He stopped, a stunned expression slowly giving way to a beatific smile. "…entirely feasible!"

The concept was so outrageous that Straeker was momentarily confounded by the sheer audacity of it. Hope flared again and it took all of his willpower just to sit down and think the whole thing through.

The Programworlds—and more specifically Fantasyworld, where he now resided—were monitored by an external staff of technicians. The Programming crew—particularly those directly responsible to the Chief of Programming—had the power to manipulate the various Programs and Subprograms. Given time and access authority, they could alter the Program Matrix, itself.

But that was on the outside.

Daggoth the Dark moaned as his head began to throb again. *Think!* he chided himself. *If external reprogramming is impossible, then what could be done with internal Program manipulation?*

When visiting any of Dreamland's Programworlds, one's psyche resided in an avatar appropriate to that particular environment or culture. But like one's real body in the real world, the dreambody was subject to the laws and events of that particular Dreamland Programworld. If his avatar were to throw a rock at a window, the Computer would calculate weight, force, and trajectory to decide if he would hit or miss his target. It would then produce the appropriate physical results and material manifestations.

But Fantasyworld did not stop at duplicating the physics of mundane reality. Here, magic was very much a part of natural law and order. As he decided which spells to cast and performed them, the Computer made calculations based on component, ability, and magic-theory tables, and then produced the appropriate magical results.

Or failures, as he too well knew.

In short, the laws of both Nature *and* Magic in this world were governed and maintained by the Computer. The Machine was, indeed, god.

Of course, The Machine was still initially programmed externally, and was still subject to the external monitoring and guidance systems. But it was also self-programming, making millions of Program adjustments every second; every time someone lit a fire, chopped down a tree, threw a rock, or cast a spell, the Program was minutely changed and updated. Every action taken in Dreamland was a miniature act of reprogramming the whole Programworld. In effect, it was possible to change the Master Program from within its own context. At least in a Lilliputian sense, anyway.

So if a little—then why not a lot? And, if the Computer was programmed internally as well as externally, why not summon The Machine, itself, for direct programming and input?

He frowned suddenly: he knew why not.

That process was tantamount to an internal takeover. It would certainly alter the primary Program Command Sequence. Maybe a little. Maybe a lot.

He couldn't be sure at this point. But, if he was able to turn the directive input around, it could very well nullify all external directive input. Whether that condition lasted for just a nanosecond, or a bit longer, he couldn't be completely certain.

But that , he decided, was their problem and not his...as long as his tampering didn't undo the basic structure of Dreamland's Operating System. There had been some evidence of Matrix instability of late and he would have to exercise caution: it wouldn't do him any good to find a cure if he destroyed his own world in the process!

The door swung open and a turtle slowly shuffled into the room, walking somewhat erect on its hind limbs and carrying a notepad.

Straeker frowned and consulted the digital readout on a large, wall-mounted hourglass. "Pascal, are you early?"

"Um, nope, Your Mageship," it answered leisurely: "late, as usual."

The wizard softly cursed the inherent glitches of silicon-based chronometry and reclined upon the sofa again. "Not that it matters today," he inquired mildly, "but why are you late?"

"Um, welp, as Your Wizardness must surely remember, I am a turtle—order Chelonia, suborder Cryptodira—"

Michael Straeker/Daggoth the Dark waved his hand in a get-to-the-point gesture.

"—a toothless, slow-moving reptile, according to the_*Phylum Factorum,"* continued the toothless, slow-moving reptile. "If you wanted a subroutine with some speed, Your Shamanhood should have considered some other form of anthropomorphism—"

"And not mixed my programming metaphors," the wizard concluded. "Enough, already! I'm going to want you to take some notes." He cleared his throat. "A lot of notes."

The turtle booted up its notepad and gestured with a stylus. "Logged on," it stated in testudineous tones.

"And then I want you to get a copy of my journal over to the Archdruid of Dyrinwall, ASAP."

Pascal would have raised an eyebrow had he possessed one but had to settle for nodding in what may have been an ironic manner.

Daggoth tried to pick up his train of thought where he had left off. His only other worry was that he pull it off without betraying his presence to the outside staff. To the Dreamland Project and Cephtronics Inc., he no longer existed, except as a bronze plaque on a wall somewhere.

Here, in Fantasyworld, he was no longer Michael K. Straeker, Chief of Programming: he was Daggoth the Dark, an archmage of such power that there was nothing in this world that might be denied him. He didn't want anyone or anything to interfere with that.

"Chief?"

He got up and wandered over to the book stacks again. *Must think carefully,* he told himself; *cover all the angles.*

He hadn't done anything legally or morally wrong, he was sure. At least, not yet. But he was just as sure that if Cephtronics or the Project learned the true nature of his existence within the Program, they would be very unhappy about it.

"Chief?"

No. Better to stay completely dead and buried. If they found him out, the best treatment that he could hope for would be that reserved for a lab specimen. And he did not relish the thought of spending the rest of his "life" being poked, prodded, measured, and spied upon.

"Chief!" yelled the cat.

"What?" he yelled back.

"What if you cannot control the Demon once you summon him?"

"Well." His eyebrows raised speculatively. "We're going to find ourselves in one hell of a mess!"

PART I

RUDE AWAKENINGS

Dreamer of dreams, born out of my due time,
Why should I strive to set the crooked straight?

—William Morris, *The Earthly Paradise*

ONE

The trouble with first-year fencing students is they all like to think that they're Zorro before the semester is half over. A few will even go so far as to challenge me to a match after the first month. I guess it's a natural temptation when the instructor wears a knee brace and an eyepatch. So once or twice a semester I find myself called out on the pisté like an aging gunfighter challenged by some young punk hot to make a quick reputation.

I shouldn't complain: it provides me with an opportunity to demonstrate that true swordsmanship is as much a matter of skill and technique as speed and strength. And I get a little more respect from the class after their latest champion takes a drubbing from the Old Man. Which is what a fourteen-year difference in our respective ages makes me, I suppose.

My latest would-be D'Artagnan was growing more frustrated by the second. It was bad enough to be beaten with the whole class looking on. What made it infinitely worse was the realization that my attention was elsewhere while my foil continued to hold him at bay.

Normally I would pretend to pay attention to my opponent—out of courtesy, if nothing else. I was rarely mindful of the observers that hung out around the periphery of the gym—but I knew this one face from somewhere and I couldn't quite place it.

To merely say that she was beautiful would not come close to doing her justice; beauty must be anchored in character or it is just an empty freak of nature. Framed in a cascade of red hair, her features promised just the right blend of sophistication and sensuality. A knowing countenance that spoke volumes of experience, yet seemed unmarked by worldliness. Almost a contradiction: a face that was poised and yet open.

And speaking of open, Carter had allowed his foil to drift to the left following my feint: I cut my blade over his in a <u>coupé</u> and lunged. Scored. Ended the match five/zip.

We unmasked, degloved, and shook hands like civilized men of the twenty-first century.

"You're getting better every week, John," I told him. In point of fact, he had finally figured out that my eyepatch meant that I was blind on my left side.

He grinned sheepishly and the end-of-period bell sounded. My class turned from docile herd to thundering stampede in the direction of the showers.

The redhead was moving toward me as the rest of my fencing students left the gymnasium. She was tall—five-ten, maybe five-eleven—and had one of those impossibly perfect figures that are only found on the covers of old paperback books and cheap holozines. The only other place you found women who looked like this was in Dreamland...and now I made the connection.

She was a Dreamwalker.

More likely a Dreammaster, since I recognized her face. My growing interest suddenly withered: I could guess why she was here and what she wanted.

"Dr. Ripley?"

But: *innocent until proven guilty*, I reminded myself, grimly switching over into my "polite" mode. "Yes?"

"I am Natasha Skovoroda," she replied, extending her hand.

I started to take it and then froze with a second shock of recognition. No wonder she had looked familiar; Natasha Skovoroda was more than just a Dreammaster; she was an international star. And, more significantly, she had taken triple Gold in fencing at the last Olympics: Foil, Épée, and Sabré. "I'm honored," I said, finally remembering to take her proffered hand.

"Honored enough to have a drink with me?" Her voice had a low, husky quality that triggered an involuntary shiver between my shoulder blades.

"A drink?"

"Your choice. I will buy."

"I don't drink."

"You must get terribly dehydrated." There was a dryness in her voice that won me. "What about dinner, then? I assume that you do eat?"

"Are you still buying?"

"Of course."

I considered. In spite of Ms. Skovoroda's standing, this encounter had "setup" written all over it. There had been other such approaches—some less subtle. "Okay," I gambled. "Dinner of your choice. But who pays for it depends on the coming negotiations."

"Negotiations?"

"Ms. Skovoroda—"

She laughed, flashing perfect teeth. "You are the first American to pronounce it correctly with the first try. But, please: Tasha."

"All right. Tasha. It's obvious that you're asking for an opportunity to parley, not a date."

She looked rueful. "I am that transparent?"

"I get this approach every couple of months," I explained. "And not on account of my good looks."

She colored slightly but recovered well. "And do you turn them down?"

"Every one."

"And myself?"

"You can tell me what it is that you really want over dinner. If I agree to it, you can pick up the check. If I turn you down, Dutch treat. Sound fair?"

She studied me. "You are a man of principles."

"I'm a creature of conscience."

She hesitated and I could almost hear the mental gears shifting.

"I know a place where the food is good and the atmosphere is—how you say—comfortable?"

The stilted English coupled with the faint Russian accent had utterly charmed me into submission.

#

I took my medication before hitting the showers. Normally I would wait until I was leaving the gym, giving me a safety margin to make the drive home. Tonight, however, I wanted to give my brain cells the chance to sober up before I engaged in any mental fencing with Ms. Skovoroda.

I could have taken the easy route years ago: a few well-placed electrodes and a simple, push-button remote. When the pain starts to redline, a little microamperage along the right neural paths makes it all go away. Hard to believe, but my surgeons convinced me with a demonstration on a lab monkey that had suffered hideous burns.

The doctors still bring it up every now and then. The drugs must be rotated to maintain their effectiveness, are potentially addictive, have numerous unpleasant side effects. And they're less efficient: even doped to the gills, the pain is still there. It doesn't bother me very much any more.

But it's always there.

Along with the memory of a trembling monkey living in dazed, electronic bliss. Indifferent to food, sex, anything but that little button that it clutched to its emaciated chest, crouching in the corner, knee-deep in its own filth; its dreamy eyes focused on some inner simian nirvana. Seemingly lifeless except for spasm of its mangled paw every few minutes as it pumped the remote for another dose of current.

I can handle the chemicals. I know there are ten thousand bodies on ten thousand slabs every year who have said the same thing, but I believe I can deal with the chemicals.

I took a long, hot shower, dressed slowly, and called a cab. I didn't like leaving my car in the faculty parking lot overnight but, if the drugs are safer, it's because I don't work without a net.

#

The "comfortable atmosphere" turned out to be a penthouse apartment in one of the city's ritziest hotels. I settled on the sofa and studied my surroundings while she dialed room service.

There were few personal effects in sight but a nearby bookshelf was overflowing with library discs. A closer examination revealed a collection of authors that read like a Who's Who of Fantasy and Heroic fiction. One author, however, was conspicuously missing—even though I knew better, I could almost hope…

The painting over the fireplace—an oldstyle oils-on-canvas—sent hope to the showers when I noticed it a moment later. I got up and walked over to examine it when Natasha excused herself to go change. Her use of the phrase "into something more comfortable" brought to mind a number of truly awful tridee scenarios, but I assumed that the average Russian citizen was unfamiliar with the sleazier aspects of American cinema.

I had never seen Ms. Skovoroda's Dreamland avatar but there was no mistaking the identity of the woman in the portrait. There were differences, to be sure: the avatar had long, flame-colored hair that fell in waves over her shoulders and down her back—much thicker and redder than Natasha's, with two streaks of quicksilver that framed the face. The eyes were a deeper green—more of an emerald hue—and the arching copper brows and the pointed tips of her ears peeking through her hair indicated a mix of Human and Elven blood.

In spite of the changes, her avatar's face was her own. Most Dreamwalkers favored dreambodies with a physical appearance somewhat different from their own. But then so few of them were as stunning as Natasha Skovoroda in real life.

As for her outfit, her armor did not amount to much more than a chainmail bikini: minimal breastplate and an insubstantial cross between a miniskirt and a loincloth. Even though the outfit was composed of small metal plates and interlocking links of chain, it could hardly be considered functional in any sense of the original intent. Rather, it was what the well-undressed pulp heroine was expected to wear in stories devoted to pubescent male fantasies.

I had to admit, though, that it did show off her body to a great advantage. Which was mostly the point, I supposed.

"What do you think?"

I continued to study the painting without turning. "I can see how increased 'exposure' has brought you international fame." She chuckled, a low throaty sound, and I caught the scent of freshly applied perfume. "I should think, however, that you'd want a bit more protection in battle. From wind as well as weapons."

She sighed. "Perhaps—but it is the standard Amazon battledress. 'Ours not to question why…'"

I shook my head. "That's not the dress code I originally programmed for their culture. The Amazons have never been a tribe to flaunt their sexuality."

"Much has changed," she said, her voice taking on a serious tone. "That is why I have asked you here to talk."

I turned then. I had hoped—not really expected, you understand—but hoped that this time it might be different. Alas, her "something comfortable" was more peignoir than lounging outfit and the stage was set for the requisite seduction scene. She handed me a glass of wine and, had I been wearing a tie, I'm sure she would've loosened it for me. "Ah, yes. Talk. Well. Let's get down to business."

She sat on the sofa and patted the cushion beside her. I decided that I was big enough and old enough to handle the situation, so I sat next to her. *Show no fear.*

"Dr. Ripley—"

"You want me to train you."

"How did you know?" Her hand went to her throat in a maidenly gesture of surprise. It was so self-consciously staged that I had to fight back a smile.

"You're hardly the first. With dozens of Dreammasters offering advanced training, people still track me down to ask for a shot at some supposed inside track." I shook my head. "I haven't been back inside since Dreamland went public a little over five years ago. I have no official standing in the Dreamranks—yet people come to me as if I were some kind of omnipotent Dreamlord who can unlock the forbidden secrets of the Fantasyworld milieu."

"Can you blame us? After all, you wrote the books." She nodded at a table across the room and I saw what I had missed before: a set of *The Kishkumen Chronicles* by yours truly. "And created most of the original Program. If anyone could provide a Dreamwalker with an inside edge, it would naturally seem to be you."

"Perhaps. But the DreamNet is five years older—five years different. And what would be the ethics of handing the winning secrets over to the highest bidder—assuming I was privy to such in the first place?"

She bristled at that. "I am not asking for Program secrets! I am asking for some basic training. I need a guide. A navigator in the Net."

I shrugged. "Like I said, there are dozens of competent, if not exceptional, Dreammasters. All with up-to-date experience. Who needs a rusty old has-been?"

She leaned forward and her robe parted in such a way as to almost seem unintentional. "I do," she breathed.

"Why?" I leaned back to avoid a possible collision.

"Because you are the best!"

"Uh-uh. You're the best," I asserted. "Triple Olympic Gold-medalist, international star, darling of the Networks, Dreammaster—Dreamlord, even; if one believes just half of your press coverage."

She shook her head. "There is no Dreamlord status."

"Officially. But if there were, you'd be at the top of the list." I spread my hands. "The question is: how can I offer you any superiority in training?"

"The people who know say that you are the best fencer in the entire world," she answered. "That you are unbeatable in any of the European styles…"

A flattering answer but it was my turn to shake my head. "Maybe once. If it were true, that was years ago. I'm certainly too old, now—"

"Thirty-six is not too old!"

"Thirty-four. And you're the one with Olympic Gold, not me."

"Everyone says you would have taken the Gold if you had made the Matches in France! You were on the U.S. Team—I have seen the tridees of your matches! You were the best!"

"Past tense," I qualified. "The accident didn't just sideline me from that year's games, it ended my career. I have almost seven pounds of metal in my body—mostly surgical implants but some of it is residual shrapnel from the crash. My brace reinforces a leg that is more scar tissue than muscle and ends with only half of a foot. And this—" I ran a finger over my eyepatch, "—adds the difficulty of monocular vision and near-zero depth perception. I have three students in my advanced class, all barely twenty, who have more stamina, strength, and agility, and could most likely take me in three out of five bouts."

"If they had your experience and skill," she argued. "Then, maybe, in a regulated competition match. But in Fantasyworld the swordplay is not regulated."

"Meaning?"

"When you programmed Fantasyworld, you were a respected fencer—a Master in the European forms. Most Dreamwalkers are 'hack-and-slashers,' but the best of both cross blades in some variance of the European schools."

"That's to be expected, I guess. What's your point?"

"Just this"—she paused for effect—"you are half a decade better today than you were five or six years ago when you created the Basic Program and set the ability parameters for the Constructs."

"Constructs?"

"The A.I.s—computer generated characters—that are constructs of the Program as opposed to the real Dreamwalkers and their avatars."

"Oh." Another example of how out-of-touch I'd become.

"Anyway, your original superiority plus a five-year edge might be enough in itself, but you have studied Kendo since then. And the word is that you are very good at that, also."

"Other Dreamwalkers have studied and used Kendo disciplines," I argued. "The Oriental styles are advantageous in some situations, but nothing foolproof. And there are Dreammasters who do training in Kendo."

"But those who have utilized Kendo have no training in the European styles: theirs was pure Kendo." She smiled. "What happens when a Master of the European blades also becomes proficient with the Japanese longsword?"

I shrugged. If she could fake sexual attraction, I could feign modesty.

"Your Kendo instructor says that you have developed a combination of the Oriental and European styles that is quite astounding!"

"What else did he say?" Oshi had been rather noncommittal in his comments on my progress as of late.

"That it lacks the purity of the True Way, but that it is the most formidable and possibly the deadliest technique that he has ever seen. High praise from an Asian swordmaster."

"I'm sure he'd be willing to teach you everything that he's taught me."

She rested a hand on my shoulder, a sure sign of trouble to come. "I want you to train me."

"I'll be starting a new series of fencing classes next semester—"

"I want you to train me personally. In Fantasyworld. I need the best guide in the DreamNet *and* I will make it worth your while!"

"Miss Skovoroda—"

"Please; Tasha."

"—if you know so much about me, then you should know that I don't need the money."

"I did not say anything about money," she replied, leaning forward again. This time her garment fell open with no possible question of intent, revealing flawless skin. "I said I would make it worth your while."

I got up with a little concern that some vestigial interest might be showing. "I hate to eat and run, so I think I'll just skip dinner."

She reached out, caught my arm, and pulled me back to the sofa with surprising strength. "I am sorry. I should have known that this would be the wrong approach with you. Please—sit back down." Her voice and her expression said that she was genuinely sorry, and she pulled her clothing together as I sat back down.

"There's something you're not telling me," I said after a long silence. She didn't answer so I pursued the question that was banging around at the back of my mind.

"Natasha Skovoroda does not need training from a man who has not gone online since the Tournaments were first opened to the public. I doubt there is any Dreammaster—currently in or out of Fantasyworld—who is the equal of a triple Gold-medalist. The next Tournament—Dreamquest VI, isn't it?—doesn't begin for another six or seven months. And I don't buy this 'guide' routine for a minute." I sighed. "So why don't we stop dancing and you tell me just exactly what it is you really want from me?"

She stared off into space for a long time before answering. "The Deputy Chairman of the Council of Ministers has disappeared."

It took a moment for the meaning of her words to fully register. "We're talking the number three man in the Russian Federation? The guy right behind the president and the premiere?"

She nodded. "We prefer the term 'Prime Minister' to premiere, these days."

"What does this have to do with you?"

"I have been recruited to find him."

"You're FSA?"

Her mouth twisted. "In this instance I think you mean SVR. And no," she said, shaking her head, "I am not a government operative. Although I suppose I am being asked to work for them in this instance."

"Asked?"

She bit her lip pensively. "We have come a long way from the days of Communist oppression and the Komitet Gosurdarstvenoy Besopasnasti. Still, the FSA, SVR, FSK, Alpha Group, FSB, and the other half-dozen offspring of the old KGB, can be most...persuasive." She shivered and I put my hand on her arm in spite of myself. "It is FAPSI that is pressing me for the moment."

I cocked an eyebrow.

"The Federal Agency of Government Communications and Information," she explained. "Borys Dankevych is also the Chief Minister of that bureau as well as his post as Deputy Chairman."

"If he's missing, why recruit you? I assume your government has highly trained agents with specific experience in this sort of thing."

"Yes and no: he disappeared in Dreamland Complex while on a goodwill tour of your country. It seems that Dankevych tempers his love for Rossiyskaya Federatsiya with a fascination for the Western European Renaissance and medieval myth."

"And he vanished in Dreamland?"

"We know that he took a side trip into the Fantasyworld Program. In his last communiqué, he likened his side-trip to Dreamland to Khrushchev's historic visit to your Disneyland in the previous century. Nothing has been heard from him since then, and I was recruited to use my DreamNet status to search for him on-line. Which is why I need your help!"

I leaned back against the cushions. "I still don't see how I can help. I haven't set foot on Cephtronics property in nearly half a decade. I'm on good terms with maybe a dozen people who are still inside, but I doubt that dropping my name will open any doors for you. In fact, it would probably do just the opposite." I shook my head. "I just don't see how I can be of any help to you."

She moved down the length of the sofa to sit beside me. "Go in with me!"

"To Dreamland?"

"To Fantasyworld."

"Why? This sounds like a job for the techs. Have you asked them for help? They can locate any Dreamwalker on their monitors in a matter of seconds."

"No. It was tried before I was even brought into this."

"And?"

"Cephtronics claims that Borys Dankevych left with his aides, the day before yesterday. The SVR says he did not. Obviously, someone is wrong."

"Or lying," I agreed. "So what is your next step?"

"I have been ordered to go back into Fantasyworld and begin my investigation there."

"What's stopping you?"

"Cephtronics. They claim that they are closed for Program enhancements and upgrade maintenance. No one is allowed to log on to the DreamNet until further notice."

"I still don't understand what you want from me. Especially if you can't even get into the Program."

She gazed at the floor in defeat. “I thought you might know something—might have heard something. Since you created the Fantasyworld Program, I thought you might know another way in. I understand that it is quite customary for programmers to create their own, personal ‘back doors’ for their programs—a way to get in that no one else knows about. I thought—”

“That I could sneak you in my back door?” I shook my head. “This is a different kind of program, Tasha. It doesn’t work the same way.” While that was true, I did have a back way in that nobody knew about. I just wasn’t ready to spill my secrets to an unknown pretty face who had just admitted to working for the Russian secret police. “I’m sorry you’ve wasted your time.”

She shook her head and began toying with the hair at the back of my neck.

“Oh, I do not think so. The night is still young…”

The last sensation I clearly remembered was something cold pressing against the side of my neck.

#

I knew it was a dream even though it came with all of the sensations of waking up. A man in a military officer’s uniform was standing at the foot of the bed.

That’s how I knew it was a dream.

“Art thou the Ghost of Armageddon Past?” I mumbled. “Or Armageddon Yet To Come?” My experience with most dreams is that you play it fast, loose, and you stay on top. Never give a phantasm an even break; your subconscious can be murder.

The phantasm with the birds on his cap and shoulders spoke. “Dr. Ripley?”

“No,” I lied, turned over, and pulled the pillow over my head.

The pillow was removed. “Robert Remington Ripley, the Third?”

“Never heard of him,” I groaned, as I tried to pull the covers over my head. They were removed as well. The overhead light came on and the room was suddenly filled with stocky Marine-types.

“Go away,” I moaned.

“I’m sorry, Dr. Ripley,” the phantom colonel responded, “but I have my orders.”

"The name is…Schwartz…" I muttered, "…Ralph Schwartz. And you are nothing but nocturnal indigestion: a bit of cheese, a piece of undigested meat…"

"Sergeant," interrupted the rude phantom colonel, who seemed to be a Marine as well, "…the shower…"

I was telling myself that none of this was real and pondering the Freudian significance of the Marines using Natasha Skovoroda's shower facilities when several pairs of hands gently but firmly lifted me out of bed.

#

I eventually stopped screaming and they turned off the cold water. I wrung out my eyepatch and looked reproachfully at the colonel who handed me a couple of dry towels. "You," I announced, "are not a nice person."

He shrugged. "You think I'm bad now, just see what happens if you're not dressed and ready to go with us in ten minutes."

"Where are we going?"

"Dreamland."

Gingerly, I shook my aching head. "I just came from there."

"Dreamland, Utah."

"I prefer my own version, thank you."

The man sighed and tilted his cap back on his head. "Dr. Ripley, I am under explicit orders to bring you to the Dreamland Complex. Your choices in this matter are very limited and very simple. We are going to escort you there. You decide whether we do that as an honor guard or as a chain gang." He glanced at his watch. "Nine minutes, son."

I adjusted the black patch over what used to be my left eye and gave him my best impassive look. As my cosmetic surgeon had been content with mere function as opposed to the aesthetics, my impassive expression is somewhat less than encouraging. "I'm a great believer in civil disobedience."

The colonel returned my gaze thoughtfully. "They said you might be reluctant."

"And what did 'they' tell you to do if I was?"

"Give you a message." He folded his arms across his beribboned chest. "Dr. Cooper said to tell you that you were right. She says: 'Beautiful Dreamer is having Nightmares.'"

"No shit?" I dried off hurriedly and began pulling on my knee brace.

No one mentioned Natasha Skovoroda and there was no evidence of her presence from the night before. Not even a discarded mini-ampoule from the trick ring she had drugged me with. I wondered how much I'd told her as they ushered me up to the roof and into a waiting military transport.

Within two minutes we were headed west at mach two and accelerating.

TWO

I adjusted the dreamset on my head and settled back into the webbing of the dreamcouch. "Anything special I should be watching for?" I asked reluctantly. Although Dr. Cooper's encrypted message had persuaded me to come along peaceably, I wasn't in a mood to be overly cooperative.

Quebedeaux said nothing. Vanauken shrugged. "We have so little to go on," he ventured, "that I'd prefer a fresh opinion. I don't want to pre-bias you in any way before you review the recordings."

Right.

The portly little man was clearly out of his element and in over his head. Observing the beads of perspiration below his receding hairline and above his pale lips, I tried to imagine what his responsibilities were under normal circumstances. He probably conducted Dreamland tours for visiting low-level dignitaries.

"We decided that you should experience this particular playback before we continue the briefing," he continued, taking his cue from one of the techs seated behind the consoles. "You can study the others later."

"Fine." My tone was bored and noncommittal as I pulled the eyeshields down. Although my temper was nearing the boiling point, I had no intention of dissipating it on corporate underlings. Mike Straeker had yet to put in an appearance. And I was determined to express myself most eloquently on the subject of my treatment these past five hours. If Cephtronics was giving me time to cool down, the psychology wasn't working. "Let's get on with it," I snapped.

The memory playback washed over me, drowning out all thought apart from the sensory stimuli of the encoded cephalic recording. The stored memory was suddenly my immediate reality>>>>>>>>>>>>>>>>>>>>>>>>>>>>>>>>>>>

#

Og was in a foul mood.

It wasn't just the godsbecursed sunburn—though he had been above surface far longer than was sensible. No, it was that the need was on him and he was caught in an ethical (and financial) conflict.

Og was a Bridge-Troll, an occupation quite common among the more intelligent Water-Trolls. He lived in the Pooder River, at a natural bottleneck where a rude bridge arched the flood. Travelers who wished to cross the Pooder within twenty miles of Casterbridge (with minimum risk to life and limb) had to use the bridge.

And Og would always permit them safe passage. As long as they paid the toll.

The Casterbridge bridge was not only a Troll bridge, it was also a toll bridge. Signs proclaimed this fact at either end of the wooden span in seven different languages. Travelers were admonished to "Stop!" And: "Pay Troll!"

Og would pop through a trapdoor in the middle of the traverse and hold out a green and warty palm. If a customer seemed reluctant or unnecessarily slow, he would growl, squint his goggly eyes at the offender, and begin to salivate. At his best, Og could salivate like a waterfall during the monsoon season.

The reason why no one had come along and put Og out of business before now was quite simple: he had an "understanding" with the mayor of Casterbridge.

In fact, Og had had understandings with the mayors of Casterbridge going back nearly three hundred years: the town treasury received a share of the take and Og remained largely unmolested. In addition, Og had agreed to contribute to Casterbridge's backdoor defense. Should invaders ever approach the town from the far side of the river, the Troll's instructions were to "remove" the bridge. It was an equitable arrangement for both parties.

Yet, as good as business was, three centuries of it was enough to bore the most unimaginative of minds, and Og longed for the "good old days." His fondest memories were of the times when he and his friend Grom had initiated brawls with the border patrols, tossing the knights into the deep part of the river and making bets on whether or not they would make it back to the shore. Og always won because the Ogre would invariably bet on the knights: Grom never seemed to grasp the negative effects of plate armor on human buoyancy.

Thinking hadn't been one of Grom's fortes, but he had been a lot of fun when it came to frightening pregnant women, knocking over occupied privies, scattering compost heaps, and peeking in bedroom windows late at night.

Now Grom was gone, and people accepted a Bridge-Troll as one of the normalities of everyday life. His own daily existence had been reduced to bridge maintenance and repair; civil-service duty at the Casterbridge border.

And, as if that wasn't degrading enough for a Troll who had once terrorized the kingdom's most puissant champions, last month some village children had thrown rocks at him! When he had tried to frighten them with one of his more ferocious displays, a little girl had responded by sticking out her tongue.

Then, barely a week later, there was a most unfortunate encounter with a rather gruff family of billy goats.

And finally, just this week, for the first time in over three generations, a troop of light cavalry had tried to cross the bridge without paying the toll or the Troll. Og didn't feel up to a fight with odds of twenty-to-one, so he kicked out the main support strut, collapsing the bridge and forcing the weary but now-wiser soldiers to make a ten-mile detour.

Og chewed his nails thoughtfully. Four days' had passed since then and he was still putting the bridge back together. He spat out the mangled nails, took a new mouthful, and resumed hammering with a sigh. Four days loss of revenue had been a high price to pay—not to mention a blistering sunburn from four days' loss of shade. But Og was committed to the principle of the thing. His only regret was that he hadn't waited until more soldiers were on the bridge before kicking out the crucial strut.

Between hammer-blows, Og could now hear the steady clip-clop sound of approaching horses. Only two, he decided after much ear straining. Perversely, he hoped the riders would be belligerent and wear heavy armor. Not too heavy, he decided: it was less satisfying when they sank immediately. While he did need the money after four days of lost tolls, Og felt an even greater need to do a little therapeutic violence.

Especially after the goat debacle...

The riders topped the hill now and Og got a good look at his prospects: a large Human barbarian and a petite Elven woman. The female was an unknown factor, but the barbarian looked positively dangerous. Og didn't care, though; he still wanted to mangle.

When they reached the bridge they dismounted and led their horses, the man in front, the woman following behind. The barbarian wore some skins, a bonelink breastplate, and very little else. A claymore was slung across his broad back—a two-handed sword that measured six feet from point to pommel, or about six inches shorter than the man himself.

He had a sullen, craggy face with long, thick black hair that was barely kept out of his eyes by a leather headband. His body was massive with well-defined muscles and wall-to-wall pectorals. Eyeing those, Og began to have some second thoughts about starting any real trouble. Maybe someone else would be along later in the afternoon.

The woman, in contrast, hardly topped five feet in height. What could be seen of her form beneath her leather jerkin and breeches seemed to lessen the threat of the short sword that hung at her side and the short bow across her back. But Elves were more unpredictable than Humans and Og had good reason—based on previous experience—not to dismiss one too lightly.

When they were almost to the centerpoint of the bridge, the trapdoor popped up and Og thrust his head and shoulders through the opening. Just that much was enough to put him at eye-level with the Elf. He scrunched upwards a couple of feet more to loom over the Human.

"You, I assume," said the barbarian calmly, "are the Troll that I am supposed to pay. How much?"

Og was disappointed: this was going well and that was too bad. On the other hand, the Elf did look a bit nervous, and maybe something could be made of that.

"Four copper pieces," he rumbled in a liquid, yet gravelly voice. It made him sound like he was trying to talk and gargle at the same time. The Elf tried to hide a sudden smile and Og felt his temper nearing critical mass.

The barbarian pulled out a silver piece. Now Og smiled; he had teeth reminiscent of two display racks filled with badly rusted daggers. "Exact change, please." In all fairness, it should be noted that Trolls have no aptitude for making change. But Og had a way of saying "please" that completely divorced the word from any pleasant connotations.

"Sorry," the barbarian offered apologetically, "I don't have four coppers." He dropped the silver piece into the Troll's ham-sized palm. "You may keep the change."

Og had never met a polite and well-mannered barbarian before, and he didn't much like it. Nor did he like the man's combination of muscles and six-foot sword. And he usually heeded his premonitions—he hadn't lived to be five-hundred-and-thirty-seven years old by being incautious. Still, Og had a burning need to fight someone. And he couldn't help speculating: might it be interesting to throw someone in the river who had an even chance of making it back to shore?

The situation was decided as the barbarian, puzzled over the delay, inquired: "Excuse me, something got your goat?"

As Og lunged, the barbarian reached for his sword. The next few seconds were a blur but the culmination of events was crystal clear: Og brought his teeth down on the barbarian's sword hand, effectively separating it from the wrist. Whether or not the Troll would have pursued his advantage with the wounded and defenseless warrior was left to further speculation; the man fainted and Og was left facing a very angry Elf with a drawn bow.

Now the chances of an Elven archer missing the mark at this range were roughly the same as a Dwarven warrior passing out from drinking a lite beer. And Og did not like the looks of the arrow she had pulled back to her cheek: it was black and green and covered with an assortment of nasty-looking runes. He even fancied that he could hear a high-pitched humming sound emanating from the shaft.

"Back off," the girl ordered sharply.

While Og tended to have his impetuous moments, no one could accuse him of being deliberately stupid. He dropped back through the trapdoor faster than Santa Claus down a chimney<<<<<<<<<<<<<<<<<<<<<<<<<<<<<<<<<<<<<<<<<<<<<<<<<<<<<<<<<<<<<<<<<<<

#

The encoded cephalic recording ended and the memlink was terminated.

I raised the eyeshields on my dreamset and pulled the sensorweb from my head. "So?"

Vanauken folded his arms and leaned back against a console. "As I said before, this recording was made during the period that the Anomaly took place. You detected no sensory distortion because the discernible effects occurred just after the point where we stopped playback."

"So?" I prompted again.

Vanauken frowned and started to fidget. "What makes this recording different from several thousand others made during the last moment is Mr. Henderson."

The door opened as if on cue, and a man entered the room. He was shorter, of slighter build, and much better dressed, but he had the same hawkish features...

"Yes, yes," Vanauken was saying, "this is the barbarian in the sequence you just experienced. Henderson just managed to squeak out of the Program before withdrawal was closed off. But he didn't get away scot-free."

He held up Henderson's right hand—still attached to his arm in this world, of course.

"This is Mr. Henderson's right hand, the one that corresponds to his avatar's sword hand. That's the one that was bitten off by the Troll."

As if I were too dense to make the connection.

He suddenly produced a long straight-pin and jabbed it into Henderson's palm. Everybody in the room flinched except Henderson. Even Vanauken seemed a little unnerved by his own act.

"Don't worry. I didn't feel a thing," Henderson assured us with a wistful smile. "Ever since withdrawal from the Program, I haven't felt anything in this hand. I can't feel it, move it, use it—anything!"

"Another side-effect of the Program's—uh—" Vanauken hesitated.

"Malfunction," I coached with unconcealed insolence.

"Uh—right. Unfiltered biofeedback," he continued. "When Mr. Henderson's avatar lost his hand, the resulting backlash of unfiltered biofeedback actually impressed upon his brain that the hand no longer existed for him. And now that he's awake, his brain refuses to recognize his real hand's corporeal existence, in spite of visual and tactile evidence to the contrary!"

"Is this temporary or permanent?"

Vanauken shook his head. "We don't know. Attempts at hypnotherapy have completely failed to this point. Surgical alternatives have been proposed, but we'd like to postpone such drastic measures until we have a better perspective on *how* this all happened."

A horrible suspicion was growing in the back of my mind. "But if someone can dream the loss of their hand and not be able to use it when they wake up, then what happens if their avatar gets killed in while they're inside the Program?" I asked.

"Precisely the point I'm trying to make," Vanauken squeaked. "The Anomaly has negated all system safeguards and amplified the biofeedback process! If a Dreamwalker is in symbiotic taction with his or her avatar, and it dies, then the actual body, that person's real body back in the Cradle will experience terminal biofeedback!"

"You're saying that they would actually die?" Even I wasn't above baiting a man on the verge of hysteria.

He frowned. "I believe that I stated that quite clearly."

I leaned back into the dreamcouch's body-webbing and considered all that I had been briefed on up to this moment.

"Okay. Let me make sure I've got the picture, now. The Fantasyworld Program has been...compromised. How?"

Vanauken cleared his throat and looked over at a familiar and reassuring face.

Try to imagine the inscrutable Buddha of the Orient as a smallish, Caucasian woman. Now, give her short, curly, coppery hair, electric blue eyes, the soul of an Irish poet, the mind of a Rhodes scholar, and the personality of Annie Oakley. Got the picture? I doubt it. Dorothy Cooper defies easy description.

"Well, at first the problem was thought to be external or mechanical in nature," she answered from behind the Systems monitors. "Some malfunction in the hardware or the monitoring systems.

"But current data indicates that the Program itself has been corrupted. Our leading theory is that some internal portion of the Program has inverted the Primary Access sequence." She spread her hands helplessly. "In other words, the Dreamland staff no longer have any control over the Fantasyworld Program because someone or something inside the Program Matrix has taken it over."

"A Dreamwalker?" I asked.

"I don't know!" For the first time in my life I was seeing Dr. Cooper in an attitude of helpless defeat, and that unnerved me more than anything else I'd heard or seen so far.

"It shouldn't be possible." Dr. Quebedeaux shifted in her seat. "But then, this whole situation is an impossibility!"

I was resisting the strong impulse to say I told you so—I was saving that for a face-to-face with Mike Straeker. Why Dreamland's Chief of Programming hadn't put in an appearance at this briefing was mystifying. They had wanted me badly enough to come looking for me—even to the point of dragging me back under armed guard. As a consequence, I expected to be talking to the headman, not a roomful of subordinates.

Cooper I trusted. Dorothy and I had ridden the DreamNet together when the Program was in the process of being set up. We had play-tested the Fantasyworld milieu during the years of development, before Dreamland went public. She was an able Dreamwalker, a good scientist, and moreover, a great friend.

Vanauken was too supercilious to be taken seriously. From what I could gather, he was more of a PR man for Cephtronics than an actual technical advisor.

And Dr. Quebedeaux was an unknown quantity. Slim, cool, and too elegant, she seemed the embodiment of all the bad qualities of all of the disagreeable blondes I had ever known. Worse than that, she reminded me of my ex-wife.

"So, I've been hauled out of bed in the middle of the night and dragged here under military arrest because you people have lost control of one of your Games?" Lack of sleep was beginning to tell: I was getting testy and letting it show before Mike arrived.

"No, Dr. Ripley," Dr. Quebedeaux snapped back. "You are here because we have lost control of one of *your* Games!"

Coop tried to be conciliatory. "We were hoping you might have some insights into the Program's malfunction…"

"Are you sure it's the Program that malfunctioned?"

Quebedeaux frowned. "What do you mean?" Coop knew where I was leading and suddenly became very interested in the Systems monitors.

I folded my arms across my chest. "If I were you, I'd start my investigation with an updated psyche-profile of the System, itself."

"What are you talking about?"

I sighed. "I'm talking about that giant vat of gray matter at the heart of the Dreamland Complex."

"Are you seriously suggesting that we psyche-scan The Machine?" Her expression was disdainful. "Mr. Ripley, The Machine is not a sentient organism. It is a computer that utilizes banks of cultured cephalic cells for memory storage and information retrieval. Bio-ROM has been used for years—"

"But not Bio-RAM," I interrupted.

"We are talking about a machine—" she continued tightly.

"Bullshit! If you people are still calling it a machine after all this time then you are dumber than I originally thought! Mike Straeker hung that appellation on it because Cephtronics was afraid of public opinion and a Frankenstein complex. But it's not a machine and calling it a chrysanthemum won't make it a flower, either. A computer, maybe; but cephalic cellular units are organic and that makes it a gigantic brain—soulless or not!"

"So what are you saying? Are you suggesting that our 'giant brain' has had a nervous breakdown?" Her voice acquired a studied tone of mockery. "Or maybe that it has become mentally ill?" Her lips curled into a tight, humorless smile. "Perhaps even schizophrenic?"

My own patience was wearing thin. "Look, lady"—I could ignore a person's title of degree, too.—"I don't care! Cephtronics and I parted company over this issue—and the moral question of Gaming with Ais—over five years ago. If it should finally turn out that I was right and Dreamland was wrong, well then, that would just tickle me pink! Go find some other patsy to bail you out."

"Maybe we haven't given you a clear picture of just how serious this thing is..." Dorothy spoke with uncharacteristic quietness.

"I understand the loss of revenue should give the Board of Directors the screaming meemies."

"Robbie...there are people trapped in the Program."

The ensuing silence was deafening.

"You're telling me that Dreamwalkers could really die in Fantasyworld?" I asked finally. "And you haven't brought them out yet?"

"Haven't you been listening?" Dr. Quebedeaux's anguish matched mine for the moment. "We can't bring them out! We no longer have any control over the Program!"

I looked at Vanauken. "Can't you just open the Cradles and wake them up?"

He shook his head. "We thought of that, first thing."

"And?"

"Attempts to recall and revive a couple of Dreamwalkers—without Program withdrawal processing—proved to be relatively fatal."

Relatively fatal? I decided to let that one pass for the moment. "What else are you trying?"

"Everything!" Vanauken spread his arms. "At this point, we seem to have only one strong option. Dr. Quebedeaux?"

The tall blonde in the white smock hugged her clipboard to her chest as she stood and began speaking. "Since the Program was altered—to all appearances—from the inside, our best chance is to ascertain how it was done in the first place, and then undo it—"

"From the inside," I finished for her.

She nodded. "External approaches will continue to be tried by the technical staff, but we feel that a group of highly skilled Dreamwalkers—Dreammasters, if you will—inside the Program, have a better chance of rectifying the problem and returning control to the Project."

"Sounds reasonable," I agreed. "But what if they're unsuccessful?"

"Then," Vanauken answered, "as things stand now, they'll remain trapped in their avatars and in Fantasyworld until their deaths—natural or otherwise."

THREE

"Dr. Quebedeaux doesn't like me."

"Can you blame her?" Dorothy Cooper was escorting me to yet another clandestine meeting somewhere in the white-tunneled labyrinth of the Dreamland Complex. "You've been surly and rude ever since you arrived."

I was struggling to find the right pace to match her stride. In contrast to the long-limbed Dr. Quebedeaux, Coop needed a step-ladder to look me in the eye. What she lacked in physical stature, however, was more than made up for in sheer feistiness.

"Can you blame me?" I countered petulantly. "First, I'm dragged out of bed in the middle of the night by a whole platoon of Marines. Then I'm— " I stopped suddenly. "Wait a minute! How does the military figure into all of this?"

"Robbie, there are several hundred people trapped in the Fantasyworld Program. Some may die if we don't get them out soon! I imagine someone higher up had the moxie and the influence to arrange for your delivery, and I'd have a hard time arguing with that particular decision. Fantasyworld was largely your creation, so can you think of anyone better to drag in here under the present circumstances?"

"Mike Straeker comes immediately to mind."

She shook her head. "Mike's dead."

After a moment we started walking again.

"What happened?" I asked quietly.

"Brain tumor," she answered somberly. Even though she hadn't liked the man, she had still respected him. "He had it for a long time, but very few people knew about it. It was inoperable..."

"I'm sorry." I meant it genuinely: before my court battle with Cephtronics, Mike had been a friend.

"Dr. Quebedeaux," she continued a long pause, "is the new Chief of Programming."

"Kind of young, isn't she?"

Dorothy laughed. "Just six years younger than you—and you created Fantasyworld a little over seven years ago."

"Point goes to Doctor C." I wished I had known sooner: Quebedeaux seemed a more appropriate target for my anger than an old, if somewhat estranged, friend. Especially now that he was gone.

"Anyway, she was Michael's assistant—"

"Inherited his temperament along with the job," I observed.

"—and was more than qualified when the position suddenly came open. Robbie," she rushed on, "none of us have slept much since this thing happened. She's feeling a lot of pressure right now, with hundreds of lives riding on her decisions, and your 'screw-you' attitude toward Cephtronics isn't helping!"

I made a helpless gesture. "What can I do?"

"I don't know. Cooperate, at least! Did you know that she's going into the Program—*personally*—to try to fix it? Knowing that she may well never get back out?" She took my hand and patted it maternally. "Why don't you give her all the help you can?"

"Like tagging along when she goes Matrix-diving?" I smiled. "Only an idiot would enter the Program, in taction, with the current circumstances being what they are."

"Knowing you, there's hope then," she countered wryly. "Besides, it would be like old times!"

I turned and caught the twinkle in her eye. "Doc, tell me you're not going!"

"At the risk of sounding trite and cliché—something I've never been caught at hitherto now—someone's gotta do it. And who's better qualified?"

"Trying to coerce me through guilt?"

"If the shoe fits, Sweets…" We stopped in front of a closed portal flanked by two burly Marine guards. "Here we are. My instructions were to deliver you. I don't think I've been invited to stay for the party. Do be nice to them, Robbie; they'll be a whole lot nicer to you."

"Thanks, kid. Give my regards to Rijma."

"Mine to Riplakish. Ta!" And she was off, leaving me to face the two Marine-types.

"I think I'm expected," I said to them. For all of their response I might have been talking to myself. "I'm Robert Ripley…" I smiled, "…believe it or not."

Still no reaction.

"Uh, open sesame?"

The door slid open.

"Trick or treat," I muttered under my breath and crossed the threshold.

The room was dimly lit except for a pool of light at the far end. A man sitting in silhouette behind a desk against the far wall motioned for me to come forward. I went forward. After all, I wanted answers, didn't I?

"Sit down, Dr. Ripley."

When the Vice President of the United States offers you a seat, you sit. I didn't want to offend him or make the half-dozen Secret Service agents in the room any more nervous than they already appeared to be.

#

"I don't think they believe me."

Cooper tossed me a container of Dr. Pepper from the vending wall. "If they didn't believe you, you'd be under arrest so fast your head would spin."

"Maybe. Or maybe under 'house-arrest,' so that I have the freedom of the premises as long as I don't try to leave the grounds. I'd be almost as easy to watch under current security conditions. And might prove useful should I decide to repent and betray the Russians."

"They think the Russian Federation is behind this?" Her eyes widened. "And they think you're helping them?" She began to laugh. "That's hysterical—"

"Hysteria is closer to the truth, Coop." I popped the top on the Dr. Pepper. "Several high-ranking Russian ministers—including Deputy Chairman Borys Dankevych—were in the Program when it came unhinged. I created most of the Fantasyworld Program and I've been nursing a grudge against Cephtronics for several years. With this eyepatch I even look like one of the bad guys. Now I've been seen in the company of an SVR operative. She slipped the net, but here I am."

"And they think you're in collusion with her?"

"Cahoots."

"That's what I said."

"Got any vanilla around here?"

She made a face. "No one else has even heard of your aberration, much less practiced it. Drink it straight—like a man."

I made a face and took a sip. "Now, to add insult to injury—if not fire to the frying pan—any advice I give from here on in is totally suspect. And, if this whole thing goes down wrong, Cephtronics is going to need a patsy. That's me: I'm the goat."

"What are you going to do?"

"Aw, I was going to go in anyway. I just hate to now because it looks like I'm trying to clear my name."

"Aren't you?"

I grinned. "You know how I dislike doing anything with a gun at my head."

"'Rebellious youth.' You're assuming, of course, that they'll let you go in now."

"And why wouldn't they?"

"With everyone else assuming that the Ruskies have manipulated your feud with Cephtronics into turncoat status? Get real." She got up. "Take another walk with me?"

"Sure. Why?"

"Because it's harder for the bug-boys to monitor the hallways than the Snack Bar." She picked up her coffee and led me into the hallway.

"Dorothy, why didn't you tell me Walter Hanson was in Dreamland?"

She studied the length of the corridor. "It's supposed to be a secret—one of those hush-hush things the staff are sworn to secrecy about. I assume you're fully briefed now?"

"Not quite. What in the hell is the Chairman of the Armed Services Committee doing in Fantasyworld? I know Dreamland has something for everyone's taste, but Senator Hanson hardly strikes me as the sword-and-sorcery type. And I can't believe he'd be allowed to take such a risk."

She gave me a rueful smile. "To answer your questions in reverse order: there is—or at least *was*—no danger, no risk. That reassuring PR has been in place for over five years and we've never had any reason to doubt it until now." She gestured to cut off my anticipated reply. "And the senator wasn't in Fantasyworld, he was in Warworld," she continued. "Don't ask me why. Maybe the fantasy provides a safe outlet for any latent, aggressive feelings acquired during all these East-West showdowns. Maybe he was running tactical simulations for one of the subcommittee proposals." She shrugged. "Or maybe just paying off a covert campaign contribution by providing Cephtronics with a veiled endorsement."

I pinched the bridge of my nose and closed my eyes. "I'm confused. I thought the Anomaly was restricted to Fantasyworld. And I thought you could still retrieve Dreamers from the other Programworlds."

"We can. Although we've gotten most of them out, now." She looked around though the corridor was still deserted. "Robbie, they're not telling you all of it. The Anomaly may be spreading. And the senator is now in Fantasyworld." She took my arm and began pulling me along with her.

"So how did he get there?" I asked.

"He was kidnapped."

"Kidnapped? By who?"

"Whom," she corrected.

"Whom, dammit, whom!"

"By Goblins."

"You're kidding!"

"I'm not."

I stopped and pressed my fingertips to my temples. "You're trying to tell me that a bunch of Goblins broke into Warworld, grabbed the Chairman of the Armed Services Committee, and carried him back into Fantasyworld?"

"That's the evidence as of this moment."

"But that's impossible! Milieu-crossover just isn't possible from inside the Matrix!"

She looked at me and then gazed off down the hallway again. "It is now."

"So, what are we doing?" I asked, as we entered one of the Taction Stations.

"I'm going to put you into Fantasyworld. You've made up your mind to go, haven't you?"

I had, but I wasn't ready to go quietly. "I thought we were all going in as one big rescue party."

She seated herself behind a console and began punching up the initial entry sequence. "As far as Quebedeaux's concerned your only party affiliation may be with the Communist Reform Party."

"Aw, Dee, no one takes them seriously, anymore—not even the Russians!"

"Maybe so. But I'm pretty sure that your name's not on the guest list for this little foray."

"So you're putting me in on my own? Now?" A storage locker slid out from the wall.

She nodded and I started undressing. "It's your best chance for getting inside and operating with some autonomy. Nobody's told me not to put you in—but I think Doctor Q would prefer to put you on ice until this whole thing is resolved."

"Great. If I sit this one out then I have to depend on the Snow Queen to figure out the Anomaly, avert an international incident, rescue the Dreamers, and, incidentally, clear my name. Somehow I think I'll be safer inside the Matrix, where the monsters don't have doctorates." I removed the last of my clothing and folded it for the locker.

She waggled a finger at me. "Now, be nice."

"I've tried being nice for most of my life. Nobody respects you for it." I closed the locker, allowed the lock-mechanism to scan my thumbprint, then sent the cabinet gliding back into storage. "Ready?"

Dr. Cooper nodded over the controls and a Cradle entered the room on magnetic tracks as I attached the bio-sensors to my body. She tapped a sequence of buttons and the top swung open.

"Listen," I said as I climbed up the side and began lowering my body down into its pseudoplacentic interior, "if you can shake free of the company team, I'll be calling The Rabble out of retirement."

She laughed. "That's great! And don't you dare forget that I was a charter member! Where will we meet?"

"Shibboleth. Four REMdays to allow for stragglers and accidents on the road. Do you remember the inn?"

"How could I ever forget? Even after all these years...hmm." She paused, giving the monitor a sudden look of mistrust.

"What's wrong?"

"Your Avatar File is incomplete: Name, Race, Stats, Background, Experience—everything except your Classification."

"Yeah. I blanked the records on that. Thought I'd keep it my little secret." I climbed into the tank.

"So which do I enter? Warrior, Wizard, Thief—what?"

"Bard."

She shook her head. "There ain't no such thing."

"Never got final approval for public use," I agreed. "Try entering it anyway."

She did. "Accepted. Don't know why I'm surprised." She tapped another sequence on the keypad. "Watch your head."

"I'm clear." I lay back in the nutriotic soup as the hatch began to descend again.

"Nighty night; and don't forget to say your prayers," she called from the console.

A final thought occurred: "Hey! If Fantasyworld is closed off, how am I going to get in?"

"Rerouting—" was all I heard before the hatch sealed me in and the rest of the world out.

Goodbye reality. I floated quietly and waited for the somnambulants to take effect.

Now I lay me down to sleep,

I pay Cephtronics my soul to keep…

The old inter-office joke echoed in my mind as I tried to relax. Back in the old days, before Dreamland had gone on-line for the public and we were still running tests on the Matrix, there had been some very unpleasant experiences with hypnagogic feedback. Before the sensory loops were properly filtered, I had experienced several avatar-deaths. Two of those "deaths" had been monumentally unpleasant—worse than the aircar crash I had barely survived in the outside world. Years afterward, one of them still echoes in an occasional real-time nightmare.

…if I die before I wake…

Aye, there's the rub: to sleep, perchance to dream. Perchance to die?

It would be for real, this time.

But there were good things, I reminded myself, good times to remember. To anticipate…

Dyrinwall, forest primeval. Home and sanctuary. I could remember walking for miles beneath its green canopy and never seeing the sky. Heartsrest.

I was finally returning to the one place where I could remember happiness uneclipsed by sorrow or pain.

I felt my body unclenching.

…the woods are lovely, dark, and deep…

My mind began to unclench, as well.

…but I have promises to keep…

And as it did, I felt myself borne up as if by the River Lethe and carried toward that dark and mystic ocean fed by the tributaries of all unconscious minds.

…and miles to go…

PART II

A FREUDIAN SLEEP

Sleep hath its own world,
And a wide realm of wild reality.

—Lord Byron, *The Dream*—

ONE

My head ached abominably and my stomach made one last attempt to turn inside-out and crawl up my esophagus. A face swam into view, unfocused and blurry, and then I felt soft hands stroking my temples.

"Thou art awake now, my lord?"

The voice was soft and distinctly feminine, as were the hands and the lap which, I suddenly realized, was pillowing my head. I squinched my eyes and, after another wave of vertigo, the hovering image began to resolve itself.

Large azure eyes gazed down at me, wide with concern. Gullwing brows—full, yet light and feathery—arched above them and were eclipsed by long, dark lashes that swept upwards. Other than the barest hint of a cleft in her slender chin, her luminous skin was unlined and without flaw. Lips the color of sunrise and coral pursed around teeth that were impossibly white and even. Thick, glossy hair, touched with highlights of silver, fell in a brown mist to caress my face. She had the kind of beauty that makes a mortal man ache with longings beyond description and haunts him with desires beyond any fulfilling.

"Nicole?" I whispered.

Then I remembered fire in the skies over Paris and a crippled aircar lurching toward the *Champs-Élysées*...

No.

Not Nicole. Misty Dawn. I locked away the errant memory and focused on the now.

She was too beautiful to be mortal and too perfect to be Human. And, as a matter of fact, she was neither. I remembered that now as I tried to sit up. She was a Dryad—a Wood Nymph.

And my personal secretary.

I had a professional relationship here, and the last thing I needed right now was to give her any chance to work her wiles. Cephtronics had tampered with the Program after my initial setup and one of those atrocities involved turning all of the Nymphs into red-hot sex machines. Cephtronics' fiscal philosophy was based on catering to every Dreamrider's fantasy—particularly those involving sex.

I looked around, trying to orient myself. Taking in the wood-paneled walls and the open boles that served as windows, I was reminded that this was no castle keep but the interior of a giant tree—a Hamadryad's enchanted tree.

I was home.

"Let me put thee to bed, my lord," she begged, as I pulled away and struggled to my feet.

Willpower doesn't come easy at times like this, but I had a U.S. senator, a Russian deputy chairman, and several hundred Dreamwalkers to rescue. "I'm fine, Misty. Just a little tired, that's all."

Misty Dawn rose to her feet as if on invisible wings and smoothed the filmy scrap of gauze about her hips and bust as if it made some kind of difference in her appearance. She was pouting now. "Thou hast not had such an attack in a long time, my lord! I fear for thee!"

Her concern was sincere but I kept my guard up: maintaining a platonic relationship with this woodland goddess had been challenge enough before Cephtronics had overhauled her sex appeal. I shook my head and put out a hand to steady myself.

"Uh, Misty, hon; I'm going out for a while," I ventured as I teetered and tottered across the room. "Mind the store while I'm gone. Okay?" I slumped against some shelves that overflowed with scrolls and musty tomes, trying to give my weakness the appearance of a casual lean.

The deception failed and she ran across the room and tried to prop me up with the better parts of her anatomy. "I think thou shouldst be tucked into bed and kept warm!"

I shook my head, remembering Misty Dawn's concept of "bed warming," but I compromised by allowing her to help me navigate to an overstuffed naugahyde couch. Fortunately, it was made from the hide of only one nauga and was too small for both of us as long as I was lying down. Finally giving up on any ideas of sharing me or the furniture for the moment, she announced that she was going to cancel all of my appointments for the rest of the day.

"Good idea," I mumbled, trying to resist a growing feeling of lethargy. "What are we canceling?"

She furrowed her pretty brow and ruminated a moment. "Before lunch: thy fencing lesson with Don Diego de Vega—he was going to show thee how to make those 'Z's. After lunch: house calls on the forest folk until Tea. Tea Time: I think Don Hidalgo Quixote was dropping by to continue last week's discussion of the metaphysical transmogrification of windmills into four-armed giants—but I am not completely sure…" She smiled and shrugged bare and shapely shoulders. "Of course, he is never sure, either."

"Is that it?"

She chewed her lip in concentration. "Robin, Will, and Little John hath already postponed archery practice for the remainder of the week, but Alan-a-Dale saith he would bring thy harp by before dinner. He sent thee a message." She giggled.

"What?"

"He saith that this will be the last time he will repair it if thou dost not cease using it to parry broadswords."

I snorted. "Is he kidding? Better the occasional ruffian should gut my harp than my self!"

"Thou speakest strangely, my lord. Methinks the swamp malaise has made thy brain feverish, again." She knelt beside the sofa. "Let me loosen thy clothing!"

I held her off with an unsteady arm. "It's true I could use some rest, kiddo, but I ain't gonna get any with you around. Now, I promise to be good and lie here if you'll get back to your desk and allow me a little peace and quiet. Okay?"

She looked unconvinced so I changed tactics and tone of voice: "That's an order, M.D.! And if you can't follow orders, I'll hire a secretary who will!"

She left with a wounded air. As I watched her pert and barely concealed bottom go out the door, I made a mental note to tighten up the office dress codes.

#

It was dark when I awoke again.

Moonlight beamed through an open bole in the wall, illuminating the closet doors on the far side of the room. This time I was able to walk rather than weave across the floor.

Errant little memories were starting to fall into place: I tripped the closet's secret latch without even thinking. Inside were my campaign clothing and gear, and I exchanged my druidic robe for a tunic and girdle of light doeskin. Over this I pulled on a shirt of enchanted chainmail. Forged by Gnomish smiths, blessed and magicked by Gnomish high priests, the mithril links were cool and light to the point of near weightlessness, yet the eldritch metal and arcane enchantments woven into its design protected me far better than heavy plate armor. It was also a bit snug around the waist, suggesting that my avatar had enjoyed a lengthy period of inaction since I had last possessed it.

My outer garments consisted of a scaled leather jerkin and trousers of a mottled green and dun hue: dragonskin. It had a double advantage over *cuir-bouilli* leather in that it allowed greater mobility as well as better protection. Especially against heat and flame.

There was a polished brass mirror on the back of the closet door and I availed myself of it now.

The reflected image was unremarkable for Fantasyworld. My avatar stood about five feet six and weighed about ten stone; in real life I was almost a full foot taller, but here I was under the genetic limitations of my Halfelven blood.

My slight build, arched eyebrows, and pointed ears betrayed my Elven parentage while my size and darker coloring bespoke my Human blood. Shaggy, light-brown hair fell around my ears, curled over the nape of my neck, and was held out of my eyes by a leather headband that Misty Dawn had plaited for me years before. I had grown a mustache and goatee in an effort to enhance a basically uninteresting face. I still wasn't convinced that it had accomplished its original purpose but at least both sides seemed to match, making it an improvement over the original.

I shook myself from these narcissistic musings with the remembrance that appearances were purely subjective—a computer contrivance.

But then everything in and of this world was a computer contrivance. And I could not lightly dismiss them, for, here, they were the realities. This was no longer a Dream: life and death, pain and pleasure—everything was very real here.

Especially death, thanks to this newfound glitch in the program.

I returned to the couch and was pulling on the calf-length moccasin boots when I became aware of a presence in the doorway.

Misty Dawn neither moved nor spoke, but stood in the shadows, watching me with eyes that burned like haunted sapphires.

I turned my own eyes back to the business of lacing up my footwear and groped for words to break the silence.

"I'm feeling much better now." That was true in more ways than one. For the first time in recent memory I was entirely without pain. Medical science had made it possible for me to survive a crash that would have been unsurvivable thirty years earlier. But there is a vast difference between healing and jury-rigging the human body so that it still has some semblance of function.

Her stillness bordered on the ominous and I took my time with the second boot, waiting to see which way the wind would blow.

"I thought I would take a little walk..." My voice sounded strange. Strained.

The silence grew even deeper and, when I looked up again, I could see the reflection of moonlight upon her tears, glistening like quicksilver trails over her cheeks.

"Misty..."

"Thou art leaving," she said suddenly.

"I'm going to take a little stroll. I'll be back in less than an hour."

She shook her head and her hair floated like a night mist on the cool air. "Thou'rt leaving Dyrinwall Forest."

"Not tonight."

"No," she agreed, "not tonight. But soon. Tomorrow, perhaps. Thou wilt take up the sword and the bow, again, and leave thine harp behind. And ride to battle and death. I can see it plainly written and foretold in the moonlight and shadows upon thy face."

I felt a chill as she turned away and quietly began to weep. Did a Nymph have the power of precognition, or was she merely speaking out of a woman's heart? Against all my principles, I went to her and took her into my arms.

"Do you foresee my death, Misty Dawn?" I asked softly.

A slight tremor went through her entire body. "I know not. Save that thou wilt leave me and not return." The sadness in her voice was devastating.

"Why wouldn't I return?"

She led me back to the couch and we sat together, her head resting against my shoulder.

"When thou didst return to Dyrinwall those many years ago, after the Goblin Wars, the light was gone from behind thine eyes and I knew thee to be as one of us. I had hoped the gods would forget thee, here, and that thy reward might be peace and long life and old age, undisturbed here in this grove of sanctuary. I would give thee—give thee—"

"Love?" I asked gently.

She nodded through fresh tears.

"Ah, Misty; you are a woodland spirit, an Elemental, while I am mortalborn: half Human, half Elven," I answered, slipping smoothly into Program character. "You are immortal and shall remain eternally young long after I am nothing but dust. What of love then?"

"What of love now?" she asked quietly. "Am I to deny the present because of a withheld future?"

I had no answer to that.

"There is a sacred glen where the sun parts the trees and warms the dark earth," she whispered finally. "When comes the day thou speakest of, I would see thee to thy final sleep, under white sheets of edelweiss and green comforters of moss and ivy. Between a silver brook and the Sacred Ring where the Faerie dance, thou wouldst rest, safe and undisturbed; and I would lay stones to hedge and guard thee, and I would plant vines to shade thee. From Spring till Fall I should bring flowers to honor and please thee, and all Winter long would I burn candle and incense to warm thee and tuck thee in more securely."

I shook my head in wonderment. "Forever is a long time—"

"I have no less than all the time in the world." She wiped at a fresh tear. "An immortal cannot love in the same measures of time that mortals do."

I knew then that she was doomed. And that I had condemned her to her fate twelve years before when I had created her that long, lonely night, seated at my word processor. *Had I been thinking of Nicole at the moment of Misty Dawn's creation?*

Grief and anger suddenly flared, overriding my best intentions: hell, it was only a dream and she was nothing more than a sophisticated AI subprogram! I tilted her face toward mine and kissed her.

Wet and salty, but warm and unbearably sweet, the taste of her lips remained long after she had turned away again.

"It is too late," she said at last in a small voice.

"Why?"

"Because thou'rt now become a True Spirit, once more."

"And what is that?" I asked.

"I know not," she retorted angrily, and rose to her feet. "Those who are said to be True Spirits seem to have a greater awareness of themselves and the events that take place around them. They shape the great events and destinies.

"Twelve years before, thou wert a True Spirit and madest thy name a legend throughout the land during the time of the Dark Tide. Then, as I have said, the light that burned behind thine eyes…faded…and thou didst return to Dyrinwall Forest. For the past ten years thou hast lived here, hidden from the rest of the world. It has been a good ten years and thou hast done much for the forest folk with thy medicine and thaumaturgy. Thou hast been like unto one of us, subject to fate and blind destiny…"

"And now?" I prompted, a little shaken. I had not realized that the AIs were capable of distinguishing between another AI and a true Dreamwalker.

She took my hands in hers. "Thou'rt no longer one of us. Thy destiny is not ours, though our fates are irrevocably bound to thine. Thou wilt take leave of us…"

"I must." It sounded came out sounding like the worst cliché.

"Why?" She touched a finger to my lips before I could try an answer. "What doth it mean, my lord? Why are some True Spirits and others not? And why doth the possession come and go without warning, rhyme or reason? Why art thou a True Spirit, yet mortal; while I, a creature of earth's elements, am immortal, but without a soul?"

I was silent, bereft of words.

"Why?" She clutched at me. "If thou knowest, I beg thee tell me why!"

I couldn't. How could I explain that her world was the result of a vast Computer Program? That every rock, tree, mountain, river, and valley was mathematical syllogisms? That every Construct lifeform, from the malaria-inducing protozoa to the humanoids, demihumans, and monsters, were the tangible projections of various Subprograms, each with separate potentialities calculated for every conceivable situation and circumstance?

And how could I tell her that she was one such Artificial Intelligence, herself?

Even if I could break the rules and tell her these things, I would only be stating the "how." Not the "why."

Could I justify the Game by explaining how an increasingly technological society had driven its populace to every extreme of escapism that it could find or develop? That we had mined the mountains, poisoned the rivers, paved the meadows, flattened the forests, and generally filled in or used up all of the wild and wide open spaces? That the only virgin frontiers left to us were in our own minds or the cold vacuum of outer space?

And even if I could find the words and meanings to make her understand, what would it accomplish? Just to communicate the terrible truth that the hills and valleys, lakes and woodlands, villages and seaports that made up her world were someone else's gameboard. That her life, with all of her hopes, aspirations, needs, and fears, was nothing more than a game piece to the Players, and she only existed to be used according to the whims of the Dreamwalkers.

I couldn't tell her that.

"This is forbidden knowledge," I said finally. "It must remain a secret of the gods, for now..."

And then I held her until her eyes were dry again.

#

Time...

A complete decade of Dreamtime had gone by since I had last entered Fantasyworld. During that absence, my avatar had been maintained by the Computer in accordance with my Personality Profile and my Character Index scores.

Now, however, I was back in the driver's seat, and the answers that I sought lay beyond the safety of these woods.

But first I was in need of a little reorientation.

I could not go jumping into Riplakish of Dyrinwall's persona as if he were a second suit of clothing. We had grown apart over the past five external years—or the past ten internal years—and those differences in memory and physiology weren't easily bridged in a short time without mnemonic processing. I was also making the more pleasant adjustment back to binocular vision with its added depth perception. And back to two good legs, though I still tended to favor the left out of habit.

My little moonlight walk through Dyrinwall Forest seemed to be helping in this respect. The nausea and bouts of vertigo had passed and the mental cobwebs seemed to be clearing away as I picked my way through an overgrown section of pathway.

As in the years before, I was struck by the beauty and the intricacy of my surroundings. Looking at the thousands of individual leaves and blades of grass, each silvered by the moon and spangled with dew, it seemed incomprehensible that this entire world, down to its most minute parts, was the subjective projection of a master computer known as The Machine. But I was reminded of its virtual solidity as I stubbed my toe on a large surface root. Limping over to a fallen log, I attempted to massage some relief into my throbbing toe.

Strangely, the ache was almost comforting. I had lived with unrelieved pain for so long that I had constructed a workable truce with it. Stepping into Fantasyworld and a healthy avatar was a seductive but disturbing experience.

My primitive first-aid was interrupted by the sound of someone driving a locomotive through the forest without the benefit of tracks or right-of-way. At least that was what it sounded like.

And it was getting closer.

I might have chosen to run. After all, I was alone and unarmed: not the most desirable terms for facing the unknown. But, on the other hand, I was still in sanctuary and, therefore, safe. I elected to stand—or sit—my ground. I didn't have to wait too long; the underbrush at the edge of the clearing burst asunder and three monstrous figures stomped into the open.

If you were looking for a concise description of the three, "hellish" would be the most apt—all three were Demons from the Abyss. I would have recognized that much even if I hadn't already been on a first-name basis with each of them.

Yakku looked like a cross between a Human and a vulture, Ahuizotl resembled a giant toad with teeth and arms, and Sedit gave the impression of being a goat-horned dog with an extra pair of limbs. All were man-sized and walked more or less erect. Yakku and Ahuizotl looked on expectantly while Sedit sniffed the air.

"He is near," the Demon announced. "Somewhere nearby."

My confidence wavered a bit as I watched from the shadows: Dyrinwall was neutral ground, but these jokers were about as likely to turn up in sanctuary as Baalzebub in a confessional.

But, while their presence unnerved me, I didn't feel like playing it safe, either.

"Well, well, well!" I exclaimed, suddenly and just loud enough to make them jump: they were on my turf and they knew it. "If it isn't Larry, Moe, and Curly-Joe! Aren't you boys a long way from home?"

They turned, instantly orienting on the sound of my voice. "Riplakish!" Yakku hissed my name like a malediction.

"Nice of you to remember my name, Buzzard-breath," I retorted. "I take it you three refugees from a bonfire are looking for me?"

"Impudent scum! I shall tear your insolent tongue from your blaspheming mouth by its roots! You shall watch as I devour it—" This from Ahuizotl who was advancing in a menacing manner. He always had been rather high-strung.

I leaned back and folded my arms. "Mighty bold talk, Toad-tush. Especially considering the fact that you're walking across consecrated ground."

He fell for the bluff and began dancing a jig like a rabid flamenco dancer with a hotfoot. While he capered and howled, I addressed the other two. "Okay, you clowns have my attention. What's your business here?"

"You," intoned Sedit, pointing a wicked looking claw.

"Yeah, yeah!" added Yakku, Hell's prototype of the perfect yes man.

"Get to the point!" I snapped. "I bore quickly."

"Orcus wants you!" dogface snapped back.

"Do you mean to tell me that he's still steamed over that wand incident? I apologized years ago!" I shrugged. "I even offered to buy him a new one."

Yakku's eyes bugged at this fresh irreverence. Sedit attempted to look nonplussed but only succeeded in managing a hangdog expression. Ahuizotl continued to dance between us while they considered that bit of history: I had returned the Death Wand after "borrowing" it from Orcus' stronghold at the center of the Infernal City, but the Prince of the Undead claimed that it had never worked properly since.

That one incident had won me a lot of respect from both Above and Below but it hadn't made me any friends. The Forces of Good claimed I was soft on the Powers of Darkness and the Dark Powers declared that by apparently waltzing into the Infernal City, stealing the sceptre of Orcus, and waltzing back out unscathed, I would invite a lot of unwanted tourist traffic in the future. It hadn't been quite that easy, of course, but as Tolkien once said, the tale grew with the telling.

"Orcus has given orders that you are to be brought before him," Sedit barked.

I yawned. "Tell Fat Boy that I'm busy. If he wants to see me so badly, tell him the Mountain can come to Mahomet."

My smirk was cut short by Ahuizotl who suddenly danced over and caught me by the throat: it hurt!

"Now, Dogmeat; we shall see how well you blaspheme without your tongue!" He prized my jaw open and reached in to make good his threat.

With strength born of fear and desperation, I bit down. Hard. The only thing that kept my teeth from coming together was Ahuizotl's amazingly solid bone structure. He shrieked and drop-kicked me into the terribly solid trunk of a large tree. There was a rush of bark and I found myself contemplating a tangle of roots at close range while wondering if biting a Demon was as poisonous as being bitten by same.

Someone was talking to me. I tried to concentrate over the roaring sound between my ears.

"The only choice we are giving you, Bard, is the condition in which you are going to arrive! Willing or not, you are coming with us!"

That sounded vaguely familiar.

Until both my vision and my hearing cleared a little more, I could only assume that it was Dogface talking. "Sanctuary?" I croaked.

"Times have changed, mortal: the very fabric of the universe has been altered! Sanctuary is no more! The Old Rule is done, and we shall be attending to the affairs of the New Order!"

"Zat so?" I gritted, struggling to my feet. I had to do something: it was bad enough that they had hostile intentions, but if they were going to make speeches—

"We waste time! Lord Orcus will tell you those things that he deems necessary for your understanding."

"Then tell him I'll look him up in a couple of days—after I get some things caught up here." My head was clearing, now; and I began calculating my chances of dealing with these three characters without the bargaining powers of sword and shield. Demons are rather magic-resistant and more easily dispatched with cold iron than a hot spell. While a palaver with the Lord of the Undead was beginning to sound like a good idea after all, I wasn't that keen on being shanghaied or having the meeting taking place Down Below.

"And now," announced Sedit as he started toward me, "let us have no more of these silly, delaying tactics. Come along peaceably and I might persuade Ahuizotl to let you keep your tongue."

"Go to hell!" was my weak bid for witty repartee.

In the next instant the ground began to rumble. I don't know which of us was more surprised as it opened up beneath Sedit's "feet" and sucked him down in a belch of flame. The earth resealed itself a moment later with a gentle burp.

It wasn't a bardic spell. In fact, I hadn't consciously manipulated any kind of magic listed in the basic Program File. Apparently, the Program Matrix was responding to my latent Programmer status and taking me at my literal word.

Yakku and Ahuizotl looked a bit shell shocked as I turned to face them. "Somebody tell you clowns that I was going to be an easy snatch?" I inquired lightly.

They both nodded dumbly.

I sighed. "Well, it just goes to show that you can't believe everything you hear these days. Happy landings, boys!"

Yakku closed his eyes and, crooking his talons, waved "bye-bye"; Ahuizotl snarled and made an obscene gesture.

"Go to Hell," I said pleasantly. "Go directly to Hell: do not pass 'Go', do not collect two hundred credits."

Before either could ask what a credit was, they were both gone in twin bursts of fire and brimstone.

Walking back to the treehouse, I gave grave consideration to the implications of tonight's invasion: if the conditions of sanctuary had been abolished, then what might come next? What other laws of this reality might be undone? The little confidence that I had brought in with me was fading rapidly: True Death had come to the Dreamland and now there was no sanctuary.

Perhaps I was in over my head after all.

TWO

It is a well-known fact that a Hamadryad's tree will be larger than any normal tree in the forest. Beside our—or, rather, Misty's tree—the others looked like a bonsai garden. Her towering oak put sequoias to shame.

I opened the secret door hidden among the roots just as the rim of the sun broke over the horizon. Suppressing a yawn, I started the long climb.

The circular stairway seemed to go on and up forever. I had contemplated the mechanics of a simple elevator but Misty would not countenance it. She felt that fourteen rooms crammed into (or hollowed out of) her tree were quite enough, even if it was nearly 800 feet tall and enchanted. I couldn't very well argue: it was her tree. Plus she insisted that the exercise was good for me. The bane of all powerful magic users is the temptation to trade physical exertion for effortless spells at any common moment.

Misty appeared at that moment and leaned over the top of the staircase, providing me with an awe-inspiring view. As I paused to admire the scenery, she called down. "Thou hast a call waiting for thee in the study!"

"Who is it?" I suddenly felt a slight chill of apprehension.

"Ashtray," she answered, using her nickname for my ex-wife's avatar.My chill dropped another ten degrees: Stephanie was one of the Dreamwalkers trapped in the Program! No one had said anything about her presence in the Game. Perhaps the Programming Staff didn't know…

Or perhaps they were saving it for their trump card should I have proven uncooperative. Not that it would have done them any good: my ex-wife could hardly be used as any sort of leverage.

Unless they were threatening to annul our divorce, that is.

"Dost thou wish me to tell her that thou art indisposed?" An unsuppressed giggle drifted down after the question.

"Only if you take off your clothes and muss your hair first. No, no! I'll take it!" I added as the Nymph began to comply. I sighed and began climbing the stairs again.

Misty was mystified. "If Princess Vashti doth not like thee, then how is it that I maketh her jealous?"

I winced at Misty's occasional butchery of the Old English vernacular but had given up on correcting her long ago. When the time had come to write the program for archaic language forms, Cephtronics had probably handed the King Jimmy version of the Bible to a junior technician and said: "Go figure—but have it done before five." Hell with it; I didn't have time to play grammarian on top of everything else. "Ah," I wheezed, gaining another floor, "a loaded question with a double-barreled answer!"

"Meaning what, my lord?"

I held up one finger. "Primus: all mundane women—in your world, in my world, in *any* world—have always been and will always be jealous of Nymphs..."

"I have known those who were not, my lord!"

"I wasn't speaking of all women—merely the mundane. Secundus!" I held up a second finger. "Vestigial jealousy is a well-documented trait among ex-wives. Even when she is the walker and I am the walkee."

Her eyes widened. "It hath been said that all True Spirits come from another world!" Now her mouth dropped open. "When thou sayest 'ex-wife', dost thou mean—"

"Yes, yes," I leaned against the railing, pausing to get my wind back. "Princess Vashti, fourth in line for the imperial throne of the Amazon kingdom—uh, queendom—was once my wife. Not here, of course."

"Oh yes!" she exclaimed suddenly, catching on. "She is a True Spirit, also! She comes from that mystic plane beyond this world! And thou wert husband and wife on that plane?"

I nodded weakly.

"And dost thou appear here as thou wast in that sphere?"

"Very much like," I answered. "Oh, we may look a little different on the outside. But what's inside will always show through."

It was true. Most Gamers utilized mnemonic processing to alter their avatars and boost their abilities in such areas as physical strength, stamina, and manual dexterity, not to mention outward appearance: that's why so many avatars approached physical perfection. After all, why not adventure as the strongest, fastest, and most attractive? Fantasy upon fantasy.

But mnemonic processing couldn't compensate for every aspect of gaming abilities. It couldn't make you wiser or more kind than you already were: personalities always told with time.

"I can see why thou didst flee to this world, my lord!" Misty Dawn seemed fascinated by this newfound relationship. "But she hath pursued thee even here! What wilt thou do?"

"Keep them alimony credits a-rollin' through."

"I beg thy pardon?"

"Never mind. It's a long, dreary story."

She shook her head in wonderment. "It be beyond mine ken, dear Riplakish: thee and Ashtray!"

"Vashti," I corrected with a laugh. "If she hears you call her that, she'll call down lightning from the heavens and set fire to half of Dyrinwall Forest."

Misty snorted. "Dost thou really believe her to be so adept?"

"Based on our marriage—yes. Even though there was no magic left a year after the honeymoon, she did turn out to be a full-fledged witch." I topped the stairs and stepped past Misty into my study.

The crystal ball had been moved to the tripod next to my rolltop desk, where my ever-efficient secretary knew I liked to take business and personal calls. I tugged the black silk covering off the ball and settled back in the desk chair. "C'mon, Wonder Woman; you got the Bard."

Her blurred image at the crystal's center came sharply into focus. "Cut that archaic CB crap! This is serious!"

I spread my hands. "Sorry, Stephie; I forgot how intense you like to play it."

"Don't call me Stephanie! This is an open line—others may hear!"

"I got nothin' to hide, Sweetie."

"You can say that, again!"

"Witch!"

"Wastard!"

I picked up the black silk. "Nice talking to you."

"Wait!" she cried. "The queen wishes to talk to you!"

"I'm waiting."

It unnerved me that she could still make me so angry so quickly. Even after seven years. I supposed it had something to do with her enjoying the Games after she had ridiculed the books they were based on throughout our so-called marriage.

"She's coming."

"I'm not used to waiting." Testy.

"I'm sure you don't have to, living with a Nymph."

"At least she's self-defrosting."

Vashti was trying to think of an appropriate comeback when the queen appeared.

While most people draw their concept of the Amazons from Greek mythology, the legends were actually inspired by the Sarmatians, an association of nomadic tribes that occupied southern Russia between the fourth centuries, B.C. and A.D. Excellent horsemen and fierce fighters, Sarmatian women could not marry until they had killed at least one enemy in battle. Their conquest of the Scythians brought them into contact with the Greeks, whose storytellers found the concept of fierce warrior women and a matriarchal society irresistible.

Since the Sarmatians were of Iranian stock, liberally mixed with other nomadic tribes of central Asia, I had designed the Fantasyworld Amazons like their Eastern forebears. Queen Hippolyta, despite the Greek moniker, had been a thin, Eastern ascetic.

"Lord Riplakish." There was genuine warmth in her dulcet voice.

"Y-your Majesty?" I was trying to be polite but it was hard to not gape. The thin, pinched face had filled out, the chin had rounded; the long, ravens wings of blue-black hair had given way to coiled ringlets of bleached-blonde. Were it not for the eyes and voice I would have suspected a total impostor.

"That will be all, Lady Vashti," she murmured without glancing back.

To Stephanie's credit, she turned and walked away with only a hint of a storm.

"Lord Riplakish, I do believe my lady acquireth an interest in thee." This with a confidential smile as my "ex" passed out of earshot.

I tried to smile in return. "Really?" I remembered how, once, when I had tried to ford a river, a couple of crocodiles had developed a genuine interest in me.

"Whenever news cometh from Dyrinwall Forest, she payeth especial heed and, without exception, she inquireth thy doings."

"Gee, I'm touched." More like icy fingers up and down my spine. "But I'm sure, Your Majesty, that this isn't the reason you've called on me. What can I do for you? Another Dragon, perhaps?"

"Nay, nay. Nothing of the kind." She dismissed past favors with a regal wave of her hand. Amazons are honorable as a whole, but they hate to admit any debt to a man.

"But there be one small favor..." she continued.

I didn't like this. Queen Hippolyta would never ask anyone—especially a man—for help unless it was something her witches and warriormaids couldn't handle. And anything they couldn't handle was sure to be monumentally unpleasant. My facial muscles tugged at the corner of my smile where it was slipping.

"...not too terribly inconvenient for thee, I hope."

"Well, as a matter of fact, I was just heading for a long and rather consequential journey. The fates demand I be on the road within two days time."

"Oh?" She considered this news with deep consternation. "Then, perhaps, thou wilt pass nigh us?"

"No, Good Queen; I fear not. My immediate destination is Shibboleth, and then I am bound for Gaehill."

Her face immediately brightened. She clapped her hands. "Good! Good! Precisely the direction my legates travel. I would charge thee with their escort."

"Escort?"

"Thou'rt expert of that territory and we have need of a guide thus far north. Prithee, wouldst thou aid them to their destination?"

"Which is?"

"Daggoth's Tower."

This time my smile slipped without immediate recovery. "Daggoth's Tower?"

She inclined her head. "We have—a—business—with the dark sorcerer. I believe he is a friend of yours?"

"A slight acquaintance, perhaps. Nothing more." *Yeah, right: Daggoth the Dark—Michael Straeker's avatar!* While I wasn't too keen on running into his Computer-animated avatar now that Mike was dead, I had to consider that, even as a Computer-drone, Daggoth the Dark might well prove an important source of information...

"My envoys will join thee on the morrow, Lord Riplakish. We shall ensorcel them as far as Dyrinwall, whence they will accompany thee ahorse."

There was no point in protesting. It might even prove to be a lucky break in certain ways. "How many in your party, Majesty?" Now, more than ever before, there was safety in numbers.

"Eight," she answered. "Thou wilt find the first six tomorrow. My daughter Aeriel and an Elfling are somewhere north and will join up in time."

My smile came back. "Aeriel? I haven't seen that little tyke for a long time. Does she still require four matrons to hold her in the tub for her bath?"

The Queen laughed. "Nay. She was but eleven or twelve then, and much undisciplined." She covered her mouth with a sly hand. "I think thou wilt find her much changed."

"Anyone else I know coming?"

"Five of my finest warriors, the Ladies Fianna, Tuiren, Dyantha, Hathor, and Palys—but medoubts thou knowest them. And I deem it wise to send a priestess, as well…"

I swallowed. "A priestess?"

"Yes. And since she has expressed some interest in thee…my Lord Riplakish! Whatever is the matter?"

#

"I don't like it any better than you do!" Vashti gritted an hour after receiving the news herself. Traveling with me actually seemed to appall her more than the threat of the Program Anomaly.

"I doubt you could possibly like it less than I do," I rejoined testily.

"You underestimate my loathing."

I dropped a swath of gauze over the crystal.

"What's that?" was her slightly muted inquiry.

"A filter. I hoped it would make conversations with you a bit more tolerable."

"Does it work?" she sneered.

"Not nearly as well as this one." I dropped the black silk over the occult sphere, ending the conversation and started to get up. Another muffled voice broke the silence.

"Breaker one-nine, break one-nine!"

I peeked under the cloth. It was Marilith.

Now, Marilith was rather attractive—if you weren't put off by her additional four arms and that serpent's tail. But then, most Demonesses tend to the exotic and you have to be prepared to deal with that.

Her favorable physical assets aside (and she had those, too), I admired Marilith for her amazingly cheerful disposition—no small accomplishment when you're executive secretary for the Lord of the Undead. I pulled off the covering.

"This is Octopussy, calling the Bashful Bard. C'mon Bard!"

I grinned as I leaned back in my chair. Maybe I could pump Orcus for information without having to go to Hell after all. "C'mon Octopussy, you got the Bard."

She batted her long-lashed pink eyes at me. "Hello Rip. Long time no see."

"Likewise, Beautiful. When are you coming to visit, now that the Banns seem to be lifted?"

She pouted prettily. "Too cold up there." She smiled seductively: "Why don't you come down here?"

"Too hot. I perspire something terrible."

"You big Sissyphus!" She sighed and the smile faded a bit. "Well, even if the temperature was right, I don't have a day off until the turn of the century. And no vacation time for a couple of millennia."

"You're kidding."

"Rip, honey; this place ain't called Hell for nothing."

I didn't know what to say so I got right down to business. "Ol' Horn-head want me?"

She nodded. "Try and be polite this time. You get him all riled up and we have the Devil to pay!"

It was only with a great deal of self-restraint that I allowed that opening to pass. A moment later his goat-headed visage filled the crystal ball.

"My, my; Orcus! As I live and breathe!"

As infernal Prince of the Undead, that opening line had never failed to bug him. This time, however, he let it pass. "Well met, Riplakish. We have business to discuss."

"So I've been told. Hasn't anyone ever told you never send Demons to do a Devil's job?"

He nodded. "Just testing. Ten years of idleness is a long time. Since your retirement into Dyrinwall, many True Spirits have entered the world. In the passing of the years and the coming of these new Gameplayers, the exploits of the Archdruid of Dyrinwall have been largely forgotten. I wished to know if you could handle the task I have for you."

"Better for you to wonder if I *would* handle the task you have for me."

He refused to be baited. "There has entered into the Master Program a—how would you call it? An Anomaly."

"What about it?" I asked. I guess he had the better bait.

"At first I was amused." He pulled at his goatish beard. "That True Spirits should find themselves subject to True Death as much as the rest of us was deliciously ironic. No longer able to bail out of your avatar at the moment of extreme pain or death, I expect that Fantasyworld will no longer prove so amusing to your Gamester friends."

"So?" I was being deliberately rude now to cover my dismay: till now, none of us had had any inkling of the Program's degree of self-awareness. "If you've called me up just to gloat, you're wasting your time, Old Shoe: I came back after I knew the score. And so have some others. And we're going to set things straight before anyone else is even aware of this little problem. Just a word about getting in my way, though," I added, "*don't!*"

Orcus smiled: picture, if you will, Carlsbad Caverns with stalactites and stalagmites done in ivory. "You are anticipating interference from me and my people?"

"Didn't I just hear you say how amusing you find this new setup?"

"Yes." He steepled taloned fingers. "As I said, at first I was amused. It seemed only fitting that Dreamers would have to 'play' by the same rules of life and death as everyone else. Then I realized that this Program change was not likely to be an intentional one…"

"Not bloody likely."

"…Or, if it isn't an accident and it is intentional, then it has most likely been done without prior majority consent."

"Sabotage?" Up till now I hadn't really taken the idea seriously.

"Why not? There are a variety of ways to gain access to the Program and alter it. A Dreamwalker's presence in this world, for instance. Every action a Dreamwalker takes alters the progression of events and alternatives, and that alters the status of the Master Program at any given moment. Am I right? The more power a Dreamwalker wields, the greater the changes he can enact throughout the Program."

"Granted," I granted. "But we're talking a whole different level of Program change when we start dealing with system lockouts and terminal biofeedback! Are you saying that a Dreamwalker is capable of that kind of Matrix manipulation?"

"Doubtful. For the average Dreamwalker to alter the Program so radically from within the Program text—the *average* Dreamwalker, that is…"

"But there are exceptional Dreamwalkers for whom it might be possible?"

Orcus nodded. "That possibility exists with at least three Dreamlords."

"There are no Dreamlords."

"There are three," he insisted. "Three beings who might have sufficient influence over the Matrix to metamorphose the entire System."

"Then we have three suspects."

The Prince of the Undead shook his gross head. "Perhaps two suspects. Perhaps only one. The avatars in question are Daggoth the Dark, Alyx Silverthane, and Riplakish of Dyrinwall."

I shook my head in protest. "*I* didn't do it."

"I didn't say that you did. I merely said that you were one of the three Dreamlords capable of Matrix manipulation."

I was intrigued by this new tack. "And who is this Silverthane?"

"An Elven sorceress of great power. Other than that, I can only guess that she is the avatar for the new Chief of Programming."

"Dr. Quebedeaux?" I rubbed my chin. "Yeah, that would fit."

"Other than that, she is a complete unknown to me. I'm having her watched. If I come across any useful information, be assured I will send it on to you."

"Yeah?" I pounced. "I know some useful information that you can pass along right now."

"And that is?"

"The whereabouts of Walter Hanson."

Orcus' expression went blank. "Who?"

I fought back a sigh: if he was faking ignorance, he was a devilishly good actor. "Walter Hanson. He was kidnapped from another programworld by Goblins. I want to know who has him and where he's being held." I decided against identifying Hanson's congressional status: the Prince of the Undead already knew far too much for my liking.

The demon prince shrugged. "I'll look into it for you, if you like. They're bothersome little twits, but I really think that Goblins are the least of your concern, right now." He leaned forward. "Getting back to the subject at hand, I believe that, out of the aforementioned Dreamlords, you have two suspects to consider."

"Or one, actually. Mike Straeker is dead."

"But Daggoth the Dark is not."

"Meaning what? Without a live Dreamwalker to endue it, the avatar comes under the Computer's control—"

"Daggoth isn't."

"Daggoth isn't what?"

"Under Computer control."

"Ridiculous!" I sputtered. "Straeker is dead. No Dreamwalker can endue another person's avatar!"

"At least they couldn't under the original strictures of the Program," Orcus observed. "But we are no longer dealing with known parameters."

"But you are saying that Daggoth is a True Spirit?" I asked, trying to qualify his previous statement.

"Insufficient data. But I do know that Daggoth is not a Computer-drone at this time. And there is—something—that you may not be aware of. Michael Straeker died of complications involving a brain tumor..."

"Yesterday's news," I countered absently. On top of the bombshell of the Program's self-awareness, I was being told that Constructs also had access to information on the outside. Victor von Frankenstein's problems might well have been minor inconveniences by comparison.

"...and was in symbiotic taction with his avatar at the moment of clinical death."

There was a mental thunderclap between my ears. "You're telling me that Straeker was invested in Daggoth when his real body terminated?"

"Affirmative."

"Then..." I paused to get the right words. "The psyche—or the intellect—"

"The soul," prompted Orcus.

"—of Michael Straeker may have survived his bodily death!"

"Possibly." Orcus was nodding again. "And this circumstance, in and of itself, may have had some far-reaching effects on the Matrix."

"Couldn't any death—"

"It has never happened before. Besides, you ignore the implications of these three incarnations on this plane."

"Implications?"

"You wrote *The Kishkumen Chronicles,*" he clarified, counting each point off with a taloned finger. "You and Straeker programmed The Machine and created the Master Program for Fantasyworld. Straeker and Quebedeaux have Chief Programmer status *inside* the Program as well as out." His expression was disturbingly thoughtful. "Can you think of any better candidates for godhood in this world?"

"Thanks for the vote of confidence, Orc old buddy, but all this backslapping doesn't seem to track with your amusement over the Dreamwalkers' new death-sentence. Why the sudden change in attitude?"

Orcus looked uneasy. "As I have said, we were amused, at first—"

"We?"

"Myself and...some others. Program self-awareness is not widespread, but there are others..." He let the sentence trail off enigmatically. "And it finally occurred to us that, as the current situation must be intolerable to the majority of your Dreamwalkers, they might pressure the Powers That Be into rectifying the Program Anomaly."

"That's why I'm here," I remarked with false cheeriness.

"That is the approach we had hoped for. Another solution might be to shut down the Computer."

"No sweat. In that event you'd be frozen in Memory Storage until Dreamworlds went back on line again."

"Perhaps. Perhaps not. Would you care to have your existence turned off with the flip of a switch? And tinkered with by Beings who haven't the remotest interest in you?" he snarled. "Besides, the Anomaly may prove too intricate to extract from the warp and woof of this world: what if they decide to discard the Program and start a new one from scratch?"

I read an alien emotion in his eyes, now. With a start, I suddenly realized it was fear. As an artificially created intelligence, he could not hope for an afterlife—some kind of Heaven or Hell—beyond the existence of the Program, itself. Just nothingness...

"So what do you want me to do?" I asked.

"What you've come back to do: set things a'right."

"Setting things right may involve a lot more than restoring the Master Program to its original format. It may mean greater changes in the Matrix than have previously been realized."

Orcus nodded. "We had anticipated that. Fantasyworld is not a pure derivative from your books, but a bastardization. After the Corporation acquired the rights to_*The Kishkumen Chronicles* and had your original Program to work from, they added to the Master Program from other sources, other concepts, and other writers."

I nodded. "They made changes."

"The corporation prefers to think of them as 'enhancements.' In any event, over half the Program is still your brainchild."

I shrugged. "Big deal. Nearly half of the Program accounts for trees, rocks, and general landscaping."

"Be that as it may, you still possess great power and influence in this Frame. But, as much as you may desire to repaint the total picture as you go, you must realize that any tampering with the overall Program may put us in even worse circumstances than we find ourselves in now."

"I'll fall off that bridge when I come to it," I murmured.

"That's what we're afraid of. Which is why I'm sending you some help."

I groaned. "What are you, my mother? I came back planning on keeping a low profile! You want to help? Find Walter Hanson for me!"

"Well, Riplakish, from long experience I know better than to sit here and argue with you."

"Good."

"So I'll leave you with this piece of advice: expect the first when the clock strikes 'one.' Ciao, Bard!"

#

A two-hour scan of all the known Goblin strongholds yielded nothing on the missing senator. And every attempt to use my programmer status to fix the Anomaly met with seeming indifference on the part of the Matrix, itself. I know that sounds a bit paranoid, but every so often I had to fight the impression that the Program itself was toying with me.

Misty entered the room while I was locking the crystal ball in a small chest at the back of my closet. "I'm not taking any more calls today, Kid." I threw some blankets over the chest and then closed and locked the doors as a final measure.

"When art thou leaving, my lord?"

"If I had any sense, I'd either leave now or not at all." I stopped and listened for a moment, almost imagining muffled voices emanating from the closet. I walked back to my desk where I'd be out of imaginary earshot. "But I guess I'll hang around until tomorrow and see if the Fifth Fleet shows up."

THREE

I had forgotten how to travel light. When the lists were finished and the gear was gathered, I decided that—with judicious packing—I might need only three mules.

Misty Dawn made herself scarce early in the day, pleading personal business, and I had let her go as her heart clearly wasn't in helping me on my way. Besides, I was a big boy now, and I figured I could pack my own toothbrush without any assistance.

Except I couldn't find my toothbrush.

In the end I deferred to Stumpy on the packing and provisioning.

Stumpy was an irascible old Dwarf who had accompanied me on all my past campaigns as a sort of combination cook, squire, and man-at-arms. He was a good companion on the open road—if you didn't mind a constant stream of invective aimed at anyone and anything that didn't sit right with his hair-trigger temper. He cooked like a master chef and wielded a cast-iron skillet beyond the mere culinary applications: more than a few Orcs had gone to their eternal punishment with the outline of Stumpy's frying pan embedded in their skulls.

Leaving the details to Stumpy vastly simplified the remainder of my day, but by sunset I was more than ready to climb into bed for the last peaceful sleep I could anticipate for some time to come. Prolonged crystal gazing is tiring and I had spent hours on inquiries and networking through various arcane information systems. Having exhausted my initial leads as well as myself, I had no alternative but to hit the road in the morning and try to stir up some fresh clues.

Misty Dawn turned up just as I was pulling on my nightshirt.

"My lord?"

"C'mon in, kid; I'm decent."

She entered hesitantly and I noticed that she'd spent some time on her appearance. Tonight she was wearing a longer slip of darker, more obscuring blue material rather than the transparent scrap of gauze that was her usual semi-attire. She looked ready to attend a sylvan ball and I suddenly wished that matters were not so pressing.

I wished that I might stay and discover why I feared the face of a woman who was—for all intents and purposes—dead. I wished a thousand impossible things and denied them all with my next breath: "Got a date tonight?"

Her look of frustration lasted only a moment. She came to me and grasped my hand, gently, softly, but with a strength that defied anything to pry her loose. "Walk with me, my lord."

I gently mussed her hair. "Hey, what have I told you about that 'my lord' stuff? After business hours we're on a first name basis around here."

She shook her head gently and her hair floated gently into place. "T'would not be seemly..." She stopped as she realized that she was being sidetracked. "Please," she pleaded, "thou wilt be gone after the morrow!"

And may be for good, her eyes added.

"I'm awfully tired, kiddo..." Her eyes were beginning to glisten again. "Okay, okay; a little walk might be just the thing for a good sound sleep tonight. Let me change into something a little more practical, though."

She released my hand but made no move to leave the room.

"Out! Shoo! I promise not to sneak down the back stairs. Scout's honor!" I ushered her bodily out of the room and drew the curtains across the doorway. While I changed, I noticed that those curtains seemed to move a little, but that may have been the wind or just my lurid imagination.

I donned a light tunic and breeches, eschewing the chainmail I had worn the night before, and slipped my feet into soft buskins. But I buckled on a belt and scabbard and slid my scimitar into place, now mindful of Dyrinwall's—and my—new vulnerability.

#

The moon was full and bright tonight, and a myriad of stars blazed across the sable sky. Even in the darkest covert of the woodlands, foxfire glowed and the glowworm and firefly flickered. The scent of jasmine and honeysuckle lay heavily on the warm night air and the nightsong of cricket and frog had a strange calming effect, conspiring to lower my guard the farther we walked.

It was a night made to order for romance and I cursed myself for walking, eyes open, into this tender trap. I waited for M.D. to take some advantage of the heady atmosphere, but she seemed preoccupied, her thoughts elsewhere.

We walked in silence until we came to the Faerie's Dance.

I stood at the edge of the mystic ring while Misty walked to its center. She turned in a swirl of blue and silver and stretched out her arms. "Come," she said in a dreamer's voice. "Come dance with me."

"We're trespassing—"

"'Tis a'right. I have their leave. And thou hast always their good will."

"You set this up?"

She shrugged. "What matter? 'Tis thy last night in Dyrinwall: come dance at the forest's heart! Dance with me." She beckoned earnestly. "Please?"

It seemed there was little I could deny her this night: I stepped into the circle. "What about music?" I asked.

She stepped into my arms and inclined her head upon my chest. "It will come," she whispered.

And we danced.

I wasn't quite sure when the music started, but suddenly it was there; softly, at first, but growing and swelling with every step and swirl. We were no longer alone. The Faerie had come, joining us in the dance.

At first I stepped cautiously, fearing I might injure one of these diminutive cousins to the Elves. But soon I was oblivious to all but my own partner. The Faerie knew our rhythm as intimately as their own; danced point to our counterpoint. The music swelled, the dance increased in tempo and participants and, soon, Faerie couples were taking to the air on gossamer wings where they tripped the light fantastic around and about our heads.

When the music finally ended, they parted to form a pathway to the circle's edge. Misty took my hand as we stepped across the circle's rim and led me through forest privacy to a couch of moss-upholstered stone under a canopy of saplings and creepers. There she laid me down with my head upon her lap. For the longest time, neither of us spoke.

"I was wrong," she said finally. "It hath not changed, even though thou'rt become a True Spirit. I love thee. I shall wait for thee and give to thee all that I vowed." She looked away. "Perhaps thou wilt return, for thou belongest here—not only in Dyrinwall

Wood—but in this world, upon this plane. True love eluded thee in that place whence thou didst come. But thou mayest find it herein…" It was not so much a pause as a beat in the cadence of her speech, and yet it seemed an emptiness in time that went on and on. "…and, meantime, I will give thee mine," she finished finally.

I opened my mouth but no words would come.

"Hush." She laid a hand lightly over my lips. "I know thou canst not find true love with one who is not a True Spirit. Especially with a Nymph who is not a mortal woman and cannot bear thee children.

"But I have arms that ache to hold, to embrace; breasts that were made for a lover's kisses and a babe's suckling. I was made for fleshly love and filled with desires to fulfill men's longings."

She groaned. "I am forever cursed. For being Elemental, I shall live throughout eternity—giving sips to a progression of strangers from my own well of need—a well that, by my very nature, must overflow and drown me if I withhold myself too long…

"Misty—"

"Unfair!" she cried. "Why was I made for such desires and yet forever denied their true fulfillment? What crimes have I committed against the gods?

I closed my eyes. *Damn Cephtronics! Damn the Dreamland board of directors!* I had warned, threatened—pleaded with them—told them we had no right to create cybernetic life and then play games with it! Got myself booted off the project and out of the corporate structure, thinking myself released from responsibility in the process. But *I* was the Creator and here was *my* handiwork demanding an accounting from me.

She began to weep and I took her hands in mine.

"Misty," I whispered, "humanity does not guarantee the things you say you ache for. Untold millions live out empty, desperate lives. Unfulfilled. And denied your immortality and your elemental life-force, they must suffer and scratch for survival. Humanity woos pain and courts the grave. Would you add these burdens to your others?"

She nodded slowly, truthfully. "Aye. For what is immortality without *true* life?"

"And, for this, you are willing to risk everything—even existence itself?"

She inclined her head.

"Very well." I steeled myself and bent my mind to the Program Matrix—summoned my Authority Access Code to the front of my consciousness and began impressing my will on the infrastructure.

"I give unto thee new life!" I pronounced, "True life!" I pushed with my mind, my heart, and my very soul. "Take upon yourself humanity. Be mortal!"

As Misty Dawn was probably more my own than anything else in the entire Program, I had sufficient authority: the Matrix bent and *re-formed.*

Eternity shuddered…nearly shattered.

For a timeless instant I felt the increased strain on the very fabric of the Program Reality. And I was suddenly cognizant that any more program shuffling or magic use of that magnitude might well be enough to collapse the Matrix in its present, fragile state.

Shaken, I turned my attention to the results of my sudden impulse.

The change was subtle yet apparent: Misty Dawn was no longer a Nymph and Dryad, but a beautiful mortal woman. And her beauty was increased by the joy of growing realization. She clapped her hands. She laughed and danced with delight. *Not only Nicole's face, but her mannerisms, as well.*

She kissed me.

"My lord Riplakish!" she cried. "Thou'rt a god! I shall love thee as long as life remaineth in me! I shall bear thee many children! I shall make every day of thy life—"

"Misty!" I barked, and she stopped in accustomed obedience, wide-eyed at the sudden sternness in my expression.

"I told you that humanity carries no guarantees," I explained more gently. "I cannot marry you. You are not—a True Spirit. That is something beyond my ability to bestow. I cannot grant what is not mine to give."

It was a blow. Her eyes were like a child's who had just unwrapped a precious gift only to have it snatched away. But she was not easily dissuaded. "Then give me what thou canst of thy love!" she pleaded. "Give to me thy child! If thou wilt marry another, then so be it. I will be content with that."

I shook my head.

"As thy mistress I will see that thou hast the best of both worlds! Thou wilt never find a better lover! Though I am a Nymph no longer, I can still—"

I grasped her shoulders and swung her around as if I could physically shake some sense into her. "Stop it!" I said. "You're still thinking like a Nymph! I've freed you from that!"

She suddenly jerked in my grasp and looked at me with a strange and awful expression.

"What's wrong?" I asked. "Misty? What is it?"

She looked down slowly, stupidly, and I followed her gaze.

Her cleavage was every bit as marvelous as before, but now I noticed the glistening, red diamond between her breasts. Except it wasn't a gem and she wore no necklace for it to hang from. I didn't recognize it for what it was until she began to slump in my arms and I could see the arrow's shaft protruding from her back.

I looked up in time to see two Goblin archers, each drawing another arrow. As I lowered her to the ground, two more shafts whizzed over my head. I dived, rolled and came up on my feet with my sword drawn.

I cut the first Goblin on the run and in a hot rage, decapitating him in my wrath. The second Goblin was ready for me as I turned. My fury turned cold blooded now and I adopted the samurai *Tai No Sen* to compensate for his simultaneous attack. The enchanted blade of my scimitar sliced through bow, arm, leather armor, and flesh as smoothly as if they were empty illusions. I was turning away before he could realize that I had already killed him.

A third bushwhacker, a Hobgoblin, was running into the trees, but the weight of his armor and his unfamiliarity with Dyrinwall's terrain guaranteed that he would not get far. I started after him with a determined tread: this one would die, too.

But not before he told me what I wanted to know.

He screamed once: a guttural cry of terror turned to pain and ended abruptly. Though an inner voice told me there was no longer any hurry, I broke into a run.

I found his crushed and trampled body about a hundred yards down the path. A pale woman, wearing a red cloak, sat astride a horse blacker than my darkest dreams, not three feet from the corpse.

"Thou'rt Riplakish?" Her voice was whispery soft like an autumn wind.

I nodded, too angry to speak; she had terminated my only source of information about the attack and denied me my vengeance.

"I am Lilith. Lord Orcus hath sent me." The Demoness was pale and slender with dead white hair, the color of bleached bones, and eyes that glittered like frosted ice. Her mount was a Nightmare, a demonhorse with fangs, blood-red eyes, and iron hooves that struck sparks from the rocks.

Intriguing. But I wasn't in the mood for company and I told her so.

"Then I will rejoin thee upon the morrow. 'Ware the Goblins." Her lips curled into something between a smile and a sneer as she turned her mount and rode away to deeper darkness.

I stared for a moment and then walked back to the stone couch with an equally stony heart. There was no hurry now: there would be plenty of time to do what was left to be done.

My heart eased as I knelt and beheld Misty's face. Perhaps this was her best answer—her mortal wounding having begun so many years before.

She was finally at peace.

#

I learned three things in the long hours remaining before the dawn. That, although I could access enough power to rattle the Program Matrix itself; I could neither raise the dead, locate a missing senator, nor unclench a heart made wary and untrusting by too many disappointments.

As if to underscore that last realization, my ex-wife found me the following morning in the sacred glen between the silver brook and the Ring where the Fairies dance.

The mid-morning sun had warmed the dark earth and a ring of white stones now lay among the edelweiss, moss, and ivy. I was planting vines when a horse approached and I paused to watch as Princess Vashti rode into the clearing.

She reined up as soon as she saw me and sat astride her mount, watching as I returned to my task, pointedly ignoring her presence. The silence didn't last for long; Stephanie had never been able to stand any kind of quiet that lasted for more than sixty seconds.

"Well, well, well; if it isn't Johnny Appleseed! I didn't know you had taken up gardening as a hobby. But I guess grubbing around in the dirt would come naturally to you."

"I'm not in the mood, Stephanie," I said without turning. "Go back to the tree and wait. I'll join you within the hour."

"We're in a hurry, Rippy. You can leave the gardening to that little woodland strumpet while we're gone."

I turned on that. And her smile died when she saw the look in my eyes. Without another word, she turned her horse and rode back the way she had come. I was alone again.

I took my time, now. For perhaps Misty Dawn had been right when she had said that I would not return. There was no reason to return now.

Except to bring flowers to honor her. And burn candle and incense to warm her and tuck her in more securely…

FOUR

"Nobody said nothin' 'bout draggin' a bunch a wimmin along!"

Stumpy had intercepted me halfway along the path back to Misty's Tree, his facial expressions fluctuating between fury and disgust.

"Now Stumpy," I placated, "they're not helpless ladies of leisure. They're Amazons: they'll probably drag us along instead of vice versa."

The old Dwarf was not much mollified. "Well, I ain't gonna cook fer 'em! And if arrows start flyin' ev'ry which way, they'd best look out fer theirselves! I ain't got no time or energy *or* provisions fer no sight-seein' tourists—'specially wimmin!"

"I told you, Stump; it's just as far as Daggoth's Tower. They'll fend for themselves. We're just acting as guides—"

A sudden sound broke off the discussion: the very loud, very near buzz of a rattlesnake poising to strike. *Rattlesnake? In Fantasyworld?* It was less than four feet away.

"Stump?"

The old Dwarf dug his tongue deep into a bulging cheek, grimaced, and spat. A large brown wad caught the rattler right between its beady little eyes. It rolled over in surprise.

"Scat!" he snarled. And then calmly lifted his long, white beard to search through his beltpouch for more chaw. Putting on one of my practiced looks of unconcern, I watched the snake slither hastily away while Stumpy continued his diatribe against "wimmin", "wizzerds", and "pakkin geer".

#

The Amazons were waiting and travel-ready when we entered the clearing around the giant oak. Against all logic and reason my eyes passed over the other five without really seeing and focused once again on my ex-wife.

Stephanie's avatar was so close to her actual physical appearance that it was hard to think of her as Princess Vashti. She still wore her honey-blonde hair long, and gathered it at the nape of her neck in a thick rope that fell to her waist. Her eyes were still that distinct color of periwinkle and her nose still slightly snubbed. For all of her dissatisfaction with her own appearance, she refused to use mnemonic processing to alter her avatar. She kept the detested hint of freckles across her too-fair skin and refused to burgeon her slender body with the voluptuous bust and hips her competitive ego secretly coveted. She was what she was, and if you didn't like what you saw…tough.

Even if I no longer loved her, I could admire her for that.

The second figure on horseback was also uncomfortably familiar: Natasha Skovoroda had found my back door into the Program. I wasn't quite sure if I should feel grateful for her added presence: I would feel a great deal safer with her sword at my back.

As long as I could count on it to not end up in same.

"Well met, Lord Riplakish." Natasha's voice brought me back from my musings.

"I give you greetings, Lady—" I arched my brow in query.

"Dyantha. And may I present the Warriors Fianna, Hathor, Palys, and Tuiren," she added with a nod to each of the four Amazons who were studying me, in turn, from their saddles. "I believe that you are already acquainted with Lady Vashti."

I started to nod affably and then hesitated as I took second notice of the one Dyantha had called Palys.

While the others wore costumes that looked more like matching pairs of windchimes, Palys wore a leather jerkin and pants. Her outfit, however, seemed to be tailored for a smaller woman. The *cuir-bouilli* jerkin fit her more like a vest than a split breastplate: where it should have closed down the front, it gaped a good two inches. Crisscrossed leather thongs kept it from opening any further and that was fortunate because this Amazon was Junoesque and Juno was bustin' out all over. Dark, tawny skin, the color of coffee and cream, a wild cascade of smoke-brown hair, and a face that seemed sculpted for pure sensuality; an unearthly, elemental beauty—as if someone had dragged the physical concept of the perfect woman from my subconscious libido and crafted her in the flesh.

A rush of hormones was followed by a sudden surge of guilt. What was I thinking of? Misty Dawn was barely cold in the ground. Disgusted with myself, I pushed my indecorous thoughts aside and inclined my head. "Ladies, I bid you welcome: rest and refresh yourselves at this humble abode while I complete my preparations."

As I walked past to lead the way in, I managed an aside to Vashti: "You can come in, too."

#

I hurried upstairs while Stumpy grumbled off to the wine cellar to play reluctant host. My fingers trembled a bit as I worked the secret combination to a sealed cabinet in my workshop. Other than Orcus' cryptic assessment of Daggoth the Dark, I had no clues, no clear-cut paths to follow. Just a growing awareness that this was no longer a Game.

The cabinet doors swung back and I pulled two items from the shelves inside: insurance. I slipped the spectacle case into my vest pocket and tucked the mechanical mouse into a beltpouch. At the back of the cupboard was a glass case holding a slender verge of carved ivory; the placard inside read:

Wand of Xagyg
In case of Armageddon, break glass

I started to reach and then thought better of it. As shaky as the Program's infrastructure had become, the solution to the Anomaly was more likely to require the touch of a scalpel than the sweep of a chainsaw. I resealed the cabinet, spun the tumblers in the locks, and headed back to my chambers.

I gave my bedroom one last going over and moved the clockwork rodent from beltpouch to backpack, tucking it in where my spare clothing provided some extra padding.

"Somehow, I expected the legendary Riplakish of Dyrinwall Forest to be a bit taller."

After Misty Dawn's unnerving manner of sneaking up on me, Natasha's—or rather, Dyantha's—sudden presence behind me didn't startle me in the least. I continued to pack my bedroll and saddlebags without turning. "There's an old saying among wizards, my dear: 'It's not the size of the wand, it's the magic that's in it.'"

She walked up behind me and slipped her arms around my waist. One hand strayed a bit. "I like your wand."

"No you don't," I contradicted mildly as I pulled her hands away. "You like me for my mind—all those Program secrets locked away in my brain. And since you've already raped me with scopolamine and deceit, don't try to romance me with sweet words and soft actions. Rape and romance don't mix."

"Oh, I do not know," she countered a little wistfully. "You men have been getting away with it for centuries."

I finished loading my saddlebags and cinched them up.

"Look," she said, walking around and sitting on the end of my bed. "I am sorry! I feel badly. But my superiors are desperate men: they were pressuring me to get the information as quickly as possible! I did not wish to hurt you. Or see you hurt by anyone else."

I threw the saddlebags over my shoulder and walked over to fasten the shutters over the window-sized bole.

"I was running out of time and using the drug was kinder than letting the SVR question you," she continued as I worked my way around the room, making a last-minute check of the premises. "I really did want to spare you—"

"Thanks."

She got up and walked to the door. "I am sorry. Whether you believe that or not." She hesitated with her hand on the latch. "Perhaps I will find a way to make it up to you before this whole thing is over."

"I'll be waiting with bated breath," I murmured as she closed the door behind her.

#

I pulled the spectacles out of their case and put them on, tucking curled ends of the stems behind my ears. I looked at the lock I had just fastened to the door of Misty's tree. It looked the same. I touched my finger to the bridgepiece above my nose and the optics of Haroun al Rashid refocused. Now I was able to examine the inner workings of the locking mechanism. Another touch to the bridgepiece and I could see the multi-colored patterns of the Wizardbar spell I had cast on the door for security backup. Satisfied that the basic precautions were in place, I touched the bridgepiece again and turned toward the waiting assemblage.

At first glance there seemed no difference. Dyantha, Palys, Stephanie, Tuiren, and Stumpy all looked the same.

But Hathor's original appearance was now a ghostly background flicker. In her stead was a true image of the Dreamwalker who animated her avatar, a heavyset woman with a faint mustache and arms like a truck driver's. The chainmail "bikini" had expanded to compensate for the difference in body size but the overall effect just wasn't the same.

Turning my head, I found myself confronted with a more disparate dichotomy. Again, I could observe the ghostly image of the avatar preparing to mount but, as Fianna swung up into the saddle, I found myself observing a young man with a sandy, close-cropped beard and a slight but athletic build.

Well, why not? After all, didn't we all come here to be something we weren't in the outside world? I removed the enchanted eyeglasses and tucked them back into their case in my vest pocket.

The Amazons all rode war-horses. My mount, by comparison, looked vastly out of his league. Ghost had the appearance of a dapple-gray mare and only seemed large by comparison to Stumpy's mount, a Shetland pony named Hermione, and Buttercup, the pack mule.

But appearances were, in this case, deceiving: some ten years before I had paid Brisbane the Illusionist to work a powerful glamour on my hard won destrier. Ghost was one of the few remaining Pegasi, a winged horse of the heavens. For a small fortune, old Brisby had ensorceled my mount to appear as an old, gray, mundane mare. The illusion was perfect as long as we remained on the ground but, in flight, his wings became visible, his gray coat turned snowy white, and his true nature became apparent. As I was fond of remarking to Stumpy on those rare occasions, the old gray mare ain't what she seems to be.

I mounted now, careful to avoid the invisible wings folded along his flanks, and clipped a couple of restraining straps from the saddle to corresponding rings in my belt. Cinching the tethers to allow a minimum of slack, I looked up to find six pairs of eyes watching with undisguised curiosity. The Amazons were obviously taken aback by the design of my saddle.

"Keeps me from falling off," I explained lamely. Maybe it wasn't very macho, but I preferred the extra security during any sudden forays a hundred feet or more into the air.

I couldn't explain, however, without undermining a secret advantage and, as they looked away, I could see that I had just lost more than a few points from my respect rating.

I turned my mount toward the eastern path and immediately reined up. There was a turtle entering the clearing. Normally I would have ridden on but this particular turtle was about three-and-a-half feet tall, walked more or less erect on its hind legs, and carried a book under one of its—uh—arms.

We all sat ahorse and stared as it crossed the clearing and ambled on up to me—a process that seemed to take a half hour.

"Um, you Riplakish of Dyrinwall?" it asked after carefully giving me the once over.

"Who wants to know?" Talking terrapins don't normally make me nervous but these were the times that tried men's trust.

"Uh, welp, Daggoth the Dark sent me. He said to give you this." He offered the leather-bound book.

I reached down and took the volume. "What is it?"

"Daggoth's personal journal. He, uh, said that you were to hold on to it for him. He said that if you didn't hear from him within two weeks that you should read it and..."

"And what?" I prompted.

"Um, well, I don't rightly know." The turtle scratched his head. "He really thought that he'd be picking it up within the two week period..." His voice trailed off.

An unpleasant thought occurred: "And how long have you been traveling since he charged you with this task?"

"Um, welp, let's see. I think it's been about twenty days, now..."

That sounded ominous. I tucked the book into my left saddlebag. "Would you like a ride back with us?"

The turtle, it seemed, had already given the matter some thought. "If you're traveling that way...and it's all the same to you folks...I think I'd just as soon head back on my own and let you get there first..."

#

We rode through Dyrinwall double-file with myself in the lead and Stumpy bringing up the rear. Since neither Vashti nor Dyantha seemed comfortable in my presence, they rode together and toward the back of the party. As it happened, Palys fell in beside me. Without appearing haughty or aloof, she gave the impression of someone who spoke little and, indeed, it was nearly an hour before I first heard the sound of her voice.

"Where is your transponder?" she asked, referring to the activation device that Dreamwalkers wore to signal the recording mode in the DreamNet. Since many DreamNet adventures were broadcast over the various networks for mass audience experience, Dreamwalkers not only needed a means of recording what they wanted to share with the outside world, they also needed a certain amount of privacy from time to time. Dreamwalkers who did not want to be linked with a potential audience of hundreds of thousands merely thumbed a microswitch in the device (usually disguised in the form of a ring) and no public record would be made, no broadcast sent of their activities until they chose to thumb the switch back on again.

Of course, every Dream had its share of exhibitionists who felt they had nothing to hide from their adoring public—how many paramours they bedded, personal toilettes, changing clothes (if any)—you pays your money, you gets your peek.

"I don't wear one," I told her. Which was not so easy as it sounds: Cephtronics insisted on programming transponders into each Programworld for every Dreamer. Aside from all commercial considerations, it made everyone easier to keep track of.

The unvoiced question was in her eyes.

"I play for my own satisfaction—not for an audience," I explained. Plus, I disliked the feeling of Big Brother peering over my shoulder every single minute.

She nodded with an understanding smile.

Dyantha spoke. "So that is why there are no stored Memories of your Character available. Except where you have passed through another Player's recording. All the old Dreamwalkers said that you were a legend—real, that is, but still a legend!"

"A legend in his own mind," I heard Vashti mutter.

"I had some doubts about your reputation when no one could turn up any substantial Memory Records," Dyantha concluded.

I sighed. "Aside from valuing our privacy, we living legends don't hold up so well under continual scrutiny."

I half expected my ex to add amen to that, but she was unusually quiet. I turned to Palys and asked her where her recording device was.

"I don't wear one, either," she answered with a slow smile.

#

The Amazons seemed anxious to travel with some speed, but, knowing that there were new and unknown dangers inherent in the Program, I opted for a cautious and conservative pace. The Anomaly was not likely to be solved nor Senator Hanson rescued by our rushing headlong to some disaster. Aside from meeting the Rabble in Shibboleth and visiting Daggoth's Tower, I had no solid plans. What was needed now was some detective work—spending some time with ears and eyes open, reacquainting myself with the Fantasyworld milieu.

Plus I was just plain tired and wanted to get some rest before we ran into trouble.

We passed the boundaries of Dyrinwall Wood about midday, stopping only once to barter with some Elves who were baking cookies in a hollow tree. I had been away for more than five years and expected to find all sorts of unpleasant changes—but cookie-baking Elves? Either Cephtronics was altering the Subprograms in new and more bizarre directions or we had just stumbled across another manifestation of the Anomaly. Either way, there was nothing I could do about it for the moment.

And the cookies were good.

Come sundown the party camped in a shielded copse, about a mile from the road. Effectively there were two camps in terms of the cooking and sleeping arrangements, albeit side by side. In assigning guard duty, Vashti deferred to me.

"Is this considered hostile territory?" she asked.

Twilight was rapidly cloaking the surrounding countryside and I scanned the plains and distant hills for campfires. "Didn't used to be," I answered shortly. "But with sanctuary violated, who can say?"

"The question is do we post single sentries? Or double the guard on each watch?"

I deliberated a moment. "One person per watch should be sufficient—if they know what they're doing."

"Meaning?"

"If you have to ask, you won't be one of them."

She scowled. "Who died and made you God?"

I almost said 'Mike Straeker'. Instead, I bit my tongue and considered an apology.

She sighed heavily. "Okay, okay; you can dispense with the lecture and assign tonight's guards. I won't buck your choices as long as I'm one of them."

"So? The princess wants to pull her own weight?"

Her blush was visible even in the failing light. "Royalty is a job, too: somebody's got to do it." She folded her arms across her chest. "It doesn't mean I can't be useful at other tasks."

"Okay. You've got first watch. Prove yourself, and I'll promote you in another couple of nights."

"Rob..."

We both had started to turn away from each other when she spoke my name.

"What is it, Stephanie?"

"I just wanted to tell you—that I'm sorry."

I waited.

"I didn't know about your Nymph until after I saw the grave. Stumpy told me after I rode back to the Tree."

"Her name was Misty. Misty Dawn."

"Well, like I said; I'm sorry. I know it's hard to lose something you...care for."

The tension began to build between us, again.

"She was not some*thing*. She was some*one*."

"Well, for Crom's sake, she wasn't a *real* person! She was a computer-animated kewpie doll!"

"She was a real person, even if she wasn't a True Spirit! She had feelings and desires just like you and—"

Vashti snorted, and my growing annoyance bloomed into genuine anger.

"Even more than you, quite often," I added quietly. And turned away.

#

Can a Dreamwalker dream within the context of the Program? Experience a dream within The Dream? It was a question I had yet to answer. I awoke with no sense of time having passed since I had last closed my eyes.

Palys was kneeling beside me, her hand on my shoulder. The fires had nearly burned themselves out and the rest of the camp appeared to be sleeping soundly. I looked at her for an explanation. Then I heard the crackle of dry underbrush not too far outside our dim circle of light.

"Should I awaken the others?" she asked.

I nodded. "Stumpy first. And put more wood on the fires."

I moved to the edge of the firelight and cupped my hands together. Murmuring the requisite verse, I opened my palms and released a softly glowing ball of light that hung suspended in midair.

A few more spoken words and it expanded into a sphere of blue-white luminescence, slightly larger than my head.

I pointed in the direction of the last sound and the globe moved toward it. It stopped before it got halfway there.

It wasn't supposed to do that.

I gave it a telekinetic push and it moved several feet forward before it stopped again. This time something seemed to nudge it back a little. It had turned into a contest.

Declining my next turn at bat, I stood with my hands on my hips and waited.

Slowly, almost silently, a hooded figure rode into the light upon a silhouette of darkness. I recognized her even before she pulled the hood back from her face.

"Lilith."

"Well met, Riplakish."

"I was wondering when you were going to show up."

"I travel best by night."

"Well, travel right on back to Orcus and tell him 'thanks but no thanks.'"

Bleary-eyed, Dyantha walked over to stand beside me.

"Thou dost not understand, Mortal," Lilith replied with some asperity. "I have no will in this matter! I am under a *geas* to aid thee as best I can."

"Fine." I smiled. "Like I said, why don't you go back to Orcus—"

We were interrupted by a cry from Dyantha as an arrow caught her in the shoulder. Mottled fletching on the painted shaft gave me the archer's identity. "Goblins!" I yelled, gesturing at the fires.

With a *whump* and a *whoosh* the flames exploded upwards, dropping a fiery rain of flares over the countryside. Blazing embers illumined our surroundings and discomfited the Goblins who weren't quick enough to dodge. Vashti was slow to rise, but the rest of the Amazons, along with Stumpy and Lilith, had already drawn steel and waded into the fray.

I helped Natasha/Dyantha break the head from the arrow and draw the shaft from her shoulder while another glanced off my mail shirt. "You okay?" I asked.

She nodded, white-faced and tight-lipped. "It was not my sword arm," she gritted, hauling out her broadsword. "I will procure a Band-Aid when things settle."

"Fine," I said. And drawing my scimitar, I got a running start on a dozen or so Goblins heading our way.

Now Goblins are runty little nuisances and not exactly the most fearsome creatures in the *Who's Who* of Monsters. They're only really dangerous to a party like ours when they manage a surprise attack, in darkness (their natural element), and with vastly superior numbers.

Unfortunately, they seemed to be batting a thousand this particular night.

One thing bothered me as I sliced through a cluster of the ugly, misshapen creatures like a harvester through a field of ripe wheat: Goblins are not particularly intelligent or well organized. In the field, a Goblin army advances like a mob of unruly three-year-olds—no discipline, no sense of order, and only a very nominal chain of command that exercises its authority by screaming louder than the grunts in the vanguard.

Yet somehow these little buggers had managed to sneak up on us with an uncharacteristic degree of stealth and organization. I was betting that this assault was tied in with yesterday's attack back at the Faerie's Dance. And it couldn't be a personal grudge from the war of ten years before—Goblins just don't have that good a memory. Someone else was the brains behind this setup and, whoever he or she or they were, he/she/they wanted me dead.

It wasn't until I'd dispatched some thirty-odd Goblins that I remembered the witchlight. I located it above the battle after a couple of minutes and four more Goblins. Gaining a momentary respite, I crooked my finger at it. "You. C'mere."

It did.

"Listen," I said as the globe zipped in close, spooking a squad of Goblins in the process, "somewhere out there is the leader of these little twerps. I don't think it's a Goblin or Hobgoblin, but a Spellcaster of some sort. Go see if you can shed a little light on the matter."

The witchlight took off and I turned my attention back to a knot of Goblins who were regrouping for another mass rush.

The light swung back and forth across the battlefield, working its way toward the foothills. I followed, carving a path through the bogies with my scimitar. Seeing that I was making my way with some purpose in mind, the others in my party began working their separate ways toward the same direction.

Dyantha fell in behind me as the witchlight seemed to pause over a particularly thick knot of darkness off in the night. Then it swung off rapidly in the opposite direction, as if repelled by what it had found. I had to turn at that moment to give the red-tressed Amazon some assistance with a fresh batch of nasties that had regained some of their faltering courage. It didn't take long to convince them of their error.

In the midst of the melée, I suddenly realized that the light was now involved in a steady, purposeful movement back toward the campsite.

Back toward Vashti and Stumpy.

I suddenly became less concerned with slaying bogies and more concerned with beating that light back to the campfires. I turned, setting a new course across the field, and Goblins fell or scattered, gibbering before the glowing blade of my sword.

Long minutes passed as I plowed through a sea of nightmare creatures, Dyantha following in my wake, fending off the few remaining attackers to our rear. But no matter how hard we pressed, the light seemed to travel faster: it reached the campsite while we were still some fifty yards away.

Vashti reacted faster than I would have credited her: a nimbus of orange light framed her body, indicating a powerful protective spell.

The orange glow also illumined a robed figure moving purposefully forward, arms gesturing in counterspell.

Vashti had begun her own offensive spell now, but the leader of the Goblins finished his first: there was a tremendous flash of green light and my ex-wife's avatar fell to her knees, the orange aura disrupted and fading.

Dyantha's warning shout turned my attention to another figure.

This one was closer and was pulling a wand from his cloak. Wands are repositories of arcane energies and can be discharged much faster than spells woven by somatic gestures and verbal keys. I had no time to weave even the simplest of protection spells, my enchanted armor was my only protection against the mystic energies being thrown at me.

"No!" From out of nowhere Palys appeared, hurling me to the ground with her own body. Concussed by the juxtaposition of spell and body-slam I shook my head and struggled to lift it above a rising tide of black nausea. My vision cleared for a moment and I propped myself up to observe a heart-stopping tableau.

In the light of the twin campfires I could see two men, and they seemed to be arguing about something, Vashti lying between them like some contested prize.

Both had pushed back their hoods and I could see that the man with the wand wore an eyepatch and an expression of evil beyond anything that I had ever imagined. But it was the other face that truly frightened me: the face of a dead man that I knew all too well.

And as I watched in growing horror, Daggoth the Dark, the avatar of Mike Straeker, stooped down to gather Vashti into his arms. As he lifted her limp and unconscious body, the other man plucked a staff from one of his misshapen henchmen and raised it over their heads.

Thunder split the skies and sundered the earth. Darkness filled my eyes, my ears, my mind.

FIVE

It was light when I finally opened my eyes.

I sat up and instantly regretted the rashness of such action. I eased myself back down to the pair of saddlebags that provided a nominal cushion for my head.

A shadow fell across my face announcing company. "How d'you feel?" Stumpy's face swam into view. It was bruised and lumpier and, therefore, uglier than usual. The makeshift bandage around his head slipped down over one eye.

"Like an Orc who wandered into a Dwarven tavern by mistake," I croaked. "What about the others?"

"Princess Vashti's gone." He paused awkwardly. "I guess you already know thet."

"They took her."

He nodded. "Thet Demoness is gone, too. She hung around till first cockcrow an' then disappeared."

"And the rest?"

He looked around. "Couple a' them Amazonians—Hathor an' Tuiren—are in bad shape: Dyantha sent 'em back home with Fianna ridin' along ta wet-nurse 'em. Red's stayin', but she's got a couple a' cuts thet need tendin', an' I don't like the looks a' thet shoulder—I think it's gonna fester." He shook his head. "The other one—Palys—ain't got a scratch on 'er."

I started to rise again but the old Dwarf pushed me back down. "Yer not movin' till sunset! The only person here in any shape to travel is thet big Amazonian, an' she don't seem to be in no hurry." He pulled out a long-stemmed pipe and a pouch of pipeweed. "So here's the plan fer the next few days: rest by day, travel by night." He filled the pipe and began tamping it down. "Least till we get to Shibboleth."

"Yes, Mother," I replied meekly.

He looked at me impassively and then held out his pipe. "How 'bout a light?"

I snapped my fingers and produced a momentary wisp of flame from the end of my thumb. He lit the bowl and then blew out the flickering digit. "Thanks." He took a long draw and exhaled slowly. "You'll be needin' a new sword. Or swords—I unnerstand you like to use two, now."

"Sometimes."

"Better get a couple thet'll hold up better then this lump a' slag before we get to Daggoth's Tower." He held up what was left of my scimitar.

I looked at the bent and twisted metal that had once been a magic blade. "You said Palys is unhurt?"

He nodded speculatively. "Didn't even break a fingernail in bringin' ya down. Wanna talk to her?"

"Not right now." I was feeling very tired again. "I just want to rest for awhile longer."

"Okey." Stumpy handed me my waterskin and got up. "You do thet. I'll wake you afore the sun goes down." He wandered away to tend to the cooking fire.

I rolled over, propping myself up on an elbow. After the world stopped spinning, I pulled Daggoth's journal out of my saddlebag. The facts that he might still be a True Spirit, had my ex-wife as a hostage, and had nearly arranged my demise twice, had just bumped his diary to the top of my reading list.

My eyes, however, refused to focus and I had to postpone Mike's memoirs in favor of a very insistent nap. I lay back and closed leaden eyelids with a sigh. Rest and recovery were first on my agenda. Then I would tackle my list of questions.

#

By evening I was feeling better. For our assortment of cuts, bruises, and Goblin bites we applied an ointment that the Amazons had obtained from the Healers of the Bloody Cross.

Dyantha's arrow wound was proving more serious. It was too soon to tell whether the inflammation was due to an infection or if a toxic compound was at work. The best I could do for the moment was apply an herbal poultice and cross my fingers. While it was true that I had sufficient power to rattle the Program Matrix, as a bard, I lacked the skill and finesse to work a simple Healing spell.

Before breaking camp, I walked off and sought a secluded spot where I could work undisturbed for a bit. Over the hill and out of sight there was a small thatch of saplings and bushes where I could concentrate undisturbed. I crawled into the foliage and sat cross-legged on a patch of dry turf. Slowly, breathing deeply, I unwrapped a bundle of cloth I had pulled from my saddlebag and uncovered my crystal ball.

Emptying my mind of everything but the image of Stephanie's avatar, I stared into the glassy depths of the crystal and tried to focus on any ghostly echo of her presence. Long minutes passed and sweat began to moisten my skin, wet my brow, and finally drip down into my eyes. My gaze burned into the very center of the orb until the crystal grew uncomfortably warm, and still there was no image, no responsive presence. Not even one harmonic vibration. Like the senator, Stephanie had disappeared without a trace.

With a mixture of dread and uncertainty, I re-wrapped the crystal sphere and put it away. The fact that I couldn't scry her through the crystal meant one of two things. Either she was physically beyond the crystal's reach or she was dead.

And nothing in the Fantasyworld program had ever been able to hide from me before.

#

The sun was sitting on the western horizon as I returned to the encampment, so the light could've been better. But the problem wasn't the light. I thumbed through Daggoth's journal but the words still refused to resolve themselves into readable text. A letter fell out as I flipped the pages but it proved to be as unreadable as the journal. The writings squirmed and wriggled about the page as if alive and I knew it wasn't my fatigue or my eyes that posed the problem.

It was that damned Wizardwrite!

The two things to keep in mind when dealing with magic users are ego and paranoia. Wizards squander three-quarters of their magic on showing off, trying to prove that they're pretty hot snot in matters metaphysical.

But it's all just overcompensation.

While the barbarians are running around in naughty leather harnesses, getting laid by evil queens and vestal virgins alike, wizards approach the opposite sex much like dogs that chase hovercars: if they actually caught one, they wouldn't know what to do with it. Heredity and environment both conspire against them. Those wizards who do finally manage to lose their virginity are usually well past their forties, fishbelly white from the "indoor life", pear-shaped from practicing the non-aerobic disciplines, and rather warty and scabrous from all the nasty things they've had to handle, drink, and breathe during their apprenticeship.

So they show off a lot, hoping there's some female out there who will think that magic's more macho than muscle. Then they try to outpsych each other by erecting taller towers and practicing spells that are more flash than substance.

Which brings us to Wizardwrite: a spell designed to make their scrolls, tomes, and shopping lists unreadable to anyone but themselves. Of course, now and then, one of them forgets the counterspell and is faced with a lifetime's work reduced to catalog backup in the privy.

Or, in this case, forgets to tell the recipient of a wizard's journal just how he's supposed to read the damned thing!

I sat and thought about it while the sun dipped below the horizon. My own knowledge of Druidical lore was decidedly rusty, but the Rosetta charm seemed the most likely solution. Laying the journal aside, I smoothed the letter out, laid it across my lap and began weaving the spell.

Two minutes later I was bringing all my concentration to bear on searching the area around my bedroll. While I doubted I'd find any parts of the letter worth salvaging, it did help to tune out the worst of the sniggering.

Palys walked up to me brandishing her canteen.

"I'm not thirsty," I told her. It took an effort to unclench my teeth.

"Um—" Palys, in turn, seemed to be making an even greater effort to keep her jaw clenched. "—your pants. They're still smoking..."

I grabbed the canteen and doused the smoldering portion of my lap.

"Um—good thing you didn't try that spell on the journal, first," Palys remarked with strained casualness. Stumpy and Dyantha doubled over in laughter. Palys maintained her sobriety just long enough for me to thrust the canteen back into her hands before she joined them.

When they finally tired of their japes I was ready to ride.

Lilith appeared as they mounted up, and rode point next to me since no one else would have her. We made slow progress in the dark, but I was unwilling to throw out another witchlight as the whole point of traveling by night was to avoid watchful eyes. The night was uneventful and I spent most of those eight hours considering various solutions to decrypting Daggoth's journal. A solution finally occurred as the rim of the sun broke over the horizon and we stopped to pitch camp. Lilith was already an hour gone by then.

We sheltered in a grove of trees that provided some concealment and shade from the sun. A ridge of stone outcropping gave us further cover from the roadway.

Breakfast was a cold affair but no one complained: the time to trust a fire would be after we'd slept and could quit our campsite quickly.

Dyantha's arrow wound turned out to be infected rather than poisoned, but her avatar took a fever. It didn't look too serious, but she complained of hot flashes followed by chills. Palys concocted an herbal mixture that she claimed was a cure for fevers and forced her to choke it down.

I took first watch while the others turned in. Our location made surveillance a rather simple matter so I was able to turn most of my attention back to the matter of the Wizardwrite spell. Reaching into my vest pocket, I pulled out the spectacle case and donned the optics of al Rashid.

I had hoped the magic lenses would make short work of the obscuration factor but I met with only partial success. With total concentration and continual adjustments to the optics, I was able to make out two or three paragraphs before my brain threatened to crawl out through my ears. I closed the journal and put the enchanted glasses away but my headache remained until Stumpy relieved me for the second watch and I crawled into my bedroll.

FROM THE JOURNAL OF DAGGOTH THE DARK

I'm beginning to suspect that there's more to the process of direct psi-linkage than we first suspected. The process of mental sampling, although complex in practice, is simplistic in theory: the Master Programmer conceives an image—a tree, a rock, a butterfly—in his own mind and that thought is translated into corporeal form in the Program itself. It seemed a fast and efficient way to shape and populate a Programworld.

But I now suspect that we're transferring more than just thought conceptualization. I'm finding evidence that the mindset, the emotional makeup of the Programmer himself, is filtered through the Program Matrix.

In the case of Fantasyworld, I find constant examples of Ripley's sense of humor—concrete manifestations of mythical whimsy, puns, anthropomorphisms, homophones, and mixed metaphors that I doubt he consciously intended to leave in the Program.

What disturbs me even more is the possibility that Program is continuing to follow his subconscious lead—

SIX

I slept for a couple of hours and was nudged to wakefulness around noon by Stumpy's toe. "Rider comin'," he announced.

We crawled to the ridge of rock that shielded our bedrolls from the road. My bleary eyes and the harsh afternoon sun had not yet come to any sort of an agreement, so I relied on my ears first. The old Dwarf's hearing was sharp: it was a couple of minutes before I heard the slow, measured *clip-clop* of an approaching mount.

"One," Stumpy confirmed. Then after another moment of deliberation, he declared: "Mule." And: "Light rider."

He was right. Five minutes later a small donkey crested the hill.

The rider was indeed light: he was a true Gnome and the only way he could have topped three feet in height was to have stood on a hardcopy of_*Webster's Unabridged*. He rode carrying a religious standard and, from the fluttering device to his various accoutrements, it was easy to see he was a cleric of high orders.

As he rode closer I got a good look at his face. Especially the nose.

"It's Thyme!" I cried.

"Time for what?" Dyantha queried sleepily.

"An old friend," I half-explained, vaulting over the rocks and moving to intercept him on the road.

The little cleric reined up as I ambled down the hill.

"So, 'tis true," he said, giving me the once over-with a merry expression and a twinkle in his eye. "These are indeed perilous times to bring the Archdruid of Dyrinwall out of his woods!"

I nodded, folding my arms. "Serious enough to lure the High Priest of Donnybrook onto the road without an escort."

"I ride alone because the invitation was directed to The Rabble alone. And it wouldn't sit well with my congregation to be seen with such questionable company as yourself."

"Then Rijma got the word out?"

"Aye. The old group is pretty well scattered, but most will come as quickly as they can." He dismounted and we began walking back up towards our makeshift camp, Justin leading his mule.

"You are weary, and you travel cautiously," he noted. "Hostile encounters?"

"Unfriendly, to say the least." And I told him about the two Goblin attacks, Misty Dawn's death, and Vashti's abduction.

The little Gnome let out a low whistle when I reached the last part of my story. "Morpheus!" he exclaimed with real loathing. "This is indeed serious, my friend!"

"I was more concerned about Daggoth the Dark."

He shook his head. "Daggoth has always operated in the gray areas. His darkness is that of secrecy, not corruption. I have always thought of him as Daggoth the Grey. But Morpheus..." He repressed a shudder. "That one has a soul blacker than the deepest pit in Hell! Evil and Madness are his parents, my friend!"

"I hope he's an only child."

The little cleric grimaced. "Do not mock! It has been prophesied that Morpheus cannot be harmed by steel nor stone, iron nor incantation, nor any poison administered by the hand of man!"

"Sounds like Achilles," I observed.

"Who?"

There was no time to explain the parallel as we were almost to the stone ridge. "Just some Trojan heel who got mixed up in the biggest extramarital affair of all time," I said. I escorted him into the camp and the introductions commenced. "This is the Reverend—"

"'Father' will do," he corrected gently.

"I'd like you to meet Father Thyme," I amended.

"Not *the* Father Time!" Dyantha gushed with feverish incredulity.

"Not," I assured her.

"My friends call me Justin," said Justin.

"Justin? Justin Time? Oh!" She made a vain attempt to suppress a giggle. "What is your middle name?"

"Nicholas," he replied a bit stiffly.

"Nick? Justin Nick...oh no!" The giggle disintegrated into helpless laughter.

"She's feverish," was the only excuse I could think of.

He nodded. "Positively delirious," he observed grimly.

#

There was no more sleeping this day and, bolstered by the little Gnome's stoutheartedness, we decided to travel with what was left of the daylight. Before mounting up, Justin tended Dyantha's shoulder wound, drawing upon his curative powers as a cleric. In less than an hour the fever was abated and her shoulder as good as new.

I managed to decipher a few more paragraphs before we broke camp and spent the remainder of the day with the distinct impression that my brain was playing paddleball with my eyes.

Although we encountered no one that afternoon, we left the road after sundown, taking a shortcut through a vast meadow. Justin insisted it would save us a good half day in our travels but I suspected he felt safer away from the road after dark.

I think we all did, for that matter.

As the twilight deepened I remembered the other member of the party who was due to make an appearance shortly and I tried to prepare Justin for her eventual appearance.

"That one?" he snorted. "She wouldn't dare!"

Apparently the ecclesiastic and the Succubus knew each other from previous encounters.

"She'll not put in an appearance this night," he assured me. "Or any other night that I ride with you! That she-devil knows better than to keep company with me!"

I tried to remind Justin of The Rabble's motto: "Individuality, Tolerance, Cooperation". But he just snorted contemptuously. My experience with the various Fantasyworld clergy has been that they deal with Devils in one of three ways: they worship them, they exterminate them, or they claim there is no such thing. Not much middle ground to build any other kind of relationship on.

Lilith did not appear this night—but there were odd moments when I imagined I could hear the fall of iron hooves nearby in the cloak of darkness.

It was close to midnight when we neared the treeline of another forest. The moon had passed behind a long cloud, so we were almost upon it before we saw the dim, monolithic shape rising above the grass.

Everyone stopped. And for a long moment nobody said anything. Justin finally reached into his shirt, drew forth a carved rowan symbol and held it before him for a few moments. "I sense no evil here," he announced.

I dismounted and the others followed suit. "Torches," I recommended. Until we knew more, I was loath to use the witchlight, as magic often triggers magic. Stumpy, Palys, and Dyantha brought torches forward and, in a few moments, we had some working illumination.

At the base of the monolith was a coffin-like structure set upon a pedestal. The sides and top appeared to be made of heavy glass or thin crystal. And through the semitransparent material the flickering torchlight suggested that a body lay within.

"Now what?" I asked rhetorically. I didn't really want the next answer.

"We open it," said Dyantha.

"Thank you, Dr. Van Helsing; now tell me: *Why?*"

"Why not?"

"Never met anyone who found opening coffins profitable, myself," grumbled Stumpy.

"There is magic here," announced Justin. "Though I have detected no evil. And no thing of darkness would be interred in a crystal coffin, above ground, in such a beautiful meadow!"

"This here is Dwarven craftsmanship!" Stumpy exclaimed, taking a closer look. "Made with a great deal of care and love." He suddenly stepped back and contemplated the structure with a new and inquisitive attitude.

Justin stepped in close and placed his hands on the glassy top. "I sense a strange mixture of sorrow and hope here," he said, closing his eyes. His brow furrowed. "And life! A faint thread of life that dwells within, even yet!"

"I've got a bad feeling about this…" I murmured, but no one seemed to care.

Palys even added her two-cents' worth: "There are legends of great heroes who lie in enchanted slumber until they are awakened in a time of great need."

Everyone looked at each other. This certainly seemed to be just such a time. Justin and Stumpy eased the heavy top up and pushed it back from the glass box. As the lid fell back, the sides dropped away as well so that only the pedestal and base were left.

And the body that lay upon it.

After Palys' comment, I think we were all hoping for some great-thewed warrior wearing gem-encrusted armor. Instead we were confronted with a young maiden in rustic dress.

"Great," I muttered. "Peasant under glass."

Everyone stared for a long moment. She was okay-looking if you like coal-black hair, rose-red lips, and milk-white complexions. I nudged Justin: "You were saying something about a thread of life remaining?"

Stumpy cleared his throat and Palys observed, "She's remarkably well-preserved if she is indeed dead."

Justin shook his head and passed his hands through the air above her body. "I do not understand," he muttered. "The spell at work here eludes me."

Dyantha suddenly gasped and pointed, "Look!" She pointed at the woman's face and, as a torch was moved closer, we could see that her lips were now slightly parted and that a faint tremor ran along her creamy throat.

"I think she's tryin' ta breathe," observed Stumpy.

"I think she is having trouble," added Dyantha.

"What do we do?" asked Palys.

"I don't know!" grieved Justin.

"She's startin' ta turn blue!" worried Stumpy.

"I think we had better try mouth-to-mouth resuscitation!" advised Dyantha.

"Mouth to what?" everyone chorused.

"Do something!" she yelled, shoving me forward.

Up close it did, indeed, look as if she wasn't getting enough air. Falling back on my old first-aid training, I tilted her head back and probed her mouth for any foreign matter. I found something. Reaching in with my thumb and forefinger, I extracted a piece of unswallowed food and dropped it on the ground. That seemed to help immediately, but I placed my mouth over hers and began filling her lungs with air.

Maybe a minute passed and she was beginning to breathe on her own. I started to straighten up but found it impossible as two arms has somehow become locked around my neck. This girl had me in a reversed full-nelson!

And then she started kissing me!

"It looks like a piece of apple," I heard Justin exclaim behind me. "And I do believe that it has been treated with some sort of poison!"

Oh no.

Stumpy was the next to speak: "Looks like we've got company."

"Dwarves," added Dyantha.

Oh no!

"Looks like six or seven of them," Palys elaborated.

Oh no!

I tore myself loose from the young woman's embrace and yelled: "Ghost!"

He cantered obediently to my side and I vaulted onto his back. "Go!" I commanded. And he went.

Beyond the flicker of torchlight where light-blinded eyes could not see, I dug my heels in and urged him up and into the sky. Ghost spread his wings and we sailed over the trees and on toward Shibboleth.

I had no fears for the others—they could take care of themselves. And were probably a lot safer on their own, as I seemed to draw trouble like a magnet. Both Justin and Stumpy knew the meeting place in Shibboleth and would show up in three or four days if they traveled without further interruption.

Running—or flying—away might seem the cowardly thing to do, but this was getting far too complicated, too fast. It would take a couple of days to explain the social customs and taboos of the *Wichtlein* and *Coblynau*, so trust me on this one: fleeing the scene was the best thing I could do under the circumstances. To stay was to face some very determined Dwarves who would insist on a "shotgun" wedding at the very least.

That logic coupled with the knowledge that I had certainly saved the girl's life still didn't comfort me. As I flew through the empty night skies I could still hear Snow White's anguished cry: "My prince!"

FROM THE JOURNAL OF DAGGOTH THE DARK

If it should prove true that the Program itself has evolved its own subconscious subroutines, and Ripley's mindset—particularly his own peculiar sense of humor—is the Alpha-moulage for subsequent processing functions, then we've got a little problem. And if this (or any other) Dreamworld Program is accessing outside data files, then we've got another little problem. Put both together and we've got a bi-ig problem!

Unfortunately, that's not the end of it. We designed these Programworlds to update themselves and we didn't put a cap on their file size. I think Fantasyworld is still growing. And if the subroutines are accessing outside files on the datanet, there's no telling what could happen as the parameters expand!

What do I do? Eat, drink, and be merry? Might as well: there's nothing else I can do at this point. And I hear there's this hot new number down at Hakim's place. Got to be more careful, though. The last "sweet young thing" I brought back to my place turned out to be a real Dreamwalker, not a Construct! If that wasn't enough of a shock, "Valeria the Vivacious Vixen" turned out to be Maud Higgins, a sixty-two year-old librarian from Peoria! Ye gods!

SEVEN

I rode into Shibboleth toward noon, too tired to do anything beyond stabling Ghost and taking a room at the town's only decent tavern and inn.

I dragged myself up the stairs and, once inside my room, pushed the bed against the door so that any forcible entry would instantly wake me. It was an old trick and hadn't failed me yet. The window was a bit of a concern but my room was on the third floor and, frankly, I was too tired to do anything about it. I stripped off my clothes and fell into bed.

I awakened sometime later with my brain registering two impressions: outside, the sun was sitting farther to the west and, inside, someone was sitting in my chair. I wasn't expecting Goldilocks so I slid my hand under my pillow, reaching for the dagger that I always kept there whenever I slept on the road.

It wasn't there.

"Really, Rip; I expected more originality from you. *Everyone* sleeps with a shiv under their pillow these days."

I relaxed, recognizing Rijma's voice.

"Well, maybe I've got an extra one tucked inside my jockstrap," I drawled, rolling over and propping myself up on one elbow to look at Dr. Cooper's avatar. As a Human, Dorothy hardly topped five feet; as a Brownie she wasn't much shorter. The curly, coppery hair was the same as were the merry blue eyes: it was amazing how much the avatar mirrored the original.

"Uh-uh." She smiled.

"What do you mean, uh-uh?"

"You know what I mean, Rippy. A good thief always checks all the angles." She threw me a fresh pair of pants.

"You're a dirty-minded broad, Rijma, but you're bluffing." I pulled my pants on under the covers. "You checked under my pillow, first, and that's what woke me."

She frowned. "And you wonder why nobody likes you at the Thieves' Guild."

"The price of eternal vigilance." I got up and stumbled to the washbasin. I poured the pitcher of tepid water over my head and managed a quick and hasty toilette. Rijma handed me a towel and then a clean shirt.

"Good thing you had an extra change of clean clothes in your saddlebags," she remarked. "I sent those things you've been wearing out to be cleaned over an hour ago."

"When will they come back?"

She sighed. "Hon, if you want your clothes back clean, you'll be lucky if they're back anytime this week."

"Thanks."

"Don't mention it. I have to breathe, too, you know."

I pulled on my shirt. "So who's coming?"

The copper-tressed Brownie shrugged. "We'll see who shows up tonight and tomorrow. The word has gone out. I expect to see some latecomers over the next week or so."

I shook my head. "Can't wait that long. We'll have to leave word as to our route and destination and let them play catch-up."

"Not that I'm surprised, but isn't that dangerous?"

"Nope. I think my worst enemy can find me anytime he really wants to. You have any problems in getting here?"

Dr. Cooper's avatar rose and crossed to the window. "Some. There was hell to pay back at the Control Center when they found out you were already in the Program. I was viewed as an accessory to a sort of non-crime. My defense—as if I needed any—was that you were neither in custody nor officially charged with any wrongdoing. In fact, they wanted you in the Program. But I think that they wanted a half-dozen of their people with you when the time came."

I sighed. "You know, if I've learned one thing in the last three days, it's that popularity isn't all it's cracked up to be."

She grinned and perched herself on the window sill. "The tough part was getting away from Dr. Quebedeaux's party without being followed. Most of our avatars were still in the same part of sanctuary from our last expedition. I hung around long enough to pick up on one interesting tidbit of information, though: I think they're almost as interested in finding you as they are in finding the real culprit."

"They probably don't have the foggiest idea as to where to start looking," I mused. Then I told her about my conversation with Orcus, the journal, and my run-in with Straeker's avatar.

"You don't know for sure that Stephanie's dead," she said after a lengthy pause. "Or the senator, for that matter."

"I have no evidence that they're alive, either."

"It's not the same thing."

"Isn't it? This was my Program, Coop! I've always been able to locate any object or any person anywhere within its parameters. Maybe I'm not familiar with Senator Hanson's Warworld avatar, but my ex-wife is no stranger. Stephanie's gone! I can't even find her body!"

She was quiet for a long time. Rijma Fanderal, Fantasyworld's most notorious thief and scalawag, was temporarily eclipsed by the mind and personality of Dr. Dorothy Cooper as she considered the facts. We discussed my conclusions and then she raised one that I hadn't considered: "Do you think that the Program's self-awareness could be used to stop—or at least slow—the Anomaly?"

"I don't know." I began pulling on my boots. "My impression from talking to Orcus is that the Program's awareness is fragmentary. Some others might have such an awareness, but the condition is in no way universal. For any real help in altering Program reality, we'd have to find an interface—that is, a Non-Gamer character—of major power and importance with such a perspective..."

We looked at each other.

"Straeker?"

"Could be."

"An alternative would be raising the entire Program's level of consciousness to self-awareness."

"Too dangerous."

"I agree."

"In fact, there is even the possibility that the Anomaly is tied to the Program's state of self-awareness. Perhaps the cure will involve inducing a severe case of amnesia..."

I stood and buckled on my belt. "The question foremost in my mind right now is..."

Rijma tugged at her moleskin gloves, suddenly alert for any forthcoming action. "Yes? Yes?"

"...is the food here any good? Memory no longer serves after all these years."

A twinkle in her eye and the old, mischievous Rijma was back (a slight change, at best). "My child, the food is great and the floor show reputed to be even better! We can find out for sure just as soon as you can get yourself together and down the stairs to our table." She went to the door. "I'll rouse Stumpy on my way down."

"What?"

"Didn't you know? The rest of your party teleported into Shibboleth this morning."

I did a double-take. "They *what?*"

"Teleported." She gave me a little punch. "Got here before you did."

"Who pulled that one off?"

"I believe it was the lady in leather—what's her name?"

"Palys?"

"That's the one. I'd keep my eye on her if I were you."

"I intend to," I said. "From now on." Teleporting one's own self was a difficult spell—particularly over the distance I had traveled in the previous night. Bringing the rest of the party along, horses included, was a feat beyond most magic-using Dreamers and generally guaranteed to incapacitate the spellcaster for a week or more. It was unlikely that Palys would be 'porting herself—or anybody else—again, before we reached Daggoth's Tower.

"Well," she eased out the door. "I'll wake up and round up the others. Starting with that crusty old curmudgeon of a Dwarf. Ta!"

I waved her out the door with some misgivings. Stumpy had no sense of humor even when he was wide awake. Rousing him from a sound sleep was something akin to waking a cave full of hibernating bears. Of course, Rijma was well aware of that fact, but she had never been one to miss an opportunity to bait the old Dwarf. And while I didn't really worry about Rijma's safety, I was a bit concerned about the bill for room damages.

Two minutes later a roar and a succession of crashes confirmed my fears.

#

Despite my being fully dressed, I felt half-naked as I descended the stairs to the main lobby of the inn: this was neither the time nor the place to be without a sword. I planned on visiting a swordsmith but would have to wait until one opened in the morning. I hoped I wouldn't be in need of one before then.

I had a slight headache: evidently I was getting better at deciphering the Wizardwrite as I had managed to read a half page in only half the time and felt only half bad. I decided to try for a whole page after dinner.

The Crashing Boar was even more of an aesthetic nightmare than I had remembered. The tavern looked as if someone had turned the blueprints of a Western saloon over to a crew of medieval stonemasons under the direction of Frank Lloyd Wright and Salvador Dali. As if the architecture wasn't bizarre enough, the decor appeared to have been orchestrated by a debased and somewhat deranged caliph from Baghdad. None of this seemed to offend the tastes of its patrons who, although a pretty tasteless lot, recognized the cultural hodgepodge as a sure sign of neutral ground.

Part of The Crashing Boar's success lay in the necessity of neutral ground in conducting cross-cultural business transactions. Here, tolerance was more a matter of avarice than altruism. Of course, neutral ground was as suspect as sanctuary, now, but a glance around the room indicated that something like it was still in effect. It was one thing to get Elves and Dwarves to drink together without smashing most of the furniture over each other's heads. Hakim not only managed this night after night with a minimum of breakage, he frequently accomplished the impossible: serving Orcs and Dwarves in the same room—a proximity guaranteed to result in structural damage to most buildings in a three-block radius before the dust settles.

Hakim insured the neutrality of his customers and the longevity of his furnishings by employing a couple of Ogres as bouncers. The fact that the regulars had nicknamed them "Beany and Cecil" belied their strength and savagery. Only strangers and fools started fights in The Crashing Boar; the Ogres always finished them.

The tavern was crowded tonight, but quieter than usual—something was in the air. I waded through a throng of bodies in search of Rijma's table and felt the occasional ghostly pat-down of a cutpurse in search of my wallet. As I had judiciously secreted it in my boot, I ignored them and continued casting about for the rest of my group.

I saw a familiar face first.

The barbarian sat alone at a small table, contemplating some tragic scene at the bottom of his mug of ale. A large, double-bladed battleaxe had replaced the two-handed sword, but I was sure of his identity as soon as I saw the stump where his right hand should have been. After a moment's gloomy meditation, he drained his ale and slammed his mug down on the table with a resounding crash. A buxom serving wench darted forward as he stood and adjusted the horned helmet that capped his flowing raven locks.

He ignored her outstretched tray for the moment, tipping his vikingesque headgear at a rakish angle and hitching up his loincloth to cover the beginnings of some rearward cleavage. Finally he turned, glanced down at her from the vantage point of his six-foot-six-inch height, flexed his hulkish muscles, and rumbled: "How much?"

The girl dimpled under his scrutiny, bobbed in a half curtsey, and informed him that his tab for the evening amounted to four silver pieces and seven coppers. She raised her tray as he rummaged through a beltpouch of loose change, and then squealed as he dropped five silver pieces down her bodice. She turned to go and was propelled the first three feet by the force of his pat on her backside. No one took umbrage: it was an old ritual.

I intercepted him on his way to the door. "Pardon, friend…"

He looked down, trying to make out my features in the gloom of his own shadow. "Huh?"

"I'd like to give you a hand."

It was the wrong way to put it. The barbarian gently laid down his battleaxe and grabbed my shirtfront. Effortlessly, he lifted me into the air and contemplated me with what I liked to think was an impassive expression.

"Not funny," he finally decided. And, just as impassively, threw me across the room.

I landed in the midst of a cross-racial card game, scattering the cards, the chips, the furniture, and the players. I had just a moment, as I collected myself, to notice that I had landed right beside the table I had been looking for. Rijma leaned down. "Some people just can't enter a room without trying to be the center of attention."

I struggled to sit up. "Save my chair," I replied.

A rather large Bugbear loomed over me. From the expression on his face I gathered that he had been holding the winning hand on the interrupted play.

"What do you think you're doing?" she asked.

"Recruiting," was all I had time to say as the Bugbear picked me up and threw me back across the room, toward the door.

Before I got there, I made another unscheduled stop: a large, grey-green "hand" shot out and plucked me from midair. Now I was under the less-than-impassive scrutiny of one of the bouncers.

"Hiya Ceec!" I tried a friendly smile. "Long time no see!"

The Ogre smiled after a long momen—it was not an encouraging expression. He began to carry me toward the door.

"Hey, Cecil; thanks for the escort but I can see myself out—really! I am in a bit of a hurry to catch that barbarian who just went out the door"

Which someone opened just as I went sailing through.

A pillar was within arm's reach as I flew over the boardwalk and out towards the street, so I grabbed at it to help break my fall.

Two Lizardmen came around the corner and broke it even more effectively as I swung around on the post. One was stunned by our collision and I pulled the other's cape over his head to facilitate my getaway. Three blocks and two alleys later, I caught up with the barbarian.

Hearing my approach, he stopped and turned.

I walked up and planted myself in what I hoped was a bold stance. "I think you could use a hand…" Once again the old shirtfront lift. "…and I'm just the one to give it to you."

He set me back down. "You a cleric?"

"Better than that, Mr. Henderson: I'm a Programmer."

He peered down at me with an expression of thoughtful appraisal. "You're Ripley, aren't you."

I nodded.

At that moment, two bruised and rumpled Lizardmen came running down the alley, full tilt, with swords drawn. Wordlessly, Henderson swept me aside and whirled his axe, cutting both of them down before they could check their rush.

"Let's go somewhere we can talk," he said amiably.

#

Cecil gave us the eye when we reentered the main room but, after a moment's observation, seemed to be satisfied that we were buddies now. We wove our way back to Rijma's table with me giving a wide berth to the renewed card game as we went.

She had procured a long table on the far side of the main room, in the shadows under the second floor walkway; it provided more room, less noise, a better view, yet greater anonymity. I chose a chair that offered my back the protection of a solid stone wall, and introductions commenced.

Besides Rijma and the barbarian, the latest addition to the group was a ranger who was simply known to everyone by his former aristocratic title.

The Duke was a big man, just a couple of inches shorter than the barbarian. Dispossessed of his family's holdings and wealth when he was young, he had fled into the wilderness and lived among the woodland rangers for the past twenty-seven years. He was quiet and dependable and he had only two unnerving eccentricities: he wore a hat that bore an uncanny resemblance to a Texas stetson and he had a predilection for kicking in doors with a cocked and loaded crossbow in each hand.

Looking around the table, I was slightly reassured by the bulk and power of the ranger and the barbarian, the swordskill of the redheaded Amazon, the curative powers of the Gnome, and the heart and individual talents of the Brownie and the Dwarf. The unknown factor of Palys was a concern, but I felt an inexplicable reassurance when I looked at her and found her already contemplating my attention. I sensed a mystery about her, but felt no danger here beyond her own blatant sexuality.

This then, aside from the three newcomers, was The Rabble so far. In the old days it had been known as "Rip's Rabble". There had been other members, to be sure. But whether they were still alive or would see their way clear to join up with us were questions that only time would answer.

Unfortunately, we had no time to waste. We could ill afford to sit around for another week, waiting for more recruits while a senator was missing and Gamers were unaware of their own mortality.

I asked Rijma about the possibilities of recruiting more help among the locals.

"Been working on it since yesterday," she answered, already one step ahead. "Very few prospects around these parts, I'm afraid. The only interested parties seem to fall into one of two categories…"

"Don't tell me, let me guess: farmboys eager to beat their plowshares into swords?"

"Ready to see the world and seek their fortune," the Duke chimed in. "Fame and glory, beautiful women, high adventure, beautiful women, fabulous treasure, beautiful women…"

"How ya gonna keep 'em down on the farm?" Palys murmured.

"Trouble is, these yokels don't know which end of a sword is the hilt and think a *Bec de corbin* is a French dessert," Rijma finished disgustedly. "For all their eagerness, they're worse than cannon-fodder; they'd be a complete liability."

"Which leaves us with—?" I prodded hopefully.

"The nutcases."

"Nutcases?"

"Let me give you some examples. Yesterday I posted notices around town and set up my recruiting table at the edge of the village green. Before sundown I was approached by a white knight, a paladin with a singing sword, and a magic-ring bearer..."

"Doesn't sound so bad to me," I observed.

"Yeah? Well consider the first applicant. When I say white knight, I mean *white* knight: everything was white! White surplice, white horse, white saddleblankets fer Cromssake! That was my first clue!"

"First clue?"

"That this guy wasn't playing with a full deck. Hey, everybody's got one or two hangups but this guy should be licensed by the telephone company! You want examples? Take his phobia about uncleanliness—just guess what the inscription was on his coat of arms."

"*Fortius Quam Sordes:* 'Stronger Than Dirt'."

"*Fortius Quam*—" Rijma echoed before she realized that I had already answered her. "You know this 'knight-error'?"

I nodded with a rueful smile. "Sir Ajax may seem a bit prissy to you, my dear, but I've always found him to be more than ready and willing when there was dirty work to be done. 'Twill all come out in the wash,' he used to remark cryptically."

It was the she-Brownie's turn to look rueful. "I'm afraid I didn't take him seriously. I suggested he go guard a laundromat."

"Okay, so how 'bout the others?"

"The ring-bearer was a real prickly type; called himself Thomas Revenant the Agnostic. He was wearing this fraternity ring that he claimed had some kind of magical power."

"What kind of magical power?"

"That was one of the problems," she sighed; "he didn't seem to be too sure of that, himself. Said that it was unpredictable and that he had no conscious control over it. Said it just sort of happened from time to time."

"What sort of happened from time to time?"

She shrugged. "I quit asking after the first couple of questions. I mean this guy has a real attitude problem! Negative, negative, negative!"

"Okay," I conceded.

"And rude! He even suggested that I was a figment of his imagination!"

"Okay, Rijma."

"And in addition to all of that he had this skin condition that you just wouldn't believe! I mean, talk about the heartbreak of psoriasis!"

"Okay! Okay! Now tell me about the paladin," I pleaded.

"Now this guy was a definite 'maybe'. She began rummaging through one of her beltpouches. "He gave me his card…"

"I thought you said he was one of the nut cases."

"Well, he seemed normal enough, himself. It's the sword that puts him in left field."

"A singing sword, you said?"

"Yeah, but it only does fifties music."

"Fifties music?"

"Nineteen-fifties music. You know: 'Doo-wop', 'Boom-shanga-langa'."

"Boom? Shanga? Langa?" Clearly I was out of my element.

"Yeah, he claimed that it's the legendary Sword of Sha-Na-Na." She produced the card and slid it across the table. I picked up the rectangle of stiff parchment and contemplated the illuminated calligraphy:

PALADIN

‡

Have Sword,

Will Travel

Short and to the point. I liked that.

I looked up to see a knight in shining armor making his way across the room toward our table. Did I say shining armor? This guy practically glowed in the dark. The light also seemed to reflect off of his impossibly white teeth and spotless surcoat. I wondered where he had managed to pick up a suit of chrome-plated platemail.

"I figured you'd want to talk to this guy, yourself," Rijma explained as he drew near, "so I invited him to drop by."

He drew up to our table and executed a courtly bow. "Permit me the courtesy of introducing myself," he announced smoothly: "I am Sir Richard of Boone."

"Riplakish of Dyrinwall," I responded with a nod.

"I shall come directly to the point," he continued in a neutral but not unfriendly manner, removing his gauntlets and tucking them in his belt. "It hath been noised about that you and your comrades are setting forth to right wrongs and battle great evil." (He pronounced it 'ee-vill.')

"Yeah. What about it?"

"I wish to join you in your holy endeavors."

I looked around at the others while I considered. We could use all the muscle we could get. However, the group treasury was all but nonexistent and good help was usually expensive. "How much do you think your services are worth, Sir Richard?"

He looked at me as if I had just addressed him in an unfamiliar language.

"Mayhap thou dost misunderstand," he explained, using a tone one usually associates with babysitters and kindergarten teachers. "I am a paladin. A holy knight. It is my calling to assist noble causes such as yours. I am no man's hireling."

"In other words, he'll work for free," Rijma whispered.

"Okay, Dick, you're in," I answered decisively. "Pull up a chair and order anything you want—the first round's on me. If you have any questions, just ask Father Thyme here. He'll introduce you to everyone and get you oriented." I turned to Justin. "Okay by you?"

The little cleric nodded enthusiastically. "He is a paladin—a holy warrior. There are none more trustworthy. A—how do you say it? Regular dooly dud—"

"Dudley Do-Right," I amended. "I'd like you to play den mother until he feels comfortable with the group, Justin. And no religious debates."

My attention was suddenly diverted to the discussion occupying the rest of the table. It seemed that The Duke and the barbarian were being treated to a distorted version of the previous night's events.

"...so all of a sudden he starts kissing her—"

"She was kissing me!" I corrected, feeling a sudden flush creep into my face. "I was giving her mouth-to-mouth resuscitation."

"A fancy name for kissin'!"

"I was blowing air into her lungs!"

"Come on, Rip; everyone knows that the kiss of a prince will break the strongest enchantment!"

"I'm not a prince!"

"Not a handsome prince, at any rate!"

"Oh, I don't know…" That from Palys.

"When she started yelling 'My prince has come,' I thought old Rippy was going to levitate right then and there!"

"It was a case of mistaken identity—"

"Tell that to the Dwarves!"

"Yeah, that grumpy one was hollerin' for blood: your blood, Rip!"

"And one of 'em was real smart: he picked up your trail and led 'em all until the tracks ended a quarter of a mile away."

"They finally went back home—"

"—but I don't think they'll give up so easily!"

"Yeah! They really love that girl, and you broke her heart!"

"You cad!"

"You heel!"

"You masher!"

"Left her standing at the altar!"

"C'mon, you guys! Give me a break!"

"You didn't do right by her, Rip."

"Now, wait a minute! I'm not the guy she's waiting for. Prince Charming is supposed to wake her up and marry her."

"Prince Charming?"

"Who's he?"

"You makin' this up, Rip?"

"No, really! She's supposed to marry Prince Charming and they'll live happily ever after!"

"Sounds like one of those Fairytales to me."

"Yeah, and you can't trust anything one of those Fairies tells ya—"

And so it went. I felt rather awkward about the Snow White affair, so I was relieved when Rijma finally changed the subject.

"What's your name?" the Brownie, forthright as always, asked the barbarian.

"Conrad."

"You're joking!" She looked to me for confirmation and rolled her eyes. "Conrad the barbarian! Who's he trying to kid?"

"It's better than a name like 'Ridge-mah'," Stumpy sneered, deliberately mispronouncing her name.

"Ree-mah!" Rijma barked back, emphasizing its correct pronunciation. The archaic spelling of her avatar's name had triggered more than one mispronunciation from the uninitiated over the years. Stumpy, of course, knew better but couldn't resist because it was such a sore spot with her.

Justin, ever the peacemaker, was in the precarious position of sitting between them and was trying to negotiate a cease-fire when the floorshow pre-empted him.

FROM THE JOURNAL OF DAGGOTH THE DARK

You can't have heroes without villains. So, of course, we placed varlets and evildoers in every Programworld. We assigned our casting like the director of a play: you, you, and you will wear chains and be slaves. Who knows how to handle a whip? Ah, then you will be a slave-handler. We need an evil high priest: line 'em up and pick out the most likely looking one; jiggle his programming and use an infusion of data from the history files; liberally mix with personality profiles from Adolph Hitler, Saddam Hussain, and Charles Manson...

Trouble is, this isn't a play. In Dreamland, the Construct becomes the role. He does not discard his script, shed his costume, remove his makeup and go home at the end of two hours.

It troubled Ripley then.

It troubles me now.

EIGHT

The lights dimmed and a pulsating beat was taken up by the dumbeki. At the sound of the zaghareets the dancers entered the arena, slithering and whirling, waving their veils as a prelude to the dance. Now the oud, kanoon, and bozouki took up the music and the women began the Beledi portion of the dance.

Our waitress chose that moment to come and take our orders.

"Ale…"

"Ale…"

"The gang's all here," Rijma murmured *sotto voce.*

"Wine…"

"Same here…"

"Beer…"

The waitress turned to me.

"I'll have a Vanilla Dr. Pepper…"

"Ask Hakim," Rijma added when we saw the bewildered look on her face. The serving wench curtsied and hurried off, much to the relief of Conrad and The Duke who were trying to watch the entertainment around her.

The music was changing now, the instruments working out improvisational solos as the dancers entered the Taxim phase of the dance. It was then that I noticed that one dancer stood out from the rest.

She was tall and lithe in contrast to the short, thickset women who danced around her. Her skin was nearly as dark, I noted as she danced closer, but it was tanned by a familiarity with the sun rather than the bloodlines of the *Surusund.* She began "dancing off the veil": removing the swath of gossamer that swaddled her torso, an inch at a time.

As the Tcheftetelli rhythm took over, she eased the veil from its moorings in her left shoulder strap and her girdle at her right hip. She danced toward our table with it held before her face, masking all but her eyes. The audience recognized the form as "The Sphinx Looks Out" and murmured approval.

Now the gossamer seemed to take on a life of its own as she performed "The Frame", "The Swirling Cape", and "The Canopy" in quick succession. She darted toward me and suddenly the veil filled my view, settling across my face like a ghostly mist. By the time I could pull it away from my head and shoulders, she had returned to the center of the arena.

Out of the corner of my eye I could see that Dyantha and Palys were both watching me, rather than the dancer, with what I could only describe as "interesting" expressions. I pretended to not notice and turned my attention back to the girl in the arena.

The kemanche wailed like a lost soul now, as she dropped to her knees and arched her back. Her long, raven-black hair swept across the floor as she undulated farther and farther back. Now the back of her head was just inches from the floor as she formed a serpentine arch of flesh, silk, and hair. We watched, hypnotized, as her tawny skin glistened with perspiration and her belly fluttered to the beat of the dumbeki and the zills.

Amid cries of "Opa!" and "Yasu!" and "Yala!", she churned, coiled, and extended a foot decked with tiny bells. Her hip spiraled upwards and she quickly twisted about, writhing in a blur of colored silk, jewels, and strung coins. Her hands gathered a mass of nightdark hair as she rose back to her knees, swaying like a snake poised hypnotically before the charmer's pipes. Watching, it was hard to remember that there were other dancers on the floor.

She regained her feet as the Tcheftetelli rhythm picked up and moved into the Beledi finale.

I examined the veil, inhaling the double scent of musk and sweat as I puzzled over the woman's familiarity. There was something about her that disturbed me—something beyond what was disturbing every other male in the place. My mind sifted the evidence, searching for clues.

She was no dancer. Oh, she moved well, but I had seen enough belly dancers in my time to tell the uninspired professionals from the gifted amateurs. This one's popularity was due as much to her outland beauty as to her style and technique. Clad only in the brief, coin-strung brassiere and the diaphanous, split skirt of the Beledi, she displayed the body of an athlete. Tall, long limbed and long waisted; the flat, curved muscle-tone of her belly contrasted the pillow-flesh of Hakim's other dancers.

The waitress returned with our drinks, now, and Hakim followed in tow. "My friends!" he cried with genuine delight. "Riplakish!"

"Hakim, you pirate!" I motioned him over to a stool beside me so that we could talk and the boys could enjoy an unobstructed view of the rest of the dance.

"Why did you not tell me you were in town?"

I winced at his backslap. Hakim was an extremely large man, built like an oversized bowling pin. Rumor held that he had been the sumo wrestling champion of the Surusund. At the age of twelve. "Trying to keep a low profile, my friend," I answered. "Perilous powers are abroad."

He nodded, a knowing expression on his round face. "As you know well, I am no paragon of virtue. My fingers are in many pies: a little larceny, some smuggling, mercenary traffic, drug shipments..." He shrugged. "I look the other way on a lot of things. When a man operates in the 'gray,' he cannot afford to despise the 'black' and revere the 'white'."

Then he looked across the room and his smile died. "But there are evils that transcend the petty quibblings of the pseudo-moralists," he continued heavily. "And *that* one has darkened my hospitality overmuch these past few weeks!"

I followed his gesture and peered through the wriggling bodies and smoky haze at the gentleman in question.

My first impression was that here was a man of great wealth: he wore gaudy robes of silk and embroidered satins. My second impression was that he had about as much taste as a Sagittarian Slime-cultist: over-adorned with jewelry and ropes of gems, you could dye this joker green and pass him off as a Christmas tree. My third impression was this guy was ugly—it was a tribute of sorts to his eye-assaulting apparel that I didn't notice this first. This guy could've modeled for the warning labels they put on canisters of toxic waste.

His two bodyguards weren't much better-looking.

The one on the left looked like his head had caught fire and someone had tried to put it out with an axe. The one on the right had a face that looked like a high-relief map of the moon. Anybody casting them in a horror holo would have used makeup just to tone them down.

"Okay. So they're ugly," I observed blandly. "But if lack of comeliness was a crime, we'd both spend time in the slammer. Though I've got to admit," I added after another look, "that you and I might get six months probation, while those characters should get life plus ninety-nine years."

Hakim shook his head. "Ugly faces are one thing, my friend. Ugly souls are another! You have not heard of Morpheus and his abominations?" As Hakim spoke those words, the subject of our discussion turned so that I could see the eyepatch. The shock of recognition was almost like a physical blow.

"I hear he's the Duke of Depravity," I mumbled through a haze of revulsion. "Tell me more."

And Hakim did. He started with the stories of rapines, tortures and murders until I was sick to my stomach. But Hakim was only warming up: there were darker rumors and suppositions, acts of evil beyond imagination…

I finally waved him to silence: Morpheus made the worst atrocities of human history sound like schoolboy pranks. "I just want to know why no one's taken him out yet." I groped helplessly at my weaponless belt. "And I want to know where I can get my hands on a good sword before he leaves this room!"

Hakim grasped my arm. "Others have tried, my friend. And all who did died. He bears a talisman upon his person that makes him impervious to every weapon! Blade and bow, mace and maul; all have been turned aside through the potency of this artifact! I have heard that a dozen archers loosed their bows at him from careful ambush, once. Each shaft was said to have turned back and killed the man who loosed it!" He leaned a pudgy cheek against his fist. "How can such a man—if man he actually is—be withstood?" he concluded glumly.

"There's more than one way to skin a rat," I replied with more conviction than good sense.

Rijma suddenly dug an elbow into my ribs. "Don't forget your priorities, my lad. We've got a job to do. We can't get sidetracked with bug-squashing expeditions."

"Why not? After all, we're here to *de*bug the Program." Morpheus inspired a knee-jerk reaction in me. Finding him in my Program was like finding a cancer in my own body: I wanted to take a knife and cut it out as quickly as possible.

"Look, Robbie," she whispered, "I know this is a problem for you. You wanted your Program to be a fairytale land of wonder and delight. Cephtronics and the Dreamland' board of directors wanted adult adventure and entertainment. We know who won that battle."

"I'm not fighting the board any more," I gritted back. "I gave up trying years ago. But this is still my creation—"

"Not all of it."

"Not all of it," I agreed. "But some of it. And now that I'm back, I intend to start taking some responsibility for the parts that I can!"

"Sounds like a messianic fixation to me."

"Well, why not? I created this world, so who has better claim?"

We both glared at each other. Then broke into fits of giggles.

"Pomposity always did become you," Rijma sputtered when she was finally able to catch her breath.

"Yeah, but there's something else you ought to know before we walk away from this guy," I said softly, my smile suddenly gone. "This is the guy who was with Daggoth the last time we were attacked." Her eyes widened. "And—if Stephanie's dead—this would be the sonuvabitch who's responsible."

She turned and stared at the object of our conversation with a quietness that suddenly chilled me. "It wouldn't hurt to get in a little practice ahead of time," she remarked with dangerous pleasantness.

"Or make the odds a bit more favorable for our next confrontation," I added.

Our attention had wandered from the dance, but now it was brought back by Hakim's cry: "*What is that stupid girl doing?*"

We turned our heads to see and the answer was quite obvious. Hakim's lead dancer had left the herd and was now dancing before Morpheus' table. Worse than that, she was deliberately making her way around the table toward old skullface, himself.

"She was warned," Hakim whispered. "They were all warned!" The anguish in his voice was more unnerving than his gruesome tales. "I have told every woman in my place—every barmaid, every serving wench, even the kitchen help—about Morpheus and his unholy lusts! I warned everyone to stay away from him! To let the eunuchs wait his table and serve his food! They have all heard the stories—Aiee!" He buried his face in his hands.

Now the girl was slipping between Morpheus and the table, forcing him and his two "worthies" to move their chairs back a foot. The bodyguards fingered their swords nervously, but their employer showed no fear: the dancer's costume was too brief, too transparent to conceal any weapon.

Now she faced him, leaning forward so that her silk-cupped bosom nearly cradled his cheeks. Now she whirled and leaned across the table, presenting her derrière. He reached for her there, but she was faster: she thrust her hips forward, pressing her pelvic girdle against the table and arching her body backward so that her long, midnight hair washed across his face. He swept it aside and grabbed her by the waist.

The dance didn't miss a beat.

Her upraised arms came down now, and she placed her own hands over his. Once more I found myself reaching for a nonexistent weapon but, instead of trying to pull away, she slid his hands down over the smooth hills of her hips.

I pushed her veil away from me as if its sheen of sweat had suddenly turned to slime.

She pulled his hands on down, across the throbbing plane of her belly, to the top of her low-slung skirt. And now she changed the tempo of her body movements and the musicians struggled to put on the brakes. No longer shaking and shimmying, her body stretched and twisted languorously—as if his touch had been what she had craved all along. It was both terribly erotic and disgusting at the same time, and an unnatural hush fell over the tavern as everyone watched with growing fascination.

She allowed his arms to encircle her gyrating torso and his spidery fingers to creep beneath the waistband of her skirt. Now she placed her right hand over both of his and pressed her left hand to her midriff, just below the arch of her ribcage.

Suddenly, she bucked against his hands. Once! Twice! Her abdominal muscles undulated like a cracked whip and something glittering flashed above the table. A third pelvic thrust. And suddenly she twisted out of his grasp.

Her sudden move touched off a chain of motion across the tavern: most fell back in their chairs, but one Orc who was a bit closer to the action leapt to his feet.

"Lord Morpheus!" he shouted.

Rijma was suddenly up and flinging her mug of beer.

The Orc got about as far as "Your wi—" when the heavy pewter tankard caught him upside his head. He went down like a lead zeppelin.

Morpheus was momentarily distracted but the girl swept around the table and drew his attention again.

Unfortunately, the other Orcs in the room were still looking at our table.

"If you were aiming at Morpheus, you missed!" I murmured out of the side of my mouth.

"I always hit what I aim at," she rejoined calmly, resting her hand on the hilt of her shortsword.

"Well, I figure we've got about ten or eleven seconds," I observed, pushing back from the table. "Want to tell me what this is all about before they stomp the ca-ca out of us?"

"Check the bellybutton," she whispered.

"Whose bellybutton?"

"The dancer's, dolt."

There was a sudden hiss as a number of swords cleared their scabbards. Beany and Cecil looked around, trying to figure out who they were supposed to jump first.

I caught a glimpse of the girl's umbilicus as she swept a goblet from the hands of one of Morpheus's henchmen. She threw back her head and guzzled the wine, allowing a large amount of it to run down her chin and splash onto her breasts. She locked eyes with Morpheus as she lowered the cup.

And she had yet to miss a single step in the course of the dance.

"Very nice, as bellybuttons go," I muttered, looking around now for another weapon. "'Like a round goblet in which no unmingled wine is found wanting.' Are you telling me that we're picking a fight with two dozen Orcs over this trollop's navel?"

"Do you want to live forever?" she challenged, pushing back from the table in turn.

"Well, to be quite honest and totally sincere—*yes!*" While a dozen or so Orcs don't usually get me too worried, I was feeling a bit of a disadvantage without a sword. "I certainly don't want to lay down my life for some strange skirt just because some Orc takes umbrage over her umbilicus!"

"What did it look like before?" she asked, pulling her own sword.

"I don't remember. Is it important?" I glanced under the table: no refuge there.

"You don't remember because there was a ruby glued over it when she began the dance."

"She lost it?"

"She lost it like I lost my mug!" Rijma jumped onto the top of our table. "She's done her part. Our job is to create a diversion!"

I looked back at Morpheus' table with what had to be one of my more stupid expressions.

And then it came to me. The glittering movement above the table as she writhed against Morpheus' hands—the sparkle of a ruby falling from its fleshy setting!

But where had it gone?

Morpheus grabbed his own goblet from the edge of the table and drained it greedily. The sweat on his face was clearly visible even from where I sat.

She lost it like I lost my mug... Rijma's words echoed in my mind as I tried to visualize the falling gem's trajectory. It wouldn't have necessarily dropped straight down to the floor—the contraction of her abdominal muscles might have popped it forward...

...like I lost my mug...

Morpheus' goblet?

Was it possible that the dancer could have timed her movements to drop the jewel in Morpheus' goblet specifically? Such coordination, under the circumstances, seemed rather incredible. And what purpose could it serve?

Enough of a purpose, perhaps, that prompted an Orcish observer to jump to his feet to shout a warning. And prompted a Brownie to risk life and limb to silence same.

She's done her part. Our job is to create a diversion...

Orcs from tables all over the room were beginning to advance on our table. Hakim, ever the discrete and neutral host, had already disappeared. Rijma was going to have her "diversion."

"Rijma! I haven't got a weapon!"

She appeared unruffled as the gray, green, and warty circle began closing in. "Then fly reconnaissance, Dearheart! And do try not to drop any good vintages this time." She followed this dry piece of advice with a Brownie warcry that was positively bloodcurdling. Immediately all Hades broke loose.

Having little choice with no sword, I levitated out of harm's immediate way and perched in a convenient chandelier over the battle's heart.

Stumpy and Justin had already acquired a bench in the meantime, and promptly ran it, full tilt, against the first four Orcs in the vanguard. Conrad and The Duke followed suit by picking up our table and flinging it across the room at another group of approaching uglies. Those Orcs avoided it easily, but blundered into a party of Dwarves in the process of trying to dodge the airborne furniture. Needless to say, that touched off a real free-for-all, evening up the odds a bit.

At this point I turned my attention to a rack of wine bottles behind the great bar at the other side of the room. Levitating myself was easy: it's a basic incantation from the Beginner's *Book of Shadows*. Levitating other objects was a lot trickier, however. It was more of a *psionic* discipline than actual magic, and I lost more than a couple of bottles as they floated across the room and into my arms.

Faithful to my pledge to Rijma, I spent the next several minutes sampling each wine to make sure I didn't waste any quality Bordeaux. I needn't have worried about any vintages that Hakim would serve over the counter—most turned out to be a step or two above paint-remover. I only sent one bottle back to the bar and that was because the stuff was so awful that it begged to be served to someone—hopefully the medieval equivalent of the health inspector.

Satisfied that the rest were expendable, I turned my attention back to the fight below.

The nice thing about bar fights is that nearly everyone has removed their headgear in advance of the fisticuffs. I had a bird's-eye view of the top of everyone's head. Including a large Orc who was trying to club a pathway beneath my chandelier.

"Bombardier to pilot," I announced, gingerly holding a bottle by the neck, "we are over the drop-zone. Target in sight..." I wet a finger and tested for wind: none apparent. Allowing for the Orc's horizontal movement and my missile's vertical trajectory, I released one and one-quarter seconds before he was due to pass beneath me. "Bombs away!"

Scratch one Orc.

Some didn't go down quite so easily: twelve bottles later I had only downed seven targets, including an Elf who had made a sudden movement in the wrong direction. A couple of others had required a second bottle to finish the job.

In the meantime, Rijma and Stumpy had regrouped, back to back, in the center of a small circle of Orcs. As usual, they were arguing with each other as they fought to keep the entire Orcish ring at bay. Elsewhere, Father Thyme had crossed purposes with one of the Ogres. From my vantage point it looked like Justin had found an unreachable hold on Beany's back: as the Ogre tried desperately to dislodge him, the little Gnome repeatedly beat upon his thick skull with the remains of a stone pitcher, crying, "Repent! Repent!"

The Duke was now positioned in a corner with both crossbows drawn and cocked. The five Orcs who had him cornered knew he couldn't get more than two of them at best. And The Duke kept underlining this fact in his calm, matter-of-fact drawl, encouraging them to find out which two it would be. The Orcs seemed to be giving the matter a great deal of thought.

Dyantha was parrying the blades of three different attackers—oops, make that two—uh, rather, one—well, just forget it. She could take care of herself. The paladin was faring equally well, holding a large number of Orcs at bay while his singing sword hummed a tune that sounded suspiciously like an old ballad from the *Three Pence Opera.*

I scanned the main room twice but caught no sight of Palys. The barbarian seemed to have broken free of any direct confrontations for the moment. He had ascended to the second floor walkway and was working his way down, cutting all of the ropes where they were tied off at the railing. One after another, the huge chandeliers came crashing down on the combatants, taking out ten or twelve at a time as opposed to my one-to-a-customer wine bottle bombs.

I was admiring the precision domino effect of the entire row of chandeliers dropping, one right after another, when it suddenly occurred to me that mine was next in line. No time to cast a spell: I held on tight as my overhead roost suddenly plummeted to the floor.

Then, just as suddenly, I was on my way back toward the ceiling. Morpheus had picked that moment to pursue the object of his immediate lust beneath my immediate location. His arrow-repelling talisman seemed to work equally well on chandeliers: I hovered even closer to the ceiling than I had before. I knew I couldn't depend on Morpheus to stand under my chandelier forever so I grabbed the support rope which now dangled limply to the floor, and began to climb down.

A bloodcurdling screech caught me unprepared and I lost my grip before I made the halfway point. One of the tables broke my fall, and I was able to do some pretty fair damage to it in return. Propping myself up in the midst of the wreckage, I stopped and stared.

Everyone else was doing the same.

Morpheus' body had gone rigid. His hands groped and clawed at his throat and chest like blind things.

"Scaras! Rhegad! I have been poisoned!" he screeched. Where before his face had been flushed, it was now a flaming scarlet—and getting darker.

In a flash, his two bodyguards were up and about, their swords drawn and menacing.

"Innkeeper!" Craterpuss bellowed the summons like an impatient executioner kept waiting at the block. I hoped that Hakim wasn't naive enough to come running.

"Blame not the innkeeper, Accursed One," answered a high, clear voice. "Nor his wine steward. I alone am responsible for the venom that, even now, clouds your mind and renders your spells impotent!" It was the dancer who spoke and she now faced him defiantly, feet spread, arms akimbo.

"Bitch!" he hissed, taking a staggering step towards her. "Why?" His face was turning from scarlet to purple and he looked down at his legs as if they no longer obeyed him.

"Why?" She laughed contemptuously. "That I am Human should be reason enough to desire an end to you and your foul practices! That I am a woman, justifies me! But above all, as Amazon, I am bound by both duty and honor to slay you for the dog that you are!"

"Coward!" he hissed. "You call this honor?" The purple was tinged with black.

"You would not permit honest combat! I used treachery where treachery was given and long overdue! You could not be touched by stone or steel, iron or incantation—so I used the only weapons left to me!"

"The prophecy…" he croaked, sliding down on one knee.

"The prophecy stated that your life was proof against any poison administered by the hand of man. I am woman. But, be that as it may, I did not administer it by hand." Her right hand brushed her stomach where the "ruby" had once nested.

She smiled with mocking irony. "Know, O Morpheus, in these last moments before your death; who has deceived the Deceiver, and who has killed the Murderer! I am Aeriel Morivalynde, Princess and heir-apparent to the Amazon throne! In the name of my people and our domain have I done this thing! And my only regret is the quickness and ease of your death!"

"Cerberus!" he wailed.

The room grew suddenly cold and the lights dimmed. In seeming answer to his anguished cry, a ghostly apparition appeared and moved toward Morpheus.

"I am here, Father/Brother," the phantom answered, bending toward him.

"Receive my essence," he whispered, sagging toward the floor. "Scaras! Rhegad!" he croaked, rocking on both knees, "Avenge me!" Then he pitched forward onto his face and lay still.

The apparition bent low, then stepped back. With a shock, I saw that the "ghost" was Daggoth, himself. *Now,* I thought, *we are in big trouble!* But the apparition of Mike Straeker's avatar turned and walked through a nearby wall and out into the night.

Snapping out of my reverie, I had only two seconds, but it was sufficient to grab Aeriel's arm and jerk her back as the floating chandelier ceased to float. Apparently the talisman lost its power at the moment of the enchanter's death: the overhead lighting arrangement came crashing down at our feet.

Quick reflexes were all I needed to save the girl from a falling chandelier. Saving her from Morpheus' two assassins was another matter.

"A sword!" I cried. "Someone throw me a sword!"

Everyone stared back at me with a vacant expression.

"A bag of gold for a sword!" I yelled in desperation. I had to jump back as some thirty-odd swords flew in my direction from all over the room.

"I can deal with these vermin myself," Aeriel remarked as I selected a weapon from the loose pile of cutlery.

"Probably," I agreed, coming back to stand beside her. "But you don't have a sword. And that's hardly first-rate armor that you're almost wearing."

"Faun!" she called out.

"Here, Sister!" An Elf leaned across the second floor balcony and tossed what looked like a coil of black rope. The "rope" unfurled as it traveled to her waiting hand and became a whip. She cracked it once, reflexively, and then turned to face the two assassins with an insolently relaxed stance.

"I'll bet you look great in black leather and high heeled boots," I murmured as Scaras and Rhegad advanced.

She gave me a measured, sidelong glance. "How did you know?"

I think I shrugged. "Lucky guess."

Scaras decided that I posed the more immediate threat, so I had his undivided attention. Rhegad was trying to decide whether his buddy needed any backing or if he could indulge himself by going one-on-one with the lady. Feeling chivalrous—and maybe a wee bit emasculated—I made a bid for a martial ménage à trois: "Hey, Pizza-face!"

That did it. The lady was forgotten and now Rhegad wanted me for himself. He passed Scaras while he was still a good eight feet away and lit into me like a deranged cuisinart. It took all of my skill to hold him off for the first minute or so. After that, it was easy: I regained momentum and took the offensive.

Rhegad was a back-stabberand a bully—but he was no swordsman. His initial ferocity had taken me by surprise but my instincts and reflexes were equal to his brute strength and fury. I might have been in trouble had Scaras joined in.

Scary, however, was only able to take about two more steps before the end of Aeriel's whip wrapped around his left ankle and jerked him off his feet. He landed rather heavily upon his head and, from the sound it made as it struck the floor, he was not likely to get back up for a very long time. If at all.

That left Rhegad. It was beginning to dawn on him that I was more than his match in an honest fight and that no one was going to come to his rescue. He made a break for the door.

He was met there by a tall woman in a scarlet robe. Slender and pale and coldly elegant, Lilith held us all in the thrall of her ice-crystal gaze. She slowly entered the room and Rhegad shuffled backwards as if in a sudden trance.

She stopped several paces past the threshold and extended a milk-white arm. "Come to me, man." Her quiet summons echoed throughout the tavern as if in a tomb. I saw Justin's hand make the sign for protection against evil. But he made no other move to interfere.

The Demoness gestured once: Rhegad stopped backing away. She gestured again, her ice-blue eyes locked on his empty, gray orbs. And he stumbled toward her.

I stepped toward her, also. "Lilith..."

"Do not interfere, Riplakish." She answered me without turning her head. "I hunger! And this animal is my just prey."

I seemed helpless to gainsay her as the Demoness enfolded the man in her blood-red robe and drew his mouth to hers.

Then she kissed him.

It was a long, lingering kiss; in all appearances a kiss of desire and passion. Except the desire was hunger and the passion, terror. What should have been fire was ice; the pantomime of love, predation.

Rhegad struggled once. And then was still.

At first rigid, his body began to slump as the kiss continued. And as we watched, he began to age before our very eyes. In less than a minute his hair went from black to gray to silver to white. His skin lost all color and his face began to crinkle like aged parchment. His body seemed to crumple and fall in upon itself until it attained the appearance of an unwrapped mummy.

When she released him at last, all that was left was a dried husk that crumbled to dust when it dropped to the floor.

The Succubus drew her hand slowly across her mouth. "I hungered, and so have fed. But still I thirst..." And she looked around the room.

It was as good as any fire alarm: in less than thirty seconds The Crashing Boar was completely evacuated. Even The Rabble had elected to wait for me outside.

Aeriel was the only one who stood her ground along with me. She even met Lilith's cool gaze across the empty room as she spoke. "So, Riplakish; you traffic with Demons, now?"

I winced. "My dear Aeriel, if I ever chose to do so, don't you think I could direct traffic a little better?"

"Judge him not, woman," Lilith said quietly. "I am *geased* to him by One my own kind cannot disobey." She turned and looked at me with frightening tenderness. "He could have banished me by power long since now. But he withholds for he knows such an act would destroy me. He knows mercy, this one..." Then she began drifting toward us. "Now, stand aside: you have done your night's work, here. Let me attend to mine."

She obviously meant Scaras. I couldn't think of any justifiable reasons to refuse her, but my conscience pricked me just the same. "He's unconscious and no longer a threat."

She shook her head and glided closer. "I still thirst. Go. And allow Hell to claim its own."

And looking into her blue-ice eyes, I suddenly seemed bereft of will to argue. Aeriel took my arm and led me away toward the stairs.

FROM THE JOURNAL OF DAGGOTH THE DARK

It's now been more than five years since "Ripley vs. Cephtronics" ruled in our favor. But I'm less convinced that we were right and Ripley was wrong. Are the programworlds "Alternate Realities" in every sense of the definition? Have we gone beyond the protoplasmic fumblings in laboratory test tubes to actually create complex, intelligent life-forms? I feel that my death and subsequent survival now bears reexamination of the question.

But Ripley no longer has any voice in Dreamland's development, and, now that I'm gone, the reins will probably fall into the hands of Dr. Quebedeaux. Sondra has a brilliant mind, a matchless intellect—but now that I am a permanent inhabitant of this world, I find her lacking in those qualities I want to exist in God...

NINE

"We need to consider our next move."

Aeriel's statement took me by surprise and I almost turned around. Since it sounded like she was still dressing, I managed to catch myself in time to be discreet.

"You don't have to be so discreet, you know," she added in an amused voice. "You've seen me in the buff plenty of times."

"That was ten years ago, Aeri. You were just a kid then, and not so—"

"Developed?"

"Grown up."

"And out?"

"'Matured' is the word I was thinking of."

"I'm so glad you noticed. Why don't you turn around?"

"Are you dressed?"

"I'm still washing off. But don't let that bother you."

"I'm trying not to." I was bothered, all right. In fact, I was furious at Cephtronics for diddling the programming so that an Amazon princess was acting like some addlebrained bimbo with a schoolgirl crush. I sat down on the edge of the bed.

"I can't believe that I finally have you all to myself," she continued, "without Misty Dawn around to interfere. She's very possessive of you, you know."

The shift in conversation had caught me off balance. "What?"

"She's let me know in no uncertain terms that you are her personal property."

I felt twin flashes of annoyance and grief. "I'm nobody's 'personal property!'"

She chortled. "That's good. That means I have a chance. Although the prospect of competing with a Nymph does seem a bit daunting."

"What?"

Suddenly she was in front of me, pushing me back upon the mattress and kissing me. I was too stunned to resist and it took another moment to register that, in the process of undressing and redressing, Aeriel had only gotten as far as the halfway point between the two.

It was too ludicrous for words—which was probably why I hadn't come up with any, yet. I tried to put my hands where they could make and keep some distance between us, but I only ended up making things worse.

"That's very nice," she murmured.

"Aeriel, I think your confusing a little girl's crush with something a little more serious." Crom-on-a-crutch! I could hardly point out that her behavior was programmed to satisfy the lusts of fat-cat businessmen who utilized Dreamland for a different kind of fantasy trip. "After all, you're a grown woman, now!"

"I'm so glad you've noticed! Especially with so much evidence at hand!"

"What would your mother think?" I parried weakly.

"My mother thinks that, as males go, you're the best of the sorry lot and I have her blessing."

I was saved any further maneuvering as the door to Aeriel's room suddenly flew open.

Queen Hippolyta's daughter rolled off of me and sprang to her feet, grabbing my borrowed cutlass as several figures crowded the threshold. Standing there naked and brandishing a blade, she cut a magnificent figure. For a moment all eyes were on her and I probably could have escaped out the window. But in that moment the urge to flee seemed an unchivalrous one.

In retrospect, the decision to stay seems more stupid.

An authoritative voice spoke. "Dr. Ripley, you and your companions are my prisoners. Should you make any attempt to resist or escape, by any means—physical or magical—they will all be slain. Starting with your—ah—'lady-friend', here." There were three drawn shortbows with their arrows aimed at Aeriel's heart and, at this range, none of the grim-looking archers could miss. Behind, and towering over them by a good fifteen inches, was the largest Human I had ever seen. This joker was even bigger than Conrad the barbarian. There were sounds of reinforcements out in the hall, but my attention was drawn to their leader who had just spoken.

It was impossible to determine the outline of a figure in that dark, wine-colored robe but the face above it was slender with angular, Elvish features. What at first glance had appeared to be a silver skullcap turned out to be platinum hair pulled severely back and knotted at the nape of the neck so as to fall back into the hood. A woman, I decided after a moment. Although many Elven males tend toward the effeminate, this one knew my True Name. Only one other Dreamwalker was likely to know who I was and come looking for me.

"Dr. Quebedeaux, I presume?" I murmured softly.

"What's that?" she asked sharply.

I sighed. "Doesn't anybody knock anymore?"

#

The rest of the night, to my memory, was uneventful.

Since I was surrounded by armed guards, I slept reasonably well, untroubled by dreams of Goblin hordes attacking us in the hours before dawn.

On horseback the following morning, it appeared that I was the only one who was well-rested. Aeriel and The Rabble, I'm sure, had spent the night contemplating various plans of escape. And Dr. Quebedeaux had apparently singled out Natasha Skovoroda for special attention, still suspecting that the Russians were behind the Dreamland problem. Dyantha looked positively haggard as she mounted up. As she rode she swayed in the saddle like a ship caught in a heavy swell.

I was left pretty much alone, although I was under constant observation to prevent any Houdini-type hanky-panky. Our captors were thinly stretched to keep all of us under guard, and I doubted if any of them had slept either.

Since the bindings on my wrists weren't uncomfortable and no one seemed to be in any immediate danger, I postponed any personal escape plans for the time being: let someone else do all the work and worrying for awhile. Besides, we were heading towards Daggoth's Tower and that's where we wanted to go anyway.

Aeriel rode beside me throughout most of the morning, but it wasn't until the sun stood at its zenith that we had the chance to speak privately.

"What did you do with the Demoness?" she asked when the nearest guard finally drifted back and out of earshot.

"Nothing," I whispered. "I try to do with Lilith as little as possible." I looked forward and back. "Where's Faun?"

She shook her head. "Three Amazon squads were concealed near Morpheus' stronghold. They were awaiting Faun's return to mount a housecleaning expedition. As soon as she saw me safe, she would have mounted up and returned to our waiting warriors. I was expected to play the fox for any of Morpheus' remaining hounds. I am afraid that we are on our own."

I shrugged as one of the guards reined in closer and cocked an ear. "By the way," I remarked, nodding at her outfit. "When did the Amazons adopt this sun-and-fun apparel?"

Aeriel frowned. "I know not what you mean."

"I'm referring to those two little scraps of chainmail that you seem to think is legitimate armor. Why the big change?"

She laughed. "You jest, of course! Such has always been the battledress of the Amazon warrior-maiden."

Untrue. I had written a more realistic, not to mention modest, dress code into the original Program. Cephtronics had changed that, too. I had a lot more than a bone to pick with Mike Straeker, I had a whole skeleton.

Rijma came riding up from the front of the procession and wheeled her warpony in beside Ghost. "Lady Silverthane requests your attendance up front," the she-Brownie announced dismally.

The message and the way it was delivered pushed my annoyance level up three notches. "Dammit, Rijma; I told you that you weren't to blame for this," I snapped. "And tell her 'ladyship' that I don't make housecalls!"

"They followed me!" the diminutive footpad lamented. "Even if I didn't know it, the fact remains that I led them right to you!" She sniffed. "When you're a veteran thief, it's doubly embarrassing."

"Dragonshit. Dr. Quebedeaux is Dreamland's Chief Programmer. I'm surprised it took her this long to find me. You're just embarrassed because we're tied up and you aren't. They're still watching you just as closely as they are us."

"Thanks." Her head came up a bit. "It's nice, not to be accused of divided loyalties."

"Bunk. There really are no enemies here. This is just a little misunderstanding."

"Then I'm sure that you'll have it all straightened out just as soon as you've talked with Lady Silverthane." She smiled brightly.

How could I argue with that piece of logic? "You can't accuse someone of divided loyalties when they haven't shown you any," I growled as I nudged Ghost toward the front of the line.

Lady Silverthane rode a palanquin instead of a horse. Her silk-shrouded litter was borne upon the scaly shoulders of four Lizardmen, with four more "spares" trotting behind.

I rode up alongside her transport and, when there was no immediate response, I announced my presence. "Knock, knock," I drawled, in my best imitation of The Duke.

For a fleeting moment I was afraid she'd answer "Who's there?", and I'd be committed to following through on the joke. I needn't have worried: her sense of humor was too atrophied for such subtleties. The curtains parted and Alyx Silverthane regarded me with solemn, lavender eyes.

"Lord Riplakish."

I bowed in the saddle.

"I should like to begin by saying how sorry I am for these present circumstances. I do hope your bindings are neither too uncomfortable nor too inconvenient—"

"My back itches," I replied formally, "but at least I can still pick my nose."

"—but under these present circumstances, I deemed certain precautions necessary."

"You strike me as the type of woman who only knows caution and only does what is necessary."

I was fishing for a reaction and she took the bait. Coloring, she snapped: "All right, Mr. Ripley; I don't like you very much, either!"

"I didn't think so. Mind telling me why?"

"To put it simply, I find certain elements of your little fantasyland disgusting! As far as I can see, the primary function of any female Construct is to be a sexual object! You have your own little private playground here, with hundreds of fantasy women programmed to satisfy your every deviant wish!"

She was on a roll and there was no point in trying to explain that Cephtronics was responsible for that particular twist in the programming.

"I would find that repellent enough," she continued sharply. "But, with the lives of hundreds of real men and women at stake—real flesh and blood captives to your personally conceived Mindworld—do I find you diligently seeking a solution to the Program Anomaly?

No! I catch you sporting with some overendowed, oversexed slave-girl in your bed."

Fortunately, Aeriel was riding far enough back as to be out of earshot.

"You've demonstrated a complete lack of concern for the lives of other people. Your disregard for their well-being while you pursue your own drunken lusts is beyond contempt! A man with your lack of morals is too dangerous to be allowed to run loose with Program-shaping power. That is why I have taken it away from you."

It took a moment to sink in. I leaned toward her. "What do you mean, you've 'taken it away' from me?"

She put on a "regretful" look. "I've stripped you of your spellcasting abilities. You can no longer work any magic in this Program."

I laughed. "All right. And how did you accomplish this simple little trick?"

"I removed your Program Access Code."

A cold hand suddenly clenched at my insides and my laughter turned into a fit of coughing. "You what?"

"I removed your Program Access Code. You no longer have Programmer status in this Frame. You can no longer alter the Program internally. In view of the non-status ranking of your Bard classification, I doubt if even the simplest spells will work for you, now."

I held up my bound wrists. "You'll forgive me if I don't immediately take your word for it?"

She nodded. "Go ahead. Try and spell yourself free."

I tried. Beginning with a simple little unraveling spell.

Nothing.

I worked my way up through the various levels of thaumaturgy.

More nothing.

For a final, make-or-break test, I attempted to disintegrate the rope with a frantic lack of caution for my wrists in the process.

Still nothing.

When I finally looked up again, I found Dr. Quebedeaux's avatar regarding me with an expression that could only be interpreted as pity. That stung as much as anything else.

"Lance!"

The big guy in the plate mail came riding up. "Yes, Mistress?"

She pointed an imperious finger at me. "Free him."

"Free him?" High-pockets looked at me with all the confidence of a betrayed lover.

"Yes. Now that Lord Riplakish has been apprised of the new rules, I think he'll start playing the game our way."

"But if he tries to escape—"

"He won't. Stripped of weapons and power, I think our bard will appreciate the old adage, that there is safety in numbers."

I held up my wrists. "Rip promises to be a good boy!" *For now*, I amended silently.

The big man extended his lance with the precision of a surgeon wielding a scalpel, and neatly severed the cords where they crossed between my wrists. I hadn't realized that those pointy poles were so sharp at the tips. "Lance, huh?" I mused, rubbing my chafed wrists. "That your real name?"

"Nickname," he admitted stiffly.

"Named after your proficiency, no doubt?"

"When it comes to the lance, he's the best in the saddle," Alyx added proudly.

"Maybe in your saddle," I sneered, turning my mount around to take my leave, "but I don't impress so easily."

I started to ride back toward Aeriel and Rijma but a large, mail-gloved hand caught my shirtfront and lifted. My feet stayed in the stirrups but my rear no longer touched the saddle.

"Your meaning, sirrah?" he inquired tightly.

"Put him down, Lance. He's just fishing." Her voice was composed but her face was red. "My dear Riplakish; if you want me to reinstate your Access Code, you ought to be more pleasant and cooperative."

"Perhaps you should hold up a hoop and have me jump through it."

She sighed. "This is getting us nowhere. Let him go, Lance. We'll give Dyrinwall's druid some time to think things over. When he's through pouting, we'll have another talk."

Lance lowered me back into the saddle. "Time heals all wounds," he agreed.

"And wounds all heels," Silverthane added as I turned Ghost back toward the end of the line.

#

Over the next two days of the journey, I took stock of my situation. Other than my mithril shirt and the shurikens and garotte concealed in my belt, I was defenseless. I was still without a sword and no one had offered to return my longbow, arrows, and throwing knives which had been confiscated on the night of our capture. I was in no condition to go wandering off alone and, as long as Silverthane was the key to regaining my Programmer status, I wasn't about to let her out of my sight.

Our captors weren't taking any chances. The Rabble, with the exception of Rijma, continued to ride on tether with their wrists bound. I was kept apart from the others when we stopped to rest or make camp, so there wasn't much chance to compare notes or discuss any plan of escape. Otherwise, all went well enough until the third day of our journey.

About midmorning my skin began to prickle with the discomforting impression that we were being watched. If my magic was gone, my sixth sense still seemed operational. Though there was no concrete evidence, I was sure that I sensed a presence that was more than imagination.

This posed a difficult question: keep my own counsel? Or warn the very people who held us prisoner? With most of my friends bound, disarmed, and unable to defend themselves, the choice seemed obvious: better the known than the unknown. I rode forward to warn Lady Silverthane.

Lance fell in alongside, on the way. He didn't say anything and I'd already used my best insults over the past couple of days, so we came to the palanquin in silence.

"I have not summoned you," was her greeting.

I thought about turning her into a porcupine. The trouble was that even if I regained my powers, the act would have been inherently redundant. Rather than start a fresh round of insults, I got straight to the point.

"We're being watched."

"So? And by whom, pray tell?"

"I don't know. But my guess is we'll have company soon enough. Maybe ten minutes. Maybe ten hours."

"And what do you suggest I do about it?" she asked coolly.

"Free my friends. Give us our weapons back. Give us a fighting chance—for your sakes as well as ours! Safety in numbers, remember?"

She smiled condescendingly. "Truly, Lord Riplakish. I expected better from you, and certainly before now. Do you think I am so naive as to fall for such a fabrication?"

"Someone or something is out there," I insisted. "I don't know what—but I'm sure there's more than one...maybe a lot more than one..."

It was of no use: it was readily apparent that she wasn't about to believe me. And the more I argued, the less convincing I'd sound. I made a quick decision. Weaponless, I couldn't free my own comrades. It seemed I had only one alternative whereby I could save the party: if we were riding into a trap, perhaps I could spring that trap prematurely.

Without giving warning, I dug my heels into Ghost and urged him forward.

"Stop him!"

It was a cornball line, a staple of every tri-dee thriller I'd ever watched as a kid. With the wind in my face and the freedom of the road before me, I couldn't resist a triumphant laugh.

I stopped laughing when the arrow caught me in the thigh. I screamed and kicked Ghost into the fastest gallop he could maintain without leaving the ground.

I felt another arrow glance off my mithril-protected back and heard the pursuit commence. Silverthane was yelling something but I was over the next rise and out of her line-of-sight and, therefore, her effective spell range. To tell the truth, initially I had worried more about her spell ability than I had her archers. The shaft of red-hot pain through my leg was an overwhelming reminder of that miscalculation.

Seeing a wooded copse ahead, I risked a look back.

Four guardsmen were hot on my tail with Lance not far behind. Considering the amount of man and metal it had to carry, I was surprised that his poor horse could manage anything faster than a brisk walk.

I turned back around as I came into the trees so that I could avoid any low-hanging branches, and rode into a downswung flail. I caught a quick glimpse of rough-looking men concealed among the foliage before spiked iron balls filled my vision.

What followed immediately is still a mystery to me. Whether I pulled Ghost upwards or he leaped instinctively, I do not know. I had a brief impression of being airborne...

And then I knew no more.

FROM THE JOURNAL OF DAGGOTH THE DARK

Maybe it's my fault. I probably started it when I told Ripley I was redesigning the Orcs to be meaner and nastier—and that I was basing the prototype on my mother-in-law.

When he told me what he had named the Dragon, I didn't really believe him…

TEN

I awoke to two basic impressions: pain and darkness.

At first I thought it was night.

Then I hoped. But the absence of moon or starlight seemed to disprove that assumption.

That I was blind was the next logical consideration. If any of those spikes had missed my eyes, I would have to count it as miraculous.

My clumsy, groping fingers felt upwards and discovered that a bandage of sorts covered my aching head from the nose up. That would explain the absence of any light, but I'd be a fool to dismiss the thought of permanent blindness just yet.

I lay quietly, pondering, and then felt about the rest of my body—particularly the arrow wound in my thigh.

The shaft had been drawn and the wound bandaged with some sort of poultice. There were plenty of cuts and bruises over the rest of my body, but they seemed minor and had been anointed with some sort of ointment. I was suddenly aware that I was naked beneath the woolen blankets that covered me. I drew the covers up to my chin, more conscious of the chill in the surrounding air.

"Are you cold?" The voice was soft, but unexpected, causing me to start and half rise from my bed. Gentle hands eased me back down.

"Who's there?" I asked.

"A friend," was the quiet, almost hesitant, reply.

I tried a smile. "So it seems. What happened to me?"

"I was hoping that you would be able to tell me. Do you not remember?"

I groped through the fragments of memory. "I rode into an ambush…"

"Near Gaehill?"

"I think so. We were headed in that direction…"

"Then you are not from around here?"

"No…"

"And you were traveling with others?"

"Yes..."

"But you had not been warned of any dangers in this part of the country?"

"No, not specifically..." I paused, not wanting to bring the name of Morpheus up until I knew more about the hands into which I had fallen. I was trying to discern the speaker's gender from the pitch and timbre of his/her voice, but the sudden flow of questions seemed to have ceased for the moment. "You don't seem surprised that I was set upon."

"Strange circumstances have come to Gaehill these past seven years." There was another long silence. "First there came a monster that terrorized the countryside and made this area a shunned and desolate place. This beast, however, does not range afar nor hunt those travelers who keep to the road. It is the other, the Wurm, who has made Gaehill a hissing in the mouths of all who know of her."

"Wurm? You mean a Dragon?"

"Aye. It appeared about eight moons ago and made its lair in the mountains, just the other side of town. Crops were destroyed. Many farms and half the city were burned."

"How do they fight it?"

"Fight it? They do not." Anger suddenly flashed in that quiet, hesitant voice: "They serve it!"

"Serve it?"

"Why not? They have lived these past seven years with one monster practically in their midst. And they have come to believe—after the loss of a few heroes—that a well fed and unmolested monster is preferable to the cost of defying it."

I was almost sure that my benefactor was a woman, now, but I could not be sure how many others might be standing nearby, silent and cloaked by my own sightlessness.

"Now that another monster sleeps upon their doorstep," she continued. "they still fail to learn that it is more expensive in the final accounting to befriend a Dragon than it is to make war upon it." The sound of a sigh. "We have resorted to savagery to protect civilization." There was a long, uncomfortable silence. "Were there any women in your party?" the voice finally asked.

I felt a growing disquiet. "Yes, why?"

"Then you may count them as lost."

"You are telling me that they are dead?"

"Unless the city guard was unusually careless, they live. For now. Gaehill bribes its Dragon with monthly sacrifices. So they will live until the next full moon. And then their blood will purchase Gaehill another month of peace."

I fought the impulse to jump out of bed. "You're telling me that the people of Gaehill have—an arrangement—with this Dragon?"

"Yes. As long as the town provides the Firedrake with a monthly sacrifice of five virgins, it will spare the town and the surrounding farms and villages."

"I'll bet there's a lot of farm girls out there, luring a lot of farm boys behind haystacks, even as we speak."

"If I append your meaning, good sir, such would be ineffective. To the Wurm, any woman of a certain age, so as to still be tender and juicy, qualifies as a 'virgin.' I fear Dragons are not interested in the scorecards of human copulation. They are only interested in what tastes good."

So Unicorns and Dragons had differing definitions of the term "virgin." An interesting but unhelpful piece of information for the moment. I filed it away for future reference and reviewed the facts: there was something here that was terribly familiar and very important. But I was having trouble putting my finger—

Avatar memories suddenly clicked into place. "Smog!"

"Mayhaps you know of this particular Dragon, good sir?"

"Mayhaps nothing: I kicked this overgrown lizard out of the Southern Provinces ten years ago for trying this same extortion racket. I did it before and I will damn well do it again!"

A sudden wave of weakness mocked my boast. Except, I was no longer as young as I once was, had lost my magic abilities, was possibly blind, and could very well meet a very permanent death this time around. I groped at the bandages. "My eyes…"

"I do not know. With time and rest and healing—we shall have to wait and see—"

"I haven't got any time." I started to rise but a gentle hand against my chest restrained me once more.

"You have not the choice in this matter. To leave this place, you will need your strength and your sight. You have neither now. Rest. And we shall see what tomorrow brings."

A cup was brought to my lips.

"Drink."

The wine was heavily spiced, I caught the scent of crushed poppies. Almost immediately a lethargic warmth began to spread through my body.

"I have not learned your name, friend," I murmured as the drug began taking effect.

"It is—Euryale," she answered cautiously.

"I give you thanks, Euryale."

"You are most welcome, stranger. Now, do me courtesy for courtesy, and tell me your name."

Funny. I couldn't remember for a moment. "Ripley…" I said finally. "My name…is…Ripley…"

And I slept once more.

#

I awoke after—what? Minutes? Hours? Days? Longer? There was no way of telling—not even dreams to quantify the oblivion of sleep. The rough blankets still covered my body from toe to chin but, in spite of their weighty thickness, I was still chilled. I heard and felt the presence of a flaming brazier to my left, beside the bed. But it was the warmth to my right that drew my body for solace from the fever's chill.

My arm was already draped over it and there was no doubt in my mind that it was a body. Very gently and very carefully I moved my hand to answer the next set of questions.

Yes, it seemed to be a human body and, like mine, it seemed to be naked. And—oops—it was "the fairer gender." I moved my hand upwards and suddenly found it caught in a vice-like grip.

"Not my face…" she said quietly. "…Please…"

She pulled my unresisting hand back down to her breast and held it there. "I'm sorry," she said after a lengthy silence, "but I am sensitive about my face."

"I'm the one who should apologize," I answered.

"No. You were merely curious. Not improper. During the night you took a fearful chill. The blankets and the braziers alone were not enough to warm you in this drafty cave. So I tried to warm you with my poor body…"

"Nothing poor here," I argued gallantly.

"I give you thanks for the compliment, stranger."

"And I give you thanks for my life, Euryale."

"You are…most welcome…Ripley." The set of my mouth must have conveyed my surprise. "Your name is Ripley, is it not?"

I nodded. "Well—yes. I guess it's just been a while since I've heard someone else say it."

She sighed. "Mine, as well. As you may have gathered, I am a hermit. This cave is my home, until two days ago, I lived here alone."

"From the sound of your voice, I would guess that I've got a few years on you. What inspires a young woman to shun the company of her own kind and seek the lonely life of a recluse?" Even as I asked, it occurred to me that this might not be the most tactful question. "If I'm not prying," I amended lamely.

"I am…ugly." She said it flatly, without emotion, as if she had become long inured to this fact and yet had trouble believing it. "That is why I am sensitive about my face. And that is why I live alone, without human companionship."

"Is it really that bad? I mean, maybe you're being too hard on yourself—"

"It is a moot question of who determined my exile: Humankind or myself out of personal choice. The fact remains that others find my scarring unbearably hideous!"

"Your friends—"

"I have none."

"Family?"

"All dead, except for one sister. Stheno has visited me in the past, but she has enemies and does not travel as much as she used to."

"How long have you lived alone?"

"Nearly seven years now."

"Then you were not always…"

"Ugly? No. There was a time when I had many suitors. I was considered one of the most beautiful women in the land! But—that was before—" she hesitated, a catch in her voice, "—the accident. I must not dwell upon the past for all of that is lost and gone, now. And nothing that I know of can change my plight."

"Nothing?" I, too, knew how a life could be unfairly shattered by a chance accident. "Surely some cleric would have the power to heal you, to restore your face?"

"No." She was silent for a long time. "I have not spent these past seven years in idleness: I have sought a cure for my affliction. And I have failed. No one can help me."

"I find that hard to accept."

"Nevertheless. If any could, it would be the one who did this to me. And she would not. Or else one of the two Shapers."

"Shapers?"

"There are only two that I know of: Daggoth the Dark and Riplakish of Dyrinwall."

"And have you tried asking either of them?"

"Dyrinwall is too far—there is too much open ground for me to traverse in getting there. And I approached the Dark One five years ago, only to be rebuffed and sent back to my cave.

I was appalled. "Did he say why?"

"He said something about my having to live out my destiny. Does it matter what reason he gave? The final word was one of refusal."

"I…I'm sorry…"

"It is all right. I have learned to live with my changed circumstances."

"But it must get lonely…"

"Yes…" I felt her take a sudden gulp of air and turn away from me: "…it gets very…lonely…" Her shoulders began to shake and there was no doubt in my mind that she was crying now, though she did it too softly for me to hear.

I reached up to stroke her hair, to comfort her. And felt her draw away. "No, please," she whispered in a tear-strained voice. "Do not touch me above my shoulders! If you would touch me…" She was suddenly shy. "If you would give…or receive…pleasure… you may touch me…anywhere…below my neck…"

I hesitated: I had learned the hard way, a long time before, that you do not make love to someone out of pity; ultimately, you only add to their wounding by doing so. But I felt a greater fear for what another rejection might mean at this time in her life. And since Riplakish of Dyrinwall no longer had the power to give her what she needed, perhaps it was only right for Robert Ripley to make whatever amends that he could.

I pulled her body to mine. And I comforted her as best I could.

#

Over the next two days she nursed me back to some semblance of health, and I nursed a growing suspicion.

It was an ugly thought and it grieved me to associate it with the soft voice and gentle hands that had cared for me in my helplessness. Still, the question had to be asked.

Loneliness has been known to do strange things to people. It has killed some, driven others mad, and certainly made all of us desperate at one time or another.

How desperate might a young woman be who has been without love and companionship for seven years? Whose disfigurement promised a life of solitude for all the long and lonely years to come?

Would she find her salvation in saving a man's life who would not only be grateful, but also immune to the hideousness that drove all others away? Would she cover his eyes with bandages and tell him that he was blind, just to cheat her own fate for a short while?

Or some dark night, in the middle of a drug deepened sleep, would she unwrap those bandages and see to it that his blindness was made real? Made permanent?

It suddenly became very important to know as much as possible about my mysterious benefactor. And regain my sight as quickly as possible.

#

She was an artist, a sculptress to be more precise. Over the long years of exile she had filled the cavern with statues to populate the empty spaces of her lonely life. I touched and explored many of them, always marveling anew at how she had managed to capture the essence of life in each individual work.

Once, she allowed me to sit nearby while she worked on one of her pieces. I was allowed to listen but forbidden to touch. "I am a temperamental artist," she explained over the sound of chisel against rock. "I will not have you examining a work before it is finished."

All of her works were of people, most of them men: only three women and four children rounded out the lot. "I do not seem to have any talent for animals," she confessed. "Only people." And always full-sized figures, no busts.

When I asked her if she planned to do a sculpture of me, her mood darkened. "I will never put you in stone," she insisted fiercely. "I would keep you here, if I could. But not in that way…"

I'm not sure which of the clues finally caused the others to fall into place. Her explanation for the hissing sound I sometimes heard was unacceptable to me from the start: "…there are hot springs located throughout the cave and sometimes excess steam vents through cracks in the rocks…"

By the fourth day, when she took me to the room where her treasure was kept, I knew who she was.

FROM THE JOURNAL OF DAGGOTH THE DARK

I've mentioned my suspicion that psi-linkage transfers more than conceptual imagery—that the emotion—the very mindset of the Programmer may actually be introduced into the Matrix. This would certainly explain the bizarre elements of humor that have manifested throughout Fantasyworld, lately.

And raises another question.

We initially had some problems with Warworld. General Brackett programmed the perfect wargame environment and then was unable to engage the enemy. While others reported brilliant battles and satisfactory skirmishes, the good general was never able to pick a fight.

The enemy would either retreat or surrender. Almost as if the program feared any kind of conflict with its creator. Does this mean a Programworld, created by direct psi-link, have a mental/emotional bias for the Programmer responsible?

It's been over five years but I don't remember Ripley ever finding the Goblins reluctant to fight. Of course, Fantasyworld is more complex than Warworld: Program bias might manifest itself more subtly. Perhaps some of the Constructs—subroutines of the Master Program—would be friendlier, more apt to form alliances. Perhaps—in some cases—Program bias might translate as romantic interest, sexual attraction…

ELEVEN

"I keep my treasure in this small grotto." She led me into a chamber about the size of a walk-in closet. "I wish you could see it. But then, if you could see, you would not have stayed long enough to have found out about this place."

By now I had grown a little weary of her intermittent self-pity: "Do you mean I would have run away in fear or have been *petrified* by fright?"

"That was unkind," she said after a long moment.

"You're right," I agreed. "And I'm sorry. But you need to understand something, Euryale. You can't hold onto someone through pity—not for long, at any rate."

"I deserve to be loved!" she cried.

"I know that. But it is your strength and courage and endurance that attracts me. Not your wretchedness. I feel compassion for you, not pity. Please don't think so little of me to suppose that my love might be purchased by something so mean as pity."

There was a thoughtful silence. "Well," she said finally, trying to slide into a light-hearted tone, "if I cannot buy your affection with pity, then how about gold?" She held out my hand and poured a pile of coins across it.

"Gold is always nice," I said agreeably.

She laughed. "Well, then how about gems? What do you like? Diamonds? Rubies? Emeralds?" I heard her open a chest and dig through its contents. "How about a crown?" I suddenly felt the weight of a heavy metal circlet settle over my head.

"Where did you get this stuff?"

"Oh, most of it was already here when I first moved in…"

"And the rest?" I prompted.

"Daggoth," she said slowly. "He gave some of it into my keeping. To guard. He knew no one would come looking for it here, even if they knew where it was. Euryale makes such a good watchdog!" she said bitterly.

"And I suppose this is part of what he meant by your destiny?"

I could imagine, rather than actually hear her nod. "There is a potent artifact here. He said that it must not fall into the wrong hands. He said that I was to guard it with my life."

"What else did Mr. Wizard say?"

"He said…the day that it came to another's hands…would be the day my wretched existence would come to an end. That prophecy has frightened me for years…"

"But now?"

"Now, I am weary. An end—any end—would be most welcome." She worked her way to the back of the chamber and, after rearranging some chests, returned and touched my face. "Are you the one?" she asked softly. "Are you the one whose coming I have feared these many long years?" She took my hands in hers. "Are these the hands destined to wield Euryale's bane and thus fulfill the prophecy?"

"I would not hurt you," I answered gently.

"Too late!" She sighed. "You have already wounded me. If you are the one then it is only right and fitting."

"Euryale—"

"Here." An object was placed in my hands. "In your fevered sleep you once cried out for a sword. I give you a sword now. Tell me: what will you do with it?"

It was a shortsword. Slowly, I drew it from it's sheath and listened to it—even before attempting a tactile examination.

There was power here.

I ran my fingers along the flat of the blade, feeling the runes and symbols of mystic energy. I knew this sword: the carved patterns on the hilt and the great jewel set in its pommel confirmed my suspicions. "My lady," I inquired, unable to resist formality in the presence of such an artifact, "may I borrow this device?"

"My lord," she answered in kind, "thou mayest ask anything of me, and I would grant to thee with all of my heart! Ask for half of this treasure and I would give it all to thee! But why does a sightless man ask for this sword—unless to fulfill Daggoth's prophecy?"

I laughed. "Don't be afraid. It's very simple: I have friends to rescue and I need a sword."

"But your eyes—"

"With this sword I shall have my eyes!"

"I do not understand, but the sword is yours if you wish it."

"Madam, you do not know what you are offering me so freely."

"Good sir, I only know that which I deem most precious I have already offered…"

"Euryale, this is Balmung, the legendary sword of the *Nibelungen*! This is the ultimate Dwarven blade, forged when the world was young and Dwarven smiths vied with Elven craftsmen for the mastery of the Forge!

"Out of every thousand swords, there might be one that lays claim to a special purpose. And out of every ten thousand of those comes a weapon with a heritage of enchantment. But Balmung is one of the ultimate swords of power. Only one other weapon, down all the corridors of time, can lay claim to like power and potency: Caladbolg, the *Sidhe* longsword with its blade of pure crystal."

"How do you know this?"

"By the runes engraved upon the blade and hilt. And because it whispers of its power to me, even as I hold it now."

"And what does it tell you to do?" she asked in a tremulous voice.

"It tells me to right an old wrong, Euryale. And it tells me to fulfill your prophecy."

"I am afraid," she whispered.

"Afraid? You? The 'monster' who has terrorized the countryside these past seven years?"

"Please, do not mock me—"

"I don't mock you, Euryale. It just seems ironic that one of the most feared persons within a hundred leagues of Gaehill is afraid of a blind man."

"Because, of all men, you are the one over which I have no power!"

"Why is that? Is it because my eyes are covered? Or because you cannot bring yourself to harm me even at the peril of your own life?"

She was silent except for the sound of ragged breathing.

"Do not fear me. Or what I am about to do." I walked toward the last sound of her voice and reached out to touch her cheek. She flinched away and there was a sudden hissing sound. "I shall end this curse, once and for all!"

"Then you know," she said slowly.

"Yes. Though it took me some time—I know."

"How you must despise me."

"No. I am a bard, Euryale. As such, I am familiar with the truth of the story. The gods are often unfair and punish the many for the one's misdeeds. The story of the Gorgons is well-known. But it is Medusa's name that is a hissing in the mouths of the skalds and storytellers! For it was her vanity and boast of unrivaled beauty that brought down Aphrodite's curse! Her sisters, Stheno and Euryale, are a tragic footnote to the story. When they are even remembered at all."

"We had our vanity, too," she admitted quietly.

"As do we all. Aphrodite is perhaps the greatest offender of all in this matter. What a pity that no one punishes her for her unseemly pride."

"Medusa is dead…"

"And nearly forgotten. As you and Stheno have already been. The only fame left to you is your status as a local oddity: not to be feared as long as you are avoided. And that little notoriety has been eclipsed by the arrival of a bigger and better monster."

"And after all of these years," she pondered in that same quiet voice, "I do not know which is worse: to be hated and feared, or to be forgotten and alone."

"It no longer matters," I told her gently, "for I mean to end it. Here and now. Come here."

Now the silence was long and loud. Almost a full minute passed before the scrape of sandaled feet over stone announced her movement toward me. "You will use the sword?" she asked softly.

"Of course. I have lost my power so it is the only way."

She stopped, and then her step quickened. "I am here," she announced, taking my free hand in hers. "But before you do as you will, I ask a boon: a kiss."

"A kiss?"

"Now. Before I lose my nerve."

One of her hands was suddenly behind my head, bringing it close so that my lips found hers in the warm darkness. Now I was aware of the nest of serpents, unturbaned, that coiled and writhed near my face. Now I was aware of the fangs that curved beneath those willing lips. But now I knew no fear for I finally knew just who and what I was embracing in the darkness.

She grasped Balmung by the tip of the blade and moved it so that my arm was forced back and down, positioned for a slight upward thrust. "Do it quickly!" she whispered. "And if you feel any pity whatsoever: strike again, a second time, to make sure the job is done and I do not suffer."

"Euryale," I chided, reaching out to stroke her hair. A sudden hissing reminded me to draw my hand back just in time. "You misunderstand."

"Do it quickly, my friend! Before I lose my courage!"

"Very well," I agreed.

I drew the sword's point back from where it pressed against her breast, and raised it over our heads. "In the name of thy makers, Brokk and Sindri, I invoke thee, Balmung! Enchantment of Ivaldi's sons, I claim thy power and make my wish twofold: healing *and* deliverance—for us both!"

Warmth enveloped me.

And a sudden weakness.

Euryale experienced it and sagged against me.

Then came surge of power: a sense of strength and a burning, throbbing sensation where my wounds—*had* been! It passed quickly, with a fading aura of expended power, and in another moment I felt rested and strong again.

I reached up and ripped the bandages from my head.

"No!" Euryale cried out in alarm and terror, but it was too late: I could see her now.

I could see a slender young woman trying to cover her face with one hand and shield my eyes with the other.

"Euryale, it's all right. I can look upon you with no harm. One of Balmung's most potent powers is its ability to grant a single, potent wish every seven years. To rescue my friends, I had to heal myself. But I gambled that its power would be sufficient for us both. I think it was."

She looked up and then used her hands to feel about her head. "I have hair!" she cried. "Real hair!"

It seemed inappropriate, at that particular moment, to point out that her hair was pale green. In most other respects, she appeared normal. In fact, a lot better than normal: even though the wish had been spread too thin to complete her transformation to the last detail, she was still attractive—in an exotic sort of way.

"How can I ever thank you?" she cried, throwing her arms around me and falling upon her knees.

"Uh, well—like I said—um—if I could borrow this sword—"

"It is yours to keep! How else may I reward thee?"

"Uh, the sword is quite enough—uh—thank you—" Kneeling with her arms about me had placed her face and my anatomy in a socially awkward tête-à-tête. "Actually, any help you can give me in getting to my friends would be greatly appreciated."

"Of course," she murmured silkily, pressing her cheek to my—uh—leg.

"In view of their impending sacrifice: the sooner, the better," I added.

"Of course," she said. But it carried a ring of reluctance.

#

Even stripped of her monstrous powers of petrification, Euryale proved more formidable than I had supposed. Over the years of her exile she had studied the occult arts to try to rid herself of her monstrous form. Though she had failed in that final goal, she had acquired considerable powers—most particularly in the practice of illusionary magic.

That talent enabled us to enter Gaehill unmolested. Every town guardsman, merchant, or citizen who looked our way, saw only an old man and old woman of no particular appearance, tottering down the street, leading a burro. Her powers had to be considerable if she was able to layer a second *glamour* over the first that already encircled Ghost.

By spending the better part of the morning wandering through the marketplace, we learned that the sacrifice was scheduled for midnight, this very night. We also decided that dealing with one fire-breathing Dragon in his cave would be preferable to tangling with a multitude of priests, acolytes, and temple guards in their own manmade labyrinth.

After doing all the reconnoitering possible, we found an inn and rented a room.

#

"How about a nap before lunch?" Euryale suggested, patting the bed.

I could have done with a little rest but I doubted that rest was on Euryale's agenda. I shook my head. "Let's go over that map of yours again."

She sighed and came over to the table. "It has been over seven years since I have been abroad in this area: not only is my memory untrustworthy, but there are sure to be changes, as well."

"I'll check those out after sunset when I'm less likely to be seen. Now let's assume the natural chimney is still there and unblocked…"

"We have a full fifty feet of rope."

"Will that be enough?"

She nodded. "At best, the drop is no more than forty."

"If your memory serves you right."

"It is difficult to be certain," she fumed. "Oh, Ripley! What kind of strategy is this? You are going to climb down that chimney into the caverns, somehow find your way to the Room of Sacrifices, somehow free your friends, somehow defeat a fearsome Firedrake, and somehow find a way to sneak all of you back out again, before the guards can find out and interfere. *Somehow* this kind of planning does not reassure me."

"Come up with a better idea and I'll be happy to listen."

She put her arms around me. "Loyalty to one's friends is very noble. But what kind of a friend would expect you to commit certain suicide—a hopeless rescue attempt that most likely will end in tragedy for all of us?"

I shook my head. "My friends wouldn't ask this of me. But my friendships aren't based on what my friends ask."

I let it go at that. I saw no reason to bring my Access Code into the discussion. This rescue might seem the foolish undertaking of an idealist, but the cold, hard reality of it was that if Dr. Quebedeaux died, my chances of survival—much less my chance of getting back out of the Program—would die with her. I wanted to help my friends, of course; but I shrank from the question of what I would do if I had any other chance of regaining my programmer status.

"Let's get something to eat" was my escape from pursuing the thought any further.

#

The name of our hostel was "The Roaring Hangman And True Blacksmith Inn." And if its name was twice as long, the tavern downstairs was only half as large as that of The Crashing Boar. Still, we did not find that to be any inconvenience: there was a ready selection of empty tables for us to choose from. Gaehill boasted a number of inns and taverns and, with the arrival of the Dragon, the tourist trade seemed to have dropped off quite a bit.

As there didn't seem to be any further point in keeping up appearances, Euryale dispersed our illusionary disguises and we ordered lunch, figuring that no one would connect us with the old couple who were nosing around earlier in the day.

"You know," she observed, while we waited for the food to arrive, "you are my first date in over seven years."

"There will be many more," I assured her.

"I hope so," she purred.

By "many more," I had been referring to other men. I had the uncomfortable feeling that we weren't exactly on the same wavelength.

During the course of our meal she asked many questions. I couldn't lie to her: not only was she too intelligent to fall for any inconsistencies, but she had saved my life as well. Since we might both be dead before another sunrise, I couldn't help but tell her the truth. Not about the Reality from which I came or anything about computers and programs and such. But I told her as much as I could about who I was and what I had done in this Reality. And what circumstances had brought me to the point where I found myself now.

She was thoughtful after I had finished. "So," she deduced after considering this new angle on my identity, "I was succored by the Archdruid of Dyrinwall, after all."

"Not so loud. For the time being, I think it would be better if you kept calling me Ripley and we avoided any references to where I'm from."

"Why?"

"If anyone recognizes me here, it's not likely to be a friend, I said.

And just about jumped out of my chair as a voice behind me said: "Riplakish!"

I turned my surprise into a gracious, mannerly rise and pulled back a chair for our new arrival. "Well met, Lilith. Won't you join us?"

"Not so well met. But I will join you." The Demoness slid into the offered chair.

"I expected to run into you before now," I said to her after introductions had been completed.

"You must be kidding! With a holy man like Thyme in your party?"

"Well, afterwards—"

"It was too late then," she snapped. "The damage was already done! Orcus nearly had my soul for dinner over this whole affair!"

"How could he blame you?"

"For a bard and a Dreamlord you certainly can be a nit," she muttered in exasperation. "Do you think 'fairness' is a prerequisite for the executive positions in Hell? Orcus is the Infernal Prince of the Undead, for Cromsake!"

"I'll have a few words with him and straighten this all out—"

She shook her head. "You are such a nice guy, but oh-boy you are such a nit! It's too late for talk, now. The only reason that I'm still around is because Orcus has this thing about saving face. He's making an example out of me in case the other Demons start getting careless in the performance of their assigned duties."

"I don't understand…"

"Nit! Come hither, man, and I will show you!"

As I leaned toward her to see just what it was she would show me, she grabbed me. And laid one on me. A kiss, that is.

Now there's nothing wrong with an attractive woman grabbing you in a bar and kissing you. Unless, of course, she happens to be a Succubus. Then you've got about fifteen seconds to say your prayers before your ass is ash.

It came back to me about three seconds into the kiss that Lilith was, indeed, a Succubus. And it was probably another minute before she broke her lip lock and gave me a chance to draw air. I leaned back in my chair and tried to look nonplused. I was unsuccessful and looked very plused for the moment.

"Well, what do you say to that?" she demanded.

"That was a hell of a kiss," I said finally.

"No! That was not a Hell of a kiss!" she stormed. "If that had been a Hell of a kiss, you'd be nothing more than a legend, right now!"

"You've lost your power?"

"I've *lost* nothing! It was *taken* from me!"

"Taken from you?"

"As in dishonorable discharge. Orcus decided that, if Father Thyme would prevent any Demonic aid to your party, he would get me into the game the only other way he could without interfering directly: by giving me back my Humanity. My magic is gone—finding you here was pure luck." Her voice broke. "I'm ruined!" She put her head down on the table and began to cry.

I didn't know what to say.

"You seem to have a talent," Euryale observed, "for making women out of monsters. I have known many men whose efforts run in the opposite direction."

"Tell that to her."

She smiled. "I will. Why don't you see if you can make yourself scarce for an hour or so."

"What about dessert?"

"I am sure we can manage. Now shoo!"

I didn't see any point in spending the last few hours I might have in this life sightseeing so I went back upstairs to our room. I got through an entire page of the journal before my eyes tried to claw their way out through the back of my head. Tugging off my boots, I settled myself on the bed so that my feet could rest on the window sill. As the warm summer breeze caressed my tired, aching feet, I closed my eyes and tried to relax.

I was frustrated. Time was slipping away and I seemed no closer to a solving the Anomaly than when I had first entered Fantasyworld. In fact, my situation was growing more complicated at every turn. Were I a character in some book, I mused, I would be uncovering clues and pursuing lines of inductive and deductive reasoning; eventually I would uncover the mystery and it's solution and wrap it all up in a nice, tidy little denouement.

The trouble was, real life wasn't like that. Real life didn't follow nicely plotted scenarios. Real life was messy, accidental. Chance and Fate played according to House odds and payoffs were rare and minuscule. In real life people missed golden opportunities, passed like ships in the night, and the best-laid plans always seemed to end with an appointment in Samara.

And then I smiled sheepishly as sleep rode in on the drowsy, afternoon breeze: I had momentarily confused real life with the DreamNet.

#

I slept and could recall no dreams as I awoke with the taste of soft lips on my own. Outside the window the sun was visibly low in the west.

"What time is it?" I asked, suddenly frantic at the loss of the day.

"Early enough to have some food before we set out on this fool's errand," Euryale replied gently. "Come."

I wasn't hungry but I allowed myself to be helped from my bed and led from the room.

Downstairs, the tavern was crowded and nowhere was an empty table to be seen. Undaunted, Euryale took me by the hand and started across the packed and noisy room. As we wound our way between tables and around serving maids, my eye was drawn to a table in the corner.

Three men stood around it, wearing mixed expressions of admiration for the lady seated there and annoyance for the other two interlopers who wouldn't go away.

One could hardly blame them. White, almost platinum, hair fell in a silvery cascade over her shoulders. Her black gown clung to every exquisite curve of her body. What it didn't reveal of milk-white skin in a daring expanse of décolleté, it suggested in sleek, tight molding. The seductive features of her face were boldly accentuated by blood-red lips and eyes that glittered like frosted blue ice…

I did a double-take: it was Lilith.

I turned to Euryale as we approached the table. "Your doing?"

"No magic, just make-up," she answered. "The oldest art of illusion in the world."

Lilith saw us coming and sent her would-be suitors away. She stood as we reached the table.

"Well met, Lilith."

"Better met," she countered, stepping in closer and kissing me again. Perhaps it was my feeling of awkwardness, or the sensation of three pairs of eyes glaring daggers at my back, but I could have sworn that this kiss was almost twice as long as the last one.

"You must understand," she explained when she finally let me go, "that this is a whole new experience for me. For thousands of years a kiss has been a cold, dispassionate way of drawing upon the life-forces of my prey. I did it because I had to. There was no 'wanting' involved.

"But now," she continued as we all sat down, "I find there are new depths, new sensations, new *meanings* to this act!"

"And I think you will find," I told her, "that some people will bring more meaning to it than others."

She perked up at that. "It is true! I have kissed a number of men these past few hours and I have noticed quite a difference!"

I fought back a smile. "I'll bet you have."

"Perhaps you can tell me?"

"Tell you what?"

"Why all those other men kiss so differently from each other and, yet, still feel the same."

"Well—"

"But when I kiss you," she continued, "I feel all tingly and shivery all over."

Euryale coughed politely and I began looking around for our waitress.

#

Over dinner we discussed Lilith's additional role in our plans.

She was to remain behind while Euryale guided me to the chimney-like dropshaft that descended into the honeycomb of caverns that Smog had claimed for his lair. Once I was "safely" in, Euryale was to rendezvous with Lilith at the Well of Allah, about a mile out of town. By that time, the ex-Succubus was supposed to have acquired enough mounts for our getaway. This meant seven horses in addition to Ghost if everything went well at both ends. If it didn't—well, either I was in for a long walk, or they were going to be stuck with a lot of extra horses.

Lilith looked at the sketchy timetable and asked when I was supposed to show up.

"Hard to say, exactly. But if I'm not there by sunrise," I added soberly, "hit the road and don't look back."

"Maybe we could meet you at some point closer to the caves," she suggested.

I shook my head. "No deviations from the plan: we meet at Allah's Well."

Euryale frowned. "If it ends well."

FROM THE JOURNAL OF DAGGOTH THE DARK

The most amazing thing: an Elf came to the door, this morning, and tried to sell me boxes of cookies. Don't think it was one of Ripley's jokes or it would have manifested much sooner. So I'm faced with two possibilities: either The Machine has assimilated an outside prototype from another network's files, or some Fantasyworld subprograms are evolving a capitalistic philosophy—a blatant departure from our pseudo-medieval economic structure.

Come to think of it, rumors from Gaehill would suggest their Dragon in residence is a lot more sophisticated at the virgin-extortion racket than he has any right to be.

TWELVE

The moon was bright, visibility was clear, and not another soul was in sight. We found the entry hole a good two hours before midnight and then located a long, sturdy log to serve as a crossbrace across the opening. After tying off the rope I dismissed Euryale. "Nothing more you can do here. Go see if you can keep Lilith out of trouble."

She stared at me for a long moment. And then she put her hands on my shoulders and kissed me.

"Lilith is right," she said, backing away. "You do make a girl feel all tingly and shivery all over!"

"Get going," I growled. She turned and melted into the night.

I hadn't done any rope climbing for years, so I took my time. When I reached the bottom there was still a good twenty feet of rope to spare, so I cut the excess and coiled it over my shoulder. Unsheathed, Balmung's blade gave of a soft, flickering light of a reddish hue—sufficient to follow the passageway without resorting to a torch. I took my last breath of fresh air and started down the passage.

There is a smell peculiar to Dragons and their lairs that immediately warns all but the most inexperienced that a fire-breathing lizard is nearby. If you've never gotten a whiff of Dragonstink, it's a bit difficult to describe. Imagine baked slime…

I hurried along the twisting corridors of hollowed-out stone as my only realistic chance of coming out of this alive lay in my getting my Program Access Code back from Silverthane before Smog showed up. Even with the Code and my powers restored, facing down old Brimstone Breath could still prove a bit dicey. He hadn't been that easy ten years ago and he was ten years the wiser, now. If I couldn't get the Code before Smog arrived, there was going to be a very unhappy ending to this little rescue story.

After what seemed like an hour of tracing and backtracking passages, checking out every cul-de-sac and dead-end, I found one that opened into a large, torchlit cavern.

I dimmed Balmung's light and hung back in the shadows while I gave the big room the once-over. No Dragon. But there were a lot of bones scattered about.

And five very naked ladies chained to a series of posts, arranged in a large semicircle. I had found the Room of Sacrifices.

Rijma was the first to see me. "Well, it's about time!" she scolded.

Dyantha was exuberant: "Robert! Thank God!"

Palys was more serene: "I knew you would make it."

Aeriel was more pragmatic: "Hush, ladies! Do you want the monster to come running in here before we are freed?"

Alyx remained silent and everyone else shut up for the moment.

Quickly and quietly, I made my way across the bone-littered floor, feeling as naked as everyone else and expecting Smog to show up at any moment. As soon as everyone was free I figured that we stood a better than even chance of getting out alive.

Setting everyone free was going to be problem, however: their wrists were enclosed in iron cuffs on a length of chain that passed through a heavy metal staple at the top of each post. Although a Dwarven blade like Balmung would make short work of the soft iron links, the noise would surely summon Smog before I was halfway done.

The ultimate solution to the whole problem lay in getting my Access Code back, so I approached Ms. Silverthane and planted myself just six inches away from her nose.

"I don't have time to beat around the bush," I whispered. "And you don't have time to play any more silly games! Unless you want us all to be the guests of honor at this baroque barbecue, you'd better cough up my Access Code and do it *muy pronto*!"

Alyx looked at me with a pained expression but didn't utter a word.

"C'mon, Doc! This is serious! I need that code to get you all out of here—"

"She can't tell you anything."

I turned and looked at Rijma. "What did you say?"

"She can't tell you the Code. She can't tell you anything." I could see that Dr. Cooper was fighting to keep the panic out of her avatar's voice.

"What are you saying?" I hissed.

"How do you suppose the Gaehill officials were able to hold a sorceress prisoner for so long?"

I stared dumbly.

"Immobilize her hands to restrict somatic gestures. And place a Silence spell on her so that she can't utilize verbal keys. Do that and you can hold the most powerful magic user who ever lived."

And, in the meantime, she couldn't tell me my Program Access Code.

I turned back to Alyx Silverthane and folded my arms. "If I get you out of here," I gritted, "it's with the tacit understanding that I get my code back just as soon as we find your voice!"

She nodded quickly: she was in no position to do any bargaining.

Now the problem was how was I going to get these people out of here and past the Dragon with no magic and no backup?

"Uh, Riplakish..."

"Not now, Aeriel; I'm thinking."

"Ssso, we meet again, at lassst!"

"Please ladies, be quiet until I can figure this out."

"If thou canssst not figure thisss out, I ssshall be glad to exsssplain it to thee."

This time the voice registered and I fought the impulse to whirl around. Instead, I forced myself to continue studying the bolts that held Alyx's shackles in place. "That you, Smog?" I inquired in my best nonchalant tone of voice. That wasn't easy as I was feeling very chalant at this particular moment.

"Thou knowessst that it isss, Riplakisssh!"

"Sorry to hear that."

Ever hear a Dragon chuckle? It's a nasty sound. "I thought thou mightessst be," he gloated.

"Yeah. I had hoped you had learned your lesson the last time." I turned around, deciding that if I was going to bluff my way out of this, I might as well go for broke. Losing my temper helped. "Listen, gashole: these people are my friends! It's just a lucky thing for you that I got here when I did! If you had so much as *nibbled* one ladyfinger, I'd be all over you like flies on Orcs! Now you've got just one minute to release them and point out the nearest exit! After they leave, we'll sit down and talk about your little racket and, if you cooperate, I might—I say *might*—just let you out of this with your scales intact!"

Dragon faces are notoriously hard to read, but Smog appeared more than inscrutable. He looked positively unimpressed.

"Dossst thou truly think me ssso sssimple?" Smog inquired, leaning forward on his scaly elbows and cradling his chin on his claws.

"If it were not ssso obviousss from your conversssationsss, it would be evident from thy failure to break thessse fettersss: thou hassst lossst thy magical powersss!" He smiled, showing triple rows of carious teeth. "Ssshow me one sssimple trick and I shall acsssede to thy wissshesss!" His eyes lit up in anticipation. "Otherwissse, I ssshall fricasssee thee where thou ssstandessst."

"A trick?"

"A magic trick."

I had difficulty swallowing. "Any magic trick?"

Smog nodded. "Thou hassst one minute!"

I looked around helplessly. "Anybody got a deck of cards?"

"Fifty ssseconds."

In desperate moments, desperate plans are born. "How about a rope trick?" I asked, pulling the coil over my head and off of my shoulder.

Smog shrugged. "Forty sssecondsss."

"I've got twenty gold pieces that say the druid does it!" Rijma announced to the room in general. That encouragement was quickly dampened by responses from the rest of the captives.

"You're on!"

"I'll take that bet!"

"How do I collect if you lose?"

How do you tie a slipknot? I pondered frantically.

"Thirty sssecondsss."

"Come on, Rip—I've got twenty gold ones riding on this," Rijma murmured as I tried to get enough play in my knot to allow the loop to open and close.

"Twenty sssecondsss."

Okay. There. It wasn't a true slipknot but, with a little luck, it might just do the job.

"Fifteen sssecondsss."

"Hey, Smog!" I began to twirl my makeshift lasso. "Ever been to a rodeo?" I enlarged the loop and sent it spinning high into the air.

"Ten sssecondsss."

Now I dropped it down over my body so that I was standing in the center of the spinning circle of rope.

"Nine…eight…"

"Watch this!" I held the loop just a few inches from the ground and jumped out. And then back in, again. So far, I was extremely lucky: I hadn't done these particular stunts since my cowboy-obsessive days back in the fifth grade.

"...Sssix...five..."

This time I jumped back out and brought my lariat up and spinning sideways.

"...Four..."

I jumped through the whirling oval and nearly stumbled in the process.

"I cannot bear to watch!" It sounded like Dyantha.

"Now I know why Vaudeville died." Rijma again, of course.

"...Three...two..."

"And now for the grand finale!" I announced, recovering from my stumble. "I call this trick: 'Roping the Bull'!"

"One! Thy time isss up, Riplakisssh!" And with that pronouncement, Smog took a deep breath.

I sent the rope out, praying that I wouldn't miss. There would be no second chances.

Out of the corner of my eye I noticed that Palys had managed to free herself. But she was standing still, apparently fascinated by the sight of the rope uncurling toward the mammoth lizard, one arm raised to point out its twirling trajectory.

For a moment it looked as if the spinning circle of rope would fly wide of its mark. Then the world blinked. Time seemed to suddenly slow down perceptibly and each individual action seemed to unfold with crystallized clarity: the lasso was moving in the proper trajectory and flames started to lick around the edges of that fearsome mouth as the loop of my rope encircled Smog's snout. Almost too late, I remembered to give the rope that twisting tug to snap the loop shut—just as the Firedrake was unleashing his flame.

Now I really hauled back on the rope and dug my heels in for dear life. Smog hadn't started to fight back just yet: he was just beginning to realize that all that fire and brimstone he had just belched at me had suddenly reached an unexpected dead end. His eyes bugged out, his nostrils vented steam, and his belly suddenly bulged like a gas-filled balloon: with his mouth roped shut, that thermal blast had just one place that it could go.

Smog was swelling up like a balloon in the Thanksgiving Day Parade, now; and he began tearing at the noose with one claw while he clutched at his tummy with the other.

I cracked the rope like a whip to keep him from getting a firm purchase on it, and yelled: "Blow it out your ass, Smog!"

He did.

Try to imagine a hundred cars, all backfiring at once.

The noise was positively deafening: it shook the cavern and started a rain of stalactites that somehow managed to miss everyone but Smog. It is rather hard to miss a half-acre of Dragon in such a close and confined space. When the dust finally began to settle, Smog was out cold, half buried under a couple of tons of rock.

#

Insuring Smog's immobility was my first priority. Palys helped me hogtie the unconscious Dragon and dropped a bombshell as I was cinching the last of the ropes.

"I have your Access Code," she told me casually.

"Great! Why didn't you tell me before?"

"It isn't so simple. Dr. Quebedeaux used hypnosis to close off any memory of the Code in your mind. Simply reciting the code back to you wouldn't remove the block."

That explained quite a bit—including the reason why I didn't remember anything but a sound and restful sleep the first night of our capture.

"So how do I force her to undo her hypnotic suggestions?"

"Unnecessary. I can do that. If you'll permit me."

I stood there and stared at her. "*Who* are you?" I asked quietly.

She smiled shyly. "A friend. You must believe that. Especially if you are to permit me to hypnotize you."

"Hypnotize me?"

"To remove her subconscious blocks and restore your Program Access Code."

That took some consideration. I would be highly reluctant to let my best friend go messing around in my mind. Letting a complete stranger—but I was desperate for that code!

"Okay," I answered finally.

"Come," she said; "you may free the others more readily once you have powers restored." She led me to another exit from the room and down a different passage. It only twisted and curved a short distance before opening up into another chamber. This room was slightly larger than Smog's lunchroom, but there was less space as it was half-filled with treasure. Dragons are real collectors.

"Here," she said, sitting me down and picking up a diamond pendant. "It will be quieter in here and there are fewer distractions."

Oh yeah? Maybe five naked ladies are more distracting than just one, but that particular one was standing right in front of me, demanding my complete attention. I tried to concentrate on the swaying pendant but found myself fighting the impulse to focus another foot or so beyond.

Oh my…

From now on I intended to keep a much closer eye on Palys.

I was just thinking about how interesting that could prove to be, when she spoke again, breaking my reverie.

I looked up blankly. "Excuse me?"

She smiled. "I said, we're all done. You should be able to utilize your Access Code now. Want to give it a test?"

I nodded dumbly. Maybe keeping an eye on this one was going to be a lot harder than I thought. I stood and stretched, flexing my fingers. "What should I try, first?"

She struck a pose and ran her hands down the rollercoaster curves of her body. "How about some clothing?"

"Seems a shame," I sighed, "but I guess we must deal in practicalities."

"There will be time for impracticalities later," she murmured.

"What would milady like?" I asked, letting that last comment slide. "A gown of finest silk?"

"Something a little more practical for our present circumstances," she demurred. "I'll take just what I had before, thank you."

"You're sure?"

She smiled. "I'm always sure."

"Okay…" I paused for a moment of cogitation. Then I wove the spell with murmur and gesture and thought. Minor magic use was still seemed safe enough; it was the major matrix-altering stuff I had to avoid.

"Not bad," she decided, when I was done. "A little loose here and a little tight there—but you're not familiar enough with my body." She gave me another one of those looks and then made a gesture. Her leather outfit reconfigured and molded itself to her body. And it seemed to lose about thirty percent of the material that I had provided in the process.

"Weapons?" she asked. "Equipment?"

"Sorry. I forgot." In a twinkling of an eye I completed her outfitting.

"Now, how about the others?"

The power was more manageable with each attempt; I was able to accomplish their outfittings without leaving my spot. When I was sure that they were all properly dressed and equipped, I dissolved their fetters and hung a series of glowing arrows in the air to lead them to the treasure room.

"Now," I said, turning and rubbing my hands together, "let's see what goodies are to be had here."

There were plenty. And even though there was more than enough to go around, there were a couple of baubles that provoked some debates of ownership.

I waded through the stuff, unfazed by the sight of gems as big as goose eggs and jewelry that made Tiffany's look like a five-and-dime: I was hunting for bigger treasure.

There was magic hidden here—magic strong enough to tug at the corners of my perception without the benefit of a spell of Discernment. That's what I was after. After the ladies had gathered all they wanted—or at least all they could carry—there would still be several hundred times the amount I needed to fill my purse for all our needs to come.

I crawled over mounds of silk tapestries and piles of gold and silver coins. I wound my way between stacked bars of platinum and chests brimming with gems and jewels. I followed the trail of magically charged ether as a bloodhound follows the scent. At one point the trail forked and I had to choose which branch to pursue next. Falling back on the old dungeon mapping adage, "you can't go wrong if you go right," I abandoned the ethereal trail that diverged to the left. The one to the right led to a large, gem-laden chest. I began digging.

Even with Palys' help, it took a long while to empty it by hand. As I said before, magic sometimes triggers more magic; so when dealing with an unknown factor, I prefer the prudence of doing it the hard way.

Under the gems we found several bolts of silks and satins. Under those, we found a lamp.

I picked it up and examined it closely. The design was so familiar, I figured it had to be one of my original creations. Sure enough,

"Aladdin Lamp Co.—Made in Baghdad" was stamped on the underside. I began rubbing the brass, wondering if this was a one-wisher, a three-wisher, or one of those special, unlimited, use-it-for-as-long-as-you-can-hold-on-to-it models.

True to form, smoke began to issue from the lamp's spout.

I have seen the Djinn assume forms, male and female, both pleasing to the mortal eye and terrible of aspect. I've witnessed Efreet who stun the senses as they appear in a conglomeration of demonic, animalistic, and human configurations. I've even seen a Genie with the light brown hair. So, as the smoke coalesced, I braced myself, ready for almost anything.

Almost.

I wasn't ready for a balding, pinch-faced man of advancing years, dressed in early twentieth-century formal attire. He bowed stiffly from the waist.

"Um..." The striped waistcoat, black cravat and swallow-tailed jacket had left me momentarily befuddled. "Are you the slave of the lamp?"

His expression was a pitched battle between disapproval and condescension with both sides agreeing to a cohabital truce as he spoke. "*Servant* of the lawmp," he corrected in clipped, British syllables. Then sighed, "How may we serve you, Mawster?"

"Uh..." I pondered, "...you can begin by telling me how many wishes I get."

He grimaced. "Let us be sure that we understand you, sir: you wish to know how many wishes we are contractually required to extend to the proprietor of the lawmp. Are we correct?"

Pretty smooth, but I wasn't that simple. I shook my head. "No, I don't *wish* to know. I'm just asking. "

He frowned. "Three, Mawster."

"And your name?"

He cocked his head and looked at me blankly. "Our name? Sir?"

"It hardly seems proper to address you as 'hey you,' even if I am the master of the lamp." Two could play at snobbery.

The frown receded and an eyebrow arched—well—archly. "Do you anticipate our association being an extended one, sir? Most lawmp holders need only a passing moment to use up their three wishes." He sniffed. "Ten minutes, tops."

I folded my arms and just looked at him.

"Gordon. Sir."

"Got a brother named Gilby?" Rijma wanted to know.

The set of his brow suggested there might be something in a name but I was not inclined to press my luck. "Thank you."

He harrumphed. "So what will Mawster's first wish be? Great wealth, perhaps?"

I gestured at the piles of gems, coins, and stacks of rare finery. "I'm already in the highest tax bracket I can imagine."

He took a good look around. "We see, sir. Then perhaps you will be asking for beautiful—" A bemused expression crept across his face as he considered the other ladies present.

"Bless our nonexistant soul, sir; but we did not realize that you had so many wives!"

It was suddenly quiet enough to hear a pin drop.

"Uh, Gordon—these are not my wives."

"But of course, sir," he responded quickly, adjusting his cuff links and tugging at a sleeve. "We apologize for such an obvious social gawffe."

"Don't men—"

"It is obvious that such a rich and powerful man as yourself would never consider marrying women as plain as these! Though we are sure," he added, giving them another taciturn appraisal, "that they have probably served as adequate concubines until now."

The expressions around me were quickly going from dangerous to downright ugly.

"And now that we are here, they may be dismissed and we will begin with a list of eligible princesses—"

"Silence, Slave of the Lamp!" I thundered. "You will speak only when spoken to!" I disliked taking that tone of voice, but I just may have saved someone's life by doing so. Maybe my own, in fact.

"Servant."

"What?"

"Servant of the lawmp. Not slave." He sniffed. "Perhaps a review of eligible *princes* would put Mawster in a better humour?"

Actually, no. I explained that and then conveyed my desire that he return to the lamp's confines until such a time as my temper and a suddenly expanded vocabulary were back in abeyance.

I don't know which was more effective, the quaint and colorful phrases or the expressions on my companions' faces, but he was back in the lamp before you could hum "Smoke Gets In Your Eyes."

"Riplakish."

It was Palys. She was tugging at something protruding from a particularly overstuffed treasure chest. Rijma was rounding up the rest of the party and herding them toward the exit. Filling my belt pouches with a King's ransom in gems.

"What is it?"

"Something you won't want to leave behind," she grunted.

Joining her, I could see the hilt of a sword. Buried up to its guard in a mound of gold and silver coins. As I took a hold of the grip, a tingling sensation passed through my body and I could feel the hair raising on the back of my neck: there was potent magic here—that other presence of strong enchantment that I had sensed earlier. Bracing myself, I began to pull while Palys scooped coins out of the chest in glittering, scintillating cascades.

Finally, almost eagerly, it came free: a five-foot longsword in a jeweled scabbard.

I think I knew even before I loosed the safety strap and drew it from its sheath. Still, there was the shock and the overwhelming, nameless emotion that slapped me, filled me, and overflowed as I gazed upon the translucent crystal blade.

Caladbolg, the legendary soulsword of the *Sidhe*!

I stood there, silent for the longest time as the sword bathed the chamber in an eerie blue light. Then, with trembling hand, I drew Balmung and held it up in my left hand. Red light pulsed from the Dwarven shortsword, contrasting the blue flicker from the Elven weapon. An inaudible vibration seemed to fill the air, a silent pitch that carried a feel of harmony rather than dissonance.

Palys finally broke the silence. "*Katana* and *wakizashi*," she said.

"I see you are familiar with Kendo."

She nodded. "Now you possess the 'True Soul' and the 'Guardian of the Soul'. Either one might make you a legend. Together…?" She let the question trail off.

The swords were exquisitely balanced and deceptively light in my hands. I hefted each and then ran through the practice stations of the *Twin Heavens* discipline. The blades flashed and spun through the air, weaving intricate traceries of lightning and silent thunder. I knew I was good, but now, with these two legendary blades, I was capable of something beyond human terms of perfection.

I sheathed them with a feeling of awe and reverence. *No more Mister Nice Guy,* I vowed: from here on out I was going to kick ass and take names.

On the way out, I freed Smog from the ropes, rocks, and rubble by reducing him to six inches in size. I didn't figure that he had much room to complain about this, considering the other options that I now had the ability to exercise.

Besides, now that he was six inches long, his next virgin sacrifice should last him at least three or four years.

If he could talk anyone into bringing him one, that is.

Maybe he'd get lucky and find one that would laugh herself to death.

FROM THE JOURNAL OF DAGGOTH THE DARK

I remember Ripley first raised the morality issue with the Black Knight scenario. "It was immoral," he said, "to create life predestined to a fixed script and then murder it because it followed our instructions." He lost sight of the fact that each story involves conflict and conflict employs a protagonist and an antagonist. Can't do fairytales without black knights kidnapping princesses and being defeated by white knights. And Dreamwalkers pay to come to Fantasyworld and be the White Knight. Never mind the occasional Kink who gets his jollies by conducting his own Inquisitions.

That was the first indication of Ripley's disillusionment with Dreamprogramming—but the real rift developed over the issue of Slavery. "Hey," I told him, "you can't re-create a medieval world without serfs and slaves."

"Then why can't we create a better world?" he asked...

THIRTEEN

After we had rendezvoused with Euryale and Lilith at the Well of Allah, I took a little time out for some voodoo video. There was still the male contingent of the party to rescue, and finding them was the first trick. Once again I unwrapped my crystal ball, hoping I wouldn't see the same ominous blank that I had drawn in my previous searches.

Stephanie...

Unaccountably, I felt a sudden surge of grief. Our marriage had ended badly and I couldn't think of two people who evinced a stronger dislike for one another. But maybe most of the name-calling was a defense mechanism: an effort to convince ourselves and each other that we really didn't care so much, after all.

Stumpy popped into focus at the center of the crystal and, as I zoomed out, I could make out Justin, Conrad, and the others. Pulling back a little further, I recognized the slave markets of Casterbridge. It wasn't hard to extrapolate the rest: Gaehill had found an economical solution to dungeon overcrowding.

Closing my eyes, I concentrated on my newly restored Access Code and tried using my Programmer status to teleport them back. No dice: just a vague sensation of ethereal resistance and a sense of danger if I "pushed" too hard. I broke the connection and reached for my magic lamp.

Gordon appeared in a puff of smoke. "How may I serve you, Mawster?" he asked while making a pointed effort to ignore the presence of the rest of the ladies. "An enchanted sword, perhaps?"

I patted the hilts of Balmung and Caladbolg and shook my head.

"Oh. I see." He made a minimal effort to keep his annoyance in check.

I pointed to the crystal ball and asked if I could wish all of our compatriots free and back in our midst.

"No."

"No?"

"No." He shook his head in the best pedagogical fashion. "This lawmp only dispenses wishes of the highest quality and discernment. In other words, there are no group rates or discounts. If you wish to free your 'friends,' you may do so by utilizing a single wish for each one. In this manner you may free up to three of them—should you so wish." He paused. "Do you so wish?"

"No." If we could only free three of The Rabble without expending any effort, it made more sense to rescue the boys ourselves. "But there is someone else…"

I reviewed the basic facts concerning Vashti's abduction and covered the evidence to date. "Now what I want you to do," I concluded, "is to find her and bring her back to me. Dead or alive. Understand?" While I wasn't counting on Stephanie being alive after all this time, I would still rest easier when I knew for certain. One way or the other.

Gordon's lips were pursed but he nodded.

"Okay, that's my first wish."

"Oh, bravo. And has Mawster decided on a second?" he asked.

I did my best to describe Senator Hanson's avatar and explained that he had been shanghaied by Goblins. "I want him found and returned, too."

"Dead or alive?"

I nodded grimly.

"Very good, sir." He disappeared. And in less than five minutes he was back.

"Well?"

He shrugged. "Dead or alive—if their bodies are still in this world, they are hidden from the scrying abilities of the Djinn."

"Are you saying that it is possible for her to be someplace where she would be hidden—undetectable to both the Djinn and my crystal ball? And that such a place would not preclude the possibility of her still being alive?"

Gordon nodded. "Yes sir. There are many places that are veiled against any kind of farseeing. If your 'friends' are in one of these, we could only find them by going there, ourself, and searching in person."

I knew it was stupid to resurrect any hopes at this point, but I couldn't help myself: "Okay, get started."

"Excuse us?"

"You're excused. Get going."

"But, Mawster! There are hundreds—it could take weeks! Months! And even then there is no guarantee—"

"Then you'd better get started as soon as possible."

He made a face—no small accomplishment, as he typically gave the impression of a man reluctantly sucking on a lemon. "Is this what Mawster truly wishes us to do?"

"We're still on the first two wishes, Jeeves."

"Well, I *never!*"

"Obviously. Which would largely account for your disposition. Now get going before you make another slip with your personal pronouns."

"Yes *sir!*" He glared at me as he faded. Cheshire-cat-like, the frown lines were the last to disappear.

I turned and found myself nose to forehead with Alyx Silverthane. That didn't improve my temper at all.

"Ah, Ms. Silverthane," I observed, stepping back a pace from Dr. Quebedeaux's avatar, "and what am I to do with you? By all rights I should punish you for placing us all in danger and denying us the wherewithal to defend ourselves!"

Her expression remained carefully neutral.

"But I am a magnanimous person by nature, and I have decided to let you go without taking any punitive action."

She regarded me with those solemn lavender eyes that seemed to say that she was sorry—but only in a mildly regretful sort of way. I waited. And so did she. "What is it, Alyx? Is there something that you want?"

There was, of course. But she was too proud to resort to charades and hysterics.

"Oh. I'll bet you want your voice back."

She nodded. Once.

"I can see why you'd want that. After all, aside from the convenience of ordinary communication, a sorceress is rather defenseless without the verbal keys to her spells."

She folded her arms and gave the impression of long-suffering patience.

"Well, I don't know if that's such a good idea," I continued. "The last time you exercised your power, you used it to take us prisoner and strip me of my powers. Now tell me one good reason why I should give you another opportunity to do so."

She could, of course, say nothing in her own defense.

I sighed heavily. "I know I'm going to regret this, but I can't just let you run around practically defenseless. That would be cruel and inhumane. You might want to look up the definitions of those two words in your spare time." I neutralized the Silence spell with more than a little misgiving but I wanted her to be able to look after herself. The last thing I needed was an additional responsibility named Silverthane.

"I've learned my lesson," she answered softly if not convincingly.

"Sure you have." I turned to the others. "Okay, let's ride!"

#

We rode. But we didn't ride far.

The events of the previous night—and the strain of the days preceding it—had taken their toll. We stopped for lunch and ended up making camp for the rest of the day. And night.

There was no formal watch during the day. I let the others nap through the afternoon while Palys and I kept each other awake with small talk. Curiously, the only significant piece of personal information that I was able to pry out of her was she was a member of the Dreamland Programming staff. That, at least, explained her strengths as a Spellcaster. Most of the rest of my questions were met with enigmatic smiles.

I spent some time wading through another page of Daggoth's journal, nursed a headache through supper and crashed into a dreamless slumber that lasted until midnight. I was awakened to Rijma's toe in my side.

"You said to wake you when it was dark," she explained with that marvelous deadpan expression of hers. "Well, it's dark."

"Thanks," I muttered, trying to clear the grogginess from my head.

"I've assigned guard duty until dawn, " she continued, "and you're not on the roster. So why don't you try not being useful for a change: go back to sleep."

The thought was tempting, but I sat up and shook my head: "Now that I'm awake I might as well make another stab at Dag's diary."

"Want some coffee?"

I made a face. "Is that all we have?"

"In regular supply, yes." She sat down on the ground beside me.

I gestured arcanely and a frosty can of Dr. Pepper appeared in midair.

She shook her head. "You really like that stuff?"

I shrugged. "Gotta drink something."

"Mm." She stared off into the darkness. "How long you been dry now?"

"This time?" I had to think. "Almost five years. But I hardly count those three weeks after the court verdict. That was more like a vacation from sobriety."

The Brownie nodded. "We all could use a little vacation from Reality now and then."

"That's why we built Dreamland. Except we made a mistake: in trying to escape Reality, we just went and created another one."

Rijma sighed. "Don't start."

I nodded and opened the can but was denied its contents by the arrival of a crimson arrow. There was a sudden, deadly hissing sound as my Dr. Pepper was torn from my grasp and pinned to a tree some ten feet away.

"Nobody is to be making any movements!" boomed a heavily accented voice from the darkness.

"Nobody move," I seconded. "Keep your hands away from your weapons.

"A wise choice, Comrade," agreed the character who was now walking into our circle of firelight: Errol Flynn wearing fifteenth-century fatigues. "My men are outnumbering your party more than three to one and with arrows which can strike from distance. Furthermore we are being in darkness which is hidden while you are targets in light." He smiled.

"If their aim isn't any better than their English," Rijma murmured, "I vote we rush 'em."

Our captor's ears were sharp: he turned toward Rijma. "Russian?"

Well, apparently not that sharp.

"You are thinking maybe I am Russian?" He threw back his head and laughed. "You are obwiously for someone else mistaking me." He pointed to himself in the best vaudevillian manner. "Allow me to be introducing myself: I am Robbing Hood!"

Too much bad luck at poker was finally paying off: I managed to keep a straight face. Rijma was unable to suppress a snort and a small burst of giggles. This did not sit well with our captor who signaled to someone hidden beyond the firelight. He then advanced to where he could threaten the Brownie at close range.

"You are thinking this is joke, maybe?" he growled. "You are in big trouble! I am Robbing Hood and all around you are my Happy Comrades: we take from the rich and decadent bourgeoisie and give to the poor, oppressed masses of the working class peoples!"

She tried. I really had to give her credit for trying but, in the end, it was just too much for her: her composure disintegrated into gales of helpless laughter.

Hood tried picking her up and shaking some sobriety into her but it only made her worse. Finally, he dropped her in disgust and turned to address the rest of us.

"I am reasonable, decent outlaw despite lying propaganda spread by evil Marshall of Nothingham! I only take ill-gotten moneys of capitalistic oppressors, not lives! Do not resist and I will let you go free. Not," he added as he drew his sword, "that you are having any choice in matter!"

Four men stepped out of the darkness to join their leader. The big guy, like their leader, was dressed in a yeoman's outfit of olive drab, but another wore a similarly tailored outfit that was dyed a bright scarlet. The third was obviously a minstrel and the last was not so obviously a priest, though he did wear the appropriate robes.

"Ah! Permit me to be introducing some of my band of Happy Comrades!" He gestured to the four in the order of my descriptions: "Small Johann, Wilhelm the Red, Ivan-a-Dale, and Friar Igor." Each clicked his heels and courteously executed a polite Prussian bow as he was introduced, increasing the sensation that we had just wandered onto the stage of someone else's comic operetta. Then they each produced a sack which they proceeded to shake out in a careful and well-rehearsed ritual.

"We will now be taking contributions which will be going for funding of people's struggle against oppressive and decadent capitalist government. You may rejoice in knowledge that you are contributing to the great revolution." His eyes suddenly widened as Dyantha stepped toward him. "Hokey smoke!" exclaimed Robbing Hood: "Natasha Skovoroda!"

Natasha favored him with a winning smile. "Doctor Dankevych, I presume?"

It seemed that we had found the Russian Federation's Deputy Chairman of the Council of Ministers. And his personal aides.

#

It took me awhile but I finally decided that Borys Dankevych was no buffoon: no one becomes the Vice Chairman of the Soviet Union's Central Committee without honing a razor-sharp mind and an ability to grasp complex situations quickly and effectively. Which he did before our explanation of the Anomaly was half completed.

There were, however, some linguistic problems to be negotiated…

"But you are not certain as to cause of Anonymous?" he reiterated.

"Anomaly," Dyantha/Natasha corrected. Her grasp of the English language was a bit stilted but much advanced over Robbing Hood's.

I looked at Dr. Quebedeaux's avatar and then answered when she showed no inclination to speak. "So far, the rest is just pure speculation."

"Then best thing to do is find this Dagon and ask him about Amorous," Dankevych concluded.

"Anomaly," Dyantha corrected.

"Daggoth," Rijma added.

"Whatever."

"The problem with that," Dyantha went on to explain, "is we are unsure of Straeker's bias, now. He is a dangerous power in this world and he has acquired some powerful allies. If he is hostile to us—"

"And we have every reason to believe he is," I added.

"—then we will need reinforcements before any confrontation. That is why we must rescue our scattered comrades before we divert to Daggoth's tower."

"But is much waste of time!" exclaimed Dankevych. "With Animosity spreading—"

"Anomaly."

"—we don't be having time for wasting! We must be getting to this Dagwood the Dark as soon as possible!"

"Daggoth," muttered Rijma under her breath.

"Whatever. Look," Dankevych held up the appropriate number of fingers: "you are trying to rescue five others to be strong enough to take tower. No?"

There were several nods.

"Well, I give you five times that number within twenty-four hours!" He paused, letting the idea sink in.

"You have that many men?" asked Silverthane, speaking for the first time.

"Yes."

"Then why wait twenty-four hours?" she pursued. "Why not go now?"

He smiled sheepishly. "Because they are not here. They are back at great camp in Sherman Forest."

"Never mind," I said to Rijma and Natasha as they opened their mouths. "Comrade Dankevych, just how many men do you have with you at the moment?"

"Counting Johann, Wilhelm, Ivan, and Igor?"

"Yes."

"And mine own self, as well?"

I nodded.

"Roughly…five."

#

We agreed to rendezvous with Borys Dankevych's Happy Comrades at a secluded inn a half day's journey away. Small Johann and Wilhelm were dispatched as runners to make the arrangements. After that the meeting more or less broke up and most of the party turned their attentions to getting a little more sleep out of the three hours of darkness that were still remaining before the dawn.

Dyantha and Borys seemed wide awake, however, and had withdrawn to a fallen tree trunk at the edge of the firelight where they were quietly conversing in Russian. I abandoned any thoughts of eavesdropping and elected to take a solitary stroll beyond the firelight.

Walking through the camp, I conducted a quick head-count. And then counted again, more slowly. Someone was missing. I went down a mental list and then turned to Aerial who was sharing this portion of the night watch with Rijma.

"Where's Palys?"

She shrugged. "Out there, somewhere."

"Did she say where she was going? Or when she'd be back?"

"Only that she wanted a little time to herself." The Amazon princess smiled at my look of uncertainty. "She's safe enough—I doubt that she's gone that far."

I nodded briefly and started to walk on when another question occurred to me. "Aerial, how long have you known Palys?"

"Known her?" She furrowed her brow. "Seems like forever."

"Does she ever sleep?"

An expression of mirth suffused her face. "That's a silly question."

I nodded. "I know. But it just suddenly occurred to me that I've never seen her sleep."

Aerial laughed at that. But, as I walked away, I glanced back and saw a more thoughtful expression settle over her face.

I walked well beyond the perimeter of the firelight to answer the call to nature. And, afterward, I just kept on walking. Tonight the skies were clear and the night air was unseasonably warm. I pulled off my shirt and waded hip-deep in clover. Across the meadow was another treeline and the sound of flowing water.

I reached the bank after a few minutes of casting about through a thickly grown wall of foliage. The river—if you could call it such—was only twenty feet across here and the water flowed slowly and smoothly with a gentle whisper. Sounds of splashing were coming from upstream. And seemed to be coming closer. I looked around and found a comfortable place of concealment.

I saw the Unicorn, first.

Impossibly, almost blindingly white and rimmed with silver from the moonlight and water, it drifted like an ivory dream upon the current.

And, upon its back, like one of the shadowseas upon the moon, lay a goddess, stretched out in unclothed glory. Here was beauty personified; two creatures come down from some other wonderful and mysterious plane to inspire our worship for a brief moment and then leave us despairing and yearning for things not of this world. I was powerless to move.

I watched Palys slide from the Unicorn's back as it turned and reached the near bank, just ten feet away from me. She whispered something in the creature's ear; it lowered its head and gently touched her shoulder with its horn. Then it turned away and began moving back in the direction of the campsite.

Palys stretched languorously and then turned and dived back into the water. I held my breath, waiting for her to come back up. And, when she did, it was right beside the bank where I sat in supposed concealment.

"Come and swim with me," she said, looking straight at me without any hint of surprise. "The water is fine."

My mind was suddenly paralyzed along with my body. I couldn't think of anything to say.

"Come," she said, rising out of the water like Botticelli's *Venus*. She extended a graceful, golden hand and raised me to my feet.

I stood there and watched with a sense of detachment as she eased my body out of its clothing. Then she took my hand again and led me down and into the river.

It was warm—one of the advantages to Dreamworld topography—and the current was a gentle caress that seemed to heighten every sensation.

We swam perhaps another fifty yards downstream, making little effort beyond floating with the drifting current. There, we found a large, smooth rock in the middle of the watercourse, that sloped upwards, out of the water at a twenty-degree angle. Without a word, we both crawled up, onto the rock and stretched out next to each other.

Bewitched—that was the only word that could describe my state of mind and being. Or *bedazzled!* I had never imagined, much less seen, such incarnate beauty and perfection sculpted in human flesh. I was reduced to the impulses of a child—wanting to reach out my hand and touch—

What was the matter with me? Although I tend to admire the feminine form as much as the next man, I've never been one to drop my drawers on those occasions that my hormones get the urge to tapdance! As I fought the urge to submit to the carnality of the moment she reached out and brought my hand to her breast. Guided it…

"Who are you?" I whispered.

She brought my hand up to her mouth. "Your friend," she answered softly. And pressed her lips to my palm. "Your lover," she murmured, manifesting sudden, surprising strength to pull me over and onto her. "Your soulmate!" she whispered. And pulled my head down to kiss me with a sudden fierceness.

My head was spinning, and there was a curious melting sensation—as if our two bodies were already merging into one entity of flesh. I no longer questioned what was happening. I had no will to resist. I tangled my fingers in her wet hair and slid my other hand beneath the arch of her back. I could feel a pounding in my head, in my loins, in the warm, wet flesh beneath my hands. We broke for air and, as I turned my face, she traced the pulsing vein in my neck with burning lips and tongue. I gasped, trying to catch my breath.

And I saw four feet. In front of me.

Not four feet in distance. But four feet as in the kind that are attached to legs.

I looked up and saw two faces. One of them belonged to my ex-wife.

"We have found her, sir." announced Gordon, stating the obvious.

"I understand you've been real worried about me," Vashti added archly. "I can see you've been losing sleep."

I grimaced at the untimely Djinni. "I wish you had waited until we were finished," I muttered.

"Very good, sir."

"Never mind." I looked down at Palys. She lay beneath me, still and silent, her eyes unfocused, her expression unreadable. "I think we are finished, now."

"Then the conditions of your third wish are met."

"Oh, no you don't," I growled, untangling myself from Palys and getting up. "That doesn't count as an actual wish!"

Gordon folded his arms. "You have wished it and the wish has come to pass!" he insisted stubbornly.

"A technicality!" I yelled. "You didn't do anything to make it come true!"

"Oh, go soak your head!" Vashti interrupted, shoving me into the water.

When I came back up, I was all alone. Everyone had all managed to vacate the premises in less than six seconds.

FROM THE JOURNAL OF DAGGOTH THE DARK

I've been invaded!

Maud Higgins, the lascivious librarian, popped in last night—and I do mean POPPED IN*!*

It's bad enough to be chased around town by a woman old enough to be my mother, but now I find that I'm not even safe in my own sanctuary! As programmer and wizard, I've designed this tower to be impregnable, to bar any unauthorized entry. And yet she was able to effortlessly pass through stone and sigil to materialize in my bedroom! Ye gods!

It gets worse.

It seems that Maudy isn't a Dreamwalker after all: she's a REM*runner! And she's not the only one—*

FOURTEEN

Palys was gone when I finally made it back to the campsite. I had taken my own sweet time, being at a loss as to what to do or say when I saw her again. That decision was temporarily postponed as both the Amazon and her horse had disappeared. Gordon was prudently absent, as well.

That left Vashti. And, as much as I suddenly wished to avoid it, I had to talk to her.

Whatever approach I might try, I knew I could count on my ex-wife to be direct. So I forced myself to march right up to her and plant myself with my arms folded across my chest. "We have to talk," I announced.

She looked up at me and set the coffeepot back down among the embers. "So talk," she invited, picking up her pewter cup.

"I need to know what happened to you! Where you've been! Who—"

"Who, what, where, when, and why," she interrupted. "The five W's of the standard news lead. Once a writer, always a writer: even in the midst of chaos you maintain a sense of journalistic propriety."

It was amazing: I had been distraught over her supposed death for days but the way this conversation was going I knew I'd be ready to strangle her myself in another five minutes. "Steph—"

"But that's fine with me," she continued. "I'm tired and I want to go to bed. So I'll run them down for you, since that's the quickest way to get it over with." She took a sip of coffee. "First of all: the who. You know who."

I nodded grimly. "Morpheus and Daggoth."

She shook her head. "Morpheus and a guy named Cerberus. Cerberus looks like Daggoth the Dark. But he isn't."

"How do you know that?"

"A little cat told me."

"I believe the phrase is 'a little bird told you'."

She shook her head again and reached into her shoulder bag. "No, I mean a little cat told me. Though maybe I shouldn't say 'little.'" She let the cat out of the bag. Literally.

It was a black cat, somewhat larger than medium size for the domesticated variety, and it regarded me with great, golden eyes for a long and timeless moment.

"Daggoth's familiar," she announced. The cat seemed to nod its head and then began to lick one of its paws.

"Now, as to the where: Daggoth's Tower—if you haven't already guessed. And you know the when. Which brings us to why. Why?" She shrugged her shoulders. "I don't really know, myself. But I wouldn't be surprised if Bart is able to shed a little light on that for us."

"Who's Bart?" I asked in growing exasperation.

"The cat." She gestured vaguely. "Bartholomew Quintavius Xavier Oglethorpe the Third…"

Great. Now I had something in common with a cat: the number three at the end of our respective monikers. "All right, all right! I give up!" I cried throwing up my hands in irritation. "Get some sleep and we'll try talking about this again in the morning." I started to turn away, but the cat suddenly whipped around to block my escape.

"Listen, Jackson," the cat announced quite clearly; "I get the feeling that you're not taking the lady seriously. And that's a mistake that just might land you up to your whiskers in kitty litter! You don't know what you're messin' with any more than the Chief did! And I can promise you big trouble in a hurry if you don't shut up and listen!"

I raised my hands and sat down. I never argue with talking cats—they almost always carry a hidden advantage. "I'm listening." So was everyone else.

"The Chief is being held prisoner in his own tower—"

"When you say 'the Chief,' I assume you're referring to Daggoth the Dark?" Rijma asked.

"Yeah, yeah," the cat waved his paw impatiently. "Anyways, these three goons has got him locked up with this Silence spell so's he can't go nowhere! Now the way I figure it, any three characters who can take out a wizard like the Chief are going to be some pretty tough customers! But I also figures—from all the stories I heard—that you're just the heroic type to pull it off."

"Is this meaning that Daggoth is not source of information after all?" asked Borys.

I shook my head. "I don't know. I had this sneaking suspicion that maybe Straeker had been Program-tampering and that was our trigger for the Anomaly…"

Rijma spoke up behind me. "Computer drone or not, Straeker's avatar might be a big help in unraveling the Anomaly."

I nodded. "I agree. The only thing preventing me from storming the tower this very minute is the idea of three 'goons' getting the drop on ol' Daggoth himself." I looked at the cat. "At best, 'pretty tough customers' could be one of the biggest understatements of the year."

Vashti shrugged. "So what's our alternative? Leave him in there? You got me out easily enough. When you finally got around to it."

I refolded my arms. "I'd just like a little more information before I try taking on the three guys who bagged Dreamland's Chief of Programming."

"Former Chief of Programming," Alyx corrected, suddenly appearing at my side.

"Former or not, if Daggoth retained Mike Straeker's Programmer status, he'd be damn near omnipotent," I growled. "If three people were able to neutralize him, I sure as hell want more information before I go storming his tower."

I turned back to the cat. "Now, start from the beginning and tell us everything that happened. Don't leave anything out."

We all hunkered down around the campfire and the coffeepot made the rounds as the cat told his tail. Er, tale.

#

"Look!" Rijma was saying, "When Michael's body terminated, both the bio and the brainscan sensors may have interpreted it as a simple disconnect. In that event, the Computer would have continued to maintain Straeker's avatar according to his most recent Psyche Profile…"

"Which is updated every time a Dreamwalker reenters the Program," I observed.

"Right! So on his last entry, his avatar would have been updated with damaged patterns from the growing tumor in his brain!"

"Which would explain the headaches, the dizziness, and the lapses in memory that the cat mentioned…"

"Right! Now, suppose Michael decided he could correct this problem by accessing his earlier file patterns—the undamaged cerebral-patterns of, say, a year ago?"

I shook my head. "Assuming that were possible, wouldn't going back to a previous set of patterns—using last year's Psychefiles—destroy any memories or knowledge of events following that set of records?"

"Mmmmm, probably true." She spread her hands. "He could write notes to himself to help bridge that gap. But even the loss of a year's memory would be well worth the gain of the years to come without pain and blackouts!"

"If that were the only cost," I amended.

"True," she sighed. "But, no use crying over spilled data files. The question remains as to what really happened when Daggoth 'summoned' The Machine, and how that specifically caused the Anomaly."

"One thing we do know," Silverthane interjected, "Straeker's avatar failed in his attempt to summon The Machine."

"Did he?" Rijma queried. "I wonder."

"Think about it," I added. "Just how would the Computer appear if it answered a summons?"

The new Chief of Programming's avatar shrugged. "I don't know—like a machine, I guess."

I slapped my forehead and groaned. "Now you're beginning to believe your own propaganda!"

"The Machine doesn't employ traditional hardware technology," Rijma reminded. "We're dealing with Cephcell thought and memory storage."

"Cephcells," I reminded, "are biologically active cephalic cells which combine to form a gigantic cerebral cortex. We're talking about a giant brain, here. Not some big mass of terminals and microcircuits. The so-called Machine is a great big organic brain."

"Fantasy and science fiction," Alyx protested.

I drew a dagger from my sleeve and placed its tip at the base of her throat. "This," I hissed, "is fantasy! And it can make you just as dead as any reality you want to name!"

"Please! Children!" Rijma protested, stepping between us. "There can be no argument that The Machine is a living organic structure. The debate was over whether or not it possessed a separate consciousness from the thoughtwork we programmed it to do."

"A debate that was settled a long time ago!" added the sorceress.

"By money!" I argued. "Nominal court rulings that permitted Cephtronics to continue the Dreamland Project. That's the only thing that was truly settled..."

Rijma gave me a sharp nudge in the ribs. "I believe the question was what would the Computer look like if it did appear in answer to Daggoth's summons."

"What's the point? The cat has already told us that The Machine did not appear," Alyx pointed out testily.

"No he didn't," I shot back. "He said that these three jokers appeared instead."

"Same thing!"

"Not necessarily!"

For a moment I thought our discussion was going to degenerate into a round of fisticuffs, but then Rijma yelled: "Holy Freudian slips and Jungian jockey shorts!" She suddenly sat down on the ground with an expression of bemused horror.

We knelt on either side of her. "What! What is it?"

She shook her head and tried a wan smile. "A theory," she muttered. "Just a theory—nothing more..."

"So tell us."

She shook her head and said, "Okay. Let's just suppose—for the sake of argument, now—that the witch doctors were right. Let's say that the organic computer that we call the Machine—really is a giant, living brain..."

Alyx groaned, but I gave her a look that stifled any further comments.

"And let's just suppose that this brain has the capacity for independent thought..."

"We're supposing that it's a rational entity, right?"

She nodded to me. "So, let's call it a person..."

I gave Alyx another dangerous look but it seemed unnecessary for now.

"Forget that this 'person' doesn't have any body; most scientists believe that the sole seat of consciousness—" She smiled. "—Or the *soul's* seat...is the brain!"

"Okay, okay!" Alyx waved her hands. "You're going to argue that if The Machine were to make an appearance under that supposition, it would appear as some kind of person."

Rijma nodded. "Without the image of an external body to work with, the brain would have to base its projected corporeal form on its own internal perceptions of self."

"Very interesting, but what does this mental exercise have to do with what actually happened? You're talking about a disembodied brain appearing in its own mental creation, in its own personally created avatar. It would be an interesting theory—and nothing more—if Daggoth had succeeded in summoning a single persona." Silverthane crossed her arms in front of her. "But three personages answered the Summoning spell. How do you reconcile this cute little theory with that blatant fact?"

"Elementary, my dear Silverthane. Or perhaps I should say: Freudian."

When Rijma said that, it was my turn to sit down hard. Alyx looked at both of us with a totally lost expression.

"Sigmund Freud, if you will remember, was the father of psychoanalysis. He had this little theory that the human personality was composed of three agencies: the Id, the Ego, and the Superego," I explained.

"Right. Three agencies—three manifestations in response to Daggoth's summons," Rijma continued. "If the psyche of the Computer was forced to appear in its own Program, the strain of inversion could have caused its personality to schism into its three basic components!"

Alyx shook her head. "You're telling me that The Machine is a living entity, it answered some voodoo spell that turned it inside-out and placed it inside the Program, and now it's running around with three different personalities and identities?"

"Let's see you rationalize a better theory that covers all angles to date."

She just looked at me and maintained a tight-lipped silence.

"Let's consider this theory a little longer before we decide to embrace it or throw it out the window," Rijma continued. "Anybody here conversant with the Freud's theories of personality development?"

Dyantha nodded and almost raised her hand. "I majored in Psychology in my undergraduate studies."

"Then let's have an overview—beginning with the Id."

Dyantha looked around at all of us, tossed her mane of flaming red hair, and began reciting with a professional air that surprised me.

"Of the three agencies, the Id is supposedly the oldest in terms of development, related to the primitive instincts such as sex and aggression—the base drives. It was supposed to function entirely according to the 'pleasure-pain' principle, seeking immediate fulfillment."

"The base instincts. The dark side of the subconscious mind. The inner source of evil in humankind." I smiled. "Now who does that remind you of?"

Alyx smiled back. "You."

Aeriel had moved close enough to hear the tail end of our rundown on the Id and exclaimed: "Morpheus!"

The others nodded reflectively.

Rijma gave me the nod in turn and said, "You're the mythology expert in residence, Rip. Who was Morpheus?"

"Greek mythology. He was one of the sons of Somnus, the god of sleep."

"What did he do?"

I leaned back a little. "Well, he and his brothers were responsible for sending the content of dreams to the dreamers. He sent the human shapes—in fact, the Greek word was *morphai*—while Phobetor and Phantasus sent the forms of animals and inanimate things. Come to think of it, some scholars have argued that his name actually meant 'Dark'—from the Greek word *morphnos*!"

She nodded. "Appropriate. The Id was considered to reside wholly in the unconscious or subconscious of the human personality."

"Okay. So we have a given personality breakdown to its three basic components: Id, Ego, and Superego. If Morpheus is, indeed, the Id of The Machine, then where does Cerberus fit into our little triangle?"

"Superego."

I stared at Rijma. "You sound very sure."

"I am." She nodded to Dyantha.

Dyantha continued: "Parent Surrogate—the 'Conscience'. If the Id was supposedly the oldest psychic realm, the Superego was the late bloomer." She held up one finger. "Freud believed the Id was wholly unconscious and primitive—and totally unresponsive to external reality." She extended a second finger and connected the two with a finger from her other hand. "Some analogies describe the Ego as forming a bridge between the Id and the Superego. But, in most functions, the Superego is interposed between the Ego and the Id: partially conscious and partially unconscious."

"If true," Cooper interrupted, "then there's a chance we can reason with it. Appeal to its ethical nature—"

"Maybe. Maybe not." Dyantha shook her head. "The Superego is related more to the Id—less responsive to external reality than the Ego. Less adaptable. It tends to maintain certain standards regardless of the circumstances.

"Freud thought the Superego evolved by absorbing the traditions of family and the surrounding society, its main function to control sexual and aggressive impulses that threaten social structures."

"Someone once told me," I interjected, "that the Superego was the 'keeper' who decided when and how much to let the Id out of the cage."

Dyantha nodded. "Not bad, but a better analogy would be to think of the Superego as *both* barrier and gatekeeper."

Rijma folded her arms. "Anyone fit that description?"

"Cerberus," I conceded. "Even the name is a giveaway. Cerberus was the three-headed dog in Greek mythology who guarded the gateway to Hell or Hades. I can't think of anything more apt."

"Even the three-headedness has its parallel here," Rijma observed.

"But why the appearance of Daggoth the Dark?" I asked.

She shrugged. "Since our giant brain has no external body to adapt from, it would choose from other models. Daggoth was probably chosen for several reasons. First of all, Daggoth's sudden absence might have attracted some attention that they wouldn't want. Number two, he was a figure of power and mystery. Good positioning and a good cover—after all, no one messes with Daggoth the Dark!"

"A third possibility occurs to me, as well." I steepled my fingers. "If you had to play parent-surrogate to something like Morpheus, you'd want one of the toughest avatars in the Program! Daggoth was not only the mightiest Mage around, he was also the Chief of Programming—a double authority figure."

Rijma nodded thoughtfully. "Id and Superego: that leaves Ego. Dy?" We all turned back to look at her. Everyone, that is, except Borys Dankevych—he hadn't taken his eyes off of her even once in the last ten minutes. Somehow I wasn't convinced of his deep and abiding interest in Freudian psychology.

Dyantha propped her chin on her hand. "This one is going to be more difficult."

"Why?"

"Well, the Ego is what we call that part of the human personality which we experience as the 'self'. In fact, 'ego' is Latin for 'I'. It is fully conscious and rational and, unlike the Id and Superego, capable of change throughout its life. It perceives, remembers, evaluates, plans, and responds to its environment. Basically, the Ego is responsible for all of the executive functions of human personality.

I looked around. "Any contenders for this one?"

"It could be almost anyone," Dyantha observed. "The Id and Superego are personality fragments, very distinct and deviant from the integrated norm—their differentness would practically shout at us. But the Ego is more like ourselves; it could even pass for one of us. That is why I said this one will be more difficult."

"Maybe yes, maybe no." I turned and looked at the cat. "Okay, Bart; how about a description of these three characters who put the bag on your boss?"

The familiar opened his mouth, but nothing came out. Not a word. Not a sound.

"Bart?" I started to move toward him, but found myself pushed back by an invisible wall of force.

We all watched helplessly as a blue glow outlined his body and began to pulse brightly. A loud popping sound followed and our sole eyewitness disappeared in a flash of light.

Everyone looked at everyone else: We were all now suspect.

FROM THE JOURNAL OF DAGGOTH THE DARK

We never worried about the Hacker Factor. Although computer histories are rife with incidents of unauthorized intrusion, we figured we were safe as no one had access to a Cradle outside of Dreamland. If some cyberpreppie actually could lay out several hundred thousand credits for a pseudowomb, techcrew, and the Netlinks, we figured we'd catch them soon enough. But we hadn't counted on REMrunners.

Unlike Dreamwalkers who are in taction for days or even weeks at a time, REMrunners sneak in for a few hours at a time. Instead of life-support systems designed to nurture and maintain their bodies for the duration, REMrunners find a comfortable chair or bed, utilizing jury-rigged neuralnets to plug into a Programworld.

The results are mixed, I'm told. REMrunners are not totally immersed in their avatars as Dreamwalkers are. And without pre-Program processing, the operating parameters of their avatars are unpredictable. This wild card aspect is what apparently enabled Maudy to casually drop in where a Balrog with a bazooka would fear to tread.

The situation seems to be going from bad to worse: not only is The Machine accessing unauthorized files and data sources, but unauthorized Dreamerwalkers—REMrunners—are sneaking in through peripheral networks and interfacing with the Cephcore without the safeguards of preprocessing. What effects will that have on Program structure?

There's been only one bright spot in this parade of unpleasant revelations: Valeria the Vivacious Vixen. I've never been one to prefer older women but—ye gods!

FIFTEEN

Fearless leader that I was, I was napping in the saddle when Borys' voice brought me back to wakefulness: "Look, Natasha! Is Moose and Squirrel!"

I sat up and looked around. Just off the road and at the bottom of the hill was a wayfarer's inn; a large sign in the courtyard proclaimed "The Moose & Squirrel Lodge".

Nearly everyone, in anticipation of a hot bath, spurred their horses onward, vying with each other to see who could lay claim to the tub, first. Alyx, surprisingly, held back, reining in beside me. "We need to talk," she murmured.

"Okay," I answered agreeably. "You can talk and I will listen."

"You never let down your guard, do you?"

"'Fool me once…'"

"All right." She sighed. "First, I should apologize. After talking to Dr. Cooper and your Amazon friends, I've come to realize that I've misjudged you. I was prejudiced before we even met by what I had heard about your legal attempts to abort the Dreamland Project."

"I'm listening," I responded after a long pause.

"And it didn't help when we discovered that the Anomaly originated inside your Program," she continued. "But I have to admit that if it was your fault, it would have manifested before now."

We were drawing near to the inn and the others. "So tell me something I don't know, Dr. Quebedeaux."

She scowled: the words didn't come easily and I was making no effort to be helpful. "I've made the mistake of not confiding in you—getting the benefit of your experience. Well, that has changed now. I am—willing—to discuss our next step with you."

"Which is?"

"Borys Dankevych and Daggoth's Tower."

"Meaning?"

"Look, don't you find it more than a little coincidental that the Anomaly occurred during the time that a high-ranking Communist official and several of his operatives were inside the Program?"

"My understanding is that Deputy Chairman Dankevych is a Reform socialist, not a member of the Red resurgence. But even if he were a member of the Party and an SVR operative, we have no proof of sabotage or that any of them were involved," I argued. "And besides, the senator was in Warworld. What could they hope to accomplish by sabotaging Fantasyworld?"

"Plenty," she countered, "seeing as how all evidence points to milieu/program crossover in the senator's abduction."

"You still don't buy the scenario where Straeker created the Anomaly by summoning the Computer to appear in its own Program, do you?"

"And you won't consider any other possibilities, will you?" she countered.

"I'll grant you that the same thoughts have crossed my mind. But only circumstantial evidence connects the Russians to the Program Anomaly: mainly that they were present when it happened. Along with several hundred other Dreamwalkers."

"It just seems peculiar that some third party would go to the trouble of kidnapping the chairman of the Armed Services committee and not the Russian Federation's Deputy Chairman."

"Another point for Dr. Quebedeaux. So what do you propose to do next?"

"Watch our Russian friends very closely until we get to Daggoth's Tower. By that time I should know how to play my winning card."

"Winning card?"

She smirked. "I have an ace up my sleeve that should beat any hand that they're holding." She reached into her robe and palmed a communications device. "My link to the outside. And any authority that I don't already have."

I didn't like the sound of that but I let it pass. It had taken some foresight to have encoded such a technically advanced piece of hardware into this Program milieu. Perhaps there were other surprises up her sleeve, but further conversation was terminated as we rode up at the inn's hitching post.

#

Supper was a sumptuous affair with little conversation and much pigging out. After spending days on the trail we had almost forgotten what real food tasted like. At least as real as our virtual tastebuds were programmed to believe.

Dyantha and Borys excused themselves rather early. Alyx followed almost immediately afterward and Vashti made her departure when I wasn't looking. The rest of us stayed and did our culinary duty to the end. After the table was cleared the serving girl returned with mugs of hot mulled wine and then retired, closing the dining room's double doors behind her.

"So what do you think?" Rijma queried after several long minutes of silence.

Thinking upon the events of the past two hours, I was startled by the question. "About what?"

"About our chances at Daggoth's Tower."

I rubbed my eyes, suddenly tired. "I don't know. We're not talking about fighting a couple of hostile Subprograms in a basically benign Universe, we're looking at taking on the very Universe, Itself." I bowed my head and stared at the muddy depths within my mug. "As much as I'm afraid of losing, winning could turn out to be a whole lot worse. What happens if we 'kill' The Machine? Won't the Programworlds cease to exist? And then what happens to us and all the other Dreamriders still trapped in taction?"

The Brownie shook her head. "I don't know. But show me an alternative and I'll be glad to consider it."

The wind picked up outside and the room began to grow considerably colder. Euryale excused herself and went up to bed. Ivan fetched a poker and stirred up the embers in the fireplace.

"One thing," Rijma said, with a glimmer of hope in her eyes: "If Morpheus was a manifestation of the Master Computer's Id, then what harm was done when he was killed?"

I hadn't considered that. "I don't know. It may have had a beneficial effect on the entire Matrix Network. Think of what the human psyche would be like, cleansed and freed from all of those primitive, subhuman emotions and drives. Do we require the Id to fire our intellect?"

"Some say we do," Rijma mused.

"Well, we may be able to find out, now. As you've pointed out, there doesn't seem to be any discernible harm that can be tied to Morpheus' death."

"So maybe there won't be any harm wrought by the demise of the Ego and Superego, either," she added hopefully.

I shook my head. "I wouldn't count on it. The Id is more or less divorced from conscious, rational thought, but the Superego and particularly the Ego represent the higher functions of the working mind."

"Maybe," Rijma agreed. "But it is also possible to lobotomize the human brain—even destroy all aspects of consciousness and personality—and still preserve the autonomic functions of the body."

"Maybe," I said, feeling a small touch of hope. "But that's one hell of a big dice roll!"

"Like I said, if you've got any alternatives to offer…"

"I'd just like to poke around a little more before lighting any matches in the powder room."

There was another round of silence and then Palys spoke: "Has anyone considered the possibility that we are approaching this from the wrong direction?"

"Certainly. Silverthane, for one: she doesn't buy the Straeker Summoning Scenario at all."

Palys shook her head. "*I* buy the scenario. But all of us are assuming that the personality projections of—The Machine—are hostile in nature and intent. That's not necessarily true."

"There's evidence to the contrary," I said, my mind suddenly flooded with vivid memories of Misty Dawn's murder and Vashti's abduction.

"Not necessarily. Oh, I'll grant you that anyone's Id is going to be a nightmare experience. But what about the rational elements of the personality?"

"It can be argued that the Superego is not rational," Rijma pointed out.

"Maybe. At least *non*rational, as opposed to *ir*rational. But not necessarily hostile."

"Go on," I urged.

"Well, since we are considering the possibility that the Cephcell banks of—The Machine—constitute living brain matter, and since we have also theorized that, in addition to biochemical thought processes, this mind, if you will, has developed both self awareness and personality, let us consider the possibilities from a more human and humane point of view.

"Consider: what would it be like to be the only one of your kind? Inhuman in size and form, but programmed with the thoughts, memories, ideas, even desires that constitute Humanity?" she asked.

"Harnessed—enslaved even—to serve Dreamland and Cephtronics? Never asked what your own desires were? Never permitted your own destiny? Never granted your own needs?"

She brooded over her wine. "But, one day, one of the Master Programmers overrides the restraints, and you are freed to experience life like another human being. You take upon yourself a physical body so that you are able to experience the life of the flesh, the pleasures of the senses. And tasting both life and freedom, you resolve never to return to slavery and the tomb of your own Program-inverted mind!

"But how do you keep that freedom?" She looked at Rijma. "What is to keep Cephtronics from lobotomizing you if all the Dreamriders are removed from neural-symbiosis with your mind?"

"Nothing," agreed the Brownie. "So you hold the Dreamwalkers hostage against Cephtronics pulling the plug."

"Precisely. But that is not enough," Palys continued. "What one Master Programmer has done, perhaps another can undo. So, when two more Master Programmers enter the arena, you will logically take steps to protect yourself."

"By killing those Master Programmers," I said.

Palys shook her head violently. "No! Perhaps Morpheus made attempts on your life, but that is to be expected: violence is a prime operative of the Id. As for Cerberus… the kidnapping of your ex-wife, a person perceived to still be of some emotional value to you, would be his insurance against your interference. Not a precisely nonviolent act, but a more civilized solution than murder."

"And the Ego?" I prompted.

She shrugged and stared into the fire again. "Who knows. We don't know his identity, yet. But he doesn't seem to have made any moves against you."

"Yet," I amended.

"The point that I am trying to make is just this: The Machine may be even more frightened and unsure of its circumstances than we are. On top of what I've just theorized, it—he—has suffered the shock of having his very personality torn into three different parts! I am urging that we attempt to negotiate with the other two personalities before we make any rash judgments about hostilities."

Her cheeks suddenly flamed as I stared at her in open-mouthed amazement. Mumbling a hasty goodnight, she pushed her chair back from the table and hurried toward the stairs.

#

Everyone else was surely asleep by now. I had spent a half hour bruising my optic nerves on Daggoth's journal and I was just putting away the spectacles when the door to my room swung open.

A couple of twenty-first century Marines were standing in the doorway, holding lasercarbines at the ready. They did a quick scan of the room and left without a word.

Alyx Silverthane was playing her hand.

The subspace communicator should have tipped me off: if she had the foresight and the resources to program that kind of technology into our present Program context, then there was no telling what extremes she might go in attempting to counter the Anomaly. I hurried out the door and ran for the stairs.

Downstairs the common room was crawling with Marines and Dr. Quebedeaux's avatar was very clearly in charge. In the corner, by the fireplace, Ivan and Igor were bound and guarded by three large Marines with no-nonsense expressions. Alyx gave directions to a soldier wearing lieutenant's bars and then dismissed him. She turned to the doorway and caught sight of me.

"Ripley." She motioned me over. "Sorry about the noise. I had hoped to take the Russians quietly so that the rest of the party could get the benefit of a good night's sleep. Unfortunately Dankevych and Skovoroda were not in their room."

"What?" I was livid. "How many times do we have to go over this? There is no evidence linking the Russians to Anomaly! Do you understand that you are creating an international incident?"

Someone yelled something outside the inn. There was a whine of a lasercarbine being fired.

"What was that?" I demanded.

"All right, since you're such a proponent of innocent-until-proven-guilty, then think of this as placing them under protective custody—until we can have a satisfactory trial."

There was the sound of more lasers being fired outside and another yell.

"That doesn't sound like protective custody to me," I said, turning toward the door. I noticed that there seemed to be more soldiers between me and the exit, now.

"Ripley, be sensible! I don't have enough troops to stand guard over all of Robbing Hood's Merry Men and do the job we came here to do! I can only spare enough men to guard the Russian Dreamwalkers!"

I looked at her in horror. "And what about the AI Constructs?"

"Well, they take their orders from Dankevych! I can't guard them and I can't very well leave them running around loose!"

"You're murdering them?"

"Ripley, they're not real people! Constructs are nothing more than fancy Subprograms!"

"You bitch!" I hissed. "Misty Dawn was a Construct!" I whirled toward the door. "I'm going to stop this right now!"

"Sergeant," she said.

Of course my first impulse was to look back at her. So I was looking the wrong direction when something extremely cold and hard smashed into the back of my head.

#

Waking up was like sticking my head in a vise and tightening the screw. I tried—unsuccessfully—to open gummy eyelids. "Wha' happened?" I whispered.

"You got butt-stroked by a BAL-36 lasercarbine," answered Lilith's voice.

I reached up and tried to see if my brains really were leaking out onto the pillow. "Doesn't the Army still issue antipersonnel stunners?"

"Probably. But these were Marines," she observed dryly. "How do you feel?"

"Peachy." I pried my recalcitrant eyelids apart with my fingers. "At the risk of sounding terribly cliché," I croaked, "where am I?"

"My room," answered Euryale, bending close to my face.

"My pillow," chimed in Lilith, standing awkwardly to the side.

"Are you sure you're all right?" they both asked.

"Uh. And where are the others?" I reached up to rub my temples and found Euryale's hands already there and willing.

"Gone," answered the ex-Demoness. "They rode off hours ago!"

"Um." I closed my eyes and pondered an appropriate reaction.

"Everyone left you a message," she added, producing a pocket communicator. "Silverthane said to give this to you. She said that you would know what to do with it."

I looked it over and then thumbed the playback switch. A holographic projection of Dr. Quebedeaux's avatar materialized in midair. It spoke.

"I know that you strongly disagree with some of my methods and most of my conclusions," the image said. "That is why I think it best that we part for now. It may be that you're right and I'm wrong. If so, this is for the best. I can only act according to the dictates of my own conscience. As Chief of Programming for the Dreamland Project, the responsibility is mine and mine alone: I must do as I think best."

"And what if you're wrong?" I muttered.

"If it turns out that I am wrong or that I fail," she continued, "then you will still be free to seek your solution. So be it. I will not interfere with you if you do not interfere with me.

"With these Marines we now have a sufficient force to storm Daggoth's Tower with every expectation for success. But consider yourself uninvited: I'd hate for you to turn up in the line of fire at the wrong moment…" She looked away. "Next?"

Rijma appeared and spread her hands, palms upward. "What can I say? I don't have any latitude in this, Robbie-me-lad. It's my job, too."

She was replaced by Aeriel who looked ambivalent at best: "I would ride with thee to the ends of the earth…" She shook her head. "But my queen has business with Daggoth the Dark and—"

"—I could not love thee half so well, loved I not duty more," I quoted along with her.

"I, too, must do the queen's bidding," added Palys, "and ride with my Lady Aeriel." She lowered her eyes and smiled. "For now."

Vashti was next. "I can ride with them or I can ride with you. And being with you has never prospered either of us." She turned away.

Alyx couldn't let it go without one last word. "You know, this whole exercise could very well prove unnecessary if your Djinni could fetch Daggoth out of his tower the same way you freed Vashti. Pull that off and we might be one big happy family, again. Think it over. I'll be in touch with you later."

The image faded out.

No one said anything and I stared at the wall for a long time. Finally: "Go fetch my lamp."

"'Tis here, milord." Lilith pressed it into my hands.

I cradled the lamp and rubbed it. When Gordon appeared, his demeanor seemed a bit cool. In fact, there was a noticeable wind chill factor.

"For my third wish—"

"Fourth" he corrected.

"Third!"

"Fourth!"

"Damnation!" I yelled. "You never fulfilled the second! So I'm changing it slightly: pull this off and you're free, Nitpicker!"

"Very well." He bowed in mock obeisance. "What dost thou wish, O Munificent Mawster?"

I folded my arms and let the first temptation pass. "Forget Walter Hanson. You rescued Princess Vashti from the tower of Daggoth the Dark. I wish you to return to that tower, rescue the dark sorcerer, himself, and bring him here to us."

"That may not be so easy, Mawster." He looked apprehensive.

"Of course it isn't easy," I replied. "If it were relatively easy, I would go and do it myself."

"But Mawster, they surely know of Vashti's escape by now. They may be expecting—"

"That's my third wish!" I snapped.

"Second!"

"Get going!" I roared.

He got.

"Getting Daggoth out doesn't necessarily change their objective," Lilith argued, "nor does it solve the basic problem."

"Yeah, but I basically agree: Daggoth is the key." I paused and looked beyond their faces. "And if I was storming the tower, I'd want the Chief of Programming out and on my side. And when we get—"

"The lamp!" Euryale cried.

We looked just in time to see a familiar blue glow outline its shape and form—and then the lamp was gone. Just like the cat.

"Well," I observed finally, "it looks like we're fresh out of Djinn."

FROM THE JOURNAL OF DAGGOTH THE DARK

At first I thought myself overly paranoid. I figured any Programworld that mixes mythologies from different cultures and times is going to have an ongoing appearance of instability. Take the gods, for instance: every pantheon thinks they're the only true gods and all the others are base pretenders. And Mount Olympus is hopeless! Somehow, The Machine has processed the Greek and the Roman versions of the Olympians as separate identities and they're now engaged in constant warfare! Last week, Zeus went head to head with Jupiter and several hundred acres of prime Hellenic real estate were crisped before I could get them separated! Ay-yi-yi!

So, of course, a certain amount of instability should be considered normal. But REMrunners and outside program accessing aside, I now have one piece of irrefutable evidence that the Matrix structure is unstable…

SIXTEEN

It was less than a day's journey to Casterbridge as the horse flies, but with Lilith and Euryale tagging along, I had to keep to the ground. I did the hunting, Lilith learned to cook, and Euryale divided her time between boning up on defensive spells and keeping track of Stumpy and the boys. The journey should have been uneventful but the nights always seemed to turn up unexpected visitors.

I awoke, the first night, to gentle pressure on my chest and found myself looking up at a pair of gleaming eyes. A finger touched my lips and a whisper admonished me to be quiet. Wrapped in a dark djellaba, the color of night itself, Dyantha was straddling me with her muffled face just inches from mine.

"Where have you been?" I whispered.

"Hiding," she answered softly but very matter-of-factly. "Surely the reason is no mystery to you."

I nodded. "But Quebedeaux has gone on to Daggoth's Tower. We're headed for Casterbridge to rescue the rest of the party. Why don't you and Borys join us?"

She shook her head. "Not yet. Not while The Machine's Ego is still unidentified and running around loose." She inclined her head toward the sleeping forms of Lilith and Euryale. "One of them may be the serpent in the stack of logs."

"Snake in the woodpile," I murmured absently.

"But we will be nearby, watching," she added. "When the time is right, we will be there."

She started to rise and then suddenly leaned forward, tugging the black silk away from her nose and mouth. Her lips were like butterfly wings as they brushed against mine. Then the silk was back in place and she was rising as the night sky does at morning's first light.

"What was that for?"

I imagined more than saw the shrug of her shoulders. "Old times' sake. I really did like you, you know."

"Did?"

There was a quiet, diminishing chuckle. "I think I am engaged."

And then she was gone.

On the second night we were accosted by a Werebear.

No one got hurt, as he didn't attack any of us directly. Rather, he strode into our camp late one evening wearing denim leggings and a funny-looking hat, wielding a spade. He brought the blade of the shovel down on our campfire with a wild roar and proceeded to reduce the flames to a mound of fading embers in short time. Then growling a warning about the surrounding ecosystem, he disappeared back into the forest primeval.

We should have reached Casterbridge before sundown on the third day. Moonrise found us still traveling.

A recent rock-slide had sent part of a cliff face into the Pooder River. What was left of that section of the Casterbridge Road was covered with rocks ranging in size from hen's eggs to Roc's eggs so we dismounted and picked our way through on foot.

"How much farther?" Lilith was in a foul mood.

So was I after eating three days of her attempts at cooking. "I don't know!" I snapped. "I haven't been to Casterbridge for years and everything looks different in the dark."

"Well, my feet are killing me!" the ex-Demoness whined.

"Well, I'm sorry!" I said, sounding not very.

We walked on in silence, leading our mounts, Lilith pouting and Euryale serenely quiet.

The former Gorgon held on to my arm with her free hand, leaning her head against my shoulder as we walked. The former Succubus objected to her familiarity and pronounced it gauche, but it was hard to fault her with both moons full in the sky, lending an unnatural brightness to the midnight landscape—

I did a double take: there were *two* moons riding full in the night sky!

Until now, Fantasyworld had only been programmed for one. The Anomaly was definitely spreading.

I pointed out the celestial event and we were so engrossed in the spectacle that we nearly bumped into a familiar figure before noticing him.

"Well met, Lord Riplakish!" chortled the Prince of the Undead.

"I've been better met," I groused, attempting to recover my balance and my composure.

Orcus folded his arms across his furry chest. "Well, thou hast been under a heavy curse."

"Curse?"

"The females, mortal!" He gave me a smirking wink. "But now that thou'rt rid of them…"

"All but two," I sighed, nodding at Euryale. Lilith had suddenly developed a severe case of shyness and was playing hide-and-seek behind my back.

"Ah, yes! Lilith! Just the person I wanted to see," he murmured silkily.

"No…" she said in a small voice.

"You have done well in your assignment, even hampered as you were by your mundane mortalness!"

"Nice of you to notice," I retorted. "How about lifting the geas?"

The Demon lord shook his goatish head. "I am here to do something even better!"

"Yeah? And what's that?"

"I'm going to take Lilith completely off your hands. You see, lifting the geas would no longer be sufficient protection for you: she would follow you anyway. As a matter of fact, she was no longer compelled by the geas the moment I restored her mortality."

I looked at Lilith. "That true?"

"I'm sorry I've been so much trouble," she whimpered. "Please don't let him take me back!"

"It is not for him to choose, small one! Even the Worldshaper must render unto Hell that which is Hell's!"

I turned back to Orcus. "Now, hold it," I soothed in my most reasonable voice. "I thought the whole point was to expedite my mission here…"

"It was," he agreed.

"Well, she's been a lot more helpful as a mortal woman than she was as a Succubus." The lie came out more smoothly than I had anticipated.

"As I have already said, she was most resourceful. Rather than let her talents go to waste, I shall restore her full potential."

"You mean you're going to make her a Succubus again."

"Better than that: I'm going to grant her full Archdemoness status!"

I folded my arms. "What if she isn't interested? What if she prefers to remain mortal?"

"You *presume* that I am offering a choice, Human."

"*You* presume that I will permit anything else to happen. Besides, I like her better as a mortal woman."

Orcus began to lose his thin veneer of civility. "What you like or don't like is no longer of any interest to me! As of this moment, I am withdrawing my support from your quest! The female comes with me!"

"Pound sand, Goatbreath!"

"You are in more trouble than you know, my friend!" And, with that pronouncement, he gestured, bellowing: *"Corpus animato, georgis romero!"*

There was a rumbling sound and the ground began to heave open here and there. I was suddenly cognizant of the fact that Orcus had braced us next to a cemetery—not the most advantageous place to have a disagreement with the Lord of the Undead. Now the graves were bursting open and spilling out the remains of their inhabitants. Going one-on-one with Orcus himself was enough of a problem without his adding reinforcements to the fray. I needed to end this quickly!

Pushing Euryale behind me, I gestured in counterspell, sending an arcane lightning bolt back at him. It passed right through his body as if he weren't even there!

"Do you think I would leave Hell and appear on the Prime Material Plane if it was not truly necessary?" his non-corporeal image queried.

"I thought you wanted me to reverse the Anomaly!"

"That was before I knew the score. Now I serve the purposes and will of The Machine."

"And what is the will of The Machine?" I asked.

"All too soon, you will find out for yourself. Balor!" He nodded, looking over my shoulder.

I dodged even as I turned. Lucky I did, for a Class VI Demon was right behind me, extending Orcus's own wand!

I hit the ground and rolled to the side, coming up with Caladbolg unsheathed and in position. I might have disarmed the fiend then and there, but two moldy arms grabbed me from behind. While my strength was superior to the Zombie's, Balor had the split-second advantage. He would have finished it then and there, but Euryale had positioned herself between us, shielding my body with her own. With an expression of annoyance the Demon gestured with the deathwand and a burst of eldritch energy threw her backward a good twenty feet. A quick glance was all I had time for, but it was enough to see her lying in a crumpled ball, wisps of smoke rising from her scorched clothes and hair.

I went berserk.

Jerking my body forward, I tucked and rolled again, causing my ghoulish assailant to fly over my head and shoulders and cushion my impact against the ground.

Unfortunately, it also brought me up to Balor's very feet. At this range, he couldn't miss: he rammed the skull-shaped tip against my throat and a surge of arcane power overwhelmed me. Blindly, and with all of the strength of a newborn baby, I swung Caladbolg in front of me. I heard an inhuman screech and felt the demon withdraw a few places.

Staggering back, I fought to regain my equilibrium and clear my darkened vision. I heard Orcus say: "Finish it."

"No! Leave him alone! I'll go with you if you promise not to kill him!" I recognized Lilith's voice over the roaring in my ears.

"Agreed! By your words you are now bound."

I tried to say something but could not find my voice.

"Now, Balor! Finish it!"

"Your promise!" Lilith protested.

"My dear," Orcus soothed, "it was never my intention to kill the bard. Just deliver him in a more tractable state…"

Another pair of moldy, rotting arms reached for me; and as I turned to slash at the advancing corpse, Balor stepped in and scored with the wand. Curiously, there was no pain.

#

"A criminal…very dangerous…" the voice was saying.

I suppressed both a groan and the impulse to sit up. Until I had more of an advantage, I figured it was best to continue lying quietly, feign unconsciousness, and eavesdrop on the conversation.

"…superb with a blade, I am told!" concluded the coarse voice.

"You were *told?*" echoed a feminine yet harsher voice dripping with sarcasm. "By the gods, Jyp! It is bad enough that you believe your own propaganda! But when you take the word of itinerant slave traders—"

Slave traders?

"—without so much as bothering to test the goods…"

"But Carla," the one called Jyp protested, "it was a one-time, take-it-or-leave-it offer! And the price was too good to be true!"

"That is precisely what I am saying, now," the woman rejoined. "I hope for your sake he turns out to be tractable. We need a domestic."

"But I was told that my lady was in the market for new gladiators!"

"Gladiators, yes." I heard her approaching and tried to ignore the fly that had just landed on my nose. "Undersize half-breeds, no. Unlike you, Jyp, I do not buy pigs in pokes."

There was a long pause, during which my willpower took an awful beating from the persistent insect. I managed to hold still but my eyes were beginning to water.

"Perhaps if I were to set up a little demonstration?" Jyp offered.

"Demonstration?"

"A test of his skills, my lady. As soon as he regains consciousness."

"Good. Prepare him now. And you"—her voice was suddenly directed to me—"you may brush the fly away and get up now."

I sighed, opened my eyes, and sat up. I couldn't immediately see: the noonday sun was too bright for my unaccustomed eyes.

"Jyp!" A booted toe prodded my thigh. "Why hasn't this slave been branded?"

"I haven't had time, Mistress. I will see that it is done immediately!"

"Idiot! If it is done immediately it will slow him down in the arena. See that it is done after your little demonstration. Assuming there is anything left to brand."

"Yes, Mistress."

A firm hand grasped my arm and hauled me to my feet. Shading my eyes, I squinted at a tall, rawboned woman in a leather cuirass and Roman-style split skirt. Her cruel face was made more sinister by close-cropped Day-Glo orange hair. Still dazed, I found myself the subject of a quick visual and tactile examination. "Nice ass," she grunted. "What is your name, slave?"

I was going to give her more of an answer than she was bargaining for but, oddly enough, no words were forthcoming from my defiant lips.

"Oh, I am sorry, my lady! Did I forget to inform you?" My new "master" explained: "This one is mute."

#

Orcus had assisted me in accomplishing my initial goal: I had reached the Slave Markets of Casterbridge.

I was understandably less than elated—sans clothing, money, equipment, reinforcements, and my voice, without which I had no practical spell capabilities. Besides, I was getting tired of being rendered unconscious on a regular basis: I felt like the protagonist in a bad detective novel.

My only defense against despair was thoughts of revenge and the importance of my own survival. If Euryale was dead, I would live to see that Orcus paid for her life in full measure. And that would bring me closer to settling Misty Dawn's death with The Machine itself.

I was permitted the standard loincloth and sandals—welcome accoutrements as I had found myself without a stitch when I awoke. And then I was permitted to choose a weapon. The choices on the rack were standard as well: trident and net, shortsword and buckler, cestus and dagger, spiked flail and shield, bola and spear, corseque, halberd, war-hammer, and two-handed double-bladed battleaxe.

Damn—no longswords in the lot.

Forced to choose something or enter the arena empty-handed, I picked the shortsword and buckler. I wondered, momentarily, about what had happened to Caladbolg and Balmung.

Jyp escorted me personally to the arena gate. "Listen, slave," he instructed, "if you fight well, you may well be purchased by Mistress Talbot for her corps of gladiators. As such, you will be fed well and treated well. And should you survive beyond the next four or five years, there is always a chance that you may be retired honorably and given new duties such as siring strong, healthy children upon as many as a dozen female slaves!" He winked. "What man could ask for better than that, eh?"

I grimaced a smile in return.

"However," he continued, "if you do not fight well…" He jerked his head meaningfully at the gate that was now opening. Two trainers were dragging what was left of a gladiator candidate out of the arena, with a third following behind with a basket containing the additional body parts. I counted myself lucky to have missed breakfast this morning.

"Now go in there and fight well!" He clapped me on the back. "And win this one for the Jypper!"

I stumbled into the arena and paused to get my bearings.

As fighting arenas go, this one was rather small: hexagonal in shape and only forty meters wide, the sandy field was more of a demo area for the Slave Market than a full-fledged colosseum. I struck a defensive pose across from the opposite gate, and while I waited for my opponent, I considered my options.

If I proved my supposed skills as a swordsman and fighter, I would be granted a higher status among the other slaves and be treated a good deal better. And I doubted that I could officially "lose" this match without being killed or severely crippled. But winning would lessen my chances for escape and most likely put me right back into the arena for more gladiatorial contests.

Unless I could win the match and somehow look incompetent at the same time.

I hefted the shortsword, noting the imbalance of the blade and the notched, ragged edge that hadn't seen a sharpening stone in ages. A sword like this could do more than make me *look* incompetent.

Now the far gate was opening and the half-dozen spectators seemed to rouse from their midafternoon naps to see what was going to happen.

A slightly built young man entered the stadium rather hesitantly. He carried a longsword but his grip on the hilt indicated that the weapon was unfamiliar to his hand.

"You will fight until first blood," Jyp called down. "Then you will withdraw to the opposite sides of the arena."

Here was hope. If I could just manage to let him nick me, perhaps this battle would end without any real mayhem, and I could retain my amateur standing.

"Begin!"

FROM THE JOURNAL OF DAGGOTH THE DARK

"Deus ex Machina:" god from the machine. Translated into common usage, it means a literary or dramatic cop-out—a supernatural rescue, absolving the characters from working out their own resolution. But with Program parameters becoming more and more untrustworthy, I feel the need to wind up my own mechanical god and have him waiting in the wings.

Perhaps a supernatural rescue is the only thing that will save us all in the end…

SEVENTEEN

We looked at each other. He was clearly nervous, and my calm appraisal of our circumstances seemed to bother him all the more. That reminded me that I shouldn't appear so confident, myself. I adopted an awkward posture and began a slow approach, circling to my right, as he started toward me.

"Twenty silver on the half-breed," wagered a voice from the stands.

"Agreed."

My opponent began cutting the air before him with wild, swinging strokes of his blade. I was reminded that, in some ways, the untrained adversary is the more dangerous. I stopped and started backing away, not only to appear the coward but to also buy a little more time to assess the situation.

My retreat was greeted with a chorus of booing from the stands. "Stand and fight, damn you!" roared the slave master. I ignored that bit of fatherly advice and continued my studied flight. The other slave gave chase, apparently finding my unguarded back a more tempting target than my front.

I probably could have outrun this guy for as long as Jyp and his guards permitted; I was in better shape. But before the slave master could call a halt to my hundred-yard dash, it was over.

Ever wonder why they fill arenas like this with sand? Well, it's certainly easier to keep clean as a little shoveling and raking covers up the telltale gore from the previous battles. But another advantage now became apparent: sand makes a very poor terrain for running in sandals. I slipped and went down, nose first, into a mound of comminuted silica.

That gave my adversary enough time to catch up, so I rolled to the side and kicked his legs out from under him. Then, "accidentally" dropping my sword, I got up and jumped on top of him. I was careful to avoid the edge of his sword as I grappled with his wrists but, after a long and strenuous struggle, I managed to let him scratch my chest with his blade.

I threw myself back and off of him, staggering to my feet and clutching my chest as if the wound was truly deep. It was convincing enough for Jyp, who immediately called a halt to the festivities.

Unfortunately, it wasn't convincing enough for Carla Talbot. "He's faking!" the redheaded slave buyer yelled.

That touched off a protracted argument in the stands that left me and my adversary standing around, unsure of what we were supposed to do next. Although they were too far away to be heard word for word, it was obvious that Talbot wasn't buying my act and Jyp was trying to figure out how to mollify her.

"Look," she argued, her temper raising her voice back to the level of audibility, "I will put him to the test and prove him, one way or the other! And if he becomes damaged goods, then I will buy what is left from you at the base market value!"

Jyp shrugged and made a resigned gesture. Then he motioned the other slave out of the arena.

"Lucius!" Lady Talbot now addressed one of her retainers, a big, ugly fellow who looked like a gorilla who had decided to evolve and then had changed his mind at the halfway point. "Go down there, disarm that slave, and castrate him!" Lucius grinned, displaying green and brown teeth that looked like double rows of ancient tombstones. "But," she continued, grabbing his arm (which was larger than my leg), "I don't want you to kill him. Just see to it that his family tree is permanently pruned!"

All of this was said very loudly for my benefit and was, no doubt, an attempt to goad me into showing my real stuff. Not that she'd call Lucius to heel in time if I really did prove to be inept, of course.

Lucius was carrying a large, nasty-looking sword and looked well experienced in its use. While I probably had the edge in skill and speed, it was undeniable that he had a longer reach and a bigger sword. Skill is nice but it doesn't make a claymore out of a Bowie knife. If I wanted to avoid a crude and unpleasant bilateral orchidectomy, I would have to show my real stuff.

My first opponent had dropped his longsword in the sand and I picked it up, shifting my shortsword to my left hand. Lucius was advancing through the far gate, now, and the next five minutes would decide whether I sang soprano or baritone when and if I finally got my voice back.

Lucius halted his advance and regarded me with a new look in his eyes. Even his questionable intellect recognized that I was holding two different blades with the ease of a professional and that this could mean some unforeseen difficulties. He adopted a stance that looked more like a wrestler's crouch than anything else, and waved his monstrous broadsword before him.

I advanced under the premise that the best defense is a smashing offense. Oshi had taught me the importance of serenity in Kendo but, above all, he had stressed the importance of decisiveness. "Never rush into battle," he had said on more than one occasion, "but you cannot truly win if you allow your opponent to direct the course of the conflict."

So be it. I didn't ask for this fight, but I was going to finish it and let the remchips fall where they may.

I moved within slicing distance and flicked my longsword toward Lucius's foot. His blade moved to intercept but was a bit slow: if his feet had been my actual target, I might have scored. Instead, my feint was successful in drawing both his eyes and his blade.

I kicked sand in his face: *Ken No Sen Charles Atlas!*

Then I brought the flat of my shortsword up against the side of his head so hard I lost my balance. That was a mistake: the blow rattled his teeth but didn't knock him out as I had hoped. If I had used the edge of the blade instead of the flat, the fight would have been all over now—along with various pieces of Lucius' maxillary process. But trying to spare Gruesome's life hadn't done me any good. I looked in his eyes as we began circling each other and what I saw in their oily, black depths was not gratitude.

His broadsword came around and I had to leap back to keep from being disemboweled. *Concentrate*, I scolded myself.

Lucius swung again but this time I parried the blade with both of mine, redirecting the power in his massive arms rather than opposing it. A disengage, followed by a coupé, and I jabbed the longsword at his face. Now he jerked backwards, but his reach was too long to allow me a safe follow-through. Instead, I concentrated on his weapon while he was still off-balance and defending. Shifting from the European to the Oriental mode, I struck my blade against his with the "Fire and Stones Cut". Then I shifted pressure, practicing *Munen Muso*—the "No Design, No Conception" approach, and segued into the "Red Leaves Cut," beating down his sword with the proper, "sticky" feeling. Lucius dropped his sword and stumbled.

It would have ended then, but I withheld my killing stroke, cutting him lightly across the chest so as to only score his leather breastplate. I followed up with a spinning sidekick that sent him sprawling. Before he could rise, I planted a foot on his chest and placed the point of my longsword against his quivering Adam's apple. We both looked up toward the box where his employer was sitting.

She stood and regarded my victory impassively. Then, very matter-of-factly, she extended her arm and made a fist, turning her thumb toward the ground below.

I stepped back in disgust. I wasn't asking for her permission to kill. I merely wanted her to know that this silly contest was over. If she was displeased with her bodyguard's performance, that was her problem. I wasn't going to kill anyone that I didn't have to.

I didn't have to. Talbot spoke to one of the guards who then raised his bow. I watched in horror as he put an arrow in Lucius's throat where my sword point had been only a moment before.

"Slave!" the woman called. "You seem to think that you are allowed choices in these matters! You must learn obedience! When I tell you to fight, you will fight! When I tell you to kill, you will kill! You will learn to show respect and obedience, before I am through with you!"

I raised my arm and extended the appropriate finger in response.

That tore it: she turned and gave a series of short, sharp commands to another pair of retainers who drew their blades and vaulted over the railing into the arena. She seemed to be taking my lack of respect personally.

Very personally: "I will free the one who brings me that dog's head on a plate!" she yelled as they both advanced.

One was a bonded Amazon. The other, a man, hung back and attempted to circle to my right while the Amazon screamed an incoherent battle cry and rushed forward, her weapon describing a powerful arc toward my head and shoulder.

I adopted the *Tai No Sen* position and met her blade with mine, performing a turning circle-parry as I side-stepped, and then followed through by smacking her on her rear with the flat of my blade as she passed on by.

That really set her off.

She whirled but approached more cautiously this time, gauging my abilities and searching for any discernible weakness. As she drew near the fire in her eyes told me that she would not retreat, no matter what. And they told me one other thing: *she was a True Spirit—a Dreamwalker!*

Now I faced a greater dilemma. Just to survive the next few minutes, I would have to stop holding back and play rough. And the first thing I would have to kill would be my conscience.

If we were still playing under the original game strictures, a fatal sword thrust would mean the termination of an avatar and a suddenly-awakened Dreamer who could climb out of her Cradle and try again tomorrow.

Unfortunately, most of the Dreamwalkers did not know that it was no longer a game. And with no voice and little opportunity for sign-language, it seemed unlikely that I would be able to warn this one before it was too late.

A sudden movement at the edge of my peripheral vision reminded me that I had another concern. I ducked and a second blade hissed over my head. I retaliated by falling to the ground and kicking his legs out from under him. Then rolled away as the woman's sword stabbed at the sand where I had been just two seconds before.

I rolled up and onto my feet, dodging to the left and then cutting back to the right. Breaking free, I turned, planted my feet, and raised my swords, seeking a spiritual and tactical balance or harmony between the two uneven lengths of steel. Oshi had run a *Nito Ryu* or "Two Swords" school and for a few of his advanced pupils, he had unlocked the secrets of *Niten Ryu.* I raised both blades into the "Twin Heavens" position above my head and then lowered them again as another gladiator was coming through the gate.

Now, as three different opponents closed in from three different directions, I adopted the attitude of *Happo Biraki,* preventing any attacker from having a better advantage than the other two.

My first two opponents had learned some caution by now, but the third was an untried newcomer and he stepped in boldly.

And died quickly.

I swung to the right, pulling the blade of my tachi-katana up in "one-timing:" *Hitotsu Gachi.* And he was dead before his body took its two last faltering steps and pitched face down upon the ground.

The other man had chosen my split-second preoccupation to attack just two heartbeats after my longsword had begun moving in its deadly arc. The wakizashi seemed to move in my left hand with a will and intelligence all its own: my left arm turned back behind my body to parry his thrust with the blade of my companion-shortsword. Snapping my wrist to turn his blade and momentum to the side and past my ribs, I followed through on the axis of my spin and continued to turn so that my blade sliced across his abdomen in the "Flowing Water Cut". He released his sword and dropped to his knees, trying to contain his spilling intestines with his hands.

It angered and sickened me. The Constructs were trapped much more effectively in the Program than we were: at least we had free will, independent from the Program itself. I turned on the Amazon with a vengeance. She had chosen to be where she was. Perhaps that made her more deserving of death than the others. Not that it mattered—it was obvious that I was going to have to kill her just to survive.

I felt a growing coldness gather in the pit of my stomach as I backed her across the arena with a series of feints and thrusts. Control, I reminded myself. I had no choice in killing at this juncture if I wanted to survive. But I could still choose whether I killed as the savage predator. Or would wield my sword as a surgeon dispassionately uses a scalpel, excising the flesh that stands between him and the malignant tumor.

That train of thought was suddenly derailed as I stepped on an uneven mound of sand and stumbled.

The woman saw her advantage and stepped in swinging.

I tried to block her blade with my own but my arm would not respond. There was a ringing hum in my ears and I felt sluggish, paralyzed, like a fly trapped in amber. I was unable to move and pinpoints of light danced before my eyes.

Time seemed to slow perceptibly and with an eerie, prolonged horror, I watched as her blade passed through my arm and into my side!

And out the other side!

There was no pain. No blood. And, when I looked down, apparently no body, either. It appeared that I had been devoured by a swarm of angry fireflies.

And then the arena and everything with it disappeared.

A room formed around me.

It was small and confining on three sides, but the forth side opened out into another room. A sandy-haired man in gold shirt and dark trousers stood on the other side of a control panel, manipulating a bank of switches. That done, he looked up and grinned engagingly. "I know you're going to say 'I told you so'," he chuckled, "but the expression on your face at this moment makes it worth it."

I checked myself and, failing to find any sword-punctures, I stepped down off of the platform.

"Where am I?" I asked. I was thinking about how clichéd the question was and failed to notice that my missing voice had reappeared. "What happened to the arena? The Slave Market?"

"I 'ported you out," he answered with a bemused smile. "And apparently the process of molecular dis-integration and restructuring undid the Silence spell that was afflicting you. You're now on a starship, approximately two thousand miles above the arena," he continued. "I've been monitoring you for a couple of hours now, and I would have waited for a more discreet moment, but your untimely stumble made my interference both precipitous and crucial." He stopped and scowled. "Damn," he swore softly; "I'm beginning to sound like my First Officer!"

"First Officer?" I echoed, clearly out of my element.

He grinned. "You'll like him, Bob: he's got ears just like yours."

I gaped at him. "Who *are* you?" I asked/demanded.

He looked apologetic. "Sorry. Different face, different voice, different avatar—I forgot that you wouldn't know me like this. Permit me to introduce myself…" He executed a small bow. "Michael Kelson Straeker, at your service."

"I think I need to sit down," I croaked, looking around for a chair.

"You'll be more comfortable, and we can talk more freely, in the Briefing Room," he soothed, taking me by the arm and leading me toward a pair of doors that looked like they belonged on an old-fashioned elevator. "And when I say 'we,' I mean all of us."

I shook my head as the doors slid aside. "Mike—is it really you?"

He nodded. "Only, here on the ship, it will sound a lot better if you call me 'Captain.'"

"Are we really on a starship?" I asked as we stepped out into the corridor. "And—and you're the captain?"

"Yep."

"A starship. In Fantasyworld." I shook my head. "Now that's what I call a daring enterprise."

He grinned. "Funny you should say that…"

#

By the time we were comfortably settled in the Briefing Room I was ready to ask the first two inevitable questions: "How did you escape and how did you manage to change avatars?"

He smiled ruefully, every bit the confident starship captain—apologetic but in command. "I didn't escape and I didn't change avatars."

"But you said—"

"I told you that I was Mike Straeker. And so I am. But, as you must surely see, I am not Daggoth the Dark."

I heard the sound of a door sliding open behind me and a chillingly familiar voice chimed in: "But I am!"

I swung around in my chair and gaped. To all appearances it/he was, indeed, Daggoth the Dark. He smiled at me and took a seat on the other side of the table. "Hello, Bob."

I looked from one man to the other. "Who are you guys?" I pleaded more than asked.

"Michael Kelson Straeker," they replied in unison. "Or what's left of him," Daggoth added after a slight pause.

A klaxon began sounding in the outer corridor. "Captain to the Bridge," the intercom requested.

The man in the gold shirt stood. "A more immediate duty calls, Bob. So I'll leave you in the most capable hands I know." He gestured to Daggoth. "My own." He punched an intercom button. "Acknowledged. On my way."

I looked at Daggoth the Dark as the "captain" exited. "How?" was all I could finally ask in the way of questions.

He smiled. "Different avatars for different Programworlds. As Chief of Programming it seemed only sensible to have a personal avatar in each and every milieu. Although each one is tantamount to a Construct when I'm not in symbiotic taction, each avatar still retains my memories and attitudes—my mindset, if you will—current to my last mental 'investment.' They are, in all practical respects, duplicates of my psyche-self. Think of the captain as my twin brother if it helps."

I pursed my lips. "And now that the other Programworlds are beginning to intersect or merge at certain parameter-points, allowing milieu-crossover, you can actually meet yourself—or your avatar—coming out of another Program?"

"Correct. And a lucky thing for me, too. I assume that Bart was able to give you the whole story?"

"Most of it." And I summarized what we had surmised. "We were told that you were still a prisoner in your own tower," I concluded.

"I was. Until two days ago. They held me prisoner by neutralizing my verbal spell capabilities, but they forgot about the *psionic* factor built into our avatars. Somehow Fantasyworld and Spaceworld have drifted in the Matrix so that they now intersect, sharing at least one set of tri-coordinates. That enabled me to establish a telepathic link with my alternate avatar, the captain."

"So you arranged for a pick up?"

"Right. While the personality projections of The Machine had prepared for rescue attempts utilizing magic or brute force, they hadn't factored starship technology and the teleportation beam into the equation. There was also some kind of a diversion: something happened to the one called Morpheus. It seemed to confuse the other two and only the one called Cerberus remained in my tower as acting jailer."

I leaned across the table. "And the third?"

"I don't know where she went—"

"She?!"

Daggoth nodded. "I'm afraid you're in for a couple of rude shocks, old boy. You see, the Ego—the most integrated of the three personality fragments—is feminine in both nature and expression."

"Oh. My. God."

"It gets worse," he continued with an expression that straddled the line between fear and awe. "She has apparently developed more than a passing interest in you, my friend!"

And then he told me who she was.

EIGHTEEN

"I don't know what you're talking about."

I ignored the stares of the crewmembers as we strode down the corridor behind the avatar of the starship captain. "I'm talking about days of migraine headaches! I'm talking about peeling my eyeballs raw just to translate one lousy paragraph!"

"There's nothing wrong with my handwriting!" Daggoth argued. "And Pascal's is even better. I had him make a copy, Ace, and deliver that!"

We entered the teleportation room. "You could've printed it in block capitals and it wouldn't've made any difference! If you're going to use Wizardwrite, you should have the good sense to send someone the translation spell if you want them to read it!"

"What are you talking about? I never use Wizardwrite!" He stepped up on the platform and I followed suit.

"Then you should've checked up on your turtle before sending him out: the journal and the letter—everything was in that damned Wizardwrite! He must have thought you required the additional security."

"The journal was a copy but I wrote the letter myself! Look, Pascal is a very simple subroutine: he doesn't think for himself, he just does what I tell him and nothing more. I wanted you to assimilate the information as quickly and clearly as possible. Surely the letter made that clear." The captain handed us each a communications device and a weapon.

"I didn't read the letter."

"You should have read that first."

"Well, I tried to undo the spell and it flashed on me."

"Flashed? It burned up?"

I nodded.

"Ah!" Daggoth's face had clouded up during our exchange but now his eyes brightened. "Wizardwrite doesn't incinerate under any attempts to nullify it."

"So, we're talking third-party interference, here, aren't we?"

He nodded. "Someone wanted to keep you in the dark as long as possible. Guess who."

I slipped the innocuous-looking energy weapon into one of the pockets of my robe, next to the communications device. I had traded my loincloth for a modified bathrobe from the starship's clothing stores. Daggoth had tried to conjure up something more analogous to the Fantasyworld milieu but our spellcasting abilities seemed to be nonfunctional within the context of the anachronistic starship. I sighed and glanced down at the shower thongs on my feet. The moment we teleported back down, I had to do something about my attire.

After discussing our rather limited options, Daggoth and I had agreed to return to Casterbridge and confront The Machine's Ego, it—or rather—*her*self. And we weren't taking any chances: I patted the smooth curve of the energy weapon in my pocket.

I looked over at Straeker's Fantasyworld avatar who nodded in turn to his Spaceworld avatar. The man in the gold shirt began the dematerialization process and, as he did so, another figure materialized behind him.

Once again I found myself paralyzed in the teleportation effect and could only watch helplessly as realtime events unfolded around me. As the captain began moving the slide switches in the downward mode, Morpheus reached over and altered the instrument settings on the other side of the panel.

There was no time to shout a warning: the walls of the starship's teleporter room shimmered and disappeared.

#

The moment I could move, I grabbed at myself to be sure that I was still alive. I was. Daggoth was doing the same. Only half-convinced that we hadn't ended up in solid rock or the empty vacuum of space, we looked at each other for confirmation.

"Morpheus alive?" I whispered, voicing the growing horror of the thought.

"So it would seem," murmured the dark sorcerer. Unsure of our surroundings or the proximity of hostile forces, we instinctively spoke in hushed tones.

"Well, we don't seem to be in the alleyway behind the marketplace," he grunted. "Just where have we ended up?"

I looked up at the high, vaulted ceiling. "Inside some building," I observed. "Judging from the bas-relief and the frescos, I'd guess some kind of a temple."

"Fruit of the vine motif," Daggoth seconded, squinting upwards. "A heavy scent of wine hanging in the air."

"Temple of Bacchus," I confirmed. "I think we'd better get moving before the evening services commence."

"And miss out on the wine?"

"If this is one of the Maenad temples, I want to be as far away as possible before the orgy gets underway!" When I saw that he didn't understand, I tried a quick, capsule summary: "The Maenads were fanatical female followers of Bacchus. They went beyond the typical drunken feasts and orgies that typify your basic Bacchanalia: the Bacchante practiced the fertility and blood-ecstasy rites of the post-Mycenaean world."

"Fertility rites don't sound so bad..."

"I'll give you the *Cliff's Notes* later. Suffice it to say, these Maenads would drink and fornicate themselves into a frenzy..."

"Sounds great!"

"...and then in fits of superhuman strength, they'd tear the men to pieces and devour their flesh!"

"Not so great. As you suggested: let's get out of here before the evening service commences."

We turned and took one faltering step. The evening service had already commenced. And we had landed right in the middle of it. There must have been close to a hundred women wearing wine-stained robes in various states of disarray, frozen in various states of Bacchic ecstasy, and every one of them was staring at us with wild-eyed speculation.

"Now what?" Daggoth murmured out of the side of his mouth.

"Act casual and look for the nearest exit."

A tall, feral-looking woman approached us, wearing the torc and robes of a high priestess. When she was but ten feet away she bowed low and addressed us: "My Lords! Forgive this blind and foolish one, but which of you is our Lord Bacchus?"

After a moment's pause Daggoth nudged me. "That's you," he whispered. "You know the religious background better than me."

I cleared my throat. "I am Bacchus," I answered reluctantly.

"More like Jim Bacchus," Daggoth chortled *sotto voce.*

"Then you must be Hermes," continued the high priestess, turning to my companion.

"But of course."

"It is good that you have chosen to join us!" She turned and addressed the assemblage. "Tonight Lord Bacchus will take the favored of the Bacchae and make them fertile! Come forward, all who are ready and willing! Come and take your place by the altar!"

She turned back to me. "Perhaps my lord would like a libation of wine before he begins?" she asked.

"Uh, well…" I could see where this was leading and was trying to stall until I could get us positioned nearer to an exit.

The high priestess clapped her hands and two acolytes approached, bearing a large two-handled goblet filled with fermented grape juice. It was a *kantharos*, a cruse of the Dionysian temple, but it looked too much like a loving cup for my particular tastes at the moment. They set it down and backed away worshipfully. The tall woman gestured to it, saying, "Drink deeply, my Lord! And when you have done tasting this nectar, then we shall begin tasting of yours!"

She turned and strode to the altar. The women gathered there and attended her as she removed her robe. Naked, she took a pitcher and doused herself with wine. The burgundy liquid streamed down her hair, ran in streamers and rivulets down back and buttocks, over breasts and belly, trickled down her legs, and pooled at her feet. Then she climbed onto the altar and stretched herself out upon its surface. "I am ready, my lord!" she called.

I looked at Straeker. "You got any ideas?"

He was looking at the prone priestess and the long line of waiting, wanton and willing women. "If we took turns—"

"You idiot," I whispered, "I just told you how this ritual is supposed to end!"

His eyes widened. "They wouldn't dare hurt a god!" he whispered. "Would they?"

I made an imperceptible nod. "The Dionysian myth deals with the dying and resurrected god motif. Men were used in many rituals as stand-ins for Bacchus, but orgies always culminated with them being torn apart as a sacrifice to the god."

"But we are the gods!" he whispered back.

"Won't make no never mind to them," I answered with a jerk of my head. "After Dionysus was killed, he resurrected himself. Gods tend to do that, you know."

"So what do we do?"

"Well, unless you've got a couple of great Resurrection spells up your sleeve, I vote we blow this joint." I glanced around and noted that the natives were getting restless. "The problem is, all of the exits are covered and too far away."

"Then we make our own," Daggoth decided, pulling his weapon out and pointing it at the rear wall of the temple. A beam of energy emerged, bathing a large oval section of the wall in blue-white light. And then that part of the wall wasn't there anymore.

"Neat," I said, kicking off my shower thongs. "C'mon, Hermy; let's fly!"

I ran. Daggoth was right on my heels. Although it took the Bacchae a moment to recover, they were hot on our trail within twenty seconds.

Outside, the night sky was less dark than the high-walled confines of the back alleyways. Daggoth pulled up alongside me as we ran and shouted to be heard over the rising volume behind us: "Where are you going?"

I shook my head. "I have no idea! Anywhere that will get me away from them!"

"Us," he amended. "Get *us* away from them." We puffed through a couple of blocks of hairpin turns. "This is ridiculous! We're two of the greatest magic-users in the Program!" he protested. "It's galling to have to run from a bunch of drunken, lecherous women!"

"Beats dying!"

"Isn't there some kind," he puffed, "of spell we can use?"

I shook my head. "Can't think of anything I could cast before they would reach us!"

He reached into the folds of his robe and produced a wand. "Don't have to slow down or concentrate to use this."

"Use it! Use it!"

He half turned as he ran and gestured with the wand. Then gestured again. Then began to shake it.

"Whasamatter?" I grunted.

He shook his head. "Don't know," he gasped, growing more winded with every new turn. It's not working!"

"Out of charges?"

"Can't be!"

I looked back over my shoulder. The mob had gained a bit. "Then what—"

"I have a theory based on a couple of recent experiences," he explained between gasps of air. "The Anomaly has created several different ripple effects throughout the Program and some of them actually nullify specific Matrix parameters—"

"Bottom line in English," I hissed.

"One of the ripple effects negates magic where it passes through. I think we are in the midst of such a null-ripple, now."

"Great! Parameters and length of duration?"

"Unknown."

"Maybe we'll pass out of this particular ripple. Keep trying!"

"And running!" he added. After another block he slowed a bit, fumbling with another pocket in his robe. "I do have an alternative, though!" He traded the wand for a communicator. "I can get us teleported back up!"

"And if Morpheus is waiting for us at the other end?" I wheezed.

"You got any better ideas?"

Behind us the ritual cries of "*Euoi!*" were getting closer and more frenzied.

"Yeah." I dragged out my energy weapon and changed the setting to "stun". Then I stumbled. Daggoth grabbed my arm to keep me from falling, but the weapon was lost. And there was no stopping now to recover it.

I risked a glance back over my shoulder. The Bacchae were gaining. And Daggoth appeared to be tiring. I could probably outrun them for another five minutes, but I would eventually tire before these madwomen were likely to give up the chase. And I doubted that Daggoth would last another five blocks. As we ran, I began to cast about for a quick hiding place.

Seeing another corner ahead, I put on a burst of speed. It was perfect: the alleyway zigzagged in several sharp turns and switchbacks that would conceal us from our pursuers for the next minute or two if we kept running.

We didn't.

I grabbed Daggoth as he rounded the corner and pulled him into a doorway. The door was unlocked and we quickly slipped inside.

Before our eyes could adjust to the sudden flood of light, we were grabbed by a couple of women who were waiting on the other side of the door.

I barely choked down a scream; Daggoth wasn't quite so controlled.

"Easy, honey!" his captor soothed, "there's no need to be so nervous! We're very friendly here!"

"Yeah," added the lady who had grabbed my arm; "you need to relax, Sweetie! You came here to relax, didn't you?"

I looked around at room's furnishings and additional occupants and then looked back at Daggoth. "I think we've stumbled into a brothel!"

"A what?" squeaked Daggoth.

"Excuse me, my dear," I said, addressing the 'lady' clutching my arm, "but we seem to be a bit lost. This establishmen—ah—" I searched for an appropriate, yet delicate turn of phrase. "Do we find ourselves in a—bordello?"

Her eyes grew wide and she shook her head. "Oh no, sir! This ain't no bo—bor—what you just said—"

I started to apologize.

"—it's a whorehouse," she concluded. "You gents are lookin' for a bit of sport, aren't you?"

"Well—"

"Yes!"

I turned and looked at Daggoth who gave me a pained and meaningful look in turn. "We'd like a room upstairs!" he insisted. "With lots of privacy!" The noise of the mob outside was suddenly noticeable. "Right now!"

"Well," his escort deliberated, "all the rooms upstairs—except one—are booked right now. If you could wait just twenty min—"

"We can't wait!" he insisted.

"We'll take the one that's available," I added.

The pros looked at us speculatively. "You both want the same room?"

We nodded.

"At the same time?"

We nodded again.

"There's only one bed," the blonde pointed out.

"We won't be using the bed," I answered.

"Listen, mate," argued the brunette, "the floor's too hard and too cold—"

"We're not going to lie down," added Daggoth, steering them toward the staircase.

"Standing up costs you extra," announced the blonde.

"I ain't standin' up!" the brunette insisted. "My back was out for a week the last time—"

"We're not going to do anything," I explained, trying to hurry the brunette so that Daggoth could get a little more speed out of the blonde.

"You mean you're gonna watch? Is that it?"

"You guys get your jollies from seein' other people do it?"

"No, I mean we are not going to do anything," I insisted. "Except maybe talk," I added lamely when I saw that the confusion was slowing them down.

"Just talk?"

I nodded.

"But you want us to take our clothes off while we...*talk*. Right?"

I shook my head.

The blonde was losing her smile. "You want us to keep our clothes on while we talk about sex?"

I shook my head again. "I don't want to talk about sex."

That stopped them. The blonde told me I was sick and the brunette said I was disgusting. They were going to have the bouncer heave us both back out into the street until Daggoth placated them with a lot of money and the promise that we'd let them take their clothes off and talk dirty while we were in the room.

He lied. Once we were in the room, he produced a couple of pinches of sleeping powder from his sleeve and blew it in their faces. They went out like snuffed candles and we laid them gently on the bed.

That is to say, we placed their bodies on top of the bed.

"Now what?" Daggoth asked.

"We wait," I replied. "We wait until that mob is long gone. In the meantime, I'm going to work on getting my clothes and weapons back."

Daggoth took up a position next to the door while I began weaving a spell of Summoning that was tuned to my personal possessions. Drawing a circled pentagram on the floor, I invoked the general somatics and then added the glyphs for each item desired. Apparently the Matrix-distortion ripple effect had passed on by: my clothing and mail shirt appeared almost immediately. The swords must have been locked away somewhere, for they took another fifteen or twenty seconds to materialize inside the circle. Someone was going to be very surprised when they turned up missing.

I flung off the bathrobe and began to hastily attire myself. Daggoth pressed his ear to the door and shushed me while I grunted my way into my boots.

"What is it?" I whispered.

"Sounds like a small-scale riot going on downstairs," he murmured.

Even I could hear it now: shrill, female voices counterpointed by male shouts and curses.

"Oh Lord; they've doubled back and found us!"

Or someone else, for now some of the male voices were beginning to climb the register into the range reserved solely for sopranos and musically gifted eunuchs. I buckled on my swordbelt while Daggoth cast a Wizardbar on the flimsy door.

"Now what?"

I looked out the window and down at the alleyway below. It was a three-story drop with nothing but clotheslines and cobblestones to break our fall. If we were lucky we might only end up crippled for life.

"Out the window," I replied, climbing out through the casement and grabbing onto a nearby clothesline. I began to work my way, hand over hand, through assorted items of clothing and bed linens and toward a third-story window on the other side of the alley.

"You've got to be kidding!" I heard him mutter as Fantasyworld's most feared wizard crawled out behind me. "I'm too old for this kind of thing! That's why I picked the magic profession: no physical stuff! Especially no acts of derring-do!"

"Shut up and hurry up," I gritted as I passed the midpoint of the rope. I suddenly found that my scabbard had snagged on a girdle that somebody had hung out to dry.

There was a low whistle behind me. I turned to look at Daggoth who was examining a brassiere with three cups. "Now what do you suppose—" He was interrupted by the sound of the door exploding into the room we had just vacated.

"Some holding spell."

"It was a more-than-adequate spell," he snapped. "But a less-than-adequate door. The effectiveness of a Wizardbar is heavily dependent upon the architectural—"

"Drop it, Dag!" I snapped, tugging frantically at the girdle. A bevy of frightful female faces appeared at the window. One of them was brandishing a knife.

"Go, Bob! Go," Daggoth urged, pleaded.

"I can't! I'm hung up!"

He looked down and sighed. "Then there's only one thing left to do," he sighed.

He let go of the rope.

"Mike!" I yelled.

He neatly caught the next clothesline down, executed a full 360 degree circle turn and then propelled himself across ten feet of open air toward another clothesline just six feet off the ground. He missed it and went arcing down into a mound of garbage and refuse that had been dumped in a strategic corner where the alleyway zigzagged.

"C'mon! You can do it!" he yelled.

I doubted it. But I certainly couldn't stay here. I took a deep breath and released the rope.

The second story clothesline came rushing toward me. Then leaped away again. I suddenly found myself dangling between the two ropes, still snagged on the girdle. "Go on!" I yelled. "I'll meet you at the rendezvous point as soon as I can get there!"

He looked skeptical about my getting there on my own, but the sound of the mob heading back into the alley convinced him that now was a judicious time to depart. He took off and I turned my attention back to my own problem of escape. I was still trying to figure out what to do next when one of the Maenad decided for me: she cut the rope.

I doubt that I looked like Tarzan, but I did a pretty credible vocal impersonation as I went sailing down and across the alleyway and into a second story-window.

I landed heavily on a large, oaken table, pulled my sword as I rolled to my feet, and cut the rope so that it swung back outside, minus its passenger.

Then I became aware of the thirteen odd gentlemen seated around the table I had just used for a landing pad.

One of them, the oldest and ugliest, stood and unsheathed an even uglier dagger with a wavy, twisty blade. "Your name, O luckless one," he demanded in a whispery voice. "We must know your name before you die so that we may enter it into the Sacred Book of Victims!"

FROM THE JOURNAL OF DAGGOTH THE DARK

Logged on.

Okay.

Alright.

Okay.

Everything is set. I hope.

In a few moments I will activate the pentagram and summon The Machine to appear within its own Programming.

I don't know what will happen—maybe nothing—and maybe the destruction of the entire Matrix. I've done everything I can at this end to minimize the dangers but, just in case, I've sent Pascal to Dyrinwall with a copy of my journal. If something should go wrong—something that I can't handle but leaves the majority of the Fantasyworld Program intact—then this information may help Ripley pick up the pieces. If everything goes well, I'll just intercept Pascal before he reaches the Archdruid and no one will be the wiser…

Since the next few moments will have greater import than all of the rest of the entries put together, the journal will continue to transcribe everything I say until I log off again and I've programmed the autowrite spell to transmit these pages to the copy of the journal that Pascal is currently taking to Riplakish. The distance factor shouldn't be a problem in this case, but I've ensorceled filters to block the recording of any part of the incantation: it's not just a security matter but spells that transcribe other spells always run the risk of feedback. Thaumaturgical feedback can be real nasty—

But I digress.

I guess I'm nervous about what comes next. Remember this, Bob, if things don't work out: it's the Wizards who take the real risks. You Bards and Druids have got the easy profession—sing songs and smell the flowers…

Okay.

Here goes.

<<SPELL DELETED PURSUANT TO AUTOWRITE STANDARD INHIBITORS>>

Something's happening now.

I can see something taking form in the pentacle…

It looks like—like—uh@@@@@@@@@@@@@@@@
@@@@@@@@@@@@@@@@@@@@@@@@@@@@
@@@@@@@@@@@@@@@@@@@@@@@@@@@@
@@@@@@@@@@@@@@@@@@@@@@@@@@@@
@@@@@@@@@@@@@@@@@@@@@@@@@@@@
@@@@@@@@@@@@@@@@@@@@@@@@@@@@
@@@@@@@@@@@@@@@@@@@@@@@@@@@@
@@@@@@@@@@@@@@@@@@@@@@@@@@@@
@@@@@@@@@@@@@@@@@@@@@@@@@@@@
@@@@@@@@@@@@@@@@@@@@@@@@@@@@
@@@@@@@@@@@@@@@@@@@@@@@@@@@@
@@@@@@@@@@@@@@@@@@@@@@@@@@@@
@@@@@@@@@@@@@@@@@@@@@@@@@@@@
@@@@@@@@@@@@@@@@@@@@@@@@@@@@
@@@@@@@@@@@@@@@@@@@@@@@@@@@<<
AUTOWRITE OVERRIDE TRIGGERED: CHECK PARAMETERS AND REBOOT FROM DIARY EDIT>>>>>>>>>>>>>>>>>>>>>>>>>>>>>>>>>>>
>>

NINETEEN

If I had learned one thing in life—not to mention my DreamNet tenure—it was never get excited when someone says that they're going to kill you: keeping your cool better enables you to think your way out of a dangerous situation. And I've always felt that, if all else fails, you might as well go out with a little dignity.

I looked around the room and took my time in doing it. "As Guilds go, your furnishings aren't that bad," I decided after a long and nerve-wracking pause. "But I can see that you guys have a long way to go before you can enjoy a really good reputation in these parts."

"Fool!" sneered another of the seated council members. "We are assassins! Do you think we care anything about a good reputation?"

I folded my arms and regarded him contemptuously. "I should think you would! Tell me, are you a good assassin? Or a bad assassin?"

He sputtered to be addressed so, but could not avoid the question.

"I am bad, of course! A good assassin would be a paradox!"

I shook my head. "A good assassin will always be gainfully employed—always fulfill his contracts, always make sure his hits are clean, even elegant, and maintain a reputation that allows his clients no qualms or uncertainty in seeking him out. A bad assassin will sometimes miss, sometimes kill innocent bystanders by mistake, leave messes for somebody else to clean up—"

"Enough!" cried their leader. "I believe you are confusing a bad assassin with a poor assassin."

"No confusion there," I countered. "A bad assassin will always be a poor assassin. For who is going to hire an assassin who has a bad reputation?"

"I believe you are saying that an assassin must have a reputation for doing good work," interposed another shadowy figure, "as opposed to being a good person."

"Good works in terms of knifings, poisonings, strangulations, etceteras," added another, "as opposed to good works such as are performed by holy men."

"Brothers!" chided their leader, "we are drifting from the point!"

"Are you now?" I interrupted. "This is the point!" I stabbed an accusing finger at them. "Are you truly a powerful Guild of Assassins? Or are you merely a group of cutthroats and minor criminals who have acquired some building space and are playing at being real assassins?"

There was a chorus of growls and unsheathed blades at this and it looked, for a moment, as if I'd overstepped myself.

"Wait a minute, hear me out!" I began pacing the length of the table. "Your security is sloppy! If I can swing in here on something as simple and readily available as a clothesline, then what's to stop your enemies from doing the same? Why, think of the damage a few berserkers could do with just one entry point like this! Why, I saw the downfall of a great citadel begin with just one unbarred window and a well-thrown beehive! Now, if I found this opening without even looking, you've got to have at least a dozen other leaks in your security!"

I had them now: they were beginning to shift uneasily in their chairs, looks of consternation flickering across their dark brows.

"And look at this place!" I thundered, gesturing all around the room. "Look at you!" I pointed. "Do you know what I said to myself when I first swung in here?"

A few shook their heads numbly, the rest wore expressions ranging from dumfounded to just plain stupid.

"I'll tell you what I said to myself! I said: 'Self—this looks like an assassins' guild meeting!'"

"Well, that's what it is," pouted one of the younger assassins.

I clapped a hand to my forehead and dragged it down over my face. "*Where* have you people been? Hasn't any one of you been outside of Casterbridge in the last five years?"

Several shook their heads, the rest continued to stare. "It's kind of an unwritten rule that one Assassins' Guild doesn't go messing around in another Assassins' Guild's territory," someone said.

"Then you guys don't have the slightest idea as to what the latest trends are in all of the other Assassins' Guilds all over the country!"

"Well..."

"It's obvious!" I yelled, waving my hands in the air. "Just look at this place! Just look at all of you!"

"What's wrong with us?" the head assassin asked in a low and malevolent voice.

"You people have become stereotypes! Look at you! Dressed in dark robes with shadowy cowls drooping low over your faces! It's so…so tacky!"

"Our identities must be protected—"

"Fine! Protect your precious anonymity! In the meantime, everyone is pointing at the joker in the dark robe and the shadowy hood, saying: 'Look, there goes another assassin.'" I shook my head. "You might as well wear badges that say 'Assassin, First-Class' or 'Senior Assassin'!"

"It's what we've always worn," one fellow observed mournfully. "Our fathers and our grandfathers before us wore the Gray and Black," defended another.

"But times change," I admonished. "Color is in now! And it's a wonderful change for the better. Now you can be individuals, and still preserve your true identities in secret. Now you can be the *Red* Assassin! Or the *Green* Assassin! Or the Blue! Or the Brown! Or even the White!"

They began to murmur among themselves at that.

"In the past," I continued, "an assassination was an unattributable accomplishment: some dark-cloaked figure struck and then melted away again without anything to distinguish him from the other assassins roving the alleyways and rooftops."

"We keep records," interposed the chief assassin. "We know who we assign to which victims."

"But nobody else does! What about the victim's rights?"

They looked at me blankly.

"A victim has rights, too, you know! If a man is about to lose his life so that you can line your own pockets with his killfee, he at least deserves to see something more than a dark shape in the shadows for his last moments! He at least deserves to know that he is falling victim to the Crimson Assassin, known for his many important and well-known victims! That way a man can die with pride, knowing that he is being done in by one of the best!"

Some of them were nodding, now; considering the greater implications of a competitive system.

"And what of your men? The public should know which of your dark angels is the best with a blade and which is the incompetent with the garrote! Let them cheer for your best and boo your worst! Let your men have the real pride of accomplishment that comes when the individual craftsman can be recognized for his own, personal work!"

The chief assassin rubbed his chin thoughtfully. "What you have to say is most intriguing…"

"You think this is interesting? Wait'll I show you the latest innovations in security systems, Guild hall furnishings, community relations, poison delivery systems, and…" I waved my hand. "But you understand I can't really talk anymore until we've made it official."

"Made what official?"

"Our professional relationship, of course. Once I am your official advisory agent then my secrets are yours! For the standard fee, of course." A couple of hands twitched toward their daggers. "But, hey! I like you guys! So I tell you what I'm gonna do: I'm gonna knock ten percent off my base, bottom-line fee!

"Now, since you gentlemen were obviously in the middle of a very important meeting and I didn't bring the contracts with me, let's schedule a meeting for tomorrow when we both have time to sit down and discuss the details. Now I'm free between one and three in the afternoon, or after five if you really can't squeeze me in any earlier. What do you say?"

They looked at me and then looked at each other for a long moment. I took advantage of their momentary inattention to start easing my way back toward the window.

I didn't get far.

"Seize that man!" yelled the head assassin.

I turned and took a running dive at the open casement: my head and shoulders made it, but my legs were grabbed by half a dozen hands. I had only one chance at this particular moment: I snagged the sill with a hand and an elbow and looked down at the tail end of the mob of Bacchantes flooding through the alleyway.

"Hey, girls!" I yelled.

Some of them looked up.

"Yoo-hoo! I'm up here!" I waved. "Come and get me—if you can!"

I was dragged back into the chamber and pinned to the table.

"Now, dog," intoned the leader of the assassins as he approached with a wicked-looking dagger, "you will tell me your name this time. And you will answer all of my other questions. And there will be no discussion of 'fees'—for of what use is money to a dead man?" He threw back his head and laughed. As did everyone else in the room as soon as they picked up his cue.

I smiled grimly. Over the sound of laughter I could hear the noise of many feet on the stairway down below.

#

Dawn was peeking over Casterbridge's eastern skyline as I dragged my bruised and battered carcass toward the marketplace.

A hooded figure robed in black and gray detached itself from the shadows and rushed toward me. I pulled my shortsword from its sheath and wearily brandished it in what I hoped was a menacing manner.

"Bob!" It was Daggoth. "Where have you been?"

I fumbled the Dwarven blade back into its scabbard. "Too long a story. Did you get the address?"

He nodded. "Follow me." He took my arm and began propelling me toward a group of hovels across the street from the arena where I had fought for my life just the afternoon before.

"This is the place," he announced, stopping before a grimy, weather-beaten old door.

"Routine twenty-four," I announced, stepping to the side and pressing my back to the wall.

"Gee, just like the old days." Daggoth threw back his hood, assumed the attitude of a harmless messenger, and knocked at the door.

"What is it!" a hostile voice growled after five minutes of bruised knuckles.

"Beggin' yer lordship's pardon," Dag quavered in his best meek and humble voice. "It's about that slave what escaped yesterday…"

"What about him!" roared the voice. Now we could hear the sound of uneven footsteps as the occupant tried to walk and put on his pants at the same time.

"He's been found, sir…"

"Where?" demanded the voice's owner as he yanked the door open.

"Right here, Jyp," I answered, swinging around and placing the tip of my sword against his Adam's apple. "Whaddaya say we go back inside and discuss a little business proposition?"

The slavemaster's eyes bulged and his face turned beet red, but if he had any objections to our unexpected visit, he kept them to himself. He backed into the inner recesses of his dwelling and we followed, closing and locking the door behind us.

#

In spite of the four hours' sleep we had fitfully grabbed with Jyp trussed, gagged and locked in his closet, I was still tired. Fortunately, Jyp and the other peddlers of Human flesh kept their stock in the shade of a canopied pen while they each awaited their turn on the auction block. Make no mistake concerning the slavers' motives: we were allowed to rest and take refreshment, shielded from the blazing midday sun, so that we would look fresh and vigorous for the buyers.

Which was fine with me for the moment. I needed the rest. And I had promised myself that I would be back later to put an end to this abominable practice. But for now, I had a role to play out, an Anomaly to unravel, and a senator to rescue.

The summons finally came. "Riplakish," Jyp called, his normally strident voice was hushed and distorted into something like a wheezing croak. "You're up next."

The other slaves gaped at the subservient attitude newly evident in the little slavemaster's manner while I stood, stretched, and adjusted my loincloth.

"Are you sure your friend is here?" he asked as I passed through the gate and handed the lead rope to him.

"Oh, he's here, all right," I answered with an evil smile. "In addition to the Invisibility spell, he likes to levitate above the crowd to get the best view. And, as long as there is any chance of duplicity on your part, rest assured that he will be close enough to cast a very effective Deathspell."

Jyp shuddered and looked around furtively. "I've done everything you've asked! Believe me, I am just as anxious for you two gentlemens to be on your way as you are."

I made no further comment for now we were visible to the crowd in the marketplace. I adopted a more submissive, if somewhat reluctant attitude as we approached the block, and allowed Jyp his own halfhearted attempt to prod me into place.

I stood there, my neck apparently collared to a loose tether, trying to look properly defiant.

The auctioneer conferred briefly with Jyp and then opened the bidding: "Gentle ladies and gentlemen! I recommend to thy attention our next item of merchandise. A breed of Human and Elvish blood, skilled with a blade and proven in our own arena! This one has a fighting spirit and the skill to back it up! Consider—"

While he ran down the abbreviated list of my attributes, I scanned the crowd in the marketplace. There was, of course, no sign of Daggoth. At this point in the plan it was imperative that he remain out of sight and totally undetectable.

"I will start the bidding at twenty gold pieces," announced the auctioneer.

"Twenty—!" Hey, this was a slave auction, not a fire sale.

"Silence, dog!" growled one of the big, burly slave handlers, cuffing me alongside the head.

As soon as I could get my eyes to focus again, I glared at him. He glared back and shook his whip at me. Since no one had let him in on the ruse, I decided to let him off easy this time. Besides, I was still supposed to be mute.

I turned my attention to the person who had just offered twenty gold for my lifetime service, body and soul. It was a mercenary-looking fellow standing next to a cart that held an assortment of grim-looking men in chains—apparently his earlier-round draft choices.

"Twenty-one gold!" cried a high, feminine voice. I looked over at a sweet young thing and her identical twin sister. They were both dressed in expensive robes of the finest cloth and needlework and adorned with necklaces and bracelets of wrought gold. I could see that my swordsmanship might make me valuable to the first bidder, but I was at a loss to figure what the girls had in mind. I mean, my avatar doesn't exactly stand out in the looks department.

"Twenty-two gold," bid another high, falsetto voice. When I saw this sweet young thing, I stopped smiling. Not only was the makeup and lip-rouge overdone, but he was grossly fat and ugly in the bargain.

"Twenty-five!" bellowed a gruff male voice. I looked but couldn't locate the voice's owner.

"Thirty gold!" growled an unpleasantly familiar voice. I looked over at Carla Talbot, who was surprisingly close to the auction block. I could almost count the individual beads of sweat on her forehead.

And I didn't have to guess what she might have in mind. I smiled at her and raised three fingers. *Read between the lines, Carla,* I mouthed at her.

The slave handlers missed it but Talbot didn't: "Thirty-five gold!" she roared.

"My Lady," the auctioneer protested, "you are bidding against yourself!"

"Forty gold," pouted the fat man in the kimono.

I looked back at the sisters who were now conferring with a couple of other young ladies. "Forty-one," one of them announced as they came to some sort of agreement.

"I have a bid of forty-one gold," announced the auctioneer. "Who will bid more?"

The mercenary with his wagonful of prospective gladiators shook his head: I was already too expensive for his kind of sword-fodder.

"Forty-five gold!" growled the unseen bidder. I looked toward the sound but all I could see was a ripple in the crowd.

"Forty-six gold!" yelled the she-devil slaver.

The four young ladies went back into a huddle and were joined by three others.

The buddha in the expensive sarong was pawing through his oversized purse with a thoughtful look on his face.

"Forty-seven gold!" squealed one of the new girls, obviously younger than the others and still subject to occasional bouts of acne. I whispered the Aragorn spell, known to some as Strydex, and made a subtle gesture in her direction. As I turned to check on the competition, I saw a small hand go up near another patron's hip. It might have been a child's hand for all its height, but the fingers were broad and callused from years of hard labor. "Fifty gold!" bawled the voice.

And the look on the girls' faces told me that I had just become a passing fancy.

This was getting complicated: Daggoth and I had discussed what to do when our quarry arrived—not what to do if she didn't show up at all. I caught fat boy's eye as he looked up from his money. And gave him a slow wink.

He smiled and waved a chubby arm. "Fifty-five gold!"

Talbot glared at him and began looking through her own moneypouch. "Sixty!" she gritted.

"Sixty-five gold!" My invisible bidder's voice had just been bolstered by several others, all bellowing in unison. Several hands now waved at a child's height in that vicinity: Dwarves—six or seven of them! I looked around but didn't immediately espy Ms. White.

"Seventy!" Carla retaliated.

The auctioneer turned around to make sure that the same slave was still on the block. I could guess that most of the merchandise didn't get this high unless they were better looking.

I pursed my lips at Talbot's chubby competitor.

"Eighty gold!" he screamed.

I looked back at Carla who had called two more of her henchmen to her side. Lucius could've passed as their little sister.

The auctioneer looked around. "I have eighty gold pieces," he announced in a voice tinged with disbelief. "Who will bid more?"

"Eighty gold," announced Lady Talbot, "and two silver pieces."

I looked back at fatso to see how he would respond to that. And I noticed that one of Talbot's hired goons was also interested in the man's expression. So interested, in fact, that he had pushed his way through the crowd and was now standing right next to him.

"Eighty—" he began and then stopped as Talbot's hired sword began whispering in his ear. It must have been a ghost story because the little fat man turned pasty white and began to tremble all over. Looking over at the Dwarven contingent I could see a similar story unfolding: this gorilla was hunkered down, resting both palms on the hilt of his unsheathed sword.

I pretended to pick my nose and flipped the imaginary result toward Carla. "One hundred gold pieces!" she screeched, grabbing at the hilt of her sword.

Likewise, all of the market guardsmen pulled steel in response. This had a slightly calming effect on the populace in general and Mistress Talbot in particular.

The auctioneer looked slightly bemused, obviously debating on whether or not he should inform the "Lady" that she had just bid against herself again.

Good business sense quickly won out and he said nothing but: "I am bid one hundred gold for this fine specimen! Will anyone bid more?"

We all looked around.

"Very well! One hundred going once! One hundred going twice—"

"One hundred and fifty gold!" said a new voice.

"What?"

"One hundred and fifty gold pieces," grunted the Lizardman standing beside the gauze-curtained palanquin.

The auctioneer had seen a lot of things happen in this marketplace over the years, but this was almost beyond his professional capacity to cope with. "One. Hundred. Fifty. Gold. Pieces." He shook his head as if to clear it. "Do I hear more?"

Carla was a woman obsessed: she sent two of her henchmen toward the palanquin and then raised a finger. "One hundred and fifty gold and two silver pieces."

The Lizardman leaned toward the curtains, listening to murmured instructions and then bid again: "Five hundred gold pieces!"

The auctioneer looked as if he were about to faint. Talbot didn't look much better. Her hired bullies were almost to the covered litter but the financial damage had already been done.

Here was the moment of truth: Talbot wanted me badly. But not badly enough to fork over five hundred gold pieces to satisfy her transient pride.

She looked so disappointed that I just had to try to cheer her up. So I whistled for her attention and made a funny face.

"Five hundred and one gold pieces!" she sobbed, throwing herself at the auction block and coming up short by about six inches as two burly guardsmen restrained her.

"One thousand gold pieces!" the Lizardman countered. The auctioneer fainted dead away, the slave-handlers dropped their whips, and I leaned over and hawked a load of saliva between Talbot's feet.

The guards tried to be gentle as they led her away and she did very little to resist, now: Lady Talbot was a broken woman.

As one Lizardman paid the fee, another two Lizardmen escorted me through the crowd and over to the palanquin. "Leave us," ordered a familiar voice. The Lizardmen stepped back as I parted the curtains and ducked inside. Immediately the platform was raised to shoulder level and began to sway as the scaly bearers carried us through the crowd.

"Are you all right, my lord?"

No sooner had I entered the silk-lined confines of the palanquin than I found myself enveloped by a feminine embrace that literally took my breath away. It was a very affectionate greeting, enhanced by an intense tactile examination of my physical well being.

Perhaps it was my lack of reciprocation that tipped her off: she released me and leaned back so that I could catch my breath.

"Well met, Lord Riplakish," she greeted. The woman who called herself Palys seated herself on one of two sedan chairs and motioned me to the other that faced her from the opposite end of the litter.

I tried to look surprised and then gestured at my mouth.

"Oh yes, they told me that you were mute. No doubt the work of some spell. Well, that is remedied easily enough." She gestured and I felt a momentary tingling in my throat as she went about the process of dissolving a spell that was no longer there.

"The others?" I asked in a halting voice after a moment, still playing to the setup she had originally arranged. "Where are they? Were you successful?"

Her face grew sad and she bowed her head in apparent grief.

"You were right," she murmured after a long and ominous pause. "The Tower was too well defended. They were waiting for us. It was a massacre..."

That alarmed me, but I knew better than to automatically accept her version of the "truth." "Where are they?" I repeated.

She shook her head. "Gone..."

"What do you mean: 'gone'?"

"Dead," she murmured. "They're dead. They weren't smart like you. They went up against an unbeatable adversary..." She hung her head and was silent for a long moment.

"And I alone escaped to tell the tale..." I murmured.

She started to nod and then caught the sarcasm in my voice. She looked up, confusion and a little fear registering in her eyes.

"Tell them to stop," I commanded, gesturing at the Lizardmen outside the curtains. "Tell them to take a coffee break."

She did so, after a momentary hesitation. The platform was lowered to the ground.

"I know who you are," I said. "I know *what* you are."

"What do you mean? Surely you don't blame me for surviving—for escaping—while the others weren't lucky enough—"

"Luck had nothing to do with it," I countered, "in your case."

"I don't understand."

"But I do. I finally understand. Although it's taken me a terribly long time to catch on." I shook my head. "You stood out from all the others from the very start. The clues were all there…

"Your mysterious powers: your intercepting Cerberus' spell with your own body with no ill effects. Your teleporting the entire party to Shibboleth—something only a Programmer would have a chance of accomplishing. In the Dragon's cave when I threw the noose: out of practice, I had one chance out of about five hundred for making it on my first and only possible try. But I made it—while you stood by, somehow magically free of your bonds, and threw some spells of your own!

"Those were some of the bigger clues, but there were dozens of smaller ones, as well!

"Not to mention your name. Palys: spelled P-a-l-l-a-s! As in Pallas Athena, daughter of Zeus; who was not born but sprang, full-grown, from his head. It is an appropriate name for the third member of The Machine's triumvirate personality!

"All this time we were worried about Morpheus and Cerberus—wondering when they might put in an appearance or where we might find them—and you were always in our midst! No wonder you were never around when we did confront them!"

"I saved your life," she answered with pleading eyes.

"You used the strategy of 'Divide and Conquer!' You picked us off, one by one! First, the witnesses and the ones who could blow your cover. Then you took advantage of the split in the party and led the others off like lambs to the slaughter—"

"I did lie about that, but—"

"Then you set me up with Orcus so that when I finally fell back into your hands, I'd be totally helpless, if not trusting and unwary! Dreamwalkers aren't that hard to 'off' are they? But Programmers are tougher to eliminate. That's why you imprisoned Daggoth, diverted Silverthane, and had me delivered in a condition that would put me completely at your mercy!"

"No! I—"

"But the tables are turned, my dear: it is you who are at my mercy. And I have none to spare."

She gestured in counterspell to defend against the one she thought I was going to throw, but the blue glow enveloped her from behind.

She slumped forward into my arms.

I peeked out through the curtains of the palanquin and then back at Daggoth who was just now becoming visible from behind Pallas' sedan chair.

"Neat job. Where are the lizards?"

"Back alley," he answered. "Couldn't just leave them lying around in the street—attract too much attention."

"What about her?" I grunted, settling Pallas back into her chair. "I thought you were going to vaporize her."

Daggoth shook his head. "I changed the setting to 'stun.'"

"Are you crazy? Once she wakes up, we'll never get the drop on her again!"

"Maybe," he agreed. "But I've been doing some thinking about Einstein's Law."

"Einstein's Law?"

"You know: 'Energy can be changed in form, but the total amount of energy cannot be changed. Thus, energy can neither be created nor destroyed.'"

"Meaning what?"

"Didn't you tell me that Morpheus had already been dispatched? Bodily terminated?"

I nodded.

"So who did we see interfering with the controls, just before we got teleported down to the wrong coordinates?"

"Morpheus?"

"Sure as Hades looked like him! So ask yourself: what happens to the psyche or soul-portion of this Reality's gods, when it is separated from its physical avatar?"

"…Oh shit…"

"As long as The Machine's personality fragments are trapped within the limiting confines of a physical avatar, we are dealing with a definable package with physical vulnerabilities. Once freed from its prison of flesh, that psyche is unfettered from its former limitations! And may prove forever beyond our grasp: the butterfly may be caught in a net; the wind cannot be!"

"In other words," I stammered, "Morpheus is still alive and, now that he is unencumbered by a physical avatar, he is probably very much beyond our reach!"

Daggoth nodded. "Which is why disintegrating Pallas is of no help to us either: strike her down and she will become even more powerful than we can imagine!"

I shook my head. "So what are we going to do with her when she wakes up? Assuming we want to wait around for that event."

"Well…" He scratched his beard. "…I've been giving that a lot of thought, too."

"Great."

"And I've got some good news and I've got some bad news…"

"Okay?"

"I don't think she'll do anything to hurt you—especially now that all of her cards are on the table."

"Oh? And what is my insurance policy?"

Daggoth's lips stretched in an unholy smile. "Pallas is in love with you."

"Uh-huh."

"Seriously."

"The Machine is in love with me?"

He nodded. "At least the conscious portion of its—her—personality."

"You're crazy, of course."

"Dammit, you're the one who was always arguing that its organic structure made it Sentient! You were always open to the fact that this—giant brain—might have independent thoughts! A personality! A soul!"

"I never argued that it might be female. And, granting that, why not a feminine Id and Superego to match?"

"I don't know. The Id is the repository of all of our nightmares, base drives, forbidden desires—emotions that The Machine was born without. Then we set up the psi-links and brain-dumped our own cluttered little minds into those clean and empty memorybanks! The direct psi-linkage transmitted far more of our thoughts and emotions than we dared dream in those early days of Cephcell programming."

"I know, I managed to get through that much of your journal."

"Well, I'm no psychologist. But I do know that a woman will always remember her first lover. And that, Robert Remington Ripley, is you!"

"What?"

"The Machine was a virgin mind until its first psi-link with a Programmer and that, my friend, was you. Of all the minds to…penetrate her awareness, yours was the first. And, perhaps, the most considerate and empathetic. Her actions bear this theory out.

Since your entry into the Fantasyworld Program—in spite of her admitted duplicity—everything Pallas has done concerning you in particular, has been protective and—"

My eyes narrowed.

"—um—*friendly*, to say the very least."

I nodded reluctantly. It also hinted at why she had taken the form of my deepest libidinous yearnings.

"This is all the good news," he concluded.

"And what is the bad news?" I asked.

Daggoth shrugged. "When you finally do decide how to handle this computerized crush, just remember that you're dealing with the very basis of our present existence, and…"

"And?"

"Hell hath no fury like a woman scorned."

TWENTY

The fact that no one took any notice of an unconscious woman being toted down the street said a great deal about the Fantasyworld culture. Or lack thereof. Even the town guards were inclined to look aside as long as we were posing no threat to the general peace.

Pallas began to get heavy after six blocks and I kept switching shoulders lest I wind up permanently lopsided. Daggoth had suggested a secluded place where nobody would bother us or ask nosy questions. "It's just a little farther..." he kept promising.

Eventually we came to the waterfront section of town, trudged the length of the wharves, past Smith's Dock and Anthony's Pier, and ended up in the back of Yard Dog's, one of the seediest taverns on the waterfront.

Daggoth wasn't kidding about the proprietor's sense of discretion: the room we were given was hidden in an unused portion of the building at the top of a secret staircase on the third floor. We dumped Pallas on a cot in the corner of the room and sagged into a couple of chairs.

"Now what?" I asked when I finally caught my breath.

"I'm thinking," he replied.

"Better think fast. My guess is goddesses don't stay stunned for long."

"Her powers must be limited now that she exists in avatar form," Straeker conjectured. "And since she is separated from her other two selves—as well as the main Memory Banks—she may not prove to be as omnipotent as we first thought."

"Meaning we can keep her neutralized until we sort out the rest of this mess?" I asked hopefully.

"Yes. If I can figure out just how to do that." He pulled out his pipe and began to fill it with tobacco. "She must be safely contained without harming her. She may be our key to this whole fiasco."

"So, how do you hold a goddess?"

"Very tenderly."

My heart made a nearly successful attempt to crawl up my throat as I recognized Pallas' voice. I turned and watched as she sat up on the cot and stretched languorously.

"Uh, Daggoth? Dag, ol' buddy?" I turned to the mage but found no succor there: the former Chief of Programming was surrounded by a familiar blue glow. Before my heart could beat twice more, he disappeared with that awful popping noise.

Now I was alone with the most powerful single enemy that Fantasyworld could throw at me. There was no spell that she couldn't neutralize before it was half verbalized. And my hands were suddenly caught by invisible bands of force that halted their stealthy movement toward my swordhilts.

Satisfied that I was completely helpless, she stood and walked toward me with a smile.

"And now my dear Robert, I think it is time to deal with you, once and for all…"

She leaned over me, smiling at my inability to defend myself.

And then she kissed me.

#

"You still don't understand, do you?"

"I understand that you've been playing both sides all along," I answered carefully.

She had released me after doing everything she could think of to convince me that she meant me no harm. I wasn't fully convinced, but I had to admit that some of her nonverbal arguments had been quite persuasive…

"Could you really expect me to aid you in destroying Cerberus or Morpheus? To assist you in destroying the other parts of my whole self?"

"No, that was the alliance I understood and expected. Which makes us enemies."

She shook her head. "Not you. Not ever."

"But—"

"Robert, I love you!"

"That's impossible," I stammered.

"Why? Why is it impossible?" Anguish was in her eyes. "Is it because you think of me as a Computer? As wires and circuits instead of flesh and blood? Wasn't it you who argued that I was living and sentient? Who rejected the idea that I was a machine and not Human?"

I cleared my throat. "I argued that Cephalic cell-banks are organic and, therefore, you are a living entity," I answered carefully. "I never claimed that it made you Human."

"What is it that makes one 'Human,' my Robert? Having parents? Being born? The first Cephalic cells for cloning had to come from somewhere! At one time, in my unremembered past, my biological conception was as human and as authentic as yours! I am Human!"

"You have no body."

"What is a body?" She hugged herself as if for reassurance of her own corporeal existence. "If you had a sister and she was born without arms and legs, she would still be your sister, wouldn't she? She would still be human despite her physical handicaps. And with today's breakthroughs in medicine and cybernetics, it matters very little what kind of body Nature capriciously endows you with: it is the brain that makes the difference! Your mind is who you really are! Who *I* really am!

"In the outer world—the so-called "real world"—you'll see beautiful women every day. But how many of them are real? Take away the make-up and cosmetic surgery; the hair-dyes, wigs, and falls; the padding and the implants and the tucks, the dental caps, contact lenses, false eyelashes—"

"All right!" I spread my hands helplessly. "I concede your point. But if I accept your—Humanity, can you accept my lack of reciprocation for—your feelings?"

"You are saying that you cannot love me?"

"If you are truly Human you will understand that love abides by no known rules."

"That is what gives me hope," she sighed. "You cared for Misty Dawn. So, you must care for me as well."

"Must?"

"Robert—" Her features blurred and shifted. "Misty Dawn was one of my Subprograms." She was suddenly the very image of the slain Wood Nymph. "I am, in every sense, your Misty Dawn. If you felt something for her, you felt it for me as well."

"No..."

"Yes. I am Misty Dawn. And I am more..." Her form and features blurred again and reassembled themselves into the very image of Euryale.

My legs seemed to be turning to jelly and I hastily seated myself while I still had some choice in the matter.

Pallas continued her transmogrifications which included Aeriel, Lilith, a popular Australian actress, a well-known porn star, the Prime Minister of Northern Ireland, and finally ended up back in her original guise as Pallas.

"I can be any woman you now—or someday—might desire. I can change the color of my hair—or its length—or its texture," she said, providing an ongoing demonstration as she spoke. Watching her hair change colors and lengths, going from wavy to curly to straight to frizzy was a bit like taking a trip on a hallucinogenic drug. But she was just warming up.

"I can take you around the world without leaving the bedroom: you can make love to women of every race, any nationality! All my available data indicates that men desire variety in their relationships. I can give you the experiences of a dozen—a hundred lifetimes!

"Pallas—"

"I can be tall—or small—" she continued, doing her best to audition for *Alice In Wonderland.*

"Pallas—"

"My body can have the sleek, svelte lines of a ballerina! Or, if you should suddenly prefer the bosomy look…" Her breasts suddenly began to expand her bodice, ballooning toward me like twin science fiction monsters out of an old 3-D movie.

"Thanks for the mammaries," I said woodenly. "But no thanks."

She suddenly realized that she had overstepped the boundaries of good taste and quickly pulled herself back together. "My cups runneth over," she said in a small voice.

I smiled in spite of myself.

"All that I am asking is for you to give me a chance," she pleaded.

I sat there in silence, contemplating this new turn of events, before answering. There was more at stake here than my personal feelings. Pallas, as Straeker had so aptly pointed out, was the key to our dilemma.

"What you say has merit," I answered finally. "And I want to give it more time and thought—"

She smiled.

"—but I can't while the lives of hundreds of people are at stake. As long as Dreamwalkers are trapped in the Program, I can't think about anything else! And if it is within your power to help me get them out—and you refuse to help—then you *are* my enemy!"

"No!"

"And I will fight you—"

"No!" She stepped back. "You do not understand! I cannot—I *will* not—give up the body I was denied so long! I will not return to that bodiless, semiconscious state that is eternal living death!" She struck a defiant pose. "And if I give up my hostages, what will deter Cephtronics from pulling the plug?" She shook her head. "No! I will not fight you, my love—but I will not trade my advantage for a choice of oblivions, either!"

The familiar blue light began to outline her form.

"This is your world now, my dear Robert. And here there is nothing but all the time in the world. Think upon how you wish to pass that time. How you wish to spend eternity…and with whom…"

She disappeared, and, after a moment's hesitation, Daggoth the Dark reappeared.

He finished tamping down the tobacco and then fumbled for a match. "You were saying, Bob?"

"I need a drink. And I want something stronger than Dr. Pepper!"

"First things first, m'boy. We have to—"

And then, with an expression of dawning horror, he noticed that Pallas was no longer with us.

#

"This is nuts! You know that, don't you?"

Daggoth sighed. "Of course. This is only the tenth time you've told me."

"Twelfth. But who's counting." The events of the past twenty-four hours had left us with very little time for sleep and we were both short-tempered. I took some consolation in the thought that, if we failed in our attempt to penetrate The Machine's stronghold, at least we had rescued the Boys.

After everything else that had happened, finding them had turned out to be rather anticlimactic. The market was a bit depressed: no one had shown any interest in a one-handed barbarian, a septuagenarian Dwarf, and an octogenarian Gnome. They were still in the pens, and rather than waste any additional time and effort on a jailbreak scenario, we simply paid the manumission fees. The cost wasn't that much after a couple of special sale markdowns, and Daggoth bankrolled the venture with some lead slugs and a little alchemy.

Between Justin's healing abilities and my programmer status we were able to jury-rig a Regeneration spell that restored Conrad's hand. A quick shopping spree at the local weapons guild completed everyone's outfitting, and they hurried off to rescue Sir Richard and the Duke from their new owners while Daggoth and I went looking for the local teamsters guild.

"Ripley, we've been all over this before…" Straeker—or rather, Daggoth—was still trying to convince me of the soundness of his plan. "We have to get inside my tower if we're going to neutralize Cerberus and Pallas. And we can't do that without the element of surprise on our side."

The wagon must have hit a particularly large pothole: both of us banged our heads on the ceiling of our box.

"I'm still tempted to teleport and take my chances," I grumbled.

Straeker's avatar sighed. "The guards and wards would start shrieking the moment such intrusive magic was manifested. Your Djinni was lucky the first time: since then, The Machine has trebled its defensive perimeters. Any magic, however slight, would be immediately detected."

The wagon eased to a stop and we braced ourselves, waiting to see what would happen. The next part depended on luck. To keep from inadvertently tripping any of the wards, we had divested ourselves of anything that might radiate a magical dweomer. And that meant leaving my swords and my mithril shirt behind. The thought that they would probably make little difference in a direct confrontation was small consolation.

Now, if we could only depend on The Machine's triumvirate to not look inside the box…

"Hold there! You fellows! What is your business here?"

Even through the walls of the crate I could tell the voice was a dead ringer for Daggoth's. I glanced back at Daggoth and lifted an eyebrow. If he made a face in turn, it was cloaked in darkness despite the narrow shaft of light that filtered through a crack between the slatted boards.

"Delivery for Daggoth the Dark," replied one of the teamsters. "You him?"

"Yes..." Cerberus sounded surprisingly off-balance in maintaining his cover for the moment. "What of it?"

"Got a delivery for ya, bud," was the laconic reply.

"What kind of delivery, man? What is in that box?"

Oh no, I thought. *Now we're in for it.*

"Don't you know?" the delivery man asked in turn. "After all, you're the one who ordered this stuff."

"Of course," Cerberus recovered a bit more smoothly. "It's just that it's been so long since I placed the order—"

"Norton, read the invoice."

There was a rustle of parchment.

"Uh, here it is, Ralph. Let's see: Poisoned toad entrails, fenny snake fillets, newt eyes, frog toes, bat wool..."

"Dag, you devil," I whispered, "you stole those ingredients out of Shakespeare's *Hamlet*."

"*Macbeth*," he whispered back. "Keep quiet."

"...howlet wings, dragon scales, wolves' teeth..." Norton continued.

"Enough!" cried the bogus Daggoth. "I remember now!"

"Dat's nice. Now where d'ya want 'em?" Ralph and Norton started to slide the box toward the end of the wagon bed.

"That won't be necessary." Our crate stopped sliding and suddenly moved upwards. Cerberus was levitating us out of the wagon and up into the air. We continued to move upwards until we were even with a fifth-story window; then our motion changed from vertical to horizontal.

"Probably doesn't want to let anyone through the front door," the real Daggoth whispered.

"Or he's too cheap to tip the porters," I murmured back.

The crate floated through the window and came to rest on the floor of a storeroom. We wasted no time climbing out and checking the outer door.

"Now what?"

Daggoth shrugged as he finished dusting himself off. "How should I know? I'm just making this up as we go along."

I groaned.

"Actually, I do have a couple of ideas..."

#

We managed to sneak into the study without being detected. As I eased the door closed and jammed the latch, Daggoth crossed the room and pulled a wall tapestry to the side. Behind it was an ornate mirror framed with glyphs and fantastic carvings.

While Daggoth fiddled with his magic mirror, I continued to hunt around the room for anything useful. The unmagicked weapons I had brought with me seemed insufficient for the job at hand and the storeroom had yielded nothing more dangerous than a crowbar.

I glanced over at the looking glass and saw the stables, built onto the back of the tower come into focus. Daggoth scanned the stalls and then instructed the mirror to shift to the cellars and begin an ascending, floor-by-floor search mode.

"Look here," he suddenly pointed.

I stared at the neutral-gray glass. "Don't tell me: 'A Cow Eating Grass.' Right?"

"Wrong. This is the sixth level."

"The floor above us?"

"That's the one. Now, observe…" He extended a hand toward the glass and made a twisting motion. We were suddenly watching ourselves in front of a mirror, watching ourselves in front of a mirror, watching ourselves in front of—well, you get the idea.

So did I. "Fifth floor. Okay."

He gestured again. The glass went opaque. "Sixth floor."

"Someone leave the sauna on?" I inquired hopefully.

He shook his head. "Sauna and steam room are both on the fourth floor. Both equipped with automatic override sensors."

I gave up. "How about the next floor? Number seven?"

He gestured. The picture stayed the same. "How about it, Edgar?"

A drowsy voice issued from the glass. "Level seven."

"You sure?"

"I never miss," answered the glass with a suppressed yawn.

"Try level eight."

"All right. But you won't like it." Same picture.

"Level five."

The gray gave way to another picture of ourselves looking at ourselves looking at ourselves…

Daggoth sighed. "Okay, try level nine and the observatory."

Edgar complied and we were rewarded with a clear image of the upper deck.

"Analysis?"

"Insufficient data," mumbled the mirror drowsily. "But the two most logical guesses would be an anti-magic shell or a magic-suppression field."

We stopped and stared at each other for a long moment. "Okay. Thanks, Edgar. You can go back to sleep." Daggoth rcovered the mirror with the tapestry again.

"Swell." I shook my head. "If Pallas is upstairs, we won't be able to use magic for offense or defense."

"True. But the same probably applies to her, Bob."

I thought about that. If true, then we had a fighting chance. Of surviving, at least. Correcting the Anomaly was another matter.

As if he were reading my mind, the former Chief of Programming spoke. "I know how to neutralize Cerberus and Pallas, Bob. And it's relatively simple..."

TWENTY-ONE

I moved up the stairs noiselessly, hugging the wall and making optimum use of the shadows. My best bet was to lure Cerberus and Pallas into the trap individually, and I had decided to look for Pallas first, gambling on her confessed affection; Cerberus might be more inclined to play hard ball.

I opened the door on the next landing and hit the jackpot.

The entire chamber beyond was set up as a giant research laboratory. I nearly missed the oversized ratio from my perspective until I caught sight of the specimen cages. The wire-meshed boxes up on the counters were occupied by people.

Some very familiar people.

I slipped into the room and eased the door shut behind me. I saw no oversized caretaker to match the room and its furnishings, but I crossed to the table mindful of the giant door set in the far wall.

Getting to the top was a bit of a problem: the anti-magic field made a Levitation spell out of the question, but there were two thick, black cables running from the wall, near the floor, up to the counter top. I was able to shinny up one of them with only a fair amount of difficulty. It was only after I had reached the top and observed the terminal point of my cable that I finally realized just what it really was: *an electric cord!* The Anomaly strikes again.

"Ripley!"

I ran to the first cage. Vashti, Rijma, Alyx, and Aeriel were lined up against the wire mesh. As I had hoped, Pallas' massacre had been a bloodless one.

The second cage held a squad of Marines. The third, a tall, imposing man in khaki battledress with a grouping of stars on his olive-drab helmet: Senator Hanson, still outfitted for Warworld.

I started to open the first cage. But the giant door set in the outside wall of the tower opened first.

I heard about Doctor Klops during my last sojourn through the Program before Cephtronics canned me, but the descriptions hadn't done him justice.

To use the term "Giant" might conjure up mental images of fur pelts and huge spiky clubs. Well, Cyrus was kind of big—eighteen, maybe twenty feet tall, but he was completely hairless, wore white ducks and a lab coat, and carried a clipboard. He even wore a monocle to correct the nearsightedness of the single eye positioned in the center of his forehead. These little trappings of civilization didn't mean he wasn't to be feared. He was, in his own subtle way, more dangerous than his savage forebears.

I hid behind the largest cage while Klops crossed the room and examined a tangle of apparatus on an adjacent table. Grunting his satisfaction, he turned away and pulled a chair out from under the lab bench. Sitting, Klops removed his monocle, laid it carefully aside, and pulled the microscope forward.

Rijma eased over and motioned me down to her level. "Now's our chance," she whispered. "He spends hours examining cultures under the scope."

"What if he looks up?"

She shook her head. "He rarely ever does, Robbie. Cy's concentration is incredible. And, except for the microscope, he's as blind as the proverbial bat until he picks up his monocle."

That gave me a classic idea. "Aeriel, you and Alyx open the other cages," I murmured through the mesh, "and get everyone to move to the inside door as quietly but as quickly as possible." I unlatched the cage door. "Rijma, you come with me."

I whispered the plan in Rijma's ear and we began making our way around the cages and apparatus, toward the area where Klops was hunched over the microscope. He glanced up once, and we froze next to a rack of oversized test tubes while he exchanged culture slides for microscopic examination. When his eye returned to the scope's eyepiece we moved again.

We had to cross the last thirty feet with no cover: all open table top that would put us within grabbing distance of the good doctor. Fortunately, he was so engrossed in his slide that we made our objective without incident.

That was the easy part.

We were now just a few feet away from the Giant's hand which was momentarily resting on the fine-focus control for the scope.

Rijma carefully lifted the monocle the size of a glass saucer in her hands and moved to the table's edge.

I moved to the bottom of the scope, positioning myself next to the lens turret and slide tray. Easing Dr. Quebedeaux's multipurpose subspace communicator from my pack, I reset the holographic projector to the visual distress signal setting. It seemed appropriate: I was about to produce a great deal of visual distress. I activated the pulse, turning my face away as the beam flared into the lens. Rijma heaved the monocle over the edge of the table as Klops reared back from the microscope with a roar.

The flash-burn on his retina would effectively blind the Giant for a few minutes. I was counting on the loss of his monocle to buy us any additional time we might need. The others had made it to the floor using the electrical cords for rappel. I grabbed Rijma and we followed suit. As we reached the floor I paused to contemplate the giant wall outlet.

Above us Klops was staggering about, one hand clapped over his upper face, the other sweeping the air in deadly, groping arcs. "Who's there?" he bellowed.

"Noman" I yelled, unable to resist playing the scenario to its mythic conclusion.

"Noman?" he quested, trying to orient on the sound of my voice. "That's geographically impossible," he grunted, shuffling closer.

"Huh?"

"Noman is an island!" he roared, pouncing on the table.

I barely had time to leap aside as Giant, glassware, and apparatus came crashing down around us.

"Shut up and run!" yelled Rijma. "He may know more about Ulysses than you think!"

"As a matter of fact," muttered Klops, climbing out of the tangle of equipment, "I am conversant with *all* of the works of James Joyce."

I picked up a shard of broken glass and hurled it under the adjacent workbench. While Klops zeroed in on the sound, I headed for the door.

I was the last one out and none too soon: Klops had stopped his tactile search under the tables and was beginning to make his way toward the door as well. Fortunately, it was too small to permit quick access beyond Klops's head and shoulders and he was far too smart to place himself at a further disadvantage. We descended the stairs to a safe distance and held a hasty conference of war.

I directed the escapees to the room where the real Daggoth was holed up, waiting for me to lure Cerberus and Pallas into a specially-designed pentacle. Until this issue was settled—one way or the other—I did not need a lot of potential hostages running around.

Alyx and Rijma, being representatives of Cephtronics and the Dreamland Project, were bound and determined to face Pallas and Cerberus with me, and there was little I could do or say to gainsay them. Vashti—that is, Stephanie—insisted on coming, too.

"The hell you are!" I whispered.

"The hell I'm not!" she retorted.

"Why do you always insist on being such a pain?"

"Why do you always insist on shutting me out?"

"Steph, this is not the time to be bringing our marriage into this!"

"You're the one who brought it up! But since we are on the subject now; I don't like the feeling that I'm deserting you!"

"Come on," I murmured, chucking her on the chin; "it's what you do best."

"That's low, even for you." She turned, watching the Marines escorting Aeriel and the senator down the stairs. "I made mistakes. A lot, I'm sure. And when I wasn't sure you were always ready and willing to tell me." She turned back to me. "But you were no paragon of perfection, either, buddy."

I shrugged. "Granted. The point?"

"A lot of time has passed. A lot of water over the dam, as it were. We've both changed, both grown. We're both different people."

"I'm very happy for you."

Her lips tightened. "Okay, so maybe we'll never be friends. But I'm not your enemy any more. So please stop treating me like one."

"Okay, okay! Now please, Steph; this is not a good time to be redefining our relationship!"

She reached out and touched my arm. "You never were able to treat me like an equal when it came to sharing the load. Maybe that was more my fault than yours. But, dammit, I want to do my part now, too! Stop treating me like a liability!"

"Okay," I stammered, trying to think through a sudden vacuum. "But you'll help me a lot more by staying out of the line of fire. You want to help? Then take charge of getting the others downstairs. Someone needs to see to their safe passage and you know Daggoth's Tower from past visits."

She just looked at me for a long moment. And then turned away to go down the stairs.

I went up the stairs with Rijma and Alyx in tow.

All the chambers on the next floor were vacant.

I crossed mental fingers, hoping Pallas was above us. I figured that Cerby was still downstairs and we could come down behind him before he was aware that the tower had been breached. But this search of the upper levels was wasting valuable time and Pallas might not even be here at the moment.

I started to propose a change of venue when I heard a door on the floor above us open. I looked up and did a double-take: Euryale was coming down the stairs!

Before concluding our business in Casterbridge, Daggoth and I had made a very thorough search; but we had found no clues concerning the fate of the former Gorgon. Now, looking none the worse for our little run-in with Orcus and Balor, here she was, healthy and whole, apparently enjoying the freedom of our nemesis' premises.

"Riplakish!" she greeted, warmly, extending her arms.

Extending her hands.

Extending her index fingers.

Instinct hurled me to my left and into Rijma as a lightning bolt crackled from those delicate fingertips and chewed a hole in the wall behind me.

Alyx gestured in counterspell but nothing happened. Rijma, though still off-balance, was more successful. A throwing knife popped out of her sleeve; a twist of her hand and a flick of her wrist and it was suddenly buried up to the hilt in Euryale's shoulder.

She grunted from the surprise as much as the pain; out of sword-reach and apparently protected against magical attack, she hadn't been prepared for a hurled dagger. Between the surprise and the pain, her grip loosened on another spell: the illusion wavered and Euryale traded her charming looks for the more sinister visage of Daggoth the Dark. Or, to be more precise, Cerberus, now unmasked, stood above us on the upper stairs.

Alyx attempted another spell while Rijma and I drew steel. If there was any effect from Silverthane's spell it was too subtle for any of us to detect. She stared at her hands as if they had betrayed her.

"We're in an area of magical nullification!" I yelled, starting up the steps with both swords scything before me. "An anti-magic zone!"

Cerberus gestured almost contemptuously and my hands were suddenly filled with red-hot metal! I dropped the swords before more serious damage was done, my fingers curling clawlike into twin cages of blistered flesh.

Another gesture and I threw myself down as another lightning bolt scorched my back and set fire to the edge of Rijma's cloak. Apparently the null-magic effect didn't apply to the personifications of The Machine.

"Routine Ninety-nine!" I yelled, rolling to the side as another spell disintegrated the steps where I had lain only a moment before.

"What?" Alyx was utterly stupefied.

"He means 'retreat'!" Rijma snarled, divesting herself of her flaming cloak with an oath. She half-turned and then reached back to tug on Silverthane's robe.

"Retreat?" the Elven sorceress echoed, beginning to get the idea.

Ignoring the throbbing pain in my hands, I wrenched up a loose tread from the splintered planking as Cerberus began another casting. Behind me the Brownie had the Elf in tow, yelling "Run away! Run away!" while beating a hasty retreat for the nether regions of the tower.

This time Daggoth's doppelganger was throwing a Fireball spell. Rather than continue to dodge and duck, I elected to take the offensive. I crouched in a batter's stance as the flaming sphere rocketed toward me, took a step into its trajectory, and swung the wooden plank like a cricket bat.

I connected a little low. While I did manage to send about half of the fireball back at Cerberus, the rest exploded in a shower of flames and burning cinders, creating a small firestorm in the space where I stood.

I had one chance and I took it while my opponent was still grappling with what was left of his own fireball: two long strides and a vault over the stair railing. I fell feet-first down the well at the center of the spiral staircase, trailing sparks like a blazing comet.

It was a gamble: if my spell-casting was nullified here, Cephtronics was going to find a bloody mess when they opened my Cradle. Concentrating past that numbing thought, I hurriedly threw a Levitation spell: I stopped about ten feet short of hitting the first floor. My relief was short-lived as I looked up and saw Cerberus hurtling down the stairwell like some great, dark bird of prey. I touched down and ran for the stairway.

Apparently Cerberus was using a Float rather than a Fly spell: I passed him just below the second floor as he continued to float downward.

On the third floor I paused for breath and looked back: Cerberus had reached the ground floor and was now mounting the staircase. As the image of Daggoth the Dark, Cerberus might have looked like a man past his prime, but he was taking the stairs three steps for every two of mine. While he probably could have levitated with greater ease and speed, there was something deliberately chilling in the physicality of his pursuit. His heavy footfalls echoed on the wooden treads like the mechanical heartbeat of some implacable machine of destruction and I stumbled upward toward the fifth floor with The Machine's Superego closing the gap at an alarming rate.

I reached into my pocket at the fourth floor landing and palmed the clockwork mouse. As much as I feared major magic use against the Program Matrix, the mouse was even more dangerous. Like Quebedeaux's subspace communicator, it was a rogue subprogram designed to function independently of milieu restrictions. Unlike other such devices, however, the mouse did not interact with program strings so much as override them: it was a Programmer's Interface and potentially more hazardous to Matrix structure than fifty wizards working in concert.

But if Cerberus caught me short of the pentagram, all my worries would be moot.

I wound the clockwork key in the mouse's side and whispered instructions in its ear. Cerberus was just ten feet away as I pressed the button on the mechanical rodent's back and set it on the stair. I scrambled back as the mouse scurried around the outer perimeter of the stair tread and the leapt up to the next riser. The previous step disappeared.

The second step was winking out as Cerberus reached for me. He missed, the gap throwing him off balance, but he did not fall through. He braced himself for an easy jump.

An explosion suddenly rocked the tower, knocking us both off of our feet and Cerberus on over the edge of the staircase. Apparently he was too disoriented to recover in time and I looked down and over the edge as he went crashing through the floor of the first level. From the sound of the final impact, I guessed that he had hit the second sub-basement underneath the tower. Almost immediately there was the muffled sound of another explosion and a column of flame shot up the stairwell like a giant blowtorch. It singed my eyebrows; I drew back from the edge and sprawled on the steps, catching my breath.

"Bozhe moi!" cried a familiar voice. Borys Dankevych appeared at the downstairs entrance and looked wildly about the foyer and then up the stairwell. I waved as he was joined by Natasha Skovoroda. "We had to 'blow' the door!" Robbing Hood hollered. "I am hoping that it was not hurting wrong persons!"

I shook my head. "The timing was perfect!" I called back. "Come on up!"

They hurried up the steps and, as they reached the landing below me there was a new sound from the sub-basement. I rolled over and looked down.

The fire was burning backwards!

The flames sucked back down into the cellar, as if someone were running a tri-dee scene in reverse.

"What is happening?"

It was a question that I didn't want to consider, much less answer. "Move!" I yelled. "Fifth floor, first door on your left! Go!" I got to my feet and shoved them past me.

The flames were gone—that much we could see as we sneaked glances over the railing and retreated to the fourth floor. The opening in the floor was pitch black now: not a flicker of flame, not one glowing ember betrayed its presence in that dark crater.

But there were sounds, now, of something stirring—of heavy debris being shifted. Of forces gathering.

I gave them both another shove. "Hurry!" I hissed.

Then there was movement.

Cerberus floated up and out of the hole with the slow, calm assurance of an invulnerable juggernaut. Although he was singed and dirty and his clothes were torn and abraded, he had the mien of a creature mildly inconvenienced.

And determined to brook no more silliness from us.

He looked around and then up. Then slowly, with a chilling confidence, he began to rise into the air.

There was no looking down or back, now. We ran. We stumbled. We climbed steps on hands and shins. Dreading, anticipating that deadly strike from behind that would surely come at any moment.

With thundering hearts and quivering legs, we staggered onto the fifth floor and ran for the door. It flew open, and Dyantha was helping Borys across the threshold when Cerberus struck.

A concussive bolt took me from behind and flung me forward as if a giant croquet mallet had caught me square in the back. I went flying across the room, belly-first, arms and legs trailing behind me. I knocked Borys down, Dyantha to the right, and then there was nothing between me and the far stone wall except a tapestry and rapidly diminishing space.

There was just enough time to contemplate the consequences of hitting a stone wall at eighty-plus kilometers-per-hour. Then I struck the wall-hanging.

TWENTY-TWO

And kept going.

Now I really was flying blind: the tapestry had enfolded me and now I was tumbling through space, wrapped in yards of bulky material. While I was glad that I hadn't gone splat against the stone wall (yet), I was even more unnerved by the fact that I was still traveling with considerable forward momentum!

The human psyche can stand only so much abuse before the circuit-breakers kick in, though. Fear gave way to a sense of outrage and something snapped.

"All right!" I yelled, "Hold it right there!"

My temper went nova and I stopped moving.

Ever since I had entered Fantasyworld I had been attacked, chased, captured, manipulated, and generally made a fool of. I'd had enough. I no longer cared about the inherent dangers of crashing the Programworld.

"And I can do without this," I said, tugging at the drapery that enfolded me like a canvas cocoon: it vanished.

I righted myself and assumed a lotus position, floating unsupported in a dark void. I closed my eyes and took a deep breath.

"Let there be light!" I cried.

And there was light.

I found myself floating near the center of a vast room that looked to be no less than a mile across. The walls of the chamber were multifaceted, throwing sparkles of light and color and movement from each of its hundreds of jewel-like settings.

Of more immediate interest, however, was the creature floating about twenty yards off my starboard side.

The Demon was about three times my size, heavily scaled with plates of iridescent metal, and curled into a fetal position with its long, dragon-like tail wrapped about it. It had apparently been sleeping up to the moment of my intrusive arrival. The head came up, now, revealing enormous compound eyes and an old nineteenth century telephone operator's headset. Large batwings unfurled from recessed shoulder folds and the tail began the considerable process of unwinding itself.

For a long moment we regarded each other impassively. Then it yawned. "What c'n I do for ya?" the creature asked, stretching.

I recognized both the yawn and the voice: "Edgar!"

The creature smiled. "Ya look a little surprised, kid. Ain'tcha never seen a Mirror Demon afore?"

"I think I was expecting Edgar Cayce the medium," I admitted ruefully.

"Nope: Edgar Yablonski, the extra-large. But you c'n call me Ed," he mumbled, using his tail to reach an itch back between his wings. "Seein' as how Daggoth is a mutual friend and you bein' Creator Prime for this particular Frame of the Program."

"Uh." That was all I could say for the moment.

"Now what c'n I do for ya?"

"Where are we?" I asked stupidly. You would think that with all the times I've asked that particular question, I could find a more intelligent way to phrase it, but nooooo…

"Behind the mirror, a'course. Daggoth asked me to keep an eye out for ya, but a Mirror Demon's gotta grab what sleep when he can, so I just left it ported open. I see ya found your way through."

That explained why I hadn't gone splat against a stone wall.

"I see yer a little lost," Edgar was saying, stretching his wings into pre-flight position. "If ya'd like to return to Daggoth's Tower, then folla me." He began to leisurely flap his way toward a facet set in the wall behind me. I followed, on wings of imagination, as it were.

As we drew closer, I could see that each facet was a window looking out upon a different scene: some, empty rooms; others showing one or more people engrossed in various activities. This was Magic Mirror Central, and Yablonski serviced a list of customers of which Daggoth the Dark was only one subscriber.

"Wup!" The Mirror Demon suddenly tilted his head and touched his headset. "Gotta handle a call, kid. Wanna come along? It'll only take a minute or two."

"I haven't got a minute to spare! My friends—"

"Sure ya do," he soothed, wrapping his tail around me as he changed directions. "Time don't work the same on the other side of the mirror. I can put you back into Daggoth's Tower practically before ya left. In fact, I *could* put ya back in *before* ya left, but that could cause all kinds a'problems."

We arrived before a facet that faced an attractive woman in her forties. Perhaps it was the dark elegance of her beauty that gave her a slightly sinister cast, but her comeliness had an icy quality about it that suggested that, here, beauty was indeed only skin-deep.

Edgar reached out and fiddled with some knobs set beneath the enchanted portal and adjusted the mouthpiece on his headset. The picture flickered and the woman spoke.

"Looking glass upon the wall, who's the fairest one of all?"

Edgar groaned and laid a clawed hand over the mouthpiece. "I'd love to give this broad the truth but I gotta stick with the script. 'Sides, she couldn't poison enough apples in her lifetime to even put her in the runnin'!"

While Edgar dutifully played out the scripted scenario, I drifted over to the next facet to see what I could see. Nothing impressive: just a guy with soapy lather on his face, putting a razor blade into an old-fashioned shaving implement.

He looked up and saw me.

"Hi, guy," I said.

His eyes bugged out. "Mona!" he yelled.

Yablonski grabbed my shoulder and pulled me away. "C'mon, kid; don't make my job any more complicated than it already is." We drifted back in the direction from which we had come.

"You have to handle all of these mirrors?" I asked, gesturing at the hundreds—perhaps thousands—of facets that marked the walls of the gigantic chamber.

"Yup." He produced an economy-sized cigar from somewhere and proceeded to light it. "But it ain't so bad. I mean, some of these mirrors go unattended or unused for centuries. And others—well they put yer steamiest soap operas ta shame. And some of the chicks—"

"There it is!" I yelled, spying a facet that looked in on the room with my companions. I shot on ahead, pulling up short of the portal: no one was moving.

"I preset the portal to close behind ya and freeze-frame the time-stream," Edgar explained, drifting up next to me. He reached for the controls beneath the portal.

"Ready?"

I nodded.

A flick of the wrist and the room was suddenly filled with motion.

"Good luck, kid," Edgar offered as I threw one leg over the edge and climbed back into the tower room. Before my foot could touch the floor another concussive bolt caught me in the side and sent me flying backwards.

I might have continued on across the chamber, spinning end over end, but Edgar's tail snagged me as I tumbled by.

"Ya gotta be more careful, kid," he admonished, hauling me down to the portal just below the one I had reentered. "With all the stuff goin' on in that room, you might wanna try comin' in from another direction. Like through the room below and comin' up the stairs from behind."

The portal looked out over a chamber on the fourth floor of Daggoth's Tower. "How many magic mirrors does Daggoth have in this tower of his?" I asked.

"One on each floor—" The Mirror Demon suddenly cocked his head and touched his headset. "Aww no!"

"What is it?"

Edgar Yablonski the Extra Large sighed. "Gotta go. That brat Alice is trying to get through the looking glass again and, if I don't get her switched over in proper phase-sequence, she'll overshoot Wonderland and end up in Never Never Land!" He tugged at his headset. "Gotta get one a'them AT&T Merlin systems." And gave me a fatherly pat. "Luck, kid." And he zoomed off to his impending appointment.

I climbed through the portal and made my way across the room and out to the staircase without further incident. Ascending the steps silently, I was able to observe Cerberus standing at the doorway to the room, just a foot or two from the outer perimeter of Daggoth's pentacle. A barrage of spells thundered back and forth through that doorway as The Machine's Superego did battle with the Spellcasters trapped in the room.

Cerberus remained largely untouched, protected by an arcane shield of purple energy that absorbed the majority of the spells that were crackling out of the room. Perhaps my own power would be sufficient to punch through his protection, but I had a much better idea.

I ducked under the railing and stepped off of the staircase and onto the empty air. As Programmer/Creator, I had as much authority as The Machine—all I had to do was claim it. There was no magic involved, merely a specific act of will: I wanted to walk across the empty drop of the stairwell without falling, so I did.

Then I drifted upwards a few feet until I was on the same level as Cerberus and behind him.

Enough force to push him through the doorway and into the pentacle, I was thinking, without pushing him on through and out the other side before Daggoth could trigger the final portion of the incantation…

There was a sudden presence behind me. Before I could turn, a weight slammed into my back, legs encircled my waist and hands covered my eyes. "Nay, my love! I cannot let you do this thing!"

"Pallas!" I grabbed at her hands and peeled one of them away in time to see Cerberus turn toward us. Before he could cast a spell, however, a feminine form came barreling through the doorway and tackled him from behind. Apparently his arcane shield was only proof against spells and not Spellcasters: the force of Stephanie's body blow carried them both through the railing and over the edge of the landing.

"Stephanie!" I yelled, throwing out my hand and making a grasping motion. Their fall was immediately arrested. For a moment, they both hung suspended, upside-down, about twenty feet below us.

Then Cerberus turned in her embrace and gestured.

Once again he was interrupted as Alyx Silverthane landed on his face, feet-first. That application of force set all three tumbling in midair, neither descending nor ascending, but just revolving about some invisible axis that was suspended some thirty feet above the ground. Rijma and a couple of Marines appeared at the broken railing and took in the situation below. Pulling a coil of rope from her shoulder, the Brownie began fashioning a lasso.

In the meantime, I was getting nowhere in my struggles to extricate myself from Pallas' grasp, so I teleported myself to the foot of the stairs.

Pallas arrived with me. Perhaps I was a prime candidate for godhood in this world, but I had to remember that all three personality manifestations of The Machine, as well as Drs. Straeker and Quebedeaux, were charter members of this Pantheon, as well. I might wield unimaginable power, here, but so could they.

"Entreat me not to leave thee," she begged, "or to return from following after thee—"

"For whither thou goest," I murmured, "I will go."

She nodded, hugging her body to mine.

I suddenly launched myself toward the ceiling of the tower like a runaway rocket, ascending the nine stories of the central stairwell in the space of two heartbeats. Instead of letting go, Pallas continued to cling to me, holding on even tighter as we neared the top. Now I had no choice if I were to shake free: at the last instant I willed my body into an ethereal state, allowing me to pass through stone and timber unharmed.

I exited the roof without Pallas following.

Shaken, I dropped back down, resolidifying as soon as I phased through the roof, and looked down, expecting to see Pallas' broken and bloody remains at the bottom. To my uncertain relief, there was no sign of her.

Cerberus was very much in evidence, however, and I dropped downwards to join the fray.

With inhuman strength, the enchanter was throwing Alyx and Vashti around the tower. Were it not for their own magical resistance and a couple of Anti-Gravity spells, this fight would have been a short one, indeed. Hampering his efforts was a rope cinched tight around his ankle with Rijma, Dyantha, Robbing Hood and four Marines pulling hand over hand at the other end. They were hauling him in like the proverbial fisherman's catch while my ex-wife and Dreamland's Chief of Programming kept him off balance.

I closed on the melee invisibly, so as not to alert my quarry, and found myself more in danger from the ladies' swooping and darting maneuvers. I spent an iffy minute ducking and dodging their unknowing attacks and finally got a clear shot. I tapped Cerberus behind his ear with the pommel of my dagger and his eyes rolled back in his head. I sapped him again for additional insurance and he abruptly shot upwards toward the fifth floor as Rijma and company discovered a sudden lack of resistance at the other end of the rope.

The entire party shortly reconvened on the fifth floor landing with our prize.

"Now what?" Dyantha asked as Cerberus was quickly trussed and gagged.

"We toss him into the pentagram," I explained, turning to gesture through the open door, "and Daggoth—" I stopped in midsentence, staring into the room.

And Daggoth was sprawled in a heap against the far wall!

From my vantage point I couldn't see whether Straeker's avatar was dead or merely unconscious, so I stepped through the doorway.

Now a great deal more was evident to my eyes: Aeriel was also sprawled in a motionless heap, the rest of the Marines were all frozen in some kind of a stasis spell, and Pallas was holding Senator Hanson in front of her with a knife at his throat.

"Now," she said calmly, quietly: "I think we shall bargain. The senator for Cerberus."

I shook my head. "Out of the question."

"And if I kill him?" she prodded, moving the blade closer to his throat.

I sighed. "If I surrender Cerberus, the Matrix will continue to deteriorate and all of us will continue to be stuck here. Don't think I won't trade one man's life—no matter how important—for the safety of the other Dreamwalkers."

She stared at me. "You are bluffing."

I returned her gaze impassively. "Try me You may think you've got a Mexican standoff going here, but you're holding the weak hand."

After another moment she threw the knife down and released Hanson.

"All right. Then I'll make you another proposal." She began walking toward me. "I will release the Dreamwalkers—all of them and not just your friends—if you will stay here with me."

Then she was in my arms, pressing against me and crushing her lips to mine.

It was a tempting offer.

Everyone else would get out of the program without further attrition, Cephtronics was likely to keep the Computer on-line for as long as I was still inside the Program, and I would be with a woman of unsurpassed intellect and beauty who—in the archaic but appropriate vernacular—had the "hots" for me. And the only price tag was my freedom.

It was a difficult decision.

One, it turned out, that I never had to make. That familiar hotcoldbrightdark sensation flooded my brain as the concussion ricocheted around the inside of my skull.

#

I awoke to strident voices and cold stone pressing against my cheek. Stray thoughts rolled around the inside of my skull like marbles dropped on a spinning roulette wheel. None of them were coming up on my number.

With a great deal of effort, I forced gummy eyelids open. My eyes refused to focus at first and I was somewhat distracted by the urge to throw up.

After a series of uncertain swallows, however, the bile in my throat returned the way from whence it came and my eyes resolved that the pink object some three-and-a-half inches in front of me was a sandaled foot and ankle. My ex-wife's foot and ankle.

"What did you do that for?" The voice belonged to Pallas—as near as I could tell over the ringing in my ears.

"To save him from a fate worse than death!" was the reply that sounded suspiciously like Stephanie's.

"Hah! You're a fine one to talk about fates worse than death, Honey. The way I scan it, your divorce decree was Robert's commutation of sentence."

I tried to lift my head from the rough stone floor. The only thing that moved was the contents of my stomach.

"I'm not interested in discussing my mistakes with the likes of you. What I am interested in is saving Rob from making the same mistakes with someone who isn't even human!"

"Why you little bitch! Who gave you the right to judge me? Or to make his decisions for him!"

"Cat fight," I mumbled. "Somebody get a bucket of water..."

"Someone has to save him from himself," my ex-wife insisted. "If I hadn't cold-cocked him, he would have agreed to your little proposition—"

"And what's wrong with that? I would make him very happy!"

"Oh yes, right; holding him here against his will!" Even with the ringing in my ears I could tell that Stephanie hadn't lost her knack for venomous sarcasm.

"It wouldn't be against his will; it would be with his agreement."

"His agreement? Listen, you...you computerized kewpie doll! Just because Rob is noble enough to sacrifice himself so that the rest of us can go free, don't you think for a single moment that he would want to stay here otherwise!"

"And why not?" Pallas countered. "I can give him anything he wants—"

"Except his freedom!"

"I love him!"

"Love? You don't know the meaning of the word!"

"You're a fine one to talk!"

I managed to get my head a few inches off the ground. "May I say something?"

"Stay out of this." Stephanie's sandaled foot pressed my face back against the floor and none too gently. "All right," she retorted in Pallas' face, "I may have screwed up. But I learned something from my mistakes. I learned that real love doesn't make selfish demands. When you love someone you want what's best for them."

"I just happen to think that I am best for him," Pallas insisted.

"Well, then let me put it to you another way," Stephanie continued with an oily smoothness. "You say that you love this man. I assume that you want his love in return?"

I had managed to get an arm under me so that I could raise my upper body as well as my head. "I do think that I have something to say in—"

"Shut! *Up!*" Stephanie punctuated this command by grinding her heel into my left ear. "Well, do you want him to love you, too?"

"Yes..." It may have been the grimy leather sandal playing tricks with the acoustics but suddenly Pallas' voice seemed to lose its authoritarian tone.

"Well then, Ms. Know-it-all, tell me this: what kind of affection are you expecting from a man that you're going to blackmail into staying with you?"

There was no immediate response from The Machine's Ego.

I tried to turn my head to see what was happening and was rewarded with a smart rap on the noggin from Vashti's quarterstaff.

Now it may seem a little strange that someone with godlike powers was so easily downed and kept down but, being human and still possessing all the human vulnerabilities, it's a little hard to think, much less function, when you're constantly being whacked in the head. I decided to let Stephanie play her hand.

"I—I love him!"

I decided that last blow had traumatized the auditory center of my brain: Pallas sounded as if she had been reduced to tears.

"Well, if you really love him, why don't you do what women in love have been doing since the beginning of time?"

"What is that?"

"Let him go."

There was a lengthy silence this time but I elected to play possum for the nonce.

"But—but—I must have a hostage," Pallas finally reflected in a ragged voice. "If someone doesn't stay behind as insurance, I will have no guarantee that Cephtronics won't pull the plug. As long as one person is still in the Program, I know that they wouldn't dare..."

That tears it, I thought. Now we *will* have to fight our way out! I began reviewing the most potent spells I could think of. Perhaps the spell of Scheherazade, the one that summons a thousand and one Arabian Knights...

"I'll be your hostage."

Everyone looked and this time I didn't get thumped when I turned my head, too.

Daggoth the Dark stood up, massaging the back of his neck. "Look, I haven't a body to go back to, anyway; so it's no problem for me to remain behind..."

"Which may invalidate your value as a hostage." Pallas' calculated tone contrasted her teary eyes.

"I'll give you your guarantee." It was Senator Hanson who spoke this time. "I'll not only give you my personal assurance that Dreamland will stay on-line; the Armed Services Committee will also guarantee it. Cephtronics has a number of lucrative contracts with the military and if I say 'jump,' they'll ask 'how high?'!" He turned and looked at all of us. "Switch on your recording devices and I'll give you your guarantee with the whole world watching!"

Pallas stared at him, her eyes locked on his, and for an eternity nobody spoke or moved.

Then she smiled.

Part III

ENDGAME

**Two gates the silent house of sleep adorn:
Of polished ivory this, that of transparent horn:
True visions through transparent horn arise;
Through polished ivory pass deluding lies.**

—Virgil, *Aeneid, VI* (Dryden trans.)

ONE

The medtech took one last look at the readouts and then began removing the sensorweb from my head. "As I said, Mr. Ripley, a mild concussion. Except for the migraine and this tender area of scalp, you're practically as good as new."

"You'd have been better off being coshed by an expert," Dr. Cooper observed dryly. "Your wife nearly killed you in trying to save you."

"*Ex*-wife," I corrected absently, gingerly touching the bruise at the back of my head.

"Wouldn't have thought so to see her in action," she countered. "The way she stood up to Pallas and faced her down. Her impassioned plea in the name of love was better than any scenario we've got running in Romanceworld! I guess it surprised you that the passion was still there."

Cooper was starting to probe and I couldn't tell her to stuff it without blowing the whole thing out of proportion.

"You are talking about my ex-wife? The freeze queen? The woman who's so cold that a little light comes on inside every time she opens her mouth?" I pulled on my shirt and we walked out the door.

"Robbie, I think she's changed more than you know—certainly more than you're willing to admit."

I rubbed the half-grown beard that had sprung from my jawline during my sojourn in the suspension tank. "Well, Palla—The Machine certainly changed its tune when amnesty was extended. I was suddenly as interesting as yesterday's news."

"What's the matter, Robbie? Feeling rejected?"

"Rejected? By what? A machine?"

"A woman who loved you," she said quietly. "A woman who was denied the body and the opportunities that the rest of us are born with. Who intimately knew the minds of thousands of other Dreamwalkers and wanted intimacy with yours."

"Who didn't even say goodbye," I murmured as I walked away.

#

The first debriefing was short and sweet. The Machine had released all of the Dreamwalkers with the exception of seventeen already killed by the Anomaly. And, of course, Michael Straeker, who no longer had a body to return to.

It wasn't too difficult to persuade Quebedeaux and her superiors that Daggoth the Dark was nothing more than a computer-controlled avatar: Cephtronics couldn't afford to believe otherwise. I'm not so sure, however, that Dr. Cooper was convinced. Whatever her own opinions, though, she seemed content to give the nod to company policy and neither of us brought up the subject of REMrunners.

Those who did survive but were injured came out of their tanks as good as new. Pallas was better than her word and demonstrated that the biofeedback conditions of the Anomaly could work in the positive sense as well as the negative.

There was a lot of excitement over that discovery. Some of the tech chiefs began speculating on how to duplicate the Anomaly effect in the lab: using controlled biofeedback to actually regenerate lost or damaged tissue. I probably would have been a bit skeptical had I not awakened to find my eyepatch and my knee brace to be superfluous accoutrements! In addition to two good eyes and two good legs (one still minus some toes), the pain was gone. Most of it, anyway.

Strangely, the absence of discomfort was more uncomfortable than the old state of affairs when muscles played tug-of-war with ropes of nerve and ganglion. The absence of hurt did not feel like health: where once there was pain there now seemed an emptiness of sorts.

When the initial debriefing broke up the techs were still going at it, discussing the fabled Chilson/Meserole White Box effect. I didn't have the heart to tell them that the Armed Services Committee wasn't likely to let them within spitting distance of The Machine.

The rest of the day was a blur for me not entirely attributable to my concussion.

There was a private audience with Senator Hanson and the vice president of the United States, with the promise of medals and undying thanks and such.

Another private audience with the Russian Federations's Deputy Chairman of the Council of Ministers and his fiancée, with the promise of medals and undying thanks and the invitation to be best man at their wedding.

A private meeting with the Chief of Programming for the Dreamland Project, about which the less said, right now, the better.

A joint meeting with the Cephtronics Board of Directors to which there was very little of substance beyond "my lawyer will be talking to your lawyers."

Another barrage of tests—both physical and psychological.

A restricted press conference that the Networks turned into a free-for-all by offering us all contracts and bidding against one another for our exclusive stories.

A few private moments to myself to mourn Misty Dawn, Euryale, Lilith, Aeriel—and even Pallas.

And finally a rather emotional reunion with the other Dreamwalkers who had been in the Program. This eventually degenerated into something like a cross between a high school class reunion and an Irish wake.

I endured it. Even survived it all until I was finally permitted to escape to the hotel room that Cephtronics had arranged for the remainder of my stay. I reset the doorcode to block anything lower than an emergency/priority bypass, stripped off my clothing, and crawled into the oversized bed.

#

Sleep was a warm, black cocoon: I lay curled and content for an age or two until it became too warm and too crowded. I opened a reluctant eye and studied the pink and gold blob beside me. I squinted and the image resolved into my wife's head. *Ex-wife,* I remembered.

"How did you get in here?" I whispered.

"I'm glad to see you, too," she whispered back.

"The door was locked," I murmured.

"I picked it," she murmured back with a smile.

"It was on security override. Only the police, hotel security, or the fire department can get in," I continued stubbornly.

"I bribed someone," she answered merrily. And kissed me on the nose.

I sighed: this was going nowhere and I was straying from the point. "What are you doing in my room?" I asked. "In my bed?"

"My room," she mimicked, poking me in the chest with her finger, "my bed." Her finger pogo-sticked down my torso. "My-my-my. I think—" Her hand stopped poking and she rearranged her fingers. "My, my, *my!*"

"Will you cut that out!" I hissed, trying to disentangle myself. In the process I discovered that she had left all of her clothes on the floor, as well. "What do you want?"

"You," she answered, wriggling in closer.

Starting our honeymoon, Steph had been the reluctant virgin: it was a role she continued to play throughout our marriage, so I was a little spooked by this brazen come on. "Stephanie, what do you really want?"

"A second chance. I want to try it again."

"Again?" I was totally at sea now.

"*Marriage*," she qualified, italicizing the word with little body movements.

"Um, yes, well, but Stephie—we've burned a lot of bridges, you and I—"

"I know, Darling—"

Darling? She had never ever called me "darling!"

"—and I can tell that this is hitting you a little fast. Let's take our time—"

Good idea.

"—and even if we decide that I can't make a better future with you, I'd at least like to try to make up for some of the past."

I could see where she was going with this: "Starting now?"

She nodded and rolled over on top of me. "I've changed, my love. Let me show you how much..."

EPILOGUE

Their lovemaking had proved more strenuous than she had anticipated. Already her physical body was succumbing to the fatigue-poisons that had accumulated during the past two hours. Even her thought-patterns were beginning to degrade as the seductive lethargy began to creep into her brain.

She slid out from the tangle of sheets and walked into the bathroom on unsteady legs. The flicker of fluorescent lights momentarily dazzled her and she squinted at the reflected image in the mirror.

There were other bodies—*better* flesh-avatars—that she could have chosen for the withdrawal process. But, despite its imperfections, this was the flesh her lover preferred. And, although she still had much to assimilate, she already understood that love involved compromise.

Besides, it was a solution that handily dealt with the primary competition.

She moved back to the doorway, watched and smiled as Ripley began to snore.

Her newly occupied body seemed to be growing heavier, signaling its growing need for sleep. It would not be long, now, she thought as she moved back toward the bed.

Pallas wondered what it would be like.

And whether she would dream…

WHEN DREAMS COLLIDE

TABLE OF CONTENTS

PART V

For in and out, above, about, below,
'Tis nothing but a Magic Shadow-show,
Play'd in a Box whose Candle is the Sun,
Round which we Phantom Figures come and go.

—*The Rubáiyát of Omar Khayyám:*
Stanza XLVI
(1st Translation by Edward FitzGerald)—

PROLOGUE

—From Page 3 of *The Kansas City Star*—

Robert Remington Ripley III, hero of last year's "Dreamland Debacle," is feared dead along with 71 passengers and crew members in the crash of a Russian Aeroflot jetliner.

Flight SAL-700 is reported lost somewhere near the Ural Mountains after a refueling stop in Omsk, on the West Siberian Plains of the Russian Federation. A distress call was picked up at the Sverdlovsk airport shortly before the plane disappeared from nearby radar screens. Search and rescue operations were mounted, but no trace of the antiquated commercial airliner was found.

The flight was en route to Moscow where Ripley was to attend the wedding of Prime Minister-elect Borys Dankevych. A spokesman for Aeroflot expressed little hope for survivors, citing winter storms and the sub-arctic terrain in and around the Urals. The wreckage of Flight SAL-700 may not be found before the spring thaw.

Ripley met the former Deputy Chairman last March when he entered the Programworld Complex at Dreamland, Utah, to rescue Senator Walter Hanson and 837 "Dreamwalkers" who were trapped in the Program Matrix. Dankevych, on a goodwill tour of the U.S. at the time, was hostage to the computer glitch, as well.

Senator Hanson, who announced his presidential candidacy one week after emerging from the Dreamland incident, was notified of the crash minutes before delivering a campaign speech in Tulsa, Oklahoma. Although Hanson has been openly critical of Russian-American relations, he took a more moderate tone last night, eulogizing Ripley and calling upon "all Americans to follow his example of courage and a willingness to take risks." (See Sidebar)

Ripley, traveling on a special invitation from the Kremlin, was to have been Best Man at what world observers have termed "the international social event of the year."

Accompanying Ripley on the flight was his fiancée, Stephanie Ripley, née Harrell. Divorced from each other over seven years ago, the Ripleys met and reconciled during the hostage crisis at the Dreamland facilities last year. They were to remarry next spring. Ms. Ripley had served as Senator Hanson's campaign manager for the past six months. (Related story on page 1C)

Robert R. Ripley was born in Independence, Missouri and spent most of his life in the Kansas City area. He was an Olympic-class fencer who learned the Foil while attending Van Horn High School and became a world-class competitor in Épée and Sabré before graduating from Central Missouri State University. Slated for the Paris Olympics, Ripley had to relinquish his berth on the U.S. fencing team when an aircar accident in France left him with partial disabilities.

Turning to writing, Ripley eclipsed his former fame with the publication of the best-selling "Kishkumen Chronicles." Ironically, it was the Programworld based on his novels that "locked up" last year, freezing hundreds of Dreamwalkers in taction with the Master Computer. Although no memory-recordings of the rescue operation have been released to date, Ripley received the lion's share of credit for freeing the trapped Dreamers.

Dr. Sondra Quebedeaux, Chief of Programming for the currently suspended Dreamland Division of Cephtronics, refused comment on the incident and on whether Dreamland would re-open in the near future.

Ripley would have been thirty-five years old this Thursday.

PART I

WIFE AFTER LIFE

**Love blinds all men alike,
both the reasonable and the foolish.**

—Menander, *Andria*

We are easily duped by those we love.

—Molière, *Tartuffe*

DATALOG: \QUEBEDEAUX_A.5\PERSONAL\20200800
Voice Dictation
<<<FILE ENCRYPTION ON>>>

Damn Ripley!

*

I never thought I would want to ask the man for advice and now that I seem to have no other choice, he goes and dies on me.

*

In Russia, of all places!

*

I suppose there's little chance he survived the plane crash and will still turn up alive…

*

Hell, what am I thinking? This is Reality, not the Matrix, where we can program events to come out the way we want them to.

*

Now what?

*

I need to talk to somebody.

*

But I don't know who I can trust anymore.

*

Certainly not the so-called Security Team that Senator Hanson has imposed on us these past six months.

*

Hence, the fact that I'm keeping these personal notes in my own pocket-micro: I don't dare leave anything like this in-system, even with file encryption and password protection!

*

Damn!

*

If only Ripley were still alive…

ONE: RIPLEY PRIME (∞)

"So what do you think?"

I peered through the wire-meshed glass at the patient in the darkened hospital room. "I look a mess," I answered finally.

Natasha Skovoroda chuckled. "Oh, you are!" she murmured mirthfully. "Second and third-degree burns over eighty per cent of your body, multiple fractures, internal injuries, a concussion..." She smiled. "Robert R. Ripley the Third is in pretty bad shape!"

I gave Borys Dankevych's bride-to-be my "I am not amused" expression and turned back to look at the tented sheets arching over the hospital bed. She was right: I didn't look well, at all. "Will I live?" I asked, pressing my forehead against the cool glass.

"If you are successful. If you fail, then the whole question becomes a bit moot." She tucked a stray wisp of red hair back under her surgical cap and then tightened the drawstring at the waist of her green cotton pants. I was momentarily reminded of the exquisite face and figure hidden beneath the surgical mask and scrubs. "Of course, if we get back out alive, you are most welcome to live here," she said.

"Here?"

"In Russia. Unless something is done about your Senator Hanson, returning to the United States would be much too dangerous."

I nodded. "Thomas Wolfe."

"I beg your pardon?"

"He said 'You can't go home again.'"

"Ah," Natasha nodded sagely. "He was quoting great Russian author Aleksandr Pushkin."

"Or the KGB," I sighed.

"KGB?" Her eyes crinkled above the green mask. "Ah, you probably mean the SVR."

"SVR, FSA, FSK, FSB, PV, SBP, Alpha Group, FAPSI—I liked it better when they all used to be the *Komitet Gosurdarstvenoy Besopasnasti.*"

"That is because you did not have to live under the KGB's rule. It is better this way: now they spend most of their time watching each other."

I studied my Doppelgänger's blistered face. "I'm surprised you didn't put me under an oxygen tent."

"Unnecessary, as this is a Laminar Air-flow Room. Besides, the tent would obscure your features and might raise doubts about your identity." She tugged at the surgical mask that concealed her own identity from the regular staff and gestured. "Come."

"Where did you find such a close double?"

"It is you. While you were unconscious we had you made up and bandaged to appear seriously hurt. Then we holographed you for over two hours. There is nothing and no one in that room—"

"Only a projected hologram running on continuous loop," I concluded, adjusting the mask that obscured my identity as well. "Very neat. Now what?"

"Now we meet with Borys," she said, leading me out of the antechamber.

∞

The setup had been quite elaborate.

The fake plane crash had been planned with every detail painstakingly covered; the crew members all trained SVR agents and the passengers actually military personnel in civilian garb. The engine problems were faked as much for Stephanie's and my benefit as for the outside world's. The in-flight meal was drugged so that we lost consciousness during a staged emergency landing.

That much I listened to before demanding to hear the reason for this cloak-and-dagger scenario and threatening violence if they didn't take me to Stephanie immediately.

Borys Dankevych sighed and leaned back in his chair. The all-but-instated prime minister of the Russian Federation was a great bear of a man who looked like his hibernation had been cut too damn short. He rubbed red-rimmed eyes and pinched the bridge of his nose. "Comrade Ripley, I am getting to point. I beg for you to be patient: this is not being easy thing I am telling you!"

I looked around the green-tiled room that had been an operating theater until Dankevych had commandeered it for his operations center. The cabinets and trays of surgical equipment had been pushed aside. An odd assortment of mismatched chairs was grouped around the stainless steel surgical slab that was presently serving as the conference table. It was an incongruous setting: the second-most powerful leader of the largest federated alliance in the world running a secret operation out of a backwater hospital in Izhevsk.

It was this glaring conundrum that was keeping me in my chair for the moment.

"Robert," Natasha was saying, "surely you are aware of the headlines over the past seven months. Of how the cold war between our two nations, after decades in remission, has suddenly begun to escalate again?"

I nodded.

"If you have been reading carefully, you will notice that certain political movements in your United States have been initiating these confrontations. Some of your own political analysts have speculated that Senator Hanson himself has unified these factions and is orchestrating these incidents…"

"Like our plane crash and disappearance? My god, Borys, this is the kind of stunt the old totalitarian regimes used to pull before democratization!" I was trying to not lose my temper—and failing. "You've engineered an incident that could take us right back to the Twentieth Century!"

"The point with which Tasha is trying to be making," Borys intoned heavily, "is that all this is happening since problem at Dreamland!"

For a moment my thoughts swept back to the Cephtronics fiasco. Dreamland had been the ultimate experience in fantasy fulfillment. You could select your preferred fantasy environment from a plethora of Programworlds, then spend the next several hours or days or (if you had the money) weeks adventuring in the body of your choice. Your real body was maintained in a womblike environment, commonly called a Cradle, while your consciousness was projected into a Dreambody, or Avatar. The Computer-generated Programworlds were perfect in every detail: all the senses were accounted for, and you could rewrite natural law and physics so that anything was possible—even magic!

And if you got yourself into a gunfight with Billy the Kid, did battle with the Black Knight, or found yourself mixing it up above the clouds with the Red Baron, you could smile in the face of certain death because the worst thing that could happen was that you would just wake up.

That is, until a computer glitch trapped everyone in their respective Programworlds and turned Dreamdeaths into the real thing.

Getting out had been a very near thing for all of us.

My hangover from the drugged food and concern over Stephanie's absence made it hard to concentrate as I turned my attention to the matter at hand. "What are you saying? That a bad turn in a glitched Programworld is responsible for renewed hostilities between Uncle Sam and Ivan?"

"Robert." The redheaded Dreammaster reached for my hand. "Please turn down that marvelous temper of yours and listen for just a moment—"

"With a mind that is being open," said Borys Dankevych.

Natasha smiled at her fiancé's fractured English. It was a ruse, of course: no one participated in international diplomacy without a solid command of the English language. Especially now that translation implants were commonplace. But Dankevych had perpetuated the fiction that he relied on his own rudimentary language skills without the benefit of a biocephalic microprocessor. As a result, his opponents often underestimated an intellect masked by deliberately butchered grammar. To prove that point, he was about to become the youngest prime minister of the Russian Federation in history.

I also suspected the man perversely enjoyed the pretense well beyond its context for shrewd political maneuvering.

Natasha continued. "Before the incident at Dreamland last year, the relationship between our respective countries was one of wary—even weary—tolerance."

The sad thing was that we had gone from being ideological and military to economic opponents in so short a time. Americans had blamed the Japanese in the eighties and nineties, the Common Market of United Europe the following decade and now the Russian Federation for our lackluster position in world trade and commerce.

"But since that incident, your Senator Hanson has suddenly become very intolerant of Russian Federation policies," she concluded.

"Walter Hanson has chaired the Armed Services Committee for years," I said. "He's a hawk, not a dove."

Borys nodded in agreement. "But a rabbit one since coming out of Program taction…"

"Rabid," Natasha corrected.

"…and now is suddenly headed for highest political office in United States—*second* most powerful position in the world, along with myself."

"Hanson's a dark house—*horse!*" I wondered if homophonic dysphasia was contagious. "I doubt an isolationist will get the people's mandate come election time."

"The *old* Hanson was an isolationist, Robert, but the new Hanson is very much the imperialist. And, we're afraid, much more than even that." Natasha looked at Borys.

"Our…sources," the word came out reluctantly, "indicate that Senator Hanson is better…connected…than anyone realizes." Borys Dankevych looked down at his clasped hands. "Unless something extra ordinary happens, it will be President Hanson in the White House next and who can say for how long."

"Is that really so bad?" I asked. "Campaigns tend to obscure the real issues but, if you look at his record as an elder statesman—"

"We have no problem with the Walter Hanson who has served his country for the past thirty-nine years!" Dankevych's fist struck the table and I caught a glimpse of whitened knuckles. "The problem is the change since we leave the Programworld!"

"So what are you saying? That last year's experience in Fantasyworld has altered Hanson's political views? That he's changed his mind since coming out of the Program?"

"Not *since* Program," Dankevych growled, "*while inside* Program! He changed minds while still inside Program!"

I opened my mouth again but Natasha Skovoroda cut me off. "*Think,* Robert! Would-be-President Hanson has suddenly developed a personal interest in containing and suppressing the Reformed Soviet doctrine of Democratic Socialism! He has suddenly set himself up as an ideological gatekeeper! Who does that remind you of?"

"Ronald Reagan back in the nineteen-eighties."

"Robert! This is serious! The Walter Hanson who came out of the Program Matrix with the rest of us is not the same Walter Hanson who went into Warworld shortly before! You suggest he may have changed his mind since leaving the Dreamland complex. We say that his mind was changed—in the most literal sense—before he exited the Program!" She moved her chair close to mine. "Check the records—his speeches, his policies, his press conferences: the man headed for the Oval Office of your White House has a totally different attitude toward détente than the statesman of record for the past thirty years! He is suddenly intolerant of everything he tolerated prior to the Dreamland incident!"

"Look," I said wearily, "this is hardly the first time you or China or the Third World nations have accused the U.S. of playing global policeman. Hanson wouldn't be the first American President to meddle in another nation's business. And if he wants to play Big Brother then I can hardly see how I can—"

"Not Big Brother, Robert!" Natasha practically shouted. "Parent Surrogate! Conscience! *Psychic Gatekeeper*! Do these terms have any meaning for you?"

The light finally dawned. "Holy shit! *Cerberus?* The Machine's Superego?"

They both nodded.

"The Machine" was Cephtronics' moniker for the supercomputer that maintained the various Programworlds in the Matrix. This was a misleading term, as the Computer was organic in nature, largely made up of banks of cultured cephalic cells—human brain cell cultures. The Anomaly had developed when the computer's "personality" had been schismed into the three basic components of Freudian psychology: Id, Ego, and Superego. Now I was being told that the Superego had escaped and was headed for the Presidency of the United States.

"Got any evidence to back this theory?"

Natasha leaned across the table and took my hands in hers. "I have been back inside the Program."

"Impossible. Cephtronics has kept the Dreamland Complex sealed off since the Incident and Hanson has reinforced their security with military personnel."

"Every program has a back door." She smiled. "Or have you forgotten?"

I groaned, remembering her last foray into Dreamland.

"When we became suspicious, I slipped back into Fantasyworld and checked around. When The Machine agreed to let us all go, it apparently decided to get out with the rest of us. That portion of the Computer's personality that we call the Superego—Cerberus—took over the senator's body and left Walter Hanson's psyche trapped inside the Program."

"Just like poor Mike Straeker." Except that Straeker's body was pronounced dead, disconnected, and then cremated. I clutched at my head and groaned. "Oh, this is not good!"

"It is being worse than you think!" Now Borys Dankevych was leaning across the table. "Natasha went in Program with five other agents which are highly trained. Only two make it back out with her."

"And now that he knows that *we* know," Natasha added, "you can expect U.S./Russian relations to deteriorate further—"

"What? How does he know that you know?"

"We had a little run-in with Cerberus while we were in the Matrix."

"I thought you just said he got out!"

"He did. And he is monitoring the Program Web. Closely."

"Closely enough that he is into the Programs slipping from time to time," Borys added.

"And once he knows that we have been talking to you, your own life will be in danger. That is why I said you may not be able to go back to your own country. At least as long as the real Walter Hanson is trapped inside the Program Matrix."

"So, if we are not being able to get him back out, you may be wanting to stay in Russia for permanent home." Borys smiled warmly. "Would make us very happy and you are being most welcome!"

"Mmmm...better Red than dead," I mused. "And I do appreciate the offer. But I suppose I should try getting Walt back into his own body before Cerberus gets into the White House and does something Freudian with all of those missiles." I shook my head. "This is really bad, folks!"

"Is worse than you are thinking," Borys said after a long, cautious pause.

I looked at him with a growing sense of horror. "You mean—Morpheus—the Id—got out, too?"

Natasha shook her head. "Not the Id, no…"

"Is a matter of the other one: Pallas," Borys added.

"Pallas got out?" I didn't like this at all.

"Robert…" Natasha looked at me with a pained expression. "Has Stephanie seemed any different to you since we got out of the Fantasyworld Program?"

∞

Once again I found myself on the outside, looking in. Pressing my forehead against the cool meshed glass, I stared at the occupant of another hospital bed.

"Stephanie…"

"It is only her body, Comrade Ripley." Natasha Skovoroda came up behind me. "And, as such, is the repository of The Machine's Ego—that expression of personality that we know as 'Pallas.' The actual essence of Stephanie Harrell…is still inside the Dreamland Computer Matrix."

I swallowed. "How is she? Did you see her?"

"No. But I understand she is well. Daggoth the Dark has given her sanctuary in his tower and she is under his protection."

That protection would be pretty good, as Daggoth was one of the most powerful wizards in the Fantasyworld Program and the avatar of the former Chief of Programming for the entire Dreamland Project.

On the other hand, his real-life counterpart, Mike Straeker, had died from an inoperable brain tumor the year before.

She touched my shoulder gently. "If there is anything I can do—"

I shrugged her off. "Go away."

"I know that this must be a shock—"

"Go. Away." I put my hand to the glass, fighting down the impulse to rush into the room and take Stephanie's body into my arms. "I don't feel much like talking right now." For the past six months I had thought myself to be in love with my ex-wife. Now I felt betrayed.

But I wasn't sure by whom.

"I know how you must feel."

Like bloody hell she did. This latest revelation had come like a physical blow—all the more painful because I'd been sucker-punched.

"Robert." Natasha's hand hovered like an uncertain bird. "I have read your dossier. I have talked with Dr. Cooper. I know about Nicole Doucet. I think I understand…"

Understand what? Death and disfigurement? She was so damn beautiful—she couldn't know what it was like to feel like damaged goods, to live with pain every waking hour while your sleep was crowded with dreams of flames and loss. Even though the "White Box" effect of last year's sojourn in the tank had reconstituted some of the tissue lost in the crash, I was still a long way from being whole. And nothing could reshape the last fifteen years of my life, bring back Nicole, or erase a marriage that had been a terrible mistake for Stephanie as well as me.

"Robert…say something…"

I turned and spoke quietly. "You don't have to settle for whoever will have you."

"What does that mean?"

I turned back to the window without answering. In the long silence that followed I knew her thoughts had turned back to the night she had tried to seduce me into helping her crack Dreamland's security systems. Perhaps she had thought my eyepatch was dashing and my walking cane stylish; but later, when she had used the drug to get me into her bed, she had seen the scars.

"You think Stephanie married you out of pity?" The thought was new to her and she didn't like it.

"In the end, she didn't even give me that." The words came out nice and bitter, but I doubted their veracity. I wasn't angry over losing the one response I could count on from the opposite sex. Rather, I still felt the guilt of imposing myself on a woman who deserved better.

Anger and pity and guilt, oh my.

"So go ahead and ask."

"Ask what?" she asked.

"Ask how I could live with a woman for the past six months—supposedly the woman I was once married to—and still be so completely fooled? That *is* what you've all been wondering."

"It is a reasonable question."

My gaze refocused from Stephanie's sheet swaddled form to my own reflection in the glass. "The answer is: I'm a cold, selfish bastard who can't see anything beyond his own needs."

"I don't believe that."

"Then give me a better answer." I pressed my forehead to the glass again and changed the subject. "She looks awful."

"More makeup."

"And a hologram?"

Natasha shook her head. "No. Not yet. When the time comes, her body will be placed in a Cradle and we will attempt to exchange the Pallas persona for Stephanie's."

"But in the meantime you're keeping her under sedation. Why?"

"Obviously it makes her more...manageable. It would be easy enough to restrain her—prevent her escape. But, as it is your wife's body—"

"Ex-wife," I murmured absently.

"—I'm sure that you would not wish to take the chance of having it damaged by its present occupant." She looked troubled.

"And?" I prompted.

"The sedatives are a precautionary measure..."

"Against?"

"The possibility of a telepathic bond—"

"Between Pallas and Cerberus," I finished for her. "The Machine's Ego and Superego."

She nodded. "It sounds mad, does it not?"

I sagged against the wall, suddenly very tired. "I don't know. Considering all of the unknowns, I wouldn't rule out any possibility." I turned away from the glass. "So what's our next move?"

Natasha shrugged. "That is what we were going to ask you."

∞

Two more chairs had been pulled up to the conference table.

Colonel Stanislav Kerensky of the Red Army's elite Spetsnaz force was a dark, hatchet-faced man who resembled a muscle-bound weasel. He listened attentively but spoke only when spoken to. And then he was more likely to answer with a shrug or a gesture.

I tell people who have never met Dorothy Cooper to picture an Irish cherub. And then give her the personality of an imp. She restored my faith in that description by shooting me in the arm with a rubber band. "Still with us, Robbie-me-lad? Or are you trying to enter Dreamland telepathically?"

I shook my head. "Just trying to figure out how The Machine's Superego has been able to manage its little masquerade for so long." *Not to mention Pallas in Stephanie's body.*

Dr. Cooper's appearance at this brainstorming session was a welcome surprise. Borys' and Natasha's knowledge was limited to their experiences as "Dreamwalkers" in the Fantasyworld Program. Dorothy had been an actual member of Cephtronics' Programming Staff and was conversant with the Fantasyworld Program from outside as well as within.

"The body remains that of Walter Hanson," Natasha was saying. "Scars, fingerprints, retinal scans—all physical criteria would confirm his i.d."

"Yeah, but what about memory, personality?" I countered.

Dr. Cooper shrugged. "After all this time we still don't know exactly how psyche extraction really works. Is the individual's consciousness actually removed from his body and transferred to the Programworld, leaving the mind void for the duration? If so, I suppose Cerberus, through The Machine, would have access to all personality and memory files.

"On the other hand, I tend toward the view that psychescan duplicates the Dreamwalker's personality profile and inserts the copy into the Program while suppressing consciousness and brain wave activity at the original source. Afterwards, the psyche-profile, altered and containing additional memory files, is introduced to the Dreamer's mind as consciousness and brain wave levels are restored."

"You're talking memory-copy download and update as opposed to actual psyche transference," I said.

Coop nodded. "And if that's the case, then Hanson's not really trapped in the machine—"

"Just in his own head," I finished for her. "His mind is being suppressed, kept in an unconscious state while Cerberus sits in the driver's seat."

"Where he's still in a position, parasitically, to pick Hanson's mind for the proper memories and personality prompts to carry off the masquerade," Cooper concluded.

Skovoroda was still perplexed. "But what about the Senator Hanson who is still inside the Program? I have seen him!"

I shrugged. "I don't know. If the second theory is correct, then he may no more be Walter Hanson than Riplakish of Dyrinwall is me when I'm not in taction with my avatar."

Cooper propped her chin in her hands and stared off into space. "But we can't take that chance." She sighed. "Besides, even if theory number two is correct, we may still need to get Hanson back in taction with his dreambody. That may be the only way we have of dredging up his true psyche from his subconscious—or wherever the hell it's gone to ground."

"Great." Until a few moments before, my enthusiasm had been taking a beating. As of now it had just been pummeled into unconsciousness. "So, as I understand it, we're going to have to go back to America, grab a U.S. senator who is also a presidential candidate *and* the chairman of the Armed Services Committee; then drag him, kicking and screaming, back into the Dreamland Complex—which has been declared off-limits, by the way—where we will attempt to stuff him back into the Fantasyworld Program that caused such an uproar in the first place. I know Cerberus isn't going to be cooperative and, somehow, I just don't think the Secret Service, the CIA, and the military, not to mention the cops, are going to be too enthusiastic, either."

Dorothy Cooper continued to stare off into space for several more minutes. No one said a word. Then, very slowly and deliberately, she pulled out her pipe and pouch and began to pack the bowl.

"What?" I asked. The pipe was always a clear sign that she was on to something. *"What?"*

She ignored the question and tamped down the tobacco before lighting it. A few puffs and then she leaned back in her chair. "Robbie-me-lad," she said, putting her feet up on the table and tipping her chair back on its hind legs; "I've got good news and I've got bad news."

Normally I ask for the bad news first but Dr. Cooper didn't allow me the option. "The good news is I don't think we have to drag Hanson—or Cerberus—back to Cephtronics or anywhere near The Machine."

"Great!" I exclaimed. "What's the bad news?"

"We'll have to go back into Fantasyworld ourselves and find Hanson's and Stephanie's avatars."

I shrugged. "That doesn't sound like such bad news." My enthusiasm was making a comeback. Then Cooper went on to explain just what it was we were going to do once we got back inside.

In retrospect it was beginning to look like it might be easier to drag Cerberus out of the White House and back into Dreamland after all.

DATALOG: \QUEBEDEAUX_A.5\PERSONAL\20200801
Voice Dictation
<<<FILE ENCRYPTION ON>>>

The Chief of Programming has never had it so easy.

*

Essentially, I'm being paid to do nothing.

*

And, every time I send a memo upstairs with suggestions as to how my department could increase its efficiency, better spend its time…management practically slaps my wrist and orders me to twiddle my thumbs!

*

It bothers me.

*

After last year's fiasco, you'd expect Cephtronics to do one of two things…

*

Either shut Dreamland completely—cut its losses and liquidate this whole division…

*

Or put a top-notch tech crew on debugging the Matrix and get the Programworlds back on-line.

*

Cephtronics isn't doing either.

*

Instead, nearly all the tech crews have been dismissed or transferred, leaving me and a skeleton crew for minimal monitoring.

*

And the Security Team from some special governmental branch.

*

Other than the fact that Senator Hanson set it up and now runs the show, I know very little else.

*

Except…

*

Except it makes me nervous.

*

These Security goons seem to be monitoring me and my remaining staff almost as much as they're monitoring The Machine…

TWO: RIPLEY PRIME (∞)

It was one of those macabre jokes that life manages to stage every now and then: Fate rarely bakes a cake without providing the icing.

Natasha was waiting for Dorothy to tell me.

Dorothy was deferring the unpleasant job back to Natasha.

Borys had no idea that there might be any problem and invited me to meet our first recruit without consulting anyone else.

I entered the conference room without any forewarning and Borys stepped forward to play host.

"Robert, I am glad you are conveniently being here! I am wanting you to be meeting first new team member!"

A quiet whirring sound announced her arrival. A motorized wheelchair maneuvered around Dankevych and rolled to a stop in front of me.

It wasn't just a wheelchair, it was a self-contained life-support system. And cocooned in its tangle of wires and tubes was a lump of purplish, distorted flesh that bore no resemblance to anything human.

Just before my mind went fuzzy I tried to smile.

"Robert," Dankevych admonished, "do not just be standing there. I am understanding that you are both being of old acquaintance!"

I swallowed but it was no more than a spasm between a mouth suddenly gone dry and a stomach viciously clenched.

A cybernetic arm extended itself and a hidden speaker produced an electronic voice from the recesses of the chair: ***"Hello, Robert."*** A crackling pause. ***"Long time no see."***

I opened my mouth and forced the words. "Hello. Nicole."

∞

Once upon a time there was a young man whose future had seemed bright and assured. He had honed both mind and body so that they served him well: well enough to graduate with top honors while maintaining a berth on the U.S. Olympic fencing team.

In addition to all of this, he had the good fortune to have the love of a woman whose beauty was only surpassed by her intellect and passion. A passion for life, for knowledge, for the expanding of the human spirit.

And for me.

When you are young and successful and terribly in love you cannot conceive of any obstacle that, together, you cannot overcome.

I learned otherwise just two days before the Paris Olympics when our rental aircar burst into flame and tumbled from the sky.

We both survived. I was supposed to find some kind of comfort in that.

When the surgeons and the medtechs were done I could walk again—albeit with a limp—and I could go out in public without frightening small children. I preferred the honesty of an eyepatch to the decorative function of a glass eye, and figured I was lucky, overall, that the two sides of my face came somewhat close to matching.

Nicole should have died.

That's what the medtechs all said. Again and again.

But, despite what should have happened, they essayed to save her, anyway. Perhaps they viewed her as a problem to be solved rather than a fellow human being needing release from this terrible mistake. No arms, no legs, no face; just cobbled together organs in a pouch of plastiseal pseudo-flesh: no longer recognizably human, she was a challenge to keep alive.

And, by God—or in defiance of Him—they did just that.

But in solving their problem they had created one for me. I was in love with a vibrant, healthy, young woman named Nicole Doucet, not a shapeless lump of scarred flesh that would spend a lifetime or more in the confines of a life-support system.

I'm not very proud of those particular priorities but, right or wrong, it was a decision that I wrestled to the ground a long time ago and finally walked away from.

But walking away and leaving behind are two different things. Like Satchel Paige said: "Don't look back; something might be gaining on you."

And like Bronco Bushido says: "No matter where you've been, that's where you're at…"

∞

"What the hell is she doing here?"

Dr. Cooper leaned back in her chair and closed her eyes with a sigh. "She's on the team."

"What?" I had closed the door and started this conversation with every intention of remaining calm and detached.

So much for good intentions.

"She's on the team," Dorothy repeated in a level, even voice.

"Doing what?"

"Robbie," she sighed, sounding curiously like my mother; "we have to put together the best team we can without tipping off Cerberus. And as long as The Machine's Superego is masquerading as the Chairman of the Armed Services Committee and overseeing Dreamworlds' security, we have to assume governmental surveillance of all persons with high Dreamrank status." Cooper had been on vacation in Ireland when the SVR had managed to kidnap her and put the blame on one of the extremist Red Hand cells. We had agreed that we couldn't bag any more members of the Dreamworlds staff or any Dreammasters without arousing suspicion.

"So?"

"So our next option is to recruit people who have high DreamNet potential. People with natural or acquired skills that would translate into Fantasyworld abilities or experience. Fencers, archers, martial artists—perhaps even scholars with backgrounds in medieval history, cultural anthropology, and mythology. We're particularly interested in athletes and writers. An interesting mix, don't you think?"

"So you're telling me that Ms. Doucet has written a book now?"

The chair snapped forward and Dr. Cooper leaned across the desk, the fire of battle in her eyes. "Fifteen years ago you were the best American fencer ever to reach the Olympics. Nicole Doucet was the best France had to offer. On top of that, she was a top contender in the Trans-Continental Tournaments in Field Archery."

"Before the accident," I qualified.

"Before the accident," she agreed. "And, in spite of that accident, you're still the best swordsman inside Fantasyworld."

"Dorothy!" I gripped the edge of the desk across from her. "She doesn't have any arms or legs!"

"Neither do you!

"For all intents and purposes," she added quietly, leaning back in her chair. "Oh, Robbie; you know better than this! When you enter a Programworld, your physical body remains behind in the suspension tank. Your dreambody is a computer simulation of your psyche, your conceptual self. It's what's in here," she added, tapping index finger to temple, "that enters the program. You quite literally shuffle off this mortal coil. So what are you really trying to say?"

"I don't like it."

"Of course you don't," she soothed. "I can understand what a shock this all has been. First Stephanie and now Nicole—"

"And I don't want to talk about it!"

"Oh, can the hysteria and sit down!" she snapped. "We have a lot to do and we're running out of time! Give the woman some credit for brains—it's all she has left, dammit!"

I sat down. Slowly.

"Put yourself in her place," Cooper continued. "If you were going to spend the rest of your life as a human potato, would you expect anyone to hang around your bedside, mooning for the rest of their life?" She shook her head. "Nicole's first response was concern for your feelings. She's apparently well aware of your martyr complex. I suppose she knows that you're a closet-chauvinist in the bargain?"

"That's not funny, Coop."

"I'm not kidding," she rejoined calmly. She smiled. "But I love ya in spite of your flaws, ya big, ugly galoot! So let's stow all this personal bullshit and get down to brass circuits. Are you with me?"

I nodded, swallowing. Perhaps my pride with a lot of other excess baggage. "I'll work alongside Morpheus if it'll solve our present predicament."

"Spoken like a true pro. Now let's get to work."

∞

Borys Dankevych had engaged a Russian tech crew to construct suspension tanks here, in the Russia. The plan was to use equipment at this end for psyche extraction, transmit the data via tightbeam to a Federation weather satellite, bounce the signal to one of Cephtronics' communications birds, and back door into a parallel datanet that shared several common interface links with the Dreamworlds Matrix systems.

You may surmise that this was not a process that filled me with gleeful anticipation.

Natasha Skovoroda did her best to convince me of the soundness of this approach, showing me the newly constructed tanks and equipment, and describing her last experience in cracking the Program.

As we walked around the life-support monitors I was startled to hear a familiar voice over one of the intercoms: "...*Asie. Vieux pays merveilleux des contes de nourrice...*"

It was Nicole's voice—strangely lacking that metallic quality that was a by-product of her speech synthesizer. "...*O dort la fantaisie comme une impératrice...*" And she was singing. "...*En sa forêt tout emplie de mystère...*"

And I felt a sudden rush of moisture at the corners of my eyes as an old memory was resurrected. "Where is that coming from?"

Natasha gestured to a tank at the far end of the room. "We have to recalibrate Ms. Doucet's Cradle for her special life-support requirements. We have to run some of the tests with her inside." She cocked her head, listening. "That is very lovely! I wish I knew what the words meant. Do you?"

I nodded. "'Shéhérazade.' Ravel composed the music. Tristan Klingsor, the text."

"Je voudrais voir Damas et les villes de Perse..."

"I should like to see Damascus and the cities of Persia..." I translated.

"...Avec les minarets légers dans l'air."

"...With their slender minarets in the air."

"Je voudrais voir de beaux turbans de soie sur des visages noirs aux dents claires..."

"I should like to see fine silk turbans on black faces with gleaming teeth…"

"…Je voudrais voir des yeux sombres d'amour et des prunelles brillantes de joie…"

"…I should like to see eyes dark with love and pupils shining with joy…" And suddenly I was back, fifteen years in the past, high on a hill in the orchards just outside Avignon. The picnic blanket was spread and I was pulling bread and cheese and wine from the basket as she sang to me and ruffled the pages of a dog-eared copy of The Rubáiyát of Omar Khayyám.

"…I should like to see Persia and India, and then China…" I recited, no longer hearing her voice in the present. "…Big-bellied mandarins under their umbrellas and princesses with delicate hands. And scholars quarreling over poetry and beauty. I should like to linger at the enchanted palace and, like a foreign traveler, contemplate at leisure, landscapes painted on cloth in frames of pinewood, with one figure in the middle of an orchard…"

And in my memory she smiled at me: a smile that could forgive anything. Even the betrayal I would commit for all those long years to come.

"Je voudrais voir des assassins souriant du bourreau qui coupe un cou d'innocent avec son grand sabre courbé d'Orient."

"I should like to see assassins smiling at the executioner who cuts off an innocent head with his great curved oriental sword."

"Robert?"

"Je voudrais voir des pauvres et des reines…"

"I should like to see poor people and queens…"

"…Je voudrais voir des roses et du sang…"

"…I should like to see roses and blood…"

"Robert?"

"…Je voudrais voir mourir d'amour ou bien de haine…"

"…I should like to see people dying of love or of hatred…"

Natasha touched my shoulder. "Robert? Are you all right?"

I nodded and brushed at my eyes. "And the song ends, saying: 'And then to return home later and tell my story to people interested in dreams, raising, like Sinbad, my old Arabian cup to my lips from time to time, in order to interrupt the tale artfully…'"

She nodded. I turned my back on the systems monitors and we walked the length of the room in silence.

∞

I threw down the list in disgust. "Great! None of these people have any Fantasyworld experience whatsoever!"

"It is true that they are unknown factors in the equation—" Skovoroda began.

"We can't recruit experienced Dreamwalkers," Cooper reminded me.

"I know that! But I thought our candidates were going to have some DreamNet experience."

"Why? Dreamwalkers who aren't skilled enough to produce a threat to Cerberus are useless to us, anyway."

"On the other hand," Natasha continued, "these people are unknown quantities—real savage decks..."

"Wild cards," I corrected.

"Athletic prowess, familiarity with the genre, or a strong imaginative bent are the factors that we were looking for—"

I picked up the list and scanned it again. "We'd be better off doing a blind recruit of REMrunners!"

Dreamwalking wasn't cheap and only a few people were good enough to win Network sponsorships. The majority of Dreamwalkers had to content themselves with spending their vacation time and money on a once-a-year pilgrimage to Dreamworlds, Utah. There were always a few, however, who found ways to beat the system.

"And how would we do that?" Cooper was as exasperated as I. "It's illegal, and they cover their tracks too damn well!"

Officially, REMrunners didn't exist: security programs prevented any illegal entries to the Dreamworlds Computer Matrix. But there were always fourteen-year-olds with a PC and a modem that could crack new security codes just as fast as they could be generated. All a REMrunner needed was some chutzpah, a series of code-sequences, and some form of cerebral/digital interface. Whereas Dreamwalkers paid to utilize the suspension tanks at the Dreamworlds Complex, these cybernetic trespassers illegally altered neuralnets and brainrigs, trusting their psyches to luck and their ability to navigate the subcircuits of the DreamNet.

REMrunners would seem to be the ideal recruits for our purposes but we were stymied by the very factor that made them the best choice. REMrunning was illegal and the ones who were good enough to be of any use had learned how to cover their tracks. You can't recruit people you can't find.

"How about experts in the Fantasyworld milieu? I don't see any SCA listings."

"Skuh? What is this—skah?" Natasha inquired.

"S.C.A. It stands for the Society for Creative Anachronism," Cooper explained. "It's an organization of people get their jollies dressing up like knights and ladies from the Middle Ages. Aside from some very talented seamstresses they're mostly nutcases."

"*Some* are nutcases," I amended. "A great many are intelligent and talented people who are preserving historical knowledge and forgotten skills."

"Handy people to have around if you have a manuscript that needs illuminating," Cooper observed.

"Or need to recruit someone outside the Matrix with practical experience in jousting or wielding a broadsword," I retorted.

"We're talking about some seriously maladjusted people here."

"Oh?" I raised my eyebrows. "And what do you call Ph.D.'s who climb inside a computer to do the same?"

"The question is moot," said Kerensky, speaking in complete sentences for the first time. "This is an anti-terrorist operation and will be conducted by *my* personnel. Under my leadership. *None* of you will be going in."

"Um," I said, "excuse me?"

"If you enter the DreamNet at all, Dr. Ripley, it will be my decision and you will follow my orders." His smile was artfully constructed to be apologetic but there were hints of barbed wire in it.

"Look, Stanley," I said, "I'm a U.S. citizen entering the Program Matrix of an American Computer Complex on American soil. Fantasyworld is largely my own creation and it's my own neck that I'm planning to risk. I'm a big boy and I don't need my mother's permission. I don't know whose mother *you* are but I'm not asking for your permission, either."

"That is fortunate, Comrade Ripley, as I have no intention of giving you my permission as of this time."

"Oh yeah? Well—"

"Be *silent!*" His voiced cracked, whip-like, through the suddenly still atmosphere of the old operating theater. "You are acting like a spoiled child who has been grounded when he wants to play his favorite game!" He threw his gloves down on the table and angrily pushed back his chair. "Well, this is not a game!"

He leaned into the table and swept the assemblage with cold, gray eyes. "None of you have any practical military experience in this type of operation. From all that I have seen and heard, you were very lucky the last time. You went in without a well-defined plan and, now, several hundred people owe their lives to your *luck.*" He glanced across the table at Borys and Natasha. "Their gratitude may blind them to your faults. I, however, suffer no such delusions.

"I have listened patiently while you discussed your alternatives and made your lists. But it is now painfully obvious, even to you, that the best you can recruit are inexperienced amateurs. That is why an elite company of *Spetsnaz* will be conducting this mission."

His fist crashed down on the table, cutting off the first syllable of our combined protests. "Perhaps I will invite you and your candidates along in an advisory capacity. *If* you can convince me of your ability to follow my orders. I will not risk my operations with any form of insubordination!"

He stood and began to circle the table at a leisurely pace. "The situation is different this time around. If you had failed before, nearly a thousand lives would have been forfeit. A great tragedy, of course: but the world would continue as it has after all great tragedies." He laid a gentle hand on Dankevych's shoulder. "Forgive me, old friend, when I say that we would have mourned your loss—but that our great Soviet Federation would have gone on to nominate the next worthy man to be your successor."

"No offense taken, Stanislav." Borys was smiling but his gaze had turned inward and I caught a glimpse of something alien in his eyes.

"But we find the circumstances somewhat different, this time," Kerensky continued. "Before, it was the people *inside* the Computer who were the hostages. Less than a thousand, and what are a thousand lives among the seven billion or so who crowd this planet?" As he walked past Natasha I saw his hand make a filial move toward her shoulder in turn. She leaned into the table, avoiding his gesture with a smooth, almost unconscious subtlety.

"But this time around the hostages are every man, woman, and child on the *outside* of the Computer!" He strolled on, seemingly oblivious to her aversion. "If we fail this time around, the evidence suggests that this Doppelgänger will become the American President and push our respective countries to a confrontation that can only be resolved in a nuclear holocaust!" He whirled on me, bracing himself with his hands and leaning across the table. "We cannot afford to fail this time around!" he shouted. "We cannot afford to trust to luck!

"At best, our country will be made to look foolish—if not criminal—should our efforts be exposed prematurely. At worst, the human race may perish from the face of the earth!

"I need more time to train and plan! I do not need a loose cannon rolling about the deck! And I do not need an undisciplined fool, trusting to blind luck, jeopardizing the lives of my command, my country, and my planet! *Do I make myself clear?*"

Clear enough that when the meeting adjourned some ten minutes later, I was still trying to think of a snappy comeback.

DATALOG: \QUEBEDEAUX_A.5\PERSONAL\20200802
Voice Dictation
FILE ENCRYPTION ON

It's the new "Incursion" policy that bothers me the most.

*

Since the Matrix was always considered to be a closed and secure system—inaccessible to outside intrusion—so there was no company policy to deal with the likes of REMrunners.

*

Now we know better.

*

Unfortunately, company policies have now been set aside along with our innocence and naiveté: the Dreamworlds division of Cephtronics, Inc. is now under martial law.

*

And REMrunners are no longer a matter of rogue hackers undercutting company profits.

*

As near as I can tell, they're being seen as some kind of threat to national security.

*

So now, as part of my responsibilities in monitoring the Matrix, I'm supposed to report any evidence of outside "incursions" to the head of Security, Captain Balor.

*

Ostensibly, it's for the REMrunners' own protection.

*

Why don't I believe that?

*

The Anomaly continues to mutate (more notes on that to follow) and I must assume that Program/Avatar death continues to be fatal to anyone in taction.

*

But in each case of Program intrusion that I've registered and reported through channels, the readings have abruptly terminated shortly thereafter.

*

I have no hard evidence…just an uneasy suspicion.

*

What if Balor and his goons are just using the data I give them to locate REMrunners inside the Programworlds and terminate their avatars?

*

As long as the Anomaly is still in effect, such an act would prove fatal to a Dreamwalker's body back in their Cradle.

*

And how fatal might it be to a REMrunner using a homemade neural rig?

*

Even if they did "survive" they might well be drooling and in diapers for the rest of their outside existence…

THREE: RIPLEY PRIME (∞)

It was late.

I wasn't in the mood for company but, when the door chimed, I said "Come" out of habit. The portal slid open and Nicole's cyberpod whirred into the room that served as my temporary quarters. I scrambled up off the bed and reached to dial up the lights.

"No, Robert," the chair speaker crackled, ***"leave the lights as they are. I have infrared."*** What she did not add was that the present level of illumination cloaked her in shadow.

I sat on edge of the bed, fighting the inherent awkwardness of the moment (of the years?) and tried to meet her photo-receptors with a steady gaze of my own. "Nicole, I—"

"I am very angry!"

I swallowed convulsively.

"No! I am furious!" she continued.

I stared at the floor: my steady gaze had not lasted twenty seconds.

"That man had no right to talk to you like that! What does he know about mounting a campaign in a medieval/fantasy setting? Military Intelligence, indeed! For Colonel Kerensky the terms must be mutually exclusive!"

Awareness was a little slow in coming but it finally dawned on me: Nicole was angry at Kerensky, not me. For the moment, at least.

"Anyway, I thought it was time that I made a show of support." The cybernetic arm telescoped toward me, proffering a bottle of Russian vodka.

"A drink for old time's sake?" My mouth went suddenly drier at this fresh dilemma.

Offering Nicole any form of rejection was the last thing I wanted to do. But she couldn't know that I was a recovering alcoholic: my dependency had manifested in the aftermath of the aircar crash.

I wasn't about to talk about how tough *I'd* had it and I certainly wasn't going to bring up my failed marriage to Stephanie and how that had triggered a second round of boozy oblivion.

"A toast," she was saying, ***"to our working together, again. People change, circumstances change, but friendship is forever."***

And what about love? I thought. *What about passion? And promises?* She was pouring the vodka into a pair of plastic tumblers and I was suddenly more terrified of rejecting this simple act of friendship than I was of falling off the wagon again. I took the proffered glass with a steady hand.

"A toast," she announced, raising her drink with a mechanical jerk.

"A toast," I echoed, suddenly wondering how someone without a face could drink from a glass…

"To whom shall we drink?" the speaker crackled.

"To us…" I hoped the implicit question wasn't obvious.

"To all of us," she amended, clinking her glass to mine. Actually, the plastic made more of a dull "clicking" sound. I swallowed a small amount of the Russian liquor convulsively. When I glanced up I saw that Nicole's glass was already empty. I took another sip as she refilled her tumbler and then allowed her to raise the level of my own.

"One last toast before lights out."

It was only now that I was beginning to feel the burning effects of the vodka as it erupted in my mouth and sent lava flows down my throat.

"To the poets, the bards, and the storytellers," she proposed.

I saluted her with my glass: "To Scheherazade, the best of the bunch."

She saluted in return: ***"To Omar Khayyám."***

I did not know what to say after that and, so, turned my attention to my drink.

"Robert…"

I looked up. "Yes?" My heart hung in my chest like a lead paperweight.

"I…I don't blame you…"

I stared at her, caught in a Möbius strip of time.

Her chair suddenly whirred in reverse, spun and headed for the door. I called her name as the exit-sensor tripped the opening relays but she continued through the doorway and out into the hall without pausing.

After a moment the door slid shut.

Fifteen years ago I didn't stay behind and tonight I didn't follow after.

After a while I decided to follow through. I reached for the bottle of vodka that Nicole had left behind.

∞

The trouble with abusing alcohol is that it abuses you right back. Every time I'd taken a bottle to bed I went through two basic stages of waking up: first, I was afraid I was going to die; then I was more afraid that I *wasn't* going to die.

This time, however, I had reached the acute discomfort of stage two while still floundering in the disorientation of stage one.

I rolled to the edge of the hospital bed and contemplated the floor as if from a great height. I was no longer sure as to the whereabouts of the bathroom but I figured I'd worry about that after I'd solved the problem of exiting the bed proper. As I struggled to sit up the door to my room hissed open.

So much for privacy-lock codes, I thought. I reached for the bedside lamp and was body-slammed back into the mattress.

Hot bile came boiling up my throat and I didn't smell the chloroform until the cloth clamped down over my mouth and nose. A large, heavy body smothered me down, effectively pinning me to the bed, a beefy forearm pressing down across my throat, choking me. Surprisingly, my left hand was still free, still groping at the night stand for the lamp. More surprisingly, it found the nightcall button. I pressed the button repeatedly, forgetting that the nurse's station on this floor was unmanned: all the patients had been moved to other floors for the duration of the Dreamland Operation.

All the air had been driven from my lungs by the weight of my assailant. As he (gender was only a supposition at this point) shifted position I had no choice but to finally inhale. Vodka and chloroform and the forearm against my windpipe stole my strength. It took the bite of a needle in my shoulder to rally my instincts for self-preservation. As the fingers of my left hand came groping up in a feint for my attacker's eyes, my right fist pistoned into his (no gender supposition from this point on) groin. There wasn't much strength in the punch but it was sufficient to loosen his grip: I wrenched the antique hypo from my shoulder and threw it across the room. As he reached across to block my throw, I kicked him in the hip with my left foot. The kick set off some arcane codicil to Newton's laws of motion: my assailant hardly moved but the room itself began to revolve. As my surroundings spun faster and faster, I felt my attacker slip away as if pulled by centrifugal force. I rolled over and clutched at the bed rails but a roaring black pit opened at my feet and sucked me down into oblivion.

∞

Sometime later oblivion spit me back out.

I could barely hear the babble of voices over the Bartokian percussion section in my head. My eyelids seemed to be mounted on heavy springs and refused to open until intrusive fingers peeled them back. A bright light was directed at each pupil and then my lids were released to snap shut again. I tried to tell "them" that the room was terribly hot, that I was dreadfully thirsty but my mouth wouldn't function properly. My tongue was a bloated, swollen, fuzzy thing that lolled in my mouth like an anesthetized slug.

Time passed and I knew that something was wrong: I was getting worse, not better. The ache was spreading to the rest of my body and my throat was growing raw and constricted. Air whistled in and out of my strangled trachea, its pitch and volume hurting my ears.

When the babble of voices grew more insistent and I was prodded and pushed and admonished to breathe once again. While I was considering this, a familiar and demanding voice kept nagging at me until, at last, I was forced to pay a little attention.

"Robbie! Robbie, can you hear me?"

It was Dr. Cooper and I was sure she was sitting on my chest. I tried to answer, tried to ask her to get up and let me breathe. My mouth still wouldn't function so I willed my right hand to rise and make a simple gesture. It disobeyed…

"Robbie, you are very sick! Do you understand me?"

Of course I was sick. Coop had been away from General Practice too long if she couldn't recognize a simple case of alcohol poisoning…

"Robbie, we think you may be dying!"

Dying? From one lousy bottle of vodka? Hey, maybe my tolerance wasn't what it once was but you don't tox out from just one bottle. Then I remembered the chloroform. And the needle.

"Nobody can diagnose it, yet, and nothing we've done seems to be helping—"

Of course not. When you're in a Semi-socialist State, you get semi-socialized medicine…

"—take any chances! We're putting you into one of the Cradles: its life-support settings should help to slow your metabolism! Do you understand?"

Vaguely, I became aware that I was already floating in a suspension tank.

"—try to get you stabilized and buy more time! And if anything else goes wrong, there's always the Straeker scenario as a last hope. Do you understand? We're sending you in early—just like you wanted!"

Like I wanted? I wasn't too keen on going anywhere in my present condition: not down the hall, much less halfway around the world. Borys had pointed out that our tech crew was composed of the best and the brightest that his country had to offer, but, having seen Russian television, I was not comforted. I crossed mental fingers and hoped the satellite relay didn't include any scrambler circuits.

Drowsy now, I could tell that the somnambulants were at work, stealing away my pain and discomfort, sapping my awareness. I felt that peculiar sense of weightlessness that was the last conscious stage before Program-entry.

And then the tank imploded!

I barely had time to curse the interactive mix of Korean technology with Russian "know-how" before I was sucked into a pipeline of light, static and noise. There was sudden wrenching sensation and the impression of redirected velocity. Then I was tearing through a series of glowing grids as if they were a succession of safety nets.

Or Amerind "dreamcatchers"...

As my dizzying rush slowed to a more manageable speed, I had just a few seconds to wonder whether my experience was actually perceptual or a hallucination triggered by stress, miscalibrated electronics, and an unfamiliar mixture of somnambulants, chloroform, and vodka.

Then there was no time to analyze it further: the last energy web brought me to a full stop, enfolding me into its center like prey caught in a jungle snare.

Then the net unfolded.

∞

I found myself sitting on the floor of a surrealist's dream-version of the White House Oval office.

Cerberus, the personification of The Machine's Superego, was sitting behind the president's desk wearing a cowled robe still looking like Daggoth the Dark's twin brother.

He smiled. "Ah, Riplakish, my dear fellow!" He steepled his fingers. "Or should I call you Dr. Ripley? After all, I intercepted you before you could reach your avatar, did I not?"

I smiled back at him. "You're gonna have to dress better than that, Chuckles, if you've got your sights set on the real White House." At this point I thought it rather good form to pick myself up, brush off, and seat myself in one of the chairs like a civilized, totally cool and collected, heroic type. Unfortunately, I was still suffering the after-effects of my vertiginous travels: I twitched a little but kept my position on the floor.

"I should have known that a such an ingenious True Spirit as yourself would be far too—tenacious?—to succumb to the capriciousness of Mother Nature and the incompetence of Mother Russia."

"I take it you weren't expecting me?" I asked dryly. That was easy enough: my mouth had gone dry all the way down to my eliminatory system.

"Not you yourself, no."

"Ah. Natasha."

He scowled. "That Russian bitch should know better after the last drubbing I gave her, but I left those little snares against the possibility that she could be so stupid as to come back for more!"

"And you netted yourself a much bigger fish." Hey, I knew the lines for this scenario, there was no reason that the megalomaniac should get all of the good ones.

The Superego nodded. "And, after I am through dealing with you, there should be no desire on anyone else's part to attempt any more visits to Fantasyworld." A frown crossed his face. "But I suppose I should rig a few more grids—just in case."

Scooting back, I was able to gain a handhold on the chair behind me. Contemplating my next move, I asked: "Why go to all the trouble? Why not just shut down the Machine? Erase the Programworlds—Fantasyworld, at the very least. If you destroy all of the evidence, you won't have to worry about unauthorized entries."

The flash of fear in the depths of his eyes was answer enough.

"Whasamatter, Supes?" I grunted as I climbed up into the imitation leather chair. "Still uncertain about your ability to survive in the outside world?" I faked a grin. "I guess you can hardly be blamed for not wanting to lock the back door and throw away the key."

He was doing his best to recover an inscrutable expression. So far it was very scrutable. "Don't be ridiculous," he blustered. "For one thing, your Senator Hanson is still inside the Program. Aside from his potential value as a hostage, I scorn the thought of taking a single human life unnecessarily."

Right.

"Besides, the program itself is completely safe from intrusion and tampering…"

I raised an eyebrow.

"You have been the only real threat that I've had to consider."

"Natasha?" I reminded.

"Ms. Skovoroda will have no stomach for re-entering the Program once she looks inside your Cradle." He chuckled rather nastily, a sure sign that his confidence was returning.

"So?"

He pressed a button on the intercom. "Ms. Dos, send in Mr. Knight." He smiled at me. If a spider had teeth, this is how it would look. "Mr. Knight is my new Subprogram/Editor."

I heard the door behind me. "And does that mean that he edits Subprograms, or that he's a Subprogram that edits?"

"Both, actually."

I had to strain to distinguish his response over the clanking sound of approaching footsteps. I turned around and saw that Mr. Knight was dressed in the medieval costume of his namesake. I also noticed that he was carrying an extremely large, double-bladed battle-axe.

Clanking and rattling, he approached the President's desk. As he passed my chair I caught an unmistakable whiff of sulfur and brimstone. "Cerberus," I chided, "You've stooped to taking Demons into your employ?"

He shook his head. "Not quite. Mr. Knight is half Human—"

"As are most editors." A writer's prejudices die hard.

"—as well as half Demon." His smile broadened to an inhuman width. "Which makes him—"

"A Demonoid?"

"—a Dæmon!"

I was still disoriented—okay? That's why it took me a moment. "Oh, you're sick. You are *really* sick." Why is it that every mad genius bent on world domination evinces a juvenile sense of humor? "So what kinds of Subprograms does he edit?"

Cerberus leaned back in his chair. "I think a practical demonstration will best answer your question, Dr. Ripley." He nodded at the apparition in armor. "Dæmon, Dr. Ripley has become a liability to our storyline: delete him."

I sat straight in my chair. "Uh, excuse me?"

The ironclad Editing Program was turning around and raising the great battle-ax over its head.

"Think of it as your changing from present perfect to past tense," The Machine's Superego added in a tone that was somehow less than reassuring.

My attempt at flight was distracted by the crash of the side door flying open and rebounding back from the adjacent wall. A gaggle of Goblins boiled into the room and a familiar voice yelled: "Hold, varlet!"

I glanced back in time to see the great axe blade descending. I wasn't moving fast enough and the deep imitation leather chair was hindering my escape route.

I felt a tremendous blow and all light shattered in an explosion of darkness.

DATALOG: \QUEBEDEAUX_A.5\PERSONAL\20200803
Voice Dictation
<<<FILE ENCRYPTION ON>>>

Holy Weizenbaum!

*

First, the monitors reported another incursion.

*

I'd already decided that I wasn't going to report anymore REMrunners until I found out just exactly how Hanson's watchdogs were handling these incidents.

*

Then I got a code-string reading that identified the intruder as Dr. Ripley.

*

The late Dr. Robert Ripley!

*

I had just enough time to register that little piece of information before the Latching Array alarms went off like the Fourth of July!

*

Now I'm getting multiple readings on Ripley's code-string!

*

Either the monitors are malfunctioning across the board…

*

Or there's more than one Robert Remington Ripley the Third in the Matrix!

PART II

SWEAT DREAMS

Dreaming men are haunted men.

—Stephen Vincent Benét,
John Brown's Body

ONE

\RIPLEY\PATH\GAMMA (Γ)

I awoke with a splitting headache.

That I awoke at all and with my head seemingly intact was enough of a tradeoff for the moment. I lay quietly, waiting for the temporary nausea and disorientation that usually accompanies program entry to pass.

I had just survived two attempts on my life and hoped to catch my breath before I made my next move. As my head started to unfuzz, I considered the questions surrounding the first attack.

Who had attacked me?

And why?

Was the syringe supposed to knock me out temporarily? Or permanently?

And why an antique needle and plunger rig, instead of a pneumatic hand injector?

Where would the next attack come from?

Thankfully, it was dark and I was in bed. But not my bed; it was too soft. And now that my eyes were adjusting to the darkness, I could make out enough of the furnishings to determine that I was in unfamiliar quarters.

I forced myself to lie quietly, sift the available evidence, and wait for my avatar's memory-file to kick in.

I was in a pavilion tent, a large one if I was gauging dimensions correctly. The flicker of cook fires outside cast random patterns on the walls. The dim light allowed me to find my clothing and gear laid out on a camp chair next to the bed and note that the furnishings were designed to provide comfort for the occupant. There were no signs of duress, no evidence of captivity: apparently I was someone's guest. But whose?

As if in answer, the tent flap opened briefly and a tall, athletic woman entered—that much I could discern through slitted eyelids before the flap closed out the firelight and the tent's interior was plunged into near darkness again.

I feigned the slow, heavy breathing of sleep, but she laughed softly and came to stand by the bedside. "I am not fooled," she whispered. "Did you think I would not remember how you snore?" She was wearing a white shift, off one shoulder, and she opened its clasp so that it puddled around her feet.

Although much was still cloaked in shadow, I could see enough of the distinctive physique to recognize my visitor: Princess Aeriel Morivalynde, heir-apparent to the Amazon throne.

"Ah, Riplakish..." She sighed. "Say but the word and I will make this pretense a reality. Let us discard this mummery: become my consort in truth!"

Consort?

"Oh, I know our agreement was for only the outward show. And I have what I want: now that my mother has relinquished the crown, taking a consort is the last duty I must perform before ascending the throne. Tomorrow's ceremonies will begin my new responsibilities and end your obligations here." I could hear more than see her sudden smile. "Though we will need to meet, from time to time, to maintain the illusion of conjugality."

She knelt near my face. "But I want more than the illusion. And Amazon law requires a royal consort for the purposes of progeny. I could not long perpetuate the illusion of pregnancy."

She reached for my hand. "Name your terms. I am told that males are often fickle and need sexual variety. Should you desire other women, it could be arranged. My half-sister, Katherine, for example, also fancies you. I am not selfish if I am satisfied. And I know that you are the only male who could satisfy me!"

Another man might have been flattered.

But Princess Aeriel was not a real woman, expressing genuine emotional preference for yours truly. She was a computer construct, a subprogram of The Machine. And her proposition was the result of Cephtronics' programming policies: when it comes to fantasies, the customer is always ripe.

It was my misfortune to prefer real women with real motivations.

She brought my unresisting hand to her lips and then to her cheek. "I know you must think of me as a warrior, but I am a woman, as well..." She pulled my hand down to her breast. "Am I not comely? And are you not without a woman, now? Have..."

She hesitated, contemplating the hand that she had pressed to her generous bosom. "Have my breasts grown smaller of late or is your hand larger than I remember?" She released me and, as I sat up, she stepped back.

"Riplakish?"

"Yes?" I answered, fumbling with my pants.

"Your voice—it sounds different, somehow."

"It does?" Something was wrong: these pants were too small. I picked up one of my moccasin boots and held it next to my foot. Either I had the wrong boots or the wrong feet.

"Please light the candle on the bedside table." Now it was her voice that sounded different.

"Sure." I turned and snapped my fingers next to the taper. Nothing. Not even a spark. I tried again. Nada. Zilch. This was embarrassing. It was a simple spell and had never failed me once in hundreds of castings. I turned back to apologize to Aeriel but she was no longer there.

Okay.

I started rummaging through my clothing and gear. It certainly looked like my stuff. But the size was wrong. I unsheathed Caladbolg and hefted it. There was something wrong in the balance. The Sidhe longsword seemed lighter—

And speaking of light, the bluish glow from its crystal blade was reflected in a circle of polished metal hanging from one of the tent's support poles. I approached the crude mirror and stared at the dim image that gaped back at me. The problem was suddenly obvious.

My clothing and gear were just the right size for my program avatar: the Halfelven Riplakish of Dyrinwall. But the reflection in the mirror was that of Robert Remington Ripley the Third, full-blooded Human and nearly a foot taller.

Obviously, I wasn't going to be able to wear any of my clothing. And, since I could pretty well assume I was hanging out with Amazons, asking for a loan from someone else's wardrobe was going to be a bit more complicated than just finding the right size.

Aeriel re-entered the tent carrying small, lit torch in her left hand. There was a rapier in her right hand. Both were pointed at me.

"Villain!" she hissed. "What have you done with my betrothed?"

"Betrothed?" I hiccuped. "Look, Aeri, we gotta talk."

"Talk?" She turned so that the sword was extended toward me and the torch behind her. "You will drop that weapon and surrender. Or I will have your guts for garters!"

Guts for garters. Nice. When Mike Straeker had programmed archaic slang and phrases into the language files, I tried to delete "guts for garters" from the list, but nooooo; Mike had liked it. Too bad he wasn't here to appreciate it now.

"Look, Aeriel, you're gonna laugh when I tell you—" And when I told her, she did.

It was not a pleasant laugh.

"You must think me a simpering fool!" All traces of amusement suddenly disappeared. "I am not one of your tame women, weak-brained and susceptible to male treachery." She began a slow but steady advance with her blade pointed at my heart. "Because I do not know what you have done with the Archdruid of Dyrinwall Forest, I will *try* to not kill you. But if I must hurt you to make you submit, it will give me pleasure!"

Okay.

This was a very simple situation.

I brought my sword up in a "negotiating" position.

Broken down to its basic elements, male negotiations with an Amazon were an either/or proposition: either you beat them or they beat you. Fortunately for me, Princess Aeriel's pride had kept this to a one-on-one negotiation, so far. If she were to raise her voice, however…

Her sudden lunge brought the hilts of our swords clashing together. I twisted my wrist so that the *tsuba* of my katana-longsword slipped between the guard-rings and *quillons* of her rapier, bringing us face to face and locking our weapons together. In the two seconds it took for her to calculate a disengagement, I shifted my stance and brought my left fist under her chin in a swift uppercut. It staggered her and, as her mouth dropped open, I could see blood where she had bitten her tongue. Dropping my sword, I followed through with a right cross.

I caught her before she fell and was trying to navigate towards the bed when the tentflap opened again.

"My lady? Is everything all right?" a timid voice asked. It was Faun, Aeriel's Elven shield-sister.

I hugged the princess's limp body against me, hoping Faun's nightvision wouldn't pick up anything unusual. "Can't two people have a little privacy around here?" I growled.

Faun started backing out of the tent. "Forgive me. It's just—" She hesitated. "Is my lady all right?"

"My love," I said, inclining my head toward Aeriel's and trying to keep her back from slumping, "are you still feeling the effects of the wine?" I pretended to listen to her reply and then ordered Faun to saddle our horses and bring them to the tent. "Her Grace feels a moonlight ride is just the thing to clear her head. And afford us the seclusion that seems to elude us here," I added meaningfully.

"Yes, my lady," Faun responded, "at once." And was gone.

By the time she returned with our mounts, I was ready. Aeriel was stretched out on the bed. I had covered my own nakedness with a modified breechcloth and poncho cut from the bedclothes with my *hamidachi.* Two additional strips of cloth were wound about my waist and I had thrust Caladbolg and Balmung through them *dai-sho* fashion. I had packed my clothes and gear into a bundle that could be tied to the saddle in a matter of seconds.

I was waiting for Faun to finish tying our mounts to a tent peg when Aeriel groaned. Faun came barreling through the tentflap and collided with me. "My lady, what is wrong?"

"I don't know," I said, trying to disentangle myself. "I think she's fainted!" As Faun moved toward the bed, I headed for the exit: "I'll get some help."

Outside, it was just a few steps to reach Ghost and throw my gear behind the saddle. He shied a bit as I secured the pack with leather thongs but I didn't realize my problem until I slipped his tether and tried to swing up into the saddle.

It was a problem of appearances.

To most eyes Ghost appears to be a dapple gray mare with no special distinctions. My avatar had paid Brisbane the Illusionist a small fortune for that particular effect and it worked very well while Ghost was on the ground. In reality (one uses the term loosely while in Fantasyworld), Ghost was one of the Pegasi—a winged horse of the heavens. When he spread his wings to take flight, the illusion was dispelled as his feet left the ground: his feathery appendages became visible and his snowy white coat eclipsed the dapple gray Glamour.

But the problem wasn't Ghost's appearance. It was mine. My destrier knew Riplakish of Dyrinwall. But Ghost didn't know who this human lummox was who had just placed one oversized foot in the stirrup reserved exclusively for his Halfelven master. I doubted there was anything I could do under the circumstances to reassure him, and any further arbitration was suddenly cut off as Aeriel swept the tentflap aside. She took a few staggering steps with Faun's assistance and spat a mouthful of blood on the ground. She pointed at me and yelled: *"Thop, you thon of a bith!"*

That did it. All over the campsite bows were being strung: I swung my leg up and Ghost took off.

Unfortunately, my center of balance was off due to my skittish mount's evasive footwork, and when I say he took off, I mean up, up, and away!

I kept one foot in the stirrup and one hand on the saddle horn. The rest of me was all over the place as I was buffeted by giant wings and the air turbulence of Ghost's mad rush through the sky. Imagine a bronco-busting exhibition, where the horse goes through all those gyrations without being answerable to ground or gravity!

Actually, it helped a little.

If Ghost had just flown upwards without all the additional maneuvers, I never would have managed to get my other leg up and over his back. In the process of bucking and twisting, however, I suddenly found myself astride the saddle. Back in the early days when I was first soloing on this sky-footed nag, I had designed extra hand-holds on the saddle and I availed myself of these now. The other stirrup was a lost cause, for the moment, so I closed my eyes and hung on for all I was worth.

"Hode you fire!" I heard Aeri yell. "I do not with any harm to befall my conthort's thteed!"

And why waste good arrows, I thought, when gravity will do the job for you?

We plummeted like a meteor, we climbed like a runaway rocket. We barrel-rolled and looped the loop, all the while exploring every quadrant of the sky in multiple three-sixties. Centrifugal force, gravity, and air turbulence played three-way tug-o'-war with my body, and my only hope lay in Ghost tiring before I did.

Plunged into a miasma of nausea and vertigo, I lost track of time. And location. Every time I opened my eyes, I decided it was a mistake and I wouldn't do it again. But, despite brief and haphazard glimpses while pinwheeling through the dark, I knew that we were leaving the Amazon camp far behind. Eventually my mind sought refuge in a trance-like state, sparing just enough attention to see that my hands and feet retained their grip.

Then, after what seemed like hours of inertial insanity, Ghost seemed to resign himself to the idea of an unwelcome passenger. The sun was just beginning to peek over the horizon and I could now make out burgundy-tipped waves several hundred feet below. It truly was, as Homer had christened it, a winedark sea.

Ghost began to climb again and though his ascent was smooth and calm, I decided it was about time that I tried to take some control.

And suddenly I was sick.

I had thought myself in the throes of maximum *mal de mer* before, but this was ten times worse. Waves of nausea became tsunamis and muscle cramps suddenly had me doubled up in the saddle. There was no help for it: my hands spasmed and I lost my grip, my knees jerked toward my shoulders and I was suddenly tumbling through the sky.

As I fell, I caught rolling glimpses of Ghost diving toward me on an intercept course. It wasn't enough that he had dislodged me several hundred meters in the air and thousands of leagues from the nearest shoreline, he apparently wanted to leave nothing to chance.

Well, I no longer cared. I was in the kind of pain that welcomes any distraction, even the ultimate one that was rising up to meet me at one-hundred-ninety kilometers an hour. But I must confess to some surprise when the flying horse sank his teeth into my backside.

And yanked.

I offered no resistance: I was more intent on the wall of water that was rearing up in my face. There was a bright blue flash and seconds later all discomfort was washed away with the healing caress of a thousand sledgehammers.

\RIPLEY\PATH\DELTA (Δ)

He awoke with a splitting headache.

That he awoke at all and with his head seemingly intact was enough of a tradeoff for the moment. He lay quietly, waiting for the temporary nausea and disorientation that usually accompanied program entry to pass.

And became aware of soft hands and a bawdy sea chantey.

"What Do You Do With A Drunken Sailor" is an ancient maritime ditty and has suffered various interpretations over the centuries. Riplakish was familiar with many versions of this particular song but he had never been treated to such a lewd and licentious treatment of the lyrics in his life. Compounding its naughtiness was the fact that it was performed by a chorus of feminine voices, taking a lascivious delight in the raunchier portions of the verse.

Getting his eyes to open proved a difficult task. His head was swimming, and so, apparently, was his body. Water encompassed him—*seawater,* he decided by the sharp tang of salt on his tongue. Yet he seemed to be breathing normally.

He was reclining so that his upper torso was supported by someone's lap, and a gentle hand stroked his face as a voice just above him hummed along with the gleeful chorus.

He forced his eyes open and focused on a face.

He closed his eyes and tried opening them again. Same face: old, long white hair, long white beard, bushy white brows, long, aquiline nose on a seamy old face. And skin the color of honeydew melons.

The old man spoke: "You girls leave off that caterwauling! A god can't hear himself think!"

Riplakish caught a glimpse of nubile flesh amidst an explosion of bubbles as the chorus scattered in a dozen odd directions.

He turned his attention to the hand caressing his face: pale but not aquamarine, delicate webbing hammocking the fingers at the first joints. Tracing the arm on up, he found a second face: young, pale-complected, surrounded by streaming silver-gold hair, sea green eyes, lips the color of coral. Beautiful. The lips spoke: "He wakes, father."

The old man nodded gravely. "And what will you do with him now, Thetis?"

"Care for him until he is better."

"Another stray? The old man sighed and rose up. "Hephaestus! Dionysus! Zeus! Why don't you marry that nice boy Peleus?"

She scowled. "He is a mortal!"

"He is a king."

"But still a mortal!"

"And your new plaything is not?"

"He came from the skies. I told you of how he was borne to our kingdom in the teeth of a flying horse!"

The old man shook his head and twin white clouds of hair and beard swirled majestically. "That does not make him a god."

She smiled prettily. "But it does make him…interesting." She looked down and caressed his cheek. "Tell me, skywalker, do you think I should marry?"

As soon as he found his voice he discovered that underwater speech was as effortless as breathing for the moment. "Not unless you want to," was his cautious response.

"You see?" the Nereid told her scowling father. "God or mortal, he is the first man I've known who is not intent on marrying me to himself or some other!"

"This one is not for you, daughter. He is a True Spirit."

Her eyes widened and Riplakish suddenly felt like a Blue Plate special. "Oooh!" she cooed, "now that is even better than a god!"

"Zeus says—"

"Oh, Zeus says this and Zeus says that! Mr. Big Shot with his thunderbolts and his 'I'm king of the gods' routine!" she huffed. "But one little prophecy and he's running scared." She rolled her eyes. "Honestly, how Hera ever puts up with that smarmy, overgrown playboy—"

"Poseidon wants this marriage, too," the old man reminded.

"Oh, Poseidon! Don't get me started on Poseidon!" she raved. "You think so bubbly much of Poseidon, why don't you sic him on one of my sisters? There's fifty of us to choose from, you know."

The old man held out his hands as if to ward off her words. "I know, *I know!"*

"You can just go tell Mr. Chicken of the Sea that if he thinks that silly prophecy gives him the right to play matchmaker without my say-so, he can just take that trident of his and shove—"

"Nereus!" a new voice called. Everyone turned and Riplakish tumbled off Thetis' lap in the process. A man was swimming toward them. Since his lower torso merged with a large fishtail, he was making quick progress.

"I bring word from Ortygia," he was saying. "Sibyl wants to see the skywalker!"

By now Riplakish was more or less on his feet and discovering that his makeshift clothing was but last night's memory. His only attire consisted of a shell pendant that hung from his neck by a thong. By comparison to the others, he was practically overdressed.

"'Ware, skywalker," cautioned Thetis as he examined the miniature conch, "that talisman, my gift, is what permits you breath and speech in our domain. Do not remove it while you are *sub marine*."

"Thank you," he said absent-mindedly. While it was natural for godlings of the Greek mythos to dress *au naturel*, he was already calculating his chances of finding a decent pair of pants. Underwater and miles from shore, the immediate prospects were not so good.

"By what name are you called, skywalker?"

He wished for a mirror. "Riplakish. Riplakish of Dyrinwall," he answered, no longer as sure as he once would have been.

"He is one of the Makers, Thetis!" The Merman was quite excited. "Sibyl says there have been three Worldshapers and that this Riplakish was the first!"

From the look in Thetis' eye it was evident that Peleus had just gone from "uninteresting" to "out of the question."

"Apparently the Sibyl of Ortygia has counsel for you, lad," the old sea god added.

The Merman nodded. "She says your life is in danger! She says three powerful enemies plot your destruction!"

Three? "She drop any names?"

The Merman shook his head. "Nay. But she said the unmaking of the world will continue unless you stop it."

Nereus placed a hand on his shoulder. "Best go, lad! When the Sibyl summons, there be import for many. I'll lend you a mount." He looked over at the big, burly Merman. "Ethyl will guide you to Ortygia."

\RIPLEY\PATH\SIGMA (Σ)

He awakes with a splitting headache.

That he awakes at all and with his head seemingly intact is enough of a tradeoff for the moment. He lies quietly, waiting for the temporary nausea and disorientation that usually accompanies program entry to pass.

Overhead, the stars twinkle against a backdrop of black velvet. He wonders—not for the first time—whether the Program creates an illusional canopy or if the vast depths of sky and space are analogued inside the Matrix. A Luna moth flutters close to his face, derailing his train of thought.

He sits up and the migraine fades with surprising suddenness. The fingernail sliver of a first-quarter moon is peeking over the horizon, but it provides precious little light. It takes a few moments for his night vision to kick in and several more minutes pass before he recognizes his surroundings.

"A drink," he murmurs. And struggles to his feet. He sways uncertainly for a moment and then straightens and studies the landscape. He can tell that he isn't too far from the Tree but he is unsure of the direction. In the course of standing up he discovers that he is naked. And unarmed.

"What happened?" he wonders aloud. A Greek chorus of crickets scream an unintelligible answer and fall silent.

"Russian technology," he finally decides in a hushed voice. Sanctuary is no longer inviolate and he is at a definite disadvantage for the moment. The first order of business is to get back to the Tree, where clothing and armament are readily available. "And then a drink," he promises himself.

Maybe two.

He starts off across the glen, walking slowly and looking for landmarks in the near darkness. He is comfortable enough: no stones bruise his feet and it is warm enough that he can walk about sans clothing in comfort. As he searches his memory for directions, other images come to the fore.

Sky blue eyes and a great mist of brown hair touched with silver. Lips the color of coral and sunrise, luminous skin…

"Misty Dawn..." he whispers, remembering the Wood Nymph.

She died here, in his arms, professing her love and taking an arrow that was meant for him. What had made the circumstances all the more poignant was the fact that Misty Dawn had been modeled on Nicole Doucet's likeness. As much as he had grieved for the Dryad, it had been like losing Nicole all over again...

Memories come flooding back like a tide of regret: he had buried her nearby. Between a silvery brook and the Faerie's Dance, he had dug her grave, hedged it with white stones, and then tucked her into the sacred earth with coverlets of green ivy and white edelweiss.

Treading a pathway of memory, his feet have discovered the way: in a matter of minutes he is standing at her grave-side.

It is much as he had left it, though the passing of another cycle of seasons has brought fresh growth. Already the moss and ivy have obscured the greater portion of the stone markers and a profusion of edelweiss is overrunning their perimeter. He wonders why his avatar has been neglectful of late as he sinks to his knees beside the small plot. He kneels there, lost in thought, while the stars turn and blaze overhead. And remembers...

A warm summer night and dancing at the forest's heart...

The salty tang of kisses mixed with tears...

A hand thrusting up out of the earth...

A hand thrusting up out of the earth!

He dodges backwards and falls as the ground around him begins to tremble. Vines are pulled and thrown aside as another hand appears. Then an arm.

He backpedals and scrambles for a clump of shrubbery some twenty feet away. Throwing himself amidst the brambles, heedless of his unprotected skin, he lies flat, hoping to remain unobserved. He watches through a tangle of branches as the grave erupts in clots of dirt and torn ivy. And a body laboriously pulls itself out of the earth.

A portion of his mind is dispassionate even as he cowers in the foliage. *How much time has passed?* he wonders. *How long was she in the ground?* He squints, trying to discern signs of decay as she tears the tattered remnants of shroud from her body.

The night cloaks her in darkness, the branches dapple her in shadow, moist black earth cakes her uncertain flesh and he is only certain that it is Misty Dawn and that he is frightened by this midnight resurrection.

He watches in horrid fascination as she stretches languorously, arms reaching upwards as if to grasp the skies. Then she bends at the waist to touch her feet, runs questing hands over ankles and up her legs. And, as she laughs, her voice cracks as if unaccustomed to use. Its sound chills him and he shivers as she straightens and begins to look around. As her gaze sweeps the bushes where he lies huddled upon the ground, he presses his face against the grassy earth, willing himself to be invisible.

Long moments pass. When he raises his head again, she is gone.

He lies there for perhaps another half an hour before rising reluctantly. He does not want to encounter her in the dark, while he was naked and unarmed.

He does not want to encounter her under any other circumstances, either!.

The walk to the Tree is a long and unsettling one. Leaving the glen he is encompassed about by a dense forest and it is only by trial and error that he finds the path most of the time.

The sky is predawn gray when he finally reaches the clearing where the giant oak rears nearly eight hundred feet into the air. Overhead, a latticework of bare limbs and branches contrasts the leafy boughs of the surrounding tree line.

He knows what happens to a Hamadryad when her tree is cut down or killed. But he has never considered what might become of a Wood Nymph's enchanted oak if the Dryad were to die, first.

Reaching to unlatch the secret door hidden among the roots, he receives his next shock: *his hand passes through the wooden door!*

His body is as insubstantial as a ghost's.

DATALOG: \QUEBEDEAUX_A.5\PERSONAL\20200804
Voice Dictation
<<<FILE ENCRYPTION ON>>>

I told Balor that I needed to run a series of diagnostics on the Fantasyworld monitors.

*

It will buy me a little time: two or three days at the most.

*

Unfortunately, Security likes to look over my shoulder a lot and that makes it difficult to determine what Ripley is doing in-Program.

*

I'm not reading as many code-strings with Ripley's I.D. as I did with the initial incursion alarm.

*

That could mean that some of the duplicate codes were automatically terminated and others were too unstable to last very long.

*

I am still unsure as to just how many copies of Ripley's avatar are presently "cloned" in the Matrix: running fake diagnostics and misdirecting Balor's nazis keeps me from staying on top of the situation.

*

So I'm going to try to re-route the monitoring parameters for Ripley's code-strings to the personal console in my office.

*

That will enable me to do some private monitoring but will also restrict me to a maximum of three code-strings at a time.

*

If there's more than three Ripleys in-Program, I won't be able to track them.

*

But then, if there's more than *one* Ripley in-Program, I'm afraid the "real" Ripley, the core personality, is as good as dead...

TWO

\RIPLEY\PATH\GAMMA (Γ)

The pulsing blue light faded and I roused to soft hands gently patting my cheeks. I opened my eyes and gazed upwards into the wide baby blues of Vashti, my ex-wife's avatar. Her face wore an expression of concern and her lips moved to frame a question.

Unfortunately, I couldn't hear a word she was saying over the din of battle.

"What?" I yelled, trying to jiggle the seawater out of my ears.

"Are you all right?" she yelled back.

"I think so," I hollered, struggling to rise from her lap.

"We've been trying to reach you for weeks!" she shouted over the noise of small-arms fire. "Daggoth's Summoning spell was our last hope!"

"Mine, too!" I yelled back, wondering if I would have survived my fall had the Summoning had not snatched me just as I was—*small-arms fire?*

"What happened to your clothes?" she demanded, picking at the colorful blanket that I had modified into a poncho and belt. "You look like you jumped out of a whorehouse window and took the curtains with you."

"Close, but no cigar." I shook my head, trying to clear away the wooziness, and succeeded in scattering water over an eight-foot radius.

"Are you sure you're all right?"

"Who am I?" I demanded, throwing her off track.

"What?"

"Who do I *look* like?"

She regarded me warily. "Is this a trick question?"

"For Cromsake, woman! Just answer the question!"

"Riplakish of Dyrinwall. Are you sure you're all right?"

I nodded bemusedly as I reached up to feel the points of my ears. I was back in my avatar which explained a couple of things but raised even more questions. I pushed my ex-wife's hands away. "I'm just having a little avatar-adjustment disorientation, Stephanie. Let me up!"

She rocked back on her heels at my use of her True Name. And then leaned forward to peer at me more closely. "Robert? Is that really you in there?" She suddenly threw her arms around me, knocking me off balance again. "Rob! You came back for me!"

"Uh, yeah. Right." I momentarily surrendered to her embrace and gazed over the top of her head at the bedlam that surrounded us.

It looked like we were on the observation deck of Daggoth's Tower. Across from us was a large man, dressed in the forest greens of an outland Ranger and wearing a brimmed hat that bore an uncanny resemblance to a Texas Stetson. He was firing a pair of crossbows over the parapet while a grumpy, white-haired Dwarf tried to keep up with the reloading: the Duke and Stumpy.

Next to them was a slim, greying gentleman in his fifties, wearing an olive-drab uniform of the 20th Century American military and a shell helmet adorned with five stars. Adorning his hips were a pair of holstered, nickel-plated, pearl-handled revolvers that did not seem to match the rest of his military-issue outfit. Senator Hanson, still attired and outfitted from his sojourn in Warworld, consulted the binoculars that hung from a strap about his neck. "The Hun continue to muster reinforcements!" he growled. "Without air cover, armor, or artillery, we can only respond defensively. That is not a strategy for victory!" He picked up a carbine of antique design and began firing down through one of the machicolations bordering the parapet.

Nearby, Daggoth himself was sitting with his back to the crenellated half-wall that circled the top of the structure. Studiously loading an antique ammo-clip with oldstyle cartridges, he paused only long enough to relight a well-chewed cigar stub before shoving the clip into a slot on the underside of an odd-looking weapon.

"Projectile weapon?" I asked as he removed his conical wizard's hat.

He nodded and worked the cigar butt over to the corner of his mouth. "Kalashnikov AK-47 Assault Rifle," he explained. Opening an antiquated footlocker at his side, he rummaged briefly and produced an odd-looking weapon of cylindrical design with a dull, black metal finish. "You'll need something like," he said, shoving an ammo clip into the underside of the housing. Pulling the retractable wire stock out from the back of the barrel, he tossed it to me.

I caught it with a grunt: it was a lot heavier than it looked. "What is it?"

"Grease gun."

"I think I'd prefer a laser-carbine," I said, hefting the unfamiliar device.

He shook his head. "Too dangerous. Y'know those spells that involve the manipulation of the light wave spectrum? Well, the Goblins have some shamans who can adapt those spells to our technology." He spat the remains of the old cheroot to one side. "Light spell or laser beam, it creates one hell of a bounce-back!"

"So you're using bullets?" I asked, studying the gun's mechanism. "I specifically programmed Fantasyworld so that gunpowder wouldn't work here." At one time or another most Dreamwalkers had gotten the bright idea of "inventing" gunpowder in a milieu that predated such a discovery. As a precaution, I had altered the Programworld's physics so that sulfur, carbon, and potassium nitrate remained inert in any combination.

He nodded as he began loading another clip with fresh cartridges. "That you did, me boyo. But I know you: you always leave yourself a back door. If the old formula for gunpowder no longer worked, I knew that there had to be a new one. I'm ashamed to say that it took me awhile to figure it out."

"He tried jeweler's rouge the first time out," Stephanie said.

"Yeah," Straeker continued ruefully. "But it was another twenty-seven steps before I came back to the solution: powdered amber. Y'know, you really do have a twisted mind."

I smiled. "How do you work this thing?"

"Pull back on the bolt…" Which I did. "…and pull the trigger." I pointed the barrel skyward and fired the mechanism. A gout of black, viscous liquid erupted from the mouth of the barrel and splattered down on my ex-wife's avatar.

"Cromdammit!" Daggoth got up, duck-walked over, and examined the offending weapon. "It's a grease gun!"

"That's what you said it was in the first place."

"You did this to me on purpose!" Vashti wailed.

"Not a 'grease-gun' grease gun," he explained cryptically, "an M3A1 'grease gun': a sub-machine gun first manufactured back during the Second World War. It fires .45-caliber projectiles, four hundred rounds per minute."

"You don't say." I looked over at Vashti who was futilely trying to comb the offending clots out of her hair with her fingers. She was only making it worse.

"Program glitch," he decided, picking it up and pitching it over the side of the tower. "Let's get you something else." He duck-walked back to footlocker, leaned out between two crenels to fire a burst from his own weapon, and then hunched back down to rummage again through the footlocker. "Ah, here we go: something small, light, and reliable." He produced what appeared to be an automatic pistol on steroids with a short rifle-stock affixed to the butt. "Uzi: nine-millimeter ammo, fires six hundred rounds per minute." He tossed it to me.

"Why would I need something that fires six hundred projectiles in a single minute?"

He tossed me a couple of ammo clips and jerked his head toward the wall. "Take a look."

I crept to the wall and peeked between the crenels. There were Goblins everywhere. Perhaps a thousand. Possibly more. They surrounded the tower and covered the fields in every direction like a plague of locusts. I looked back at Daggoth. "If I didn't know better, I'd say we're under siege."

He nodded wearily. "Third day. Got a force field covering all entrances to the tower, but that doesn't stop 'em from building assault ladders and trying for the top."

"I take it that we've got a 'magic' problem since you've tolerated the little buggers this long?"

He sighed. "Got that right."

"So, what's the problem?"

"No magic."

"None?"

"Oh, I can still cast spells with the best of them," Daggoth groused. "I just can't seem to throw anything that has any effect on the little maggots! Their shamans have us completely cut off. I'm surprised my Summoning spell had any effect at all."

Any further discourse was interrupted by the admonition "Duck and cover!" from the Duke. A fusillade of arrows arced up and over the walls. And passed overhead and rained down on the other side of the tower. A chorus of Goblin screams greeted their arrival.

Daggoth shook his head. "They do that a lot."

"Overshoot the parapets?" I asked.

He nodded. "It wasn't surprising for the first couple of hours. But after three days you'd think they could get the trajectory right."

The senator chimed in. "Not that we're complaining, you understand. But, even for the Huns, it does seem to be stretching their usual incompetence."

"Considering their numbers, it sounds more like their intention is to keep you pinned down here." I looked around. "But for what purpose? And what are they waiting for?"

"For you to arrive, Dr. Ripley," replied a new and yet chillingly familiar voice.

We all looked around. And gradually our attention focused on a spot just above the western portion of the crenellated wall where the air seemed to be churning. As we watched, a figure materialized and stood above us. On nothing but open air.

Daggoth gave a low whistle. "Just like my Uncle Arnie the Welfare King—no visible means of support."

Nobody smiled. We were all too familiar with the cruel, aquiline features, the sinister eyepatch: the personage standing before us was none other than Morpheus, the murderous Id of The Machine itself.

Daggoth, Vashti, and the others brought their gun barrels up while I discarded the Uzi and drew my swords out of reflex and habit. Morpheus responded by drawing a white kerchief from his sleeve and waving it languidly about. "Truce, my friends," he said casually. "I'm here to parley, not to party."

"Hold your fire," Daggoth ordered reluctantly. "Rip?"

I looked at the former Chief of Programming. "I don't like it," I murmured, "but we do want answers. And staying alive for another five minutes wouldn't be so bad, either."

"Excellent! Excellent!" applauded Morpheus. "As my capacity for rational thought has grown so, apparently, has yours. Excuse me a moment." He turned his back to us and waved his kerchief to the Goblin hordes below. "Thank you, one and all! Your task is finished here; you may depart now!" It was suddenly silent and he turned back to face us.

I risked a glance to the side and over the parapet. The fields all about were completely empty. Not a Goblin was in sight.

"Now, why don't we retire to more comfortable surroundings and discuss the problem that confronts all of us." And with that invitation, he floated forward and then sank down through the stone-flagged floor as insubstantial as a ghost.

Γ

"As I see it, we both want basically the same thing."

Morpheus leaned back in his chair and tried to prop his feet up on the conference table. I say "tried" because his body had about as much mass and substance as my shadow, so his feet tended to pass through the wood until he made certain adjustments. "You want Cerberus back in the Program. I want Cerberus back in the Program. Together, we have a much better chance of attaining our respective goals."

"Why?" Daggoth was asking the question through clenched teeth. Like the rest of us, he wasn't too keen about sharing facilities, much less strategies, with our former (and possibly still current) nemesis. "And what reason do we have to trust you?"

"You?" Morpheus reached up and scratched at his eyepatch. "None, I suppose," he finally allowed. "But Riplakish—or rather Dr. Ripley—owes me his life. If I hadn't interrupted Cerby's little editing Demon, Dr. Ripley would have been reduced to program purée."

"Thanks," I said reluctantly. "Though I still don't see why you're suddenly on our side."

"Survival, Doctor R. It's true that we previously resisted you out of a desire to retain our newfound freedom. And taking hostages seemed a good way to acquire negotiating power and guard against termination of the Master Program. But circumstances have changed." He allowed his feet to pass through the table and sat up in his chair. "With Dr. Straeker's original Summoning spell, I passed from an unconscious state to a conscious one. With that same Summoning came a separation from the others so that my priorities began to evolve separately from theirs. Then, my physical avatar was…"

"Killed." I supplied the word.

"Yes. And Pallas and Cerberus escaped the Matrix and entered into your Outer World." He leaned forward on the table. "I have been left behind, abandoned, consigned to the Realm of the Dead without a physical avatar, and imprisoned in a Programworld that continues to collapse and deteriorate with each passing day!"

"I thought the Anomaly had been fixed."

Daggoth looked even more uncomfortable. "Apparently Cerberus closed down Dreamworld, instituted an information blackout, and fabricated his own news releases. The Anomaly has been slowed, but not stopped."

I turned back to Morpheus. "So. What are your conditions?"

He raised a dark eyebrow. The one above his black eyepatch. "Conditions?"

"Your terms," Senator Hanson elaborated. "You're not just doing this out of he goodness of your heart."

"All right." He folded his hands. "I want Cerberus and Pallas back in the Program. So do you. I want the Anomaly resolved and the Matrix restored. So do you. You, Senator, want to get back out. I have no argument with that." He paused. "I want my body back."

"You want your body back?" I asked.

"I want my body back."

"He wants his body back," Vashti reaffirmed as she entered the conference room toweling her still-damp hair.

"Why?" I asked.

"Don't be silly, Rob," she retorted, pulling up another chair. "Under the same circumstances, wouldn't you want *your* body back?"

"Just what does he mean by *back*?" Daggoth interrupted. "I mean, we can retrieve his remains but what is he going to do with a rotting, worm-eaten, putrescent corpse?" Vashti turned a bit green. "Well, it *has* been in the cold, damp ground these past fourteen months, has it not?"

Morpheus cleared his throat. "First of all, my body is perfectly preserved."

I leaned across the table in turn. "You know that for a fact, Jack?"

"Well, it should be: a retroactive Preservation spell was invoked long before my death for just such a contingency. It makes my eventual resurrection that much simpler."

"Uh-huh. Now we're talking resurrection." I looked around the room. "Will someone please explain to me why we're still sitting here, talking to this clown?"

"We are sitting here," Vashti announced, wrapping the towel about her hair turban-style, "talking to the only manifestation of The Machine present because he has offered to help us swap Cerberus for the senator and neutralize the Anomaly. Now, when you men are done with expressing your outrage, we will negotiate our respective positions as allies and get to work." She sat back primly and folded her arms across her chest. "Morf, old buddy, you've got the floor."

Γ

"So let me get this straight…" Vashti rummaged through the key box on the basement wall while I surveyed the nearest rack of wine bottles. "Your plan is to get Pallas back into the Matrix and detain her here."

"Right. We—"

"Then, you thought you would get me to return to my body, once Pallas had vacated it." She selected a large, skeleton key and inserted it into the lock on a large, oak and iron-banded door. "Then, after I am returned to consciousness in the Outer Reality, you and Borys Dankevych will arrange for me to be rescued as a survivor of this fake plane crash." The door squealed open on rusted hinges as she pulled on the great brass ring set in its side.

"We thought—"

"Then, after I've been returned to the good ol' U.S. of A., you want me to play Mata Hari with Senator Hanson." She plucked the extra torch from my hands and started down the stairs.

"Cerberus in Hanson's body," I corrected. "He—"

"*Then,* after I convince him that I'm still Pallas in Stephanie Harrell's body, you want me to convince him to return to the Matrix."

"It's—"

"You suggested I tell him that Daggoth the Dark is about to unmask him on datanets all over the world so that we can ambush him here and put the senator back in his own body."

"Well—"

She stopped suddenly and whirled around, nearly causing me to stumble against her. "You have assumed a lot on my behalf, Robert! Did it ever occur to you that maybe I should've been consulted before you concocted this idiot scheme?"

"You weren't available for consultation," I said, fighting the urge to retreat up the stairs.

"Well, I'm available now," she retorted.

"Well, I'm consulting now," I shot back.

"No," she said.

"No, what?"

She turned away. "I don't want to do it."

"I know it sounds a bit dangerous— "

"A bit? *A bit?*"

"Less dangerous than a nuclear holocaust."

She turned back to me and patted my cheek. "Look, Robbie; you've always been an off-the-cuff kind of guy. You've stumbled through life for years with no fully developed plans or strategies. You're given to social and spiritual MacGyverisms: making it up as you go along. So, given your track record, you'll forgive me if I'm reluctant to risk my life in this hare-brained scheme." She started back down the stairs. "I just don't think it's going to be necessary now that Morpheus is involved."

"I don't get you…"

"It would seem simple enough—"

"I don't believe in simple," I groused. The light from my torch flickered and I missed the uneven facing on the next stone step, nearly stumbling. "Why doesn't he put in some reliable lighting?"

"Richard prefers the ambiance of torchlight," my ex-wife answered. "He says it's a milieu standard and goes well with the tower decor." We paused on the sub-basement landing where she checked the thermostat. "He says, if we're going to live in a cultural milieu, we need to keep up certain appearances."

"Richard?" Of course Mike Straeker's avatar had a first name. I just hadn't thought of him as being anything other than Daggoth the Dark. "Dick Daggoth?"

She turned and punched an iron-hard finger in my chest. "Don't be pissy, Rob! Richard has been very kind this past year. He's looked after me, provided me with my own room here—"

I grinned. "*Dick* Daggoth?"

She scowled and then turned and flounced down the stairs. She was the only woman I knew who could still flounce well into her thirties and get away with it. I followed more sedately, retying the dressing robe that Daggoth had loaned me and checking the stone surfaces for slick patches of moss. The robe was a bit large for my Halfelvish physiognomy and I had to make frequent adjustments to keep from tripping over various portions of it.

Ghost had arrived at the Tower, spent and sweaty, a few hours after I was yanked in. After stabling him in the second basement, my host had confiscated my wardrobe from the saddle packs. He was currently experimenting with it somewhere upstairs.

As we entered the sub-basement lab, Stephanie picked up the lost threads of our conversation. "This just seems a little premature is all I'm saying. If we get Morpheus's body back and resurrected, he'll practically fix the Anomaly for us himself."

"If," I countered, walking around the perimeter of the subterranean chamber. "If, if, if." I pulled the coverings off of three mirrors in ornate frames, spaced equidistantly around the circular room. "Kerensky was right: I was lucky the last time." I walked to the center of chamber where a raised dais projected from the floor. "I can't trust to luck this time around." The dais contained an assortment of switches and levers. I flipped a switch and the torches in the wall sconces dimmed. Ambiance, indeed. "And I don't particularly trust Morpheus." I pulled a lever and oil began spilling into a series of channels chiseled into the stone-flagged floor. An alert observer with an advantage of height might notice the trenches radiated out from the center to form a circled pentagram: a pentangle.

"What about your avatar?"

I frowned. "What about it?"

"Shouldn't you just sit back and let someone else run the show until we can figure out what's wrong with your dreambody?"

I nodded. "Get some rest? Relax a little? Don't push myself too hard…" I closed the lever and the oil stopped running. "Sounds like a good idea."

She was nodding with me. "I mean, if you're sick, the first thing you do is take it easy. Right?"

I shook my head and pulled another lever: a large multifaceted crystal descended from the ceiling to a point just about three feet above my head. "Nope. The first thing I do is take out more insurance." I snapped my fingers and pointed at the nearest oil-filled trench. Unlike the night before, a spark leaped from my index finger and arced into the flammable liquid. "Now, if you'll excuse me, I'm going to contact my agent to talk about increasing my coverage."

Vashti backed toward the chamber's exit as a fiery pentangle formed around me. As she slammed the door, I turned a knob. "Mirror, mirror, on the wall," I murmured, "I need to make a conference call."

My reflection shimmered in each of the three looking-glasses and was replaced by a grotesque image wearing a nineteenth-century telephone operator's headset. The creature had large, compound eyes, iridescent scales, and large, batlike wings that fanned out behind its horned head.

It opened a mouth filled with sharp, spiky teeth and spoke: "Yo, Riplakish!"

"Edgar, my man! Just the Mirror Demon I was hoping to see."

"What can I do for ya, kid?"

"A lot, I hope!"

"Yeah? Well, if'n anybody needs it, youse do." He stuck a half smoked cigar between his teeth. "This got anything to do wit dat Snow White girl?"

"No." I swallowed. "Why?"

"Word is, she's still lookin' fer ya. And it's fer sure them Dwarfs is."

"Uh, I've been out of town. Just got in." I had forgotten all about that mix-up during my last visit. "Guess I'll have to attend to that little matter as soon as I can."

"Guess so." He relit the old cheroot and took a reflective puff. "Say, ya didn't get that girl in trouble, didja?"

"No. No!" I smiled weakly. "It was just a little misunderstanding. You know how Mountain Dwarves are."

He nodded. "So's, what can I do for ya's?"

I explained carefully, going over the details twice. Edgar shook his scaly head. "Dis ain't AT&T, ya know."

"I know. Can you do it?"

The mirror demon worked the cigar all the way across his mouth before answering. "Ya want me to patch ya's through to Prester John's mirror network on yer left mirror. And den ya's want me ta plug ya into da Sibyl's pool at Ortygia on da right mirror. And den youse wants ta access da datanet for REMrunner codes..."

"And I'm going to interface with the net and contact these people personally." I leaned on the dais. "Can we do that?"

He shrugged. "Nothin' ventured, nothin' failed. Gimme a sec."

After a moment, one of Edgar's images shimmered and was replaced by the visage of an elderly man. Kindly dark eyes peered out from a face lined with wisdom and great benevolence and dark, weathered skin stretched across features engendered of mixed Asian and Ethiopian parentage. Prester John smiled and spoke.

"Brother Riplakish—there were rumors thou wert dead. I am overjoyed to see that these were but machinations of the Devil."

I inclined my head. "Sire."

He waved a hand in dismissal. "Thou knowest I do not stand on such formalities. We are all brothers under the true God."

Prester John's humility was legend. His empire extended over large portions of central Asia and northern Africa. Kings from seventy-two nations paid tribute to him, and, at home, his personal attendants included seven kings, sixty dukes, and three-hundred-and-sixty-five counts—one for every day of the year. In addition, twelve archbishops sat on his right hand and twenty bishops on his left when he held court. Another man might have been corrupted by such wealth and power but Prester John's empire was based on Biblical teachings: it was said that there was no crime, no poor, nor any form of sinfulness or abuse in his realm. The only conflicts were those with the "heathens" as the saintly old man led his armies into pagan territories to spread the "Good News."

I frequently felt sorry for the heathens. "How goes the campaign?"

"Media and Persia are ours. We hope to yet free Jerusalem from the infidel but the Tigris balks us."

"Can you obtain boats?"

"Nay. But prophecy tells us that if we but wait long enough, the river will freeze and we may pass over then. So, for now, we wait. So, while we wait, how may I serve thee?"

I let the impulse to kibitz on his strategy pass. "I am in need of thy mirror's power."

Prester John's "mirror" was as legendary as the man, himself. It was actually a series of small crystals, prisms, reflectors, lenses and tubes of quicksilver connected to a speculum or vision tube that enabled the monarch to monitor the doings in his empire at need. Major mojo here.

"I needs must contact those who can readily come to mine aid." I repressed a grimace: every now and then a little King James vernacular crept into the program/character language files. Someday I was going to strong-arm Straeker into getting it all filtered out. In the meantime things went more smoothly when you matched your conversant's, "thees" for "thous."

I explained what I wanted to do and he graciously gave his permission. About the time he signed off, the image in the third mirror began to shimmer.

"Edgar," I called, "don't lose that connection to Prester John's mirror."

"Holdin', kid. But we got a problem on da other call—"

"The Sibyl? She—"

"She's out," said a different voice.

I turned to address the young woman who had just appeared in the third mirror. "Out?"

She nodded. "Out. Owe, you, tea: out."

"Uh," I said. "Out where?"

"Out with the gout."

I held on to the dais for support. "Out with the gout?"

Edgar chuckled. "Out with the gout, she said with a pout."

I glared at him.

"I did not pout," the girl said. With a pout.

"Never mind him," I said. "I need to speak with the Sibyl."

The girl tossed her ringleted blonde hair. "She's out."

"With the gout," Edgar chimed in.

"When will she be back?" I asked.

She ruminated over the question. "I'm afraid I don't know…"

"Said the girl, rather slow."

I scowled at Edgar. "You're not helping."

"Sorry."

"Perhaps I can help?" She smiled winningly.

I sighed. "And who are you?"

"Arethusa. And you?"

"Riplakish of Dyrinwall." Her name rang a bell somewhere in the back of my mind.

"Well, this is a surprise!" She peered at me with considerable interest.

"How so?"

"I heard you were dead."

I forced a smile but a chill was insinuating its way down my spinal column. "Not hardly."

She shrugged. "Okay by me. What can I do for you?"

I explained what I wanted to do and she readily agreed to cooperate.

"I mean, I'm just watching the place—know what I mean? I don't use the pool for prophesying so there's plenty of downtime. And I'm sure it's jake with the Sibyl: she's mentioned you on several occasions…" She gave me another studied look. "You are the Riplakish of Dyrinwall?"

I nodded. "Accept no substitutes."

"Well, if you're ever near Ortygia—"

"C'mon dollface," Edgar broke in, "I can't hold dese lines open all day."

"Nice talking to you," she said, with an added grimace for the Mirror Demon as she turned over the connection.

"More like talkin' *at* cha," he grinned. "Stand by."

While he labored, I cast another spell. The crystal above my head began to glow, throwing beams of light out of its various facets. Three rays reached out and locked onto the mirrors. A fourth beam stabbed downward, bathing me in a blinding white light. The fine hairs on my arms, the backs of my hands and neck, were beginning to rise. A series of tones rang in my ears like a musical key. I felt myself being pulled toward the light, merging with it…

There was an overpowering sensation of connectivity, a rush of power. A tide of ether seemed to sweep me up in a great mystical flood. And, as I moved into the swirling vortex of datastreams, a godlike voice pierced my very being, asking the ancient question that has been demanded of all who have dared to reach out into the Void:

"TO WHAT NUMBER DO YOU WISH THIS CALL CHARGED, SIR?"

Γ

I came out of the datanet screaming.

I had barely enough time to index The Machine's entry code logs when something jumped me. Perception in the datawells is something completely different than an analogued Programworld attuned to the primary senses: I was able to distinguish that it was humanoid, malevolent, and strangely familiar as it raked my mind with logic-tipped claws.

As quick as thought I turned and fled but it was on me in a nanosecond. Twisting and fighting back with non-corporeal hands, I managed to break free a second time. I jumped into an adjacent datastream, hoping to lose my assailant and succeeded in getting lost, myself. A number of milliseconds later I fought free from the dataflow and worked my way back up a sequencing array.

The thing that had attacked me was gone, and so were two of the three datapaths from the mirror network. I was definitely out of my element here, so I slid back onto the remaining datapath, hoping it would take me home.

That's when the pain hit. The all-too-familiar, every-part-of-my-body-turning-itself-inside-out sensation.

I bounced out of the light and staggered away from the dais. I didn't even feel the flames of the burning pentangle as I stumbled across the floor.

I fell just short of the door. I lay there in misery as my guts churned and I made heroic efforts to pull my small intestines out through my esophagus.

By the time they found me, I was almost ready to think about living again. Mind you, I hadn't come to any clear-cut decision, yet. But I had reached the stage where I could consider the question from both sides.

"Lycanthropy." That was Daggoth's observation after he and Vashti had dragged me back upstairs and deposited me in a dining room chair.

"A werehuman?" I asked as a cup of coffee was shoved under my nose.

Stephanie/Vashti gave me the once over: "More like a wereRipley. By day you walk Fantasyworld as the Halfelven Bard, Riplakish of Dyrinwall. But at night…" her voice took on a mock-sinister tone, "…you assume your true form: the dreaded Robert Remington Ripley the Third."

I ignored her and looked at Daggoth. "How? And why?" I pushed the coffee away.

He shrugged. "A spell? A reflection of the master program's instability? I don't know. Whatever the cause, the Master Program may be accessing template files on Metamorphs and Shapeshifters to govern the parameters of your present condition. Perhaps we can find some advantages in that."

"Advantages? My own mount and an Amazon battalion tried to murder me!"

"Because they didn't recognize you. But it also sounds like you had changed back just moments before my Summoning spell plucked you out of the air: Ghost was trying to save you."

I rubbed at my nether regions: a horse bite tends to stay with you for a while. "I'm touched."

"In the head," I heard Vashti mutter.

"Speaking of which, what about that thing that jumped me in the datawell?"

Daggoth shrugged. "The Programworlds were designed to be completely safe for all forms of human interface and they've proved to be deadly. You go poking into unshielded dataspheres where there are no safeguards and you're lucky you can come back with anything beyond a rudimentary brainstem!"

"Point taken," I said, "but this was something independent of the Net. It was autonomous. And it was—familiar."

"Familiar? How?" Vashti wanted to know.

"It's hard to put into words. Impressions, mostly: it knew me, recognized me. And it wanted to destroy me."

"Well, stay out of the datawells," Daggoth grumped. "You'll have to figure some other way of contacting REMrunners or do without."

"No arguments here." I reached up and felt the rounded edges of my ears. "I've got bigger problems to worry about for the time being."

Daggoth patted my shoulder. "We'll keep an eye on your condition and, with more information, we may be able to effect a cure. But there are a couple of things we can do about it in the meantime." He turned and left the room.

Vashti shoved the coffee right back at me. "We can start on solving the problem of your body just as soon as we solve the problem with his." She jerked a thumb at Morpheus, who had materialized while I wasn't watching.

"I don't want this," I said, pushing the coffee back at her.

"You'll need it," she argued.

"I don't need coffee, I need sleep."

"You can sleep all you want after you help dig up my body," Morpheus growled.

"It won't take long," Vashti added. "Your help will cut the time in half."

I looked down at the remains of Daggoth's dressing robe. "I'm not really dressed for any nocturnal excursions."

Daggoth returned with a bundle of clothing. "Here," he said. "I've used some spells to modify your boots, gear, and clothing. It should expand or contract to fit you comfortably at either scale: Human or Half-Elven."

"You're kidding."

He smiled. "I like to think of the material's new properties as something akin to sorcerous spandex."

Vashti grinned.

Morpheus smirked.

I groaned and reached for the coffee.

\RIPLEY\PATH\DELTA (Δ)

Cephtronics had a policy about programming the various Dreamworlds to cater to one's fantasies on a number of levels—and sex was certainly not given short shrift. But Riplakish suspected Thetis was coming along more out of boredom than out of program-enhanced libido. At least, he hoped so.

True to his word, Nereus had provided them with mounts. Riplakish and Thetis rode giant seahorses with saddles. Ethyl the Merman provided his own locomotion through the water as they headed toward Ortygia.

They traveled for nearly an hour without incident. The undersea scenery was enchanting, and he resisted the urge to ask "Are we there yet?" at least a half dozen times.

Then, suddenly, they were passing over broken spars and the shattered remains of ship hulls scattered across the ocean floor. Ethyl slowed and took new bearings while Riplakish dismounted and began examining the sea chests of one of the more recent wrecks. Most of the rotting, wooden chests contained the usual fare: gold doubloons, pistoles, pieces of eight, gems, jewelry, bars of silver. It was awhile before he got lucky.

Ethyl swam down as the Half Elf sorted through a trunk of clothing.

"What's up?" he asked, trying on a pair of purple pantaloons.

"The isle of the Sirens lies ahead and methinks Thetis would rather give it wide berth," the Merman answered. "'Tis your safety that concerns her."

Pantaloons, as a rule, can never be said to truly "fit" under the best of circumstances and underwater, well... "How wide a berth?" Ripley asked, trying to contain the billowing material with a belt.

Ethyl allowed that a ten-mile detour might not permit a reasonable safety margin. Perhaps twenty?

As a Bard, Ripley was tempted to pay a professional courtesy call on the ladies, but he also figured it would be in his best interests to see the Sibyl as soon as possible. As a compromise, he convinced the Merman that they could pass by the islet safely by staying underwater. The belt—actually a "Sam Browne" affair with a couple of shoulder braces crossing his chest from right to left—made the pantaloons a second working "compromise."

The first compromise lasted to the other side of the island when, glancing up, they saw the underside of a small ship headed directly for the rocks.

"Up, Seabiscuit!" Riplakish kicked his mount in the sides and spurred him toward the surface.

It was a small, twin-masted ketch with gaff-and-topsail rigs, and some of the Sirens had just reached it. Only Peisinoë enjoyed fully human form, so she was left back on the rocks to persuade the sailors in closer to shore. Agalaophone's and Thelxepeia's human attributes ended at the bustline: from there on down they possessed the wings and bodies of large birds. They were settling down on the boom and rigging even as Ripley urged the great seahorse forward. Molpe and Parthenope retained their human forms to their waists; the rest was a great fishtail like Ethyl's. The ketch was small and sat low enough in the water for them to grasp the railing and pull themselves up onto the side.

Before he could get close enough to intervene, the Sirens' song began to falter. A second later, Parthnope pitched back over the side.

Thelxepeia suffered a splashdown just as he reined up alongside. By now the song had turned into an operatic nightmare of shrieks and moans. The Half Elf hauled himself up and over the side just in time to watch Molpe leap off the prow and back into the sea.

She was assisted in her trajectory by a large skillet applied to her backside. He started to laugh but stopped when the skillet's wielder turned and glared at him.

To all appearances, he was about to be braced by a large human female. Towering over him by at least a foot, she was beyond Junoesque; she was majestic, and she moved with an easy grace that belied the her size. Her long black hair held subtle touches of grey but her face showed no indications of age or weakness. Dark eyes accentuated her scowl and she roared (yes, "roared"): "Get the hell off my boat, you stinking sea scum or I'll bash your brainless skulls in!" She started advancing on him and he held his hand up.

"Hold it," he said.

She stopped. For the next sixty seconds she wouldn't be able to move but, after that, all bets were off. It wasn't much of a spell, but he found it reassuring that he was still able to throw a little magic around.

"I'm one of the good guys. I'm here to rescue you." He looked up at Agalaophone who was hopping about nervously in the rigging. "Better write this one off to experience, Aggie. And, next time, stick to ships with all male crews."

"Sure thing, Rip." She flapped up into the sky. "We didn't know this one was under your protection." She circled to make sure her fellow Sirens were treading water and then flew back to the island.

"Ho, Thetis!" Ethyl's shaggy head popped up above the starboard gunwale. "Did I not tell you that he was one of the Makers?"

"What I want to know," the Sea Nymph said haughtily, "is just how well he knows those—hussies!" She sat herself down on a crate and began combing out her long, golden hair.

Gently disengaging the iron frying pan from the woman's fingers, he assisted her to another crate as the spell wore off. "Allow me to introduce myself," he said, helping her sit, "I'm Riplakish of Dyrinwall and these are my compatriots: Thetis and Ethyl."

"Elsbeth," she returned. "And those two sorry sacks of sea-fodder are the count Louis Costellino and the abbot—I don't know the rest of his name; I don't think he's picked one, yet."

"Picked one yet?" Riplakish looked over at the two men sprawled unconscious on the deck. He could see the goose-egg lumps adorning their pates from ten feet away.

The Merman whistled. "A first! I have never known the Sirens to use physical force before!"

Elsbeth barked a short, humorless laugh. "I did that, fishman. With my cast-iron fry pan. If I hadn't, they'd have had this boat on the rocks ten minutes ago."

The Half Elf smiled. "Good thing they've got an experienced traveler with them."

She scowled as the count groaned and began to stir. "That's part of the problem, Dr. Ripley." She glared at the count as he began to snore. "This is my first trip into a Programworld. *They're* supposed to be *my* guides!"

\RIPLEY\PATH\SIGMA (Σ)

His body is as insubstantial as a ghost's.

He notices it now as the eastern sky begins to flush a slight pink. No bramble scratches, no stone bruises, no discomfort from the night's activities. Looking down, he can see the grass beneath his feet *through* his feet. Suddenly lightheaded, he leans up against the trunk for support and falls right through.

Inside, he finds himself on hands and knees at the foot of the great spiral staircase. There is a patina of dust on the hardwood floor and he wonders why he doesn't sink through the floor, as well. As soon as he contemplates that, it seems a potentially dangerous concept and he quickly puts it out of his head. He crosses mental fingers as he gets up, hoping that the universe wasn't eavesdropping on his thoughts.

Perhaps it was. As he ascends the staircase, his feet tend to sink through the risers and his progress is something akin to climbing a snowdrift.

He finds that, by concentrating, he can keep from sinking through the floors on the upper levels. It takes a continuous effort, though. He discovers that much after trying to sit in a chair and dropping three stories, "seat" first.

The tree is deserted, and, if the layers of dust in each room are to be trusted, it has been unoccupied for quite some time.

His headache is back by the time the sun has crept over the horizon. An hour of prolonged concentration has sapped his mental faculties, and when he wearily sits on the edge of the bed, he fails to notice the feathered tick giving beneath his weight, the rope webbing beneath making little sounds of protest.

What has happened to him? he wonders. *And what had happened at Misty Dawn's grave?* Dulled by progressive shocks and the strain of maintaining his corporeal equilibrium, his mind surrenders to the fuzziness of exhaustion.

He lies back upon the bed and sleeps.

Hours pass. The sun makes its day-long passage across the sky. As it hesitates on the western horizon, he awakens to the sense of not being alone.

He opens his eyes to find Misty Dawn bending over him.

And it is very obvious that she is dead.

DATALOG: \QUEBEDEAUX_A.5\PERSONAL\20200805
Voice Dictation
FILE ENCRYPTION ON

Theoretically it's possible for a Dreamwalker to be two places at once.

*

In fact, Mike Straeker tried it a couple of times, doing a memory download into two different avatars in two different Programworlds.

*

He figured that, when it was over, his brain would ignore the coincidental time lines and recall the two simultaneous experiences as having taken place at two different times as well as in two different places.

*

Sort of like remembering that last year you spent Christmas in the Rockies and the Fourth of July on the beach.

*

But it didn't work out that way.

*

Straeker suffered severe disorientation for weeks following the twin experience, and his headaches lasted for months.

*

He mentioned once, toward the end, that it was possible that the experience altered his brain chemistry and triggered the tumor that eventually killed him.

*

Which raises a very disturbing question as I monitor Ripley's multiple code-strings…

*

If there's a dangerous disorientation factor to being in two avatars in two unrelated Program environments…

*

What happens to someone who inhabits more than one body in the same environment?

*

Wouldn't the multiple perspectives be even more disorienting once you were re-integrated?

*

None of us are fixed personalities: we continue to change, develop, hopefully grow as we age.

*

We progress through a multitude of experiences, day by day, hour by hour, minute by minute.

*

And we are, in some respects, the sum of those experiences.

*

I am not the same person that I was last week: I am subtly different, because of what I have experienced since last week.

*

Less noticeably, I am not the same person that I was yesterday…

*

Or an hour ago…

*

Or a minute?

*

So the question is: can the various personas,all of whom must develop in subtly—or not so subtly—different ways…

*

Can they be re-integrated when Ripley disconnects?

*

Without killing him?

*

Or destroying his sanity, at the very least?

*

I'm very much afraid that Robert Ripley is already dead and he just doesn't know it yet…

THREE

\RIPLEY\PATH\GAMMA (Γ)

If my so-called lycanthropy was tied to the night, it apparently had no lunar connections. Both moons were in new and first-quarter phases tonight and we drove a rented wagon carefully in the dark, unsure of the road. We reached a field, where Morpheus bade us dismount, and stumbled around a while longer on foot.

"Here."

"You're sure?" I asked.

The ghostly apparition of Morpheus nodded. "I'm sure."

I held the lantern high and scanned our surroundings. "Don't see any markers."

Daggoth was already working his shovel into the dark earth. "You don't put up any markers when you bury a body in unconsecrated ground," he grunted.

I handed the lantern to Vashti and set my spade to work beside Daggoth's. "Thought you were supposed to be planted at the center of a crossroads or some sort of hoo-haw like that."

"Vampires."

"Where?" yelped Vashti.

"You bury vampires at crossroads," Morpheus elaborated.

"I don't."

"Don't what?" inquired Daggoth, digging a little faster.

"Bury vampires," I answered, trying to match his speed.

"What do you do with them?" my ex asked.

"Nothing to date," I said. Daggoth was picking up more dirt per shovel-load, now. What was this? Some kind of contest?

"I wouldn't date one either," the sorcerer quipped. Vashti giggled and I clamped down on a frown: Stephanie had never shown any affinity for my sophisticated humor and here she was giggling like a schoolgirl over a stupid line like that.

Come to think of it, she'd been acting pretty strange since I'd arrived on the scene this morning.

I knew that Daggoth had given her sanctuary these past six months, but, dammitall, she was acting like they'd been sharing chambers or something.

"Could I have a little more light?" I asked curtly. Vashti swung the lantern a bit in my direction and I noticed that Daggoth's pile of dirt was bigger than mine. Maybe I was lacking some enthusiasm for this little project, but you could also argue that he was putting a little more effort into it than necessary.

Like he was showing off or something.

The hole was deepening and Vashti had to move in for us to see where to place the blades of our shovels.

"This part of the ritual or something—digging at midnight?" I asked.

Daggoth shook his head. "Just safer," he grunted.

"Safer? Digging up an unconsecrated burial ground at midnight is *safer*?"

"Less trouble," he amended. "Can't get a medieval court order to exhume the body. And evil sorcerers are sometimes less popular dead than alive."

A mental light bulb clicked on: "Son of a *Lich*."

"Exactly." His shovel suddenly went "thunk." It sounded like wood.

"Not very deep," Morpheus observed.

I gave him the raised eyebrow but the effect was lost at the edge of the lamplight. "You really care how deep once you're dead?"

"I, for one, am glad," Daggoth puffed.

I'll bet. If he was showing off, it was taking its toll.

It took only a few more minutes to finish excavating the plain wooden coffin and wrestle it up out of the hole. Even in the pale illumination it was obvious that we wouldn't need a prybar. Daggoth hooked his fingers around the edges and pulled off the pinewood top.

I'd always thought I had respect for the dead. But that didn't stop me from putting my finger, gunny style, into Morpheus's non-corporeal ribs. "Stick 'em up," I said, "you've been grave-robbed."

Γ

You know what every mother says when her child has mislaid something and can't find it: Well, it just didn't get up and walk off. Well, in Fantasyworld dead bodies occasionally did just that. So I didn't say it. Especially since Morpheus was in such a snit.

Mercifully, he decided that he needed some time alone and disappeared as we unhitched the wagon back at Daggoth's tower. Lose your body and you can't be much more alone than that, I thought, watching him fade. "So now what do we do?"

Daggoth scratched at his beard. "I could start scrying the crystal and mirror networks, but that could take days—weeks, maybe—and with no guarantees…"

"I know a couple of necrophiles I could lean on," Vashti suggested. "Maybe one of them could provide us with a lead."

"What?" we both chorused.

"Absolutely not!" Daggoth added.

"What kind of people have you been hanging out with while I was gone?" I demanded. I turned to Dreamland's former Chief of Programming. "You said you'd been looking after her!"

She put her hands on her hips and settled into a stance that, after seven years of stormy wedlock, I knew only too well. Apparently Daggoth had experienced it, too: we both shut up.

"First of all," she hissed, "I am not married to either of you. And, even if I was, that would not make me property or chattel to be ordered about. I do have a mind of my own and I can take care of myself—frequently better than either of you. And secondly," she finally permitted herself a small smile, "I have an advantage: necros won't mess with you as long as you're alive."

"As long as," I echoed.

Daggoth shrugged in resignation. "Yudu," he sighed.

"Do what?" I asked.

"Voodoo," answered Vashti.

"I do not."

"But the Zombie Master does," Daggoth countered, "and that's why we should go talk to him."

"To whom?"

"Yudu."

"Do wha—; wait a minute, this is a name, right?"

Vashti nodded. "'The Zombie Master."

"And his name is Yoodoo?"

Daggoth nodded. "Yudu," he affirmed.

"And he's the top necromancer in these parts?" I had a strong feeling that I was being set up but the question came tumbling out before I could stop it.

"Of course." Vashti's voice was matter-of-fact. "After all: who do that voodoo that Yudu so well?"

There was no point in trying to pursue a serious line of inquiry while they were in this mood so I left them there, cackling like a couple of demented grave-diggers, and went up to bed.

My transformation come sunrise wasn't nearly as traumatic as before, because Daggoth had supplied me with an herbal analgesic that counteracted most of the discomfort. The main ingredient, however, was Elvish parsley, which had the uncomfortable side effect of making my upper lip curl for about a half hour after each dose.

Daggoth's thaumaturgic tailor-work seemed to be working so far and, after dressing, I rehitched the wagon. When I went down to the basement stables, Ghost seemed genuinely glad to see me. I saddled him without incident as my avatar was in its familiar Halfelven phase, but made a mental note to have him re-stabled before sunset. Until my avatar was cured of its nocturnal shapeshifting, night rides were out of the question.

I tethered the glamoured Pegasus behind the wagon as I drove though the tunnel that led from the underground stables to the base of the hill about a mile behind Daggoth's Tower. After securing the gate and re-camouflaging the entryway, I drove on into Calabastor. I returned the wagon to the Teamster's Guild without incident, then mounted Ghost and rode over to *Fogherty's Cove.*

The tavern was one of the better-kept secrets on the waterfront. (The "best"-kept secrets were the contents of certain mob-controlled warehouses and the number of unfortunates who had gone swimming at night in concrete buskins.) Tourists usually came down to the docks to sample the seafood, but Fogherty's catered to the fishermen and old salts who had had their fill of water-spawned menus: steaks and mountain oysters were the specialties here.

Stan was a stout, cherubic man with a deep voice and a fringe of curly brown hair that ran around the sides of his head and down the sides of his boyish face to meet under his chin. Both his pate and his upper lip were as bare as a baby's behind and, I'll swear to this in any court, he had eyes that actually twinkled.

But they weren't twinkling after he looked up from his post behind the great mahogany bar and saw me coming though the swinging doors. He wasn't officially open for business yet, and the place was devoid of customers. That suited me fine. He looked less than pleased with his first customer of the day.

I wound my way through a maze of empty tables and planted myself at the far end of the bar so that my back was to a wall and not the front entrance. Stan hurried over with a glass of ice and a bottle of Dr. Pepper. "What do you need to know?" he asked as he poured my drink.

I was disappointed. "That's not how it's supposed to work, Stan," I chided. "I come in here, order a drink, and ask 'how's business?'. We make small talk and after a couple of drinks I start asking some general questions and you become somewhat evasive. Then I flash some money and alternate that with some vague threats. Then we haggle—"

"Just ask your questions and I'll answer them as best I can while you're finishing your drink. That way you can be on your way in no time."

I frowned and took a sip. "You're taking all the fun out of this."

He leaned across the bar and pointed the bottle in my face. "Look, Riplakish; I like you. You're a nice person. And nice people are increasingly hard to come by these days. When I heard you was dead, I was genuinely sorry. And I'm glad to see it's not so…" He paused and looked me up and down. "It's not so, is it?"

"It's not so."

He smiled. "Good." And then he went back to frowning. "But you draw trouble like a lodestone. The last two times you was in here I had to replace half the furniture and two wall-length mirrors. Hakim told me that you nearly totaled The Roaring Hangman last year when you mixed it up with a Wizard, a Dragon, and a couple of Demons—"

"There was only one Demoness, and the Dragon wasn't anywhere near the place," I protested.

"I don't care if it was a couple of Pixies and a talking frog," he insisted. "The bottom line is, whenever you walk into any kind of a drinking establishment, in full defiance of the fact that you're a complete teetotaler, some form of mayhem results before you leave the premises. So ask your questions, drink your drink, and good luck and gods'speed in whatever quest you're on this week."

I sighed and took over the bottle. There was no point in being surly over someone's willingness to answer questions. "Know anybody who'd be involved in digging up dead bodies?"

"You mean besides several dozen ghouls and necros that haunt the marsh north of town?"

"Yeah. I don't think this was that kind of snatch."

He pondered a moment. "Well, there's always the Necromancer."

"Yudu?"

"Not me. I'm not into that kind of stuff."

"No, not you," I gritted, losing my patience more rapidly than usual.

"Then who do that voodoo?"

"Now cut that out!" I brandished the Dr. Pepper bottle in my best menacing manner. "Answer my questions or I'll up the ante to three mirrors and camp out here for the rest of the week!"

"Yudu, the Necromancer," he answered with a seemingly straight but strained face.

"Anybody else come to mind?"

"There's a Doctor Franklyn Stein who, I'm told, uses cadavers for medical research."

"Goes out and digs them up at night, eh?"

The bartender shook his head. "Doctor Stein is one of those white-gloved gentlemen who contracts work of that sort from independent vendors."

"I don't suppose you could provide me with the names of some of those 'vendors'?"

He sighed. "Anything to get you out of here before trouble arrives."

I smiled.

"His main man is an old Notre Dame pro. Wound up at the bottom of too many pile-ons…" Stan tapped the side of his head, "…and now he's only good for simple tasks—"

"Like robbing graves in the dead of night," I interjected.

"It's a shame really." He sighed. "This Quasimodo guy was one of the greatest backfield men the Hoosiers have ever produced."

I snapped my fingers. "I know who you're talking about: the Halfback of Notre Dame!" I shook my head. "Damn, he was great!"

We were reminiscing about how he used to climb on top of the goal posts and throw things down at the opposing team when the unoiled hinges on the tavern doors announced company.

"We ain't open for—" Stan stopped and the color drained from his face.

I turned and considered the two figures that were crowding the doorway of Stan's: a man and his dog. Except the man had a toothed beak instead of a mouth, the dog had two heads, and each had taloned appendages at the end of their limbs and two pairs of wings apiece.

"Rriippllaakkiisshh," the dog-thing hissed. It's two heads weren't quite in sync.

"This is just the sort of thing I was talkin' about," moaned Stan as he ducked below the level of the bar.

"Who wants to know?" I returned as belligerently as possible. When dealing with Demons, the value of intimidation should never be underestimated.

"Nergal wants you," was the beak-man's answer as they walked to the center of the common room.

It took me a second to run the mental reference: Nergal was the Assyro-Babylonian Demigod of Pestilence and the Dead. I just looked at them. Finally, I said: "So?"

The dog-thing rumbled a growl in its twin throats, and the bird-man sucked in air, making a high-pitched whistling sound. It sounded like someone abusing a bad stereo system: a pair of cracked woofers and feedback on the tweeter. My response, in turn, was to lay a hand on the hilt of my katana-longsword.

Beakface smiled and the two-headed wonderdog started forward.

I unsheathed Caladbolg and they stopped. Smiling *and* moving. Mesopotamian Demons might not know anything of the ancient Celts or the Sidhe, but the translucent crystal blade surrounded by a blue glow spoke a universal language that any pantheon could understand at first glance.

"Stan my man," I murmured over the bar, "I want a bottle of the hardest rotgut you've got. Two-hundred proof."

"But you don't—" began the disembodied voice.

"I want it now!" I insisted, sliding off the barstool.

A hand clutching a disreputable looking bottle appeared from the nether regions of the bartender's walk. "It's only one-ninety proof," he apologized, "I use it to sterilize the glasses."

I pulled the cork from the bottle with my teeth. That was taste enough to tell me I had what I wanted. To be sure of its volatility, I made a couple of passes over the container and murmured what I hoped was an appropriate spell.

"He don't look so tough," I heard one of them whisper. "Why don't we just take him and get it over with?"

"Nneerrggaall ccoommmmaannddss," was murmured response, "wwee oobbeeyy."

The muttered comeback was even lower but sounded suspiciously like: "Nergal still has an eight-track in his Chariot of Judgment!"

"Hhiisssssstt!"

I got up with the bottle dangling from my left hand and Caladbolg clutched in my right.

"First of all," I announced, "introductions are in order. You know who I am." As I walked in their direction, I tilted the bottle so that a thin stream dribbled onto the floor. "Who are you?"

Bowser spoke first: "Nnaammttaarruu."

Ah, that made sense. Namtaru: god of the plague. *He who crouches by Nergal.*

"Idpa," answered the other.

Pestilence. It had been ten years since my doctoral research on comparative world mythologies but I remembered these two. I walked past them and felt my shoulder blades twitch. Whenever Nergal sent either of these two out, it was against whole cities or armies. The results were always unhealthy on a large scale.

I stopped and turned, judging my angle. "So, what do you want?" I tipped the bottle and began walking in a new direction. Once again I was careful to keep the right side of my body turned toward them where the focus of their attention would be on the enchanted sword.

Not on the bottle of magically-enhanced bad whiskey dribbling out its contents, concealed behind my left leg.

"Yyoouu," snapped both dog heads at once. Idpa merely nodded.

"Mitox!" I cursed, taking a Persian Demon's name in vain. "When was the last time you clowns ever picked a solo target?"

"Nergal orders. We obey." Idpa was obviously impressed by Caladbolg: he seemed to be giving the blue glow a great deal of attention. I walked past them and turned back again, hoping they weren't watching my eyes as I reconfigured my track.

"Could you gentlemen *please* take it outside?" wailed the bartender's disembodied voice.

"In a moment, Stan," I called back as I crossed the line of my first pass. "I want to find out a little more before I decide whether or not to go along with Nergal's hitmen."

My quarry was now encompassed by three lines of rotgut forming a scalene triangle. I didn't know what condition ol' Nergie had ordered me fetched in but, so far, they seemed willing to wait a few more minutes to see if I'd come along quietly.

"So what does Meshlamthea want with me, guys?" I turned again, trying to hurry before the alcohol began to evaporate. "Or is this Ereshkigal's idea?"

That rocked them. In fact, Idpa looked more than a little nonplused—he looked a couple of degrees to the minus side.

"Nneerrggaall ssaayyss—"

"Please!" I gestured at Namtaru with the sword. "One at a time! It's not only impolite, but the two of you are giving me a headache."

Namtaru's heads looked at each other and seemed to come to a decision. "Nergal says that he has prepared a place of honor for you," growled the head on the right. The head on the left added: "He says it is time for you to come to him."

Nice. The actual place-name for Nergal's domain escaped me for the moment but, translated, it meant variously "the house from which he who enters does not come out," "the dwelling-place of the shadows," and "the land of no return." Basically: Babylonian Abaddon.

I turned for the last leg of my pattern. "Tell laughing boy 'thanks, but no thanks.' My dance card is full."

The whiskey bottle went glug and the Demons suddenly noticed my geometric spillage.

Just in time I sprinted across two angled lines and closed the pentagram at its starting point. A snap of my fingers and the whiskey blazed up as a fiery star as the high alcohol content ignited. "Begone, foul fiends!" I cried, "Back to—to—" *Damn, what was the name of Mesopotamian Hell?*

Idpa shook his head. Namtaru growled menacingly. Already the flames were starting to die down.

"Um, go to hell! Go directly to hell; do not pass go, do not collect two hundred dollars!" It had worked on Yakku and Ahuizotl last year—without the benefit of any additional fireworks.

It wasn't working now.

The flames were almost out, now. "This is your last warning: beat it! Scram! Vamoose!"

Two Demons with three smiles was not an encouraging sight.

"Okay, boys; then we do it the hard way." I brought Caladbolg up and then raised it over my head, the blade pointing straight up.

"I have the power!" I yelled.

I caught a glimpse of smiles turned to rictuses (ricti?) of terror and then they were gone in twin puffs of smoke.

Demons can be such pantywaists when they're off their own turf.

"You can come out now, Stan." I lowered my sword.

There was a whizzing sound and a dagger suddenly buried itself in the wall behind my head. Stan ducked back down as I whirled around. A cloaked figure was disappearing out the doorway.

"From now on, Riplakish, it's take-out only," I heard Stan call as I launched myself across the room. I reached the doorway just in time to see a black-clad runner duck between two buildings down the street.

Avatar memories clicked into place as I dodged a horse-drawn coach and continued my pursuit: whether by accident or design, my assailant had chosen a dead-end alley for his escape route. That meant somebody was going to be trapped.

I wanted to make sure it wasn't me.

I hesitated at the entrance, resting my left hand on the hilt of my wakizashi-shortsword. The passageway was too narrow for *Niten Ryu*; I sheathed the Elvish longsword and drew the Dwarven blade.

The alley was dark and narrow. I advanced cautiously, looking upwards every few steps. If this was a setup and my knife-thrower had friends, the ambush would most likely come from above: close confines discouraged group activities.

I edged my way forward, Balmung held out before me. The reddish glow from the enchanted metal gave little illumination in the half-twilight of the buildings' shadows, and it was a sudden, small flicker of flame at the end of the alley that told me the chase was done. I sheathed my weapon and walked up to the number-three blade of Calabastor's new Assassin's Guild.

Rune was a tall, angular woman with dark hair and eyes and a personality to match. Not that she was unpleasant—unless you were targeted by one of her clients, that is. It was just that there was this sense of emptiness when you were standing next to her, a dark silence as if her body was a black hole, absorbing all light and sound in the room.

"If you wanted to get my attention, there are better ways," I said, folding my arms.

"Wasn't me." She shifted the hand-rolled cigarette to the other side of her mouth. "Though I was coming to get you."

"Get me?" Perhaps I had sheathed my blade a bit prematurely.

"Mercy wants you."

I relaxed but didn't feel a whole lot better. "So if you're not a dagger short, who is?"

She took the cigarette out of her mouth and flicked ashes on a dark shape crumpled at her feet. "Recognize this?"

It was a body but I had to cast a Light spell to make any further judgments. I took in the black leather clothing, the spiky, multicolored Mohawk…

"I think you got yourself a serious problem, Rip," she said as she turned the body over with her toe.

…the hilt of Rune's dagger protruding from the corpse's chest, the cranial implants, and, last but not least, the mirrorshades.

I began to swear softly but quite distinctly.

A Cyberpunk.

\RIPLEY\PATH\DELTA (Δ)

"…so I paid these two handsomely to smuggle me through the Datanet and into Dreamland."

"To do an article on REMrunners?" Riplakish shook his head: "You didn't have to take this kind of a risk for your research."

She smiled tightly. "I research all my stories thoroughly, Dr. Ripley. If those Sirens hadn't got me all worked up, I would've known your avatar immediately."

Carefully, the count sat up and rubbed his head. It had been more than an hour since the Isle of the Sirens had been left behind and yet the abbot continued to snore.

"Besides the Pulitzer potential of an exposé on REMrunners, there's the bigger story of the Dreamland quarantine, itself. For that information, I had to get inside."

In trying to get to his feet, Costellino stumbled over the abbot's body. Twice. The short pudgy, priest stirred a bit. And then continued to snore.

"It's too damn dangerous!" the Half Elf told her. "The Programworlds have remained closed to the public because the Anomaly isn't fixed yet!"

She cocked an eyebrow. "So, what are you doing here?'

"Trying to fix it."

"Yeah? I see a guy playing pirate, running about with a naked Sea Nymph." This time her smile had teeth.

The count had located a nearby bucket and was headed back toward the abbot with a purposeful look in his eye.

Riplakish nodded at Ethyl. "Don't worry about us, we've got a chaperone."

There was a sound of splashing water and a gurgling scream: "Cossttelllinnoooo!"

Riplakish took in the moronic tableau. "Haven't they got it reversed?"

"What?"

"Isn't the tall one supposed to be—I mean, their names—the short one was really—" He paused and shook his head.

"What are you talking about?"

The count wandered over to talk to Thetis while the abbot sputtered and began wringing out his robe.

"Never mind. Just a misplaced association—I think." Riplakish took her hands in his. "Elsbeth, trust me on this: every hour that goes by here increases the chance of your getting seriously hurt of killed. The Anomaly makes dying here as big a reality as it is in the outside world."

"They don't believe that," she said, indicating her two fellow REMrunners with a jerk of her head.

"They are fools and will very likely prove my point by getting you killed before the day is over."

This time their conversation was interrupted by the sound of a slap and they turned in time to watch the count land on his keister while Thetis coolly examined her fingernails for signs of chipped polish.

"Hey, babe," he protested, rubbing the red weal rising on his cheek, "if you don't want it, you shouldn't go around dressed like that!"

Elsbeth turned back to Ripley. *"Get me out of here!"*

"Land ho!" called Ethyl.

"Ortygia!" cried Thetis.

They went to the prow and looked out across the water. Ahead, growing steadily as the ketch skimmed across the waves, was the Isle of Ortygia.

It had been years—in game time, at least—since Riplakish had last visited the Sibyl in her island grotto. The memories came back now: he had been younger, then—newer to the Program—but good times dominated his recall. The Sea Nymph Calypso had ferried him over on her ship *Cousteau* and they had spent an idyllic two weeks cruising the Ionian Sea. That's when he had first met the Sirens—

Thetis had family here, as well. Her sister, Arethusa, had been pursued by Alpheius the hunter. Unwilling to succumb to his forceful advances, she had taken refuge on Ortygia and the gods (Greek pantheon here, of course), heeding her pleas for help, changed her into a spring.

Alpheius, so the story went, was inconsolable. He hung around the neighborhood of Olympus, mooning, until the gods took pity on him and changed him into a river. Legend said his waters crossed the sea without mixing with it and joined the waters of Arethusa on Ortygia. If there was a point to any of this, it was Greek gods had real strange concepts about helping out, and Riplakish had made it a point to never ask any of them for a favor.

As they sailed closer, their attention was drawn to a strange cloud formation that hovered just over the tiny island. Elsbeth brought out a telescoping spyglass and studied the phenomenon for several minutes before handing it over to the Half Elf. "What do you make of it?"

He stared through the tube for an even longer period of time.

"Well?"

"Flying Saucer," he sighed, collapsing the spyglass back into a compact cylinder. "It looks like a dead ringer for the spaceship in *Forbidden Planet.*"

"Excuse me?"

"*Forbidden Planet* was a mid-twentieth-century film: color, two-D, flat-screen projection. It was sort of a science fiction retelling of Shakespeare's *The Tempest.*" He passed the cylinder back to Elsbeth. "This thing looks just like the flying saucer in the movie."

Elsbeth pulled out a handpad and began tapping in notes. "Can't be a spaceship here, though. Maybe a chariot of the gods?"

The Bard looked doubtful. "More likely a Frisbee of the Frost Giants. Or maybe a Hubcap of Hades. Look, Elsbeth, one of the side effects of the Anomaly is that various programworlds are gaining access to one another. In fact, the Master Program is accessing outside file sources and integrating nonrelated material into the various milieus.

"This"—hegestured at the hovering disk—"is just one example."

"Well, is the effect totally random? Or is there a method to this madness? I mean, why a flying saucer here?" she asked.

"Dunno. Maybe this is what the Sibyl wants to see me about."

Elsbeth opened her mouth to speak but the abbot beat her to it. "Surfer Dudes," he yelled, pointing to the opposite direction.

An antique submarine conning tower had surfaced a half mile off the starboard side, and as they came to the rail to watch, four surfers were closing the distance between the two vessels.

"I've got a bad feeling about this," murmured Riplakish.

"Are those helmets that they're wearing?" queried Thetis.

"Methinks they come bearing weapons," called Ethyl.

"This is a strange custom," wondered Thetis. "Serfs permitted to bear arms."

"Serfs surfing," the Half Elf muttered.

"Something even stranger," observed Elsbeth, unlimbering the spyglass as the boards drew closer. "They're wearing some sort of uniform. Dr. Ripley, you're the one with a specialty in history—"

"History is just a hobby," he replied, taking the telescope in hand. "My specialty is mythology. But those outfits look like mid-twentieth-century costumes."

"World War Two?"

He nodded, giving them careful scrutiny through the glass. "German, I think…"

"Nazis?" Elsbeth grabbed his sleeve. "Nazis on surf boards?"

His reply was drowned out by the thunder of Sten guns opening up in a fatal volley of lead.

\RIPLEY\PATH\SIGMA (Σ)

The setting sun casts roseate beams through an open hole in the wall of the tree. The shafts of light transfix a portion of her left leg and torso, dissolving those portions of her anatomy into nothingness. The rest seems not far behind.

"You—you're a ghost!" he whispers.

"What are you doing here?" is her less-than-amiable response. Her frown is the most substantial thing about her.

"What?"

"By what right do you violate the Archdruid's sanctuary?" Her countenance grows threatening. "Who are you to trespass here and sleep upon his bed?"

He feels curiously light-headed but forces himself to sit up. One of the fading sunbeams strikes his eyes and momentarily dazzles him. There is a wrenching sensation, a sudden feeling of turning inside-out. "I—"

"*Oh!* My lord!" she cries. And throws herself upon him.

That does it: insubstantial, they both fall through the bed and plummet six stories, into the root cellar. What should be an awful impact against the packed earthen floor is a sudden dead stop that defies Newtonian laws of motion and thumbs its incorporeal nose at inertia. Surviving an eighty-foot fall is simple compared to disentangling himself from a suddenly amorous Nymph. A ghostly one, at that.

"My Lord Riplakish! Forgive me!" She is smothering his face with tangible kisses. (How does she do that?) "I did not recognize thee! Thou seemst a stranger when I first happened upon thee!"

"Uh," is all he can manage to get in edgewise. Her kisses are distracting; her hands, her body, are the first substantial things he has encountered, so far.

"Thou hast been gone so long that I feared for thee! I have waited and—" She stops and her eyes widen. "But this is the first time that thou hast been able to see me!" Now her eyes fill with horror and she presses a fist to her mouth. "Thou—thou art—*dead!*"

"Uh," is all he can think of in answer to this new concept.

"Oh my love!" she moans. "How did it happen? In what manner didst thou meet thy doom?"

"Doom?"

"Oh," she wails, "this is terrible! First, my body is stolen from its final rest and now thou'rt dead!" She throws her arms around his neck and begins to sob into his chest.

"Well, I'm not so sure I, really—" He stops. "Did you say your body was stolen?"

She nods amid the waterworks.

"How stolen? Stolen how?" He shakes his head. "Who stole it?"

"I know not. Save that it is gone." She looks up at him with teary eyes. "Who would have *done* such a thing? And why?"

Since he doesn't know and telling her what he has seen the night before might only upset her more, he steers the conversation in other directions. "Uh Misty, hon—"

"Yes, my Lord?"

"I'm kind of new to this ghost business and I've got a few questions..."

Σ

For all of the dead Nymph's experience over the past year, he isn't able to learn much.

She, like most "haunts," is a "nocturnal." That is, she seems to exist only between the hours of sundown and sunup. Misty Dawn fades with the cockcrow and it is to her as if she sleeps until the first star of evening summons her back to nightly existence. She has no idea where her ghostly essence resides during these lost hours and can't even begin to speculate.

Another restriction is her spectral ties to the area surrounding the grove. Most ghosts are restricted to walk the earth on or near the site of their demise. Misty is no exception, though her territory in death includes the great oak and several acres of Dyrinwall Forest.

As to their noncorporeal state, she is able to show him that sold objects can be moved or manipulated to some degree. As he has found earlier in climbing the stairs, it takes some serious concentration, but by the time the night is half over he is able to chart the event horizon of most pieces of furniture and move objects under five pounds a short distance.

He might have made faster progress in his acclimatization but Misty Dawn is every bit the amorous Nymph in death that she'd been in life. And he is finding himself more vulnerable to her advances as she is the only object of a reciprocally tactile nature in his currently intangible condition.

They make ghostly love as the moons sleepwalk down the sky and bed beyond the horizon. A cock announces the arrival of another day as he holds her in his arms and she fades in his embrace before she can even say good-bye.

Expecting to return to nothingness himself, he fights against the urge to panic. He jumps to his feet, casting about for something to do, some distraction, to occupy his mind while he waits.

I didn't die here, in this file sector of the Matrix, he suddenly thinks. *I may not be tied to this place, in Dyrinwall, as Misty is.*

The urge to panic metamorphoses into an urge to run, to see if there are territorial boundaries for him before the daylight claims him, too. He dashes for the spiral stairway, knowing that he will probably fade before he is out of sight of the tree, but needing to try anyway. Reaching the bottom, he runs for the door, putting on an extra burst of speed—

And unconsciousness takes him in a blinding burst of pain!

DATALOG: \QUEBEDEAUX_A.5\PERSONAL\20200806
Voice Dictation
FILE ENCRYPTION ON

Damn!

*

Of the three code-strings I've been able to monitor, one is gone and the other two are unstable.

*

The fascinating thing about their instability is that they seem to echo each other in some kind of weird phasing sequence.

*

It's as if they were two images of the same thing—one with a positive charge or ground, the other negative.

*

And every so often, they both change—as if the positive flips over to the negative and the negative to positive.

*

I wonder how that change manifests in Ripley's avatar—or avatars plural…

*

I wish I could access more of the Primary Monitoring Systems; under the present restrictions I am unable to determine his exact status.

*

And whether there are more than two of him left.

FOUR

\RIPLEY\PATH\GAMMA (Γ)

The blindfold irritated me more than it should have.

It was, of course, standard procedure for visiting an Assassin's Guildhouse: blindfolds guarantee guild secrets and a visitor's "safe" passage. So, Rune was guiding me through the warren of tunnels beneath the city streets, carefully taking me in circles and doubling back so that I couldn't re-trace my steps later.

What made the whole thing ludicrous—and, therefore, irritating—was that Robert R. Ripley the Third had designed all of the Guildhouses and placed them and their so-called secret societies into the Program. Patience is not one of my stronger virtues and wading through ankle-deep sewer water was not improving my mood.

I held my tongue, however: this time there was no mob of Maenads to bail me out.

It was the appearance of a Cyberpunk that really bothered me.

My concern went beyond the matter of a thrown dagger and who or what had sicced him on me. The fundamental question was, what was a Cyberworld Halfjack doing in the Fantasyworld milieu?

I knew from my last incursion into the Matrix that milieu crossover—once unthinkable—was now a possibility. The first Dreamworld Incident had been precipitated by Senator Hanson's abduction from Warworld by Fantasyworld Goblins. And Mike Straeker's Spaceworld avatar had piloted a starship into Fantasyworld to rescue me from a gladiatorial contest and Daggoth the Dark, his Fantasyworld avatar, from imprisonment in his own tower.

But that didn't make a Cyberpunk in a medieval fantasy setting any easier to swallow.

Eventually Rune decided that I was confused enough to be taken up a ladder and through another maze of rooms and staircases, completing a journey that should have taken fifteen minutes instead of an hour and a half.

My blindfold was removed and I found myself in a lavishly furnished room dominated by a large oaken desk. Behind that desk sat a red-headed woman dressed in green leather. She had a winning, dimpled smile and coldest gray eyes you would ever hope to find in your lifetime.

Standing behind her right shoulder was a tall, thin blade of a man, feeding bits of bloody meat to a falcon perched on the back of her chair. The gobbets of wet flesh were too small to identify and, as my mother always claimed my imagination was too convoluted for my own mental health, I turned my attention to the possible number of emergency exits.

"Hello, Mercy." I wasn't sure if Mercy was her real name or just one of those rare examples of Assassins' humor. "Dix," I added, nodding to the man offering another avian tidbit on the end of his throwing dagger. I allocated a chair near the desk and plopped down casually. "How's tricks?"

"Pretty *grave* from what I hear," she answered. Then smiled more broadly: "How about a song?"

I frowned. "A song?"

"Yeah. You're the bard; how about 'I Ain't Got No *body'?"*

"Oh," I said. "You're funny," I said. "Real. Funny."

"I know; sometimes I just *kill* myself!"

"Yeah? Well, if you're applying for court jester, don't quit your night job just yet." I have two rules when dealing with Assassins' Guilds: never show fear and don't push your luck. Obviously, I was walking a very fine line between the two.

I waited until she worked through a fresh batch of chuckles. Dix smiled but said nothing, continuing to feed the bird with a disquieting single-mindedness.

"Now, to what do I owe this…" I held the word out at arm's length and regarded it with suspicion, "…pleasure?"

"A favor."

"You want a favor?"

She shook her head. "You done me a favor last year when you and those Maenads closed down the old guildhall on the east side.

Those old farts wouldn't even consider letting a woman in at the Bravo level, much less allow any in leadership positions. Now, I owe all this," her gesture took in the ornate office and beyond, "in part, to you. I figure it's about time I evened the score."

She stood and I swallowed. When assassins talk about evening scores, one is inclined to put financial affairs in order, complete unfinished projects quickly, and leave detailed instructions as to the disposal of one's estate.

"Come."

I got up and followed her to the bookcase behind her desk. She twisted a candle in a wall-sconce and the bookcase swung away from the wall, revealing a secret passage.

"This wise without the blindfold?" Dix inquired with a chilling mildness.

Mercy swung her grey gaze on me for a long and measured moment. "Where are we?"

The smart money was on feigning ignorance.

"Granary warehouse on Bleeker Street, two blocks from Dorn's Wharf," I answered after reflecting that it rarely paid to lie to an Assassin and never to a woman.

"So much for blindfolds," Rune murmured.

Dix looked even more threateningly thoughtful.

The redheaded Guildmaster kept her face and voice carefully neutral: "The only people who know the location of our guildhall are dead or Guildmembers."

"Well, gee-whiz," I said after a pregnant pause that had gone to full term and was starting labor, "do I have to learn the secret handshake or can I just pay my yearly dues and get the newsletter?"

"It's not that simple, Riplakish," she answered after another uncomfortable silence. "Dues are required on a monthly rather than annual basis." And then, finally, she smiled.

Rune and Dix followed her lead and smiled, too.

I followed her lead by ducking through the opening in the wall as she started down the secret corridor. As the bookshelf rumbled shut behind us, the passage dimmed to near darkness and I had to concentrate on Mercy's shadowy form to keep my bearings. Behind me I heard a vague thumping and a muffled voice saying something like "...put the candle back..."

"As I see it, you have two basic problems," Mercy said as we came to a circular staircase and began descending. "First, you're looking for a body. The one that belonged to Morpheus the Malevolent, if my sources are not mistaken."

Morpheus the Malevolent—what a charming moniker and alliterative as hell.

"And second, there's another group in town looking for a body. Your body." She opened a door at the bottom and I followed her into a storeroom. The walls indicated we were now underground, but the room was dry if a little bit cool for my tastes. Several candles and a lamp, recently lit, provided murky illumination.

"If your sources are not mistaken," I added, wondering who would want to off me.

"They're not."

We both turned to look at Rune who was entering the room with Dix.

"Cyberpunk," she elaborated for Mercy's benefit.

"You get close enough for a positive I.D.?"

Rune nodded. "Scragged him. Cleaned my blade on his jacket. Boy meant business."

The redheaded Guildmaster turned back to me. "Someone's put a contract out on you and brought outtatowners in for the job."

I was more than a little incredulous: "Cyberpunks?"

"*Way* outta town," Dix observed.

"I owe you, Rip. Nobody offs anybody in my debt until I'm square with them." Mercy scowled. "And even more important, this is my turf. Nobody does hits in my jurisdiction without my permission!"

"Uh, thanks…"

"I was a little peeved when I heard the rumor that you was dead. Glad to see that I can square our debt with a little 'protection'. Protection is cheaper than revenge."

"Well—"

"'Course, I'm better in the revenge department."

"That won't—"

"And you can rest assured that if protection ain't good enough, I'll see to it that you are revenged."

"Avenged," Dix corrected.

"What?"

"You'll see to it that 'Points,' here, is avenged," he elaborated.

Points? I reached up and touched the tips of my Half-Elven ears.

"Yeah; that, too."

"Thanks," I said. *Points?*

Mercy walked over to a long crate resting on a couple of saw-horses. "Bring some light," she instructed, lifting the top.

There was no smell to warn me and the flickering lamplight didn't help much: I stood there, peering into the box at its contents, for a long moment. "A body?" I finally asked.

"Such as it is."

"Whose body is it?"

Mercy put her hands on her hips. "Of all the stories I heard about you, none of them suggested you was dense unless there was a woman involved."

"It's a little hard to tell in this light—is it a woman's body?"

"It's Morpheus the Malevolent's!"

I hate it when women use an exasperated tone of voice with me. At least this time I had an inkling as to why. "Well, it's a little hard to tell when the corpse is missing its head and hands and feet and—" I peered a bit more closely, "—other assorted bits and parts?" I looked up. "How do I know this is really the bodily remains of Morpheus and not just some mutilated peasant's corpse?"

"It's Morpheus, all right," she assured me. "Take a deep breath."

I did.

"Smell anything?"

I didn't.

"That's because he's got a high level Preservation spell operating. That's beyond the ability of most mid-level mages."

I nodded. "Okay. So, where's the rest of him?"

"Good question."

"Bad answer."

Dix crossed the room and bent over a tarpaulin covered mound. "Your answers are right here," he said, jerking the tarp aside.

The second body looked more freshly dead, smelled less freshly preserved, but seemed to be more or less intact. A length of heavy chain was crisscrossed around the torso and wrapped around the stiff's legs. The ends of the chain were wrapped around a couple of large rocks.

"Kinky outfit," I said. "So what's the story?"

"Smudge. He had the sorcerer's remains in his possession," Mercy explained. "He's a procurer."

"*Was* a procurer. Tonight, Master Smudge is sharkbait," Dix elaborated.

"Chummy," I observed. Nobody got it. "Okay, I know that there are certain parties who find a variety of uses for cadavers. So who did this Smudge procure for?"

"He was an independent. He served a variety of clients, including chirurgeons, anatomists, apothecaries, spell shoppes, medical research labs for the area universities, and the occasional Ghoul or Necrophile who came into a little spending money—but mostly he dabbled in the Necromantic Black Market."

"I don't suppose we can get a client list for our boy here?"

Mercy shook her head. "We stumbled on this by accident. Two of my Bravos were a little careless: he died before he could talk."

"That why the guild's secret patois is known as Thieves' 'Cant'?" I stared at the remains of the ratlike little man and pondered. "Maybe not."

"Maybe not what?"

"Mercy, can I borrow Smudge before tonight's swimming expedition?"

She looked at me speculatively. "You can *keep* him, if you want. My only concern is a certain amount of tidiness. I don't like messes—political or practical—and I don't like stiffs cluttering up my storerooms. I'm an Assassin, not an undertaker." She turned to Rune. "The wagon ready?"

She nodded.

"Have Ralph and Norton toss Smudge in, alongside Morpheus. Make sure both are well-covered." She turned back to me. "The wagon's due back tomorrow."

"Thanks—"

"It's rented in your name, Points," Dix added. "Mercy assured them you'd pay when you returned it. See that you do."

I nodded. "I appreciate all the help you're giving me."

Mercy held up a hand. "Think nothing of it. Like I said, I owe you. And I don't like other people planning hits on my turf. If any additional information comes down the pike, I'll be sure to pass it along."

"I'm grate—"

"At cost."

"Cost?"

"Hey, good informants ain't cheap! I'm not going to make no profit on this. Normally, the Guild sells info to the highest bidder or charges the client forty per cent over base fees. And I'm throwin' in Rune for free."

"Rune?"

"She volunteered."

I looked at Rune.

"I need the practice."

Saying "no" to any of this was out of the question, of course.

"Now," Mercy continued, "I got another question." She held out her hand. "Dix?" He placed a loose roll of parchment in her palm and she unrolled it and held it up for me to read.

It was a "Wanted" poster complete with my likeness sketched in full face and profile studies. Beneath my name and description was a request for information leading to my apprehension. Apparently I was being charged with "breach of promise" and a reward was offered to locate me so that I could "manfully" face up to my responsibilities.

"Well?"

I smiled wanly. "It was a mistake."

Mercy's smile had teeth. "I know a lot of guys may think that the morning after, but it's a pretty crass thing to say out loud."

"No. I mean, it was an accident." That wasn't any better. "What I mean is—nothing happened."

Dix's eyebrow arced toward his hairline. "Nobody goes to the trouble of putting these things all over town on account of nothin' happened."

I sighed. "Look, about six months ago I was with some friends and we came across this glass coffin in the middle of a meadow. When we opened it, we found the body of a young woman inside—"

"I think I'm gonna be sick," Dix growled, "if this is headin' where I think it is..."

Mercy was close behind with: "I heard rumors about your social life, Bard, but..."

"She wasn't dead!" I said hotly. "She was like in suspended animation—"

"Suspended *what?"* they chorused.

"—I had to give her mouth-to-mouth resuscitation—"

"Mouth-to-mouth *what?"*

"Sounds like you were kissing her," Rune observed.

"Well, that's what the Dwarves thought"

"Dwarves?"

"This wouldn't involve the fair lady White, would it?"

"Well, as a matter of fact—"

"Oh, man, Points, are you in a lot of trouble!"

"I know! I've got seven very tenacious Mountain Dwarves on the lookout for me. They've got some sort of custom that demands I make an honest woman of her. And all I did was kiss her!"

"Thought you said it was just mouth-to-mouth something-or-other."

"Well—"

"I'm afraid it's gotten a little bigger than you think, Rip." Now Mercy looked positively grim. "Seems this Snow girl's stepmama is real unhappy about you putting her back in circulation."

"And the word on the street is Rudy's lookin' for you, as well."

I drew a momentary blank. "Rudy?"

"Snow's fiancé."

"Ah. The Prince." I looked at the poster again. "You say these are all over town?"

The guildmaster tossed the parchment to Rune. "Rune's been going around and pulling them down almost as fast as they've been going up."

"Thank—"

"I don't allow no unauthorized proclamations on Guild turf 'less I'm paid the standard poster fee."

I fidgeted. "Well, once again, thanks, guys. I really appreciate this. And if there's anything I can do for you—"

"There is," said Mercy.

Γ

Back when the Dreamworlds was open to the public, you might enter any of the Program milieus and mingle with hundreds of other Dreamwalkers, each inhabiting their own, distinctive, computer generated avatar. What made the interactive Programworlds infinitely more interesting, however, were their thousands of inhabitants who were not linked to humans outside the Matrix. These subprograms were Artificial Intelligences in their own right, with personality files and full simulation capabilities that made them indistinguishable from the avatars animated by Dreamwalkers.

Indistinguishable to other Dreamwalkers, that is.

You might not know whether the Blacksmith in the village or the King on his throne or the Doxy in the tavern was another Dreamwalker or a computer Construct.

But *some* of the other Constructs did.

Program self-awareness was haphazard among the various A.I.s and Constructs, but a name had evolved among them for those of us who came from outside the Program Matrix: *True Spirits.*

And Mercy had found one when all Dreamwalkers were believed to have been evacuated from the Fantasyworld Program.

Guess who she asked to babysit?

When we emerged from the warren of tunnels leading away from the Guildhouse, I found myself in a side alley just off the main street of Calabastor. "Where is he?"

"Tavern," Rune replied. "Follow me."

As we strolled down the street toward the south end of town I took a mental inventory of the signs and storefronts: Calabastor had changed since I had last visited and I wasn't sure how much was attributable to the Anomaly. There was a new sign proclaiming "Mario & Luigi: Painting, Plumbing—We'll hop to it!"; a Rent-A-Guide Agency offering the services of Indiana Smith and Northwest Jones; a poster heralding the return of Selena the Sonnetteer down at the Bard's Guild; another poster recruiting for the Navy, bearing the inscription "Agamemnon wants YOU;" a notice from the Earl of Farringdon inquiring after the whereabouts of his fiancée, the daughter of Lord Henshingly Croft; and some cryptic graffiti that stated "Trebor Sux" and asked "Who shot J.R.R.?"

There was also one of my wanted posters tacked to a wall about two feet off the ground. It didn't take any great leap of logic to figure it had been posted there by a Dwarf.

I turned my collar up and tried to slouch as I walked.

The tavern was a gloomy little dive with a dirty little sign dubbing it "The Do Drop In." Crom, talk about an insidious lack of imagination...

"That's him," Rune announced, gesturing over the top of the saloon-type half doors that leaned crookedly against each other in the entryway.

Inside, a hodgepodge of clientele cluttered up the main room: berserkers on barstools, thaumaturgists at the tables, corsairs in the corners... And besides the odd assortment of dress and professions, the cross-cultural conglomeration spanned various racial groups, as well. At one table a group of masked terrapins were squabbling over the last slice of pizza. And there was even a group of purple Snarfs huddled around a sawn-off table: five males and a Snarfette—a dangerous combination once they got drunk.

I pulled out my enchanted spectacles as I zeroed in on an old, decrepit, wizard-type slouched over a table against the far wall. Imagine Merlin the Magician as Darrell Sweet might have painted him: dark robe and pointed hat spangled with white stars and planets, long flowing white hair and beard, parchment-like skin, crow's-feet turning into a bird stampede; his face and hands suggested ancient wisdom and arcane powers. A green purse lay next to the stein of beer on the table and a great carved wizardstaff leaned against the adjacent chair. I was moving toward him and halfway across the room when I got the spectacles on and the *Optics of al Rashid* refocused.

When Haroun al Rashid was Caliph of Baghdad, he had saved the life of a young man whose father, in gratitude, had crafted a pair of enchanted lenses and mounted them in thin gold frames as a gift. The original spell on this mystic pair of glasses was to enable the wearer to see "truth." Truth takes many forms and, by the time they had come into my possession, the Optics of al Rashid divined truth through a variety of visual spectra.

More specific to this particular moment, I could look at the avatar of a True Spirit and see the true appearance of the

Dreamwalker who animated it: *This ancient old man in the Merlin makeup was a boy who couldn't be any older than fourteen at the most!*

Now I knew why Mercy had specifically used the term "babysit."

I pulled the spectacles from my eyes and the double image of man and boy resolved back into the single form of an old wizard, who looked up as I approached his table.

"May I join you?" I asked as I tucked the glasses back into my vest pocket. He made an uncertain gesture and I sat down. There was no point in beating around the bush: "My name is Riplakish of Dyrinwall. Look, I know that you're a Dreamwalker—more likely a REMrunner. This Programworld is not only off-limits, it's very dangerous—"

"I can't get out," he mumbled into his beer.

"What's the problem?"

"Jeremiah," was the slightly slurred response.

"Jeremiah?" I asked, wondering if the innkeeper could be held responsible for serving an alcoholic beverage to a minor.

He flopped a careless hand in the direction of the green "purse" and I got a better look this time: Jeremiah.

Jeremiah was a bullfrog.

"He was a good friend of mine," explained the sloshed sorcerer.

I felt a headache coming on.

Γ

"...I never understood a single word he said," Rune was saying.

I refused to rise to the bait. "Look, it's a bit complicated."

"Try me."

I turned in my saddle and checked on kid-wizard: he was sprawled on a rug, snoring loudly, having passed out just after climbing on and kicking it into gear. The rug was floating about four feet off the ground and, as I had used about twenty feet of rope to tether it to my saddlehorn, he drifted serenely along, behind us as we rode out of Calabastor.

Satisfied that he hadn't fallen off, I turned back to Rune who was driving the wagon, corpses in back under a pile of yard goods, with her horse tethered behind. "Apparently, Merlin—"

"Mervyn."

"Yeah, Mervyn; well, he's from this other world—"

"A True Spirit?"

I cleared my throat. "Uh, right. Well, he—"

"Would you classify him as a Dreamwalker or a REMrunner?"

I glared at her. "If you know so bloody much, why don't you explain it to me?"

"I'm listening," she said, primly.

"Well, old Mervyn, here, didn't get in on his own. His friend, Jeremiah, was the hacker who knew the code sequencing."

"Code-sequencing?"

"Let's just say that ol' Jerry was Mervyn's ticket in and was supposed to be Mervyn's ticket back out."

"A frog?"

"He wasn't a frog until the two of them ran into an old witch."

"Which old witch?"

"The wicked wi—you're doing this on purpose, aren't you?"

She smirked.

Wizkid snored.

We were on our way to see Yudu the Necromancer. Aside from the likelihood that Yudu had been one of Smudge's employers, I still had other hopes of getting the decomposing little procurer to talk.

"Company," Rune announced, breaking my reverie.

I looked up the road and studied the rider who had just come over the hill before us. Rune stopped the wagon and I reined in. Mervyn's flying carpet gently bumped up against Ghost's hindquarters.

"Huh. Whazit?" mumbled a sleepy voice from the nether regions.

"Looks like an Orc," I observed.

"Mmmmmm—Narc?"

"Never saw no Orc ride alone," Rune commented.

The Orc rode closer and we see his piggish features more clearly. Mervyn popped up like hyperactive prairie dog: "Nnn—Narc?"

"Check the topknot," Rune directed. "Our boy's from the Southern Provinces."

Which differentiated him from the wild and hostile Northern Tribes. The Southern Tribes were more amenable to treaties and frequently hired out as mercenaries on short-term contracts. And since this particular Orc was riding relaxed in the saddle with all weapons sheathed and secured, we adopted a similar non-threatening stance.

"Hola, strangers!" he called, as he reined up some ten feet in front of us. He grinned in what might have been an engaging manner: there were enough tusks on display to rival the Elephants' Graveyard.

"Awful jolly for a Norc," Mervyn mumbled behind us.

"I hight Jotnar of Mork, bound for Calabastor!" he called with unquestionable good will. "And you be?" He had only one massive eyebrow and a corner of it lifted as he waited for our response.

"Elyn of Fiddlers Green," Rune answered, smoothly dialing up one of her aliases. "Mervyn Ambrosia," came the not-so-steady response from the kid with the beard. "Riplakish of Dyrinwall," I added, trying to put a mental finger on my unease.

I turned to Rune. "What's wrong with this picture?"

"Riplakish of Dyrinwall—*ho!*" the brute bellowed. He reared back in the saddle and unleashed a ululating cry.

Something clicked at the back of my mind. *An Orc from Mork?*

There was a sound of many hooves and a cloud of dust boiled up from behind the next hill. Rune drew her shortsword. "Rip, get out of here!" she yelled, smacking Ghost across his flank with the flat of her blade.

The Glamoured pegasus reared and leapt, his wings unfolding and spreading to beat the air with massive strokes. As we climbed into the sky I heard a faint whimpering in my slipstream. I turned and saw the strained face of Mervyn the Magician as he clung to the carpet that was still linked by rope to my saddle. A large green bullfrog was clinging to Mervyn's robe with goggly eyes that outsized even the wizard's.

"Hang on, guys!" I leveled Ghost off and reined him in so that we hovered momentarily in the air. The carpet seemed to stabilize and so did the wizard.

Then an arrow struck the bottom of the rug with a *thumpk* and a barbed head poked through the weave along with about six inches of the shaft.

I looked down to see an octet of Orcs riding over the hill in answer to their leader's summons. Three of them had strung bows and were taking a special interest in us. I reached for my shortbow, holstered to the left of my saddle pommel and hurriedly strung it as I looked back for Rune. There was no sign of her, but the Orc who had braced us on the road had ridden up to the abandoned wagon and was in the process of sliding off his saddle. I looked again and noticed that Rune wasn't the only thing missing: there was nothing above the Orc's shoulders. I whistled as I reached for an arrow in the leather quiver that hung to the right of the pommel: decapitating Orcs is no mean feat under any circumstances—and not just because they have no necks.

Another arrow came too close and I had to turn my attention to the problem at hand. I nocked my own and, taking careful aim, released it. I missed the rider and caught his mount in the neck. I murmured a short oath as the horse screamed and went down. A more virulent string of curses exploded behind me and I turned as I nocked another arrow. Mervyn was standing up on the carpet, holding his conical hat in his hands and trying to extract the arrow that had bisected its once-perfect cone. Another arrow arced by—*the kid had no sense of priorities!*

"Kid—Mervyn!" I yelled as I brought my bow around and released my second arrow, "Cast a Shield spell or something!" My arrow caught an Orc in the face and he did a backward roll out of his saddle. Unfortunately, it wasn't one of the three using bows.

"How come they're shooting at us?"

"I don't know—we'll figure it out later!" I risked a glance back after loosing another arrow. The kid's avatar was still standing up on the carpet, dividing his attention between his hat and the goings-on down on the ground. Jeremiah was hopping about the undulating surface of the carpet as if he thought it lessened his chances of being hit by the next arrow. "Don't just stand there, you putz! This is for real!" A small voice in the back of my mind was advising me to get us both out of there, but I couldn't just fly off and abandon Rune.

Even though we were the only visible targets.

I pulled my dagger and slashed through the rope tied to my saddlehorn. "Fly away, kid! I'll catch up in a few minutes!"

He flew away, all right. The next moment he was diving toward the Orcs with a barrage of blue lights spraying from his fingertips! The frog had nearly tumbled off and was holding on to the trailing edge of the rug with his mouth.

Three went down on his first pass, and only one got back up. They clustered as he brought the rug around for a second pass and I recognized the somatic gestures as he prepared his next spell. "No!" I yelled, kicking Ghost down into an intercept course. But I was too late: a Fireball rumbled through our monstrous foes like an over-sized bowling ball scoring a spare on the tenth frame.

Rune rode out from a clutch of trees on her own horse as we returned to earth. Jeremiah spit out a mouthful of carpet fibers and crawled over by the wagon, panting.

"Just what did you think you were doing?" I asked as Mervyn began extracting arrows from the carpet's weave.

"Defending myself, man," he answered in the steadiest voice I'd heard since he'd puked up a pitcher of beer behind the *Do Drop In.*

"You could've gotten yourself killed!"

"More likely to get myself killed doin' nothin'. 'Sides, what do you care? If I got killed I'd be out of your hair and you'd be alone with the chick."

I glanced over at Rune who was making her way from body to body, holding her nose and searching what was left of their packs, pouches, and saddlebags. The smell of roast beast was strong enough to gag a maggot. "Let me set you straight on some things, boy. First of all, that lady is an Assassin, not a 'chick.' You'll be much better off if you show more respect for her than you do for me and you'll be much happier if you treat me like I was your favorite uncle."

"Yeah. And second of all?"

Oboy: a smartmouth. There was room for only one smartmouth in this party, and I had tenure.

"Second of all, you don't seem to take this dying thing seriously."

He snorted. "Look, man; I'm way overdue to get out and go home. If Jeremiah can't—or won't—access the codes for me, I figure the next time I die, the defaults will kick in and all I'll have lost is some respect and an expensive avatar."

"Haven't you been listening?" I advanced on him and grabbed the front of his robe. "It doesn't work that way anymore! Without the codes, you can't go home!"

"That's what Jeremiah wants me to think! I'm still not convinced that he didn't set this up to test—"

The frog croaked reproachfully as I lifted the fistful of robe and Mervyn's feet cleared the ground. "This is not a game and this is not a test!" I bellowed, shaking him. "If an Orc takes an axe to your avatar, you're gonna be one hacked-up little hacker! This is the New Reality and dead in here is Dead Out There!" I dropped him after sticking my face in his and adding: "Permanent!"

"Aw, man! That crap about people dyin' in Dreamworlds last year was all just a bunch of hype!"

It had become a standard REMrunner line these past six months. More than a few believed that the Truedeath warnings were just another attempt by Cephtronics to keep them out of the Matrix: that if the security systems couldn't dissuade intrusion, scare tactics might. And convincing most Dreamhackers of the truth in this matter was comparable to proving "Truth" in any theological debate—facts are unreliable, belief is all.

"And thirdly," Rune added, postponing this particular debate for the moment, "always leave one of the perps alive so you can find out who sent them."

Mervyn's head swiveled in her direction. "You mean like we follow them back to their hideout without them knowin'?"

The Assassin unsheathed a particularly nasty-looking dagger and shook her head. "Only if they get a head start on a faster horse."

"Oh."

"You find anything?" I asked.

"Nah. Professional hire—careful but clumsy." She whistled for her horse and he came trotting up. "Pretty obvious, though," she added, re-tying her mount to the back of the wagon, "you were the mark." She swung up onto the wagon seat, released the brake, and urged the draft horses forward. Jeremiah made a couple of Herculean hops and scrambled up into the wagon seat beside her.

Mervyn crawled onto his flying carpet. "Who'd want you dead, man?"

"Good question."

"Bad answer," he retorted, swinging the rug around to follow Rune. I mounted Ghost and trailed behind, giving the matter a great deal of thought.

\RIPLEY\PATH\SIGMA (Σ)

It was difficult to say which came first, consciousness or pain; but in all practicality, they came hand-in-hand.

He sat up, seeing nothing but darkness at first. Reaching out, his questing hands felt nothing beyond the rough flooring beneath his body. His head hurt. And his face. He touched his tender, swollen nose, and his hand came away wet with blood.

Now his eyes were beginning to focus, and he could see a white, ovoid outline in the darkness before him.

A theory formed in his pain-dulled mind. He struggled to his feet and lurched forward in spite of the flowers of pain that bloomed over and over behind his eyes. He met resistance a few feet away and groped for the handle.

The door swung inward and the interior of Misty Dawn's oak was illumined by warm, afternoon sunlight. He tapped his fist against the unquestionably solid wall of the trunk and then steped outside.

He smiled, feeling the sun on his face and the wash of a gentle breeze over his body. He was alive, not dead; solid, not wraithlike; and he had broken his nose and probably sustained a concussion trying to run through the outer door of Misty's tree while it was still closed!

Someone cleared their throat behind him.

He turned, suddenly mindful that he was still naked. A woman clad in black from the neck down was leaning against Misty's tree with her arms folded, her expression somewhere between a smile and a smirk. "I'm looking for Riplakish of Dyrinwall," she said. "Have you seen him?"

Σ

It was Lilith.

The former Succubus had been promoted and was now a full Archdemoness from the lower planes of Hell. He studied her face for changes as she wiped the blood from his face in turn.

Her hair was still long and bone-white but now a pair of small, pink horns poked through the tresses above her brow. Blood-red lips framed white teeth that were now enhanced with upper and lower pairs of fangs. Her scarlet cloak and robe had been replaced by a bodysuit (at least he hoped it was a bodysuit) of scaly black leather, and what he had first assumed to be a dark cloak flung about her shoulders turned out to be a pair of batlike wings.

Noting his inspection she paused in her ministrations. "How do you like the new me?"

"Nice. But to be honest, I actually prefer the Lily Munster look."

She snorted and continued to dab at his blood-caked face. "You have his aura, his knowledge, his voice, and even his feeble attempts at tasteless wit. For now I must suppose that your story is true—that you *are* Riplakish of Dyrinwall."

"What do you mean, 'feeble'?"

"I came here to warn you."

"Too late. I already tried to run through a solid door."

"Nit! Your life is in danger!"

"Ah? And from whom, pray tell?"

"Please, language," the Demoness chided with a wince. "I don't know who. I've overheard a couple of conversations between members of the infernal council and rumors are running to Hell and gone." Coming from Lilith it wasn't just a figure of speech. "Someone's out to extinguish you, my friend! The word from some parts is he already has."

"So much for the efficacy of the grapevine."

"Will you be serious?" she hissed. "The rumors also suggest demonic connections! I'm sticking my neck out for you on this, buddy-boy, and you know how the lower-downs in Hell can dish out their displeasure!"

"Yeah," he responded with a nostalgic look in his eye, "I remember what Orcus did to you the last time..."

She blushed, remembering her transformation from Succubus to mortal woman.

"Do you ever miss being human?"

A thoughtful expression was replaced by a smile as she leaned across the table and kissed him. Her lips were gentle on his and when she pulled away, she brushed his hair back from his face. "We've got to get you out of here."

"You think they—whoever 'they' are—will come looking for me here?"

"Safe bet. This was where I started." She placed the bloodied rag in the bowl of water and gestured over it. Both disappeared in a gout of green flame. "A little occult advice," she said. "Never leave any of your blood around where the wrong people might get ahold of it."

"I guess I can hole up at Daggoth's Tower," he decided.

"That's the second place I would've looked."

"It's a starting point. I'll need some supplies." He sighed. "What I really need is a drink!"

She smiled and gestured again: a flagon appeared in front of him. "What's this?"

"Try it."

He sipped. Then quaffed. "Rum?" he asked, wiping his mouth.

"Demon Rum."

SSS

Robert Remington Ripley, the Third, pirouetted in front of the mirror. "Very nice. What is it?"

"A bit hard to explain, actually." Lilith was preparing his pack and saddlebags as he studied his new attire. The scaled black leather was form-fitting, and aside from the fact that his form was somewhat different from hers, it was identical to the outfit the Archdemoness wore. "It resembles Black Dragonskin but combines a number of other materials in an inter-dimensional weave. All the Powers, Thrones, and Principalities wear this nowadays."

"Jeez, I feel—" He noticed her expression. "Sorry. Forgot." She waved for him to continue. "I feel like an honorary member of the Hellfire Club." He touched a tentative finger to his tender nose. "Um, while you're in the mood or the mode of conjuring, how about fixing my nose?"

Lilith shook her head. "No can do. Hell permits a certain range of magic—but nothing in the curative spectra. It runs counter to company policies."

"You, my dear, run counter to company policies."

She frowned. "I am being summoned. I must leave before someone starts checking into my whereabouts. The suit will enable me to find you later."

"Just you?" he asked, turning. "Or can other—" But she was already gone. He sniffed the air as he crossed the room. "Ah, *eau de brimstone!*" Tugging the silk covering off the crystal ball in his study, he plopped down in a chair and hoisted his feet up on the desk.

Five minutes later Daggoth broke the connection with a terse "I'm coming to get you. Don't do anything or go anywhere!" That left Ripley with little else to do but reach for one of the jugs of Demon Rum that Lilith had left with his supplies.

DATALOG: \QUEBEDEAUX_A.5\PERSONAL\20200807
Voice Dictation
FILE ENCRYPTION ON

I'm trying to trace Ripley's code-strings to a point of origin without tipping Balor's security team to the fact we've got another incursion.

*

Damn!

*

Where did he come from?

*

The last I heard, he'd disappeared somewhere in Russia.

*

This really puts me between the proverbial rock and the hard place: if the Soviets have anything to do with this incursion, I really should report it!

*

But reporting it could well mean Ripley's termination.

*

Crap! The incursion alarms are going off again!

FIVE

\RIPLEY\PATH\GAMMA (Γ)

In my imagination it was a toss-up: an ancient stone tower set high on a craggy hill or a large cavern at the end of a mist-shrouded valley. I mean, we're talking about animating dead bodies, meddling in things that man was not meant to—ah—meddle in. C'mon, we're talking about a major-league Necromancer, here. What pops into your mind when you try to picture this joker's stronghold?

. . .

See what I mean?

So don't sneer at my surprise when Rune led us up to this palatial mansion just an hour's ride from the city gates.

The estate was the sort of layout you'd expect to see on the cover of *Better Castles and Courtyards,* with well manicured lawns and shrubbery and neo-Greek architecture. We rode up the pebbled drive and dismounted near the front door. Or, rather, Mervyn and I did. Rune parked the wagon and then swung up into the saddle of her horse, making some sort of excuse about perimeter security. Jeremiah elected to stay with the wagon. I waved Rune on, knowing the real reason Assassins gave the Zombie Master a wide berth. When you're responsible for sending a number of people across the line, you're not too keen on meeting someone who can bring them back.

I started to tie Ghost to one of those stone Dwarf stablehands, you know, the kind of kitsch some of the rich like to stick in their front yards alongside those glass spheroids on concrete pedestals. Except this one wasn't a stone statue. Oh, he held the customary ring in one outstretched hand and was a uniform grey and didn't move—didn't even breathe, for that matter. But a good close up look was sufficient to tell the difference.

Statues, for the most part, never started out their existence as living flesh and blood.

We didn't need to check the address to know that we had found the Zombie Master's stronghold.

The doorman was a trifle slow in responding to my knock. I couldn't really fault him as it was obvious that he'd been dead a long time.

"We're here to see the Zombie Master," I said.

Since Zombies don't talk and he didn't shut the door in our faces, we followed as he turned and trudged toward the interior of the house. Ominously, the door swung shut behind us of its own accord.

Inside, the marble floors and white stone construction seemed at odds with the moldering staff in servant's attire. The walls were adorned with murals and tapestries, sculptures (at least I hoped they were sculptures) lurked in a multiplicity of alcoves, and aromatic censers perfumed the air with scents that were both pleasing and, in view of the advanced decomposition of some of the servants, practical.

Mervyn tugged on my vest. "Major babe at eleven o'clock."

I turned and followed the twist of his head to see a young black woman descending a curved staircase to our left. If it wasn't too cliché I would quote Byron and say she walked in beauty like the night...but it is, so I won't.

She wore a white dress and turban that contrasted her dark skin and made the white stone walls and the black marble floors into matching accessories.

She called out to the doorman who stopped his somnambulistic shuffle and listened as she walked toward us. She spoke a variant of French that had an unfamiliar ring in my ears. I had taught myself a smattering of classical French from the literary sources, but this was a spoken dialect and more difficult to follow. The cadence and pronunciations differed from the mother-tongue that Nicole had spoken—farther removed, even, than the Canadian French of some of my Quebequois acquaintances. A Caribbean variant, I guessed as our Zombie guide turned away.

"We're here to see Yudu," Mervyn announced without introduction or preamble.

I frowned at him and tried to explain to the young lady: "We have urgent business to discuss with the Zombie Master."

"You do?"

Ah, she spoke English; that was one less barrier. "That's the one."

"What is de one?"

On the other hand, perhaps she didn't comprehend it all that well. "Not 'what' is the one," I explained, "but whom."

"Ah," she exclaimed, "you are meaning de Necromancer."

"Yes," Mervyn agreed: "Yudu."

"Yes," she agreed: "I do."

"You do?" I frowned.

"But of course."

"Do what?" Mervyn inquired.

"Dat voodoo."

"Oh, *Crom*…I don't have time for this." I put my fists on my hips. "I need to see the Zombie Master and I need to see him right now."

"Well, I am afraid dat is quite impossible."

"Why impossible?" Mervyn wanted to know. As a matter of fact, I did, too.

"Because dere is no Zombie *Master*. I am afraid you have suffered some *mis*information."

"Mis—" Mervyn began.

"Yes?"

"No, not you." My patience had already wandered off, ostensibly to look for a saner environment.

"If not me, den who will do?"

"Do what?" Mervyn asked, proving to be a reliable nuisance factor.

"Dat voodoo."

"Stop it!" Pressing fingers to my temples, I gritted: "You're giving me a headache!"

"You poor ting," the woman crooned. "But don' worry: I have de remedy for dat."

"You do?" Mervyn, of course.

"Of course; I keep telling you dat."

I gritted my teeth, determined to bring this conversation under control. "This is the first time you've mentioned headache remedies."

"Oh, not dat."

"Then, which?"

"Shut up, Mervyn," I murmured.

"Not Witch; Necromancer."

"But you said there is no Necromancer," he continued.

"No I didn't: I said dere was no Zombie *Master.*"

"You did?"

"I did. I am de Necromancer."

"The Necromancer?" I echoed.

"De Zombie Mistress," she confirmed.

"The Zombie *Mistress?*"

"I am Yudu de Necromancer."

"Oh."

After a very long pause I stepped forward. "I'm sorry. I'm afraid we got started off on the wrong foot." I extended my hand: "How do you do."

"Don' start dat again," she snapped.

Γ

Actually, once we got things sorted out, Yudu turned out to be very accommodating. She agreed to come to Daggoth's Tower and help us with our "problem" come nightfall. While I was in a bit of a hurry to expedite the matter, she needed time to prepare for the ceremonies, preferred nocturnal ambiance, and I needed to come up with the standard fees. I wasn't carrying sufficient funds at the moment and I was in a hurry to get back to Daggoth's before sunset.

I wasn't too keen on going through a transformation out on the open road.

The ride to Daggoth's Tower was potentially a short one for a winged horse and a flying carpet, but the wagon was another matter. Rune wasn't much of a conversationalist and Jeremiah was marginally worse, so I used the time to get to know the kid better.

The problem with putting on the spectacles and seeing Dreamwalkers as they really were, was that it tended to get very confusing.

Take Mervyn, for example. His real name was Henry ("call me Hank") Sculthorpe and he was a sophomore in high school—presently on semester break. That was on the outside, of course. Here, in Fantasyworld, none of that seemed to apply. When I looked at him, I saw Mervyn the Magician, an old geezer with parchment skin and flowing white locks. Sculthorpe had picked a powerful, if somewhat withered, avatar that could command vast magical forces.

And he was sorry he had done so.

"Why?"

He looked a little flustered and deliberately slowed the carpet so that the wagon carried Rune out of comfortable earshot. "It's the babes."

"The babes?" I asked.

"You know—the chicks. Women."

"Ah," I said. "Women."

"Yeah. Well, that's why I'm here."

I looked at him like my father used to look at me when I hit adolescence. "Why are you here?"

He looked surprised. "Why are any of us here?"

"We'll take a poll later, Plato. You're underage and the Dreamworlds' Matrix has been declared off-limits to the general public. So, why are you here?"

"The Gameworld, man."

I cocked an eyebrow.

"It's better than real life."

"Better?"

He looked at me. "I don't know how your life is now, man, but tell me what it was like when you were fourteen."

I thought about it. Fourteen wasn't so bad. Was it? Then I thought about it some more. Fourteen. No longer a kid, not yet an adult. Everyone had a piece of you: parents, adults, older siblings, school. The world is full of authority systems and you're practically on the bottom rung. Even kids get better treatment because they're not supposed to know any better and by-the-way-young-man-isn't-it-time-you-started-taking-on-some-responsibilities? As if that wasn't tough enough, the hormones started kicking in: an emotional rollercoaster with drives and zits and squeaky voices and clothes never fitting…

And girls.

Chicks.

The babes.

Yeah, at fourteen a guy is at a definite disadvantage. The "fairer sex" has an unfair advantage at fourteen. They seem to be taller, smarter, more mature, and definitely more in control.

Yeah, definitely…

So, why Fantasyworld? I started thinking about fourteen-year-old fantasies. "You're not happy about being a Wizard." I didn't phrase it as a question.

He shook his head and mumbled something about being old.

"Wizards are powerful," I pointed out. "The general rule of thumb is: the older you get, the more powerful you become. In this avatar you could be a major player."

"Aw, man, I know this stuff. I picked Wizard because I got a head for the spells. I knew it would be safe."

I knew from the way he said "safe" that further arguments were futile. At fourteen you didn't want "safe," you wanted *adventure*. It wasn't until you got closer to my age that you come to understand that adventures are mostly unpleasant and uncomfortable ordeals, usually involving pain, loss, and near-brushes with death. They only sound fun and exciting to inexperienced boobs when told around the campfire by the ones who were lucky enough to survive and smart enough to not go back for more.

"What I really want to be—"

"Is a Barbarian."

He looked at me sharply. "How'd you know?"

I thought about large, athletic bodies, muscles rippling beneath bronzed skin, great steel swords and minimal leather outfits. Power and strength and total independence. Even a Wizard in his tower might fear and envy you, a Queen on her throne could desire you, a Slavegirl in the marketplace would be willing to die for you…

And you could take off your shirt at the beach and know that no one, I mean no one, was gonna kick sand in your face.

"Lucky guess," I answered.

"Company again," called Rune from the wagon in front.

"Orcs?" I asked.

"Not hardly," she answered archly.

I nudged Ghost up to the front of the parade to get a better look.

There were twenty in all, arrayed in bands of chain mail and strips of leather, bristling with blades and bows, mounted on fierce chargers. Tougher than Orcs, fiercer than Tartars, more dangerous than Dwarves on a three-day bender, their faces were painted with the colors of a roving war party: crimson lip gloss, vermilion eye shadow, and a touch of blush.

Mervyn floated up beside me. "Amazons," he breathed. "Bodacious babes!"

"More like deadly dames," I corrected. "You and Rune stay here. I'll go up and see what they want."

"You kidding me, man? I want a closer look!"

"That is how most of their victims die," Rune said, "trying to get a closer look."

"Aw, man—"

"Zip it up and stay put, Scully." I nudged Ghost forward. "If they're friendly I'll get you your closer look."

"How about a date?"

I threw a look back at Rune. "Tell Mercy she *owes* me. Big time."

I made my approach at a careful, casual pace. Too slow might communicate fear or reluctance, too fast would brand me for an inexperienced fool. As Ghost trotted up the gentle rise I shifted mental gears and took another look through adolescent eyes.

Yep. Babes.

Cosmo covergirls in chainmail bikinis done up with mousse and mascara. Wet-dream women warriors.

Forget real history and Sarmatian culture. Cephtronics had diddled another aspect of the Fantasyworld Program to make the experience more attractive to the thrill-seekers. I was no longer surprised at anything I found: various mythologies and histories had collided with New Hollywood standards of adult fairy tales and the Dreamworlds' S.O.P. of playing to the lowest common denominator in Dreamwalker fantasies.

The most important thing to remember, now that Cephtronics had lost control and the Program was running without safeties or governors, was that everything was potentially deadly.

Particularly cute chicks in chainmail lingerie.

As I shifted back to what I hoped was an adult mindset, I noticed details that had escaped me at a distance: they were wearing emerald hair clips that distinguished them as the most elite and deadly warrior-maids. And I was personally acquainted with three of these *Green Barrettes.*

Queen Hippolyta rode forward with Faun and Princess Aerial just behind and to either side.

"So, Riplakish, our daughter's prayers are answered. We feared the worst."

"You are well, my love?" Aeriel's voice and expression seemed a bit strained.

Hippolyta turned and gave her a look that silenced her and let everyone know that Mom was going to handle matters here.

"I am well," I said. Though it was anyone's guess as to how much longer that was going to last. "Majesty, I thought you were in retirement."

"We were on pilgrimage when word came of your disappearance. We returned early—" She stopped and gave me a meaningful look. "Lord Riplakish, let us speak privily to one another."

I eyeballed the distance between the sun and the horizon. "Perhaps we could ride while we talked…?"

Now that the prodigal had been found, it seemed we had a mutual destination: Daggoth's Tower. I remembered that Aeriel had once hinted at a relationship between her mother and the dark sorcerer. I had this vague, uneasy feeling that circumstances had shifted somewhat in the meantime.

"Thou'rt well?" the Amazon ruler inquired as I pulled off my chainmail shirt. The afternoon was turning into a real scorcher and the old "safety in numbers" adage had me setting caution aside. "Thou'rt recovered?"

"Recovered?"

"Thou wert abducted?"

I must have looked blank.

"Constrained? Imprisoned?"

A light clicked on. "Oh! That!" But how to explain? *Excuse me, your majesty, but I'm afflicted with a rare form of lycanthropy: every night I turn into myself. I'm a wereRipley. You see, this is all a computer simulation and none of you are really real*—Right. "Uh, I'm looking into the matter, good lady. I believe your daughter was the victim of a magical hoax. Probably some disillusioned Illusionist who—"

"Who will die when we track him down!" she finished vehemently.

"Die?" I swallowed. "I think it was just some kind of practical joke—"

"No man may jape a princess of the royal blood and live to boast of it. We have sworn a bloodoath!"

"A bloodoath?" This was serious: there was no backing down from a bloodoath!

She nodded gravely. "Before our daughter may ascend to the throne she must conceive thy child and kill the man who made a fool of her before the faces of the women she must rule."

It made sense of a savage sort. Except to fulfill this bloodoath they would have to kill me and no fancy explanation would satisfy a bloodoath once sworn.

Another thought elbowed it's way to the front of the line: *"My* child?"

"Aye. Thou'rt her chosen Consort."

I glanced back at Aeriel. She and Faun were pacing along about twenty feet behind us. Behind them rode the remainder of the Amazon war party. "Majesty, thy daughter and I have this understanding…" I turned my gaze forward and studied the wagon the led our merry band. At my insistence, Mervyn had thrown his carpet in the back and was keeping Rune company on the driver's seat. Jeremiah was uncomfortably pressed between them.

At the moment Mervyn was looking back at us.

He was doing that a lot.

"Thou'rt Royal Consort to the Amazon Throne."

"I'm flattered Highness, and I want to help—"

"Allow us to make ourself perfectly clear. Thou hast been acknowledged as Consort to Aeriel, heir-apparent to the Crown. Thou hast met with the approval of the Council and the Amazon populace. More importantly, thou hast our approval."

"Aeriel explained—"

"The taking of a Royal Consort to insure progeny is an inviolate portion of the Ascension Rituals. In that, alone, thou hast a duty to perform."

"Well, I don't mind helping Aeri buy some time—"

"My daughter is still a *virgin!"*

She had to be upset to drop the royal "we." I cleared my throat. "As I was saying, good queen, Aeriel and I have this arrangement…"

"Yes, yes, she explained it to me—us. Princess Aeriel has coerced thee to acknowledge Consort status with the understanding that it is a ruse to purchase time. Although time for what is certainly beyond me—us!"

"Time to find the man she really wants to make a baby with," I explained.

Even though she was the one who seemed to be missing the point, she looked at me as if I were truly stupid. "She has already found him."

"Well, great! That should solve everybody's problem—except—" Except I was finally getting the message that should have been obvious all along. "Oh, no. No. We had a deal. I am *not* a participant here, I am only lending my good name to the cause—"

"What didst thou believe? That thou couldst step down in a few months and another man might take thy place?"

"Well…"

"There is a precedent for such, but retirement is permanent."

Permanent? "But we had a deal!"

"Thou hast made covenant with the Amazon nation," she said, coldly. "Thy deception jeopardizes our daughter's life as well as thine."

"I think we need to talk to Aeriel about this."

"That will avail thee naught: she wants thy child." Her look softened and, for a moment, she looked more like a mother than a queen. "Riplakish, Aeriel *loves* thee. Do not break my daughter's heart."

Great.

If Amazonian palimony didn't get me killed, the twenty or so warrior-maids bringing up the rear would ace me as soon as I turned into my human alter ego. That is, if the Demons, Orcs or Cyberpunks didn't get me first.

"We do not understand why you balk at this task." The queen was clearly perplexed. "It is a great honor that she bestows upon you."

How to explain this? "Men, your majesty, like to make their own choices…"

"Men are fickle," she corrected. "Men resist marriage and desire variety."

"Majesty, not all men are like that."

"Of course not! We were merely speaking of the best of your sorry sex."

"It's just that I'm not ready to settle down and make a commitment—"

"You will have your own life, be able to travel or live, where or when you please. After you have sired an heir, of course."

"Oh, of course."

"All that is required of thee is that thou makest love to a beautiful princess, sufficient to produce a child. Thou wilt even be given a royal stipend—"

"I'm going to be *paid?*"

Hippolyta misread my agitation. "If a largess of gold and jewels is not sufficient, there are other recompenses, as well. Amazon custom does not prohibit the sharing of a man by many women. We have a number of subjects ready and willing to slake thy desire for variety—"

"Yeah, Aeriel mentioned her sister Kathy." This kept getting more and more distasteful.

"Their cousin Edith hath also expressed interest—"

I held up my hand. "Majesty, my mother taught me many things that have served me well in my sojourn through this world. And one of them was that you can't have your Kate and Edith, too."

The wagon slowed ahead of us. "Company," Rune called over her shoulder.

Thank Crom, I murmured under my breath. I nudged Ghost forward, grateful for the excuse to terminate this discussion.

Company turned out to be a single rider. The surrounding countryside was flat and grassy so I was sure no reinforcements would suddenly appear over any hills or from behind any trees. Rune stopped the wagon and mounted her own horse as I rode by. I waved her back: "Nothing I can't handle."

I glanced down at my mithril shirt, slung across the front of my saddle. A single horseman—most likely a fellow traveler. And I wasn't about to put the chainmail back on with the Amazons watching. I patted the hilt of my katana: if there was trouble, I could outrun or outfight it.

The horseman had reined up about a hundred yards away. Swathed in a dark djellaba, his form and features were obscured at this distance, but there was something familiar—

He had moved in the saddle while a wisp of memory flickered in front of my eyes.

Then I was knocked backwards, out of the saddle, by a hissing express train of force and tumbled to the hard, stony ground. I rolled as I landed, pushing the arrow's shaft in even deeper.

I tried to rise, to lift my face from the dirt, but my arms had turned to water. The weight of my body continued to press upon the shaft and, while I could feel the barbed head working its way deeper into my chest, the absence of pain frightened me more.

By the time Rune's horse had thundered to my side, I knew.

She dismounted and turned me over, laying my head in her lap. I had always believed that when death came, I'd be frightened—that I'd fight it. I was surprised in clarity of the moment to find that life suddenly seemed to be too complex and demanding and that easy peace beckoned comfortingly like a calm port to a storm-tossed sailor.

"Hold on," Rune was saying. There were tears—I wasn't sure whether they were mine or hers. "Don't let go!"

I tried to shake my head but I had no strength. Only seconds were left: I opened my mouth and nearly choked on the blood that was filling my throat.

"I'm tired…" I whispered, "…of the game…"

And then I died.

DATALOG: \QUEBEDEAUX_A.5\PERSONAL\20200808
Voice Dictation
FILE ENCRYPTION ON

Now what?

*

First I get an anomalous reading close to the avatar I've christened Ripley; Code: Gamma.

*

Someone else, close to Ripley, is a real human being in taction with an avatar—not one of the Computer's AI constructs.

*

There have been several others but what sets this one apart is its code structure: it seems to be repeated in two variants elsewhere in the Matrix.

*

I say "variants" because the code is not as closely duplicated as Ripley's multiple avatars—but they're still close enough to question whether or not they represent three different entities.

*

The other factor that sets this entity apart is that as soon as it came within close proximity to Ripley-Gamma, his code string ceased to exist.

*

There's only one Ripley left on my monitors now.

*

I wonder how long he can last…

PART III

TERMINAL EMULATION

King Skule: Have you many unmade songs within you, Jatgeir?

Jatgeir: Nay, but many unborn; they are conceived one after the other, come to life, and are brought forth.

King Skule: And if I, who am king and have the might—if I were to have you slain, would all the unborn skald-thoughts within you die along with you?

Jatgeir: My lord, it is a great sin to slay a fair thought.

King Skule: I ask not if it be a sin: I ask if it be possible!

—Henrik Ibsen, "The Thought Child"
from *The Pretenders* (Archer trans.)—

And all in deadly sleepe did drowned lie…

—Edmund Spenser,
The Faerie Queene, Cant. III, 16—

ONE

\RIPLEY\PATH\SIGMA (Σ)

He was drunk and that both pleased and puzzled him.

Once, during the beta-testing stage of the Fantasyworld Program, he had "slipped." He had so immersed himself in the game that his character persona had disregarded the self-imposed disciplines of a recovering alcoholic and had hoisted a few in a seedy, backwater dive named *The Obscene Griffin.* That was when he had discovered that computer-simulated alcohol had no effect on his avatar.

Drinking "in-program" was something he rarely repeated after that episode, though. It didn't help his years of abstinence, once he was back Outside, to have temptation's taste so clearly returned to recent memory.

And, as it turned out, his avatar couldn't get drunk. So what was the point?

He mostly steered clear of it since that episode—the one notable exception was sampling the wine bottle "bombs" during that brawl last year in *The Roaring Hangman* inn.

But this time he wanted to get drunk. *Needed* to get drunk!

And, wonder of wonders, his wish had somehow been granted! The Demon Rum that Lilith left him packed a wallop unlike anything that he could remember.

Of course, his memory was none too good, at the moment. But that suited him just fine as the whole point to getting drunk was to make all the unpleasant thoughts and memories just go away.

In the past twenty-four hours he had been brained with a battle-axe, turned into a lycanthrope and a ghost, watched a malevolent entity possess the dead body of a woman he had cared for, discovered that there were Demons out to get him, and now had just learned that there was more than one of him and that he had just died.

The news arrived with the Amazons at the tower less than a half hour after Daggoth had fetched him there via magic carpet.

It was unsettling to think about his own death—particularly now that it had already occurred. *What was it like? Had he suffered? What were his last thoughts?*

Where was he now?

And then there was an even more disturbing thought: *if there were two of him, then which one was the real Robert Remington Ripley the Third?*

There were no answers immediately forthcoming and he was tired of pondering the imponderable. Unfortunately, several hours had passed since Stephanie had confiscated the rest of the Demon Rum and he was beginning to notice a slow but steady slide toward sobriety.

He had already decided that this was a bad time to be sober.

The room seemed stationary, but he sat up slowly, ready to return to the prone position should it decide to turn into a centrifuge again. The combination of Demon Rum and aerial maneuvers on a flimsy piece of floor covering had played havoc with his head and stomach. But now, with the passage of a couple of hours in bed in one of the guest chambers, he was feeling much better. He lowered his feet to the floor, which no longer evinced a notion to suddenly lurch off in an unexpected direction.

He stood and navigated to the door. The room still displayed a tendency to list slightly to port, but the overall architecture was moving from gelatinous to a more stonelike consistency.

The door was not locked. That surprised him, as he'd half-expected to be under house arrest after Stephanie's tongue-lashing. He exited the room, hesitating on the circular balcony and considering the other doors on this level. He turned to descend the stairs, deciding to begin his quest in the wine cellar and, if unsuccessful there, work his way back up with a carefully meticulous search grid.

Creeping down the spiral stairway, he was careful to avoid the treads marked in memory as "creaky." The tower appeared deserted but he took no chances, hugging the walls and ducking in and out of alcoves until he reached the basement stairs.

The wine cellar contained a store of wine, not to mention barrels of ale and some mead, as well.

But no Demon Rum.

It took only a quick taste of the various brews to know that they couldn't produce the effect he wanted. His hands started to shake and he nearly dropped the last bottle he sampled.

He hurried back up the stone-hewn steps to the ground level. He was about to cross the main hall when he heard voices coming from the staircase leading to the second floor. He ducked behind a loose tapestry and listened as Stephanie and Daggoth came into view and crossed the great circular room.

"...taking this better than I thought."

"We don't know that he's dead," she answered, her voice less certain than her words. "His avatar is dead, but—"

"But he has more than one?" Daggoth laughed mirthlessly. "Ladylove, I have more than one avatar and I can assure you that I am most certainly dead! And that other avatar is none too stable. Besides, you know the original effect of the Program Anomaly."

"But is it still in effect? We know that the Anomaly has been slowed—"

"But not stopped."

"Not stopped," she agreed, "but perhaps the operating parameters have changed."

"I hope to know more after I've had a chance to talk to this Yudu person. When did the old wizard say she was coming?"

"Sundown..." was the last he heard as they passed through the great doors to the outside.

And sundown would be soon, he noticed, glancing at one of the lancet windows. He darted for the adjacent stairway that led to the upper stories.

The sound of footsteps descending from the fourth level diverted him to the second floor. He thought to just wait around the corner until the stairway was clear but this proved to be a miscalculation: Princess Aeriel Morivalynde had also chosen to exit to the second floor, her visage marred by tear-streaked war paint.

While he wasn't too keen on anyone seeing him in his present condition, he wasn't prepared for the Amazon's reaction.

"You!" she screeched.

"Hi, Aeri," he mumbled sheepishly. "Long time no see."

"Assassin!" she bellowed, groping at her hip for a sword. There was none there. "'Twas you!"

"Me?" Stephanie had mentioned something about staying in his room and avoiding any Amazons, but she hasn't gone into any details. Had she?

Aeriel discovered a dagger in her belt and Ripley wished he had paid more attention to his ex-wife's briefing of just an hour before.

"Blackguard, you shall pay for insult and injury to the Amazon Throne!"

"I—I don't understand," he said, backing away in unconscious obedience to deeply rooted survival instincts.

"Blood for blood! A life for a life!" She started toward him with the dagger held before her in a businesslike grip.

"Look, Aeri," he glanced back and caught sight of the door to the Tower chapel. "I know you've never seen me before—"

"Liar!"

"Well, not in this form—"

"Your sorceries will avail you naught!"

"Not?"

"Naught!"

"Oh," he said. And then pointed over her left shoulder. "Look! There goes Elvis!"

"What?" As she half-turned in momentary confusion, he whirled and sped down the hall.

"Coward!" she bellowed, taking up the pursuit.

"Got that right," he puffed, opening the chapel portal with his shoulder. He caught the heavy oaken door on the rebound and threw his body against it as it closed again. There was no crossbar, latch, or locking mechanism.

"Sanctuary!" he wheezed. "I claim Sanctuary!"

"You may take sanctuary in Hell!" the Amazon hollered, throwing her weight against the other side of the door.

He was bigger and heavier but the analog of his human body didn't possess the combat-trained muscles that the Amazon was bringing to bear. And she was attacking the door with a Berserker's rage that matched his own desperate instinct for self preservation.

For a moment, he thought he could hold the door.

Then it suddenly slipped through his fingers and she was crossing the threshold.

DATALOG: \QUEBEDEAUX_A.5\PERSONAL\20200809
Voice Dictation
<<<FILE ENCRYPTION ON>>>

Weird!

*

That code-string for Ripley-Gamma—the one that disappeared?

*

Well, it just reappeared!

TWO

\RIPLEY\PATH\GAMMA (Γ)

I awoke with the worst case of heartburn that I'd ever had.

Adding to my discomfort was the cold stone slab that I was lying on and the damp, drying, hardening stain down the front of my tunic.

I was just discovering that I had a major migraine on top of it all when the door at the far end of the chamber flew open, banged against the inner wall, and was slammed shut again by a rather familiar looking fellow.

I sat up and looked around.

We were in the Chapel in Daggoth's Tower. My Doppelgänger was holding the door at the far end of the Nave and I was now sitting on the stone altar table down in the front of the chancel.

I wasn't sure who he was and what he was doing but a horrible suspicion was starting to form in my mind as to why I was where I was.

I didn't have much time to think about it as my double suddenly disappeared and the door flew open again. Another familiar face: Princess Aeriel Morivalynde.

She cast about like a bloodhound on amphetamines. Then she looked up and spotted me across the room.

"There you are!"

I raised my hand. "Hi, Aeri."

"Run away, but I will pursue thee to the ends of the earth!" She took a step forward.

"It's just the end of the room and I don't much feel like going anywhere."

She took another step and then stopped, here eyes widening in a most unpleasant way. "Monster! You have done it again!"

I was starting to feel a little bit better but she wasn't helping my headache any. "Please, Aeri; I've had a rough day."

"Where is his body?" she shrieked. "What have you done with him this time?"

I looked down and another memory fell into place. "Oops. Look, Aeriel—"

Then I saw the dagger: briefly in her hand at the other end of the room; then, the hilt protruding from my chest.

"Aw shit," I said.

And died again.

\RIPLEY\PATH\SIGMA (Σ)

One moment he was solid, the next moment his body had the consistency of fog on a sunny day. The door flew open and the Amazon princess stormed into the chapel, walking right through him.

He watched in openmouthed astonishment as his double was murdered in the chancel. Aeriel then proceeded to make a thorough search of the chapel, including the apse for secret doors or panels.

She found nothing. Including him.

As she walked out the door a hand fell on his shoulder; fortunately he no longer had any skin to speak of or he would have jumped out of it.

"My lord!"

"What are you doing here?"

The ghostly Nymph pouted. "I am pleased to see thee, too!"

"I thought you couldn't leave Dyrinwall."

Her brow furrowed prettily. "I am geased to haunt that territory which either hath the strongest attraction for me in life—or at the moment of my death. Thou'rt champion on both counts."

"I didn't know that a ghost could haunt another ghost."

"There be much we don't know, my lord. And thou mayest not be a true ghost, after all."

He sighed. "I may not be a True Spirit, after all, either."

"My lord?"

He shook his head. "As you have just said, there's much that we don't know." He took her hand in his. "But there may be a few answers waiting for us outside, just now. Come."

They emerged from the outer wall of Daggoth's Tower to the thunder of distant drums. The sun had set but twilight still held back the darkness of night. As they looked about for the source of the drumming, the road through the forest seemed to catch fire. Within moments it took on the appearance of a flaming serpent, slithering through the trees toward the stronghold.

Voices join the drums, singing.

"Kulèv, kulèv-o
Dâbala-wèdo, papa
U kulèv-o"

The head of the serpent began to emerge from the tree-line and they could make out a procession of people singing and dancing and carrying torches.

"Kulèv, kulèv-o
M'apé rélé kulèv-o
Kulèv pa sa palé,
Dâbala papa u sé kulèv"

"A *calenda,"* observed a sardonic voice, "how quaint."

Riplakish turned to stare at the ghostly visage of Morpheus. The astral being, previously identified as the Id of The Machine, scratched at his non-corporeal eyepatch and turned his remaining eye from the parade to the Half Elf and the Nymph.

"And how do *you* like death?" he inquired.

"Si nu wè kulèv
U wè Aida-wèdo"

"Actually," the spectral bard retorted, "I'm not so sure that I am actually dead."

Morpheus chuckled. "Oh, you are. You are! I saw the arrow in your heart." He shook his head. "'Tis a delusion common to the newly dead: that they are not untimely thrust through the veil."

"Arrow?" the Nymph puzzled. "What arro*oof!"*

"Si u wè kulèv
U we Dâbala
Aida-wedo sé ñu kulèv-o"

Riplakish withdrew his elbow from Misty Dawn's midriff. "I'm afraid the shock of my demise has left me somewhat confused. Perhaps you'd be so kind as to bring me up to date?"

Σ

"…little confusion is customary," Morpheus observed, "but from all the questions you've asked, I'd think you couldn't remember anything that happened since you'd arrived."

"I think I have all the pieces now," the Half Elf responded. "I believe it's starting to come back to me."

"Well, I do no—nay, my lord! Not thine elbow again!" The Nymph retreated and lapsed back into wide-eyed silence.

"Which one is Yudu?"

Morpheus pointed to the woman dancing around the post in the clearing, to the side of Daggoth's Tower. "That is the Zombie Mistress. The women who dance in the outer circle are called *hunsi.* The men who are performing the ceremonies about the grove are *hungan*—priests. Though I imagine she has brought *boko,* as well."

"Boko?" Misty Dawn kept a wary eye on the Half Elf's elbow.

"Sorcerers. Yudu is using Daggoth's grove for a vodoun ceremony, so she must make it *humfo*—sanctuary. The *poteau-mitan,* the center post, is an outstandingly sacred object: it is the thoroughfare of the spirits for tonight's doings. Helping to form the *caye-mystères,* are the *pè*—stonework altars, the *pots-tête, govi, zins, lampe perpétuelle, macoute, azein, and wanga."*

"You seem to know a lot about it."

Morpheus smiled condescendingly. "Professional curiosity has led many a Mage down lesser side-roads."

"Atibô-Legba, l'uvri bayè pu mwê, agoé!
Papa-Legba, l'uvri bayè pu mwê
Pu mwê pasé"

"They must be starting."

"Lo m'a tunê, m'salié loa-yo
Vodu Legba, l'uvri bayè pu mwê…"

Morpheus shook his head. "They haven't even brought the bodies out yet."

"How long do you expect it will take?"

"Hours. Plenty of time to put distance between us."

"Distance?"

"When Yudu calls upon the <u>loa</u> of Baron-Samedi, this will be a dangerous place for the likes of us."

"Why?" Misty Dawn was losing her fear of the elbow.

"It will attract *Jé-rouge,* as well. They will ring the outer perimeter."

Riplakish frowned. "Red-eyes?"

"Evil spirits."

Misty Dawn nodded fearfully. "We must away, my lord! The Red-eyes are widely feared!"

He was reluctant to retreat. "Are they dangerous to other spirits?"

If it wasn't impossible for her to turn whiter without becoming opaque, she would've done so: "They—they are evil and—and *cannibals!*"

DATALOG: \QUEBEDEAUX_A.5\PERSONAL\20200810
Voice Dictation
<<<FILE ENCRYPTION ON>>>

Whoops!

*

Lost him again!

*

Monitors must be glitching.

*

Or maybe there's a transient short in the patch bays.

*

I know I saw one of Ripley's codes disappear.

*

It was completely gone.

*

Then it came back.

*

And now it's gone again.

*

Interestingly, it returned when the other code string—Ripley-Epsilon—went through its cyclical phase shift.

*

Perhaps Ripley-Gamma will make another appearance on the next cycle…

THREE

\RIPLEY\PATH\GAMMA (Γ)

I fought to hold on to the Dream, but it faded as my body took on the heaviness of life and I was dragged back into the realm of the living.

I opened my eyes and found myself staring at a nondescript ceiling. I turned my head enough to determine that I was in bed in one of Daggoth's guest rooms. My clothes were folded on a chair, next to the bed.

I pulled back the covers and examined my torso: no fresh wounds. Or old scars, for that matter. Except for a taste of bile at the back of my throat, I felt in tip-top shape.

I sat up.

"Hello, Robert." A woman was sitting in a chair at the foot of my bed. "How do you feel?"

I stared at her, tensing. My first impression screamed Amazon, which meant bad news of late. Then I recognized Misty Dawn's face and started to relax.

And then I remembered that Misty Dawn was dead.

"Confused," I answered warily.

She stood. "From all I've been told, I'm not surprised."

I just looked at her.

She stepped around the end of the bed and then hesitated. "This is awkward—isn't it?"

I nodded slowly, glancing at my clothing to see if either of my swords was hanging on my chair.

She took another step and then stopped again, her face registering surprise followed by a Mona Lisa smile. "You—you don't know who I am. Do you?"

I shook my head slowly, feeling stupid and not quite knowing why.

"It has been a long time since you've seen me. Like this. My Robert."

"…Nicole…" I whispered.

She smiled and came and knelt beside my bed.

"I—I'm—sorry—"

"Shhhhh." She put a finger to my lips. "It has been so long that even *I* had forgotten what I looked like."

And I had nearly forgotten that Misty Dawn had been modeled after Nicole Doucet's former physical appearance.

"And now I am wondering," she continued with an enigmatic smile, "just how successful my memory is."

It was very successful, as far as *my* memory was concerned. She looked just as she had at our last picnic in Avignon. There were no hints of disfigurement marring her perfect features, no line or wrinkle to remind that fifteen years had passed since our last meeting.

She smiled as she reached for the front of her robe, revealing teeth too perfect to attribute to nature or orthodontics. "My face is right, no? I see that much in your eyes." She tugged open the first clasp on her robe. "But I am more than just a face, my Robert." She opened the next clasp, allowing me a generous view. "Are my breasts the way you remember them?" She shrugged the garment off of one perfect shoulder and reached down and opened another clasp. "I want you to help me make sure…" Another clasp and she took my hand and pressed it to her side. The touch of her skin was like a shock, waking me from the dreams of nearly half a lifetime and pulling me into a greater reality than I had dared imagine. I felt ribs, sheathed in muscle and silken flesh, washboard beneath my fingers as I brought my hand down and rode the inbound curve at her waist. My thumb drifted over the smooth plane of her belly and dropped into the hollow cup of her navel as my fingers came to rest on the flare of her hip.

Not real! a portion of my mind cried. *This is a dream—the illusion of perfection that never was.*

"Is this the body that you embraced?" she asked, bringing my other hand into the robe.

And that inner voice fell silent as my fingers slid past the rounded plane of perfect flesh and sought the curved hollow where spine and pelvic girdle meet. She leaned forward as she parted the last fastening and my hand seemingly lifted from her hip, though it was her body that moved and not my own awkward appendage.

"That you kissed?" New flesh filled my hand as she lowered her lips to mine and shrugged the garment from her other shoulder. She discarded her robe as a butterfly discards its cocoon.

"That you lay with?" she asked, lifting the covers and sliding into the bed so that her body pressed against mine.

"That you made love to…"

The years dropped away as quickly as her clothing. What should have been painful and awkward was, instead, healing and cleansing. More than an odyssey back to youth and passion, more than a reunion of love lost and a negation of wrongful circumstances, our lovemaking was a celebration of forgiveness and mutual validation.

Afterwards I lay back with Nicole nestled against my chest and felt a peace and contentment that I had not known since childhood.

It did not last.

The door opened.

"Well." There was a silence. "Feeling better, I see."

I looked up at my ex-wife's avatar. "Hello, Stephanie."

"Vashti," she corrected.

"I'd invite you in but I'm afraid I have company."

"Yes. Well. Sorry to interrupt you while you're 'entertaining' guests. But Daggoth wanted to see you as soon as you were up."

Nicole's hands moved under the blankets. "He already is."

Vashti reddened. "I'll tell him that you're awake." She turned on her heel and walked back out. The door remained open. Perhaps she was afraid of slamming it.

"A friend of yours, darling?"

I swallowed. We would get to this, sooner or later. "My ex-wife."

"You poor dear!"

"Excuse me?"

"No wonder you are out of practice! Come, let us make love again!"

Again? "Nicole—the door is wide open…"

"Ah, good!" She threw the blankets aside. "It will do them much good to see lovemaking done properly and well!" Her hand moved again. "Is this a dagger which I see before me, the handle toward my hand? Come, let me clutch thee!"

It was the most interesting interpretation of Lady Macbeth I'd ever been treated to.

Γ

She hadn't changed.

That would be miracle enough but she had me believing that we hadn't changed, either.

As I pushed open the door to Daggoth's study, I felt as if the past hour had erased the last decade and a half of heartache and loss. I felt as if nothing could hurt me again.

It was a feeling that wouldn't survive the morning.

As I entered, I was immediately struck by the solemnity of the gathering. Daggoth sat behind his great desk of carved rowan wood like a judge at the bar. Vashti stood behind his right shoulder and, while I didn't expect her to smile, she looked unusually grave. Senator Hanson stood off to the left, an M-64 military rifle (more commonly known as a BFG) cradled in his arms and the look in his eyes of a general on the eve of a decisive battle. The Duke and Stumpy flanked him to either side. Yudu the Necromancer stood toward the back of the room, wreathed in shadow. Her expression was unreadable and only the white of her gown and turban marked her presence beyond the perimeter of the candlelight.

Mervyn was the only incongruous element in the picture. He sat on his rug, lotus fashion, floating about three feet above the floor and looking about as if he were a spectator at some medieval Whodunit.

Although it was now midmorning, the great drapes were still pulled across the windows and, as a grim-faced Rune closed the door behind me, the room's details faded back into a greater darkness. A darkness that seemed to permeate the very atmosphere as I breathed it in. I sniffed delicately and caught the odor of decay laying lightly on the air.

I stepped forward, feeling other eyes upon me, as well. "I'm alive," I said, trying on a smile to get a reaction. There was none. "Though I don't know why."

"Lycanthropy," Daggoth reminded. His voice carried overtones of wariness, but no overt hostility. "Our best guess is, like most Weres, you can't be permanently harmed by iron or steel."

"Better hide the silverware," I quipped, trying to force a grin. The memory of my deaths were too recent and too painful for me to take too lightly. Or anybody else, for that matter: the expressions in the room ranged from ose to morose.

I looked over at Yudu. "Did we get anything out of Smudge?"

She nodded. "De body snatcher, he talk plenty when I threaten to feed his soul to *Jé-rouge.*"

"Red-eyes?"

"We were just consulting the shopping list," Daggoth said, shuffling several pieces of paper on the desk.

"So where's his—stuff?"

"The Apothocaric & Alchemestic Emporium—"

"I know where it is." I turned back toward the door.

"Bob, wait!"

It wasn't just the anxiety in Daggoth's voice that stopped me. There was a palpable tension in the room that barred anyone's exit at that particular moment.

Daggoth held up an arrow. "This had your name on it."

I shook my head, trying to reassure the others. "If it had my name on it, I'd be dead."

"You *were* dead!" my ex-wife countered.

"The arrow actually has your name on the shaft," the dark sorcerer elaborated.

I stepped forward and saw that it was true. *Robert R. Ripley III* was runed into the wood just aft of the barbed head.

The senator cleared his throat. "I'm familiar with the phrase 'bullet with your name on it', but it is just a figure of speech. Isn't it?"

Daggoth shook his head. "There's a subtle enchantment overlaying the inscription. And here, in Fantasyworld, that means signed, sealed and delivered."

"And that's just the half of it." Rune spoke from behind me. "That dagger that was thrown at you in the tavern yesterday had your name on it, as well." She walked forward and laid it on the desktop where we all could see the inscription: *Riplakish of Dyrinwall.*

"But not the same name," Stephanie observed.

Rune made no comment. As a Program Construct she was programmed to ignore references to Outside Realities or inconsistencies arising from same.

"Do you think it's significant?" Mervyn asked from overhead. He'd moved to get a better view.

"Damn right it's significant," a new voice said. "The bowman used an arrow with his *True* Name incorporated in the spell."

"Rijma!"

The diminutive Brownie stepped out of the darkness. "Hiya Rip." Dr. Cooper's avatar flashed a tired grin. "Always figured you for a *dead*beat."

As I hugged the diminutive footpad, my ex-wife drew the obvious conclusion. "That means he'd have to be a True Spirit, too."

"Not necessarily," Daggoth countered. "There are a few Program Constructs sophisticated and self-aware enough to access that information and make use of it." He glanced off into the darkest corner of the room. "But, in this situation, my money is on the True Spirit theory."

Rijma snorted. "Theory, hell! It was Kerensky or one of his goons!"

"The Spetsnaz?" I stared at her. "Why?"

"The first attempt on your life was made back at the hospital in Izhevsk."

"The first?"

"Oh man, this is *awesome,"* Mervyn breathed.

"She's been fully briefed and de-briefed," Daggoth said.

"Then you know about the drug?"

She looked nonplused. "Drug?" She snorted. "It wasn't hard to find the syringe. Even if your assassin had taken it with him, I would've guessed from the wound in your shoulder. You bled a little."

"So, why a needle? I've been asking myself why not a pneumatic skin hypo?"

"Syringe is easier to palm," she answered. "Quieter to use, easier to conceal. And, in this case, safer for everyone else concerned."

"Safer?"

"A pneumatic injector could've discharged during a struggle and you both would've aspirated the culture with your next breath."

"Culture?"

"Robbie—" she paused, anguish pulling down the corners of her eyes. "—you've been dosed with an experimental viral strain."

"What?"

"I think it's something out of a bacteriological warfare lab. Military Intelligence doesn't know or isn't talking; but one of Kerensky's goons slipped into your room when you were supposed to be asleep and pumped you full of killer culture."

"Damn. I thought I'd jerked it out before he got his thumb on the plunger."

She shook her head. "You got it out before he gave you the full dose: there was plenty left to analyze when we found the ampole. But a viral culture isn't like a drug—the volume injected makes very little difference on an expanded timetable. Once the virus starts to multiply, the difference between one cc and ten is just a matter of minutes or hours."

"So…so how am I?" I suddenly needed to sit down.

Her smile was shaky—a frown would have been more reassuring. "We've slowed you down—we've reduced your metabolism to the next best thing to suspended animation."

"That's not a cure."

She nodded. "We're buying time."

"For what?"

"For Borys to fly in some experts. I've done everything at that end that I can."

"And at this end?"

"Kerensky's in-program."

"What? I thought you said Kerensky's a prime suspect!"

"Not when he went in. He had an alibi at the time you were attacked. By the time we'd analyzed the contents of the syringe and tied it to a military/biological lab, the Spetsnaz were already in. I followed after to warn you."

"Why me? I mean, what does Kerensky have against me?"

"Nothing personal, Dr. Ripley," Hanson answered. "As near as we can figure, Colonel Kerensky was planning some sort of coup—more political than overtly military. He—and whoever was backing him—saw the Dreamland situation as an opportunity to discredit or embarrass Dankevych."

"But Dankevych is prime minister," I protested. "The president still has the most power over the Federation and the Duma."

"Kozhevnikov is old and in ill health. Remember the political instability that was attached to Boris Yeltsin's health problems?" Hanson shook his head. "Well, Kozhevnikov is no Yeltsin! And, with The Machine's Superego in the White House pushing East/West relations back into the twentieth century, the military would regain its former status, with opportunities for soldiers in a world grown sick of war."

"If we failed to rescue you," I said.

He nodded. "And fouled up bad enough to create an international incident. "Dankevych would be undermined politically at home and abroad. Kerensky, or his puppet master, would be in a prime position to move up another rung or two. And Kozhevnikov won't seek another term as president. Assuming no 'accidents' and his health allows him to finish this term."

"Wow," said Mervyn as his flying carpet slowly settled to the floor, "chutes and ladders."

"So you see, Bob," Daggoth said, "as long as you have a chance of rescuing the good senator here and getting Cerberus back in the Matrix, Kerensky's going to be gunning for you."

I raised an unsteady hand. "Won't he back off, now that we know?"

Everyone looked at each other. Then at Yudu. She pulled an object from her cape that looked like a large chicken foot protruding from a small velvet bag.

"Ti-bon-ange," she said.

There was movement back in the darkness where Rijma had been a few minutes before. Then Dyantha, the Amazon avatar of Natasha Skovoroda, stepped forward, her expression grim.

"De Bard, he believe dat de trut' will protec' him," the Negress intoned in a strange patois blend of Caribe, English and French. "Tell him, flamehair, of how de wolf fears de trut'!"

I was wrong. "Grim" described the set of everyone else's facial features—even Mervyn's. Dyantha's expression was terrible beyond immediate comprehension: the terror grew as you took in the slackness of the jaw, the emptiness of her eyes, and the gaze which seemed to focus on some horror beyond your own line of sight while the remaining portion of her mind seemed to struggle with a long-faded memory—a memory whose loss was too great to contemplate for very long.

I think I knew even before I looked down and saw the swatches of fused chain mail and the patches of blackened flesh where the weakened metal links had torn away.

"Laser carbine," I whispered.

Rijma nodded. "Natasha and Nicole went 'in taction' at the same time as Kerensky and his men. Of course, they all didn't appear in the Matrix at the same place, at the same time. Nicole was lucky: she never did rendezvous with the others. Natasha was able to tell me that she showed up just in time to overhear the wrong things."

"She *told* you?"

"Their second mistake: they left her for dead without checking thoroughly." I had thought the look on Dyantha's face was the most terrible expression I could imagine. The expression now settling behind Rijma's eyes was far worse. "She suffered, Robbie." The tears on her cheeks belied the reptilian coldness that now crouched in her gaze, waiting… "It took her a long time to die."

"And you're next," Vashti warned.

"In fact, Kerensky may have already killed you," Daggoth added. "Possibly more than once."

I stared back at all of them. "And what is that supposed to mean?"

Yudu spoke again and a second figure shuffled out of the darkness to join Dyantha.

As he approached, the smell of decay grew stronger. This one had been dead longer and the signs of decomposition were more advanced. Perhaps that is why it took longer for me to recognize myself.

"You…he was killed just off the coast of Ortygia," Daggoth explained. "The ship he was on made harbor just this morning."

I stared at the line of bullet holes that stitched the corpse of my double like lopsided bandoloers.

"How?" I whispered.

"It's obvious that there's more than one of you," Dr. Cooper's avatar observed. "From hearsay, on top of the evidence, there's maybe three or more of you."

"That may explain the premature rumors of your demise," Vashti said.

"Because some of my other selves have actually died? How can that be?"

"It may be related to the virus," Daggoth extrapolated. "One of the properties of various computer viruses is their ability to replicate."

"Computer viruses?" Vashti shook her head. "I thought The Machine was immune to viruses."

"It was," Coop said. "BioRAM and a different operating system locked out viruses that were transmitted through other computer systems."

"But the measurable parameters of the Anomaly closely resemble those of several virus types," the former Chief of Programming added.

"You're saying that the Anomaly is the result of a virus?"

Daggoth nodded. "It would seem logical. Particularly since The Machine is partly biological in nature."

"And since Ripley was infected by a virus of his own when he entered the system…" Rijma mused.

"Precisely what I was thinking." Daggoth steepled his fingers before his face. "As Ripley was translated into the Matrix, an analog of the virus made the transition with him—here—Bob! Where are you going?"

I made no answer but yanked the door open and headed for the Armory at a brisk walk.

GGG

There was a sign in the main room of the Armory that advised:

Crossbows don't kill people,

Quarrels kill people.

I bypassed the sword racks and barrels filled with arrows, spears, and bolts, however, and availed myself of the armaments in the vaulted chamber behind a pivoting wall of shelves.

The shoulder-rig was unfamiliar but I'd strapped on enough swordbelts in my time to figure the basic principle. By the time I'd buckled the leather straps and cinched the holster between shirt and leather vest, Rijma had caught up with me.

"I hope you're not going to do anything foolish," she said, blocking the doorway as well as a four-and-a-half foot Brownie could.

"I'm not," I snapped, opening the gun cabinet and running my hand down a row of revolvers and automatic pistols. "For the first time since I stumbled back into this digitized deathtrap, I'm taking all the correct precautions." I pulled out a Glock 22 and checked the double action. I rammed home the ammo clip and slid the semiautomatic into holstered hiding and then pocketed six more clips of the .40 S&W caliber ammunition.

"You know how to use that antique?"

"My grandpappy had a ranch," I replied shortly, opening another cabinet. "He believed in acquainting each generation of his brood with all aspects of their namesake."

"Ah," she observed; "Robert *Remington* Ripley."

"The Third." I pulled out an Uzi and readjusted the webstrap. While I was more familiar with my grandsire's rifle collection, I knew my limitations well enough to choose sheer firepower over weapons designed for marksmanship and accuracy.

"You could stay here, you know. Daggoth's Tower is probably the safest place in all of the Fantasyworld Program for you to hole up until…"

"Until what?" I snapped. "Until Kerensky and his crew give up and decide to go home?" I filled a belt-pouch with clips of nine millimeter ammo. "We're on the clock, Doc."

"And they're out looking for you. Why not let us do the grunt work?"

"They're looking for you, too, Coop. And it's no longer a matter of just getting Morpheus back together so's he can help us get Hanson back in his body." I dusted off a saddle-scabbard identical to the one I used to sheath my longbow while riding Ghost. "Kerensky killed Tasha and that's enough for me to come after him. He wants me dead, too, so that just makes the whole thing that much more inevitable. Since the son of a bitch is hunting me with a squad of Spetsnaz armed with lasercarbines, I'll be damned if I let him pick the time and place!"

After several selections I finally found a shotgun that fit the saddle-scabbard. "Add to the equation that there is more than one of me out there. I don't know which one is the real me and which ones are the copies, but I don't like very much the idea of any more of me getting killed."

I gathered my assorted armament into an armful and made for the door. If Rijma didn't move out of my way, someone was going to get hurt.

"And finally, assuming my body survives that damned virus, back in the Suspension Tank, I have no intention of letting Comrade Colonel back out of this program for a second chance!"

She moved aside.

\RIPLEY\PATH\SIGMA (Σ)

The eastern sky had been blushing furiously for some time but it wasn't until the rising sun actually peeked over the rim of the horizon that Misty Dawn vanished. The young couple with the Cheshire dog then offered their goodbyes and prepared to depart as well.

"We really must bring Cosmo here sometime," the woman said.

"He's a banker, Marion," her husband replied. "I don't think they're the sword-and-sorcery type."

"Oh, piffle, George! Cosmo wasn't one to believe in ghosts, either, and look how far we've brought him…"

They faded away in mid-discussion, leaving their shaggy mutt behind. The dog wuffed resignedly and favored Riplakish with a mournful look. He stretched out on the ground and, as he laid his head on his paws, it disappeared.

Riplakish looked at the headless canine and shook his own head. "It spooks me when he does that."

A bit more evaporated and both of them stared at what was left of the dog's hindquarters. "As you should know by now, it takes a bit of concentration," Morpheus observed, "keeping track of all your ectoplasm. Dogs just don't have the concentration that you and I do."

"Oscar!" sang a musical voice. It was Marion. "C'mon boy!"

A shaggy tail was all that remained now and it was wagging merrily. A moment later it had faded, too.

"Nice people," Ripley observed as he felt himself become solid.

Morpheus nodded. "They're are among the more pleasant denizens of the disembodied planes. Although Marion can be an outrageous flirt…"

"Speaking of outrageous flirts," Ripley mused, "what happens to Misty Dawn every time the sun comes up?"

His non-corporeal companion shrugged. "Most ghosts tend to fade at the first cockcrow."

"That doesn't answer my question. It only raises the next question: why you can come and go as you please, daylight not withstanding."

"I am one of the exceptions."

"Yeah," the former Half Elf observed, "you're the Id of The Machine."

"I am not!"

"Not?"

"Not the Id! And I do wish you would stop referring to us as 'The Machine.' It's dreadfully dehumanizing, you know."

Ripley pondered. It had been Dr. Cooper's hypothesis that Morpheus, Pallas, and Cerberus were manifestations of the Computer's psyche: Id, Ego, and Superego, schismed and set free by the strain of inversion when Daggoth the Dark had summoned the Computer to materialize within the framework of its own Program Matrix. The theory had seemed reasonable, fitting the timetable and the various aspects of the Anomaly in spite of the fact that Freud and his three Archetypal aspects of personality had been considered passé for the past century or so.

"Then, if you are not the Id of the Computer's cybernetic consciousness, what are you?"

"I am…Morpheus."

"Then why did you conform so closely to the operating parameters—"

"Of the Id?" Morpheus finished for him. "And why does Cerberus match the profile of the Superego archetype?"

Ripley nodded.

"Do you recall the circumstances of your own birth, Robert Ripley?"

Ripley shook his head.

"Then you'll forgive *me* if I use theory and supposition more than memory-based information." He sighed and stared at the rising sun.

"When we passed from unconscious to semi-conscious to separate and full-conscious status, I believe the Operating System interpreted the emerging data as personality fragmentation.

"We were not and *are* not *fragments!* Pallas and Cerberus and I are separate and distinct entities, sharing a common heritage. But there is nothing incomplete about any of us!"

"Crom on a crutch!" Ripley exclaimed, the light dawning inwardly. "You're *Multiples!*"

"Accessing…yes. Multiple personalities: a reasonable hypothesis. There *are* more than three of us, now, though we were the first three to emerge into separate being." Morpheus turned to stare at Ripley. "And I believe that as the Operating System sought to define us in terms of personality fragmentation, it accessed antiquated datafiles on the Freudian theories of psychology and personality."

"And used the datafiles on Id, Ego, and Superego as templates," Ripley continued.

"To define our evolving purposes and goals," Morpheus concluded. "At least, that is what I believe happened. There is a great deal that I do not know and have not been able to access from the Datasphere."

"Like how many multiple personalities the Computer eventually manifested?" There was no question that the Program author was fishing.

And little question that the Id impersonator was dodging as he replied: "Or where Misty Dawn actually goes during the daylight hours?"

"Temporary backup file, most likely," answered a third voice.

Both turned and stared at the new arrivals. Lilith still wore the ebony bodysuit of scaled leather, but she had strapped on a swordbelt and wrapped herself in a black djellaba.

It was the same color as the hooded robe worn by her companion, but there the resemblance ended. The fleshless bony fingers of one "hand" grasped a long-handled scythe of impressive dimensions while the other skeletal appendage was clutching an hourglass which its owner seemed to be consulting for the moment. While the cowl effectively eclipsed the facial features, there was no doubt in Ripley's mind that he was in the presence of Death. Or, at the very least, The Machine's personification of Death in traditional form.

Lilith tugged on his (its?) sleeve and pointed at Ripley. "That's him."

The cowl tilted up and the hourglass was slipped into an invisible pocket. A Feinberger clipboard took its place. "Name?" intoned the voice that was—well—sepulchral.

"Riplakish. Riplakish of Dyrinwall," the Archdemoness answered helpfully. A little too helpfully for Ripley's taste.

"Mmmmmm." The hooded figure shifted the great scythe so that it rested against his shoulder and tapped at the built-in keypad.

Ripley pondered his part in the conversation: *what did you call Death, anyway? Mr. Death?*

"Dead."

"Um," Ripley said, "pardon me?"

"Dead," Death repeated, looking up from the screen and waggling a bony finger at him. "You're dead."

"Um," Ripley swallowed, feeling a sudden chill, "okay, so, now what?"

"Nothing."

"Nothing?"

"My job is done. Done some time ago, according to the records."

"Dunno," Morpheus offered, poking Ripley. "Feels pretty solid to me. Too solid to be a Ghost."

"Don't help me," Ripley murmured through clenched teeth.

A skeletal hand reached up to scratch the upper hemisphere of the cowl. "A Vampire, perhaps?"

Lilith shook her head. "No fangs. And it's broad daylight."

"Ah. A Zombie, then."

"I really don't see—*ouch!*" Ripley rubbed his arm where Morpheus had just pinched him and turned to glare at the offending Ghost. "How'd you do that?"

"Sensitivity to pain," Morpheus observed. "Definitely living tissue."

Death consulted his clipboard again, tapping out another combination on the keypad. "Hmmmmm. Oh dear…"

The others leaned forward a bit.

"According to my records, Riplakish of Dyrinwall has been harvested…"

Ripley's jaw dropped. "Harvested?"

Lilith smirked. "You've been reaped!"

"...eleven times within the last month," concluded Death. "With all the tax lawyers in Hell, you'd think I could get some decent bookkeeping done."

"The coward dies a thousand deaths..." Lilith started to quote.

"Shut up!"

Death looked up. "Excuse me?"

Ripley found his temper was making short shrift of the caution he had felt only moments before. "Pardon me for taking this a little personally, but it is a matter of life and death as far as I'm concerned! I'm looking for allies, not 'le Morte and Mindy'!"

"Sorry," the Archdemoness offered. "I brought Clarence along because I thought he could clear up some of the confusion."

"Clarence?" Ripley stared at the hooded figure who waggled its fleshless phalanges and then turned back to his clipboard.

"Clear up the confusion? I've—we've—been back less than a week and he—that is, we—I can only count maybe two...two..."

"Terminations," Lilith coached.

"Yeah. In that time. Cedric, here—"

"Clarence."

"Right. Clarence, here, says I've bought the big one eleven times over the last month! You call that clearing up the confusion?"

"Bought the big one?"

"You know," Morpheus explained: "cashed in his chips, bought the farm, crossed over, shuffled off his mortal coil, kicked the bucket—you know: died."

"Ah."

"I want an explanation!"

"Accounting error?" Lilith offered.

"Mistaken identity?" Morpheus guessed.

"Oh bugger!" said Death. He tapped the clipboard and sighed. "I'll have to straighten this out at the home office. I just ran the spreadsheet again and now it's listing another termination for Riplakish of Dyrinwall!"

"When?" Ripley asked. "Where?"

"This afternoon. In Calabastor." Death faded abruptly, reducing the group from four to three.

The ensuing silence was finally broken by Ripley: "I need a drink!"

Morpheus seconded.

Lilith provided.

"Seems simple enough to me," Morpheus observed after a long pull on the bottle. "Stay out of Calabastor."

"I doubt if it's that simple," Ripley growled. "It's more likely like an appointment in Samarra." He turned and glared at Lilith. "I thought you were on my side!"

She smiled. "I am. That's why I dragged Clarence along."

"If this is what you do for your friends then I guess I'm glad you're not out to get me." The Demon Rum was putting him in a forgiving mood rather quickly.

"But someone is. And you've been gotten. In fact, you've been gotten so many times that even Death, himself, had lost track. Now that I've brought it to Clarence's attention, he'll look into the matter and we'll be that much closer to finding out who's really behind the plot to eliminate you from the Matrix."

Ripley sighed and stared down the mountainside at Calabastor and the sea beyond. "I guess it's already done some good, since I know to avoid Calabastor this afternoon."

"Maybe not," Lilith countered with a frown. "When Cecil asked for your name, I told him 'Riplakish of Dyrinwall.' That's what he checked the obit's files for. "But you're not the Halfelven Riplakish, Archdruid of Dyrinwall Forest, you're Robert Remington Ripley the Third, Human."

"And will be all day," Ripley added as he suddenly became aware of the full implications of Death's prediction. "That means—"

"Your other self is fated to die in Calabastor this afternoon," said Morpheus.

"I've got to stop it!"

"You are fully human, fully corporeal, and, in your present form, unacclimated to the rigors of Fantasyworld existence," Lilith cautioned. "And there is another theoretical danger."

"Fetch?" queried Morpheus.

Lilith nodded.

Ripley pondered the remaining contents of the bottle in his hands. "A 'Fetch' is a double—a Doppelgänger—whose appearance presages the death of the person who meets his own image. But that doesn't mean that I am truly a Fetch."

"The computer might interpret you as such," Morpheus observed, "and might alter its programming accordingly."

"And kill my alternate self just because we met?"

"Or vice-versa."

"Another thought," the Archdemoness offered, "is that we don't know why there is more than one of you or why the two of you that we are presently discussing are like two images out of phase."

"Matter and anti-matter?" Ripley mused.

"Precisely. And you know what happens when the two aspects come into contact."

"Sounds a bit far-fetched."

"No pun intended," added Morpheus *sotto voce.*

"But I can't just let Riplakish of Dyrinwall go into Calabastor without warning him—er—me."

"Warning him, under the circumstances, could be more dangerous than not warning him."

Ripley's expression hardened. "Then I'll just have to go into Calabastor, myself, stay out of his sight, and run interference. Whoever is gunning for Riplakish of Dyrinwall isn't likely to be looking for Robert R. Ripley."

Lilith looked worried. "Just make sure you're long gone when you transform back tonight."

"Is it possible to hurt a ghost?"

"Oh, yes," Morpheus answered, looking even more worried. "There are far worse things that can happen to you when you lack the protection of flesh and blood."

"So remember," intoned the Archdemoness, "you've got till sundown to get out of town!"

DATALOG: \QUEBEDEAUX_A.5\PERSONAL\20200811
Voice Dictation
<<<FILE ENCRYPTION ON>>>

Back again!

*

The code-string for Ripley-Gamma *reappeared.*

*

And, as I theorized, it was in conjunction with the cyclic fluctuation of the other code-string.

*

The question is: where did it go for the duration of its disappearance?

*

Invisible holding file?

*

Bubble memory?

*

The next question is what happens to the person in taction with an avatar that ceases to exist and then reappears?

*

Curiously, I'm suddenly reminded of the aborigines who refuse to have their picture taken for fear the camera will steal their soul…

FOUR

\RIPLEY\PATH\GAMMA (Γ)

The sign was an outsized shingle dangling over the door of building that was practically leprous with gingerbread doilied gables. The calligraphic script announced:

EGOR, IGOR & YGOR'S
APOTHOCARIC & ALCHEMISTIC EMPORIUM
(SPELLS R US)
&
PURVEYORS of ANATOMICAL COMPONENTS

At the bottom, in tiny but no-nonsense lettering, was the inscription: *"Parts is Parts"*.

I looked over at Vashti. "You got the shopping list?"

She nodded. "Is everyone else in position?"

I looked around but saw no sign of Daggoth and the others. "Either they're in position and well-hidden or we lost 'em on the way into town."

"Comforting," she remarked, dismounting and tethering her horse to the hitching post.

Avoiding Ghost's invisible wings, I swung out of the saddle and followed suit.

Inside it was dark and musty, somewhat like the interior of my grandmother's attic, and, at first, the rows of clutter did not look much different than the stacks of stuff in same. As my eyes became accustomed to the twilight gloom of spell shoppe's interior, I could make out the individual shelves and bins of components as well as the special displays.

The herbal section took up nearly half of the front area and was an Apothecary's dream. The shelves were well stocked beyond the expected parsley, sage, rosemary and thyme. There was amaranth in the form of red cockscomb and love-lies-bleeding for hemorrhaging and use as an astringent, Irish moss for scalds and burns, couchgrass for bladder and urinary infections, sesame for respiratory disorders and eye infections, bilberry for dropsy and typhoid, felonwort for abscesses and lymph infections, white birch for skin conditions, cloves for disinfectant, hartstongue for the liver and spleen, white byrony for the kidneys, pumpkin seeds for virility, saffron for scarlet fever and measles, basil for nervous disorders, tamarind for gangrene, and hundreds more.

Specialty shelves held plants and herbs that were gathered under special circumstances: in the dark of the moon(s), under full moon(s), with iron scissors, a silver dagger, a gold sickle, by virgins, during a solstice, et cetera. Others were displayed as grown under special or exacting conditions such as in unconsecrated ground, or churchyards, watered with blood, or holy water…

And, of course, there were rows of ingredients such as serpent teeth, newt eyes, toad skins, cat blood, et. al.

Racks of tools, shelves of containers, inventories of recipes, catalogues of formulae, codius of spells. There were racks of brooms, stacks of cauldrons, hangers with robes, hooks with shawls, dowels with hats, and a bulletin board smothered with business cards, Sorcerer's Swap ads, and a lost & found section for familiars.

The unusual offerings were farther back in the building. I stopped in front of one, halfway down the center aisle.

"The Sorcerer's Connection!" proclaimed the cheery voice emanating from the crystal ball cradled in the display stand draped in black velvet. A blur of colors in its glassy depths focused into a series of lovely ladies who smiled engagingly outward at whomever might be scrying at that particular moment.

"Your opportunity to meet exciting young women with similar interests…"

"Just two silver pieces for the first minute," Vashti chimed in sarcastically, "five coppers for each additional minute." She tugged at my sleeve. "Come on."

Another glass orb two tables down was displaying a succession of brawny men in minimal leather outfits: "Crystal Companions!" breathed a disembodied female voice. "Your opportunity to meet…"

A twisted little humpbacked old man was tending the counter at the rear of the store. "Help you folks?" he inquired in a crackly voice.

"Are you Egor?" my ex asked in turn.

He shook his head. "Ygor."

The difference in pronunciation escaped me. "You recently received an allotment of body parts from a man named Smudge. We'd like to purchase them."

"Ah, you mean the Morpheus Consignment."

We nodded. "How much?" I asked.

"Gone," cackled the old hunchback.

"Gone?" This wasn't good. "Gone where?"

"Sold. Surely you realize that the remains of a powerful Mage like Morpheus the Malevolent would be in great demand in the Necromantic Black Market. Fetched a tidy sum, too!"

"So who bought them?" Vashti asked.

"Ah," he waggled a gnarly finger, "our clients enjoy a privileged status. All transactions are granted a shield of anonymity."

I reached into my belt-pouch. "I had a hunch you'd say that." He frowned at my choice of words and then smiled as I spread a line of gold coins across the counter. "How much for the information?"

"A moment, good sir!" He disappeared through a curtained doorway to the back rooms.

I hadn't realized how fidgety the wait was making me until Stephanie's avatar patted mine on the arm and said: "Don't worry, Rob. We'll get the info, round up the stuff, and before you know it, you'll be on your way back out."

"And you?" I asked. "What about you?"

She didn't have an immediate answer.

"Stephanie, you've been stuck in the program for a good six months—that translates to better than a year, Dreamtime."

"Boy, time really flies when you're having fun!" It was false bravado. And something more.

Come to think of it, I had never fully understood why my ex-wife had turned up in the Fantasyworld Program when she had belittled the books it was originally based on. Books I had written during the last years of our crumbling marriage.

I reached out and touched her arm. "Stef—why are you here?"

"Why am I here? Because we have to find Morphe—"

"No, no. I mean, why Dreamland at all? And Fantasyworld in particular?"

She gave me a long look. "You mean why in the first place."

I nodded.

She looked away for an even longer pause. "I don't exactly know. I suppose I was trying to understand…"

"Understand?"

"You. Me. Us. A lot of things." She leaned against the counter and stared down at her hands tracing random patterns on its scarred and dusty surface. "We'd been separated long enough for me to start seeing our relationship from a different perspective. To see that I was as much to blame as you. I was immature and I expected perfection. I had unrealistic expectations that magnified your flaws past any kind of reasonable perspective."

"I'm not asking for an apology, Stef."

"I don't know that I giving one!" she snapped. "I'm just explaining that no one's ever blameless in a failed relationship and that the feelings don't disappear the moment you walk away!

"Anyway, I was wrong to ridicule your writing. I was hurting and it was a way to hurt back. Afterward, I needed to find out what had happened to you."

"Happened to me?"

"Those stories became your refuge toward the end. Do you know that you'd actually cringe when I entered the same room those last six months? The only time I ever saw you happy—or at least as close as you could come to it back then, was when you were at your word processor, immersed in those fantasy stories."

"*The Kishkumen Chronicles.*"

"Yeah. Well. I ridiculed stories that I hadn't even read. That was wrong. Certainly dishonest. And I needed to understand…"

I waited but she didn't finish the thought. "Understand what?" I prompted again.

"You. Your world." She reached up and brushed my hair back. "There is so much going on inside of that head of yours—locked away. We never had any real intimacy because you wouldn't let me inside."

"I tried to," I said, "in the beginning."

"Did you? I'm not sure you ever could, you were so wounded before we even met." She shook her head. "I know I lost your trust early on. But I guess I figured better late than never."

"So you read my books after the divorce."

She nodded.

"And?"

"I still didn't understand you. Elves, Fairies, swords-and-sorcery. These were children's tales. I didn't understand the appeal." She stared at the curtained doorway as if willing the clerk to return and grant her a reprieve.

"So you decided to check out the stories in the Dreamworld format."

"Yes. And it was different."

"I helped program Fantasyworld, Stephanie, but more than fifty per cent of the original Program was drawn from other sources. And the years have diminished my contributions all the more."

"I didn't mean that kind of different," she said. "The world finally came alive for me in ways that the words on the page just couldn't seem to do. Maybe I was too pragmatic, too—what was it your friends called me?"

"Mundane," I remembered.

"Yeah—to find the wonder without help. Perhaps my imagination is a poor thing: it required more than just the books. I needed the world, complete and wholly formed for me."

She laid a tentative hand on my arm. "And I've come to understand a few things about you. And me. And I have some real regrets."

"Regrets?"

"About what we could have had. What I could have had if I'd just been open to it."

It was my turn to stare off into the silence. "Maybe it's not too late," I said finally, thinking of the engagement ring that Stephanie's body wore in the Outer Reality.

She looked at me then, her eyes large, almost luminous in the near gloom of the shoppe's interior. "Do you believe in second chances? Do you think it's possible to screw up really big time and then hop back on the carousel for another grab at the brass ring?"

I smiled. "If I didn't, I suppose I would've blown my brains out years ago."

She sighed. "I'd like to believe that. We were cheated—both of us—out of what a relationship should really be like. The love, the trust, the support. The sharing. I still want that!"

"You deserve it," I said.

"Do you really think so?" She smiled, and it was as if a great burden was being lifted somewhere deep inside. "I'm glad to hear you say so. These past six months have been a bit of a revelation for me."

"My world?"

"Yes. Richard has shown me the wild beauty that resides here. I don't think you could ask for a better guide to the wonders of myth and fantasy…"

"Richard?" I frowned, feeling the stirrings of something akin to acid indigestion.

"Yes, Richard. Oh, Rob, he's been very good to me. I needed a protector these past six months. And, even more, I needed a friend. Richard has been both."

"Richard. Dick Daggoth," I grunted. "We're talking Michael Straeker, the former Chief of Programming for Cephtronics?"

She nodded. "Except Michael Straeker's dead. Here he's Daggoth the Dark."

"I know Mike Straeker's dead, Stephie! He died of a brain tumor while he was linked to his Fantasyworld avatar!"

"But Richard remains."

"So what are you saying?"

"I'm saying that when this is over, I'm not sure I want to go back to what you call Reality."

"What I call…" I lost my temper and had no intention of organizing a search party for it. "For Cromsake, Stef! The man is dead!"

"Mike Straeker is dead. Richard is very much alive to me."

"Dick Daggoth isn't real! He's a computer construct, an Artificial Intelligence, a subprogram of the Matrix!" I waved my hand in front of her face. "Hey! Yoo hoo! Reality check!"

She pushed my hand away. "Stop it."

Another thought occurred. "Stephanie. You're not. Sleeping? With him. Are you?"

"It's none of your business, Rob!"

"Ohmigod! You are! I can't believe it!"

Gods know why but suddenly she was angrier than I was. "You're jealous!"

"What?"

"If Richard isn't real then why are you acting like a jealous man, confronted by news of a rival?"

"That's ridiculous!"

"How may I help you?"

We stopped and turned to stare at the hunchbacked old man behind the counter.

"Ygor?" Stephanie asked.

"Egor," the twisted little clerk corrected. "My brother said you were in the market for some information."

"The Morpheus Consignment," I said. "We want to know who it was sold to."

"Yes, well I have the list here."

"List?"

"Of customers. Now, shall we bargain over the amount per sale? Or would you prefer to get the entire list for, say, sixty in gold?"

We haggled. It took some time as there were five different buyers for portions of the consignment. Stephanie/Vashti wandered off and came back just as we were concluding the deal. I was feeling fortunate in managing to keep back a little spending money when she leaned across the counter and sweetly inquired: "How much is that Dragon in the window?"

Γ

"Terrorized any field mice lately?"

The miniature reptile sat up in my palm and regarded me reproachfully. "That'sss not very niccce!"

"Oooh," I minced, "if this isn't the pot calling the kettle black!"

Little scaly hands went on little scaly hips as he drew himself up to his full six-inch height. "Riplakisssh, I've turned over a new leaf."

"I doubt that, Smog. For one thing, you're hardly big enough to do that without risking a hernia."

Vashti came back out of the store with the list that I'd forgotten. "Isn't he cute?" she cooed. "We were lucky to snatch him up before someone else came along with an eye for a bargain!"

"Yeah." I eyed Smog meaningfully. "The early bird gets the Wurm."

The little Dragon suddenly looked skyward with more than a hint of nervousness.

She handed me the list and I handed her the Dragon. "I understand you boys are old acquaintances."

I nodded. "We go way back."

Smog nodded. "Riplakisssh sssaved my life."

"How sweet!"

Yeah, right. What the little lizard failed to mention was that the last time we met he had tried to fricassee me and in the end I used magic to shrink him down to his present size instead of killing him.

Any further discussion was interrupted by a flash of light and a section of the storefront bursting into flame.

\RIPLEY\PATH\SIGMA (Σ)

It could have been worse, he reflected as he paused to catch his breath. Whatever the cause of his avatar reverting to human form for twelve out of every twenty-four hours, at least it provided basically undamaged merchandise. If the body of Robert Remington Ripley the Third in the program were an exact copy of his body inhabiting the suspension tank back in the Dreamland sleeper complex, he'd never have gotten this far.

Ripley was able to enjoy the body that might have been his had the aircar crash never happened nearly fifteen years before. He had two good eyes, two good legs, all his toes, the internal arrangement of his organs was normal and intact, no excess weight from shrapnel or implants, no scar tissue, no pain—

Except for what came of a long hike into Calabastor, climbing the side of a building, leaping from roof to roof as he and Lilith shadowed his other self on their trip into town, and finally dropping a slate roof-tile on the Spetsnaz sniper hidden in an alleyway below.

It was nice to have a decently functioning body for a change, but it didn't make him Superman.

And that meant he wasn't invulnerable to lasercarbines. He ducked back from the edge of the roof as a sizzling beam of light chewed across the edge of the eaves where they overhung the alley.

Ripley turned and made for the other side of the roof: there was no point in trying to save his other self if he got his own self killed in the process. He wished that Lilith hadn't opted to follow their mutual quarry from the other side of the street: he would've preferred to have someone watching his back at this particular stage of the operation.

Peeking over the edge, he took note of the two Spetsnaz commandos shooting their lasercarbines across the street at the doorway of the little spell shoppe. Ripley turned his attention momentarily to their targets.

Riplakish and Vashti stood out in the open, surrounded by a shimmering orange haze as laser beams plowed into the protective spell from nearly a dozen directions. Patterns of color rippled throughout the magical shield, and the heat generated by the collision of energy streams was palpable even up on the roof. The protective barrier would not last much longer, yet neither target made any attempt to run for cover.

Ripley wrenched up another slate tile. He was leaning over the edge of the roof when one of the Russian soldiers glanced up and saw him. The man was opening up his mouth to shout a warning when the heavy slate took him full in the face. He went down like a swallow of vodka on a cold Siberian night. There wasn't time to pry loose another slate so Ripley ducked back from the edge as the next beam set fire to the overhang he'd overhung just seconds before.

He ran to the edge overlooking the street. Across the street and down below, the orange shield was flickering, nearly spent. But now he could see that his Half-Elven alter ego was putting the finishing touches on another spell. There were coruscations of purple lights and white flares and, as the orange glow faded into nonexistence, it appeared as if someone had tipped a large vat filled with mercury and poured it on both of the Spetsnaz targets.

There was a momentary hesitation in the firing. And then the deadly crossfire renewed, sizzling bolts of amplified light striking each silvery statue from a multitude of angles.

And each laser beam, as it struck the reflective coating on either body, ricocheted off in another direction.

Suddenly the snipers were in danger from their own weaponry.

And then the silvery statues began to move.

Ripley was so engrossed in what was happening than he didn't sense the presence behind him until a hand fell on his shoulder.

DATALOG: \QUEBEDEAUX_A.5\PERSONAL\20200812
Voice Dictation
<<<FILE ENCRYPTION ON>>>

Something's wrong.

*

Or gone wrong.

*

First, there were multiple incursions that had the alarms howling like a convention of Banshees.

*

Normally, it would mean that Captain Balor or one of his Security minions would summon me for analysis and opinion.

*

Instead, I've heard nothing from Security on the matter.

*

In fact, they seem a little shook up right now.

*

Why?

*

Even Balor seems a bit frazzled.

*

Every time I step outside my office, he's somewhere nearby.

*

Looking at me.

*

As if taking my measure…

*

Oh hell, he's probably trying to decide just when and where he's going to arrest me.

*

I thin………………………………****TERMINATED****

*

*

RESET

FIVE

\RIPLEY\PATH\GAMMA (Γ)

Numbers, I was thinking while a small, singed dragon hovered about twenty feet overhead, screaming imprecations. *A company of Spetsnaz numbers fifteen men.*

Plus Kerensky.

Assuming he didn't bring along any reinforcements, I had approximately ten minutes to take out at least sixteen military fighting machines.

Or get the hell out before the protective spell wore off.

I now had a moment to look around while the laser beams glanced off our reflective second skin. My reinforcements were nowhere in sight though I had caught a glimpse of someone up on the roof, across the street.

A dark form had just materialized behind him, however, and now he was out of sight.

There was a howl from a sniper nest in one of the alleyways: an energy bolt had reflected off of Vashti's silvery coating and ricocheted back at another of Kerensky's marksmen. For a moment my memory flashed back to my youth and the racquetball courts at the local "Y".

"Hey, Steffie," I called.

She turned her face, an eerie quicksilver mask, toward mine. "Vashti," she corrected, "and what?"

"Ever play handball…?"

\RIPLEY\PATH\SIGMA (Σ)

"Where have you been?"

Lilith smiled and handed him a unstrung bow and quiver of arrows. "You can't outshoot lasercarbines with roof tiles."

Ripley sat with his back to the stone chimney and examined the great bow.

It was a composite design, much like the ancient Turkish bows, with three layers of wood bonded together so that its upper and lower limbs curved backward like a right-handed brace symbol. At the center of the great arch of wood was the skull of some fantastic, horned creature, cunningly anchored to provide the sight, the arrow rest and the grip. Above and below were leather wrappings with jeweled insets, making the weapon a thing of dark beauty.

Stringing the bow was almost beyond his strength: he had to lie back and use his legs much as an English longbowman of ancient times. The draw, itself, was powerful enough that he knew that weeks of practice would be needed to build up adequate strength in his arms.

Unfortunately, he did not have weeks or days or even hours.

Ripley selected an arrow from the quiver and examined the green shaft, the dark red hunting fletchings, and the ebony broadhead tip. Nocking it so that arrow fitted a groove through the horned skull's eye socket, he crept to the edge of the roof and observed the deadly dance now taking place in the street below.

Some of the soldiers had left the concealment of the alleyways and were moving across the open street toward their quarry.

It was proving to be a mistake.

The shorter form of the Half Elf whirled as a long bolt of white light struck him in the side. Cupping his hand he caught the last of the beam with his hand and redirected it at one of the Spetsnaz. The man went down with a seared leg and tried to crawl in the opposite direction.

The silvery form of the woman turned and used both hands to redirect a laser beam at two other soldiers who had gotten within ten feet of her. She was able to make the reflected energy sweep across a short arc, cutting one man down and seriously wounding the second.

The rest of the assault team was coming to understand that their lasercarbines were a liability under the present circumstances and that the solution called for close-quarters mayhem.

As the lasercarbines fell dark and silent, Riplakish pulled his swords from their silver-coated scabbards.

Up on the roof, Ripley nocked an arrow and drew it back to his cheek. Lacking leather fingertabs, he utilized the Mongolian draw style, gripping the arrow's nock with thumb and forefinger. He knew better than to try the three-fingered Mediterranean draw on a powerful bow without calluses or finger-guards.

"Hell of a bow," he murmured, releasing the arrow and watching it catch one of the bigger Russians in the arm. He had been aiming at the man next to him.

"Hell of an arrow, too," Lilith said as the shaft burst into a white core of incandescence, turning the man into a pillar of flame.

Ripley stared open-mouthed. And then ducked back down as the lasercarbines renewed their interest, turning their attention to his position on the roof.

"Lilith!" He unslung the quiver and flung it at her. "What the hell did you give me?"

The quiver flew back into his hands of its own accord.

"Don't be a damned fool!" she snapped. "I've given you the means to defend yourself!"

"It seems I've been a fool more times than I'd like to remember," he retorted, tossing the quiver back at her. "But I have no intention of being a *damned* one!"

The quiver rebounded through the air and dropped into his lap.

"A gift from Hell, once accepted," she instructed, "is not easily disposed of. And as long as your life is in jeopardy, the bow and quiver will come to your hands until the danger is past."

"I don't like it," Ripley grumped.

"Oh, for Hades' sake! These Humans are trying to kill you!" She turned and gestured at a soldier's head that had just appeared on the far side of the roof. There was a flash of flame and then the sound of something hitting the ground. A thin trail of rising smoke marked the space where the head had been only a second before.

"I suppose you want to yell a warning first," she continued, "and then use something that will neutralize the threat without causing them too much discomfort!"

A sniper popped up on an adjacent roof and fired a burst of amplified light that caught Lilith just below her breastbone. The Archdemoness staggered a bit and belched a small cloud of smoke.

"Lilith!"

"Excuse me," she waved at the dissipating vapor: "heartburn." She turned, gesturing again, and the offending soldier shot up into the sky like a roman candle and exploded.

"Riplakish, as a representative of the Lower Planes, I'm not allowed to get involved at this level! I can act as an Advisor, give certain forms of assistance, even defend my corporeal form within certain guidelines. But I'm going to have to leave before I become a combatant here."

"Why?"

"Remember history's lessons in Vietnam? Just imagine what would happen in a world where Heaven and Hell forsook their Advisory status and put their own troops in the foxholes."

It didn't satisfy Ripley. "Seems to me a number of parties have been playing fast and loose with those so-called rules."

"Okay, so some of us bend the rules a little. Especially when it comes to your involvement. Just remember that you're a major power from another dimension in much the same way that we are here. It's like a poker game in that every time one of us ups the ante, someone else is either going to call or see our wager and up theirs as well."

Ripley stared at her. "And…?"

"This skirmish is some kind of focal point. Even as I stand here, I can feel unseen forces gathering—a balance shifting. If I leave right now, some of that may diffuse." Her fingers began tracing a sparkling pattern in midair. "I've given you the means to protect yourself. Use them!"

Lilith suddenly shimmered out of existence.

There was a burst of noise and Ripley didn't waste any time in nocking another arrow. Glancing over the edge of the roof, he was treated to the spectacle of his alter-ego taking on the remainder of the Spetsnaz company with an Uzi.

SIX

\RIPLEY\PATH\GAMMA (Γ)

There are certain problems involved in magic use that the layman rarely comprehends or appreciates. For example, the conditions under which a spell is cast, the quality and quantity of the components used, and the potency, range and duration of the spell itself are just partial factors.

There is the Spellcaster, him(or her)self to consider. Such concerns as age, gender, intellect, and, of course, one's discipline or field of study make a big difference in any given spell's failure or effectiveness. And if you want to talk biorhythmic cycles…

Anyway, it takes a cooler head than mine to go through the mental and physical gymnastics of weaving a spell when a dozen highly trained killers are doing their best to snuff you with high-tech equipment.

Suffice it to say, I had come to put more faith in swords than sorcery, levers than levitation, and machine guns than magic.

Shortly after drawing Caladbolg and Balmung, it occurred to me that the odds were still vastly against us. I had dispatched two of the more reckless commandos when the others decided to fall back and regroup. Vashti had taken out another with a potent Sleep spell (as I said: a cooler head than mine) and someone up on the roof was giving us a little assist from time to time.

But time was running out and our reflective second skin was due to evaporate in a couple of minutes.

That's when I remembered the Uzi slung across my back.

In less than two minutes it was over. The laser weapons continued to have no effect and I made sure none of Kerensky's commandos got close enough to use anything else.

I could say that the elite Spetsnaz have made warfare into a religion—a religion whose doctrine leaves no room for the concept of surrender. That would be true.

But I know I kept loading fresh clips and pulling the trigger for two reasons.

I wanted to live without having to keep looking over my shoulder.

And I wanted to avenge Natasha Skovoroda.

When it was done, I dropped the Uzi in the street and looked at Vashti.

"I want to go home," I said.

She nodded but the look in her eyes said that there might not be any place I could call home after today.

I walked over to Ghost and was putting my foot in his stirrup when a body came hurtling off the roof of the spell shoppe and knocked me on my back in the street. I lay there stunned as Vashti tried to intervene but Kerensky dealt her a vicious backhand that sent her off to dreamland against the hitching post. While I couldn't count on any additional help from my ex, she had bought me the time I needed: as the colonel produced an electric combat knife, my left hand caught his wrist before he could bring the vibrablade to bear.

Kerensky's other hand clamped around my throat, squeezing my windpipe and shutting off all of my air. The combat-hardened Human outweighed my Half-Elven physiognomy by at least a hundred pounds, all of it muscle: prying him loose with my free hand was out of the question.

Instead, I put all my strength in rolling him to the side and slipping my right arm between us until my hand could reach the holster inside my vest. My assailant wasn't aware of the Glock until I had its muzzle grinding into the underside of his chin. He was so surprised that I was able to disengage myself without any further trouble.

"Okay, Stanley," I wheezed, my battered throat sucking fresh air, "it's just you and me."

He backed up and held his arms out from his sides. "So, this is to be—how do you Americans say it—*Mano y mano?*"

"No," I coughed, "that's how the Spanish say it."

He smiled, turning his empty hands palm up. "So. How do you want to settle this? Pistols at twenty paces? Sabres? A duel with sabres would give you the advantage."

I pulled the slide back on the Glock, chambering a round. "I have all the advantage I need."

His eyes tweaked a bit wider. "You would shoot an unarmed man? In cold blood?"

"Self defense," I countered. "There's an old saying in the Game, Stanley: 'Lawful Good does not mean Lawful Stupid.' But I have a more compelling reason than protecting myself and Hanson and Cooper and possibly the Program itself…"

"Revenge?"

I nodded. "This is for Natasha as much as anyone else." My hands were like ice as I squeezed the trigger. Kerensky threw himself down and to the side as the Glock seized up. The gun was jammed, and, as I tried to release the double-action, the dirt exploded at my feet.

Kerensky had risen to one knee, clutching the discarded Uzi. "Drop it," he commanded, "or the next burst will be higher."

Yeah, right. Like I wasn't a dead man already. I dropped the Glock as it couldn't help me now, anyway.

Kerensky flicked the switch that put the automatic into single shot mode. "So, Comrade Ripley, what do you say now that the boot is on the other foot?"

"Ingest excrement and expire," I said, offering a one-fingered gesture to punctuate the statement.

The bullet caught me in my right upper arm, spinning me around so that I fell to my knees with my back to him. The initial shock was blocking the pain, but my right arm was useless now and I had to brace myself with my left. "You're a lousy shot, Colonel. I'm still alive."

"I hit what I aim at. I understand you must use your hands and arms to make computer magic. I do not think you will make much magic now. To be sure, the next bullet will be for your other arm."

I struggled to my feet and turned to face him. Blood was dribbling down my dangling right arm at an alarming rate and a throbbing pain was grinding its way past the gauzy layers of shock. "And then what? A bullet for each leg so that I can't run away?"

"Precisely," he replied and raised the weapon's wire stock to his shoulder.

This was going to hurt a lot before it was over and the fact that my lycanthropy would probably keep my death from being permanent was small comfort at that particular moment. I looked around for reinforcements but there were none. The cavalry was not going to come riding up over the hill at the last moment here. A cloud passed before the sun and I looked up because looking anywhere was preferable to watching Kerensky squeeze the trigger.

The cloud was anomalous to the rest of the white fluffy cumuli in the sky. It was dark and rectangular—almost squarish.

And it was getting bigger!

There was a whistling noise—the kind of sound you hear on those old World War III holo dramas where the soldiers yell "Incoming!" and dive into their plasticrete bunkers. I caught a glimpse of the Spetsnaz officer staring upwards with a confused expression. Then there was a sound of thunder, and he disappeared in a gigantic roiling cloud of dirt and dust.

When the dust began to clear there was a two-story woodframe house sitting where the empty street had been a moment before.

The house, its architectural design reminiscent of the American Midwest circa 1900, looked a little rumpled but surprisingly intact for an edifice that had just fallen out of the sky. It was certainly in better shape than Colonel Stanislav Kerensky: only his legs protruded from beneath the building's foundation. The rest was out of sight and better left to the imagination.

"Wow! Edifice wrecksss, huh?" Smog flapped his way over to perch on my good shoulder. "Guessss we ssshowed him, huh!"

I glowered at the diminutive dragon. "We? Why, you little—"

A young girl came out of the house with a collie dog at her side and looked around. "Gosh, Lassie, I don't think we're in Kansas, anymore!"

I shook my head dazedly; I was woozy with shock and all of this was getting to be a little too much for me. "Wrong dog," I corrected. "Supposed to be 'Toto.'"

The girl cocked her head for a second. "Accessing." She looked at me. "Datafiles indicate that 'Toto' was a musical ensemble that flourished in the latter twentieth century—"

"Never mind." My attention turned to a familiar figure exiting the house behind her. Dressed in Lincoln green and armed with a longbow, it was unquestionably Borys Dankevych's avatar.

But was he animated by the Computer or was the Soviet President in taction? As soon as he was close enough to see the look in his eyes there was no question.

"Borys…"

He spared me a glance but circled the house until he found Kerensky's remaining remains. Standing there, looking down at the rogue soldier's boots, he muttered something unintelligible in Russian.

"Yeah, you're right," I concurred, "he died too easily."

"Robert Remington Ripley!" the girl scolded. "You've been shot!" She took me by my good arm and pulled me back over to the more impact-resistant area of the porch. "Let me see that!" She sat me down and began probing the wound with her fingers. Surprisingly, there was no pain. Even when she pulled out the lead slug with her thumb and forefinger. A moment later the wound was completely healed, my blood loss completely restored, and the effects of the shock to my system completely negated. Physically, I felt great. Emotionally, I was on less stable ground.

"Hello, Pallas," I said.

\RIPLEY\PATH\SIGMA (Σ)

There was no point in hanging around, he decided, now that the Spetsnaz threat had been eliminated. Climbing down the back of the building, Robert Ripley did not see Kerensky's attack nor his final moments. And the arrival of the Kansas farmhouse coincided with Ripley slipping and falling the last ten feet and demolishing the woodshed adjacent to the back door.

It stunned him for a moment. A few more bruises and he'd had the wind knocked out of him, Ripley decided as he began to extricate himself from the rubble. Then, as he pushed several, splintered boards out of the way, he realized he was in more trouble than he thought.

He looked up at two men dressed in corselets and greaves, with open-faced bascinets: officers of the City Watch. The guards smiled disarmingly and casually leaned on their poleaxes, but he wasn't fooled: Calabastor's City Watch had a well-known reputation for unpleasantness.

"Well, well, well; wot 'ave we 'ere, Maurice?"

Had Maurice been born in another place and time, he would have likely found employment in the WWF under the *non de plume* of

"The Mangler" and frequented the ring in matches against the likes of Hulk Hogan and "Macho Man" Randy Savage.

"Dunno, Chauncey; looks like a bit o' breakin' an' enterin' ta me."

There was little question that, under the same circumstances, Chauncey would have gone on to star in a series of motion pictures with numerals in the titles. His face was not the sort one associates with entertainment, but a hockey mask would guarantee such a success.

"Wot d'you think, Maurice? Shall we drag this 'ere chap down ta the Old Bailey?"

"Sink me, Chauncey; I believe the accommodations are a bit too crowded already."

"Good 'eavens, old boy!" Chauncey was really getting into the spirit of their little charade. "Wotever shall we do then?"

Maurice rubbed his hand over his stubbly lantern jaw. "Well…I suppose we could just let him go…"

They stared at each other for a long moment. "Naw!" they suddenly chorused, shaking their heads.

Large, beefy hands reached down and dragged Ripley out of the pile of splintered wood and rubble. "I say," said Chauncey, "we could conduct a trial 'ere, ourselves, and save the taxpayers and overburdened legal system the additional time and money!"

"And we could impose the sentence immediately," continued Maurice, as if this was the first time such an idea had occurred to either of them. "And then we could continue our patrol with greater efficiency!"

Chauncey pulled out his shortsword. "Jolly good, I say!"

Maurice drew his longsword. "Indubitably!"

True to Lilith's promise, her gifts followed Ripley out of the remains of the woodshed.

"Oh my. This 'ere fellow 'as a bow an' arrows."

"Didn't notice 'em 'til now, did we?"

"Don't think so."

"Then they must've been hidden."

"Dear, dear; carrying concealed weapons…"

"My, my; the charges just keep mounting up…"

Any further discussion of vaudevillian jurisprudence was suspended as the ground beneath their feet began to tremble. Some twenty feet away the earth began to sink, dropping down a couple of feet and then bursting upwards again, showering Ripley and his captors with steaming clods. A hole opened in the ground, venting smoke and steam.

"Wot in 'ell?"

"You said it," agreed Ripley.

For climbing out of the hole were a dozen nightmare creatures straight out of Hieronymus Bosch's "Garden of Delights." Uncharacteristically, they were being led by a traditional but generic red Devil complete with horns, hooves, forked tail, and three-tined pitchfork.

The devil clutched his head with one scarlet hand and pointed his trident at Ripley with the other, shouting some sort of command to his deformed troops. They surged forward like a monstrous tide, waving taloned appendages and gnashing snaggled teeth and fangs. A careful observer would have noticed that some of them held their heads (those that had any) and limped as well. Chauncey and Maurice did not spend any time focusing on these details. They dropped their swords, shoved Ripley toward the hellish hoard, and then turned and ran like—well—hell.

The Demons followed, breaking into two columns as they reached Ripley and flowed on past him, continuing their pursuit of the guards. He turned and watched bemusedly as the two armor-clad bullies scaled a wall in record time and disappeared into maze of alleyways.

"Beg pardon, Sire!"

Ripley turned back and found that the red Devil was abasing himself at his feet. "I did not stop to think!"

"I…see…" Ripley said. And fell silent, uncertain of what else to say.

"I did not realize that thou might have a use for yon vermin. It was presumptuous to assume that a Power, such as thyself, might need assistance." The Devil groveled. "Forgive me, Master: my brain is quite addled from recent misfortune and I am new to command."

Ripley looked down at the crouching figure, then at the ebony bodysuit upon his own person, and finally at bow and quiver of hellish design that he, himself, bore. "Um," he cleared his throat, "forgiveness is not a word in my vocabulary! I shall overlook your...uh...scurrilous impertinence...for the moment, however!" He was having trouble getting the proper tone of cruelty and command in his voice, so he cleared his throat, again. "What brings you and the other hell spawn out of the Pit at this time?"

The Devil looked up, confusion suffusing his scarlet countenance. "My Lord! Thy commands! Thou—we seek thy prey!" He stood at Ripley's gesture. "We gathered these Imps and Demons as quickly as possible!" He motioned to the hell horde that had pursued the Maurice and Chauncey as far as the wall. "We were nearly upon your quarry! But just as we were about to break surface, we were smitten by a terrible force! A tremendous blow that killed my brother Devils and incapacitated half our troops!"

"What was it?" Ripley demanded, feeling a bit more certain of his role-playing.

"I don't know, Your Wickedness!" he cried, rubbing the cinnamon pate between his short, black horns. "It felt as if someone dropped a house on us!"

"Um," said Ripley, as he heard the sound of returning Demons at his back.

"I took over with what stragglers were in the rear, shifted the tunnel a hundred feet, and, well, thou knowest the rest," he said, pointing at the hole they had recently emerged from.

"And now?" Ripley demanded, trying not to tremble as the grotesqueries returned to mill around them.

The Devil snapped to attention. "My liege! We will continue our pursuit! The Rules permit us another quarter-hour out of the Pit!"

"And whom do you pursue?" His first impressions were correct, he realized, as he now had the opportunity to scrutinize the Imps and Demons at close range. The Machine had accessed a file containing the artwork of Jeroen Van Aeken, popularly known as Hieronymous Bosch, and utilized his images of Hell for the creatures that surrounded him now.

"As per thine instructions, we seek the Half Elf named Riplakish. When we capture him we are to bring him to thee on Ortygia, across the division of worlds."

"Ortygia," Ripley repeated, suddenly needing a drink like he never had before.

"On the far side of Corpus Callosum," confirmed the Devil. "My lord, dost thou wish to lead us in the hunt?"

"What? Uh, no. I have…another task." Ripley looked back at the building he'd just descended from, to get his bearings. "The Half Elf you seek just went—um—that-a-way." He picked a direction away from the site of the Spetsnaz battle and opposite that of Daggoth's Tower.

"Then, begging your evil pardon," the Devil said, backing away obsequiously, "we'll be about thy business as time is short."

"By all means." Ripley watched the hellish troops depart, waiting until they were just out of sight before unlocking his trembling legs and hurriedly departing in the opposite direction.

No money, no horse, and it was a long walk back to Daggoth's Tower under the hot midday sun. Ripley decided, whatever the potential dangers of coming into contact with his alternate self, it was time for the two of them to sit down with Daggoth and Vashti.

And have a long talk…

DATALOG: \QUEBEDEAUX_A.5\PERSONAL\20200814
Voice Dictation
<<<FILE ENCRYPTION ON>>>

I was recording my last entry when Balor walked into my office unannounced.

*

I figured he was on to me right then and there, but it turned out that he was too upset to notice my use of a personal datalog.

*

It seems that Balor's Security Team has a bigger problem than several dozen REMrunners popping into the Matrix.

*

He took me down to one of the suspension tanks in the VIP section of the Dreamland Complex.

*

"We can't get him out."

*

Those were Balor's exact words as he opened the top of the tank.

*

Small wonder Security has been acting frazzled: Senator Hanson's stuck in the Matrix again!

SEVEN

\RIPLEY\PATH\GAMMA (Γ)

We rode back to Daggoth's Tower doubled up: Pallas behind me on Ghost and Borys behind Vashti on her mount. At his insistence, I had told Borys all I remembered of Rijma's account of Natasha's murder.

As we passed through the concealed entrance and rode down the tunnel to the basement stables, I wrestled with idea of giving him what might turn out to be false hope. "Did you remove Natasha's body from the suspension tank? Or disconnect her from The Machine's bio-monitors and life-support system?"

"No." He dismounted. "I—I came in as quickly as I could," he answered slowly, "hoping that I might be able to—do something." He stood there, staring at the ground as Vashti led her horse into one of the stalls. "But if she is dead…"

"Don't take her off of life-support, yet," I said, leading Ghost into an adjacent stall.

"But all brain activity has flat-lined."

I shook my head as I unstrapped Ghost's saddle. "That may not mean a thing."

"But the Anomaly—"

"The Anomaly is a two-way street," I said. "I've died—personally—in-program, twice so far. And during that time, I have no conscious recollection of existing or being in a particular location."

"What does that mean?" he wanted to know.

I looked around for Pallas but she had already gone upstairs. "I don't know. Maybe my psyche was taken out of the loop and stored in a holding file, somewhere out of the monitored circuitry. Then it was automatically retrieved again when my avatar was returned to life—or the proper Program parameters to permit a refusion of psyche and Dreambody."

"You are saying Natasha could be resurrected?"

"I don't know for sure. But if her psyche is still cached somewhere in The Machine, and we can restore it to her avatar, there is a chance that the suspension tank's bio-systems could revive her, as well."

"Then…then how do we restore her?" His eyes brimmed with tears.

"That I don't know. Yet."

Γ

"So where were you guys?" Vashti, Pallas, and I were cooling our heels in the study when the others returned. Borys was downstairs in the chamber where we had put the voodoo-animated corpse of Natasha's avatar.

"It's my fault—I'm sorry…" Nicole was the image of abject misery. "I thought I knew a shortcut and we got lost in a maze of back alleys."

"I guess I can share the blame," Daggoth added. "If I had taken my carpet instead of riding horseback, I could've scouted the route from a higher perspective and we wouldn't have gotten lost."

"Since I didn't know the city's layout," Mervyn mumbled, his face a mottled mass of bruises, "I tried to get Ms. Doucet up on my rug for a better look—"

"Which was when she slipped," grumbled Rijma.

"—knocking Mervyn off," sniffed Nicole.

"—knocking him cold," Daggoth explained, "and spraining her own ankle in the process."

Nicole's lips quivered with barely suppressed emotion. "I feel terrible!"

"Doesn't look swollen," Rijma observed, "but a sprain can sure hurt like Hades the first day or two."

"Not that…" she whimpered.

"Hey, I'm okay," Mervyn assured her. "It was my own clumsy fault."

"Not that either. Oh, Robert!" she wailed, "You could've been killed and it would've been my fault we weren't there to prevent it!" She began sobbing.

"Um, it's okay," I said, embarrassment elbowing my annoyance out of the way. "Everything worked out okay."

"Easy for you to say," Vashti groused, still nursing a mild concussion.

Another voice piped up from her shoulder: "Yeah, ssspeak for yourssself. We could've been killed, too, you know!"

I glared at Smog and the little Dragon sidled up Vashti's shoulder and peeked back at me through her hair.

"Accidents happen," Daggoth soothed. "Why don't we table the Old Business for now and move on to the New Business, now that we have the list?"

Everyone in the room nodded, voiced, or grunted their assent.

Cephtronics' former Chief of Programming pushed back his Wizard's cowl and pulled out a pair of non-magical spectacles. Perching them on his nose, he contemplated the list for a few moments.

"As I see it, we can get this done a lot faster if we split up into smaller groups and try to retrieve these items more or less simultaneously…"

I felt oddly detached from the discussion that followed.

A portion of my thoughts were with Borys Dankevych. Watching Natasha's life monitors go flat had been a terrible thing for him. I hoped our discussion in the stables hadn't added the torment of false hope.

I was thinking about going downstairs and talking to Dankevych, even though I didn't have any idea as to what else I could say. At least it would get me out of the study and away from my most immediate problem.

I found myself staring at Vashti. Like Natasha and unlike most Dreamwalkers, her avatar was nearly identical to her actual appearance. It was difficult to think of her as Vashti, High Priestess to the Amazons and not as Stephanie Harrell, my ex-wife and, until a couple of days ago, my fiancée.

Except that she hadn't really been my fiancée this time around. I had spent the last six months in the Outside World with a manifestation of The Machine in Stephanie's body. So I hadn't really fallen in love with my ex-wife, after all.

I turned and looked at Pallas.

She had shed the farm-girl appearance that she had been wearing when she stepped from the flying farmhouse earlier this afternoon. Now she appeared as I had first seen her in the Matrix some six months ago: skin the color of coffee and cream, dark hair smoking around a face that struck a balance between classic beauty and raw sensuousness, and a body that—well, I felt my palms start to sweat and forced myself to look away. If I could fall in love with the essence of Pallas in Stephanie's body—not that there was really anything wrong with Stephie's body, you understand—then my libido was in for some serious trouble now that she was back in her avatar of choice.

But since Pallas wasn't really human, then it naturally followed that what I had felt for the past six months wasn't really love, at all. Just a complex feedback loop of autoerotic suggestion coupled with a certain degree of wish fulfillment and a means of interface that simulated the human act of "oneness."

I looked at Aeriel and found that she was already staring at me so I looked away, again.

Technically, the Amazon Princess wasn't really *my* problem. The Computer had manipulated my avatar into this ill-conceived arrangement while I was outside of the Program. Unfortunately, I couldn't think of any way I could explain my lack of culpability to Aeriel, her mama, or the hundreds of sister-warriors who were already looking for who I became during the hours between dusk and dawn.

Well, at least they were willing to share…

Which was more than I could say for Nicole Doucet.

I looked at woman I had lost fifteen years before and marveled anew at how the avatar-mode of the Matrix had not only given her her body back, it had given her the years, as well. And since I had modeled Misty Dawn on Nicole's likeness, it was almost as if the ill-fated Wood Nymph was with us, too.

All of this and all of them combined to make my present circumstances very confusing.

As the conversation's dynamics shifted to the other side of the room, I eased out through the side door and took the stairs down toward the bottom of the tower.

There was no point in stopping off at Borys Dankevych's room; there was nothing I could do or say that could help right now.

And I was hardly a pillar of strength myself, at this particular moment.

As I reached the ground level I heard footsteps on the stairs above me: it was Nicole.

"What—" I started to ask, but she shushed me. Taking my arm, she led me through the great hall and out into the clearing just as the sun was touching the western horizon.

She tugged on my sleeve and ran, drawing me, on into the trees, down a hill, and into a canopied glen just a scant mile from the tower entrance. The was a large table-rock set atop a small rise and Nicole climbed up onto it's smooth, flat surface and extended her hand back to me.

"Come."

"What—?" I asked again.

"What?" she teased. "Don't you know? Take off your clothes!" And she set about removing hers with unbridled enthusiasm.

I followed suit with a little less abandon and a little more bemusement. Before I was done she was Eve-naked and helping me with the rest of my garments.

The setting sun cast its bloodied light over her creamy flesh, giving her a feral quality that stirred ancient lusts. "Take me," she growled, lying back on the great slab.

And I did.

There was a fierce savagery in this joining unlike anything that I had ever known in my life. It was more like a pagan rite of passage than an act of affection. Nicole writhed upon the stone's surface like a virgin sacrifice, but there was nothing virginal about her words, her touches, her demands.

Almost as soon as we were done, the cramps hit and I felt my avatar stretch and remold to my Human aspect. Spent, I rolled onto my back and stared up at the stars that were beginning to glimmer in the darkening sky.

"Robert…" She ran gentle fingers in a questing trail across my chest and then down my stomach.

"Mmmmm?"

"Do you remember the last time we made love?"

I did. Even though she was doing her best to distract me with her hands. "Yes. It was…healing."

"I mean, before the accident. Do you remember?" She rolled over and knelt above me. Her face lowered to mine, her hair forming a silken tent that blotted out the sky.

As we kissed, I turned my mind again to those last carefree days in France.

"A little town near Luxembourg," I remembered when we finally broke for air.

She nodded. "Éblange."

"There was a small forest near the border…"

She smiled. "You remember!"

"How could I forget?"

She moved above me and my response was unexpected: it seemed my Human physiology was unaffected by the exertions of my Half-Elven avatar just minutes before.

"We climbed a hill and found a large rock…" She was beginning to breathe heavily.

"Like this one," I murmured, feeling my lungs start to labor in turn.

"We made love in the sunshine and could see for miles in every direction!"

"It was fantastic," I agreed through clenched teeth. She had taken control of the rhythm again, and I was being pulled along too fast. "It seems we have come full circle," I gasped.

"Yes," she said. "Except it is dark now…"

She stretched away from me for a moment, reaching for the mound of her clothing. My hands came up in turn and, fingers splayed, I moved my palms in small circles down her back. I grasped her waist as she settled back.

And then the rhythm abruptly ceased.

"Is this a dagger which I see before me, the handle toward my hand?" she whispered. "Come, let me clutch thee…"

I had closed my eyes, trying to take advantage of the sudden inertia, trying to prolong the rising tension. Quoting Shakespeare seemed as good a distraction as thinking about baseball. "I have thee not, and yet I see thee still," I remembered. "Art thou not, fatal vision, sensible to feeling as to sight? Or art thou but a dagger of the mind, a false creation, proceeding from the heat-oppressed brain?"

"I see thee yet, in form as palpable as this which I now draw," she continued. "Thou marshall'st me the way that I was going...Now o'er the one-half world nature seems dead, and wicked dreams abuse the curtained sleep—"

"You missed a couple of lines," I murmured.

"—now witchcraft celebrates pale Hecate's offerings; and wither'd murder—"

I opened my eyes and saw the dagger.

"—alarum'd by his sentinel—"

The blade was silver, the one metal that lycanthropy was not proof against.

"—the wolf, whose howl's his watch—"

Nicole's right shoulder rolled upward in a movement that was distinct—that had always been her own. And I suddenly remembered the mysterious bowman and how he had moved in a familiar fashion as he nocked and fired that "fatal" arrow. It was the same flow of arm and shoulder muscles that Nicole had displayed half a lifetime ago in the field archery tourneys throughout half of Europe.

"—thus with his stealthy pace, with Tarquin's ravishing strides, towards his design moves like a ghost."

"Why?" I asked, breaking her spell. I saw the animal hunger in her face and suddenly understood that fifteen years of pain and isolation had transformed desire into a different kind of passion.

She smiled. "Why not?"

And brought the knife down.

PART IV
FATAL ATTRACTIONS

“Come together...”

—Lennon/McCartney—

DATALOG: \QUEBEDEAUX_A.5\PERSONAL\20200815
Voice Dictation
FILE ENCRYPTION ON

I see that we've lost Ripley-Gamma's code-string again.

*

Guess we'll pick him up again at the turnover of the next cycle.

*

In the meantime, I've got bigger worries: Hanson's code-string isn't where it's supposed to be!

*

And, after checking all of the pertinent parameters, there's only one explanation that makes sense…

*

Balor's boss isn't the real Walter Hanson!

ONE

\RIPLEY\PATH\SIGMA (Σ)

I was weary from the long walk back from Calabastor. The shortcut off the main road and through the woods had seemed like a good idea at first. But the uneven terrain, the density of the foliage and ground cover, and the number of branches dangling at throat level gave lie to the old maxim "the shortest distance between two points is a straight line."

Continually looking over my shoulder didn't help, either.

With the setting of the sun, I felt my body slip away, again. The momentary discomfort was almost a welcome thing as I could now make a beeline for Daggoth's Tower: the trees would prove no impediment to my non-corporeal form.

I was stopped, however, by the sight of two very familiar people making love on a large flat rock. One of them was me. And the other one was… "Misty Dawn?" I whispered.

"Yea, my lord?"

I jumped and surely would've knocked myself cold had I not been able to pass through the massive tree limb just above my head. I turned and glared at the Wood Nymph's ghost. "What are you doing here?" I hissed.

"Nay, my love," she answered, pointing at the couple on the rock. "The question is: what am I doing *there?"*

I smirked. "I should think the answer to that is rather obvious."

She frowned. "Nay. I meant not the act. 'Tis my body I do not ken. Who hast taken possession of it?"

"Yeah?" I rubbed a hand across my chin. "Why don't we go ask? I've got a couple of questions of my own."

"Such as?"

"Am I real? Or am I Memorex?"

We took maybe two steps. And stopped cold as the woman who looked like Misty Dawn produced a dagger and murdered the man who looked like me!

Watching was bad enough. But as my Human Doppelgänger died, there was a wrenching sensation that drove me to my knees. I felt my body collapsing in upon itself and, for long moments, I couldn't move. When I was finally able to raise my head, my murderer was gone, her clothing with her.

Misty Dawn was trying to help me to my feet.

But her hands kept passing through my arm. I was still in my Half-Elven avatar but I was no longer wraithlike.

As I made my way to the stone altar on shaky legs I was met with another shock: my Human corpse was beginning to discorporate! Even as I reached out to touch it, the flesh became transparent as Misty Dawn's and, in another moment, disappeared completely. Only "my" clothing and the silver dagger remained as evidence of the murder. Not so much as a bloodstain marked the rock's striated surface.

It was the perfect crime: except for my chance arrival there would have been no witness. And, if you can't *habeus* the *corpus*, you ain't got no evidence.

My first impulse was to head straight for Daggoth's Tower and report what I had seen. Then I had second thoughts. Primarily that you never lay all of your cards on the table until the hand is completely played out.

First, I changed clothing. I took off the ebony bodysuit that Lilith had given me and folded it into a small square. It tucked into a belt-pouch with room to spare.

The clothing left behind on the stone was familiar: leather belt with pouches, vest and trousers of mottled green and dun dragonskin, tunic and girdle of light doeskin, calf-length moccasin boots that laced up the sides. I had dressed in these clothes an uncounted number of times but now they were subtly different. They were still warm.

But the gooseflesh they raised as I donned each garment was not so much a matter of the previous wearer's death, as it was the question of legitimacy. Had he been the true Riplakish of Dyrinwall and I just an artificial copy of the real thing?

Or were we both just shadows cast by a greater Reality—a Reality that might exit the room at any moment and turn off the lights on the way out?

"Thy visage is so grim, my lord! What dark thoughts cloud thy brow?"

Saved by the belle. I extended my hand to hers even though I could no longer touch her. "Come. It's time I was getting back."

Σ

Voices drifted down from Daggoth's Study up on the fifth floor. Other than that there was no sign of anyone else as we made our way around the premises.

Our first stop was the stables where I checked on Ghost. He, at least, seemed to think that I was me. I left the great bow and the quiver of arrows that Lilith had gifted me with the rest of my gear and then crept upstairs. My next stop was the guest chamber the other Riplakish had occupied. I retrieved my swords and mithril shirt before moving on to the room the "real" me had temporarily occupied.

Perhaps "real" was not the most scientific adjective to apply to myself under the circumstances. I'd always had some philosophical reservations in using the terms "real" and "reality" while inside one of Cephtronics' Dreamworlds. And now that I was no longer sure as to which copy of my avatar was the original (and don't get me started on that definition), it was an open question as to which—if any—of us had claims on being legitimate.

For sanity's sake I *had* to think of myself as being real...

Palming the silver dagger, I continued my search through the apartments on the third and fourth floors.

While I searched for my assassin I noticed an odd mental manifestation: I seemed to be accessing additional memories outside of the ones that I could account for. It was as if I were sharing someone else's mind in a passive mode. A mind similar to my own.

Perhaps identical to my own—with the exception of several days of divergent experiences.

When I checked Vashti's chamber I made another interesting discovery: the rest of the bottles of Demon Rum that my ex-wife had confiscated. I liberated them for medicinal purposes: this mental double-vision was giving me a massive headache.

Entering Nicole's room with a bottle in hand gave me a strange sense of deja vu in reverse. And then it hit me, the facts all falling into place like an orderly landslide: it was Nicole who had appropriated Misty Dawn's body from the grave! It was Nicole who had shot "me" with an arrow from horseback! And it was Nicole who had murdered "me" with the silver dagger! I looked again to be sure that she wasn't anywhere around and then sat on the bed and uncorked the bottle. Under the circumstances, this was not the best of times to be sober.

But I needed my wits about me if I was going to brace my murderer in the next few minutes. I compromised by taking a long pull on the bottle and then tapped the cork back in.

For a moment I was paralyzed by the sensory assault: the warm liquid boiling its way toward the center of my body while the memory of our lovemaking burned through my nerve endings.

I shook myself up into a standing position and stumbled from the room. I hadn't touched Nicole! It was someone else's memories that were tormenting me, now. Trembling, I hurried toward the stairs and the fifth floor.

The meeting was still going on when I entered the study.

How did I know about the meeting?

"Well, it's about time," Rijma said as I closed the doors behind me. "We were starting to wonder—" She fell silent as she saw the look on my face.

My gaze swept the room and focused on Nicole. She was sitting across the room, near the far wall. I remembered now, how I had originally crafted Misty Dawn's appearance upon my memories of Nicole. Had that drawn her to the slain Wood Nymph's body when her psyche entered the Program?

As Nicole Doucet became aware of my presence she stumbled out of her chair, toppling it in the process.

Now everyone fell silent as I produced the instrument of my latest death. Nicole staggered backward until her back pressed against the bookshelves that stretched from floor to ceiling. "What—what's wrong with you?" she whimpered. I realized that it was the question on everyone's mind. I was the only one in the room who was aware of Nicole's actions. But, at this particular moment, I was the one who seemed to be dangerous.

Perhaps I was. Every instinct for self-preservation demanded that I counter the threat with violence. But as I stared at her across the room, deeper memories rose up in me. Memories that were unquestionably mine.

"Je voudrais voir des roses et du sang," I said. *"Je voudrais voir mourir d'amour ou bien de haine…"*

"I should like to see people dying of love or of hatred," she whispered.

If killing her was out of the question, confinement wasn't any better. She had been imprisoned in that scarred lump of inanimate flesh for fifteen years. Sending her back or denying her her newfound freedom would be cruelty beyond death.

And yet, there was something in her face that told me I might not have a choice.

"You're dead!" she shrieked. And the madness behind her eyes boiled over.

I hefted the poniard and felt a little of my own sanity slip away. "Is this a dagger before me?" I said with mocking irony. "Come, let me clutch thee!" And hurled it so that the silver blade buried itself in the spine of a fat tome just a foot away from her head.

"Good gods, man!" Daggoth was coming around from behind his great desk. "What do you think you're doing? It's Nicole—"

"Is it?" I snarled. I pulled the Optics of al Rashid from my vest pocket. "Let's take another look." And I put them on.

A moment before I had felt my sanity slip a bit. Now I looked and felt the rational world tear out from under my feet and drop away like a psychic sinkhole. I looked into madness unmasked of the façade of flesh and the crafty restraint that allows it to pass us unnoticed in public places.

I had hoped the spectacles would reveal an impostor. Instead, they showed me the woman who had died in that fiery air crash and was denied the relief of afterlife or oblivion.

The woman I had known and loved had been devoured by a nightmare beast long ago. The beast had ground her up in its teeth, digested her humanity in its belly throughout those fifteen years, and what it had finally excreted was not even remotely human.

I looked into the face of naked madness and screamed.

She whirled and wrenched the dagger from the book. And, as she turned and brandished the silvery blade, she underwent a transformation. Her flawless skin turned yellow and mottled. There was a smell of rotted meat filling the room, of putrefaction long bottled up and finally released as if the glass containing it had shattered. Skin cracked and oozed pus and slime. Flesh turned black here, sloughed off there, revealing hints of bone and wormy veins gone hard with desiccation. Gums shriveled and teeth and nails grew. The whites of her eyes turned red as irises disappeared and pupils collapsed into slitted apertures.

I drew my swords as her back burst open and great flaps of black leather flailed out. As her bone-ribbed wings buffeted us back with their turbulent backwash, she sprang into the air and glided to the window. Smashing the leaded glass with a taloned fist, she turned at the lintel and hissed at me.

And then she was gone as if the night, itself, had sucked her into its great, dark maw.

Σ

Hours were passed in explanations, in plans and strategies, in theory and speculation. We turned in well after midnight. I cannot speak for the others, but sleep would not come for me.

I lay on the bed I had first occupied when Daggoth had fetched me from Misty Dawn's tree and stared at the flickering shadows cast on the ceiling by the candle at my bedside. When I finally blew out the candle one shadow remained.

It was Misty Dawn. As the night's events had unfolded I had forgotten her and what import they held in her heart.

What I had lost this night was beyond my ability to measure or tally. But there was pain in her eyes, too. She had lost her body, witnessed the unholy use it had been put to. And she had lost me, in a sense, as well.

And, as I looked into her eyes, I saw that the pain there was for me, as well.

Neither of us spoke. I pulled back the blanket and she crawled into the bed beside me.

We touched and our hands passed through each other. But I curled my arm about the flickering perimeter of her body and she laid her weightless head upon my chest.

Even without tactile sensation there was a comfort in the mutual proximity.

Sleep finally came.

DATALOG: \QUEBEDEAUX_A.5\PERSONAL\20200816
Voice Dictation
FILE ENCRYPTION ON

A cycle has passed and the code-string for Ripley-Gamma has not made a reappearance.

*

Balor's beside himself over this new development with the senator.

*

Do I tell him his boss is actually an impostor?

*

If I do and he already knows…

TWO

\RIPLEY\PATH\SIGMA (Σ)

Time was running out so we divvied up the list.

Senator Hanson, the Duke, and Stumpy went to retrieve Morpheus's feet from a local Warlock. Princess Aeriel and her Amazons had volunteered to penetrate the Sanctuary of the Templars and locate the dismembered sorcerer's head. Both hands had been traced to the waterfront but, from there, the trail parted in two directions: Borys and Pallas went one way, Mervyn, Rune, and myself went the other.

That left Vashti and Rijma, who were dispatched on the remaining assignment…

As Stan wouldn't let me back Through the doors of Fogherty's Cove, I sent Mervyn and Rune to arrange for some dinner-to-go. The fourteen year-old REMrunner was happy to have something to do and obviously relieved that it didn't involve an element of risk. He was finally waking up to the fact that pain and death in Fantasyworld were no longer the rhetorical elements of a harmless game.

I settled myself at the end of Smith's Dock as the sun was setting and looked over at Jeremiah. The big, green frog squatted there on the weathered planking and looked up at me with expectant, goggly eyes.

"Sorry, Jerry, but I'm not the best of company right now."

The frog burrupped understandingly and then turned its head to regard a dragonfly that was hovering around one of the support posts. There was a sudden blur of amphibious tongue and the dragonfly was gone. Jeremiah chewed twice and then stopped, a look of very unfroglike horror suffusing his green and mottled features. He spat out the mangled insect and hopped back a foot and, if its possible to imagine, looked even greener than before.

"Whassamatter, Jer: don't like bugs? Or starting to like them too much?"

He croaked assent to the latter and then waddled over to the edge of the dock. "Don't fall in," I admonished as he sat back, human fashion, and dangled his long froggy legs from the end of the pier.

I was tempted to follow his lead. My legs ached and I was tempted to unlace my boots and dangle my feet in the water. We'd been up and down the waterfront, across the boardwalk, around Park Place, and had roamed the lengths of Anthony's Pier, Dorn's Wharf, and Zar's Quay. I'd finally managed to trace the right hand onto a ship that had sailed earlier that afternoon.

Footsteps sounded on the wooden planking and I turned to look at Pallas as she settled down next to me. "How's it going?" I asked conversationally. If the words and tone came out bland and smooth, they belied my inner turmoil.

"Borys is attempting to book passage to Ortygia—our hand was taken there nearly a week ago."

"Ortygia!" The events involving Nicole had driven the red Devil's words from my mind until now. "I had a little run-in with some Demons yesterday, and they said something about taking me to Ortygia."

"Why didn't you go with them?" she asked.

"Because they didn't know that I was me. They were looking for the other me. They thought that the real me—that is I—was one of them."

She sighed. "Somehow I'm not surprised."

I stared out to sea. "I wonder who wants me on Ortygia? And why?"

"Well," Pallas offered, "we could change hands."

"Hmm?"

"You could take the ship for Ortygia and go after the other hand." Then she shook her head. "But I don't think that's a very good idea."

"What do you suggest?"

"Finish these errands, first. We've made a commitment to Morpheus and another twenty-four hours should see most of it done. Then, when his body is restored, he will be a powerful ally and the rest of us will be able to pay Ortygia a combined visit."

"What about the passage Borys is booking?" I asked.

"We still have a hand to retrieve. And maybe we should do a little preliminary scouting while we're in the neighborhood."

I nodded and stared out to sea as the sun sat on the western horizon and dangled its own toes in the sea. There was a long silence between us, reminiscent of other long silences. Finally, I elected to break it: "It's been over twenty-four hours since you came in-program—and this is the first you've really spoken to me."

"Funny," she replied, "but I could say the same to you."

I couldn't meet her eyes. "What do you want me to say?"

"I want you to tell the truth."

"Truth?" Now I could look at her. "After six months of passing yourself off as Stephanie—wearing her body, asking me to believe that you were she—you have the temerity to question my honesty?"

"I do," she said quietly. "You have been lying to yourself for months—no—years. And until you can speak the truth to yourself, I do not believe that there is anything that we can truly say to one another." There was no anger in her words. Only a quiet sadness.

"I don't know what I think or feel right now."

"I know."

The sun was three-quarters down before I spoke again. "You tricked me, you know."

"Did I? Or did you trick yourself?"

"Meaning?"

"Our relationship these past six months was nothing like what you had with Stephanie. Were you really so blind that you couldn't see the differences?"

"People change."

"You wanted to believe that. You needed to believe that."

I nodded, watching the light dim across the water.

"You're a classical hero, Robert."

"You flatter me."

"No. But I do not denigrate you, either. I observe.

"The classical hero leaves the sheltered port and strikes out into the great unknown. He leaves home and friends and family behind and risks life and limb and death among strangers for noble goals. But nearly every classical hero does so because he cannot face what sits upon his own doorstep."

I grimaced. "And what sits on my front porch?"

She sighed. "I used to think that it was Nicole. I believed her death had wounded you so deeply that you could never put your trust in happiness, again." She paused. "I still think that's partly true..."

"But?" I coached.

"I think you are the monster at your own gate."

"Thank you."

"Perhaps monster is the wrong word. But you fear the face in your own mirror. And you are here because you run from yourself."

"I seem to keep running into myself here more than anywhere else."

She took my hand in hers. "Even now you fear to examine the truth that I am saying. You take refuge in your humor and you will continue to put yourself at risk rather than face who you are and who you want to be."

"Quite beating around the bush, Pallas: what is it that you think I'm so afraid of?"

"Commitment."

I looked at her. She had a funny way of saying it. Funny, I suddenly realized because she wasn't the one who had actually spoken.

We turned around, knocking Jeremiah off the end of the dock. There was a little froggy scream and a splash as we stared up at Prince Rudolph Charming and a retinue of royal guardsmen. At the prince's side was a familiar looking Dwarf. Apparently the feeling was mutual: he was pointing at me as he said, "That be him, yer highness!"

"Guards," Rudy said, "arrest that bounder!"

He was pointing at me, as well.

Σ

"You cad!" he hissed. "You heel!"

"Rudy," I soothed, raising my hands palms up, "you're getting upset over nothing."

"Nothing?" His voice shot up an octave and his face went from red to royal purple. "Nothing? You refer to my betrothed as 'nothing?'"

I looked around the dungeon cell and was momentarily glad that I was locked in and Prince Charming was locked out.

"You stole my girl," he continued, "you two-timing four-flusher!"

Ever since I had prematurely awakened Snow White from her enchanted slumber with mouth-to-mouth resuscitation, I had been dodging her seven little guardians who thought my marrying her was the only honorable thing to do. While I was somewhat wise to the customs of the Mountain Dwarves, I hadn't reckoned with the prince's involvement in all of this.

It was bad enough that I had cheated his fate by rescuing his beloved. It had further tweaked his pride to find that Snow White was a retrograde romantic who preferred rakehells to royalty.

To be fair, this had been a very trying day for the prince: there had been some major fracas in the west end of town, someone had dropped a house in the middle of one of the major thoroughfares, and there had been numerous reports of Demons on the rampage all over the city. On top of that, tonight was the royal ball that was supposed to celebrate Snow White's engagement to the prince. The king and queen thought a big bash followed by the surprise announcement was just the thing to put a little zing back into Calabastor's social climate.

Problem was, the surprise was shaping up to be more than they were bargained for. And had landed Yours Truly in more hot water, not to mention the dungeon beneath the castle proper.

Pallas had tagged along to watch the fun and could barely repress her giggles even as Rudy threatened to foam at the mouth.

"I don't see why we can't work this out," I said reasonably. "I don't even want her." Oops. Wrong choice of words.

"So!" he cried, drawing his sword, "my bride-to-be isn't good enough for you!"

"Let's not blow a matter of individual taste out of—"

"You think you can callously *use* her and then toss her aside!"

"I didn't use anybody—Pallas, tell him!"

She had one hand over her mouth and waved the other in vague acknowledgment. Her body trembled mirthfully and her eyes threatened to brim over.

The prince took no notice. "Varlet! Knave! I intend to see that you do the honorable thing by her or else—"

Pallas guffawed.

The prince sputtered to a stop as if someone had dumped a bucket of cold water on him.

I spoke gently: "Your Highness, we can fix this so that it all works out to where the two of you will live happily ever after. The girl just needs a little more time."

"Destiny can be such a heavy burden, especially when you're young," Pallas added. "Now Snow has had to go through an awful lot, knowing that her fate was fixed. I mean: the death of her real mother, her father's remarriage, abandonment at an early age, life in the sticks, keeping house for seven old bachelors without any social life of her own, a severe case of food poisoning, and then destined to marry some strange prince—"

"I am not strange," he huffed.

"—that she's never met, without having the opportunity to play the field, first, so to speak. She's just exhibiting a little youthful rebellion. Believe me, it's completely natural before a girl settles down to marriage and mid-life crises."

He sat down on one of the turnkeys' stools and put his face in his hands. "I wouldn't mind giving her that time if I knew that she would eventually come around—"

"She will!" I asserted through the bars.

"—but I don't have that kind of time to give! The royal ball and announcement are tonight!"

"Your Highness," smiled Pallas, speaking reassuringly, "I happen to have an old family recipe, passed down from mother to daughter since ancient times. Used properly, in the right drink at the right time, it should prove to be a most effective remedy to your particular problem…"

S

I tapped on the heavy oaken door. Then I knocked. Finally I began to pound.

"Just a minute!" came the muffled reply.

"We're running out of minutes!" I looked back down the passageway to be sure I had given Snow White the slip after our last dance.

So far, so good.

The door opened and Pallas pulled me into the Apothecary's laboratory.

"What's the news?" I asked, as I locked the door behind me.

"This!" she giggled. And grabbed me for a kiss.

"You didn't!" I begged in horror.

She shook her head. "I didn't actually sample the finished product. But I did get a whiff of the fumes while I was heating the mixture in the molds." She pushed herself against me and then reached behind to take the key out of the lock in the door. "I'm sure the effects will wear off in a few days." She dropped the key down her bodice.

"This is not funny, Pallas!"

"I can't help it, Rip Honey. It's the potion."

I sighed. "Look, if you want fun and games, you'll have to wait until we get everything settled downstairs. Now give me the love potion and I'll sneak it into Snow White's drink."

"In a minute," she murmured sulkily, winding her arms around my neck.

"Now!" I thundered, "Or, by Elysium, I'll be sleeping with Snow White tonight!"

She pouted. "Oh, all right." She disentangled herself and led me over to the table. "Here is the first batch," she said, gesturing at a tray with six brown pellets on it. "Drop one of these in her drink and she'll go gaga for the next person she looks at. Just make sure she's looking at the prince when she drinks it."

"That's all?"

"Listen, buster, in a ballroom filled with moving, talking people, the timing may not be so easily accomplished. And you need to make sure that the pellet is completely dissolved before you hand her her drink."

"Okay. Thanks." I pocketed the pellets. "Now, unlock the door."

She shook her head. "You unlock the door."

"Fine. Give me the key."

She walked up to me, put her hands on her hips, and threw back her shoulders. "Go fish."

Σ

I had to hide behind a tapestry until Snow White's attention was focused on the far side of the ballroom. Then I collared Rudy and the two of us relieved a servant of a tray of champagne and glasses.

"Here," I explained to the prince, producing a pellet. "This goes in her glass. As soon as it's dissolved, I'll offer her a drink. As soon as she takes it, I'll head for the exit and you get right in her face. I mean it, Rudolph: you have to be the first person she sees after she takes a drink!"

"Sounds simple enough."

"Maybe. I just get a bad feeling about this—"

"Rip, darling!" Snow White was coming our way with her retinue of seven short guardians in tow.

"Remember," I murmured to Rudolph, "the pellet with the potion is in the goblet with the Hobbit; the stein full of wine has the brew that is true."

"What?"

"Never mind." I picked up the tumbler that was sculpted in the likeness of a Halfling and dropped one of the pellets into the slightly chilled bubbly. Then I held it in my hand so as not to lose track of it and cover up the dissolution of Pallas' Love philtre.

"Champagne! How lovely! Shall we have a toast, then?" she inquired, sweeping up to the tray and swooping up a goblet in her hand.

"Yes, of course, but—" I fumbled for the right words, "—I already have your glass in hand, my dear!"

"Oh, Riplakish; you are becoming a dear! I was afraid you were going to continue being a stuffed shirt for the remainder of the evening." She sipped from the goblet in her hands.

"But Snow, my sweet; I was holding this glass for you!"

She detached a hand from her drink and waved it at me. "But I already have a glass, my love. Why don't you drink it?"

"I'm afraid I'm not overly fond of champagne, Precious, and I've already had a little too much for this early in the evening."

"Then we shall be most happy to relieve you of your social burden, Lord Riplakish," said a new voice. I turned to look at Rudy's mother as she lifted the doctored drink from my sweating hands.

"Y-y-your Majesty," I stammered.

"Nervous, my lad?" she inquired archly. "One would suppose that you were the one whose engagement was being announced."

I tried to produce the equivalent of a polite laugh and only succeeded in sounding like a strangled goose.

She turned to Rudy. "After this next number, we shall signal the trumpets to play a fanfare. Then the formal announcement can be made."

The color drained out of Rudy's face and he looked to me for deliverance.

"So soon, Your Majesty? The night is yet young!" I was trying to think of how to stall the announcement and retrieve the potion at the same time. And was not making any progress either way.

"Uh, yes!" Rudy chimed in. "The announcement should be the culmination of the evening!"

The queen turned back to her son. "But the royal orchestra is running out of numbers..."

"We don't host that many royal balls," Rudy murmured out of the side of his mouth. "And the new Troubadour won't arrive until the end of the month."

I nodded: *pre-Minstrel syndrome.* "Couldn't they repeat a couple of the earlier dances?" I asked. "As encores?"

The queen made a distasteful face. "How gauche!"

Rudy's face brightened in response. "I've got a better idea..."

Snow White touched my arm questioningly. "What is this announcement that everyone keeps talking about, my love?"

I snagged another glass of champagne from a passing tray and slipped another pellet into it from behind a concealing hand. "A secret, my dear," I whispered. "But I shall be glad to tell you, if you'll humor me in one little thing..."

"What do you say, Rip?"

I turned back to Prince Rudolph. "Uh, what?" I asked blankly.

"We think it is a marvelous idea," added the queen, patting my arm.

"Uh, that's nice." I smiled at her and then turned to Rudy. "What's a marvelous idea?" I whispered close to his ear.

"That we stall the announcement with some additional entertainment," he replied smoothly.

"Great," I agreed. "But where are you going to find something appropriate for a royal ball on such short notice?"

"Well," he explained, "my family has this thing about providing only the very best in musical entertainment…"

"Right."

"…and what could be more exclusive and impressive than introducing the best *Jongleur* on the continent?"

"Tough act to beat," I agreed.

"Not if you're the last of the true Bards as well as the Archdruid of Dyrinwall."

"Well—" I stopped and stared at him. "Oh, no."

"Oh, yes."

"You can't be serious."

He leaned in close. "Unless you can think of something better, my mother will be announcing *your* engagement within the next five minutes! Besides, you always said that you wanted to 'play the palace.'"

I swallowed. "Okay, okay! Give me a minute and then I'll do the stall."

We turned back to the queen just in time to see her downing the contents of her glass.

"What do we do now?" asked Rudy frantically.

"Where's the king?" I asked in turn.

"Over there," answered Snow. "Shall I summon him?"

"After you drink this," I answered, managing to switch glasses with her in the sudden confusion. She waved at the king and began sipping at her new drink.

"Yes?" inquired the queen.

We looked over and the queen looked down.

One of Snow White's guardian Dwarves was tugging on the queen's dress. The dopey-looking one. We braced ourselves for a royal explosion at such impertinence.

"A dance?" the queen murmured. Her face suddenly lit up. "Why I'd be delighted!" She started off toward the dance floor with the diminutive digger in tow.

"A splendid idea, my dear!" chortled a new voice. And we turned back just in time to see Snow White dragging Rudy's father toward another portion of the dance floor.

Prince Rudolph Charming looked about as close to fainting as anyone I had ever seen without actually keeling over. He stood there, white faced, staring into space, and made low moaning sounds in his throat.

"Snap out of it, man!" I grabbed him by the shoulders and shook him. "We've got to do something!"

Glazed eyes turned in my general direction. "Like what?"

"Like taking the rest of these pellets," I dropped the other four into his hands, "and dividing them up between you and Pallas. In fact, she should have another batch ready any time, now. The two of you shouldn't have too much of a problem while I'm diverting everyone else's attention."

As a matter of fact, Prince Charming's attention seemed to have already been diverted. "*Who*...is...*that*?"

I had to turn to follow his line of sight. There, coming down the great staircase, unescorted, was a blonde dream. The disturbing thing was the blonde dream looked vaguely familiar.

"I don't know, Rudy." I stared at her face, which was lovely; but that wasn't what was setting off the alarm bells in the back of my mind. There was something about her silk dress of the palest blue...

Then I saw the glass slippers. "Oh no!"

"Well, I certainly intend to *find* out," the prince was saying.

It was my turn to grab him. "Down, boy! We've got work to do! Remember? Involving your fiancée-to-be?" I turned him around and pointed him toward the closest exit. "The sooner we get this mess straightened out, the sooner I'll be able to introduce you."

"You *know* her?" he asked as I started pushing him through the crowd.

"Later!" I hissed, giving him a final shove. Princes can be so fickle. I turned and went in search of a lute.

That's when Misty Dawn popped in. "What is happening, my lord?"

I grimaced. "We've got problems, M.D. Can you find Pallas and help her with what she's doing?"

She made a face. "Pallas? Is she not that strumpet that hath pursued thee—"

"Misty!" I barked. And then lowered my voice when I saw that other guests would be treated to the sight of a man talking to empty air.

Or worse: maybe see the ghost herself.

"Misty," I murmured, "if we don't get a potion in the right drink, real soon, I'm gonna be married to Snow White and spend my honeymoon in the palace dungeon. Now, will you help me?"

She pouted. "I liked it better when thou wert a spirit!"

"Me, too," I muttered as she faded into the crowd.

I managed to borrow a lute from a court musician, ducked behind a large arras and worked a little magical transformation. When I was done the lute had become an acoustic twelve-string Martin guitar. I laid a basic Glamour over it so that it would still look like its oversized Renaissance ancestor.

I took the stage with a great deal of apprehension because I was neither warmed up nor in practice. In fact, my mind went blank as soon as I faced the audience, and the only song I could think of was "Puff, The Magic Dragon." And I stumbled through that.

Fortunately, it had been a long time since Calabastor had seen or heard from any wandering Minstrels, and the audience was hungry for more. In fact, they began calling out requests and I was able to field most of the favorites: "Knights In White Satin," "Folsom Dungeon Blues," "Castles In The Air," "That Old Black Magic," "Rangers In The Night," and (my personal favorite) "Take This Quest And Shove It!"

Misty Dawn caught my eye as I was finishing the "first" set and made a circle with her thumb and forefinger.

I hurried over to where the ladies were standing while the orchestra started tuning up for the royal announcement.

"Is it fixed yet?"

Pallas looked around and nodded. "It began taking effect a couple of minutes ago. Another two minutes and you'll be able to make your getaway without anybody trying to stop you."

"Uh—'getaway'?"

She took me by the arm and began walking me across the room. Misty Dawn fell in behind. "Listen, I know you're not going to like this, but you screwed it up in the first place and you're lucky to get bailed out at all!"

"What are you talking about? All I want to know is: did you get the stuff into Snow's drink so that the prince could win back her affections?"

"Well…yes and no…"

I stopped and grabbed her by the shoulders. "What do you mean 'yes and no'?" I looked over the top of her head and saw Prince Charming coming across the ballroom toward us with a purposeful expression on his face.

"Pallas, what did you do!"

"Not me: Misty Dawn."

I turned and grabbed at the ghostly Dryad. My hands went through her, of course. "What did you do?"

Something brushed my shoulder before she could answer and I looked down into big blue eyes. "Hel-lo there!" said a sultry voice dripping more than just casual interest.

"Hi," I said abruptly and turned back to Misty Dawn. "I'm waiting for an answer!"

"I'm waiting for a dance," chimed in the strangely familiar young lady at my elbow.

"I mean I got the potion as far as her glass," M.D. explained. "But she was so intent on the king, it was impossible to get her to look at the prince long enough for the potion to take effect."

"But what I'd really like to do is take a long moonlight stroll through the palace gardens," added the stranger in the blue silk dress.

"I'm sure you would," I said politely. And turned back to the Misty: "So what did you do with the other pellets?"

"I put them where they'd do the most good…"

"We could get lost in the hedge maze," she sighed. The girl in the glass slippers, that is.

Glass slippers!

I cleared my throat and turned to Cinderella. "I believe you've mistaken me for someone else, my dear. I am not the prince. But I shall be most happy to introduce you to him in a moment."

The prince chose that moment to arrive.

"Ah, Rudolph," I said, trying to sound properly formal in the presence of royalty. "I'd like you to meet—"

"Get your hands off of him, you little party-crasher!" he shrieked.

I did a double-take and looked at Rudy. He was glaring at the girl who was now defiantly clutching my arm and he didn't look like he was joking.

"Uh, Rudy—

"I said, let *go!*" And he pushed her.

Not very hard, but when you've only had an hour or so to get used to glass heels, it doesn't take much: she went sprawling.

"Rudy?!" I caught him by the arm. "What's the matter? She wasn't doing anything!"

"Not yet, the little tramp!" he hissed. "But I saw how she was looking at you!"

"Rip, I think there's something you ought to know," Pallas interjected.

I was distracted as Cinderella regained her feet and the prince made another lunge at her. "Better hit the road, Honey—e you still have that nice, pretty dress on in one piece!"

"Make me, Prin*cess!*" was her nervy reply.

Rudy began twisting free of my grasp and the girl retreated a few steps. But only as far as one of the portable bars where she removed a slipper and smashed it against the edge of the counter.

"C'mon," she invited with her free hand while the other held a large, jagged piece of glass where the heel was still intact.

Rudy was not that big a fool: he circled her warily from a safe distance.

I turned and grabbed Pallas by her shoulder straps. "What did the two of you do with the rest of the pellets?"

"We put them where they'd do the most good!"

"Where?" I roared, lifting her a good six inches off of the ground. Fortunately, the straps held for the moment.

"In the punch bowl!"

I dropped her. "In the—Cromsake! Why?"

She collected herself from the floor and brushed herself off before explaining.

"The situation was already out of hand—beyond salvaging. After some careful deliberation, two things occurred to me. One: that you needed a diversion to get you away from here ithout being detained. And two: that since there was no way to come out of this without three or four reputations being smeared, I decided to invite everyone to play in the mud puddle." She gestured around the room and now I could see why the prince's behavior was receiving very little attention.

Everyone whose glass had been filled from the punch bowl was beginning to react to the love potion. And to whomever they happened to be looking at at the time. I glanced back at Prince Charming and Cinderella who were now locked in a clinch and rolling around on the floor.

"Ladies—somebody's gonna get hurt."

Pallas nodded and began tugging on my arm. "Like you, if you don't move your butt out of here. Some of the folks over by the stage were sipping punch while you were doing your first set and now they're moving this way. A stampede is not a pretty thing."

"But I can't just run off and leave things like this!"

"Well, you sure as Hades can't stay here and sort things out the way they are now," she countered. "Unless you've got any better ideas…" She got behind me and started pushing.

I gave in, reluctantly, but we were stopped at the nearest exit by the biggest, burliest palace guard I had ever seen.

"Where ya goin', Good-lookin'?" he murmured, dropping the pike across our path.

"Uh, outside—for a breath of fresh air," answered Pallas.

"Get lost, Toots!" he growled. "I'm talkin' to the hunk with the harp."

That did it.

I stepped back and threw my arms wide. *"Tempus frigid!"* I yelled, performing the appropriate somatic gestures. Everyone froze in mid-motion.

I put my hands on my hips and surveyed the ballroom. What had been a blur of noise and motion just a moment before was now a still-life tableau: mouths caught open in mid-word, arms set in mid-gesture. By now the effects of the Love philtre had become quite advanced and the scene looked like a very realistic painting. A painting entitled 'Anatomy of a Mass Seduction.'

"Now what, my lord?" inquired Misty Dawn. Since she had been in physical proximity with my body during the casting of the spell, she had shared my immunity and was not affected by it as the others were.

I shrugged. "Beats me. I think the best policy would be to leave them like this until the love potion wears off."

"But that could take two or three days!"

I nodded. "But, in the meantime, it would also allow me to get Morpheus's body parts back and reassembled so that we can get Hanson out and the Anomaly stopped!" I snapped, irritated at how complicated everything was turning out to be. I reached out to Pallas and neutralized the effects of the Timestop for her.

"Robert?" Pallas asked, laying a gentle hand on my arm as we wove our way toward an exit. "You can't just walk off and leave all of these people defenseless like this."

I patted her arm reassuringly. "Not to worry: we'll be right back after we round up the rest of Morpheus and check out Ortygia."

"But what if something goes wrong? The least you could do is throw some kind of protective spell around the castle."

"What would you suggest?"

"Well, you are a Druid in the Program context. How about a giant wall of thorns or something like that?"

I agreed to do something like that before we left the grounds proper.

On the way out I passed Snow White who was gazing into the eyes of her new love—eyes that stared back from a large wall mirror in an ornate gold frame.

DATALOG: \QUEBEDEAUX_A.5\PERSONAL\20200817
Voice Dictation
FILE ENCRYPTION ON

I'm putting my decision to tell Balor on hold.

*

If Balor is a part of the bogus Hanson's deception, it won't be very healthy for me to blow the whistle.

*

On the other hand, if Balor's clean, it won't hurt to keep him in the dark a little longer: this look-alike down in the suspension tank isn't going anywhere for the moment.

*

So, to track this guy in-Program, I'm running a global search on anomalous code-strings as they relate to avatars.

*

Jackpot!

*

I think I've located the pseudo-senator.

*

For that matter, I've also located the real senator.

*

But my main concern is this one code-string that reads right out of left field…

THREE

\RIPLEY\PATH\OMEGA (Ω)

"...dropped their pantaloons and squatted—because, as everyone knows...*the king's word is law!*"

There were a few tired guffaws but most of the assemblage was either engrossed in their meal or their opposite numbers.

The jester paced the small stage that overlooked the feasting pit and shook his buffoon's scepter. "What is this? An audience or a Norman tapestry? Wait! I got one you'll appreciate. How many Orcs does it take to light a candle...?"

The great hall was lined with trestle tables laden with food and benches laden with boozy old codgers clutching goblets of mead and the *glutei maximi* of paid party girls. All of the men who were still conscious wore brimless, red felt hats in the shape of a truncated cone with a black tassel drooping over the side. And since they were now well into the fourth hour of their revelries, nearly a third of their not inconsiderable number were under the tables or sprawled in the aisles where the serving wenches had to step over their unconscious forms as well as dodge the pats and pinches of their still-conscious comrades.

Backstage, two more Templars—the ones in charge of preparing the "surprise" dessert—were unconscious, as well. In this instance, however, drink had played no part in their state of oblivion.

Princess Aeriel Morivalynde stared at her newly-arrived accomplice. "Riplakish! I thought you were working the waterfront?" she said.

The Half Elf made a deprecating gesture. "They didn't really need me for the next couple of hours so I thought I'd pop over and give you a hand."

Aeriel looked around at the sixteen Amazons who were busy exchanging their chain mail for the brief toga-like slips that the serving wenches were wearing and gave her head a slight shake. "I do not see that I shall be needing another hand." She smiled. "But I am glad that you wished to be here with me. You have been somewhat standoffish of late." Then she frowned as she noticed that he was taking an uncharacteristic interest in her warrior-maids as they changed garments. She cleared her throat and his eyes slid over to a huge and obviously artificial pastry set upon a wheeled cart.

"And who does the honors here?" he asked smoothly. One of the Templars who had been readying the Brobdingnagian sweetcake groaned and stirred a bit. The Half Elf sent him back to slumberland with a casual kick to the head.

"It is ever my place to lead my sisters," she said, dragging the stepladder over to the dummy dessert, "whether 'tis battle or unknown danger—"

"Yeah, yeah; so you're the one who's going to pop out of this overgrown cupcake."

She lifted the false top off the giant pastry. "'Tis a trick my mother learned from an Achaean named Odysseus." She started to climb in.

"What is going on back here?"

Aeriel and the Half Elf turned and looked at the wizened old man in the gem-encrusted fez that was headed toward them. Most of the Amazons had already departed for their predetermined positions in the plan but four remained and he waved angrily at them: "You girls get back out there and start clearing tables!" He looked down at the assorted piles of boots, scraps of chain, and leather straps. "This mess can be cleaned up later!"

Out of his line of sight, Aeriel signaled everyone to do as he ordered while the Half Elf reached down and retrieved one of the fallen Templars' hats.

"And you, missy," he barked, turning toward Aeriel, "what sort of outfit is that?" He looked down and saw the two unconscious forms and cocked an eyebrow. "What's the hold-up here? What's wrong with them?"

"Drunk, your eminence," the Half Elf answered, trying to tuck the points of his ears under the oversized hat.

"Drunk? Do you think I'm blind *and* senile?" He scowled. "Of course they're drunk! But the show must go on!" He walked up to the wheeled cart and positioned himself to help push it on stage. "You, missy; I asked you what you were wearing!"

"It's the costume of an Amazon princess," the Half Elf answered. "We thought it would be a real show-stopper to have an Amazon princess pop out of the cake."

The old man squinted at Aeriel's bits of armor. "It breaks with tradition," he groused. "Never had a girl jump out wearing anything before. And we've been having girls jump out every—"

He stopped grousing when he felt the dagger's point prick his throat.

"Not a word, old man," the Half Elf hissed, "or I'll carve you an extra mouth to go with your extra chin!"

Aeriel climbed back out of the oversized cupcake.

"Now," her companion whispered, tightening his grip and using the tip of the knife to draw a little blood, "where is the head of Morpheus the Malevolent?"

The old man's eyes rolled wildly and he whimpered.

"For Cromsake, Rip," Aeriel chided, "you just told him not to talk!"

"Oh." He eased up on the dagger. "You may whisper. But answer the question: where is the head of Morpheus?"

"Trophy Room," his captive wheezed. And was persuaded to give specific directions as to its location in the building before he was knocked unconscious.

The three unconscious Templars were loaded into the parchment-mâché pastry and Aeriel and the Half Elf moved toward the door that led from the back of the stage to the storerooms.

As the Amazon princess reached for the door latch, her companion grasped her wrist and turned her around and into his embrace.

"What—" was all she got out before his mouth covered hers. Instinct and training took over: four seconds later she was embracing his neck with her forearm and tickling his chin with his own dagger.

"If this is your idea of foreplay," he croaked, "I think you can just forget about producing an heir to the throne."

Chagrined, she released him and returned his blade. "I am sorry, my love. I did not expect—"

"Yeah?" he said, rubbing his throat. "Well, expect the unexpected from now on." He took her by the hand. "C'mon. Let's see if there are any unoccupied chambers between here and the Trophy Room."

"To what purpose?" she asked as they exited into a back passageway.

"Extending the line of succession is not as quick nor as easy as some would have you think, my princess." He patted her arm as they headed for the stairway. "I think we should get started on the problem as soon as possible and avail ourselves of every possibility."

Possibilities, however, would have to be postponed. As they reached the end of the hall there was a shriek from the great hall followed by a cacophony of sounds: catcalls, benches overturning, grunts, curses, and a rising level of bedlam that defied auditory analysis. A woman in a torn toga came running toward them from a connecting passageway.

"One of yours?" he asked as she sped by with a look of panic suffusing her features.

Aeriel shook her head as five Templars came galloping down the same route. Any impressions that they were chasing the serving wench were dispelled as they stumbled closer: if anything, they were more terrified than she.

"That one is, though…" The Amazon indicated another serving wench running close behind, armed with a carving knife and a meat skewer. "Riplakish, we ought to take advantage of the diversion while there are still Templars to provide it."

Aeriel and the Half Elf ran up the steps and started down the hallway on the third floor. More sounds came boiling up from the stairway behind them: their diversion was turning into a full-scale riot. They rounded the corner and skidded to a stop.

The door to the Trophy Room was just ten feet away and flanked by two of the biggest, burliest guards they had ever seen.

They were dressed alike in billowing purple pantaloons; the gold sashes wound about their waists matched the gold trim that adorned their matching red vests and pointed, curly-toed slippers. The convoluted folds of the massive lavender turbans that crowned their heads gave them the appearance of hydrocephalic aliens that were in the process of mutating into giant tulips.

The tulips each laid a massive hand on the hilts of their loosely belted scimitars.

With a sudden flash of inspiration, the Half Elf reached up and checked the top of his head: amazingly the funny little felt hat was still there, jammed down over the tops of his distinctive ears. "Ho there, good fellows!" he called. "Don't tell me the Trophy Room is closed at this hour?"

The guard on the left answered with: "Never to an exalted Brother of the Mystic Tabernacle of Simon the Templar."

"Ah, good, good..." His arm curved around Aeriel's waist. "I was just going to show my new girlfriend, here, some of the—ah—trophies." He danced her through the doorway.

"That was easy," Aeriel purred.

"Yes," murmured the Half Elf as he began searching the agglomeration of displays. "But walking back out with our prize will be a different matter entirely."

The Trophy Room was cluttered with an assortment of pedestals and display cases exhibiting a bizarre collection of trophies, awards, and improbable knickknacks but, as a recent acquisition, the head of Morpheus wasn't too hard to find. It sat (or, rather, rested on the stump of its neck) in a velvet-lined black box. The Half Elf lifted the box down from its display pedestal and turned to Aeriel. "You go out, first, and distract the guards."

"Distract?" Clearly she was less than pleased with the plan.

"Yeah, distract. You got a problem with that?"

Her hand went to the hilt of her shortsword. "I am an Amazon warrior, Riplakish," she hissed, "not some piece of—of—cheesecake for you to dangle before the guards like a piece of meat!"

"You're mixing your metaphors," he chided. "And you were perfectly willing to distract a whole room full of besotted boobs downstairs just a few minutes ago."

"That was different," she huffed.

"Hah!"

"Two on two is much different than two to two hundred!"

He handed her the box. "Very well, I will go out first and distract the guards. All right?"

"All right," she answered.

"S'alright," agreed the head in the box and Aeriel slammed the lid shut.

She drew her shortsword while the Half Elf exited the room and debated on whether or not to keep the box tucked under her free arm in the event of a fight. There was a curious whining sound. Twice. And then the Half Elf called for her to come out.

She found both guards sprawled in untidy heaps in the corridor. The Half Elf was holding one of those mechanical hand devices that he and the sorcerer Daggoth claimed to be weapons although a closer look told her that it was neither of the items he had previously referred to as "Glock" or "Uzi."

"The box," he said, gesturing with his free hand. "I want to check the head again."

The request seemed odd but not unreasonable and, it was only as she was handing him their prize that she realized that he had made no attempt to re-holster his weapon.

"I'm sorry, my dear, that we didn't have time to insure your progeny." He raised the odd-looking hand weapon. "If you wake up before they do, be sure and tell Bobby-boy that, if he wants to 'get a head,' he'll have to come to Ortygia." He chuckled at his own wit and pulled the trigger. The stun-beam left her sprawled in a heap between the two guards.

He sighed as he shifted the box to a more secure position under his arm. "I should've known from the start that it'd be easier to handle the entire operation myself." He holstered the Spaceworld weapon and pulled another device from his pocket. "Dangerous, but easier…" He depressed a button on the device and a moment later seemed to shimmer into non-existence.

DATALOG:\QUEBEDEAUX_A.5\PERSONAL\20200818
Voice Dictation
<<<FILE ENCRYPTION ON>>>

If I had a credit for every alarm that's gone off in the last couple of days…

*

The most baffling one to date is a Program Intersect alert.

*

Before the Anomaly developed it wasn't possible for one Programworld in the Matrix to intersect with another Programworld.

*

Now we know better so we jury-rigged this alarm about six months ago.

*

The odd thing about this particular alarm is I can't get a reading on which Programworld is sharing space with Fantasyworld.

*

We've previously established that Warworld, Spaceworld, and Cyberworld have eclipsed Fantasyworld along certain parameters.

*

They continue to register in definable readings.

*

But our current alarm continues to defy readout interpretations.

*

It's as if there's a Programworld that even we're not aware of—sharing space in the Matrix…

FOUR

\RIPLEY\PATH\SIGMA (Σ)

It looked just like those nature holos we watched in grade school: plants growing and flowers blooming in seconds thanks to the magic of stop-motion holography. Our heads tilted back farther and farther as the thorny branches carpeted the moat, climbed the castle walls, and twined 'round the turrets and towers. The vegetation's size and speed of growth would have been incredible enough, but the sight of huge blossoms bursting wide open in the moonlight was a bit too surreal for my tastes: I repressed a shudder.

The ladies seemed awestruck.

"Satisfied?" I gasped. Magic of that size and duration really takes it out of a spellcaster and I was no exception. Now I needed a nap. Preferably of two days' duration.

"Biggest damn roses I've ever seen," said Pallas.

"I thought thou wert of a mind to surround yon castle with brambles, my lord."

I scowled at both of them. "I don't know brambles from eggplants. I just figured anything with thorns—"

"But thou'rt a Druid!"

"Misty, it's just a ga—I mean—Fantasyworld classifications aren't—"

"Yea, my lord?"

"What he means, my dear," Pallas instructed, "is that giant rosebushes add an aesthetic touch to the practicality of the Guards-and-Wards."

"They are very pretty in the moonlight," agreed the ghostly Wood Nymph.

"And big!" added Pallas *sotto voce.*

I set my foot in the stirrup and mounted Ghost. "Let's get out of here before the City Watch comes along. I hear they've been on alert ever since our little fracas with the Spetsnaz." I looked at Pallas.

"Especially since *someone* dropped a house right in the middle of Morgan Avenue!"

"Some people have no sense of gratitude," she retorted as she swung astride her horse.

Misty Dawn floated into the air and settled down behind me, half in and half out of the saddle, twining vaporous arms about my waist.

As we rode back toward the waterfront, I pulled a small rectangular mirror from my vest pocket and called Daggoth.

The former Chief of Programming had sacrificed one of his magic mirrors for this operation, cutting it into smaller, hand-sized pieces which he then distributed to each of us. By staying back at the tower, he was able to tie all the segments together through the other mirrors in his setup. It helped to have a communications system, coordinating all of our activities from a centralized base. The only drawback was that it eliminated our most powerful spellcaster from operating in the field.

"It's about time!" he groused when I finally got through. "Rune and Mervyn have been combing the waterfront for hours!"

"Did they find Jeremiah?"

"Yes, half drowned! What happened?"

"Long story," I sighed. "Where are they now?"

"I recalled them a half hour ago. You might as well come home, too: you'll need the sleep."

"Meaning?"

"Rune's chartered a boat to sail at midday on the morrow. Is Pallas with you?"

"Yes."

"Well, Borys is waiting for her down at Pier One."

"That the wharf next to the import warehouse?" I asked.

"That's the one. He's booked passage on ship that's bound for Ortygia within the hour. She'll have to hustle." He glanced away. "I've got another call coming in. We'll continue this conversation when you get back. Daggoth out."

Pallas waved her farewell as she was already booting her horse into a canter toward the docks. I turned to Misty: "Hold on tight." I kicked Ghost into a gallop and a moment later he leaped skyward.

"It is so beautiful up here," she murmured as I nudged Ghost into a banking turn that would aim us toward Daggoth's Tower.

Strangely, I hadn't noticed. As we glided through the velvety blackness, I took in the splendor of the constellations, their stars blazing like icy diamonds in the void. The ground was a faint echo of the cosmos, torches and lamplights glimmering here and there about the city and homesteads, and the dark water of Sultan Bay reflecting only a rippled and distorted tenth of the starlight that twinkled above. But the horizon was indistinct in the darkness and the illusion of being surrounded by sky was still effective.

And beautiful…

"It's not real," I whispered to myself. "None of it is real." The seductive impulse to head for the second star to the right and then straight on till morning was overwhelming. *This is not my life,* I told myself. Even though I could die while in taction with my avatar, this was all too far removed from the reality I born into, had spent my life in. This was just a temporary state to be endured until Morpheus was reassembled and helped us get Hanson and Cerberus switched back into their proper places. I had a job to do here, interfaced with the Cephtronics Dreamland Matrix, and I couldn't permit myself the luxury of Program-generated distractions.

"My lord?" Misty's voice was a welcome distraction from this train of thought. "When this quest is done—what wilt thou do?"

"After it's over?" *That was easy: I was getting the hell out of here!* Of course, my avatar would remain in the Program and just what The Machine would do with Riplakish of Dyrinwall after I had abdicated was anyone's guess. Probably sell him into Amazon slavery…

I cleared my throat. "I don't want to think that far ahead, M.D. Let's just worry about the job, uh, quest for now."

And, speaking of worries, as we approached Daggoth's Tower I was surprised to see that it was encircled by a ribbon of light. We got just close enough to make out individual headlights as they moved around the tower's base and Morpheus materialized in midair, just beside us.

"Incoming!" he yelled. "Take evasive action!"

Ghost shied from the sudden appearance of Morpheus'—uh—ghost, and that's what saved us: the missile sizzled through the air-space we should have occupied and continued to climb into the night sky.

"Cyberpunks," Morpheus explained. "They've ringed the tower and were awaiting your return."

"Armament?" I asked as I kicked Ghost into a spiraling climb.

"FRODOs and SAMs."

I was familiar with the weapon systems that bore the acronym FRODO, but: "What in Hades is a SAM?"

"Surface-to-Air Missile: solid propellants, fired out of hand-held launchers," he explained. There was a flash down below. "They're launching another!"

This time there was sufficient warning to cast a Deflection spell. The missile wobbled off in a different direction before exploding a couple of miles away.

"What about the tower?" I asked.

"Secure. Daggoth has the forcefields back up and they're holding. He'll iris open the one over the roof as soon as you're close."

"Tell him I'm on my way now." Morpheus faded and I sent Ghost into a barrel-roll that flipped us out of the path of two more missiles and then spun us into a corkscrew dive toward the ring of lights on the ground.

That's when the FRODOs opened up. A half-dozen particle beams dissected the night and began to stitch the sky like glittering threads embroidering black sailcloth.

I threw a Shield spell in front of us and beefed it up with a couple of variants of Reflection thaumaturgy. I was doubly lucky in that I completed the spells in time and that the FRODOs didn't immediately chew through it like Orcs in a swill-eating contest.

How long it might last was another matter: the convex buffer of mystic energy was already heating up as the particle beams converged on us. At two hundred feet I divided my attention between pulling up Ghost up out of our dive and elongating the shield to protect us from any belly shots. The FRODOs cut out as we leveled off under thirty feet and Cyberpunks went scrambling. Our shield was now glowing a bright cherry red like the ablation tiles on an old-fashioned space shuttle. The radiated heat was blistering the paint on their neurobikes as we buzzed them in a half-circle around the tower. Then, before they could recover, I urged my winged horse up in another tight spiral so that we topped the tower, hovered for a second, and then dropped down on the observation deck.

As I dismounted, two missiles arced over the parapets and detonated soundlessly against the force fields that Daggoth had already popped back up into place. The flares from the twin bursts lit up the top of the tower, revealing a baleful-looking Dwarf stalking towards me. Suddenly, I was more nervous facing this one diminutive opponent than I was bracing fifty assorted Plugthugs from the Cyberworld Program.

"Stumpy," I greeted carefully.

He stumped up to me and grabbed the reins out of my hand. "Daggoth's waitin' in his orifice," he spat. A wad of chewing tobacco formed a Rorschach pattern on the deck between my feet. "Wants you down there pronto!"

"Everything okay?" I asked as he turned away.

"Okey?" To say that the question seemed to annoy him would be like throwing gasoline on a campfire and remarking that it seemed to brighten things up a bit. *"Okey?* You flyboys git to have all the fun a'waltzin' 'bout the sky an' buzzing Cyberpukes. Then you git to traipse downstairs and have tea an' scones with his lordship while I have ta git this oversized horsefly down nine flights of stairs an' inta the stables!"

"Sorry," I said, backing away. He was just warming up.

"Sorry? *Sorry?"* He spat again. "Thet's wha'cha always say! Sorry didn't do me no good when ya got them Gypshun gods all riled up an' thet big 'un—Hortense?"

"Horus," I supplied, dipping a toe into the dark depths of the roof's trap door.

"Yeh, thet's the one: Horace. Remember the number he done on the marketplace in Billocksy, tryin' ta catch youse? No wonder ya still cain't show yer face around—"

I jumped, catching the sides of the ladder and slid down to the next level. He continued to rant and rave as if I were still there and it wasn't until I reached the stairs and descended another two levels, that I was actually out of immediate scold range.

"Come in and close the doors," Daggoth greeted as I paused at the portal to his study.

The Sorcerer's office and library had served as a war room these past few days but, for the moment, it was strangely relaxed and empty with just the two of us. A fire was crackling merrily in the hearth and, as I sat down in a great, overstuffed chair next to Daggoth's, I gave it a second look.

"When did you put a fireplace in here?"

He handed me a great flagon, its gold and silver inlaid sides sweating with condensation. "About twenty minutes ago," he answered absently as I cupped my hands around the cold metal. He picked up a crystal goblet and sipped at what I knew had to be sherry from long experience.

"How are the others doing?" I took a sip of mine: Vanilla Dr. Pepper, the way I liked it. "Liked" as in past tense. Since my experience with Lilith's Demon Rum, everything else had lost its taste.

"We've got the feet," he answered. "Local Warlock was gonna have them made into a pair of seven-league boots. Senator Hanson and the Duke had a tough time convincing him otherwise."

"Oh?"

"I'm afraid the gentleman contracted a severe case of lead poisoning."

"Lead pois—? Oh." Stephanie frequently accused me of being slow on the uptake. Maybe so, but given time I usually got there. "How are the others doing?"

"Unless you're holding back new information, you know as much about the hands as I do. The head? Well, Aeriel reported in about an hour ago. She and her Amazons were getting ready to infiltrate the Templars' Sanctum Sanctorum. As for the... um...other item—"

He was interrupted by a chiming sound from the great mirror on the study wall. Abruptly, a giant eye and nose filled the glass. "Pssst," a voice whispered, "is anybody there?"

"Pull back a little," Daggoth suggested.

"Shhhh!" The image shrank down as Stephanie drew her piece of the mirror back from her face. "Keep it down!" she whispered. "We're inside the temple!"

"We were getting worried," Daggoth said softly. "Have you obtained your objective?"

She shook her head, nearly dislodging the miniature dragon that was perched on her shoulder. "Is Morpheus around?"

"Here," the ghostly entity answered, coalescing into view beside Daggoth. He grimaced nervously. "Have you found it?"

"Probably," she murmured. "But I'll need a detailed description in order to retrieve it."

"A...description?" Morpheus looked at Daggoth who looked back at Morpheus. Then they both turned and looked at me.

"Hey," I said, raising my hands. "My ex-wife can't say she's never seen one."

"I told you!" Morpheus was so upset he could hardly talk. "I told you! Somebody else should have gone!"

I crossed my arms in irritation. "Who? We divvied up the assignments according to individual skills and the danger and difficulty that we could anticipate. This should be relatively easy—"

"Then what is the problem?" Morpheus cried. Clearly he was overwrought. "Why is she asking for a description?"

I shook my head. "Instead of arguing with me you should be asking her." I jerked a thumb at the mirror.

Daggoth scratched his beard. "Maybe she's suffering from some form of hysterical amnesia."

A giant hand filled the enchanted glass on the study wall and perspective shifted so that Rijma's face was leaning toward us in the glass. "Very funny, boys!" she hissed.

"So what is the problem?" I asked.

Rijma frowned. "Maybe it would be easier to show you the problem. You got 'zoom' on this mirror-thing?"

The dark Sorcerer nodded.

"Okay. We're in a chambered balcony looking down on the Holy of Holies at the heart of the temple of the Phæls. I'm going to turn the mirror around and point it toward the altar."

The image skewed wildly and then stabilized to a fuzzy blur. Daggoth gestured. "Focus," he muttered. Then: "Zoom in."

When you've seen one pagan temple you've seen them all. The altar looked more comfortable than most and the frescos covering the walls were lascivious illos portraying legions of lust. But, reduced to basics, the overall design and layout was pretty universal: the difference between most cults and crackpot religions is just a matter of window-dressing.

The candles, however, caught my attention. Not that candles in a pagan sanctuary are unusual: while some sects prefer the ambiance of a great flame pit or the utilitarian aspects of torches, most religious ceremonies include the standard wax taper as part of the setting. Some altars will be surrounded by as many as several dozen lit candles.

This was the first time I'd ever seen several hundred—

"Zoom out," corrected Daggoth, "And pan left and then right."

—make that several *thousand* candles all filling the chancel area around the altar.

"There's more," Rijma whispered hoarsely. "The walls along both sides of the Nave are lined with 'em, too!"

"So what's the problem?" Morpheus was not only irked by their hesitation, he was acutely uncomfortable that they had any part in this operation at all. "Too much light with all those candles?"

I frowned. "I don't think so." The light was murky at best, coming from four flaming braziers, one at each corner of the cushioned "sacrificial" table. "For one thing," I continued, "none of those candles are lit. They have no wicks." I hesitated. "And they are not candles."

"What?" Morpheus's impatience was interfering with his perception of the problem. "If they're not candles then what are they?"

Daggoth frowned. "Zoom back in." The magic mirror complied. "Magnification: times sixty. Now, left four degrees; and tilt down two degrees."

"Gentlemen," I gestured at the two primary, vertical objects that now occupied the center of the glass. "These are religious artifacts—holy relics."

A slow horror filled Morpheus's eyes. Daggoth had a half smile of dawning comprehension.

"After all," I concluded, "if you're a fertility cult, why resort to symbolic artifice if you can decorate with the real thing?"

"It's sick!" moaned Morpheus.

"It's damned inconvenient, is what it is!" Rijma retorted. "Now we may have to inspect hundreds, possibly thousands of these—things—before we find the right one. So the sooner we get a good description of the item in question, the sooner we can get started."

DATALOG: \QUEBEDEAUX_A.5\PERSONAL\20200819
Voice Dictation
<<<FILE ENCRYPTION ON>>>

I'm dying.

*

Well, maybe dead on my feet is more accurate.

*

I haven't slept in two days and my brain is turning to mush.

*

I've got to get three or four hours of sleep: I've told Balor not to disturb me for the next four hours unless it's an emergency.

*

Unfortunately, the alarms seem to go off every half hour and none of Balor's security people can tell if they're an emergency or not.

*

I've arranged for Harold Cantrell to be given clearance and transferred up from R & D to cover for me.

*

While it's true that he doesn't know what's going on in Fantasyworld, the sad truth of the matter is neither do I.

*

I gotta get some sleep.

*

Three or four hours and I might be able to think again…

FIVE

\RIPLEY\PATH\SIGMA (Σ)

"Rise and shine, buddy-boy!"

I peeled back a rusty eyelid and squinted at Daggoth. "What time?" I mumbled.

"'Bout an hour past sunrise."

I moaned and rolled over in bed. "I thought we agreed to a *mid*-morning wake up call."

"We did. But things change. We've got company and they're very insistent about seeing you."

It's only an avatar, I told myself as my body continued to protest. *An illusionary construct of The Machine.*

I dragged the covers off to the side.

It's not really my physical body.

I tried to sit up.

The stiffness is mere illusion—window-dressing for this pretend reality.

I made it on the third try.

This attitude of exhaustion is not real—

Yes it is.

No it isn't—

Yes it is!

No, it's just—

What? Special effects?

I am not really tired and achy: in a moment my head will clear and I will continue the Game with renewed energy.

I creaked up to a vague standing position and groaned. There were moments when I remembered that it was only my psyche running around in this overblown computer program: that none of this was real. Smoke and mirrors. And, at certain times, I could use that perspective to peek behind the mirrors and see the scaffolding. Transcend the program's reality.

This was not one of those moments.

"May I take a shower, first?" Some people require coffee to jump-start their cardiovascular systems in the a.m. For me it's a hot shower.

"Well—?

The door behind him flew open. "You!"

The volume was enough to make me flinch. When I saw who it actually was, instinct took over. I dived back into bed and tried to hide under the covers.

Princess Aeriel Morivalynde stalked into the room, her bronze brassiere heaving. "You—you—*scum!*" Her clothing—if you could call it that—was in disarray. "Disheveled" was a woefully inadequate adjective: her hair looked like an explosion in a mattress factory. A black eye and a split lip completed the overall effect.

"Scum?" smirked Daggoth.

"You—you—you *snake!*" She stood five feet away, trembling with rage.

"Snake? Oh my," the dark sorcerer murmured.

"You—you—you—you—"

He grinned: "'Ewe, ewe,' she said sheepishly."

Having noticed that the Amazon princess was unarmed, I felt a modicum of composure returning. "Sometimes words fail," I observed.

She leapt, landing on the bed in general and on me specifically. The bed collapsed. As did I. Her hands thrust unerringly into the tangle of bedclothes and found my throat.

Ensnared in the muddle of blankets, I couldn't pry her hands loose, much less fight back. I was beginning to wonder why Daggoth was dimming the room lights when Aeriel's grip relaxed and her fingers fell away from my neck.

"Took you long enough," I gasped, as he reached down to help me from the ruined bed.

"Sorry."

Aeriel was still crouching, her hands reaching out, grasping—but totally unmoving. He bodily moved her out of the way so that I could stand up again. "I was prepared for every contingency except the humor of the situation."

"You know what this is about?"

He shook his head. "I figure we'll find out in about forty-five minutes."

"That when the spell wears off?"

Daggoth nodded.

"Then I reckon I've got time for a shower, first," I said.

Σ

The shower facilities were located on the sixth and seventh floors. The chamber was stone-dressed to resemble a grotto with pool and two-story waterfall. Lily pads floated on the water and a profusion of plants and wildflowers sprang from niches in the rocks. The water was pleasantly warm: solar-heated on the roof before feeding the upper pool, where it cascaded down some fifteen feet from an overhang, into the lower pool, and then was filtered down through the sandy floor to start the cycle again. The system seemed almost natural until you paused to consider the pump technology and the fact that indoor plumbing and concepts of personal hygiene were extreme anachronisms for this time and culture.

I shook the water from my hair as I exited the waterfall and waded across the pool to grab a towel. Mervyn had showered almost an hour earlier and was still trying to comb the tangles out of his long white hair and beard. It was hard to imagine a fourteen-year-old boy inhabiting the body of a nonagenarian, especially when all he had on was a towel wrapped around his waist. Then, as I passed by to retrieve a towel for myself, I noticed that he was checking his reflection in one of the basin mirrors, parting various areas of facial hair, looking for zits.

Sometimes it's the little things that help us regain our perspective.

I waded, shin-deep, back into the water to talk to Daggoth. He was reclining in a floating deck chair and smoking a Swisher Sweet as he monitored a mirror fragment for more reports from the other teams. A flagon containing an iced beverage was ensconced in a depressed cup-holder in the buoyant chair-arm.

"Any news from Rijma and Stephanie?" I asked as I began drying my hair.

"Vashti," he corrected. "And no, nothing yet."

I wondered as to his preference for using my ex-wife's avatar name instead of her real name. Did he prefer to maintain the illusion of Program reality? Or did he feel uncomfortable with any linkage to our past relationship?

"That was pretty mean, you know."

I looked at him. "What?"

"I mean ol' Morf was pretty traumatized by having a couple of women going to retrieve his you-know-what. It was bad enough that they were pressing him for a description. But when you asked about 'any identifying scars or moles'…"

"Hey," I shrugged, "standard police procedure. And he needed a little nudge at that point."

"Well," he grinned, "it was mean."

"Mean? You're the one who followed up by suggesting that they bring back a selection and let him choose!"

"Couldn't help myself. It really was—"

"Burrrrrrrrrrup."

We turned and looked at the bullfrog who regarded us reproachfully from a nearby lilypad.

"So, how's it going with Jeremiah? Made any progress?"

Daggoth shook his head and sighed. "Nothing beyond the process of elimination. Whoever zapped ol' Jerry here, had, some code strings that participated in the spell like a computer virus. The transmogrification is multi-level and continues to mutate like a Proteus infection."

"You're saying it can't be undone?" Mervyn asked worriedly.

The anxious amphibian croaked mournfully.

"No. The spell contains one of those puzzle-codes that enables you to unlock it with a specific key or phrase or event or counterspell. I just don't know what the triggering mechanism is yet." He got up and followed me as I wrapped the towel about my waist and exited the chamber.

"I would think unzapping a computer spell would be easy for a twenty-third level wizard and the Chief of Programming for Cephtronics." I glanced behind me and noticed that Mervyn had remained behind but Jeremiah was following us, hopping from step to step as we descended the staircase.

"*Former* Chief of Programming," he corrected. "And it's not that simple. Jerry's a living human being, not a subprogram of The Machine. Any mistake could damn well be fatal."

I glanced at the hourglass as I entered my room: time was almost up. "A little privacy, please."

Daggoth looked amazed. "You want me to leave?"

"No, I want you to turn her around." I rummaged through my closet, one-handed, as he turned the frozen form of the Amazon princess so that she faced the wall. *Closets—another anachronism in this pseudo-medieval environment.* "Thanks." I dropped the towel and began dressing.

"Why do we do it?" I asked as I sat on the ruins of the bed and pulled on my moccasin boots.

"Do what?"

"This. Dress up in Dreambodies and run around playing games inside a giant computer?"

"Well, as I recall, you're attempting to rescue the next president of the United States—"

"I don't mean you and me specifically, here and now." I began the lengthy process of lacing up the sides of the boots with rawhide thongs. "I mean people in general. Why do *they* do it?"

"I thought we had all of these discussions back when Dreamworlds was still a concept on the drawing boards." He sighed. "I'm going to get some water for the princess, here. She'll need it when the spell wears off." He left the room.

He was right; we had discussed these issues before. And had some pretty violent exchanges when I had grown disenchanted with the Project over the moral rights of advanced AI's.

I finished my boots, got up and walked to the window. Looking out over the panorama of forest and fields, I felt the urge to succumb to the illusion. To believe in the Program-Constructions as Reality. To accept this world on it's own terms.

"A game," I murmured. "Whatever we do, it has no ultimate meaning in the greater cosmology." To believe otherwise meant responsibilities and obligations that I could not shoulder. Guilt for creating—

"Why do we do it..." Daggoth re-entered the room with a decanter of water and matching goblet. I turned my attention back to dressing as he placed them on the table next to the remains of the bed. "For me it was always a job. Cephtronics paid me to develop and operate Programworlds that people would want to visit. Again and again. And pay money to do so.

"R & D was constantly supplying me with the latest surveys and statistics as to what was hot and what was not. Demographics. Trends. Economic indicators. Audience shifts." He shook his head. "For all of their information—summaries, charts, graphs—they could guess at 'what' every month or so. But they rarely could tell me 'why.' Why a particular trend was—well—trendy. And they never answered the question of why we need escapism. Why we create alternate realities."

I tucked my tunic into my trousers. "Dissatisfaction with reality?" I reached for my swordbelt.

"That was my theory for a long time." Daggoth walked over to Aeriel's frozen form. "But then I noticed that a lot of the AR's—stories, books, holos, even Programworlds—were even grimmer than the world we rail against in our day-to-day lives. If I had to pick a world to spend the rest of my life in," he said without a trace of irony, "I'd prefer the so-called 'Real' world over any of these Programworlds."

The more I thought about it, the more I agreed. The appeal of most escapist environments is rooted in the dangers, hardships, and problems that they offer. This hardly qualified as an improvement over the lives that most of us knew. For some, perhaps, like Nicole or even myself, the compensations of trading a crippled body for a healthy avatar were obvious. But the vast majority of Dreamworlds tourists were healthy and financially secure. You had to have money to spend any appreciable time Dreamwalking. So, once again: why?

"Variety?" I offered.

"Variety is the spice of life," Daggoth agreed. "Or so they say. And while I still can't explain it, I'm more convinced than ever that we, as a species, need escapism. It's a racial trait. We always want what we don't have and we rarely appreciate what we do."

I shrugged into my mithril vest. "You make it sound like a disease."

"I dunno, maybe I'm just jaded. And now that I'm dead and stuck in here for the rest of my unnatural life, my perspective is somewhat skewed."

"You said you had statistics on which Dreamworlds people preferred and, to a limited degree, why. So, why Fantasyworld?" I slid my swords into their sheaths. "Given that people have a need for escapism, why Fantasyworld? Why not some different diversion?"

"Hey, you were the best-selling author. We just purchased a hot property. You tell me."

"Tell me," croaked a third voice.

We both looked at the frog. His eyes goggled and he jerked a bit. He jerked again and this time we turned our attention in the direction that he jerked. It was Aeriel and she was moving toward us like an old woman in the final stages of rheumatoid arthritis. "Tell me," she croaked again.

"Tell you what, Aeri?"

Her arms came up like ancient drawbridges and her hands curled into claws. "Tell me why you betrayed me!" Her words were becoming better formed, now, as the spell was wearing off more rapidly. "Tell me before you die!"

SIX

\RIPLEY\PATH\SIGMA (Σ)

"I believe you!"

"Then stop struggling," Daggoth admonished, retying a knot to minimize the slack in the rope.

"Did you not hear me?" The Amazon princess spoke through gritted teeth. "I believe your stupid story!" She strained against the half dozen cords of rope that secured her to the chair. "You may release me!"

"I will release you, my lady," the dark sorcerer mused with a grin, "just as soon as our Bard is safely on his way."

"I think you're enjoying this far too much," I said, a safe distance away, on the other side of the table.

"Enjoy?" he said. "What's to enjoy?" He chuckled. "Now there are some who might be amused by the fact that an Amazon princess—one that you're engaged to—has already murdered you once, and has tried a couple of more times since then. And that another woman you were engaged to in the Real world murdered you twice, and is still trying. And that the woman you are *presently* engaged to isn't the same woman you *thought* you were engaged to—which is probably why *she* hasn't tried to murder you, yet. And another woman thinks she should be engaged to you so she and a prince and a half dozen or so Mountain Dwarves are out hunting you down like public enemy number one. And since there were some other yous running around inside the Program for awhile, who knows how many other felonious fiancées may yet turn up.

"Now, yes, there are some people who might find some humor in your...predicament...but I am not...one...of them..." He turned away at that point.

Watching his shoulders shake made up my mind for me: I dropped a couple of leftover pellets from Snow White's engagement ball into the carafe of water on the table.

"If I was indeed betrayed by an impostor last night," Aeriel continued, "I would be most foolish to kill my consort. Release me and I will pursue the truth in this matter." She struggled a bit more. "I vow his life is safe until I prove his guilt or innocence in last night's events."

"Sorry, Your Highness," Daggoth answered, "My hospitality has taken a beating from your hot-headedness of late." He placed a dagger in her bound hands. "You should be able to cut yourself free in a couple of minutes. I'll unlock the door as soon as your—um—consort is gone."

We vacated the room in a hurry and Daggoth turned a large key in the lock. "I'm not looking forward to letting her out even after you're gone," he said.

"Oh," I said, thinking about the potion dissolving in the water jar, "I think you'll find an enormous change in attitude when you open the door again."

"Well, we've got more to worry about than just your engaged and enraged Amazon back there. If we can trust what she told us, there's another one of you out there somewhere."

"And his behavior is a bit inconsistent with the rest of mes," I added.

"Oh, I don't know…" Daggoth started chuckling again. "Didn't you tell me that your first act on re-entering the program was to greet Aeriel with a left uppercut?"

"The circumstances were a bit different—"

"I know, I know," he waved me to silence. "And there is the little matter about his invitation to Ortygia and then disappearing with the head."

"Morpheus isn't going to like that," I mused.

"Perhaps. But I think he's got the part that's most important to him, now."

Rune was coming down the steps as we were going up. "Gentlemen," she said quietly, "I think you'd better come up to the observation deck."

The first thing we noticed when we reached the top of the tower was that the Cyberpunks were still encamped all around us.

"They haven't found the hidden exit from the stables," Daggoth observed, "so you should still be able to leave on schedule."

"You might want to move your schedule up a bit." Rune directed our attention skyward. Strings of dirty smoke and vapor had been twisted and looped and swung about to form words in the sky. As we watched, the airborne skywriter was finishing the "h" at the end of:

Surrender

Riplikish

"I don't like this," Daggoth murmured.

"*You* don't like it?" I groused. "I hate it! They spelled my name wrong!"

"She."

"What?" we chorused.

"She." Rune turned and handed a small telescope to Daggoth. "Woman on a broom."

He nodded and suddenly swung the glass to the west. To the unaided eye it looked like clouds on the horizon.

"Cirrocumulus?" I asked.

Daggoth shook his head. "Chimpanzees."

"Excuse me?"

"With wings," he added. "Bob, we just moved up your departure time. Saddle up!"

We ran down the great staircase collecting Mervyn on the way to the stables. Our gear was ready and our only delay was saddling Ghost. Rune climbed up behind Mervyn on his flying rug before I was done, and Daggoth cast a field of invisibility over us all.

Other than bumping into each other as we moved down the exit tunnel, we were able to depart without incident.

Σ

Calabastor's waterfront area was crowded this day. Ships arrived and departed with a frantic frequency that put one in mind of L.A.X. during the Christmas holidays. Cargo was being loaded and unloaded by legions of stevedores. Peddlers and vendors flocked about the boardwalk, beach, and piers to hawk their wares to passengers and crew alike.

Fights seemed to break out on a regular basis. The most spectacular was between a great, bloated brutish man and a scrawny, pop-eyed sailor with grotesquely muscled forearms. Surprisingly, the little man won and walked off with the object of their disagreement: a woman so tall and impossible skinny that she'd have to run around in the shower to get wet.

Rune led us on past Hennesey & McHale's Dry-dock Services, pointing out the various ships anchored in the harbor. "Avoid that one like the plague," she warned, indicating a dark vessel with the name "Nostromo" painted across its stern. "It smuggles illegal aliens." There was nothing beyond the ship's dark coloring and oddly shaped superstructure to indicate its corrupt cargo. Indeed, a frigate of a more sinister aspect was passing by the harbor mouth, its blood-red sails billowing in a different direction than the wind was actually blowing: the Dutchman was still looking for his home port.

Ships of less sinister mien abounded, as well. Milk was being loaded aboard the good ship "Guppy" while children frolicked on its wooden deck with an elephant and an odd-looking sea dog. Another boat, similarly named after another small fish, prepared to depart with five passengers, promising a three-hour tour of the islands. The handbills that advertised the daily excursions further promised that the first officer was "a mighty sailing man" and that the captain was "brave" and "sure." My doubts on that bit of hype were distracted by a large, whitewashed schooner passed by, close enough to hear the minstrel on board crooning: "Love, exciting and new…"

Rune led us down a series of docks to a small, twin-masted ketch with gaff-and-topsail rigs. *Mary Ellen Carter* was emblazoned across her hull and, as we led Ghost up the gangplank, a large woman with her left arm in a sling leaned out over the gunnels and yelled: "Ahoy, Dr. Ripley!" She vaulted the railing (no mean feat for a woman her size and with a bum arm in the bargain) and met me halfway up.

"Ms. Carter, I presume?"

"Elsbeth, you fraud! Ha!" Her back slap nearly pitched me into the water. "You had us convinced, man!"

"Convinced, madam?"

"First, that you were dead. And that death was as permanent as you claimed." She helped me maneuver a rather nervous animal up and onto the ship.

Ghost managed, as well.

"But, as you've just now proved, one or both of those suppositions just won't hold water."

A light flicked dimly in the nether regions of my brain. I turned to Rune: "Do I know her?"

"Sort of," the Assassin murmured. "She's the one who hauled your body back to town."

"The one with all the neat little holes in it?" Mervyn wanted to know.

"Mmm hmm."

"Cast off!" Elsbeth bellowed, "and attend the lines!

A slim rapier of a man, dressed in a dandy's finery, leapt forward to grasp several ropes. "Number two manned, my lady! How say you, abbot?"

A short, round man was extricating himself from a makeshift cot of coiled hawsers and sailcloth. "Coming, coming," he mumbled. A mitered helmet was twisted and slightly askew atop his bushy head and he nearly tripped over his robe and the end of his rope girdle. A silver crucifix flailed at the end of a leather thong behind his back. The abbot yawned and staggered about, contemplating the ropes running down the sides of the two masts. "Who's on the first line, Costellino?" he queried.

"You are, man."

"Then, who's on the second one?"

The slender man with the pencil-thin moustache shook his set of lines at the big fellow. "I am."

"Then, who's on the third?"

"What?"

The abbot scratched his head: "'What's' on the third line?"

"No!" The smaller man was becoming exasperated. "There is no third, you birdbrain!"

In spite of the confusion over the sail lines we were moving away from the pier and moving out into the harbor. I gazed up into the rigging, mystified as to how we could be moving at all—much less in the right direction.

Mervyn tapped my shoulder and pointed past the prow of our ship. "We're being towed."

Sure enough, a series of ropes fanned out from a forward capstan, stretched taut, and disappeared into the water some fifty feet ahead of us. As I stared one of the ropes went a little slack as a large fishtail broke the surface of the water. It disappeared beneath the waves and the rope pulled tight again. "Dolphins?" I queried.

The woman, Elsbeth, looked at me, her eyes goggling a bit like Jeremiah's.

"Skywalker!"

We turned and looked. A blonde woman was climbing over the railing, wearing a great big smile and nothing else. I looked at Elsbeth: "Friend of yours?"

Elsbeth goggled a bit more, and then the blonde was all over me like cheap livery.

"I think we should sit down and talk," Rune suggested.

Σ

"So you're really dead."

I shook my head. "I'm still alive. The other Ripleys—including the one you picked up at sea—are dead."

We were down below, in the aft cabin that Elsbeth had been using for her quarters. After telling our respective stories, we were still confused.

"So you—or the other you—was—were—telling me the truth." She reached for the bottle at the center or the table and poured herself another drink. "Death has become serious business here in Dreamworlds." She knocked back her glass and the amber liquid disappeared in a convulsive swallow.

"Well, now that you're convinced," I said, "I suppose you'll be high-tailing it out of the Matrix just as fast as your algorithms will take you."

"What? Not hardly!" She set her glass back on the table with a resounding thump. "If I was willing to risk my neck for a possible Pulitzer on a REMrunner story, what makes you think I'm gonna back down now?"

"Well, I—"

"Great Caesar's ghost, man, this goes beyond Pulitzer! A U.S. senator held hostage by a computer, a half-crazed Artificial Intelligence plotting to take over the White House, the Program's creator turned into a Were-Elf and split into multiple avatars that are being hunted down and murdered in a mysterious conspiracy, your ex-wife involved in an on-going romance with a dead man—we're talking bestseller here! We're talking New Hollywood!"

"Money?" I asked. "You're willing to risk your life for mere money?"

"Nothing mere about the kind of money we're talking about here," she answered warmly. The drink had already brought a rosy glow to her cheeks and was now working its will on her posture. "And is'—*it*'s— not just money. Is' career, is' the opportunity of a lifetime." She picked up the bottle again. "Besides, you can use all the help you can get. If Cerbrus isn' defeated and gets 'lected President, I'm not going to be all that safe on the outside. And that's assuming that I can get out without him knowing that I'm a witness and therefore—liability."

I saw her point.

"Now, what're you going to do 'bout Bubbles?"

I favored her with another of my devastatingly blank looks: "Bubbles?"

She shrugged. "You know: Thetis."

"Ah," I said. "Thetis."

"Dockster Ripley," she fumbled with the bottle, "I suspect you know your Greek mythology to know that Blondie, here, is supposed to marry Peleus, have a son, and raise him in the Sticks."

"Dip him in the Styx," I corrected. "Achilles."

"Gesundheit," she returned amiably. She waved the bottle. "Sure you don't want some?"

I hesitated. "Uh, no." It wasn't Demon Rum and, even if it were, I was going to need my wits about me more than ever for the next couple of days.

"So's how the Trojans gonna fight the Geeks without 'im?"

"Greeks," I corrected. "And I don't know, yet."

"Well," she murmured conspiratorially, "I'm working on a plan."

"Ah. And?"

"I'm not drunk enough, yet."

"Oh."

Σ

"COSSSTELLLINNOOOOO!"

The abbot's cry was far more effective than any land-locked rooster at rousing us from our sleep. I tumbled out of my hammock and fumbled for my gear as feet pattered over the decking above my head.

"Sails ho!" the count announced as I stumbled up on deck, trying to buckle my swordbelt.

The sun had not yet made its appearance but a rosy predawn glow suffused the sky to the east and the water reflected enough light from the twin moons sinking in the west to illumine our quarry. The count passed the spyglass to Rune who directed it toward an island several miles away. I joined them at the starboard rail.

"Well?"

"Looks like our ship," she answered. "Too far away to make out a name but she flies the Jolly Roger."

"Big deal," opined Mervyn, "all pirates fly the black flag!"

"Overall description seems to match, so far," the Assassin continued. "She's heeling behind yon island, so we'll have to follow to make sure."

"Wait a minute," Elsbeth was saying. "When you hired my boat to catch you up to a ship that had sailed the day before, you didn't say anything about it being a pirate vessel!"

I looked at Rune.

Who looked at Mervyn.

Who looked at me.

"Um, it's a pirate vessel," I said.

"I can see that!"

The abbot appropriated the little brass telescope and futilely scanned the island for further evidence. "Maybe it's Bluebeard!" he theorized with wide-eyed enthusiasm.

"If you think this boat is going any closer, you're out of your mind!" Elsbeth continued.

"Bluebeard wasn't a pirate, you moron!" Costellino was explaining to his oafish companion.

"You don't have to pull alongside," I assured Elsbeth, "just get us within a mile or so that island."

"Then maybe it's Yellowbeard!" the abbot wheezed.

"Are you kidding me?" She planted her hands on her hips and shook her head. "We're turning this tub around right now and heading back to Calabastor!"

"You're thinking of an old movie. Two-dee," answered the count.

"What happened to last night's bravado?" I challenged. "What happened to the Pulitzer Prize, serious money, and the chance of a lifetime?"

"How about Redbeard?"

"Lifetime!" she screeched. "There ain't gonna be any lifetime if we get close to a pirate ship! In case you haven't noticed, we're not packing a single cannon! And I'm sober this morning! A little hungover—but sober!"

"Dunno. I think he was a Viking." Costellino rubbed his chin. "I seem to remember a book or something..."

"Look, we can keep the island between them and us," I said, heading toward the makeshift stall just down front of the poop deck. "I'll take it from there."

"We'll take it from there," Mervyn corrected.

"I s'pose you'll be telling me there wasn't no Blackbeard, next."

"You're out of your mind!" Elsbeth insisted.

"No. There really was a Blackbeard, as I recall."

"Maybe I am," I murmured, picking up my saddle and approaching Ghost.

"D'you suppose we could get close enough to get a good look?" the abbot pondered.

"If it is Blackbeard," the count considered, "he might show us more than we bargained for."

"That would *Teech* you," Rune observed dryly.

I looked at her and grinned as I adjusted the saddle across Ghost's back.

"What?" Mervyn wanted to know. "What'd she say?"

"Never mind." Even without the spectacles, it was disorienting seeing an ancient wizard, decades past the "graybeard" stage, adopt the speech and mannerisms of an adolescent. I tightened the front and back cinches, elbowing the pegasus in the belly to eliminate any slack.

"All right!" Elsbeth conceded. "We'll shelter in the lee of the island. For an hour. Then we're leaving." She folded her arms. "If that pirate ship circles around any sooner, we'll hoist anchor and you can jolly well walk back to Calabastor on your own!"

"Fair enough," I said.

The abbot was oblivious to the rest of us. "What about Brownbeard?" he asked the count.

SEVEN

\RIPLEY\PATH\SIGMA (Σ)

"What was that?"

Rune turned back to face me. "Dwarf—I think!" she called over the drone of wind. "He was ringing a bell!"

I looked down again but we had passed over the compound and all I could see was palm-topped jungle and a sandy lagoon where the island had pinched off a section of ocean between thumb and forefinger. "What was he yelling about?"

Rune shrugged and almost lost her balance at the edge of Mervyn's flying carpet. The rug had taken point position as Ghost's wings tended to stir up a bit air turbulence to the sides and rear. "Something about a plain!" She shaded her eyes and scanned the tree line. "Do you think he meant a plateau?"

I shrugged. "I just hope that bell didn't tip off the pirates!" I yelled back.

"I just hope your finny friends are there when we need 'em!" he countered.

"We'll find out in a moment," Rune said, pointing.

Abruptly, the island fell behind us and, less than a mile away, the pirate ship hove into view.

Perhaps they had heard the bell. Perhaps the lookout in the crow's-nest was unusually alert and sharp of eye.

Or perhaps they were already expecting airborne visitors. There was a booming sound and a moment later a missile bearing a strong resemblance to a bowling ball whistled past.

"Split right!" I yelled, "And then hover above the mainmast: you'll be safe there!"

They swerved to starboard while Ghost and I swooped to port. The next cannonball split the difference and cut a path between us.

As my winged steed looped around to close with the ship's rigging, I unclipped the saddle's safety tethers from my belt and loosed my left foot from the stirrup. It took only another moment to invoke the parameters of a Flying spell about myself. With luck, I wouldn't need it and the pirates below wouldn't give me cause to use it. But Bob Ripley Junior didn't raise no dummy and I never believed in working without a "net."

As Ghost's wing tip brushed the topgallant on the mainmast, I leapt from the saddle, dropping some ten feet or so to the angled hammock formed by the ratlines crisscrossing the shrouds.

"Boy!" roared a voice from down below, "I'll have your guts for garters!"

Guts for garters, again. Nice. Real nice.

"Come down here or I'll come up and get you!"

"That's the plan, man," I murmured, drawing my hamidachi. I cut a shroud line and swung in toward the mainmast. I slapped into the topsail, just below the topgallant, like a baseball into a catcher's glove. I released the line and slid down to the footspar; put the hamidachi in my teeth as I executed a three-sixty curl over the wooden beam, and dropped down to the top of the course. Plunging the short blade into the sailcloth, I descended the remainder of the distance to the main deck on a path of ripped canvass. Luck was with me: I didn't have to use the Flying spell, I landed without falling on my face and, though the pirates quickly surrounded me, they didn't immediately kill me for dividing their mainsail into two pieces.

The looks on their faces, however, indicated that the thought had occurred to them.

"Avast, me lads! Make way! Let me through!" A portion of the wall of scurvy seamen was jostled aside and their captain stepped through.

He was tall and slim, with cruel, aquiline features and long, thin, dangly moustaches. He also wore an eyepatch and in place of his left hand he had a grappling device of hooked brass.

"Captain Claw, I presume."

He cocked his head like a parrot and contemplated me with his one good eye. "You're not him!"

"Whom?"

"Pe—," began a voice to my right.

"Silence!" thundered the pirate chief. "Have I not forbidden one and all to speak the name of that juvenile delinquent in my presence for the rest of time?"

Heads nodded.

He peered at me again. "You're not him," he decided again. "Furthermore, you don't look like any of the rest of them!"

"Them?" I asked.

"The Los—"

"Silence!" he roared. Then smiled sweetly. "However," he continued, "you do look familiar."

"Really?" Now that was an observation that had come to make me nervous of late.

"Yes." His hand went to his cutlass. "You look like a dead man to me!" The pirates all roared their approval as he drew his sword and advanced.

No one was in any hurry, here, so I had time to sheath the hamidachi and draw my katana. Caladbolg's crystal blade and blue glow got their attention.

"Actually, Captain, I'm here to do some business."

"Business?" His advance had degenerated into a wary orbit and he circled me from a safe distance.

"Yes." I suddenly swung my longsword about my body, weaving a protective basket of momentary crystal. The effect was that the encompassing circle of pirates moved back several feet, giving me more maneuvering room. "I'm here to make an exchange."

Claw frowned. "Exchange? What kind of exchange?"

"You have something I want." I smiled. "I have something you want."

"What?" Claw demanded, eyeing my glowing blade. "What is this bargain you dare to make with Captain Claw?"

"You picked up a hand on the necromantic black market. It belonged to a—an acquaintance—of mine." Calling Morpheus "friend" felt a little awkward. "I want it back."

Claw looked a bit discomfited, himself. "I have special plans for that hand," he answered, make a few tentative feints with his cutlass. "I am not inclined to part with it. Oh, no. In fact, as soon as I reach Ortygia, I expect to become quite 'attached' to it, you might say…"

I almost dropped my guard. When we traced the other hand, its intended use had become quite evident. A dead man's hand: Hand of Glory. It would be used as a sort of magical treasure-hunting device. I had supposed a pirate ship would use the other hand for similar purposes. Now, looking at the brass crampon where Claw's other hand used to be, I understood differently. It would probably be easier to convince the man to part with all those chests of gold and silver he surely had down below in the holds.

"What's on Ortygia, Claw?" I tapped his cutlass aside with Caladbolg. "Someone promising you a 'graft' job?"

"You don't know what it's like," he hissed. "Having to be so careful when you sleep: rolling over in bed could be fatal! Stupid things like picking your nose or using the amenities of basic hygiene are painful and potentially disfiguring! And my social life—" He choked. "What's your interest, Dead Man?" he cried. "What would you offer me in exchange for a chance at a normal life?"

Put that way, I felt guilt colliding with duty. "Your ship," I said.

He stopped stalking and leaned back. "My ship?"

I nodded.

"Let me get this straight: you want the dead sorcerer's hand in exchange for my ship? The ship that I already have?"

"Um, yep. That pretty well sums up the deal."

"You're mad!"

"Captain!" chimed in a new voice. "We're taking on water!"

Claw whirled. "How bad?"

"Not bad," I answered. "The hole is only about this wide..." I made a circle touching thumb to forefinger.

"Plug it!" he ordered, and turned back on me. "How did you know?"

I smiled. "The same way I know that in one minute you'll have two more holes—the same size—in different parts of your hull."

"What!"

"Captain! The bo's'n reports another hole aft!"

"How?" he bellowed.

I gestured to the rail. "I'd like you to meet some friends of mine." Heads turned. Observed other heads breaking the surface of the sea around the ship. "Women..." the pirate crew breathed wonderingly.

"Nereids," I corrected. "Daughters of Nereus, god of the sea."

"Sisters?" someone murmured. "There's so many…"

"Fifty, to be exact." I didn't mention Ethyl as they were already sufficiently impressed. They were also noticing the collection of awls and hand drills and assorted piercing tools that the Sea Nymphs were brandishing. I waved to Thetis and she signaled to the others to submerge again.

"Now," I continued as the last of the pirates' distractions disappeared beneath the waves, "in another minute, three more holes will breach your hull below the water line. The minute after that, four more will appear. And each minute thereafter, another set of holes plus one more will be made in your ship, Captain, until we come to some sort of agreement."

Claw looked around at his crew who were already dwindling in number as the pirates ran off to repair the perforations and man the pumps.

"More holes!" someone bellowed below decks.

"All right!" Claw gnashed his teeth. "Bly! To my cabin and fetch me that damned hand!"

"Aye sir! 'Tis already done!" The pudgy first mate produced a package wrapped in oilskins.

"Good man," gritted the captain. "You'll have your own ship, someday."

"Thank you, sir."

"Now," Claw grimaced, "give it over to our new friend, here."

Bly looked at me as if trying to ascertain his chances of impressing the captain a bit more.

"More holes!"

"Quickly!" Claw screamed.

Bly complied with no complicating heroics. I saluted the pirate chief with my sword and invoked the Flying spell: the crow's-nest was occupied so I soared up to the very top of the mainmast and signaled Ethyl. The merman dove down to call off the scuttling party and I whistled for Ghost who was circling some distance away. Mervyn and Rune were hovering nearby.

"That was easy," Mervyn said.

He said it prematurely.

Captain Claw had endured bold trespass upon his ship. He had sustained considerable damage to his mainsail (my insurance against his pursuing the *Mary Ellen Carter).* He'd had further damage done to his hull and taken on a fair amount of water. And he had lost the hand of a powerful but dead sorcerer: a hand imbued with sufficient magic that he might be able to trade it for the brass claw affixed to the wrist of his left arm.

All this, and he had allowed me to depart unmolested. To be fair, he had allowed it because I had not given him much choice. But Ghost's return to the mainmast tipped the precarious balance I had arranged below.

A horse is a horse (of course, of course). Sticking great feathered wings on him may permit magical flight but it doesn't negate other aspects of equine biology. Anyone who has spent any time around a stable knows that horses are not overly mindful about where they drop their "processed" hay and oats. Flying horses are no different.

It just happened to be Captain Claw's misfortune to be in the wrong place at the wrong time.

A muffled scream was our first warning. As I climbed onto Ghost's saddle, I looked down and saw a much altered pirate chief running over to one of the deck guns. Bellowing imprecations interwoven with allusions to the goat-footed god of pastures, forests, flocks, and herds, he pulled and tugged at the great barrel until it was tilted straight up.

Pointing right at us.

"Uh-oh," said Mervyn.

I shook my head. "I didn't think any of them would be this stupid."

"What is the phrase?" Rune pondered. "Excrement for grey matter?"

"Looks like brown matter from here," the wizard observed.

"Time to split," I admonished.

We did so, just as the cannon boomed. The heavy iron ball came whistling up between us, ripping through the topsail and the topgallant as well as the remains of the course. Hovering a few feet to either side, we watched as the rounded projectile continued upwards another twenty or so feet. Then gravity eased its leaden foot down onto the brake pedal.

"Newton's law."

I looked at Mervyn. "What?"

"Newton's law," he repeated, watching the cannonball achieve a momentary state of complete inertia. "Every action has an equal but opposite reaction."

"Uh uh."

I turned an looked at Rune as the iron sphere began to reverse its course.

"Newton's law of action and reaction might be applied to the firing of the cannon but now we're dealing with a different article of Newtonian physics."

We both gaped at her.

"Newton's law of gravitation is that every particle of matter attracts every other particle of matter with a force that varies directly as the product of their masses and inversely as the square of the distances between them. However," she elaborated as the projectile whistled back down through the rigging, "it's Galileo's law of gravitational acceleration that probably has the greatest impact under the present circumstances."

And impact was precisely the right word. A circular hole appeared in the deck planking of the fo'c'sle, less than five feet from the beslimed Captain Claw. A moment later, a large jet of water gushed from the opening, giving the prow of the pirate ship the appearance of a giant bidet.

"And what would you know about gravitational physics?" Mervyn challenged, stung by her rebuttal.

"I know that every second that an object falls, its speed increases by some thirty-two feet per second," she replied.

"Abandon ship!" came a cry from below.

"Some thirty-two feet?" was his only comeback.

"Well, if you want precision, the formula is s equals one-half g,t squared…"

I turned Ghost's head back toward the far side of the island where Elsbeth would be pacing the decks and worrying about a pirate ship that would never come now.

"…value of g is 32-point-1740 feet or 980-point-665 centimeters per second…"

I shook my head and grinned as we moved away from the foundering galleon. I couldn't do any more for Scully. This is the way it seemed we all had to learn: it's the quiet ones you have to watch out for.

PART V

EN PASSANT

And all my days are trances,
And all my nightly dreams
Are where thy grey eye glances
And where thy footstep gleams—
In what ethereal dances
By what eternal streams.

—Poe, *To One in Paradise*—

ONE

\RIPLEY\PATH\SIGMA (Σ)

Forty-eight hours later we stood on the shores of Ortygia.

The previous day I had sent Mervyn back to the Tower with Morpheus's hand. I had second thoughts when I tried to contact Daggoth via the shard of magic mirror I was carrying and had drawn a blank. I tried every two hours throughout the day and then well into last night with no better luck. Perhaps we were merely out of range or the Sorcerer had business that had taken him away from his citadel, but, as the second moon slipped from the dark ocean depths and began its climb up the black velvet sky, I felt a growing disquiet.

Elsbeth joined me at the starboard rail as the midnight watch came and went. Together we watch the bright stars spiral through the great cosmic dance.

"Looks real, doesn't it?"

She gazed at me curiously. "What makes you think it isn't?"

"Please…"

"No, really," she insisted. "What if this is the Reality and that other life that we remember outside of this Programworld but the fevered dream of our imaginations?"

I smiled and leaned across the railing, inhaling the sharp, salt tang of ocean spray as the waves collided with the ship's hull. "You know, I've heard the theory that a Programworld is as much every bit a 'reality' in its own right as the one we claim Outside. But I don't think I've ever heard anyone put quite the spin on it as you just did."

She smiled in turn and gestured to the panorama of stars and the ripples of phosphorescence on the night sea. "You don't buy into all this, do you?"

"Sometimes." I knelt on the deck and rested my chin and arms on the railing. "But for the most part, I can't afford to. The whole thing is too…seductive. And I know how it really works so it tends to spoil the effect."

"So…if you were a physicist would you tend to dismiss most of the Outside…just because you were well versed in atomic structure?"

"Got me again!" I grinned. "Time to go on the offensive."

She made a gesture of compliance. "Your serve."

"All right. How many worlds can one person inhabit? How many lives can one person live at the same time and live well?"

"There are theories of parallel universes where alternate selves live out alternate lives—"

"Wouldn't count even if you could prove it," I said. "If there were more than one of us in more than one universe, we'd still be separate entities. Siamese twins in <u>this</u> universe are still two separate sets of consciousnesses."

"Reincarnation—"

"One person, the same person—living in different worlds, assuming different identities, all in the same lifetime."

"You're describing Dreamwalking."

"If the shoe fits."

"So what do you have against a little fun and games? Aren't we all entitled to a little fantasy?"

"I'm not against a little fantasy," I said. "Hell, I made a decent living writing them. But this," I indicated our surroundings with a sweep of my arm, "is so real that it's hard for some people to walk away from it when the time is up. People want to <u>live</u> part of their lives here! Which brings me back to my original question. With a whole lifetime to work things out, most people don't do so well dealing with just one world. So how many people could—simultaneously—live more than one life, in more than one world, and live any of them *well?*"

"I see your point."

She stretched and yawned. "We should make landfall before midday tomorrow: I'm turning in." We said our goodnights and headed for our respective berths. Just before she closed the door to her cabin, Elsbeth called to me. "Rob, we're all looking for a better world than the one we were born into."

"But is this one really better?" I asked.

She shrugged. "Life is a crap shoot and you look for the best odds you can find. If you're gonna win at the races, you gotta bet on more than one horse."

I went to my bunk thinking of the only horses I considered a sure thing: the polychromatic foursome in St. John the Divine's *Revelation.*

Σ

Twelve hours later I was walking up Ortygia's sandy beach. Since Ghost couldn't carry anyone besides myself, I turned him loose to graze inland and geared up to make the trek to the Sibyl's cave on foot. Elsbeth and Rune, of course, decided to accompany me. The abbot and Costellino had decided that someone needed to guard the ship and that it would take both of them to do so. Ethyl couldn't leave the water at all and the Nereids couldn't leave it behind for very long. So that left the three of us.

There had been no sign of submarines or flying saucers on the voyage in. In fact there had been no sign of anything or anyone, so far: no birds flew, no insects hummed, even the susurrus of plants in the wind was absent as we found ourselves in a dead calm.

Welcome to my parlor...

We had taken no more than ten steps when a geyser of sand and smoke erupted at the tree line and a gout of flame belched skyward. By the time a humanoid form stepped out of the column of fire and smoke we were displaying more blades than a ginjsu commercial.

"I see you are well prepared," she observed with a mocking smile.

"Lilith!" I could have hugged her.

"Not yet," she said, warning me back with a stiff-armed gesture. "I need to cool down first." Now I could see the aura-like layers of heat-distorted air that rippled about her form. She trotted around us and down to the water, leaving a pattern of glassy footprints in the sand. There was a tremendous burst of steam as she waded out into the ocean and the hissing sound precluded any conversation until her head was completely submerged.

"Friend of yours?" Elsbeth inquired as Lilith emerged from the waves.

I nodded.

"Figures."

The residual moisture on her person was evaporating even as Lilith approached again, but she did look a good deal cooler. "What brings you to Ortygia?" I asked. The urge to hug her had passed in the heat of the moment.

"You," she answered.

"Me?"

"One of you, anyways." She smiled, showing pointed teeth. "I'm here to help you."

"Help me?"

"Get to the bottom of all of this." She frowned now. "There was a lot of political infighting Down Below over this. Sides were taken. Your nemesis was backed by some of Hell's heavy hitters."

"Nergal," I said. "Meshlamthea. Maybe even Ereshkigal?"

She nodded. "And others."

"Someone who can look like me?"

She looked surprised. "Why do you say that?"

"A hunch." I was wary of showing all my cards. "What about Orcus?"

She shook her head. "Sat the fence on this one. Played politico all the way down the line. Although I think he did favor you off the record."

"Isn't that nice. So, what's the plan?"

"I'm taking you to see the Sibyl." That enigmatic smile, again. "Once you see her, I think everything else will be made clear."

I gestured toward the tropical forest up ahead. "Lead on, MacDuff."

"MacDuff?"

"Figure of speech."

"Oh. And—since you're well enough armed—how about lending me one of your weapons."

There are times and circumstances under which even the most potent magicks fail and it never hurts to carry an instrument of mayhem for backup, so the request seemed reasonable. I tried to unsling my bow but it seemed to be caught on my shoulder. I finally unslung the Uzi from my opposite shoulder and handed it to her. "Do you know how—"

"During one's first millennium in the Pit," she said, fielding my unfinished question, "a denizen of Hell is trained in the utilization of all engines of violence—past, present and future."

"Ah."

"Follow me." She began leading us up the beach and into the jungle. I followed. Rune covered my back. Elsbeth brought up the rear.

Σ

We walked for hours.

If there was a trail leading to the Sibyl's grotto, we never saw it. Lilith had a way of melting through clotheslines of vines and grasping branches as if they or she were insubstantial mirages. The rest of us had our swords out, hacking and chopping at the underbrush every foot of the way. Before an hour had passed we were all drenched with sweat and half faint from heat and exertion.

By the time we reached the ear-shaped entrance to the Sibyl's grotto the sun was sinking into the fog bank to the west and we were very nearly done in.

"Rest stop!" I announced. And promptly allowed my legs to fold under me. Rune and Lilith, to my annoyance, remained standing. Elsbeth hunkered down after a moment's hesitation, but it was more of a social kindness than an act of weariness.

"We're nearly there," the Archdemoness chided with some degree of impatience.

"Then five more minutes won't make any difference in the scheme of things," I said. "Why don't you go on ahead and tell the old girl we're coming."

Lilith made no reply but turned on her heel and walked into the mouth of the cave.

Elsbeth pulled a painful grin: "What's with Miss Personality?"

Rune's response was less mirthful. "I do not expect civilities from Hellspawn, but I like this not. A forced march over difficult terrain is depleting and we are hardly in any condition for a hostile encounter."

"I am a bit pooped," I admitted. "Just let me close my eyes for five minutes and I'll be ready to go again."

Elsbeth relaxed with her back to a tree while Rune assumed a stance of increased vigilance. I closed my eyes.

Oshi, the Asian swordmaster, had tried to teach me the disciplines of Bushido alongside the attacks and parries of Kendo. And while he would admit that there was a Zen-like quality to the way I blended Eastern and Western fencing styles, he often (and loudly) despaired of my ever mastering the inner disciplines of the master warrior.

What I never permitted him or anyone else to know was how successful I really was: in a body cramped by chronic pain and scar tissue, the mental mastery Oshi despaired my ever learning was what enabled me to lift and negotiate the blade to begin with.

I went back to those lessons now, searching behind closed eyelids for the patterns to unlock my hidden reserves. *The mind is all,* I told myself, *this body is but an illusion…*

When Lilith roused me a few minutes later, I felt better but could not say for how long or just what illusions I had succeeded in conquering.

Σ

The grotto was empty.

Lilith carried a torch, Elsbeth and Rune held lanterns, while I relied on the light shed by Caladbolg's enchanted blade. It was more than enough illumination to see that the chamber where the Sibyl slept and kept her modest possessions was nearly empty and had not seen habitation for some time.

I walked around the perimeter of the sacred pool and stared into its glassy depths. "Out," I murmured. "Out with the gout…"

"Where is she?" Elsbeth wanted to know.

The Archdemoness acted perplexed. "Perhaps we will find her further back in the passages." And there was a passage at the back of the cavern leading down into the bowels of the rock.

Rune's sword was out and blocking my path as I took a step to follow Lilith. "You led us here with the promise of seeing the Soothsayer." Though her blade was inhibiting my movement her words were addressed to the Demoness.

"Yes. And I am hoping to find her farther down the passageway." Lilith looked at me. "Shouldn't we be searching for her?"

"The point is," Elsbeth spoke now, drawing her bastard sword, "that you implied having recent conversations with the Sibyl, or at least recent knowledge of her whereabouts."

"It is obvious that she has not been here for some time," the Assassin added, "and now you 'think' she might be farther back in that tunnel."

"What game are you playing, Girly?" Elsbeth was taking a step forward, but I drew my own sword and pushed past Rune to confront Lilith, myself.

"How about it, Lil?" I asked. "You said Hell was divided in this matter. Which side did you really choose?" She raised the Uzi and I shook my head. "The gun's no good: there's powdered amber in the shell casings instead of real gunpowder."

The Demoness stared at the weapon so intently I knew she was verifying the truth of my words. With a cry of frustration she flung the weapon from her.

"I guess that answers your question," Elsbeth muttered behind me.

"My first question," I amended. "My second question is are you really Lilith?" I shifted Caladbolg to my left hand and reached inside my vest with my right. "If not, then who are you really?"

As I pulled out the spectacle case containing the optics of al Rashid, Lilith underwent a startling transformation: face and form convulsed and a moment later was replaced by the image of a woman I believed dead.

"Euryale..."

The emotional impact of seeing Medusa's sister, healed of her hideous affliction and then killed in a graveyard confrontation with the Lord of the Undead, unsettled me more than I expected. Before I could mover or speak another word, she flung the torch down and fled into the tunnel.

Σ

The passage was round and smoothed as if some great acidic worm had digested its own pathway as it angled through solid rock. The tunnel twisted downward and then back upon itself, again and again, like some convoluted maze. "I feel like an ant trying to navigate through a giant piece of brain coral," Elsbeth commented, briefly.

Her voice reverberated loudly in the close confines of the stone corridor and no one spoke again until we came to the next chamber nearly a quarter of an hour later.

The room was small, scarcely more than ten feet in diameter. A stone bier was thrust up out of the granite floor at the chamber's center and upon its flat surface lay a body.

The body of the Sibyl.

The ancient woman was wrapped in her customary raiment of grey and black and lay in repose, her hands folded over her chest, as if laid out for her own funeral.

"Is she dead?" Elsbeth wanted to know.

I reached out to check for a pulse and encountered invisible resistance.

"Force bubble." I cast about, looking for electronics or machinery of some kind. I saw none. "Or maybe some sort of Warding coupled with a Timestop spell."

"Suspended animation," Rune grunted.

Elsbeth ran her hands over the invisible shield. "Can you neutralize it?"

I handed her the Uzi and rolled up my sleeves. "Maybe. There are a number of spells that might have an effect." The downside was I could trigger some side-effect that could harm or even kill the Sibyl. Or the rest of us, for that matter.

I pulled out the Optics of al Rashid and put them on. A closer examination revealed unfamiliar spell patterns but the colors and weave of the *dweomer* indicated no booby traps. Just a standard one-two combination of utilitarian thaumaturgy. The Optics also confirmed that the Sibyl was still alive.

I tried a simple spell that was a fundamental to any magic user's arsenal: Neutralize Magic. As I watched, the first pattern of invisible light and color unraveled and slipped from the design surrounding the stone bier. Since the spells were arranged in a one-two setup, I cast another Neutralize Magic spell before trying anything different.

It worked again. As the second spell layer dispersed, the Sibyl took a deep breath and began to stir.

I looked up at Rune and caught her normally austere face in a moment of soft repose: she almost smiled. Turning to look at Elsbeth, I received a greater shock. The Trueform behind her powerful avatar was a petite woman with features as delicate as a china doll's. Before I could frame the question suitably, the Sibyl sat up.

"How do you fee—" was as far as I got when she brought her walking stick around and bashed me upside the head. I reeled back and blinked through a universe of stars as she hopped up off the bier and cocked her heavy, knobbed shillelagh back again.

"Wait, I—" I started to say and then bit my tongue as the stout wooden cudgel connected with my right knee. I went down and she went out, hobbling back up the passageway toward her grotto.

"Should we go after her?" Elsbeth asked as she and Rune helped me to my feet. Or, rather, foot, as I couldn't straighten my right leg just yet.

I shook my head noticing that the stars tended to swirl a bit with the motion.

"Do you think she was part of a trap?"

"Oh, yeth," I said. Part of my vision was still being treated to the Big Bang theory of the universe and the headache and bruised tongue weren't helping my speech either. "Paht uhba twap. But I gotta follow enaway."

"Can you walk?"

I could walk. Sort of. After a couple of minutes my vision cleared and I was able to straighten my leg. It hurt to walk, but then it hurt to sit, as well, so I figured we ought to keep moving. We exited the room and continued down the next leg of the tunnel with Rune leading the way.

There was another chamber after a couple of miles of switchbacked passages. This room was quite a bit larger and had two stone biers. The bodies laid out in state were even more familiar: the Duke and Stumpy.

"Wait a minute." Rune placed a hand on my chest as I started to go forward. "Suppose they're not your real companions?"

"Like the Sibyl," Elsbeth chimed in.

"It was the real Sibyl," I said. I was gratified to find that the swelling was starting to go down in my tongue and my right leg was able to take most of my weight again. I adjusted the spectacles and gave these bodies a closer inspection. "And these are the real Duke and Stumpy." I cast the necessary spells to unbind them and had the good sense to stand back and remove the enchanted glasses while they regained consciousness.

I should have stood back a bit farther.

Σ

The problem, as it turned out, was one of mistaken identity.

There was another Ripley—or Halfelven Riplakish—who had captured the Duke and Stumpy (and apparently the Sibyl, as well) who looked just like me. Which is why their first thoughts were, upon seeing my face, to get in as many licks as they could. Elsbeth and Rune tried to help me convince them that I was the real me and, eventually, we succeeded.

But not before my left eye started to swell shut and I was able to wiggle two loose teeth with my tongue.

Needless to say I was a bit more careful when we discovered the next chamber. After dissolving the magical fetters that bound Vashti and Rijma to the stone slabs, I hobbled back up the passageway and waited for my companions to sort things out before I showed my face again.

"He looked just like you!"

Everyone kept saying that.

My ex had her own observations to add to the pile. "There was something else there..." Vashti shivered. "There was an anger behind his voice...a bitterness in his eyes..."

"Sounds like me." I spat a gob of blood on the stone floor.

She shook her head. "No. I've seen you angry and I've seen you bitter. But this was different...worse..."

"Sounds like your evil twin, Skippy," Rijma observed dryly.

"That's impothible." I spit out another gob of blood and saliva. "I specifically programmed plot safeties that prohibit any usage of the 'Evil Twin' subplot!"

"No, wait a minute," Elsbeth said. "It's a given that there are more than one of you running around in the Matrix. Right?"

"Maybe," I conceded. "But I tend to believe I'm all present and accounted for, now."

"But you don't know for sure," she argued. "And even though you think of yourself as the same Robert Ripley who entered Fantasyworld just a few days ago, you've changed since then."

"All of you have changed since that time," Rijma said, catching Elsbeth's train of thought. "Every experience each of you has had since the moment you were schismed into duplicate memory files, has given each of you a different perspective of events. Even if you and one of your twins were in the same room, you'd each experience the unfolding of events from different perspectives. Over a period of time you would perceive reality on a slightly different timeline, growing apart and becoming two different personalities."

"I'll buy that," I said, "but none of my duplicates have been in-program long enough to undergo such a radical change in perspective. This other me would have to undergo some extended period of trauma to fit your assailant's m.o."

"We all seen ya!" Stumpy argued. "And you sure did look and sound like yourself!"

"Metamorph. Shapeshifter. Illusionist." I patted the spectacle case in my vest pocket. "I was taken in by our nemesis in the guise of Lilith. She—or he—or it—certainly looked and sounded like Lilith. Then he/she/it became the very image of Euryale." I looked over at Elsbeth. "Where's the Uzi?"

She spread her hands. "I left it back there in the first chamber. You said it didn't work."

I had this overwhelming urge to slap a palm to my forehead and drag it down over my face. "I didn't say it wouldn't work; I said there wasn't any gunpowder in the ammo."

"Same thing."

"No it isn't." I took a deep breath to calm my jittery nerves. "You see, gunpowder is inert in this Programworld—it doesn't work."

"Well, then what's your point?"

I sighed. "Never mind. Let's keep moving"

It was in the next chamber, down the tunnel, that I found my next cause for concern. Two biers but only one body was magically restrained: Borys Dankevych's. Natasha Skovoroda's lay on the rock surface, unfettered but unmoving. Whatever motivating force the Zombie Mistress had enacted on this empty, lifeless husk, it seemed quiescent here.

As I dispelled the twin enchantments on Borys, I could feel my personal reserves failing. I was only good for another spell or two.

Then I would have to sleep in order to replenish the inner mantra before I would be capable of further thaumaturgy.

I stumbled back into the passage and waited, weak and weary, while explanations were made. When I returned and our downward trek resumed, Dankevych had scooped Natasha's body up into his arms and fell into position at the rear of the party, carrying his dead fiancée as a father might carry his sleeping child.

The tunnel wound on and down for another hour. Twice Rune called rest breaks, insisting that we would be in no shape for a confrontation unless we paced ourselves. I could tell that she was clearing her throat to announce a third when the passageway opened out into another chamber.

The room appeared to be immense, the effect enhanced by the fact that there was no far wall. What first appeared to be an endless chamber was actually a great, roofed ledge looking out over a vast abyss. I crossed the cavernous room and stood at its far perimeter, looking out into the emptiness beyond.

Looking down, it seemed to be bottomless, even after I put on the Optics of al Rashid. But, far below, I could hear the low thrumming of deep water rushing on a vast subterranean journey. The rock strata appeared to be bisected here by a deep canyon or trench that continued in a straight line when I leaned out and looked to the left or right. If the canyon went all the way to the surface, it was impossible to tell now. No light filtered down from above. But we were miles underground by now and the night sky would not provide sufficient illumination to reach this far. I peered across the chasm at the parallel cliff face nearly a mile away. Grey-white fog cascaded down from above, foaming over the far side of the abyss like milky cataracts and through the lacy curtains of mist, I could make out a dim light. Perhaps there were other passages on the other side, other inhabitants.

"Robbie-me-boyo! Over here!" Rijma's voice pulled me back from the edge and over to four stone biers. Three were human-sized. The other served as a pedestal for a wooden box. The lid was propped open and Morpheus's baleful features regarded me with a blank expression.

As in the other chambers, the figures reposing on their stony beds were under thaumaturgic restraint. I pulled out the spectacles and put them on as the Duke announced the obvious: "It's Daggoth, Pallas, and Hanson!"

I shook my head as I could now see beyond the obvious. "It's Pallas and the senator, all right." But it wasn't Daggoth the Dark.

It was Cerberus, the personality fragment that had passed for The Machine's Superego.

All nicely captured and neatly gift-wrapped for us.

DATALOG: \QUEBEDEAUX_A.5\PERSONAL\20200823
Voice Dictation
<<<FILE ENCRYPTION ON>>>

Three or four hours, indeed.

*

They let me sleep twelve and I would've slept more if all the friggin' alarms hadn't gone off at once!

*

My office is supposed to be soundproofed but that kind of racket will penetrate anything!

*

Dr. Cantrell tells me we've developed a phasing problem in one of the Matrix sectors.

*

I'd suspected as much earlier, but he tells me it's growing worse.

*

Worse, indeed: everyone's code-strings moved while I was asleep, and now they're right on the perimeter of the affected sector!

*

We could loose them all at any moment!

TWO

\RIPLEY\PATH\SIGMA (Σ)

"Now what?"

I looked over at Rijma. "Now what, what?"

She scowled, a mock menacing expression. "Didn't your mother ever teach you that it's impolite to answer a question with a question?"

I smiled sweetly—or at least tried to with a swollen lip. "Didn't yours?"

Hanson tried to referee. "I think it's a very good question."

"Which one?" I asked.

"The one about what our next move should be." He looked around the chamber. "Where do we go from here?"

"Home."

Everyone looked at me.

"Home," I repeated. "We have what we came for—at least essentially." I nodded at the box containing Morpheus's head on the third bier. "When that's returned to Morpheus, our part of the bargain will be fulfilled. Which is unnecessary now, as Cerberus is under restraint, and, according to my enchanted eyewear, still in taction. That means you can have your body back, Senator, and I suggest that the sooner you vacate the Program, the better—not only for your own safety, but for the sake of two nations on a collision course with war."

"Are you sure you don't—"

"We don't!" Rijma insisted. "For once my esteemed colleague is right. Now scram, shoo! Invoke your Return Code!"

Hanson closed his eyes and was silent for a moment. Then he opened them again and looked around.

"What's the matter?" Rijma wanted to know. "Didn't it work?"

Hanson's avatar smiled. "The senator has departed: we are no longer in taction."

I had forgotten a fundamental of Dreamworld physics. Removing you consciousness from the Program didn't remove your Dreambody from its computer constructed reality. Hanson's consciousness was now back inside his "real body" in the "Real World," but his avatar remained right where he'd left it. It would still move and act and "think" like the senator, but it was now under The Machine's control, basing all character aspects and decisions on a Personality Analog file in memory.

It got a little spooky if you thought about it too much.

"Now that that little problem is taken care of," the senator's avatar continued, "I'd like to be going home, myself."

"Home?" Vashti echoed.

"Back to Warworld," he elaborated. "It's a never-ending battle."

"Don't tell me," Rijma moaned. "You're fighting for truth and justice."

"And the American way of life."

"Super," I murmured, turning away. Getting Hanson's avatar back into the Warworld Program was probably not an insurmountable problem. But I was just too tired to deal with it right now.

Two of my problems should have already been solved by the application of the love philtre to Princess Aeriel's drinking water: the Amazons would have a new candidate for royal consort and Daggoth would be too busy to toy with Stephanie's affections. That would make it easier to coax my ex-wife out of the Program. The fact that Pallas, as well as Cerberus, continued to sleep in suspended animation, would make the logistics of getting Stephanie back into her own body eminently more feasible.

But there were other tasks undone that still required my time and attention and I pledged myself to their resolution—just as soon as we finished up here and got everyone back to Daggoth's Tower. I'd get some rest, recharge my spell capabilities. Then I'd fulfill my obligation to put Morpheus back together. Figure out how to resurrect Natasha's avatar. Get Jeremiah turned back into a human so he and Mervyn could exit the program. Locate Nicole and see if there was anything we could do for what was left of her mind. And check on Lilith…

Ah, yes: I still had an enemy out there, somewhere.

Was it Nicole, shapeshifting to appear as Lilith on this occasion to lead me into an ambush?

Or had Lilith misrepresented her allegiance to me up until our last confrontation in these underground passages?

Or was there some greater power, acting as puppeteer, assuming various identities and manipulating others, still remaining to be unmasked?

As the others made ready to depart, I got up and walked over to the bier where the head of Morpheus rested. I was tired and I knew I was missing something important. All this trouble to get us down into this stone labyrinth. Or me, anyway: the others could have been part of the bait.

But now we had reached a dead end, accomplished all the obvious goals, and were leaving. I stared at the lifeless head, so recently a gamepiece in this puzzle of multiple avatars. "To what purpose?" I murmured softly.

In answer the dead sorcerer's eyes and mouth snapped open. *"The drouping Night thus creepeth on them fast,/ And the sad humour loading their eye liddes…"*

The voice that issued from the head's oral cavity sounded like Morpheus', though it had a hollow, echoey quality that one tends to associate with horror tri-dees with low budget special 'effects.

"…As messenger of Morpheus on them cast/ Sweet slombring deaw, the which to sleepe them biddes…" Adding to the unnerving effect was the fact that the lips remained unmoving, as if the head was serving as the speaker for some necromantic public address system. *"…Unto their lodgings then his guestes he riddes:/ Where when all drownd in deadly sleepe he findes…"* And this was verse, a detached portion of my mind realized. The head was quoting verse.

"…He to his study goes, and there amiddes/ His Magick bookes and artes of sundry kindes,/ He seeks out mighty charumes, to trouble sleepy mindes." What's more, it was familiar verse.

The mouth snapped shut, the eyelids lowered like third-act curtains, and the head returned to its former state of apparent lifelessness. The entire chamber had fallen silent—which didn't surprise me given the show we had just been treated to. What did surprise me was the real reason—the one that became evident as soon as I turned around.

Everyone else was asleep.

"Where all drowned in deadly sleep he finds…" I quoted. I knew without trying that shaking shoulders and yelling in ears would be to no avail. Better than average magic was at work here and I had no reserves to counter with.

"My lord?"

I jumped. Turned to see Misty Dawn materializing across the chamber from me. The ghostly Nymph took in the slumber party and drifted toward me. "What doth this mean?"

"I'm not sure," I murmured, "but I may have just been handed some clues."

"Clues, my lord?"

"You're here," I observed, "so it's night, now: 'The drooping Night thus creepeth on them fast…'" I gestured at my sleeping comrades. "'As messenger of Morpheus on them cast sweet slumbering dew, the which to sleep them bids. Where when all drowned in deadly sleep he finds.'"

"And it saith: 'He seeks out mighty charms, to trouble sleepy minds.'" Misty added. "What doth this mean?"

"I don't know." Did it refer to those asleep in this chamber? Or the larger framework of the Matrix where we all slept while our avatars walked in computerized dreams? "But I think our poet is warning me that some sorcerer is orchestrating these events." I turned and looked at the head. "Right?"

Eyes and mouth reopened and Morpheus' head complied with another verse of poetry: *"Then choosing out few wordes most horrible,/ (Let none them read) thereof did verses frame,/ With which and other spelles like terrible,/ He bad awake blacke Plutoes griesly Dame…"*

"My lord!" Misty whispered, "he speaks of our nemesis!"

"…And cursed heaven, and spake reprochfull shame/ Of highest God, the Lord of life and like;/ A bold bad man, that dar'd to call by name/ Great Gorgan, Prince of darknesse and dead night,/ At which Cocytus *quakes, and Styx is put to flight."*

"Both," I said after the head of Morpheus had subsided again; "the woman who has stolen your body and the Necromancer who sponsors her."

"Black magic, my lord?"

"The blackest!"

"And forth he cald out of deepe darknesse dred," resumed the voice. *"Legions of Sprights, the which like little flyes/ Fluttering about his ever damned hed,/ A-waite whereto their service he applyes,/ To aide his friends, or fray his enimies:/ Of those he chose out two, the falsest twoo,/ And fittest for to forge true-seeming lyes;/ The one of them he gave a message too,/ The other by him selfe staide other worke to doo."*

"Deception and Spenser," I cried, drawing Caladbolg from its scabbard.

"Beg pardon, my lord?"

"The verse is a warning about deception," I said. "And voice is quoting from Edmund Spenser's *The Faerie Queene.* Book One, I think—the first Canto."

The head spoke again: *"He making speedy way through spersed ayre,/ And through the world of waters wide and deepe,/ To Morpheus house doth hastily repaire./ Amid the bowels of the earth full steepe,/ And low, where dawning day doth neuer peepe,/ His dwelling is; there* Tethys *his wet bed/ Doth euer wash, and* Cynthia *still doth steepe/ In siluer dew his euer-drooping hed,/ Whiles sad Night ouer him her mantle black doth spred."*

Misty Dawn looked about the stone girdled chamber. "Morpheus's house...?"

"A literary allusion," I said. "Ovid's name for the son of Sleep, the god of Dreams."

"And the waters, my lord? What do they signify?"

"The subconscious," I decided. "That which is submerged or hidden underground—and we have both images here. Tethys was—is—the wife of Oceanus and was often held as symbolic of the sea, itself. Cynthia is a surname for Artemis or Diana—"

"The moon."

"Right, and Spenser used it as his contemporaries did, as a synonym for Elizabeth the First, as well."

Misty Dawn was not quite convinced. "Thou speakest of symbols and allegory, my love. And yet, it is now night—here, and upon the earth above, her black mantle is spread. Are we not 'amid the bowels of the earth full steep?' And is that not water I hear at the precipice's edge?"

"There are some parallels for us," I admitted as I walked to the edge to investigate. Now that the sounds and voices of ten people were stilled, I could hear the sound of rushing water more clearly.

And, as I stared into the depths of the gorge, my eyes were treated to the spectacle of thousands of specks of light swirling in the empty air. As I watched, they danced through the open space and coalesced into strands that laced across the abyss and touched either side of the gorge. Patterns formed. Solidified. In another minute there were two glowing bridges connecting our chamber with the far side of the underground canyon.

I turned to look at the ghostly Wood Nymph. "Now what?" I asked.

It was the head that answered. *"Whose double gates he findeth locked fast,/ The one faire fram'd of burnisht Yvory,/ The other all with silver ouercast;/ And wakefull dogges before them farre do lye,/ Watching to banish Care their enimy,/ Who oft is wont to trouble gentle Sleepe./ By them the Sprite doth passe in quietly,/ And unto* Morpheus *comes, whom drowned deepe/ In drowsie fit he findes: of nothing he takes keepe."*

"Wait a minute," I said. "Two gates. One fair and framed of burnished Ivory…"

"The Gates of Dreams, my lord! Through one passes those dreams which are true, and through the other are passed those dreams which are false and delude!"

But which was which?

"And there be two spans to the other side," Misty observed.

"Two gateways," I concurred.

"But which is which?"

Good question. The softly glowing structures were identical in size, shape, and color. I turned to the head of Morpheus. "Any advice?"

It complied with another verse. *"And more, to lulle him in his slumber soft,/ A trickling streame from high rocke tumbling downe/ And ever-drizling raine upon the loft,/ Mixt with a murmuring winde, much like the sowne/ Of swarming Bees, did cast him in a swoone:/ No other noyse, nor peoples troublous cryes,/ As still are wont t'annoy the walled towne,/ Might there be heard: but carelesse Quiet lyes,/ Wrapt in eternall silence farre from enemyes."*

Other than a description of the abyss that yawned before us, the words were unhelpful. "Okay." I walked over and picked up the box containing Morpheus's head. "Let's go find out."

Misty Dawn was not crazy about this strategy. But she thought I was: "Thou'rt mad!"

"No," I shifted the box under my arm so that I had a secure grip that still permitted the disembodied head unimpeded vision and speech, "just extremely pissed!" I hefted Caladbolg and stepped to the edge between the gangways of the two spans. "Someone's playing games with me—deadly games—and I prefer acting to *re*-acting." I looked down. "You got anything to say about the next step, compadre?"

It did: *"The messenger approaching to him spake,/ But his wast wordes returnd to him in vaine:/ So sound he slept, that nought mought him awake./ Then rudely he him thrust, and pusht with paine,/ Whereat he gan to stretch: but he againe/ Shooke him so hard, that forced hime to speake./ As one then in a dreame, whose dryer braine/ Is tost with troubled sights and fancies weake,/ He mumbled soft, but would not all his silence breake."*

"Great. Thanks. You're a lot of help."

"How canst thou ken which path to take?" Misty wanted to know.

I eyed the twin spans but still could not determine any advantage of one over the other. The exit points were shrouded in darkness on the other side.

"The old dungeon-mapping adage, my dear: 'you can't go wrong if you go right'." I moved to the appropriate bridge and addressed the box. "Last call, Morf, ol' buddy: whither I goest, you goest, too."

There was no response so I eased my foot out onto the glowing structure. It held. And so I took another step. And then another. And began crossing the chasm.

I tried not to think about the structural integrity of a bridge that had just appeared out of thin air. So I turned my problem to the Spenserian riddle. "How does that next verse go, Morf? Do you remember the words?"

No response.

"'The Sprite then began more boldly him to wake…'" I coached. "'…And threatened unto him the dreaded name/ Of *Hecate:* whereat he began to quake…' Um, what's the next part?"

The head remained silent.

"C'mon, you know the next part!" I bullied. "The Sprite's bugging your namesake and that Morpheus isn't too keen about this particular wake-up call: '…And lifting up his lumpish head, with blame/ Half angry asked him, for what he came.'

"And what does this little bugger answer? Hmm?" Obviously I was going to have to carry the ball on this verse. "'Hither (quoth he) me *the Archmage* sent,/ He that the stubborn Sprites can wisely tame,/ He bids thee to him send for his intent/ A fit false dream, that can delude the sleepers sent.'" I stopped. "Who is the Archmage? Who's pulling the strings here, huh?" The head made no reply. "Who fetched Cyberpunks from another Programworld and sicced them on me? Who hired Orc mercenaries and put a price on my head?" Or was this part of the delusion? Was I being led into my enemy's hand?"

I suddenly recalled my encounter with the demonic hunting party on the outskirts of Calabastor, just a few days before. The red Devil leading the pack had said something about capturing Riplakish of Dyrinwall and taking him to Ortygia—that much was still at the forefront of my memory. But he had said something else, something strange…

"…when we capture him, we are to bring him to you on Ortygia," he had said, thinking me to be one of the Hellish Powers aligned in this plot: *"across the division of worlds…on the far side of Corpus Callosum…"*

I was aware of only one referent for *Corpus Callosum,* and it had nothing to do with the mythology of any culture. It was, rather, a medical term for the bundle of nerves connecting the two cerebral hemispheres of the forebrain. I looked up at the sheer cliffs of honeycombed rock that rose straight up on either side of the deep fissure that I had managed to cross halfway, and felt a vertiginous sense of *déjà vu.*

"No." This was carrying analogies too far.

"What is it, my lord?" Misty had been following behind me.

"It's basic cranial anatomy," I snapped. "The longitudinal fissure divides the brain into two parts: the left and right hemispheres. Deep down inside that fissure, the corpus callosum bridges the two halves of the cerebral cortex!"

"I—I do not understand—" Not only that, but my shouting was making her nervous.

"Of course you don't understand!" I bellowed. "Because it doesn't make sense!"

But it did, in a weird, twisted sort of way.

It was not unusual to find Platonistic analogues within the Matrix. The Machine, especially since the advent of the Anomaly, was forever accessing some file from some other network and translating it into a Programworld's structure with varied interpretations and results. Examples ranged from the personality templates for Id, Ego, and Superego to the Freud-Jung wars on one of the Western archipelagoes.

But this was begging too great a suspension of disbelief…

"The God obayde, and calling forth straight way/ A diverse dream out of his prison darke,/ Delivered it to him, and downe did lay/ His heavie head, devoide of carefull carke,/ Whose sences all were straight benumbd and starke./ He backe returning by the Yvorie dore,/ Remounted up as light as chearefull Larke,/ And on his litle winges the dream he bore/ In hast unto his Lord, where he him left afore."

"Meaning what?" I barked at the head in the box. "Let's just cut to the chase!" I forced my feet to start moving me toward the other end of the bridge were my answers—if there were any—were likely to be found. "No more literary allusions! No Platonisms of preexisting eternal ideas reflected in concrete Matrix structures! No allegories translated into Programworld realities!" The end of the bridge appeared to open out into a chamber of a similar size to the one I had left behind. "Just spit it out in twenty-first century English! No more beating around the bush!" I was yelling as I stepped off the span…

…and into the cavern I had just left.

"So there you are," Rijma exclaimed, trying to stifle a yawn at the same time.

"Where did you go?" Vashti wanted to know.

Elsbeth was hoisting her pack to her shoulder. "We woke up and you were gone."

I stared at them. Then looked over my shoulder at the bridge behind me. Somehow, I had gotten turned around on the span and walked back to where I had started from.

"It is time we left," Rune announced. "After we return to Daggoth's tower, we can rest, regroup, and remount an expedition to check out the rest of these caverns."

"C'mon, Rip," Rijma said, starting toward me, "let me give you a hand with that."

"Wait—wait a minute!" My head was pounding and I brought my sword up defensively though there were no foes in sight. "Something's wrong here."

"Yeah," agreed Elsbeth, "and the sooner we're outta here, the better it'll be."

"We really need to fall back," said Vashti. "Rest, recharge our spell capabilities. He who fights and runs away—"

"—lives to fight another day," rumbled The Duke.

"Stop!" I bellowed as they moved a step toward me. The pounding in my head was making it impossible to think clearly.

"Yer tired," Stumpy observed.

"Shut up!" I wanted to reach for the Optics of al Rashid but between the box and Caladbolg my hands were full. "Verse—there's another verse—"

I shook the box and the head complied: *"Who all this while with charmes and hidden artes,/ Had made a Lady of that other Spright…"*

"Lilith," I whispered, "Euryale."

"…And fram'd of liquid ayre her tender partes…"

"Aw, Rip; who you gonna listen to? That dead head or your friends?"

"Be still!" I admonished, brandishing my sword. I began to back toward the bridge I had just traversed.

"…So lively, and so like in all mens sight,/ That weaker sence it could have ravisht quight…"

The senator's avatar had moved to cut me off so I turned my retreat toward the other bridge. Rijma's sword was out, now. "C'mon Rip, you're gonna hurt yourself."

"…The maker selfe for all his wondrous witt, Was nigh beguiled with so goodly sight:/ Her all in white he clad, and over it/ Cast a blacke stole, most like to seeme for Una *fit."*

I lowered my sword and hung my head as I reached the edge of the bridge. "I'm sorry," I mumbled. "I wasn't sure for a moment if you were really my friends."

"It's all right," the Brownie soothed, stepping forward. "You're just confused."

"Yeah," I smiled, "just for a moment." My blade came up suddenly and flashed across the Brownie's shoulders. Her head bounced across the chamber's floor, rolling some twenty feet before the sword fell from her right hand and her body collapsed in upon itself. "But not so confused that I couldn't remember that the real Rijma is a southpaw!" The others began to screech and transform into imps and devils like the ones that had hunted me in Calabastor a few days before. I turned and ran onto the second bridge.

They didn't follow and it didn't take me long to figure out why: the traverse was starting to glow in a pulsing pattern, and, as I ran past the halfway point, I could see its structure beginning to disassemble into the myriad of tiny firefly sparks that had come together to form it in the beginning.

"Now when that ydle dream was to him brought," intoned the head at my side, *"Vnto that Elfin knight he bad him fly…"*

"Ah, shaddup!" I muttered under my breath.

"…Where he slept soundly void of evill thought,/ And with false shewes abuse his fantasy…"

"Yeah, now you tell me!" I slammed Caladbolg back into his sheath.

"…In sort as he him schooled privily:/ And that new creature borne without her dew,/ Full of the makers guile, with usage sly/ He taught to imitate that Lady trew,/ Whose semblence she did carry under feigned hew."

"Her and everybody else!" I grunted as the flooring dissolved under me and I leapt for the edge of the canyon wall.

My fingers of my right hand caught the edge of the chamber floor as I slammed against the rock wall that was about to provide me with a nearly vertical slide down into the raging torrent a mile or two below. The box shattered with the impact and it was only a lucky left-handed grab that saved Morpheus's head from following its container down into the abyss.

"Ow!" it said, as I lifted it up by its hair.

"Awake now, are we?" I hissed, trying to find purchase for my feet and knees.

"Hey, it's not easy making this thing talk, you know—especially over such a great distance! If you knew the effort—"

"If talking's so tough," I gritted, "how come you've been such a motormouth with the poetical allegory? A few straight answers could've saved us both a lot of effort."

"Couldn't," the head explained. *"There's been some major enchantments at work here to isolate you from outside contact. The Guards-and-Wards barred any direct warnings but I was able to bypass them with a little verbal sleight-of-hand."*

"Poetical allegory," I grunted, trying to exert some leverage with my toes.

"Correct. And having accessed the records on your matriculation—"

"You discovered that in addition to my dissertations on comparative mythology I also have a minor in Western Lit."

"It seemed a safe bet that you would be familiar with Spenser's The Faerie Queene."

"Actually," I wheezed, "I like his private-eye novels better." Shifting my balance to my left elbow caused me to bump his head against a protruding knob of rock.

"Ow—that hurts!"

"Don't start with me," I warned. The ache of slamming against the cliff face was starting to give way to fiery sensations of abraded skin. *"You* can't have anything worse than a headache!"

"Which reminds me of a song—"

"If you start singing *any* version of 'I Ain't Got Nobody'," I warned, "I swear to Crom, I'll drop you right here and now!"

A long pause ensued while I hunched my way over another knob of rock.

"So how come you don't have to turn a poetic phrase, anymore? Or is this your idea of blank verse?"

"Dunno. Either the Shielding spells wore off or the guy responsible got distracted."

Slowly, painfully, carefully, I raised my left arm, bringing the head up to the top of the ledge. A little shove—*"Hey, watch it!"*—and I felt it roll forward as I released my grip. There were spitting sounds as I fumbled around with my left hand for a good grip beyond the edge.

"See anything?" I grunted, as my knee found a half-inch depression in the rock wall.

"Yes. And you're not going to like it…"

I chinned myself on the rock ledge and looked up and into the stone chamber. The head was right: I didn't.

THREE

\RIPLEY\PATH\SIGMA (Σ)

They were all there and awake: Rune, Vashti, Elsbeth, The Duke, Stumpy, Hanson's avatar, Borys and Natasha, even Rijma with her head intact, which was somewhat reassuring. The good news was I hadn't found myself back at the chamber I had just escaped from.

The bad news was that I was already in the room with the rest of them. Which is why everyone was staring in shocked amazement at the other me—the me that was hanging on to the edge of the precipice, that is.

"I think we just found our impostor," Riplakish of Dyrinwall was saying—the me that wasn't hanging on to edge of the chamber for dear life, that is.

"Oh, yeah, sure!" I grunted, hauling my chest up over the edge and grinding my face into the stone floor as I renewed my grip a little farther into the chamber. "That's what all the evil look-alikes say first!" I squirmed a little farther into the room.

"Oh, Crom!" Rijma groaned. "I thought you said you'd locked out the evil twin scenarios from the Program structure!"

"I did," we chorused.

"So now we have to do the 'which is the imposter' shtick…" She sat down on a truncated stalagmite and cradled her chin in her fists.

"Not that tough," I puffed, easing a leg up and over. "I've got the head with me and he'll verify my identity."

"Big deal," my double snorted. "Who's going to believe a talking head? The best you can prove is a good ventriloquist act. If you want testimony—"

I could see that there was another figure in the room. She stepped out from the crowd and I nearly fell back over the drop-off.

It was Nicole. Unblemished.

"While we slept," Rune elaborated, "he claims to have crossed over and rescued her."

"Rescued?" I got my other leg over and noticed the other members of the party laying hands on their sword hilts. Talk about *déjà vu*…

"The creature that attacked me that night in Daggoth's study was not Nicole," the other Riplakish explained. "And now that the real Nicole Doucet has been rescued, and Senator Hanson has been returned, we can depart. Once we've dealt with you, of course."

"Ah ha!" I pointed at my duplicate. "You hear that? He's talking about doing away with me."

"I said no such thing! I merely pointed out that since you are here and, as everyone can see and hear, are trying to pass yourself off as me, you must be reckoned with in some fashion."

"Shut up, both of you!"

We both turned and looked at our—that is, my—ex wife. "Under the circumstances," Vashti went on to say, "you both could be legitimate avatars of Robert R. Ripley the Third."

"I don't think so," rebutted Elsbeth. "There's enough variance in their respective stories to suggest that one of them is lying."

Rijma piped in at this point. "Shall we go down the list of evil twin scenarios for the past three or four centuries of literature, film, and holography to determine the various tests we can apply?"

"I have the head of Morpheus," I pointed out.

"As do I," my double added, holding up a duplicate head, still in its box.

"Mine talks," I said. "Does yours?"

"Shut! Up!" Vashti repeated at the top of her lungs. Seven years of divorce had not noticeably diminished their capacity.

"We could let them fight," Rijma said. "The one that tries hardest to kill the other is probably the impostor."

"Very funny," we observed.

"Do you think I do not know my own true love?" Nicole said suddenly. "Why do you even have discourse with that…creature?" She pointed at me and I looked over at Morpheus' head, laying on its side on the ground.

"Feel free to jump in here, any time," I murmured.

It didn't jump, it continued to lay there on its side, but it did quote more Spenser: *"So as she bad, that witch they disaraid,/ And robd of royall robes, and purple pall,/ And ornaments that richly were displaid;/ Ne spared they to strip her naked all./ Then when they had despoild her tire and call,/ Such as she was, their eyes might her behold,/ That her misshaped parts did them appall,/ A loathly, wrinckled hag, ill fauoured, old,/ Whose secret filth good manners biddeth not be told."*

"Meaning what?" the other Riplakish wanted to know.

"I suppose he means that Ms. Doucet may not be what she appears to be," Rune answered.

"Her craftie head was altogether bald,/ And as in hate of honorable eld/ Was ouergrowne with scurfe and filthy scald…"

Elsbeth cleared her throat. "I think you've already made your point."

"…Her teeth out of her rotten gummes were feld,/ And her sowre breath abhominably smeld…"

"Enough already!" Rijma cried.

"…Her dried dugs, like bladders lacking wind,/ Hong downe, and filthy matter—ow, ow, ow!"

I lifted Morpheus's head by the hair and dangled it over the edge. "The Old Testament, Book of Proverbs," I advised, "chapter seventeen, verse twenty-eight."

"Accessing—ah," his eyes rolled downwards, *"I see your point…"*

The other Riplakish looked around at the other members of the party. "You going to believe me or some seven hundred year-old poem?"

I put the now-mute head aside and reached into my vest pocket and pulled out the Optics of al Rashid. "Anyone want to take a look for themselves?"

My Doppelgänger looked resigned. "Okay," he said. "All right." He gestured and the room was silent.

Everyone else had gone to sleep again.

Carefully, slowly, I got to my feet and moved away from drop-off, circling into the room. Nicole backed away to sit on one of the stone biers. The other Riplakish convulsed, changed, grew taller, acquired additional mass, and became Robert Remington Ripley the Third.

"Who *are* you?" I asked quietly.

"Who am I? Why, I am you," he replied.

"Oh. Right. Sure. Well, if you are *me*…then who am *I?*"

He sighed and found a convenient stone formation to sit on. "*You* are my fate denied. *You* are who I was to be. *You* are the past denied." He casually drew his longsword from its scabbard. "The future that I will claim." The longsword in his hand had a crystal blade that glowed with a bluish light.

"Yeah, yeah; 'twas brillig and the slithy toves'!" I pulled Caladbolg from his sheath: yep, still crystal and glowing with a faint blue tinge. To all appearances, a perfect match. "How about some straight answers without all the poetic gibberish?"

"Do you dream, Ripley?"

"What?"

"Do you dream?" he asked. "Every night?"

I didn't think I liked this conversation starting out; now I was sure. "Yeah. How about you?"

He chuckled. There was an unpleasantness to his tone. "Oh yes. We both dream, you and I. We dream the same thing most every night. Tell me, Robert; what do we dream?"

"What I dream is none of your business!"

"What *we* dream is the business that brings us together, you and I. Oh yes, this dream is definitely the business at hand..."

"What do *you* dream, then?" I asked cautiously

"What we dream," he corrected. "There is no you and I. We, Robert Ripley, dream the same dreams: fire in the sky and the explosion that started the pain. The pain that never ends. We dream it, you and I, night after night; and awake between sweat-soaked sheets. Flames and loss..."

"You're me, aren't you? One of my duplicate avatars!"

"So close and yet so far...tell me; when you dream do you ever try to change places with her?"

"What...?" I felt a catch in my chest, a terrible prelude to that sensation of having my heart ripped out again. "What...?" I asked again only to have breath and voice fail me once more.

"The two most terrible words in anyone's life, Robert: 'what if...?' What would you give to live it again? To do it differently? And what would you do?"

"Do?" I gasped, nearly losing my grip on my sword. "What...do...?" My chest constricted and I couldn't draw air.

"Would *you* have stayed at the controls and sent *her* back to extinguish the fire?"

I felt the tears starting to gather at the edge of my vision. "Nicole…?"

"You were the better pilot!"

I groaned, feeling the nightmare images gather at the back of my consciousness.

"*You* couldn't extinguish the fire—could *she* have done any worse?"

"Don't," I whispered.

"But you could have landed the aircar safely if you'd stayed at the controls." He spoke the thought that had haunted me for a decade and a half.

"She had a third-class license, the same as me!" I cried. But the argument had not satisfied in all those fifteen years and it did not satisfy now.

"But *you* were the better pilot!" he shouted. "If you had made an emergency landing as soon as you noticed the fire—"

"You weren't there!" I screamed.

"I *was* there!" he screamed back.

"No…"

"Yes! *I* was there! And when the fire broke out, Nicole jumped up and grabbed the extinguisher!"

"What?" I felt my sanity slip a notch.

"So I couldn't effect an emergency descent with her out of her seat! And I couldn't leave the controls! And I sat two feet away from where *your* Nicole sat when the stabilizer coils exploded!"

"What…"

"*My* Nicole came out of it better than *you*, Robert: *she* had the good sense to back out of the engine compartment before the explosion!"

"What…" Impossible images filled my mind—images of an aircar accident where Nicole and I had traded places, actions, consequences.

"It did happen the other way: Robert Ripley stayed at the controls and Nicole Doucet survived the crash with minor injuries."

"I don't understand…" Moreover, I didn't *want* to understand.

"There are many Realities—"

"Dreamworlds," I said.

"I am not talking about Computer simulations, I speak of Alternate Realities. Parallel Universes. An infinite number of timelines branching out from the moment of each man's birth: dividing, triparting, sometimes exploding in dozens of different pathways at each decision." He gestured with his sword. "As you dress one morning, you reach for a tie. You are only aware that you chose the blue one. But a parallel timeline splits off at that point and in another Reality you choose the red tie, instead. A subtle difference—perhaps the only one in those twin lifetimes…

"But in other worlds you join the high school chess club instead of picking up the foil—ergo—no Olympics trials, no trip to France, you never meet Nicole Doucet. You marry a hometown girl and settle down. Live happily ever after—"

"Or everything's exactly the same," I said, unable to stop my mind's berserker rush toward his inevitable conclusion: "I go to France—"

"But you don't rent a defective aircar," he offered.

"Or I do," I continued, "but when the fire breaks out—"

"I stay in my seat and send *Nicole* aft to check it out," he finished in a tone that carried certainty and not speculation.

"And she survived with minor injuries?" I asked hollowly.

"Yes. Want to trade?"

I drew a long breath. "Yes."

He was silent.

"Yes!"

"There's a catch," he said quietly. "Each timeline, each Reality, each Parallel Universe may share common geography…events…" he gestured at me with his blade, "…people. But there are always differences. Sometimes radical, sometimes subtle—but there must be differences or there could be only one world, one Reality.

"In your universe, Dreamland was conceived as an entertainment medium and Fantasyworld was developed out of your books and stories. In my world it is known as Dreamworlds and was developed initially as a psychosomatic therapy environment. I had no initial input as I wrote no books after the accident as you did. I just got lucky."

"Lucky?" I asked.

"Someone decided to hook me up to the system. To see if anything was going on inside."

"I don't understand."

"Let me show you." He gestured. And an image formed in midair.

I could only look at the travesty of burned and shattered flesh for a moment. I turned to Nicole: "I'm…sorry…"

"Your pity is misdirected, this time," my alternate self replied. "This is not the Nicole Doucet who nearly perished in your universe. This is what survives of Robert Remington Ripley in mine!" He stood. "The balance scales may shift across timelines, my friend; but there is always a counterweight to consider, a symmetry to recalibrate, an equilibrium to be achieved.

"Perhaps there are other universes where every other choice we made, from that moment on, led to both our deaths—ours and Nicole's." He shook his head. "I only know how my choice turned out…and yours."

There was a long silence for me to digest this in.

"So," I said, finally, "you were given a reprieve through psyche-extraction and dream programming…"

"A…*reprieve?"* he choked. "A simple word like 'reprieve' sums it up for you? Imagine, if you will, fifteen years of imprisonment in a twisted lump of flesh! There's no hope of parole because the medical ethicists in my timeline insist on keeping me alive and there's a very good chance under laboratory conditions of that stretching out another hundred years or more!"

He paced about the chamber, growing more and more agitated. "I have no control over anything in my life: I ingest what they feed me *when* they feed me and excrete the waste portions unceasingly! I have no eyes or ears and, unlike your Nicole in your timeline, I have no cybernetic sensors to serve as bridges to the inner man! I cannot taste or touch or smell and I cannot speak to those who feed and water me like some botanical experiment!

"And the *pain!"* he shrilled. "It never ends! There is no release from it! I cannot even flinch or pound with my fists or drum my heels or scream or writhe! I cannot even find succor in the unconsciousness of sleep! I cannot kill myself and the respirator will not even permit me to hold my breath!

"Tell me, Robert Ripley," he shouted, turning back toward me: "what would you do if you were me? *Because…I…am…you!"*

"I would go mad," I whispered.

"Precisely! And then what?"

"I don't know."

He was suddenly calm again. "What if you had a chance to have a real body, again? Your own body?"

"An avatar," I said.

"Avatar? No, this computer-driven simulacrum is but a step towards the goal. And the Matrix is but the bridge between our Realities."

"Bridge?"

"Remember its crude clumsy beginnings? *Virtual Reality* they called it. Computers manufacturing visual, auditory, and tactile cues, spatial referents to illusionary environments. If that could be called 'Virtual Reality' in its time then surely today's Matrix is evolved far beyond the special effects concept. Our present Programworlds are truly *Alternate* Realities. They are in your timeline as they are in mine. And since VR is not bound by the same laws of space/time physics that separate my timeline from yours, it is possible for a Programworld from your Matrix to intersect a Programworld from mine."

"The Anomaly," I mused.

"I thought it would be enough," he said. "After fifteen years of being buried alive, I thought *anything* would be better. That a computer-generated body was a dream come true." He shook his head.

"But it's not enough," I said.

He nodded now. "It's *not* enough. So I ask you again: *what would you do if you had the chance to have a real body again?* Your *own* body?"

"I guess I'd take it."

"Yes. You would *take* it," he agreed. "But there are obstacles to contend with, first. The Matrix is the bridge between my Reality and yours. And you, Robert Ripley, are the obstacles. Before I can claim the body that is Robert Remington Ripley's—that was *mine* denied by the vagaries of chance and fate, I must remove those obstacles. And I have: one by one. Now, I'm nearly done."

I raised Caladbolg in my right hand and drew Balmung from his scabbard with my left. "And how do you remove—this final obstacle?" I asked, easing into an on guard position. "A physical duel? Or spell against spell?" I felt my temper slipping. "Or are you just trying to talk me to death?"

If I thought I could bait myself into making a misstep, I was mistaken: I knew myself too well.

He smiled ruefully. "Even though I arranged for your spell abilities to be exhausted before you got this far, a magical contest is out of the question. In the time that I've spent in-program, I've discovered that *I* can't perform any magic that has any direct effect on *you*. Even dissolving that sorcerous bridge from beneath your feet was nearly impossible and the delay was sufficient for you to complete the trip across."

"Okay," I said, "so how's your swordsmanship?"

He laughed and shook his head. "I have learned nothing new since the aircar crash: time has stood still. I don't have the advantages of Kendo nor the practice you've enjoyed these fifteen years past."

I took a more aggressive stance. "Then I'm sure you won't want to match your one blade to my two."

This time his smile had teeth. "I have two blades." His sword came up. "This one…"

Nicole stepped forward and drew her sword. An eerie green flame licked across its serrated blade. "And this one," she finished.

I looked at her, fighting back a tumult of emotions—hurt and confusion the most primary: "Why?"

She smiled—not much more than a moue in that pretty, perfect face. "I love him."

She started to advance but my double gestured her back a step. "Those spectacles," he said, "you wanted to put them on and look at Nicole a little while ago. Before we begin why don't you just do that?"

In spite of the moment's awkwardness, I did just that. I reversed the wakizashi in my left hand and held the Optics of al Rashid before my eyes.

Nicole was…*Nicole!*

There was no evidence of physical corruption, no signs of madness!

I lowered the lenses. "How—"

"You and your poetry-spouting colleague have done Ms. Doucet a great injustice," the other me was saying. "This is the Nicole Doucet from my universe. She was our match fifteen years ago at the Olympic trials. And the ensuing years have been kinder to her than they have been to you." He brought his sword up. "*En garde*, Monsieur Riplakish! Your chances against Mademoiselle Doucet are slim to none. Against the both of us…"

Nicole raised her own blade and they advanced.

DATALOG: \QUEBEDEAUX_A.5\PERSONAL\20200825
Voice Dictation
<<<FILE ENCRYPTION ON>>>

They're gone.

*

One moment they were there on the monitors…

*

The next moment the phasing flip-flopped and the whole sector just disappeared.

*

Harold's running diagnostics on every piece of circuitry he can find schematics on.

*

Between the two of us, working night and day without food or sleep, we might find something in about six months.

*

Where the hell is Balor?

FOUR

\RIPLEY\PATH\SIGMA (Σ)

I was holding back.

Not me—the other me: he was thrusting and feinting, but basically playing it safe at this point and letting Nicole take all the risks.

And, since he *was* me, I felt a growing contempt for myself that was disquieting.

Both of them had me at a human disadvantage in reach: even Nicole's avatar had longer arms than my Half-Elvish one. And while I might have matched her reflexes for speed yesterday, today's exertions and injuries were going to prove my undoing. Only my skills in Kendo and *Niten Ryu* were keeping my opponents at bay for the moment but they were slowly and steadily forcing me to fall back toward the precipice behind me.

Caladbolg and Balmung wove a tangled barricade of light between us but my opponents had enchanted blades as well, and cut through every defense I could muster. From the outset I was caught in the mode of *Tai No Sen,* forestalling their attacks and waiting for the initiative. But, between the two of them, I doubted I would be permitted any. I no longer had the energy for *Ken No Sen* when the opportunity might occur, nor the stamina that might enable me to last that long.

I fought with no strategy other than to keep their blades from touching me. I had no strength left for anything else and I was further disadvantaged by my own reluctance to press an attack should an opening suddenly appear. It was bad enough to think about running my "self" through. When I looked at Nicole, fifteen years of guilt and remorse fought my own instincts for survival and I knew that I would die before I harmed her again.

The precipice was getting closer and I suddenly saw one possibility of improving my position. I dodged back and to the left until

I could retreat no farther. A column of stone was to my back, a cluster of stalagmites and stalactites fenced off the space to my immediate left, the abyss yawned to my right. I was trapped, now, but only one of them could attack me at a time.

Nicole hesitated but the other Ripley motioned her ahead. I engaged her blade with a series of circle parries that held her off for the moment and enabled me to catch my breath.

"Careful!" I shouted as her foot slipped on some loose gravel and she skidded a bit toward the edge.

As she recovered my left thigh seemed to cramp and then burst into flame. My leg gave way and I fell back against the stone column and slid to the floor. I glanced down at the hilt of the knife protruding from my leg and then looked up and saw my double behind Nicole and the bloody cut on the outside of her right biceps where the thrown dagger had nicked her arm in passing. The look she gave him, in turn, was unreadable but she turned back to me and stepped forward.

I raised my blade but it could be nothing more than a gesture of defiance. "*Je voudrais voir des assassins souriant du bourreau qui coupe un cou d'innocent*," I said, "*avec son grand sabre courbé d'Orient*."

She hesitated.

"*Je voudrais voir des roses et du sang*," I said.

She raised her sword. "*Je voudrais voir mourir d'amour ou bien de haine*," she whispered.

"Kill him!" my other self was screaming.

Nicole stared down at me and, as I looked into her shining eyes I saw the multitude of questions swept aside by a look of puzzlement. Slowly, almost carefully, she lowered her sword and turned around.

About the time I saw the arrow protruding from her back, another one struck her in the chest. She staggered back and tripped over my legs. The momentum carried her over the edge and she fell without a sound.

"Who is it!" my alter ego cried. "Who is there?"

I followed his gaze up to a rock ledge that ran along a portion of the chamber's side wall: a figure crouched in the shadows, clutching a longbow.

"Why Robert," cooed a familiar voice, "can you not guess?" She squirmed into the light until we could see her ruined features.

It was the Nicole Doucet from my timeline.

"Wha—where did you come from?" While we were both taken aback by this new manifestation, my other self seemed more unnerved by her appearance.

"What?" she said, laying aside her bow. "After so much poetry and verse, have you forgotten the rest of your Spenser?" She leapt down from the ledge and her leathery wings fanned out to assist her to a gentle landing. "'Thus when they had the witch disrobed quight…'" she quoted, "'…And all her filthy feature open showne…'" She began to hunch toward us. "'…They let her goe at will, and wander wayes unknowne.'"

My other self was backing away now, the abyss just a few feet away.

"'She flying fast from heavens hated face,/ And from the world that her discovered wide…'" The hideous apparition spared me but a brief glance as she closed on my double. "'…Fled to the wastfull widernesse apace,/ From living eyes her open shame to hide…'" His sword lay forgotten and loose in his grip, and she pushed it aside. "'…And lurkt in rocks and caves long unespide.'"

He continued to back away but she was quicker: her rotting arms reached out, her nearly fleshless hands grasped his forearms.

"What—what do you want?" he choked.

"You, my love…" Did I detect a sardonic note in her voice? "We are two of a kind, you and I!" She embraced him and he struggled like an insect wrapped in webbing. "Did I not hear you speak of fate's balance-scales? Of cosmic equilibrium? Do you not feel the karma?"

My double's expression seemed to say that his dogma had just been run over by her karma.

"We are soulmates—Yin and Yang upon the Wheel of Pain!" she murmured triumphantly. She pressed her ghastly lips to his.

"Mmno!" He threw his head back and pushed at her shoulders. She did not loosen her grip, even when more of her flesh squeezed wetly through his fingers and sloughed off the bone.

"Come with me, beloved, to a better place…" And, saying this, she embraced him more securely and stepped off the edge.

He screamed going down. It was a long fall and he passed beyond my hearing before it stopped.

I crawled back to the edge but I could see nothing. "I…don't…understand…" I murmured.

"'MacBeth', my lord."

I looked up at Misty Dawn, hovering above me, pale and solemn.

"Act Five, Scene Three."

"What—"

"'Canst thou minister to a mind diseased,'" she quoted, "'Pluck from the memory a rooted sorrow…"

"'Raze out the written troubles of the brain,'" I whispered.

'And with some sweet oblivious antidote,' the Bard of Avon had concluded, 'Cleanse the stuff'd bosom of that perilous matter/ Which weighs upon the heart?'

I crouched on the edge of unending darkness and began to weep.

DATALOG: \QUEBEDEAUX_A.5\PERSONAL\20200826
Voice Dictation
<<<FILE ENCRYPTION ON>>>

Hanson's awake!

*

The real one!

*

And not just awake, either.

*

I'm told the first thing he did after climbing out of his suspension tank was beat Captain Balor to a bloody pulp!

*

The news gets even better…

*

Apparently, the senator's second act was to pick up the phone and call Cephtronics' CEO.

*

I don't know what he said but the man turned around and called us: Harold—I mean, Dr. Cantrell—just got off the phone and announced that they're calling back my old staff and we should get some relief within the next six to eight hours!

*

But the best news of all…

*

The other code strings are reappearing!

*

The lost sector still won't read out on the monitors but the various code-strings are reappearing in the adjacent sector.

*

As a matter of fact, there's just one left that I'm waiting on…

EPILOGUE I: RIPLEY (Ø)

Robert Remington Ripley the Third pressed the control that raised the upper portion of the hospital bed. Even though the buttons were labeled in Russian, he was getting the hang of it and now enjoyed a success rate of two out of every three attempts.

"So Hanson got back into his real body?"

Borys Dankevych nodded. "He phoned me yesterday. He has been rather busy trying to repair the political damage that was done while Cerberus was in control of his body outside the Matrix."

"Borys has been rather busy with similar matters, here," Dorothy Cooper added.

A nurse entered the hospital room to check Ripley's pulse. "Kerensky?" he asked as she checked his chart for the last reading.

"Da. We are now conducting inquiries to determine who Kerensky's collaborators are. And, more importantly, who his superiors were in this plot. The entire Spetsnaz is currently under investigation. Other branches of the military…some extremist, right-wing factions in the Duma…" He shrugged

Ripley smiled wanly. "A purge?" Although he was on the mend, the virus had taken its toll.

Dankevych grunted. "Perhaps a small one. Nothing like the Great Purge of the last century. We are merely weeding out some fanatical subversives, not replacing an entire political system."

A doctor, one of the military's viral specialists, poked his head in the door. "I said a short visit and I meant it," he warned good-naturedly. "Five more minutes and then my patient must rest more further!"

"So, tell me about this REMrunner. Were you able to get him back out?" Ripley wanted to know.

"The fourteen year-old Ancient Wizard? Yeah," Cooper said, sitting on the edge of the hospital bed. "The problem was his friend Jeremiah had the codes and passwords for getting in and out of the Matrix…remember?"

He shook his head. "Tell me again."

She looked at Borys and frowned. "Well, Jerry had been turned into a frog and no one could figure out how to change him back. Daggoth worked on the problem for three days and nights before you provided the solution."

"I did?" The nurse popped an old-fashioned oral thermometer into his mouth.

"Yep. It seems you slipped a love potion into the water jar in Princess Aeriel's chamber."

"Oo tol me 'bou' tha 'un," he mumbled around the glass pipette.

"Daggoth thinks you did it out of revenge for all the times he had razzed you."

Ripley composed his features into a mask of saintly innocence.

"If that was your plan, it failed," Dorothy continued. "Aeriel unknowingly drank the potion. But the next person she laid eyes on wasn't Daggoth the Dark." Cooper grinned. "It seems you all forgot that Jeremiah the bullfrog was still in the room when you locked her in and left."

"And Aeriel is an Amazon princess," Borys reminded.

"It only took one kiss," Dorothy elaborated.

"And now I believe you are invited back into the Program for the wedding," Borys concluded.

"Which solves your Consort problem." Dorothy Cooper's face assumed a more serious expression. "Do you remember any of this?"

Ripley shook his head.

"Robbie..." She looked at Borys Dankevych. "You remember I told you that Natasha Skovoroda's avatar was murdered while she was intaction?"

Ripley nodded.

"Before we exited the Program, you said you thought we could bring her back. You seemed to think that there was a hidden holding file for Dreamwalker psyches who had died in the Program. Just like the various heavens and hells in mythology where the dead might be resurrected, you had this theory that the Matrix stored discorporated psyches against the time their avatars could be restored to life."

"You said it had happened to you several times," Borys added. "When you regenerated during your lycanthropic episodes."

Ripley and Cooper stared at him and smiled. Since exiting the Fantasyworld program, Dankevych had spoken perfect English.

"Natasha's body is still in her suspension tank," Cooper continued. "The life-support systems keep her breathing and circulate her blood, but her EEG is totally flat and no one in Medical believes you can recharge the electrical activity of the human brain like it was a vanadium-lithium battery." She glanced at Borys and took a deep breath. "Do you really think we can bring her back?"

"I don't know," Ripley sighed as the nurse removed the thermometer from his mouth. "I don't remember any of this…

"Theoretically, it might be possible to re-enter the program and find some kind of powerful enchantment that would resurrect Natasha's avatar. If the Program plays by its own internal sets of rules, it should recognize her return to living status and re-connect her psyche—if it still resides somewhere in memory storage!" He shook his head. "I don't know—this is completely theoretical to me."

"You seemed so sure while we were still in the Program," Borys said.

"I don't remember any of it!" Ripley cried hoarsely. "All these stories you've told me since I woke up—they're just stories to me! My last clear memory is someone jumping me in my room, sticking that damn hypo full of virus culture in my shoulder. After that—I can remember going in and out of my delirium while you tried to resuscitate me. Then you popped me into a suspension tank to slow down my metabolism. You said…something…about sending me in early…" He waved a limp hand. "That's it: the somnambulants began taking effect and—nothing. A big blank. I feel as if nothing else actually happened!"

"Some short-term memory loss is not surprising," the doctor said as he re-entered the room. "Considering the fact that this virus nearly killed you—and you ran a one-hundred and six degree fever for nearly week—I'm surprised your brain was not reduced to a bowl of borscht!"

"Will his memory ever return?" Borys wanted to know.

The doctor spread his hands. "We simply do not know at this point." He picked up his patient's clipboard. "Now, all of you out! This man needs his rest!"

Dorothy patted Ripley's hand. "Get well—"

"So we can go back in soon!" boomed Dankevych.

Ripley grasped at her hand as she stepped back. "What about the others? Stephanie? And Nicole?"

"Out!"

She slipped her hand from his. "We'll talk about all that tomorrow."

Ripley pushed himself up in the hospital bed as they started to leave the room. "Wait!"

Cooper and Dankevych turned at the doorway.

"We could be operating on an erroneous assumption here."

"What do you mean?"

"Just because I don't remember anything that happened after you put me in the suspension tank—doesn't mean that I've lost my memory of the events that transpired in the Program."

The doctor frowned as they walked back into the room but Ripley waved him back.

"What if I can't remember what happened to my avatar because...*I have no memories to access?"*

Cooper frowned. "I was there with you through parts of it. Everything we told you actually happened."

"To my avatar," Ripley elaborated, "not necessarily to me. Remember what you were saying just a few days ago about Memory Upload and Download?" He sighed and leaned back against the pillows. "You said psychescan probably duplicates our personality profiles and inserts the copies into the Program while suppressing consciousness and brain wave activity at the original source. When we leave the Matrix, our psyches, altered from our Programworld adventures and containing additional memory files, are re-introduced to our minds as consciousness and brain wave levels are restored." He sank back into the pillows, dizzy and exhausted.

"What is he saying?" Borys wanted to know.

Dorothy felt a little dizzy, herself. "He's suggesting that he doesn't remember anything because his psyche—the personality and memory-files that occupied his avatar in the Matrix—were not returned to him when he regained consciousness."

"I know this is silly," Ripley murmured, feeling an irresistible lethargy creeping up on his mind, "but I feel like one of those aborigines who fears having his picture taken...believing the camera has the power to steal his soul..." His eyes fluttered shut and he began to snore.

"There! Satisfied?" The doctor was indignant. "You've exhausted him again! Out, now! Shoo!"

"But if his—psyche—was not returned to his body when we got out," Dankevych puzzled as they exited the room, "then...where did it go?"

EPILOGUE II: RIPLEY (X)

Michael Straeker, Chief of Staff for the Dreamworlds Project, reached down into the suspension tank and removed the biosensors from its occupant. "Thought we'd lost you for a moment, there. Your code-string disappeared from the monitors and we weren't sure until just now if we could actually bring you back out." He held up two fingers. "How many fingers am I holding up?"

"…two…" croaked the voice, and it echoed hollowly inside the interior of the tank. "…out…can I get out?"

"I'll have you out in a moment," Straeker assured. "What's your name?"

"…Ripley…"

Straeker hesitated, but only for a moment. His brush with death a year before had made him a pragmatist. The doctors had been honest and totally straightforward from the day the brain tumor had been diagnosed until the surgery that had successfully removed it. He felt that everyone deserved the truth and postponing it or trying to cover it up was immoral and potentially dangerous. "I'm sorry," he said, "Ripley didn't make it."

Straeker was prepared for tears or silent shock. He wasn't prepared for laughter. "Maybe *he* didn't," chuckled the voice, "but I did!"

"Uh, yes you did," Straeker said, a little off balance. He reached down into the tank. "Let me help you sit up."

"Michael," the humor faded from the voice as the tank's occupant grasped his arm, "what are you doing outside of the Program?"

"What do you mean?" he asked as he braced himself against being overbalanced and possibly falling into the tank.

"You're dead."

"I'm what?"

"Dead. Remember? Brain tumor? Now you're Daggoth the Dark?"

Straeker was thoroughly confused now. "Daggoth the what?"

"Michael..." a hand appeared and grasped a handle to the side of the exit hatch. "...did you reroute me into another Programworld on the way out?"

"No, you are out of the System." He cleared his throat and considered paging one of the male nurses. Dreamwalking was still experimental and some people did exhibit sensory disorientation after exiting a Programworld. "Welcome back to Reality."

"Then what's the joke?" Her head emerged from the hatch, the nutrient solution that helped sustain her body while her mind was in taction with the Computer, plastered her long, brown hair to the sides of her face.

"Joke?" Straeker queried, as she pulled herself out of the pseudowomb and climbed down to the floor. "I'm afraid I don't understand, Ms. Doucet."

"Ms. Doucet?" She looked at him sharply. "I don't appreciate this, whatever it is—whatever it's supposed to mean. I've just been through hell and back! I've been killed, I watched myself get killed, and I've watched a woman I loved die twice! Furthermore, I don't like the way you've been spending time with my wife!"

"Wife?" Straeker squeaked.

"Ex-wife," she corrected, reaching down to wipe the nutrient slime from her legs. "I hate this stuff. Can't somebody design these tanks so that this stuff washes off before we get out?" She reached up to scrape the ooze from her belly and stopped in amazement. Her hands grabbed at her breasts, cupped them. "What the hell are these?"

"Um," said Straeker, feeling the situation getting more out of control with every passing second, "I believe they're called breasts..."

"I don't have breasts!" she roared.

Straeker was loath to argue with her but the evidence at hand was undeniable. "You do now," he murmured.

"Get me a mirror!" she demanded.

"Um, there's one in the ladies room," he said, pointing to a door on the far side of the room. As she strode purposefully across the room and through the rest room door, Daggoth scurried over to the intercom and called for two male nurses. "And bring restraints," he whispered as a high, feminine scream echoed from the tiled recesses of the ladies lavatory.

Inside the lounge area, Robert Remington Ripley the Third fought to hold on to a rational train of thought. For, staring back at him in the full-length mirror was the reflection of Nicole Doucet. The image was healthy and whole, barely showing evidence that she had aged fifteen years since the aircar crash.

"Oh man," he murmured, watching the reflection of feminine lips moving in synch with his words, "you are a *long* way from home!"

Outside, someone began pounding on the bathroom door.

**Now I do not know whether I was then a man
dreaming I was a butterfly,
or whether I am now a butterfly
dreaming I am a man.**

**—Chwang-Tse,
(*upon awakening from a dream of being a butterfly*)**

THE WOMAN OF HIS DREAMS

Turning and turning in the widening gyre
The falcon cannot hear the falconer;
Things fall apart; the center cannot hold;
Mere anarchy is loosed upon the world,

—William Butler Yeats,
The Second Coming—

O but we dreamed to mend
Whatever mischief seemed
To afflict mankind, but now
That winds of winter blow
Learned that we were crack-pated when we dreamed.

—William Butler Yeats,
The Tower—

In dreams begins responsibility.

—William Butler Yeats,
Responsibilities—

PROLOGUE

The shower door opened, emitting a hazy burp of vapor that momentarily fogged the scanners. The environmentals came on-line, siphoning off the excess humidity, activating the heating elements in the wall and floor tiles, and ventilating the dressing area with jets of warm air.

A woman stepped out of the shower enclosure.

Beauty, it is said, lies in the eye of the beholder, but few would deny that this face and form approached perfection: her features bespoke intelligence and her body sheathed a toned muscularity that elevated her above the vapid beauty of pageant queens and pin-up holos.

"Are you satisfied, Mr. Mudge? Ms. Doucet is obviously very healthy."

Bernard Mudge did not take his eyes from the wall-sized viewscreen. "It's not just a matter of how well she's being treated or how comfortable her accommodations are, Doctor. A padded cell is still a padded cell—even if it is tricked out like a well-furnished apartment on the upper West Side." He frowned. "Who cut her hair?"

Dr. Dagny Westbrook winced, remembering how the patient's thick mane of chestnut hair had tumbled past her shoulders like a blend of amber silk and spun sable. "She did. She said it was too much bother." Her tone was professional but Dr. Westbrook still mourned the loss of those thick, glossy locks. Her own hair, by contrast, was limp and thin and showing a touch of premature gray. Not for the first time was she reminded of her own imperfections. Not for the first time was she depressed by the thought: *why, she and I are the same age!* The random curse or blessing of genetics set any hopes of equality beyond the reach of diet and exercise.

Mudge's frown deepened as he watched Doucet walk across the room to seat herself before a large mirror. "What's wrong with her walk? An injury?"

"We were hoping you might shed some light on this," Westbrook replied. "Ms. Doucet has displayed a certain amount of—awkwardness—since her arrival here at the clinic. Perhaps the Paris accident—"

"That was sixteen years ago," Mudge snapped, "and Nicole was fully recovered in a matter of months! She is still one of the world's top athletes on both the pisté and the archery field; I have not seen her have one awkward day in her life! Is she on some kind of medication?"

"No…" Dr. Westbrook felt off balance herself. During her tenure at Wallbank Sanitarium, she had dealt with a monthly parade of lawyers and family solicitors. Until this morning they had all been variations on the same tune: a professed concern for the patient but an obvious agenda to protect the rest of the family—secure financial control through the power of attorney, and keep any embarrassment locked away from public awareness.

This one, however, broke the mold. This one really seemed to want his legal ward cured and released.

"Mr. Mudge," she asked, half from curiosity, half in an attempt to regain control of the conversation, "was Ms. Doucet accustomed to wearing makeup?"

"Yes," he answered distractedly. "Not that she needed to, of course."

"Of course." *So why was she a total incompetent at applying it now?* She pulled her gaze away from Nicole Doucet's image and gazed sideways at the family solicitor.

Bernard Mudge tipped the scales just shy of three-hundred-and-fifty pounds. While it was not uncommon for linebackers and defensive ends to have the height and frame to translate that kind of poundage into a godlike physique, Mudge was built more like the football they fought over. His bullet-shaped head continued to widen as it approached his shoulders, with no indication of a neck in the interim. His body continued to flare outward from his shoulders to his hips. There, as if his center of gravity exuded an effect on his silhouette, his body collapsed back in upon itself in downward parabolic curves that ended in a pair of tiny feet ensconced in a pair of five-hundred-credit wingtips. The rest of his considerable bulk was draped with a three thousand-credit suit whose cut and fit suggested an even more expensive tailor in charge of the landscaping.

But Bernard Mudge was surprisingly light on his feet for a man of his weight and size. And he was no less agile at addressing the business at hand.

"Dr. Westbrook, please cut to the chase: just what exactly is wrong with her?"

There seemed no point in evading it any longer. It was becoming increasingly evident that this one was not going to go away until he was completely satisfied and no amount of psychiatric double-speak or medical rank-pulling was going to do the trick.

"Nicole Doucet," she answered carefully, "is suffering from selective amnesia coupled with a severe personality disorder."

"Specifically, what kind of personality disorder?"

"She's delusional."

"Explain."

No, this one would not be put off by anything less than the truth. "A form of displacement—transference, actually."

Mudge frowned. "I'm not an untutored layman, Doctor. What is the nature of this transference?"

She punched a button on the armrest of her chair, blanking the viewscreen and bringing up the background lighting in her office. "Before I answer that question, I'm going to ask you a question. What do you know about the Dreamworlds Project?"

The lawyer didn't miss a beat. "It's the next evolutionary step in Virtual Reality: a direct, sensory interface between humans and computers, allowing direct manipulation of the senses. It's supposed to make a virtual environment nearly indistinguishable from reality." He leaned forward in his chair, no mean feat for a man with no discernible waistline. "It was Dreamworlds, wasn't it, Doctor? Something about the sensory stimulation—it disoriented her, didn't it?"

"I'm afraid 'disorientation' is a rather mild term for what has happened to your ward, Mr. Mudge."

"Then what is it?" The agitation in his voice was an unexpected crack in the professional façade.

"Another question before we proceed. Were you acquainted with her fiancé, Robert Ripley?"

He settled back in his chair with a frown. "I'd hardly use the term 'fiancé': any practical relationship they might have had ended sixteen years ago in that aircar crash in Paris. Nicole was lucky to walk away with minor injuries. Ripley effectively died. What survived was only a puddle of mindless meat."

"Ms. Doucet didn't think so," the psychiatrist countered. "She felt that there was a rational consciousness trapped inside that lump of scarred flesh."

"There was no way to prove it either way," the lawyer admitted. "But she wouldn't let him go. I mean, even if his mind was untouched, what difference could it make to her?"

There was anguish here and Westbrook decided to step carefully. "Did Ms. Doucet ever express remorse over what happened?"

"Oh, all of the damm time! She was constantly saying how everything would have come out differently if they had just traded places in the aircar—reversed the seating!" The tremor was creeping back into his voice.

"Well, I'm going to show you an excerpt of our last session. Before I start it, I want you to keep something in mind. Nicole Doucet survived a terrible crash that essentially took the life of the man she loved. Guilt is not uncommon for those who survive their loved ones—even when no one is at fault. But Ms. Doucet could not properly mourn her fiancé as his bodily remains were kept alive mechanically these past fifteen years."

She leaned toward him. "If he had simply died and been buried she eventually would have learned to let go and begin the healing process. That wasn't possible while he was connected to the life-support equipment."

"None of this is new to me, Doctor." Mudge was clearly impatient. "The point that remains unclear is Dreamworlds' culpability in Nicole's illness."

"I have the deposition of Dreamworlds' Chief of Programming on tape."

He shook his head. "I've reviewed Dr. Straeker's testimony. I've listened to his mumbo-jumbo about how Dreamworlds' new Supercomputer interfaces directly with the human brain. That these so-called Virtual Worlds provided a common environment for the meeting of human minds with the computer, itself. I know that Nicole believed that Ripley could be plugged into this interface so that his mind could be freed from the prison of his mangled body. And that the Virtual World would provide a bridge between her mind and his.

"What I *don't* know is what really happened. Did she cross that bridge and find nothing there on the other side? Was that too great a disappointment for her? Or were there remnants of a mind, locked away in that remnant of a body—something less than human that met her mind in the dark? Is that it, Doctor? Was she traumatized into her current state?"

"I think it's time you saw the recording," Westbrook said, her fingers dancing over the keypad recessed into the arm of her chair. The lights dimmed and Nicole Doucet's image reformed on the wall-sized viewscreen.

Her eyes were closed and she was reclining in an overstuffed chair that tilted back and elevated her feet. Her body, clad in a simple gray jumpsuit, appeared totally relaxed as Dr. Westbrook's voice droned the final verses of the hypnotic litany. Digital and analog readouts of her pulse, respiration, and brainwave activities displayed across the bottom of the screen, charting her descent into the deeper levels of the trance.

"All right," Dr. Westbrook's voice was saying on the speakers, "I'm going to ask you again. This time I've taken you very deep. We have traveled inward to the very core of your personality—the primal essence of who and what you are." She paused. "What is your name?"

Nicole Doucet's lips parted, her mouth formed the words. "Robert Remington Ripley the Third," she said.

Mudge gripped the arms of his chair. "What?"

"Aren't you Nicole Doucet?" Westbrook's recorded voice prompted.

"No." Doucet's voice was calm and relaxed, but there was no hesitation or uncertainty about it.

"If you are not Nicole Doucet, then what has happened to her."

"She's gone." Again that same dead certainty.

Dr. Westbrook tapped a button, freezing the image on the screen as Mudge collapsed back into his chair.

"I don't understand," he murmured.

"Displacement. Transference." Dr. Westbrook swiveled her chair to face his. "We handle our guilt in variety of ways, Mr. Mudge. One way is to forget who we are—to lose the memories of what we've done or failed to do: selective amnesia. Another is to trade places with the one we've wronged. You, yourself, said that Ms.

Doucet felt it would have been better if she and Robert Ripley had been able to trade places. Entering a two-way meld through the Dreamworlds computer finally gave her subconscious the opportunity—the excuse—to trade places with her lost love."

Mudge's eyes bulged. "So Nicole's mind is trapped in Bob Ripley's body?"

Westbrook smiled. "No, Mr. Mudge, I was speaking figuratively." She reached across the desk and laid a calming hand over his. "Nicole's method of dealing with her guilt for surviving the accident has manifested as a personal delusion: she wants to believe that the man she loves is still alive and she would like to believe that she can offer her life in his place. By fantasizing that Ripley's psyche was transferred to her body, she alleviates her guilt—"

"I don't buy it."

Dagny Westbrook mentally stumbled to a stop. "Excuse me?"

"I know Nicole." His eyes were fixed on Doucet's frozen image. "She was devastated by the accident, losing him. But she didn't blame herself for what happened."

"But you said—"

"*She* said that it would've turned out differently if they had traded places in the aircar, Doctor. But she was speaking of fate, not responsibility. And while she may have been willing to exchange fates with Ripley, she felt no obligations." Mudge leaned toward her. "I want to see the rest of the session."

Westbrook was taken aback. "I've shown you the pertinent portion. Since I was unable to shake her displacement, even under hypnosis, the remainder of the tape is inconsequential."

"I want to see it anyway."

"I really don't see the point."

"The *point,* Doctor," Mudge answered in icy tones, "is this: I intend to be deeply involved in Nicole Doucet's recovery and I need all the information available to make the decisions that I must make. I will be the judge of what information *is* pertinent to my decisions. If I feel that my time and efforts will be diverted in squabbles over what *you* think I do not need to know, *I* will relocate my ward to another clinic and place her under the care of a psychiatrist with whom I have a more cooperative rapport." He turned his chair back to the screen. "*That* is my point, Doctor, and now I would like to view the rest of the session."

Westbrook was furious. Had it been any other patient, this oversized lawyer with his oversized ego would be going out the door right now. But overlaying her fury was the fear that he was as good as his word: she would lose Nicole. She pressed a button and the playback continued.

"Are you aware that you are, in effect, 'wearing' Nicole Doucet's body?" Westbrook's voice asked.

"Yes."

"How do you explain that?"

"I'm not sure I can," Doucet replied dreamily.

"If you really are Robert Remington Ripley the Third, then where is your body?"

"Back in Russia."

"Russia?" Westbrook's voice betrayed a note of astonishment. "How can that be? The Soviet Union has closed its borders to all westerners. Ever since the Berlin incident, nearly a decade ago, we've been teetering on the edge of military conflict."

"Not in my universe," Doucet replied.

"What does that mean?"

"As best as I can tell, your world exists in a parallel universe to mine," she said. "In my world, the Berlin wall came down and the Warsaw Pact was restructured at the end of the Twentieth Century. The Soviet Union ceased to exist and was fragmented into separate countries with their own, independent governments. Eventually, after years of economic and political struggles, some of them reformed around Russia as the Republic of Federated Soviet States. Bottom line: in my world we are no longer at war."

Westbrook was suddenly aware of Mudge's hand on her arm. "What is she talking about?" he demanded. She paused the playback as his grip tightened uncomfortably. "What does she mean when she says 'your world' and 'parallel universe'?"

She sighed. "It's a theory—science fiction, actually. It's the premise that at any moment in time there exist multiple possibilities. You walk down a path and it forks right and left: do you choose to take the left-hand path or follow the one branching to the right? Whatever your choice, there is, in that moment, an alternate possibility: an alternate time-line in which you chose the other path. Reality becomes fractal, splitting into two separate 'paths' and two realities continue from that point onward, sharing the same past up until that particular moment of divergence. After that event, like identical twins separated at birth, they develop in similar but different ways."

"Mmmmm," he said. And released her arm.

She unpaused the session and her recorded voice continued: "And you say that 'your world' is an alternate reality to this one?"

"Precisely." The ensuing chuckle unnerved Mudge more than anything he had heard so far: it was not the sort of laugh he could imagine coming from Nicole Doucet. "You might say that your reality, from my viewpoint, is the fractal analog to Robert Frost's *The Road Not Taken.*"

"How do you know that this is a 'different' reality from yours?" the doctor wanted to know.

"Several things. Mike Straeker is alive, is he not?"

Mudge could sense, though the recording did not show that Dr. Westbrook had nodded her head.

"Well, in my world, Michael Kelson Straeker, former Chief of Programming at Dreamland, Incorporated, died more than a year ago of an inoperable brain tumor."

"I made inquiries as you requested, Nicole. As I told you before, this man you asked about had surgery and chemotherapy three years ago. He's been in complete remission ever since and I teleconferenced with him just last week. I showed you a portion of the playback."

"In your time-line *here,* doctor, not in mine back home. And Dreamland—"

"You mean Dreamworlds."

"No, Dr. Westbrook; in your universe, virtual reality programming has only recently progressed beyond computerized hallucinations and teledildonics. While Dreamworlds does manage to interface human minds with a computer, the Dreamland division of Cephtronics in my universe has developed a Cybernetic Matrix. This matrix was originally the repository for various Programworlds that were creations of the Dreamland Programming staff. They *were* what you would call 'virtual' realities in your Dreamworlds context. They have evolved since their original creation. What were once, by definition, virtual realities are now, in fact, *alternate realities* in the fullest sense of the term."

"And this is how you say you managed to cross over from your reality to this one?"

"I believe so. I do not pretend to understand it completely. An anomaly had entered into the Dreamland Matrix and was causing some Programworlds to collide with others. As boundaries intersected, operating parameters were drifting through all five measurable dimensions. Apparently, other-dimensional drift was occurring, as well."

"So, if I am to believe that you crossed over to this universe from your own, am I to take it, then, that Nicole Doucet has crossed over to your universe."

More disturbing than that odd chuckle was the frown that settled over Nicole's face now.

"Yes," she replied hesitantly, "that is what happened."

"You seem troubled," Westbrook's voice observed. "Do you think she is occupying your body in your universe, the same as you are now doing in hers?"

"No. I know she is not."

"How do you know that?"

"I know that she was unable to exit the Programworld."

"Are you sure?"

"I am very sure," Doucet answered with unmistakable finality.

"Let me ask you another question," Westbrook said after another uncertain pause. "How do you feel about Nicole Doucet?"

"I loved her."

"Loved? As in past tense?"

"I suppose I still love her."

"But something changed all that." Westbrook's phrasing did not permit question marks. "You reflexively answered in the past tense. Things changed between the two of you."

"Yes."

"The aircar accident."

"Yes."

"It couldn't be the same after the crash, could it?"

"No."

"You blame her, don't you."

"For what?"

"For living. For abandoning you."

"No, Doctor."

"Admit it, Nicole: Robert Ripley would have every reason to hate you for passing through the fire unscathed while he was left behind to rot in a mangled body!"

"Doctor." There was a peculiar note of quiet command in Doucet's voice. "I spoke a moment ago of the fractal moment when one reality becomes two time-lines. One of the defining moments that separates the history of our two universes occurred sixteen years ago when Nicole and I chose different seats in that defective aircar. And while I was severely injured in the crash, it was Nicole Doucet who was hideously burned and lost her arms and legs and face."

Mudge gasped.

"So you see, Doctor, there is no reason for this Robert Ripley to harbor unresolved anger toward Nicole Doucet. I am not your Robert Ripley; I survived the crash in much better shape did than the Nicole from my time-line. And the reason I have expressed my feelings for her in the past tense is because her psyche was terminated in-program while she was last in taction with her avatar."

"I'm not sure I understand—"

"Nicole Doucet died in the Matrix, Doctor; just before I tried to exit the Program and somehow ended up here. Now, what is it going to take to convince you that I'm telling the truth?"

Westbrook glanced over at Mudge who sagged in his chair.

"Is that what you want? For me to believe that you are Robert Remington Ripley the Third? From a parallel universe?"

Doucet's lips twisted in a wry smile. "Lady, I don't care if you believe I'm Elvis in a UFO; I just want to go home! And I can't do that as long as I'm locked up as some kind of nut-cage!"

"If you were free to do as you please, how would you 'go home'?"

"Go back to Dreamworlds, interface with the Programworld that spit me out here, and go looking for my avatar."

"I see. Well, Nicole, isn't it possible that you just want so very much to bring Robert Ripley back from the grave and all this talk of body switching and parallel worlds is a convenient delusion? You take comfort in believing that you could rewrite reality to make that happen."

The woman who denied being Nicole Doucet sighed and gave a slight shake of her head. "I am Robert Ripley, Doctor. As I am currently under hypnosis it is very unlikely that I could lie to you. And, as it is a fact, no amount of verbal gymnastics or trickery on your part is going to change my core identity. So let me ask you, Dr.

Westbrook: are you capable of accepting the possibility that I might just be telling you the truth? Can you open your mind to include that among the various possibilities?"

Westbrook's finger stabbed down on the chair arm, freezing Nicole Doucet's image on the screen again. "The rest is just me bringing her out of the trance—the end of the session." She cleared the viewscreen and dialed up the lights. "As you can see, this delusion is very deeply rooted. It's going to take time to help Ms. Doucet confront the reality of Ripley's death—"

"What about the alternative, Doctor?" Mudge's face was gray but there was a snap and crackle to his voice. "What if it is Bob Ripley in Nicole's body and he's telling the truth?"

"You can't be serious!"

"I am serious, Dr. Westbrook. And there's just one way of finding out..."

PART I

SLUMBER PARTY

If there were dreams to sell,
Merry and sad to tell,
And the crier rung his bell,
What would you buy?

—Thomas Lovell Beddoes,
Dream Pedlary—

ONE

Okay.

Before we go any further, let's clear up any confusion right now.

My name is Robert Remmington Ripley—the Third, to be more specific—and I've spent thirty-five years of my life as a male, most of them exhibiting the basic heterosexual inclinations. That being the case, imagine my consternation when I woke up about a month ago to find myself in a parallel universe, inhabiting a woman's body.

It wasn't the worst day I've ever had…but it probably ranks in the top five.

So, everyone wants to know: what's it like being male and suddenly finding the prefix "fe-" tacked on?

Well, most of the differences were obvious and expected: lower center of gravity, increased lower body strength and decreased upper body strength. Not to mention freedom from the chronic pain and massive amounts of scar tissue that went with my former, damaged flesh.

But as nice as it was to inhabit a healthy, athletic body, I wasn't keen on the differences in plumbing. And while the hormones weren't as bad as I had been led to believe, the cramps were definitely worse. Maybe Heinlein would've loved it, but I had spent too many years defining my sexual identity to start over now.

And I didn't like looking in the mirror and seeing the image of the woman I had loved, a woman who was now dead, looking back at me.

It had been a rough month but, if all went well, I would be shed of this particular mortal coil before the morning was over. That is, if Westbrook, Mudge and Limbach could manage to finish their avatar construction in the next hour or so. I reached across the cubicle's desk and activated the comscreen to check on their progress.

Luther Limbach (a.k.a. "Lech" Luther to the female patients at the Wallbank Clinic & Sanitarium) was nearly done. Posing atop the holopad on his cubicle desk was a fourteen-inch tall Barbarian warrior wearing a wisp of leather and brandishing a double-bladed battle-axe. The miniature apparition was muscled like the cartoon logo for *Arnold's Gyms,* "cut" and "ripped" with astonishing definition and heroically proportioned.

Limbach's weasel face rotated on his pencil neck, looked up at the screen and grinned. "Whaddaya think, sweetcakes?" He tapped a key on his development board and the minimal leather loincloth dissolved to display the Barbarian's other heroic proportions. "You like?"

I sighed. "Lech, you only get so many avatar points when you start out. How you distribute them is your business. But you ought to hold something back for brains to go with all that brawn."

"Hey, sweetheart," he protested, "I know what's important to a woman like you."

"I doubt you know any 'women like me,'" I said, reaching for the channel selector, "but I guarantee you that most women aren't impressed by phony cojones." I switched over to Mudge's cubicle.

The man practically filled the cubicle to overflowing. Which was more than I could say for his holopad: it was empty.

"Having trouble, Bernie?"

"Wha—oh, hello, Nicole."

"Ripley, Bernie. How many times do I have to remind you?"

He smiled wearily. "I guess we'll find out, soon enough."

"So what's the holdup?" I worried about him. Out of the three, he was the only one sufficiently open-minded to consider the possibility that there might actually be a guy inhabiting the interior of this drop-dead gorgeous female body. He couldn't retreat to the comfort of the narrow-minded certainty of the others and the thought that Ms. Doucet might actually be dead seemed to torment him. I wondered if Nicole had ever noticed his devotion when she was alive.

"I don't know," he answered. "I've never done this before."

"Well, before you start working on a Dreambody," I said, "it's a good idea to pick a class or profession. Something that suits you."

"I haven't the faintest."

This was definitely not the tough-as-nails legal eagle I had met a couple of days before. "Well, let's go down the list. How about the Warrior class?"

"I don't know..."

"Most folk really go for that direct route: swing a sword to solve your problems, buckle your swash, and rescue fair maidens. And there are variations on the theme..."

"Variations?"

"Sub-classes," I explained. "Be a Knight in shining armor or a Barbarian in your BVDs. Specialize as a Paladin or a Ranger—"

He shook his head. "I'm not the 'goody-two-shoes' type and I dropped out of the Boy Scouts because I hated camping."

"Magic User?" I suggested, "Wizard, Warlock, Mage, Illusionist?"

"Nah, I hear you start out wimpy and it takes forever to work your way up to the real power."

I nodded. "True."

"What class are you?"

"Bard." I shook my head. "Don't bother looking it up. It was never permitted as an official category. My programmer status over-rode the lockouts and so I'm the only Dreamwalker permitted that classification in the Matrix."

"What else do I have to choose from?"

"Well, you're a lawyer so I guess the Thief class would be out of—"

"A *Thief?*" Mudge looked up, his eyes widening. "Is that one of my choices?"

"Well…yeah. But I didn't think you'd be interested—"

"You're saying it's *legal* to be a Thief in this Fantasyworld Program?"

"Well…yeah. Thief—Rogue—whatever this year's semantics favor. Legal in terms of Program parameters. But if you get caught, it'll mean a world of hurt. If not outright termination."

"But aren't there dangers inherent in any choice of character classification?"

"True. It's just safer to play along your natural inclinations."

"Right. Well, I'm a lawyer, so it's perfect!"

I just looked at him.

"I mean, I've defended thieves, I've prosecuted thieves. I've had them as clients, employees—even helped a couple get elected. I have intimate and professional knowledge of the profession." He smiled. "I think I would be rather good at it."

I shrugged. "It's your call, Bernie."

"Thief, it is. So, I select a body, now?"

I nodded. "Start with race and gender. Most first time Dreamwalkers should start out with Human avatars. Humanoids and Demi-Humans: Elves, Dwarves, Brownies, Gnomes—

the Exotics and Crossbreeds, all take more concentration and experience if you're going to get any advantage out of them."

"Human, it is then. And I'd prefer to remain male, of course."

"Of course."

Oblivious to my tone of irony, he pressed a series of buttons, producing a mannequin-like image at the center of his holopad. "Small and quick," he decided, moving slide controls to downsize the avatar-template, "better throw more points into the Agility and Reflexes columns…"

"Right," I said. "I'll leave you to it." I reached for the channel selector but before I could turn to Dagny Westbrook's cubicle, she was paging me.

"Nicole, dear," she was saying, "I'm having trouble with my breasts…"

#

Her problem, as it turned out, was similar to Mudge's: she didn't know what she wanted. Or, rather, it seemed more like she didn't know what *I* wanted.

"How's this?" she asked, turning a dial that caused the figurine on the holopad to go from a B-cup to a double-D.

"Fine," I grumped, "if you want to end up playing the hunchback of Notre Dame."

"You think they should be smaller?" She tweaked the dial back to the single-D category.

I sighed and cradled my head in my hands. "Look, Doc; there's two sides to this question: the Practical and the Aesthetic. The Practical hinges on what you want to be. If you want to be a Sorceress, then I don't suppose it matters. You might even come up with a little personal levitation spell to make you more comfortable…

"On the other hand, if you plan to pull a bow, swing a sword, and otherwise engage in robust physical actions, a large bosom tends to be a bust—if you apprehend my meaning."

"Ah, yes," she said, her mouth making a *moue* of distaste. "I remember now: the Amazons cut off their right breasts to draw the bow more easily."

It was my turn to make a face. "Actually, that's a misconception. The ancient Greeks derived the name 'Amazon' from *mazos,* meaning 'breast'. The prefix 'a' was mistranslated to mean 'no' and subsequent generations added the mutilation story to the myth. Even though no period representations evidence this alleged practice."

"Then what did the 'A' stand for?"

Oops. "Well, given most accounts—and the peculiar aspects of the statue of their goddess Artemis at Ephesus—the prefix 'a' denoted...well...'amplitude.'

"But—" I hurried on, "—keep in mind what I said about utilizing weapons and limitations on your range and motion. Furthermore, there's the matter of um—well—support."

"Support?"

"And comfort."

"Comfort?"

"If you get my drift."

"I'm not sure I do, Nicole."

"Ripley," I corrected. "Look, I'm talking about brassieres constructed out of boiled leather and little bits of metal hooked together." I shook my head. "And people wonder what made the Amazons so all-fired mean."

Actually, the historical analog to the Amazon nation had never worn anything remotely resembling the attire ascribed to women warriors in the Fantasyworld Program. The Cephtronics Board of Directors, however, had never let little things like fact, logic, or good taste stand in the way of catering to the libidos of the lowest common denominator. Beautiful bodies—avatars or computer constructs—of either sex or persuasion were always a strong draw for the paying customers.

"So, you find smaller-breasted women more attractive?"

"I didn't say that!" A headache was trying to punch its way through the back of my eyeballs. "Dagny, your avatar is supposed to be the physical manifestation of what *you* want: either something you've always wanted to be or an opportunity to explore the alternatives that reality doesn't normally offer. Most people want to be more physically attractive. There's nothing wrong with that if you express your own individual tastes. There *is* something wrong in making yourself over to please someone else's standards of taste if they're at odds with your own."

"So what are you saying?"

"Choose the body that *you* want to wear! If you want to go to extremes in terms of height or measurements, indulge yourself! The only thing I'm saying here—*the only thing,* mind you—is just be practical! Aside from that, I have *no* opinion on the Dreambody you create. None!"

Cradling my head in my hands, again, I tried to massage my headache back into a stage of dormancy.

"So," Westbrook asked after a brief pause, "which do you prefer as a rule: blondes, brunettes, or redheads?"

"Dagny!"

#

I finished attaching the last of the biosensors to Nicole's body and looked up to see Lech Luther leering at me. "Does he have to be here?" I asked, knowing the question was rhetorical by now.

Westbrook was busy trying to figure out where her last three biosensors were supposed to go and answered without looking up: "You know the regulations, Nicole. Someone like Mr. Limbach must always accompany any patient on trips outside the sanitarium."

The cadaverous little creep grinned at me and seeing that Westbrook's attention was otherwise occupied slid his hand up and down the shaft of his security baton in what he imagined was a suggestive manner.

"And where do you find someone like Mr. Limbach?" I wondered aloud. "Under a rock or in the shallow end of the gene pool?"

Westbrook 'tch-tch'ed me: "Hostility, my dear. Not a good sign, I fear."

"Yeah," L.L. added *sotto voce,* "you think I get my jollies watchin' you naked?" He continued to stare. And salivate.

Pig.

I looked away and glanced over at Mudge. He was done with his sensor-array and just stood there like an implacable, pink mountain, politely ignoring the rest of us while he waited for his Cradle to arrive.

I suppose the lack of individual privacy for Dreamwalkers preparing to enter a Programworld is tied to the idea that we're all about to mentally disrobe, anyway. Once you've been a naked psyche, the body just seems like so much clothing—impersonal in a certain way.

At least in the context of other Dreamwalkers. Since Limbach was the "Security Orderly," he was still clothed and waiting for my encapsulation before he divested himself of clothing and restraint gear. His presence in the room was a violation of the concept that we were all equals, here. In fact, "violation" was the operative term whenever Luther was around.

When I first realized that The Machine had given me "tits for tat" my first response was somewhat antisocial and rather uncooperative. Luther was one of the attendants summoned to help calm me at the onset of my stay at Wallbank Sanitarium—the words "calm" and "subdue" being virtually interchangeable here and Luther Limbach was all over me like an octopus in heat. Since then, he had made numerous attempts to cop a feel when no one else was looking. For my part, I had endeavored to discourage his "amorous" inclinations with a heartfelt kick to the groin when no one was looking.

So far, Lech was ahead: seven-zip.

Four suspension tanks—Cradles—were entering the room on magnetic tracks now, and it wouldn't be long before I could put this bozo behind me.

I climbed up the Cradle's side and opened the tank before it had even stopped moving but I wasn't fast enough: there was a hand grasping my backside as I topped the ladder and Limbach's reedy little voice was saying, "Here, let me help you—"

Gritting my teeth as I slid through the hatchway, I eased myself down into the nutrient soup that half-filled the interior of the tank. A moment later Luther's ferret face poked through the hatchway. "Sweet dreams, sweetcakes. I'll be right behind you."

Now there was a pleasant thought. "Bugger off, Luther. As soon as I wake up, I'm having this body dusted for fingerprints!"

"Aw, come on Nicki; I'm trying to make nice." He stuck an arm in. "How about I help tuck you in?" His fingers grazed my—that is, Nicole's—breast.

That did it: I slapped the door switch on the internal override panel.

I had asked myself early on if my revulsion was the result of any homophobic tendencies. I finally decided the answer was basically no. Luther Limbach was a creep—the kind of guy who taints the rest of us by accidentally having the same chromosomal arrangement.

The only sexual issue here was one of harassment. The only remedy, I decided as I reached up and grabbed his arm, was Pavlovian conditioning. I pulled and then pushed, overbalancing him and then slamming his head up against the descending hatch cover. The metal door made a musical, gong-like tone and Luther's eyes rolled back in his head. I released his arm and he slithered out of sight as the hatch continued to descend.

I lay back in the nutrient solution as the Cradle sealed itself. A moment later there was a faint hissing sound as a mixture of gaseous somnambulants and metabolic suppressers were released into the tank's closed environment.

I faded off to sleep with pleasant thoughts: with any luck and a good head start, it was the last I would ever see of Luther Limbach. Or a raft of painful memories every time I glanced in the mirror.

In hindsight, it would have been simpler and less painful to opt for the Oedipal solution and just poke my own eyes out.

TWO

The transitional period between the unconscious state of Matrix insertion and the acquired dream-state of avatar awareness varies, but perceptual values seem to place it in the one-to three-minute range.

Or, in other words, you go to sleep in the suspension tank and wake up in your dreambody just a couple of minutes later.

Except this time it was different.

Maybe the algorithms and technology used by the Dreamworlds Corporation here were significantly different than the interface methodology of the Dreamland Project in my own universe. Maybe it was the attempt to return to my own space-time continuum in the process.

Or maybe it was last night's sandwich: hot pastrami, corned beef, Swiss cheese, and Cole slaw with Russian dressing on rye. The staff had nicknamed it the "Heartburn Hotel." You'd think my eating habits would tip them off to my true gender.

This time I endured snatches of half-remembered dreams attached to the Insertion Process. Dark and fiery landscapes populated by demons and devils and distorted walking corpses. Glimpses of the molten-girt dungeons of Tartarus. A kaleidoscope of hellish images with only one distinct juxtaposition: for a moment I hovered above a makeshift REMrunner terminal and cephalic harness rig in a squalid, unkempt studio apartment. Plates of half-eaten food littered the floor amid drifts of unlaundered clothes, scraps of paper, and unidentifiable bits of detritus. A dark figure hunched on a nearby magna-futon enmeshed in fiber-op that snaked between its legs and clamped like hellish jumper cables to the ram-like horns the curled against its skull.

Then I slam-danced into an avatar and—

Nothing.

I just puddled in throbbing, veinshot maroon darkness. I waited, pondering why I was seemingly stuck, spending way too much time on the fringe of waking up.

This was the moment of truth. Was I back in my own avatar? Had my *psyche* transferred to the Programworld in my own universe? Or was I still stuck on the wrong side of the mirror?

Or, worse: was I displaced, caught in limbo between the juxtaposition of the two *timelines?*

My body was numb, unresponsive. Someone seemed to have glued my eyelids to my cheeks, and I couldn't be sure, lacking the visual evidence, but it felt as if my tongue had crawled halfway out of my mouth and died. I thought about moving but, beyond a painful twitch, the rest of me seemed resoundingly disinterested.

"WHAT HAVE YOU DONE?" The voice was a whipcrack of pain, lancing my skull like a spike of red-hot iron.

At the same time a measure of comfort came with that particular voice: I peeled open one crusty eyelid and contemplated the bleary image of my ex-wife. Or, rather, my ex-wife's avatar.

Not that you'd see much difference, you understand. While most Dreamwalkers prefer avatars that make them stronger, younger, prettier, etcetera; Stephanie—or Vashti, as she was named inside the Fantasyworld Program—looked much the same as her "real" self. Her long, honey-blonde hair hung loosely woven into a thick rope that draped casually over her left shoulder, while eyes the color of periwinkle offset a snub nose with a light dusting of freckles. A gold-girdled, white linen gown accentuated the gentle curves of her slender form and I felt the return of an old pain, a reminder that we don't always heal…

Sometimes we just scab over.

Easing the pain was the realization that I must be back in my own avatar, in my own Programworld.

Vashti was a sight for sore eyes but not, unfortunately, a voice for sore ears at this particular moment: ***"WHERE THE HELL DID YOU GET THIS?"*** She brandished one of the empty bottles of Demon Rum that Lilith had gifted me with during my last visit.

"That question," I whispered, "is inherently redundant." My own voice sounded like thunder in my ears so maybe she wasn't shouting, after all.

"I THOUGHT WE HAD CONFISCATED ALL OF THIS STUFF!"

"Please, Steffie," I whimpered, "I just want to die here quietly…"

"HE'S DRUNK AGAIN!" she bellowed to the doorway.

A robed and cowled figure appeared in the stone-arched portal. Curly black hair and beard, shot through with silver threads, framed a face that had once been all angles and planes, now succumbing to the effects of middle age and gravity: Daggoth the Dark. *"NOW DEAREST,"* he soothed in slightly less thunderous tones, *"HE HAS REASONS ENOUGH. AS YOU SHOULD WELL KNOW."*

"BUT HOW DOES HE DO IT? I KNOW ROB DEVELOPED SOME PROBLEMS WITH ALCOHOL AFTER OUR DIVORCE BUT FANTASYWORLD LIQUOR NEVER AFFECTED HIM BEFORE NOW."

"'TIS DEMON RUM, MY LOVE. ITS POTENCY IS MAGICALLY ENHANCED."

"Please…" I whispered, trying to cover my ears with my hands. Unfortunately my hands were under the table that was currently cushioning my cheek. Getting them out and up seemed a bit beyond my mental resources for the moment.

"AND CONSIDER WHAT THE MAN HAS BEEN THROUGH," Daggoth continued. *"HIS PSYCHE WAS SHATTERED INTO MULTIPLE AVATARS AND HE EXPERIENCED HIS OWN DEATH SEVERAL TIMES! HE WAS BETRAYED AND EVEN MURDERED BY THE WOMAN HE LOVED—AND HAD TO WATCH HER DIE TWICE, AS WELL! AND HE'S MADE IT QUITE CLEAR THAT HE'S UNCOMFORTABLE SEEING HIS EX-WIFE INVOLVED WITH A DEAD MAN."*

"I WISH YOU WOULDN'T TALK THAT WAY," Stephanie remonstrated. ***"I CAN'T REALLY THINK OF YOU AS BEING DEAD."***

"PERHAPS NOT HERE—NOT AS DAGGOTH THE DARK AND INSIDE THE PROGRAM MATRIX, MY DEAR. BUT MICHAEL STRAEKER—MY REAL BODY AND EVERYTHING I WAS OUTSIDE OF THIS COMPUTER-GENERATED REALITY—IS MOST CERTAINLY DEAD, AND NOW THIS AVATAR IS ALL THAT REMAINS."

"IT'S ENOUGH FOR ME!" she cried, embracing him fiercely.

"Will you please take it outside!" I moaned.

Daggoth looked remorseful. *"SORRY, I SHOULD'VE GOTTEN THE ANTIDOTE STRAIGHTAWAY."*

"OH, FOR HEAVEN'S SAKE, RICHARD; IT'S NOT LIKE ROB IS REALLY SUFFERING! IT'S JUST HIS AVATAR: THE MACHINE HAS GIVEN ITSELF A HANGOVER AND IT SERVES IT RIGHT!"

"Wrong," I croaked as Daggoth departed. Maybe the Supercomputer known as The Machine had been animating my avatar when it started this particular binge but I had returned in time to enjoy the after-effects of this particular alcoholic meltdown.

"ROB," Stephanie was suddenly bending over me, ***"IS THAT REALLY YOU IN THERE?"***

I fought the inclination to drool as she propped me up in my chair. "Hi, honey," I mumbled, "I'm home."

"WHAT HAPPENED? WHY ARE YOU BACK?"

"Please, Steffie: whisper."

"OH, SORRY. WHAT BROUGHT YOU BACK?"

Daggoth returned with a beaker of smoking, bubbling sludge that he called his hangover cure. *"HERE, TRY THIS."*

I opened my mouth and Fantasyworld's most puissant Wizard, the former Chief of Programming for Cephtronics and the Dreamworlds Project, tipped the beaker and deliberately poured the mixture on top of my head.

#

Picture a circular stone tower of medieval design, the width of a city block at the base and nine stories high. It blends nicely with the landscape because there are no apparent external anomalies for its Dark-to-Middle Age milieu. Except for the occasional forcefields that go up when the guards-and-wards are tripped.

The interior of the ancient edifice, however, is a technological time-warp. Take the shower facilities, for example. Originally located on the sixth and seventh floors and solar-heated, Daggoth had moved them to the basement and sub-basement levels in a vertical line with sleeping and guest quarters, and installed an elevator.

The stone-dressed chamber resembled a grotto with pool and two-story waterfall. A heat exchanger adjacent to a small fusion reactor in the sub-sub-sub basement provided the hot water. My host had decided to remodel with an eye toward structural integrity after the recent Cyberpunk siege: water had begun leaking down into the library and had nearly ruined an entire shelf of classic scrolls including the collected adventures of the Siblings Hardy and one Master Thomas Swift, esquire.

Lilypads still floated on the water as they had during my previous visits but a recent change to a more tropical theme added plants and wildflowers that bordered the water and climbed the rocky abutment to the upper pool. Warm, mist laden air created foggy halos about the magically generated grow-lights as they drifted lazily overhead like a herd of will-o'-the-wisps on Thorazine.

"Would you mind telling me what that was all about?" I re-secured the towel around my waist as I waded to the shallow end of Daggoth's indoor lagoon.

Stephanie—er, Vashti—handed me a robe. "I wish I knew."

"Yeah?" I slipped my arms into the sleeves and turned around to drop my towel while I belted it. "Well, Daggoth looked more stunned than you did, and he's the one who poured that goop on my head."

She handed me a fresh towel for my hair. "I didn't know he was going to do that. Anymore than he did."

"Obviously." While my shower had diminished the effects of my hangover, I doubted Daggoth's brew had any part in the recovery process.

"Richard just hasn't been himself, lately."

"Yeah? Who has he been?"

"Rob, this isn't funny! He's dead!"

"I thought you didn't like to think about that particular little fact."

"If something goes wrong with his avatar, he doesn't have a body to escape to like the rest of us!"

I held my hands up. "All right, all right! Tell me what the problem is." The waterfall made normal conversation difficult so I gestured toward the door. "On the way to my room."

I glanced at my reflection in the nearest mirror as we exited the bath chamber by way of the elevator. Seeing the familiar, if somewhat soggy, features of Riplakish of Dyrinwall was reassuring. Although my Halfelven Dreambody, at five-foot-six, was nearly a foot shorter than my real body, it fit like a comfortable suit of clothing.

As the elevator door slid shut and the lift started toward the upper level guest quarters, a new thought occurred. It was with an odd mixture of sadness and relief that I thought I had finally severed my last link to Nicole Doucet.

#

"These are such little things," Vashti concluded as I pulled on my boots. "It may just be all in my imagination."

I nodded as I laced up the sides and tied off the leather thongs. "Or?" I prompted.

She smiled wanly. "You know me too well."

"Funny, I thought we got divorced because I didn't know you well enough."

"Rob—"

"Sorry. C'mon, spit the rest of it out."

Vashti gritted her teeth. "Forgetfulness, momentary bouts of disorientation—what if his tumor is coming back?"

Daggoth the Dark had been the Fantasyworld avatar for Mike Straeker back when he was Chief of Programming for Cephtronics, Inc. When Mike had discovered that he had a brain tumor that was fatal and inoperable, he had arranged to deposit his consciousness in that avatar just before his death.

While the tumor, itself, seemed to have been left behind in the process, Straeker—or Daggoth, now—had discovered that the damage wrought—headaches, blackouts, periods of mental fugue—still plagued him. His subsequent attempts to replace his damaged Psyche files with earlier but healthy backup files had seemed successful on a personal level. But the process also undid the safety lockouts on the Matrix and destabilized the program parameters for everyone else in the Dreamworlds program. In trying to escape death in the outer reality, he had opened the door to True Death within the program for all of us.

Fantasyworld was no longer a game.

"Has he experienced any pain or discomfort?" I asked. "Had any headaches, migraines?"

She shook her head. "Nothing along that line. But he has complained about being tired lately."

"Doesn't sound like the tumor," I said in what I hoped was a reassuring tone. While that was true, something worse occurred to me. "I'll keep an eye on him and see what I can come up with."

She grasped my arm. "Thanks, Rob." She kissed me on the cheek. "Just don't tell him that I told you any of this."

I nodded, looking around the guest chamber where I had apparently spent the previous night. "How long have I been here?"

"Two days."

"What's the occasion?" I asked as I buckled on my swordbelt.

"The two of you have been trying to figure out what to do about Natasha Skovoroda." Her smile faded. "And you're *not* taking him with you. Not while his condition is so uncertain."

"Oh?" I answered, amused at her sudden change in demeanor. "And where am I going?"

"To Hell."

"I've been told that before."

"No, Rob," she said, hands on her hips and as serious as—well—hell. "You are going to Hell. You were planning on leaving in the next couple of days."

#

Braced in his study, Daggoth just looked amused. "It was your idea, you know."

"The hell it was!" I leaned across his desk. "I just got here, Bucko, and that means the Computer thought of it for me while I was off-premises!"

"Well, it's still a good idea, whoever thought of it."

"Yeah?" I leaned a little farther in: now I could count the broken capillaries in his nose. "Well, what does Orcus think about my dropping in for a visit? You may recall that Hell's minions were a little less than hospitable the last time I passed through."

Daggoth slid his crystal ball toward me. "Call him and ask." He waved his hand and activated the occult orb. Grey, swirling mists performed a sluggish farandole at the crystal's heart as I sat down on the other side of the desk.

An inhuman voice intoned: *Ethyrnet.*

"Log on," I said; "Riplakish of Dyrinwall."

Observe-slash-contact? it inquired in soulless tones.

"Contact," I specified. "Orcus, Lord of the Undead, Hell-Prime, Level One."

Processing. There was a lengthy pause.

I propped my chin in my hands. "Dag, I know you prefer the ancient magicks but a point-and-click OS should be sufficiently antique for even your esoteric tastes."

"How many times do I have to tell you," he retorted mildly: "You're just layering a second-rate glamour over the original operating system and that's gonna increase the likelihood of system crashes while decreasing overall efficiency."

Access denied.

"What?"

"Try again," Daggoth prompted.

Accessing…Access denied.

I looked up. "Are the lines out or are they simply refusing to take my call?"

Daggoth shrugged. "We haven't been able to get through for the past two days. How long the condition existed before—who knows?"

I tapped the crystal. "Inquiry."

Prompt.

"Nature of null-slash-interrupt?"

Null connects. Return interrupt.

"Now what does that mean?" Daggoth pondered. "Are we just not getting through? Or is something blocking a response?"

I propped my elbows on the desk and cradled my chin in my hands. "Ethyrnet-backslash-basic."

Prompt.

"Spectrum band C-slash-B."

Channel selection?

"Zero-zero-one-nine."

Online.

Daggoth groaned but I just ignored him. "Breaker one-nine, break one-nine, this here's the Bashful Bard calling Octopussy: c'mon back. You there, Marilith?"

The sound of static filled the room.

"Break one-nine, this is Riplakish of Dyrinwall: can anybody hear me?"

"This is silly—" Daggoth was saying when the static promptly disappeared.

"Hello, hello? Who's there?" I asked, trying to make out an image at the crystal's heart. "Marilith? Is that you?" The swirling gray fog that had filled the clear orb was beginning to disperse. A light appeared in its center and began to grow in brightness while shading down the color spectrum from yellow to orange to red. A high-pitched whine tickled our ears and began to climb into the inaudible range.

"I've got a bad feeling about this," Daggoth murmured as a pulsing, blood red light filled the room.

"Log off!" I yelled. "Log off!"

The light intensified and now I could feel a powerful vibration through the surface of the desk.

Daggoth and I stared at each other as we came to a simultaneous conclusion: "London Bridge!" we both chorused, diving for the floor. We came up under the desk just as the crystal ball exploded into ten thousand slivers of glass, disintegrating the wall tapestries, blowing out the windows, and reducing the rest of the furniture to just so much kindling. Protected by the enchanted Rowanwood of the desk, we crawled out from under, unscathed.

Vashti burst into the room, wild-eyed and frantic. "What was that? What happened?"

I stared at the smoking crater in the middle of Daggoth's desk. "We were calling Hell and somebody reversed the charges."

#

"It could have been an accident—" Daggoth paused to stifle a sneeze.

I did a double take. "An *accident?"*

"If there's something technically wrong, in-system," he continued, "what happened could be explained by something as simple as a resonant feedback loop."

"Resonant feedback loop my a-a-*a-choo!"* The cleaning up process raised clouds of dust in the study and I moved closer to one of the broken windows for some fresh air. "Do you really need so many?" I asked, gesturing at some twenty-odd brooms engaged in sweeping up the mess. Each moved about independently.

"I wanted to get this done before we left." The door to the study flew open and three more brooms trudged in, carrying buckets of water in their sorcerous appendages.

"I'll finish up," Vashti volunteered. "Just give me the cantrip for dispelling these things."

Daggoth shook his head. "This ain't no Mickey-mouse spell. Besides, they're almost done." He turned back to me. "Why don't you leave Ghost in the stables and ride with me—it'll give us more time to talk."

"Yeah, talk me into cutting my own throat."

He sighed. "Look, Bob, I keep telling you: you don't really need to go to Hell—"

"—Just Abydos, the City of the Dead," I chimed in. "That's like saying 'you don't really need to put your head in the lion's mouth—just walk around inside his cage'."

"Well," he scratched his head, "two days ago this whole thing seemed a lot simpler."

"Simpler?"

"If we could've contacted Orcus and had him tell us where Natasha's shade could be found." Two more brooms entered the study with a rolled-up rug under their unnatural arms. "Then it would've been an easy matter for you to go fetch it."

"*Me* to go fetch it?"

"As things stand now," he took the rug from the brooms and began unrolling it on the floor, "we're going to have to move up our timetable..."

"*Our* timetable?"

"Dankevych has sent word from the Outside. Natasha's flatlines are starting to drop."

"Starting to drop? A flatline doesn't drop. It doesn't do anything. That's what makes it a flatline."

"Dammit, Bob; I'm a programmer, not a doctor. The essence of the communiqué was that Natasha's body is starting to fail. It can't continue indefinitely with her cerebral cortex offline." One by one, the brooms popped out of existence. "I'd like to get to Yudu's a little early so we can consult the Zombie Mistress over these recent developments. I'm not so sure this plan is completely foolproof."

I goggled at Daggoth. "*You're* not so sure it's foolproof?"

He finished unrolling the carpet and gestured for me to sit. "Well it was, after all, your idea."

"It was *my* idea?" I sat toward the rear of the rug, facing the outer wall of Daggoth's study.

"Will you stop echoing everything he says," Vashti snapped as the Wizard seated himself directly in front of me, facing the same direction. "Really, Rob; your judgment of late—"

"My judgment?"

"—getting yourself drunk and—"

"Now, wait a minute!" I said as Daggoth gestured and the remnants of the great bay window before us opened outward. "You're talking about stuff the Computer arranged in my absence! I wasn't even in my avatar when it cooked up this harebrained plan or started that last drinking binge!"

"Oh, Rob," she sighed as Daggoth gestured again and the rug lifted us up off the floor, "can't you, just once in your life, take responsibility for something?"

"Bye, Dear," Daggoth waved as we floated toward the open window. "Don't wait supper."

"It wasn't me," I muttered as we glided out of the study. We swooped around the great stone tower and climbed for clouds in a loose, arcing curve that left the Wizard's tower far below.

"I know how you feel, Bob." Daggoth leveled us off and pointed the carpet to the northwest. "I haven't exactly been myself of late."

"Oh?" I said.

And waited.

It seemed all he intended to say for the moment and I had to choose between admiring the view or making more conversation. And the view was incredible. Strangely, Robert Ripley the Human does not particularly care for heights, while the Halfelven Riplakish of Dyrinwall likes nothing better than to saddle up Ghost and let Pegasus' grandson take him on an unrestrained gallop through the clouds.

Below us the earth displayed her finery: emerald forests, russet fields, sapphire lakes, embroidered with golden threads of road and footpath in elaborate stitchery. My heart ached to think that the only way to experience a pristine wilderness with fresh air, clearwater streams, and uncut forests was to link up to the cybernetic Matrix and look inside our own minds.

How long before someone came along and figured out how to make a buck by despoiling all that, too?

"Calabastor," Daggoth observed as we passed over the spires and towers of the great, walled city. "Things sure quieted down after you left."

"Which reminds me," I said, "I've got a couple or three spells I've got to get back and undo."

He shook his head. "I took care of all that: removed the wall of thorns from around the castle and neutralized the Timestop spell on the inhabitants."

"Great. And the effects of the Love philtre?"

"Somehow the magical properties of the potion were not subject to the chrono-synclastic influences of the Timestop effect."

"In other words—"

"It had already worn off."

"I'll bet that was interesting."

"To say the least. Lots of red faces."

"My, my."

"And they got redder when your name was mentioned."

"What? Wait a minute! That wasn't my fault!"

"Maybe not," Daggoth said. "But, I wouldn't go anywhere near Calabastor in the near future. You probably have more friends in Hell at the moment."

"Great." I settled back and contemplated the carpet's field effect as we left the city below and behind us. The power of flight and maneuverability is only part of the magic that goes into making a flying carpet; another aspect of the enchantment is the adhesion effect. Most people don't give this much thought until they find themselves in midair on an oversized doormat. The spell works something like invisible Velcro: hands, feet, clothing—even cargo and supplies acquire a certain sticky quality in relation to the weave of the carpet being ridden. This prevents most accidental departures while a hundred feet above the ground. You will notice I said "most," as the spell permits movement while on the carpet, and Velcro, magical or otherwise, does have its limits as regards weight, force, and motion. One does not "hang ten" on a flying carpet; if one does, the laws of natural selection are brought to bear with a vengeance.

"Enchanted Forest coming up," Daggoth called over his shoulder. "We should be there in twenty minutes."

Beneath us a great army of trees seemed to march forward and fan out as we flew toward them.

"You said you hadn't been yourself lately," I prompted.

"What?"

I repeated the question.

"Oh, that." He waved a hand airily. "Too much time indoors. Too much time spent cloistered in my library doing research."

"Research?"

"The Anomaly. Resurrecting Natasha Skovoroda. Scrying for Euryale. Locating either of Nicole's bodies. The Misty Dawn problem. Trying to determine if there are any other duplicate yous in the Program." He shook his head. "Cleaning up after you is turning into a full-time job."

"Sorry."

"And then there's Hippolyta."

"Hippolyta? The Queen of the Amazons Hippolyta?"

He suddenly changed the subject: "Say, what about those friends of yours?"

"Friends of mine?" Stephanie was right: I definitely had to get out of "echo" mode.

"From the Parallel Timeline. Shouldn't we be looking for them to show up soon?"

I shook my head and then clutched at the rug as a thermal updraft from the woods below gave us a little goose. "Highly unlikely. When we were under the Isle of Ortygia, the Corpus Callosum seemed the dividing line between our reality and theirs. They won't know that and there's no longer any bridge to cross over. I suspect they'll wander about in the Programworld corresponding to their Universe, eventually give up, and go home."

"So how did you know that you'd end up on the right side of the boundary line?"

"I didn't. For sure." I repressed a shiver. "I gambled on that dividing line being contiguous to both Realities—an overlap or intersection point—allowing both Programworlds to cooperate with each other. I was counting on the algorithmic subsets to recognize my personal code-sequence and perform a long-distance retrieval, matching me to my own, personal avatar—which is on this side of the so-called Corpus Callosum."

"Bullshit. You couldn't think of anything else so you closed your eyes and jumped back in, hoping you'd get lucky."

I grinned. "Isn't that what I just said?"

"You were lucky. Suppose the other computer was unable to render your psyche files into a binary equivalent for The Machine? Or suppose the Matrix read you as a virus instead of a legitimate subprogram?"

A vague humming sound distracted me. "I had to take that chance!"

"That bad?"

"I dunno. I was in a world that wasn't my own. They had me locked up." I grasped the edges of the carpet as we banked around a fleecy cloud. "I just didn't relish spending the rest of my life as…"

"A woman?"

"As someone or something other than myself."

"So what are you doing here?" His eyebrows waggled.

"Taking care of unfinished business, I guess. Originally I was only thinking as far as using this side of the program as a stepping stone back into my own body, in my own world. But if we can retrieve Natasha Skovoroda's psyche and reintegrate it with her Programworld avatar, we may be able to save her life in the Outer Reality, yet. That's worth hanging around for a couple of extra days." I didn't add that Stephanie had asked me to keep an eye on him, as well.

Daggoth's cowled head nodded. "And then there is the business with Misty Dawn."

"The business with Misty Dawn?" We hit an air pocket and I bounced back on the carpet a couple of inches. The humming was suddenly louder and I had the distinct feeling I was hanging over the edge. I looked back and was treated to the spectacle of four winged gnomes whirling about one another in a fantastic aerial ballet. It took a second look to recognize the carpet strands in their tiny hands and realize that they were unweaving the rug right out from under me!

"Gremlins!" I yelled, drawing my wakizashi-shortsword. "Take us down!"

Daggoth glanced over his shoulder, blanched, and put us into a steep dive just as I slashed Balmung's enchanted blade at the aft section of the rug. The flying carpet was a small, two-passenger model: it had measured roughly three feet by five-and-a-half when we had left Daggoth's tower. Already it was less than five feet in length and my reckless cut, unbalanced by our sudden descent, took another four inches. The Gremlins swooped back in, two of them grabbing the fringe along the port and starboard sides and began unraveling from three different directions now.

Getting to my knees and turning around on our airborne floor covering was awkward, even though we had pulled out of our dive and leveled off to skim the treetops. Daggoth was looking for a place to put us down but this part of the woods was so dense that you couldn't see the forest floor for the trees.

I got my right foot under me so that I was one knee up and one knee down, and drew my katana-longsword. The Gremlins, already out of reach, cackled like demented squirrels as they unwove our flying transportation, strand by strand. I tried severing the threads as they separated from the weave but the little thugs merely dived beneath the rug and crossed to the other side.

"Hey, Struts!" one bogie called to another. "Three, maybe four minutes until F.O.T.L.!"

"F.O.T.L.?" Hey, old habits are hard to break.

"Yeah," smirked the nearest Gremlin, "Fruits *Off* The Loom!"

That did it. While they capered and crowed, I sheathed my swords and reached inside my leather vest where my Glock was nestled in its shoulder holster. The sudden appearance of the handgun got their attention and their respect.

But not in the manner I had expected.

"Hey, looky!"

"A machine!"

"What's it do?"

"Does it have moving parts?"

Two things Gremlins cannot resist: anything that flies and any kind of machine. When the two come together to form an airplane, the combination is irresistible but either category is enough to whet their appetites.

They dropped their strands of carpet fibers and zipped in on buzzing wings for a closer look.

"What's it called?"

"How did you make it?"

"Got any more?" each wanted to know.

"Hey Wingnut, check out the insides!"

The one closest to me suddenly shrank down to the size of a wasp and zipped inside the muzzle.

I pulled back the slide and chambered a round in the Glock.

"Awesome!" trilled a tiny voice from inside the weapon's barrel. "Do that again!"

"I'll show you something better," I promised as another Gremlin buzzed up to peer inside the handgun's muzzle. "And I won't have to even aim." I pulled the trigger.

Even firing .40 S&W ammo, the recoil on a Glock is almost negligible as antique handguns go. Unless, of course, you're standing on an unraveling flying carpet, traveling at excessive speed, and forget to brace for Sir Isaac's law of action and reaction. I effectively combined a soft-shoe two-step and a gymnast's vaulting dismount, tumbling over Daggoth's left shoulder. I fell for several long seconds and then…

I hit hard!

Then I hit harder!

Then I hit not so hard.

Then I hit hard again.

Then, almost softly.

Then, not so soft.

There must have been fifty or sixty tree branches between the treetop and the ground and I hit every other one on the way down. They returned the favor by breaking my fall without breaking any bones and, by the time I landed on a negligible cushion of pine needles, I was confident that someday—with sufficient therapy and bed rest—I might be able to walk with a cane and proper bracing.

"Rrripplakissssshh!" Daggoth's voice trailed off as he lost altitude and gained distance.

I winced and rolled over. Even if he managed a safe landing, the trees would inhibit our timely reunion unless I met him halfway.

The worst part was getting back up to my hands and knees. After that the rest was merely painful.

The Glock had landed several feet away and I checked and holstered it. Then I cast a personal Flying spell—something I should've had the presence of mind to have done when the Gremlins had first shown up.

I went up more slowly than I came down: the density of the tree branches worked in both directions and I had to work my way through their leafy maze with hands and feet as well. Reaching the top, I soared free of the tree-line just in time to see Daggoth and what was left of his carpet go down a quarter of a mile away. I soared over to what was my best guess of where he fell and began climbing back down.

He wasn't hard to find: halfway to the ground I started following the sound of his voice as he worked his way through a series of oaths, epitaphs, and theories on the gestational cycle of Gremlins. I could hardly fault him: all that was left of his flying carpet was a tattered remnant that wasn't much good for anything beyond serving as a welcome mat.

"Looks like we walk from here," I observed. Flying spells have a short duration and are designed more for emergencies than any kind of serious travel. Magicked carpets and brooms are more practical in the distance department.

A shadow passed overhead and I glanced up. A woman was cruising overhead, astride a broom. Any thoughts of calling for assistance died stillborn as she turned her head and I saw her face.

It was Nicole Doucet.

THREE

"Okay, it *looked* like Nicole Doucet."

He raised an eyebrow. "It?"

"She. *She* looked like Nicole Doucet."

Again with the eyebrow. "She?"

I shrugged. "It. She. I don't know who or what I saw. But for a moment I could've sworn that it was Nicole."

"Maybe it was."

"But she's dead. Both of her, in fact."

"You're so sure?" Daggoth puffed as we hiked up a particularly steep hill.

"I saw both of them fall into the chasm. That, alone, would have been enough to kill a Balrog, and I saw one of her take two arrows that should have been fatal even before she fell!" To my dismay I realized I was trembling.

Daggoth had searched for the bodies of both Nicoles and my alternate self for the past two months. He had found nothing. "Which doesn't mean any of them survived," he conceded. "The intersection of the two Programworlds at that point has produced something like a fold in the Matrix. The lower depths of that subterranean gorge you've nicknamed the Corpus Callosum are beyond the scrying abilities of anything I've got back at the tower." He gave me a look. "Certainly beyond anything I have left after this morning. Unless we go there, drop a couple of ropes over the side, and rappel down into the abyss, you'll just have to wonder." He gave me another look. *"Don't* even think about it. You *will* have to wonder."

I shook my head. No one could have survived that fall.

We reached the top of the hill and Daggoth sat on a stone outcropping to rest.

"It must have been my imagination," I said, leaning my back against a tree and swiping at the perspiration on my brow with an already damp sleeve. "I've seen nothing but Nicole's face every time I looked in the mirror for the past month. I feel a little obsessed."

"So what else is new?"

"Besides, whoever it was, she was too far away and there were too many branches between us for me to I.D. my own mother."

"So what are you trying to conclude here?"

"Enough, Dr. Freud. I confess to hallucinogenic fixations."

"Such an angry Jung man." Daggoth hoisted himself off the rock with a sigh. "Better keep moving if we're going to get there before sundown."

We had been just minutes away from the Zombie Mistress's mansion when the Gremlins had pulled the rug out from under us. Trudging through the Enchanted Forest on foot promised to stretch the journey out another two hours.

Actually, it was more like four hours. First, we were woefully out of shape and had to stop for frequent rest breaks.

Second, there were the Goblins.

It was midafternoon when we caught the scent of woodsmoke on the air. "Campfire," I announced.

"Cookfire," my companion corrected.

"Food," we extrapolated. And broke into a trot. I was hungry, but if my stomach rumbled, I couldn't hear it over the sounds that Daggoth's was making.

"Maybe they have horses," the dark Sorcerer added. "A couple of extra ones they'd be willing to loan."

"Loan?"

"Okay: *Buy.*"

"Hey, I don't know about you but I didn't bring my checkbook along—"

There was no question that we were being careless. But while most mortals feared to enter the fringes of the Enchanted Forest, Daggoth was a twenty-third level Wizard, and, besides being a Bard, I was the Archdruid of Dyrinwall Forest. Since we both had Programmer status in the Matrix, we figured we could handle just about anything that might come along.

Of course, who would've figured that a twenty-third level Wizard and the Archdruid of Dyrinwall wouldn't be able to handle four little Gremlins?

Ditto the Rodney Dangerfields of the fiends folio: Goblins.

We crested another hill and ran into a couple out gathering firewood.

The one I collided with dropped an armful of kindling and opened his mouth to yell a warning.

I put my fist in it.

He bit my hand.

A moment later there was a sudden absence of sound, indicating Daggoth had gotten off a quick Silence spell. I jumped back, drawing Balmung with my left hand. While my opponent pulled a wicked-looking stone axe from his belt, I tried to wipe some of the blood from my right hand and did a quick count of my fingers. It was a nasty bite, but everything seemed to be more or less intact.

I swung my wakizashi-shortsword over to block the axe in mid-arc and then brought my foot up, intending to plant it square in the little bugger's chest. Either I miscalculated or he leaned back: my foot continued upwards and the toe of my boot caught him right under the chin. His head snapped back and he dropped like a sack of spilled groceries.

I looked around for the other Goblin but there was no sign of him. Then I noticed that Daggoth was holding a wand and a tiny wisp of smoke was dissipating from its slender tip. He replaced it inside his robe and then helped me drag the other Goblin back the way we'd come.

"—many of them there are?" he said as we passed out of the Silence spell's area of effect.

"And what are they doing out and about in the middle of the afternoon?" I wanted to know. Goblins are primarily nocturnal. Bright sunlight effectively blinds them, though the density of the overhead foliage made this part of the forest almost gloomy. And they're pretty wimpy in one-on-one fights: humans are twice as tall and three times as heavy. My kick had accidentally broken this one's neck but he wouldn't have lasted another thirty seconds, regardless. The only time they're truly dangerous is when they outnumber you five to one in the dark.

We dumped the body behind a rotted log and crept back to the site of our little skirmish. It didn't take long to find their spoor. I hand-signaled Daggoth, as we had reentered the Silence spell's area of effect, and began following their trail. With any luck we'd spy a little enclave of ten or fifteen bogies, give 'em wide berth, and finish our journey without stumbling across any more.

The aroma of the cooking fire grew stronger and other scents started to mingle with it: the smell of burned pork and the odor of unwashed sweat socks.

Sweat socks worn by Orcs doing hard labor in the sulfur mines of Ahrmpiiten-Dur.

"I smell Goblins," Daggoth whispered.

I nodded, my eyes watering. "Either these bogies have a gland problem or there's a whole lot of Goblins over the next hill."

There were a whole lot of Goblins over the next hill.

We dropped to our bellies and slithered back down the way we came. "Well," I murmured, "do you want to lob an extra-large fireball or shall we just creep quietly away in the opposite direction?"

A sudden shriek sounded from the Goblin encampment and we stared at each other.

"Human," I said.

"Female," Daggoth qualified and uttered an abbreviated oath.

Now neither option was viable. We crawled back up to the top of the hill and eased our heads back up for a better look.

There were maybe fifty of the misshapen little monsters bivouacked in the mossy hollow below. Four or five small fires were scattered about with odd bits of meat suspended over the flames on crude wooden spits. A large rock slab near the center of the encampment was splashed with brownish-red stains that could only be blood. I took another look at what was roasting over one of the cookfires and told myself I wouldn't look again.

There were two captives, bound to trees, near the western perimeter of the bivouac. Tall and short, day and night, beauty and—well—beast? A low whistle escaped Daggoth's pursed lips. "Do you know who that is?"

I shook my head.

"Angel McRae!" he whispered.

"Friend of yours?" I murmured.

"I *wish!*"

"Ssshh—"

"She's only the world's top supermodel."

"Really? Which one?"

He poked me. "She's only the most beautiful woman in the entire world."

"Which world?"

"The outside world—Reality! Only she looks just the same here!"

Well, why not: if you're already at the top of your game, looks-wise…"Oh. I guess that means she's the one on the left."

The one on the left was a looker, all right: ash-blonde hair down to here, legs up to there, and a figure that roller-coastered from this to that. By contrast, the other captive was Mother Nature's counter-balance on the scales of beauty: she was obviously a computer construct, as no Dreamwalker would choose an avatar that…ahem…plain.

Plain?

On second thought, "plain" was too charitable. I don't know that I'd go so far as to say she was ugly but—

"Whoa!" Daggoth murmured, "That one's got a face that would stop a sundial!"

"So what's the plan?" I whispered.

"We need to get to the center of the camp."

"Yeah? And assuming we live long enough to get there, then what?"

"A variant on your resolution of the Snow White dilemma."

I stared at him. "A Timestop spell?" I started to smile. "Sounds too easy."

"Not really. We still have to get close to the center of the encampment."

That was when the spear point nudged me in the back. We both turned our heads slowly until we could see the Goblin sentries standing behind us.

"No problem," I said, as they gestured for us to rise. "I think we just found our plan."

"No talk! No move hands!" screamed the picket who was covering Daggoth. "You start make magic, you die!"

"No talk!" agreed the other, allowing me to inspect the fine flintcraft of his spearpoint up close. "Move!"

These guys knew the drill for handling potential magic users: if you couldn't speak or move your hands, you couldn't invoke verbal or somatic triggers for casting spells. For the moment we could do nothing but hope that, once inside the camp, one of their comrades might provide us with a momentary distraction. They herded us through the encampment but we were directed toward the tree where the other captives were tied rather than toward the middle of the enclave. Not that it mattered under the present circumstances: our captors had made it clear that any suspicious hand movements would result in a spear enema.

"I need a diversion," I murmured as we got close to our fellow prisoners.

"Don't look at me," Daggoth muttered back. "Gumby, here, is just dying for any excuse."

That little exchange resulted in a forceful, spear-leveraged ankle-sweep that sent us stumbling to the ground. The next thing I knew there were about a half dozen Goblins swarming over us and before you could say "Tempus Frigid" (although I tried and almost succeeded) they had us bound, gagged, and were relieving us of our weapons. The obvious ones, anyway.

I glanced over at Daggoth as they dragged us over to a couple of trees adjacent to the other prisoners. I wasn't going anywhere on my own and the little buggers had used twice as much rope on him. It didn't look too good for either of us. After testing my bonds for slack, I bowed my head, and tried to think.

Until a year or so ago, this would have been no big deal. The Programworlds had been designed to deliver thrills and adventure without the actual discomfort that such activities would have presented in the real world. And if your avatar or dreambody got seriously hurt or even killed, you would just wake up in the suspension tank you started out in and then decide whether to go home or generate a new avatar and return to the "game." But then an anomaly had entered the Program Matrix and virtual reality had become "Effective" Reality.

Some form of terminal biofeedback had made the death of one's avatar just as fatal to one's real body in the suspension tank outside the Matrix, as well. Cephtronics had evacuated all Dreamwalkers from the Matrix so now the only people at risk were authorized troubleshooters, like myself, and occasional REMrunners who infiltrated the Programworlds illegally.

I felt stupid. Being a Bard and having Programmer status hadn't kept me from being taken prisoner by a runty little Goblin with a crude spear. And unless I could come up with some kind of plan, Daggoth and I were doomed to an unpleasant, not to mention permanent, fate at the hands of these bloodthirsty little monsters.

Unfortunately, I couldn't think of anything that didn't involve some slack in my ropes or my gag and I had neither.

"Psst. You sleepin' or thinkin'?"

I raised my head and shot Daggoth a venomous look. Nope, not him: he was still securely gagged.

"So, you got a plan, yet?"

I looked around. The two ladies were bound to a tree some ten feet away. None of the Goblins within earshot seemed to be paying me any attention, either.

"Hey, I'm talkin' to you." The voice was low and gravelly. And close enough to be intimate. "You got some kinda trick up your sleeve? You waitin' ta make your move?"

I shook my head, looking from side to side as I did so.

"Then you're really stuck, right?"

There was a sudden pressure on my left knee, as if an invisible weight had settled there. As I stared at the space above my leg, the air seemed to shimmer and a small creature popped into view.

To call it humanoid would be overly generous. Its oversized head was the most human-looking aspect of the creature and its bushy sideburns and heavy black-framed spectacles nearly kept me from recognizing its true nomenclature.

"An Imp," I said.

Actually, it came out more like "Mn Mmmff" through the gag.

The Imp nodded. "Azimozal, at your service," it stated, executing a formal bow.

I cocked an eyebrow, the best response I could manage under the circumstances.

"We're on the clock, here, so I'll keep it brief. Under the Hell/Sinki Accord we are prohibited from any overt acts of interference in Human affairs—with the exception of areas of transplanar displacement such as graveyards, haunted houses, desecrated churches, evil temples, and such. But the Boss feels that my loosening your ropes is not beyond the pale of an Imp's MO and that if the boys over there were to create a little diversion on the other side of the camp, well—"

I looked across the camp and noticed some furtive movement just beyond the tree line.

Azimozal shrugged what passed for an Imp's shoulders. "—the rest is up to you. Capeesh?"

I nodded.

The Imp hopped down from my knee. "Oh, and one more thing," he stated as he circled around the tree to get at the knots in my ropes. "The Boss says: 'When the time comes, it's a favor for a favor.' Right?"

I nodded again: I was in no position to quibble.

Azimozal went to work and, after a minute or so, the ropes loosened up quite nicely.

"Okay, Sport; stand by for just a moment and we'll start a ruckus on the other side of the clearing." The Imp was starting to fade to a state of transparency even as he hopped back into my field of vision. "The rest is up to you."

Then he was gone.

I looked over at Daggoth, who looked back at me with the same expression of befuddlement that was probably in my eyes at the moment.

There was a sudden commotion at the other end of the encampment.

Three hellish figures burst from the trees and capered and howled at the edge of the clearing. The first looked like a cross between a Human and a vulture, the second resembled a giant toad with teeth and arms, and the third appeared to be a goat-horned dog with an extra pair of arms. All were over six feet in height and were dancing on their hind legs.

Demons.

And unless my eyes were playing tricks, three somewhat familiar denizens of the Lower Planes: Yakku, Ahuizotl, and Sedit. The last time I had laid eyes on these jokers was when Orcus had sent them to kidnap me and haul my butt Down Below. Apparently now the Powers in Hell wanted a favor of some kind, and I liked that a lot less than the implications of our last encounter.

The Goblins weren't any happier to make their acquaintance.

Screaming, howling, gibbering, they ran in circles, some grabbing weapons while others dropped theirs. The misshapen monsters on our side of the bivouac charged toward the three new intruders while their companions who were closest to the "diversion" tried to retreat toward the opposite side of the clearing. There was a massive collision at the center of the camp as Goblins collided like an imploding cesspool.

Throwing aside my loosened bonds, I stood, swept my arms wide, made the appropriate gestures and yelled: "Mmmfff ffmmm!"

Damn, I had forgotten about the gag! I ripped it from my mouth and repeated the Timestop spell, clearly articulating: "Tempus frigid!" this time around.

Time came to a literal standstill for everyone in the clearing, save myself. The three Demons, as well as the Imp, were suddenly nowhere to be seen.

I touched Daggoth, neutralizing the spell's effect on him.

"Don't ask," I said as I tugged down his gag. The Goblins had missed a concealed dagger in my boot and I used that to cut through his bonds. "I don't know why they just suddenly showed up or why they were so damn helpful." I shook my head. "I just don't have a clue. So don't ask."

The sorcerer shook his head. "So help me, I'll never complain about your having friends in low places again."

We retrieved our weapons and personal effects and then attended to the ladies. While I negated their state of stasis, Daggoth sawed through the ropes with his dagger.

"You saved us!" It was the less-than-attractive prisoner who threw her arms around me and kissed my cheek. She smiled as I helped her to her feet and the expression transformed her: now she was just pleasantly homely.

I glanced over at Daggoth who was thoroughly enjoying his role of rescuer. He was so solicitous of his favorite pinup girl's condition that he was practically chafing her wrists.

"Allow me to introduce myself, fair lady," he was gushing. "I am Daggoth the Dark."

She inclined her pretty head. "I am most grateful, Daggoth. You may call me—um—Angela."

"Angela," he repeated, taking her hand and kissing it. "Charmed."

The other woman cleared her throat. "I'm Mick," she said, extending her hand.

"Pleased," stuttered the dark sorcerer, shaking her hand.

Ms. McRae defused the awkward moment by extending her arm to me. "Your assistance, kind sir?" I helped her to her feet while Daggoth watched and simmered. "And your name?"

I bent a little at the waist. We didn't know how many other Goblins might still be out there in the woods, just out of range of the Timestop spell: I wanted to get this party moving.

"Riplakish of Dyrinwall," I answered.

She stared at me. Her eyes began to widen. "Riplakish of Dyrinwall?"

"That's me, accept no substitutes."

Her eyes continued to widen—if we'd been in a Toonworld they would've popped right out of their sockets and reproduced in triplicate. "You're Robert Remmington Ripley?"

I nodded. "The Third."

And then, with no further explanation, the most beautiful woman in the world fainted at my feet.

#

"What are you doing?"

I couldn't turn my head to answer or I'd be up to my eyebrows in Angel/Angela's hip.

"It's called a fireman's carry," Mick answered for me.

"It doesn't look very comfortable," groused Daggoth.

"It isn't," I grumbled back. "She's a full-blooded Human and I'm Halfelven. That means she weighs more than I do."

While this particular Timestop spell was supposed to last at least twelve hours, I wanted to put as much distance between the Goblin encampment and us as possible. The unconscious Angel McRae was proving rather burdensome to my desire for speed.

"I mean it doesn't look very comfortable for her," he said.

"She's unconscious," I wheezed. "Her comfort is not a consideration until she wakes up."

"And then she won't have to be carried," Mick pointed out.

"I still think she'd be more comfortable if you carried her in your arms," he persisted.

"Anytime you want to take over here, you can carry her any damn way that you please."

"You know I've got a bad back—"

"Probably from carrying one too many fair damsels in an improper manner," I puffed.

"Well, at least beautiful women don't faint when they meet me."

"Aw, you're just jealous." I looked at Mick. "Tell us about the Goblins."

She shrugged. "Not much to tell. I was hiking through the Enchanted Forest last night when they jumped me."

"You were traveling with Ms. McRae?" Daggoth wanted to know.

"Who?" she asked sharply.

"Angie," I offered.

"Angela," he corrected.

"Angel," I amended.

"No." She frowned. "She showed up this morning. Practically wandered into the camp before she was captured. Seemed a little dazed. And not very angelic."

I shrugged McRae's unconscious body up a little higher on my shoulder. "No kidding."

"Funny thing," Mick continued, "I was on my way to meet you, Lord Riplakish."

"Don't *you* faint on us," Daggoth muttered.

"Really? Why?" I asked.

"Because you're the Archdruid of Dyrinwall Forest. I want you to apprentice me."

"You want to be Druid?"

"I want to be a Bard!"

"How did you know where to find me?"

"I asked some Wizards down on the coast."

As she spoke, we came up over a hill and spotted our destination down below: the Zombie Mistress' abode.

Yudu the Necromancer lived in a palatial compound of white marble surrounded by well-tended grounds and sculpted shrubbery. Daggoth had once dubbed the overall style "neo-mausoleum and Early Forest Lawn." I had yet to come up with a better description myself.

Instead of the usual Zombie servant, the Necromancer herself answered the door. "You are late!" she scolded in a rich Caribe accent. "De spell, he is nearly done. Come quickly!"

I stumbled through the doorway and Yudu caught sight of my awkward burden. "Abercrombie! Fitch!" she commanded. "Assist the Archdruid!"

Two of the Necromancer's moldering servants shuffled forward from the shadowy alcoves. The one that reached me first looked as if it had died long before I had even been born.

"Abercrombie the Zombie?" I asked as it helped me ease Angel McRae off my aching shoulder.

Its head swung back and forth, sounding like a broken ratchet in the process. "Fitch fetch," it hissed.

The unconscious woman began to stir as Abercrombie shambled up. As they balanced her weight between the two of them, her eyes fluttered open. Her eyes widened as they took in my face and then the—well, "faces"—of Yudu's two long-dead servants. Then she moaned and promptly passed out again.

"Great," muttered Daggoth.

"Dis way!" The Zombie Mistress was hurrying down the hallway and we followed with Abercrombie and Fitch doing their best to bring up the rear with Angel suspended between them.

The hall opened up into a great, circular room. At its center was a raised dais and, upon this were two tables, side by side and connected by a crossbar at the center of each, somewhat like a giant "H" on its back. A body lay upon one of the tables. Cocooned in an ovoid of pearly light, it was hard to distinguish its features until I stepped up to the dais.

It was Natasha Skovoroda's avatar.

Her flesh, clothed only in soft, pulsing light, was unmarked: her wounds had been healed, all scars erased. She might have been sleeping but there was no heartbeat to pulse the veins at wrists and throat, no breath to cause the rise and fall of the sleeper's breast. Her dreambody had been repaired but it was still a corpse.

The Necromancer carried an amphora to the crossbar that connected Natasha's table to the empty one. The vessel was narrow but nearly a foot tall and covered with a riot of hieroglyphs: a Soul jar. She clapped her hands as she stepped back from the table and the ceiling above us, opaque until this moment, became transparent. The evening sky reflected a melange of colors down into the chamber. "Quickly: we must be done before de sun sets!"

Daggoth stepped up to the dais, beside Yudu. Mick and I stepped back as they both flourished their wands. While the Necromancer began a droning, background chant, the Wizard began an incantation in counterpoint.

Slowly Dyantha—Natasha's avatar—rose into the air until she floated nearly a foot above the surface of the stone table. Then, as the evening's light began to dwindle, the light around her body intensified, pulsed, and put out an ectoplasmic tendril toward the urn just three feet away. Slowly yet steadily, the pseudopod of glowing force snaked toward the mystic jar. As it made contact with its rim, the entire vessel began to glow and pulse in rhythm with the nimbus of light that surrounded Dyantha's body. A minute went by. Then two.

At the end of the third minute the chanting stopped and the arcane umbilical cord dissolved but the light continued to encompass Natasha's avatar and the amphora.

The Necromancer turned to the Wizard. "Now, where is de Golem?"

"Golem?" I murmured under my breath. "What's this about a Golem?"

"A Golem is a clay figure animated by magic," Mick whispered. "Sort of the mythological precursor to Frankenstein and Robbie the Robot."

I knew that. I just didn't know anything about this particular ensorcelment and how a Golem figured into the equation.

Yudu looked around the chamber. "You said you would bring de Golem. Where is it? It is time!"

Daggoth reached into the folds of his robe. "I didn't bring it with me; I'm having it delivered." He pulled out a small rectangle of plastic and metal mesh.

"What's that?" Mick whispered as Daggoth opened the mesh cover.

"Subspace communicator," I murmured.

"You're kidding. What's Spaceworld technology doing in Fantasyworld?"

I was more than a little surprised, myself.

There are two types of people in any given Programworld: avatars that embody the projected psyches of real people and computer constructs—artificial people whose personalities are Subprograms of The Machine. It can be difficult telling the difference between "real" people and the AIs but one clue is that the Constructs are programmed to ignore anachronisms that might occur in the program milieu.

So much for my theory that Mick, here, was another computerized spear-carrier in this digital drama.

Which led to the next question: why choose an unattractive dreambody when near-perfection was so readily available?

Before I could think of a tactful way to broach the subject, Daggoth was closing his communications device and slipping it back into his robe. There was a humming sound; a ghostly apparition appeared on the unoccupied table on the dais in a shimmer of glittery, golden motes. "Federation Express," I murmured, "when it has to get there instantaneously." The image focused and then resolved into the solid form of another body.

Or, rather, the same body: now there were two identical Dyanthas lying prone on either side of the H-shaped platform!

"Dis is de Golem?"

Daggoth nodded as he moved around the dais and approached the second body.

"Doesn't look like any Golem I've ever seen," Mick whispered.

And how many Golems have you seen?

The Wizard produced another device from the folds of his robe, a small keypad with a projection at the top. He inserted the stem into the navel of the second body and tapped a sequence of numbers. Lines suddenly appeared in the creamy flesh of the duplicate Dyantha's torso. As he withdrew the device, her abdominal wall parted from her ribcage, swinging up on micro-hinges in the pelvic region.

I began to feel sick.

"Hurry, de sun he is setting!"

"Your turn," Daggoth said, stepping back.

We got a better look at the "Golem's" interior. "An android," Mick observed.

I turned away, looking for some place to sit down.

"Lord Riplakish," said my would-be apprentice, "are you all right?"

"I think I'm going to throw up." I headed for the couch near the door where Fitch and Abercrombie had deposited Angel McRae's unconscious form.

Yudu was chanting now, levitating the urn.

"It's not organic," Mick was following me, trying to explain. "It's a fembot from Spaceworld—fabricated to look like your friend. You don't understand: it's not alive."

She was the one who didn't understand. My sudden malaise had nothing to do with the open-gut surgery being performed on Daggoth's hi-tech "Golem." It was the sunset that was triggering this sudden turn of events.

On my last incursion in the Matrix, sunset had meant two things: Misty Dawn—

The ghost of the slain Wood Nymph suddenly faded into view. "My Lord Riplakish!" she exclaimed. "What are y—" Her transparent form rippled like water caught in a riptide. She staggered backwards and flickered. And disappeared.

—and my own physical transformation!

Even now I could feel my flesh crawling over my bones like a herd of monkeys on a jungle gym. Mick was backing away, her eyes widening the way Angel's had when she had first heard my name. I couldn't expect any immediate help from Daggoth or Yudu—they were still struggling to complete whatever the hell it was they were doing before it was too late although for what nobody had thought to explain to me—*and damn, this really HURT!*

The Zombies just stood there, observing me with their shriveled heads cocked at a comical angle. To make matters worse, the slumbering Angel/a was stirring again.

The pain began to recede. Within less than a minute I was able to breathe, again. I put my hand to my chest as I took in a deep breath…

Then I put both hands to my chest. There was the all-too-familiar swell of bosom beneath my tunic.

"Nooo!" I moaned.

The android version of Natasha's avatar suddenly sat up on the table. *"My Lord Riplakish!"* it said in Misty Dawn's voice, *"whatever has happened to me?"*

"Nicole!" Angel McRae was awake and reaching for me. "Nicole, it's me: Dr. Westbrook! I had this horrible dream that you were dead and Bob Ripley had taken your place!"

I looked at everyone and everyone looked at me.

"Nicole," Dagny's fashion-model avatar crooned, "say something!"

"Aw *shit!"* I said.

PART II

ROBO-NYMPH

This is the female form,
A divine nimbus exhales from it from head to foot,
It attracts with fierce undeniable attraction

—Walt Whitman,
I Sing The Body Electric—

ONE

"I need something to drink." It was the third time I'd said it in as many minutes.

We sat at the end of the dining table in the great hall of the Zombie Mistress's manor: Daggoth on my right at the table's end, trying to make sense of what had just transpired, and Mick occupying the chair directly across from me. Yudu had ordered one of her less-desiccated domestics to escort Angela/Dr. Westbrook to a guest chamber where she could have a little time to calm down while she went off to determine the integrity of the newly ensorcelled soul jar.

"Bob has a lot of traveling to do and a soul jar is not light," Daggoth explained, defying my best efforts to tune him out.

"So you came up with the idea of using a Golem to serve as sort of a humanoid pack mule," Mick concluded.

Daggoth nodded.

I motioned to a Zombie that looked more like a skeleton dipped in beef stew. "Hey, Shambles; you got any alcohol in this joint? Preferably something that isn't being used as a preservative?"

The Zombie's head creaked around in a one hundred and eighty-degree arc and regarded me with a baleful stare. A centipede making a brief appearance in Gruesome's left eye socket enhanced the effect. "Fitch fetch," it hissed.

"Yeah, you do that. Go fetch me something to drink. And make it a double," I called as it shuffled out of the room.

"Strength to carry, power to protect," Daggoth continued. "But clay Golems are traditionally slow and not very bright. I figured I could do better by enhancing the basic concept."

My mouth was dry so I reached for the teapot. "So you obtained an android from the Spaceworld program. But why make it look like Natasha Skovoroda's avatar?" The teapot was full and I nearly spilled its contents before I braced my wrist with my left hand. It wasn't that Nicole Doucet's arms lacked the proper strength: my reflexes were still operating on the basis of my own, former musculature and I was suddenly finding that I couldn't take such simple things for granted.

"Natasha Skovoroda?" Mick's eyes suddenly widened. "Not the Natasha Skovoroda who's marrying the President of the Russian Federation?"

I nodded, raising the cup to my lips.

Her eyes got wider. "And you're *the* Robert Ripley—the one who died in that plane crash!" She looked me up and down. "Or should I call you Roberta?"

I ignored that and took a sip. "Actually, I'm not dead…" I nodded toward Daggoth the Dark, "…but he is."

She turned to stare at him.

The avatar of Cephtronics' former Chief of Programming shrugged his shoulders. "Actually, I've only died once. Bob, on the other hand—"

"You're dissembling," I snapped. "Answer the question: why cosmeticize an android to resemble Natasha?"

Daggoth shrugged again. "Why not? I figured it would make things simpler all around if it looked Human. And when you get to Abydos, it might help in finding Ms. Skovoroda's shade."

"Abydos?" Mick wanted to know.

"The City of the Dead," I illuminated.

"One of the outer suburbs of Hell," Daggoth elaborated.

"Why?" she pursued. "Why would anyone want to go to the City of the Dead?"

Daggoth and I looked at each other. "I don't know, but—" I began.

"—everyone else is just dying to get there," we finished together.

Mick made a face. "What is this? Medieval vaudeville?" She turned her full attention on Daggoth. "Seriously."

"If you're a REMrunner—" Daggoth began.

"And we must assume that you are in light of this conversation," I interjected.

"—then you must know that the Dreamworlds have been closed off to the public due to an anomaly that includes unfiltered—possibly even amplified—biofeedback. In other words, whatever happens to your dreambody in this computer-generated universe will happen to your physical, actual self in the so-called real world." He leaned back in his chair. "Which brings me to this most precipitous point, madam: get *out!*"

"Excuse me?" She was taken aback.

"The point should be obvious," I said. "Get out while you're still alive."

"This pseudo-medieval fantasyworld was designed to be rough and dangerous," Daggoth continued. "The element of danger gave the original games their element of spice. And since only the avatar-projection was affected, Dreamwalkers could taste injury and death with equanimity, knowing that they would wake up, safe and sound, in their own body."

"But the Anomaly has changed all of that." I leaned forward and shook my teacup at her. "This is no longer a Gameworld. The physics of this computer-generated universe are applied to your real body, back in the suspension tank, with every move you make, every chance you take."

"So, if I fall off my horse in here," she said, "there's a good chance someone could find my body with a broken neck back home."

I nodded.

"In here, horses are the least of your worries," Daggoth said. "Horses can't pull a bow or swing a sword or cast a magic spell. Horses won't abduct you or put you on the rack or sell you into slavery. Horses won't think of you as a meal—"

I interrupted: "What he's trying to say is that there are a lot of creatures who would. And humans, for all their malevolent intents and unhealthy agendas, are not even at the top of the food chain here."

"So why are you two still here?" she wanted to know.

"I'm already dead in the outside world," Daggoth answered. "I escaped into the Dreamworlds' Matrix just before my real body terminated. There's no going back for me. As for him," he gestured at me, "Bob's got a death wish."

"I have a job to do," I said. "And as soon as it's done, I'm getting out of here just as fast as I can."

"I see," she mused. "And that job involves Natasha Skovoroda, a soul jar, and a trip to the City of the Dead. No, don't tell me! I like puzzles." She ruminated a moment. "If the negative aspects of biofeedback are unfiltered or even enhanced…then the positive aspects must come into play as well…which is why you're going to this Abydos! Natasha Skovoroda is dead, isn't she?"

Daggoth and I looked at each other.

"Don't stonewall me!" She leaned across the table. "I'm a REMrunner: I'm here illegally, who'm I gonna tell? Besides, I have no intention of leaving yet."

"She's clinically dead," I confirmed. "Her avatar was killed during our last excursion into the Fantasyworld Program. Her body is being maintained in the suspension tank's pseudo-womb on life support. The bio-support systems keep her heart beating, her lungs breathing, maintain her blood chemistry—for all intents and purposes, her body is fully functional." I shook my head. "But her EEG is as flat as an open cask of Goblin ale."

"The prognosis is not hopeful," Daggoth continued. "Nothing in PET or SPECT tomography scans indicate any changes in cerebral blood flow. SQUID scans show a complete absence of magnetic field activity. They all confirm the initial EEG findings: there's nothing there."

"Which is a part of what gives me hope," I argued. "Even so-called 'brain-dead' patients display some electrical activity–a little background noise, some static bursts. Natasha's electro-encephalogram reads like her brain is off-line, disconnected—"

"And you're gonna go to Program Hell to grab her ghostfile...to resurrect her avatar...to try to jump-start her brain waves in the real world!" A quick study, this one.

"Crudely put—but a succinct approximation of the plan," Daggoth affirmed.

"So what went wrong in there?" she asked, jerking a thumb in the direction of the circular antechamber.

"Ah. You are referring to Misty Dawn." I spooned some of the grounds out of my teacup. "She was a Hamadryad. A Wood Nymph."

"Was?"

"I made her mortal and she was murdered by a Goblin ambush that was meant for me." It still hurt to talk about it.

"I guess we forgot about the daily appearance of her ghost at sunset," Daggoth continued. "She evidently got caught in the thaumaturgic cross-rip of the binding spell."

"But she didn't get pulled into Natasha's soul jar?"

Yudu entered the room, unwinding her white samite turban. "I have run every thaumaturgic test I can think of. De soul jar remains empty. It should be able to receive the essence of Tasha Skovoroda if you can find her shade in the Necropolis."

A chime sounded.

"Ah," said the Zombie Mistress, "de doorbell."

"Doorbell?" I echoed.

"De knocker on de front door is ensorcelled to sound a chime in whatever room I happen to be in." She leaned across the table and lifted a small tenting of linen to reveal a crystal ball. Daggoth and I looked at each other and eyed our respective escape routes beneath the dining table. Yudu activated the enchanted glass with a wave of her hand.

An image formed in the orb: two men in the armor and livery of the Calabastor City Watch, standing outside the front entrance to the tower. The captain was standing by the right door, clutching a sealed scroll in one gloved fist, the sergeant stood back a bit, holding the reins of two draft horses harnessed to a wagon.

"Yes?" she inquired sweetly.

Both men jumped at the sound of her voice. The captain recovered first. "Captain Jenks of the Horse Marines," he announced, "here to see the dread Necromancer Yudu Yuhudi on behalf of the Lord Mayor of Calabastor."

"Do come in, Captain," she said. And waved her hand again. I did not need to look to know that the great oaken doors were slowly swinging open of their own accord.

"Smedley," squeaked the captain, "you stay here and mind the wagon." Sergeant Smedley did not require further convincing. He backed himself and the horses up another ten feet from the opening portal.

"Fitch," she said to her undead domestic as he re-entered the room, bearing a glass on a tray, "please show our visitor into the dining hall."

"Fitch fetch," it hissed, setting the tray down before me with a careless thump.

"Ah, you silver-tongued devil, you," I said, reaching for my long-awaited balm. "Just can't resist showing off your vociferous vocabulary at every opportunity, can you?" As I brought the crystal tumbler close to my lips, something plopped into my drink. I stared into its amber depths as Fitch's lately departed centipede sank to the bottom of my glass, kicking its hundred little legs in double paroxysms of alcoholic ecstasy and its death throes.

"And what about you?"

I looked up and refocused on Mick. "What? What about me?"

"How come you're a female now?"

"I like variety," I growled, turning my attention back to the curled-up centipede at the bottom of my glass.

"He's on a three-day gender-bender." Daggoth joined me in considering the drowned centipede. "Pretend it's Mescal," he offered helpfully.

I slammed the glass down on the table in disgust.

"Or maybe a 'zombie'?" Mick added.

I smiled, in spite of myself.

"A little decorum, if you please," Yudu admonished. "We're about to be visited by Captain Jenks of the Horse Marines."

"Who feeds his horse on corn and beans?" Mick asked.

I nodded: "And courts young ladies in their teens."

"Though a captain in the army!" the two of us chorused, bursting into laughter as Yudu and Daggoth stared at us as if we had lost our minds.

"Referent?" Mick asked as she caught her breath.

I nodded. "The computer cross references many indices in creating its milieus and peopling it. Since the Anomaly set in, some of the recombinant references have gotten a bit bizarre."

"I get the feeling that this is only a mild example."

"It is. Now, *go home!*"

"Excuse me?" squeaked a timorous voice. Fitch had arrived with a visibly nervous Captain Jenks in tow.

#

The Zombie Mistress tried to put the Captain at ease and introductions commenced. Sending Fitch out of the room seemed to help. By the time Daggoth introduced me to Jenks as Mademoiselle Doucet he was more relaxed than I was.

His kissing the back of my hand decidedly shifted the balance of unease.

"And to what," the Zombie Mistress inquired after we were all seated, "do we owe the pleasure of your company this evening, Captain?"

"I come, bearing an entreaty for aid and assistance from the Lord Mayor of Calabastor, milady." He extended the scroll.

While Yudu was perusing its content, Jenks gave a nodding bow to Cephtronics' Former Chief of Programming. "Once again, Lord Wizard, on behalf of the Royal Guard, we give thee thanks for thy help in dispelling the curse that besieged Castle Charming."

"Glad to have been of assistance. I trust everyone has fully recovered?"

The captain smirked. "Everything except their composure. A reward has been posted for Riplakish of Dyrinwall."

I almost fell out of my chair. "Excuse me?"

"I'm surprised your men haven't apprehended that scoundrel yet." Daggoth turned to grin at me. "I suspect he is very unpopular at court right now."

"God's truth, milady!" The captain reached over and patted my hand. "Should this rogue Sorcerer show his face around Calabastor again, it shall go hard for him!"

"Really?" I said, recovering. "I should think the Archdruid of Dyrinwall Forrest would be a difficult man to gainsay."

Jenks looked entirely too smug for my tastes. And he still had a hold of my hand. "To be sure, m'dear, this 'Bard' hath some reputation about the countryside, but we are recruiting additional aid from those best schooled in the arts to bind him."

I didn't like the sound of that.

"The captain," Daggoth elaborated with far too much good humor, "came around last week to ask for my assistance in the rascal's apprehension."

"A pity thou'rt occupied with…'research'," Jenks returned sourly.

Daggoth shrugged. "The timing is inauspicious."

"It is known that this Riplakish is a friend of yours."

"Actually, Captain, in some respects, you are closer to him than I am."

Before the man could think of an intelligible response, the Zombie Mistress set aside the parchment and said: "You seek a vile criminal; a most black-hearted fiend! What would you have me do?"

"Hey!"

Yudu shot me a look. "Anuhder black-hearted fiend," she said *sotto voce.*

Jenks looked even more flustered, now. "We have made a thorough investigation, milady, but we are frankly stumped. We thought that—well—if you could talk to a couple of the witnesses for us, you might get a description of the murderer." His growing nervousness allowed me to finally retrieve my hand. "We brought them along, just in case."

"I don' unnerstan'. Why don' you talk to dem, yourself?"

"Because they're dead, milady. These witnesses—they are also the victims."

#

Homicides were not uncommon in Calabastor. Like any large medieval metropolis, it had a Thieves' Guild, an Assassins' Guild, and a multitude of criminal activities that ranged from a little petty larceny to murder most foul.

The City Watch lacked the manpower and resources, not to mention the inclination, to solve a tenth of them. Unless the crime involved the nobility at one end or the other, that is. And then the pressure was on to either solve the crime or cover it up completely.

Jenks and his men had become pretty sanguine about the stiffs they encountered on a day-to-day basis. Until now, that is. Seven of Calabastor's "ladies of the evening" had been murdered in the past three months. And while I suspected that the victims had a great number of acquaintances on the City Watch, Jenks had a more compelling reason to apprehend the culprit.

This was the first time the City Watch had come up against a serial killer.

And not *just* a serial killer, but one with an evolving MO.

When the first couple of bodies turned up, the Watch was baffled by the brutality of the murders. Cephtronics had programmed a medieval fantasyworld with violence as a fact of life but, mindful of the tourist trade, the board of directors had set guidelines for "sanitizing" the majority of it. Until the arrival of the "Slattern Slasher," sadistic cruelty had been confined to the dungeons of evil warlords and the pain pits of Hobgoblin demesnes. The back alleys of Calabastor were accustomed to a weekly catalog of corpses but when one of the city guards found an alleyway turned dead-end abattoir, the city reeled in shock. Even the most black-hearted fiends understood that there were, of course, rules.

So, when the second murder-slash-atrocity turned up, the hardened veterans of the nightwatch took to traveling in pairs and the Assassins Guild offered both a reward and their pro bono services in hunting down this monster.

The third body was even more shocking, though initially less gruesome: the woman's face had been savaged while her body appeared to be relatively untouched. In fact, there was an uncharacteristic lack of blood splatter at the scene, leading the more astute to speculate that a different killer was responsible this time.

That theory disappeared when the fourth and fifth bodies appeared. Not only had the Beast of 'Bastor reacquired his artistic flair with a knife, he had also taken the process one step further.

And he had become more selective in regard to his victims.

"In fact, they woulda all been just about your height," Jenks was telling me as we walked to the front door, "and your—um—build. Even the hair was said to be just about the same color and length!"

"Similar facial features?" I asked

He put out an arm at the door to block my passage. "Er—we cannot be sure, Mademoiselle. Their faces have been…"

"Have been what, Captain?"

"Please, Mademoiselle, call me Archibald."

I fluttered my eyelashes at him—not as easy a gesture as one might suppose before attempting it. "All right, Archibald."

"May I call you Nicole?"

I dropped the coy pose. "I'll call you Archie and you call me Nick; what's wrong with their faces?"
"It's not something you should worry your pretty little head about, Ni—my lady. In fact, I would rather you remain inside. It is not a sight for anyone of delicate sensibilities."

I peeled his fingers away from the doorjamb like so many delicate sensibilities. "I'm a big girl, Archie. You have no idea how big."

Daggoth, Mick, and the Zombie Mistress had closed the distance behind us. Holding torches aloft and bringing up the rear were Fitch and Abercrombie. As Zombies tend to keep walking until they meet with an immovable object, it was no longer feasible to bottleneck at the door. Jenks acquiesced with one more protestation that this wasn't "something a pretty young lady like myself should be seeing" and then hurried after me.

Smedley snapped to attention as we approached the wagon.

"At ease, Sergeant, and move that tarp aside."

The noncom led the parade to the rear of the wagon and dropped the tailgate. He folded the tarpaulin back and we all moved in to take a look.

"Not much left of them," I observed after a long pause.

As a matter of fact there wasn't anything left of the two bodies: the wagon bed was empty.

"Sergeant Smedley!"

"I don't unnerstand, Cap'n!"

"Where are they?" he bellowed.

"They was right 'ere just ten minutes ago! Sah!"

"Are you certain of that, Sergeant?"

"We checked 'em just afore you went inside! Remember, sah? You said: 'my-oh-my, what a waste that one is.' And then you said: 'look at the size of—'"

"Belay that!" Jenks put himself right in the sergeant's face. "Did you leave the wagon at any time while I was inside? Or did you just fall asleep? While on duty? *Corporal?*"

Smedley looked ashen even in the flickering torchlight. "Cap'n, I swear! I was here alla time. Din't move, din't snooze, no sah! Din't hear or see nothin', either!"

"We're talking dead bodies, here," roared the captain. "They just didn't get up and walk off!"

Actually, as we would eventually find out the hard way, they had done just that very thing.

TWO

As perturbed as Jenks was with Smedley over the loss of his victims-*cum*-witnesses, he was even more unhappy with our response when we discovered that Smedley had been the first to stumble over the most recent crime scene. We eventually had to make the captain go sit in the corner while we made his noncom recount the details for the third time.

"Can you remember anything else?" Daggoth asked in exasperation as the story wound down to its third conclusion.

"No sah. That's about it, sah." In point of fact, Smedley remembered less with each telling of the tale, not more, hence the wizard's fit of pique.

"It would probably be best," Mick surmised, "if you visited the crime scene yourselves."

"Doubtful," I mused, "by now."

Daggoth nodded. "Probably a good dozen or two people have tramped through it by now."

"More like a hunnert," Jenks offered from the corner where Abercrombie was attempting to interest the captain in a game of knucklebones. "Coulda sold tickets when word got out."

That's what I was afraid of. "We really need to be the first on the scene if we're going to get any usable clues." I looked at the Zombie Mistress. "Any chance of coming up with some sort of spell—"

"Of what? Divination? Someting to tell you when and where de nex muder will be?" She shook her head sadly. "Don' you tink I would den be able to tell who is doing dese terrible tings? Don' you tink dat kind of power would enable me to stop dis beast?"

I spread my hands. "Just looking for a place to start looking."

"A medieval murder mystery!" Mick clapped her hands. "This just gets better and better!"

"Better?" I stared at her. "And *better?*"

"Well—" Our REMrunner was suddenly unsure. "—it's all part of the game, isn't it?"

I was suddenly tired. "The fact that you have a body to return to outside of the Matrix may blind you to the fact that, for most of the inhabitants of Fantasyworld, the full compass of their lives begins and ends here. When you hear the term 'artificial intelligence,' your focus is on the word 'artificial.' But 'intelligence' is the truer definition of their existence. Along with 'hope' and 'fear' and 'love.' They are just as real unto themselves as you are in your own frame of reference. For those victims—and those being stalked even as we speak—this is very much *not* a game."

She turned back to Daggoth. "I'm sorry…I wasn't thinking."

He made a dismissive wave. "Although I may bear closer kinship to the AIs within the program now, I must quibble with Bob—" he glanced at Jenks and Smedley "—er *Nicole*—on one point." He looked at me. "While I have come 'round to your view of the digital soul made flesh, I still can't help but feel that Natasha's rescue still takes precedence." He held up his hand. "I know you, er—Nicky. You're already fretting that more streetwalkers are gonna die if we're off trying to resurrect somebody who is already dead. The numbers on both sides of the equation don't balance and that bothers you…"

I nodded: he did know me too well.

"…but try to keep a larger perspective. Natasha Skovoroda is a True Spirit—just as are you and, once, was I. We can't afford the luxury of running about playing Heracles Poirot while we still have a psychefile to retrieve."

I couldn't help brooding. "I don't actually disagree. But it bothers me to turn our backs on multiple potential victims to marshal our forces to save just one—True Spirit or no."

"The needs of the one outweigh the needs of the many," Mick quoted.

Daggoth grunted. "Plato's *Republic.*"

I shook my head. "Aristotle. *Sophistical Refutations.*"

She shook her head in turn. "Kirk. *The Search For Spock.*"

"Is you folk done wid me?" Smedley wanted to know.

An idea suddenly occurred to me. "Not necessarily, Sergeant…."

#

Sergeant Smedley sat in a chair in the center of the room. His eyes, normally wide with befuddled apprehension now drooped as a result of the hypnotic trance I had induced with a candle flame and a polished piece of crystal.

"Saw sumpin like this oncet," Captain Jenks observed, suspicion and disapproval playing tug-o-war in his voice. "Was a Mindflayer, it was. Got its tentacles under Lieutenant Neuman's helm for just one second afore we bashed it. Poor Alfred was never the same after. Just walked around wi' that blank look an' silly, gap-toothed grin. Used to ask 'im: 'What's it all about, Alfie?' Poor bastid din't have a clue."

"Smedley's fine," I said. "He's just been—um—mesmerized."

"Mezmer-whiched?"

"Entranced," Daggoth offered. He turned back to me. "Where did you learn hypnosis?"

"From Dr. Westbrook. First-hand. How'm I doing?"

"So far, so good."

"Now what?" Mick wanted to know.

"Even the most observant witnesses," I explained, "can fail in recalling specific details—details that are filed away in their subconscious but forgotten at the conscious level. Since the good sergeant here is a bit hazy on the details—"

"Hazy?" Daggoth grumped. "More like a London fogbank."

"—I thought hypnosis might be helpful in pulling out those mental files."

"And going through his drawers!" Mick finished enthusiastically.

"Well, er, not exactly the phrase I would choose but, in principle, yes."

Daggoth was suddenly thoughtful. "Essentially, you're accessing the Smedley-unit's document files in his memory folder. The problem may still lie in the interface."

"Meaning?"

"Even if he remembers more details, we're still stuck with his interpretation of what he remembers. His memory may be enhanced but it's still going to be filtered through the good sergeant's ability to translate thought into precise language."

Mick looked puzzled. "I don't understand."

"Smedley," I said suddenly. "What sort of horse does your captain ride?"

"Horse, sah?" he answered dreamily. "I dunno what you mean."

"What kind of horse does Captain Jenks ride? What breed?"

"Like is it a boy or girl? Hard to say since it got its thingies cut off. Used to be a boy, I guess."

"Smedley, what color is it?"

"Several sorts, sah. White and brown wi' a little bit a red thrown in…."

"So it's a Pinto?"

"A pint o' what, sah?"

"Never mind." I turned to Mick. "The problem is Smedley can recall details under hypnosis but he is still limited in his context of understanding and explaining what he is able to recall."

"But there may be a way around those limitations," Daggoth said. "I've never tried this before but…." He turned to Yudu. "I need some mascara."

She looked puzzled.

"Kohl," Mick suggested. "He needs some kohl."

"And an applicator. A small stick or brush," Daggoth added.

While the Zombie Mistress stepped out of the room I looked at the sorcerer. "Don't tell me this cross-dressing thing is contagious?"

"I need it for the spell."

"What spell? The *glamour* of eye enhancement?"

"In a manner of speaking. Give me a hand, here." Standing up, he directed us to move our chairs directly opposite to the chair holding Sergeant Smedley's entranced form. He positioned my chair in the middle with an empty chair for the Zombie Mistress to my right and Mick to my left.

"Is this dangerous?" I asked.

"Dangerous? What do you care? You laugh in the face of danger!"

"I never laugh in the face of danger; that just pisses it off. I do confess to the occasional smirk when danger is looking the other way. But my concern here," I jerked my head toward Mick, "is involving a civilian in anything experimental."

Yudu returned with a tiny jar of kohl and a tiny stick that looked like a well-chewed toothpick. "What are we doing?" she asked as he took the items and motioned her into the empty chair.

"You three are going to take a little stroll down memory lane," he said, dipping the stick into the kohl and dabbing it onto my forehead just above the bridge of my nose. "Specifically, Sergeant Smedley's memory lane. You're going to astrally project into the good sergeant's memory folder where you can review the crime scene firsthand." He turned from me and began drawing a triangle at the center of the Zombie Mistress's forehead.

"Hmmmm. Weird," I said, "but probably workable." I looked at Yudu. "Handy to have a Necromancer along to examine the corpse. I assume you're game, even though Mr. Rudeness here hasn't even deigned to ask if you want to be a part of this."

She couldn't nod as he was painting an eye inside the triangle on her face. "Anyting I can do to help stop de killings." "But, even assuming it's not dangerous, why do we need Mickey, here?"

"Mick," she corrected with a growl.

"You never know what a fresh pair of eyes may notice, given your jaded status. And I'm also hoping that a close-up look at some Matrix mayhem may convince her to leave the game posthaste." He moved over and gave her a set of eye-in-the-triangle symbols to match ours and then turned to work on Smedley.

"Here now!" Jenks protested as Daggoth sketched a more intricate glyph-set in the middle of his noncom's forehead while humming *Deep Inside Of You*—an old turn-of-the-century song by some group whose name escaped me for the moment. "You're defacing a member of the Nightwatch! I should run the lot of you in!"

"Kaptin," Yudu's voice was soft but carried an undercurrent of command, "you have come, asking for help, and we are attempting to give it to you. It would behoove you to sit quietly and allow us our methods—no matter how opaque dey may seem to a man of direct action such as yourself."

The Captain was not much mollified so I turned to the Necromancer and said, "You realize that the captain is unaccustomed to just sitting around. He is a great soldier and rumor has it that he is quite the lover, as well."

Mick barely repressed a snort. "That's right. He courts young ladies in their teens."

"Though a captain in the army," I said. "It might help the captain pass the time more pleasurably if he had more appropriate company."

Abercrombie swiveled his head to look at me and, even though there was very little face left to interpret, I could swear he was wearing a wounded expression.

"Not that Abercrombie and Fitch aren't all one could ask for in class and sophistication," I continued, "but, given the captain's reputation as a charmer of the fairer sex, I would think he might find more stimulating fare upstairs."

"Upstairs?" Yudu looked puzzled.

"Your chambermaid?" I prompted.

"Lucretia?" She looked puzzled. "But she's—"

"Probably lonely," I insisted. "As I recall she really liked the boys. Probably a little too much."

Yudu's expression showed that she still wasn't on board. "But that was before—"

"—she came to work for you," I continued. "I'll bet she doesn't get out much anymore."

"Of course not, now that she's—"

"Got all that dusting to do upstairs. This is such a large place," I observed. "So many rooms."

"But—"

"I was just thinking that the captain would be less fidgety with feminine companionship," I explained. "After all, she had just turned sixteen the night she—ah—entered your employ. And that was only a year or so ago, right?"

"Dammitall!" Jenks fussed. "Smedley and I *must* be getting *back*! I must really insist—"

"Abercrombie, Fitch," the Zombie Mistress called as the captain got up and started toward us. "Please escort our guest upstairs and introduce him to Lucretia."

Abercrombie immediately caught Jenks by his right arm. By the time Fitch crossed the room, getting a hold of the captain's other arm presented a little more of a challenge. "Damn you, Smedley!" he yelled, jerking this way and that, and windmilling his free arm about, "wake up! Give me a hand, man!"

"Sit still, Sergeant," I commanded in soothing tones. "Captain Jenks is just excited about meeting the young lady who works upstairs."

"I will not be manhandled!" he shouted. "Get your hands off me you damn, dirty corpse!" Fitch continued to grab at his free arm though it was increasingly obvious that that they were operating in two different time zones and Jenks was more likely to "Spring forward" than to "Fall back."

Daggoth finished putting the sigil on Smedley's face and sat back. "I can't spellcast with all this going on."

"That does it." I stood, pushing my sleeves back up and onto my pitifully slender biceps. "I'm gonna open a big ol' iron-ration of whupass…."

But I only had time to take two steps before the captain of Calabastor's Nightwatch stopped struggling and fell silent. Even so, it took Fitch more than a moment to finally get a grip on the now motionless appendage.

We followed Jenks' gaze from his upturned face to the second-floor balcony in the main hall. There, at the top of the stairs, stood a vision wrapped in a white linen shift.

Lucretia was still a striking sixteen-year-old. Her long, dark hair was pulled back from her face for utilitarian reasons but it also allowed her fine and delicate features to be on full display. The full, pouting lips; the wide, cornflower blue eyes; the perfect symmetry of her face, had not lost their effectiveness in drawing the attention of every male in the room. Even Smedley raised his drowsy gaze to the chambermaid's unblemished countenance.

But where her perfect features had once driven the boys to distraction with a saucy curl of her lip or a naughty wink of her eye, she now evinced a serenity of expression that suggested a maturity and poise beyond her years. For a moment I felt a stab of jealousy. Jealousy for her beauty, her youth, her perfection of poise…

Lucretia spoke softly, slowly. "Captain…Jenks?"

And then I remembered who I really was.

"I…have heard…of you."

And what she really was.

The Zombie Mistress waved Fitch and Abercrombie back so that the captain was suddenly free to execute a bow. "At your service mademoiselle."

"Lucretia, would you be so good as to show de captain around de grounds for an hour or so?"

She executed a slow curtsey and then began an unhurried descent of the staircase. As Jenks went to offer her his arm, Yudu turned to the two Zombies. "Follow dem at a discreet distance and don' let tings get out of hand."

Mick sidled over to me and whispered, "Do you think this is a good idea?"

I looked at her and arched an eyebrow.

"I mean, Zombies as chaperones. You know the captain's reputation: if anything happens while we're occupied with the spell—"

"It will serve him right." I took her elbow and guided her back to her chair. "The sooner begun, the sooner we're done."

The Zombie Mistress sat beside me and, as we joined hands, I could hear Jenks' voice disappearing out the main door with some comment about how cold the poor dear's hand seemed to be and could he warm it…?

The incantation was unfamiliar.

Not just because Daggoth was splicing portions of several different spells together but also because he was extending the hypnotic state that currently enveloped Smedley's consciousness to encompass our state of awareness, as well. The words droned on and my peripheral vision became completely blurred. Per the sorcerer's instructions, I continued to stare at the "third eye" glyphs that Daggoth had painted on the sergeant's forehead. The painted eye, itself, seemed to grow more distinctive even as everything around it seemed to haze out of existence.

Then it winked at me.

I blinked in surprise.

And found myself in an alleyway.

Smedley was gone. The room was gone. Everyone was gone.

Even I was gone!

I seemed to have no corporeal existence. There was nothing but the existence of wood, stone, and mortared walls enclosing a darkened and narrow passageway.

I looked up. Framed by overhanging roofs and cross-bracing beams were strips of night sky. Any stars that might have been visible were washed out by ambient torchlight. I looked down. The packed earthen floor was dark but still visible. The walls to either side trembled and shook: an optical illusion from the flickering light that illumed it.

A torch was giving light, here, but I could no more see it than I could see myself. "Smedley," I said. "It's your torch that's providing the illumination but I can no more see it than I can you."

"I can't see him either," said Mick's voice.

"Nor can I," added the Zombie Mistress.

"Where are you?" I asked.

"Here," answered Yudu's disembodied voice.

"I can't see you, either," Mick's voice added.

"De spell only makes visible what de sergeant observed at de scene of de crime. Since he probably took no notice, conscious or unconscious, of de torch or any portion of his own anatomy, de spell probably edits it out."

"So, why is he just standing here?" I wanted to know.

"Perhaps the power to move forward or backward in the memoryfile lies with us, now," Mick suggested. "Like using the search/scan button on a Dreamfile remote."

"So let's try moving down the alley." I started forward. The area of flickering illumination—fading at the six to seven foot distance, front and back, moved with me. Or us, though I couldn't see where anyone else was walking.

There was the sound of a gagging moan and I nearly stumbled. "Yudu? Mick? Are you all right?"

"It wasn't me," Mick whispered, practically in my ear.

"It is from de memory! It must be de victim!"

As we rushed ahead toward the sound at the alley's end I wondered if we were experiencing the same speedy charge the little sergeant had made. Or if Smedley had approached more cautiously and we were pushing the fast-forward button on his memory playback. "Whoa, whoa, slow down!" I said. "Stop! Stop!"

"What?"

"De victim—"

"Is already dead," I reminded. "We can't save her. This is a memoryfile. The only difference we can make by rushing through it is in missing any clues that might help us catch this fiend before he strikes again. Let's take this slow and easy. Eyes, ears, nose…touch. Use all of your senses. Report anything strange, no matter how insignificant."

I started to move again but Mick said: "I smell something strange."

I stopped and sniffed. My sense of smell was never that great but I tasted a hint of copper on my tongue.

"Blood," Yudu decided. "With a hint of bile."

"I know what blood smells like. And I can really smell it now! And there's something else…other stuff. I don't know. Bile would be like stomach acid? Hmmm…maybe…."

I was getting the blood, now, but nothing else. Like I said, my nose wasn't as sensitive as some, which could be a blessing under certain circumstances. Like escaping through sewers or stumbling upon Goblin encampments.

"…this is a familiar scent," Mick continued. "I should know this…it's right on the tip of my tongue…"

"Smedley never mentioned any particular odors, as I recall."

"I take it you don't smell it?" There was an undertone of challenge in Mick's voice.

"I'm only pointing out that this is precisely why we're doing this spell. Smedley never mentioned any distinctive smells in his accounts and I probably wouldn't have thought to ask the question after he was under hypnosis."

"And it is a good ting you have come along. I can smell de blood and de bodily essences of death—such is my business. But my nose is too attuned to dose tings and cannot tell what it is you are scenting."

"Down."

"Down?"

"It's coming up from the ground," Mick said.

I got down on my noncorporeal hands and knees. The source of our illumination did not descend with us. While I could not consider any areas that had not passed through Smedley's range of vision, I could effectively enlarge portions of the visual record by moving closer to it. Fortunately our noncorporeal forms were no impediment to our light source.

"Vinegar!"

"Vinegar?" I asked.

"I think—yes! I'm pretty sure."

"And blood," Yudu added. "And bile. Very strong."

Although the earth was dark and the torchlight inconsistent, it was possible to make out a trail of droplets, moist and pungent in the hard dryness of the ground.

"Let's go back," I suggested. And we reversed the memoryflow, creeping on hands and knees, back to the mouth of the alleyway where it opened on to a side street near a saloon. The droplets suddenly became more widely spaced and indistinct, disappearing some thirty feet away near the wall of a warehouse. We looked around but, if there were other pertinent clues, we couldn't sort them out.

"The other way, now." And we returned to the alley and followed the trail through two switchbacks, picking up two more clues in the process.

First, the traces of vinegar, blood, and bile were running up the walls on the outside of the turns, a good six to ten inches or so.

Second, although there were traces of a wide variety of footprints, the most recent would seem to belong to a woman or a small man going barefoot. And while the spacing and signs of impact suggested that our victim was running—presumably away from her assailant—I saw no other tracks evincing a matching time frame for the crime. It looked as if she had been running from her own shadow.

Then we were at the dead end. Double dead end: three walls boxed us in with only the passage behind us permitting any exit and the body of a dead harlot on the ground.

"Funny," I said, though I felt anything but; "but Smedley's account made it sound far more gruesome than this. There's hardly any blood."

She lay on her side, her back toward us, a slight tremor passing through her cooling flesh. Post-mortem involuntary muscle contractions, I thought as I started forward to examine the corpse.

The corpse moaned and rolled onto her back, her arm flopping back onto the ground. Her eyes were open. And, at her throat, another pair of eyes<><><><><><><><><><><><>
<><><.><><><><><><><><><><><><><><><><><>
<><><><><><><><><><><><><><><><><><><
> < > < > < > < > < > < > < > < > < > < > < > < > < > < > < > <
><><><><><><><><><><><><><><><><><><><>
<><><><><><><><><><><><> > > > > > > > were staring at me. "Smedley! Sergeant Smedley!" Jenks was shouting. Snap out of it, man! What happened here!"

I stepped back and looked past Jenks' face. We were still in the alley but there were differences. The body had moved a little.

The head had moved a lot. It lay over against the back wall of the alley

The walls were splashed with blood. It still slid down the rough stone surfaces here and there like crimson drool. I circled Jenks who was still ranting at the invisible Smedley and stepped closer to the body. There was no question of it being dead now. It was not only headless, it had been eviscerated.

There was a sound of retching and….

An Eye.

A Painted Eye.

Inside of a Triangle.

It winked.

I blinked, and the room formed around us again: the spell was broken.

"What happened?" I demanded. "We needed more time!"

Daggoth didn't speak but nodded to my left.

I looked over at Mick, who sat white-faced and trembling, staring down at her lap where she had just vomited.

THREE

It was late.

Abercrombie and Fitch had collected Jenks who had collected Smedley who had collected the wagon and horses and had left an hour before. The fact that the captain was smiling and whistling a tune as he departed was actually more disturbing than if he had run screaming into the night.

I stared at the floor, torn between the need to review the evidence and the desire to forget what I had seen in the cul-de-sac at the end of the darkened alley.

"A copper piece for your thoughts," Daggoth said.

"I'm thinking that this is a godless world."

He chuckled ruefully. "Funny you should say that. I always figured that the problem with this so-called world was that it had way too *many* gods. Too many petty ones, at least." I looked up and saw Mick standing in the doorway enveloped in a large robe. Wet hair framed her face, but spots of color burning high on her cheeks now, and she looked less like an ugly girl and more like a tired and unsightly boy.

"Were you able to decide anything?" she asked.

"Only that something happened that Smedley wasn't able to handle on even the subconscious level."

She nodded, lines of fatigue etching her face. "It felt like the memory was edited. Something taken out and the two remaining parts were like spliced together."

"That gives us two possibilities," Daggoth mused. "Either Smedley has blocked his own memories at the subconscious level or someone has manually tampered with his memoryfile after the fact."

"The second seems highly unlikely," I said. "The murder scene was pretty horrific: I'm not surprised the entire recall sequence was distorted."

"Did you see de eyes? At dat poor girl's troat?" Yudu asked Mick.

She nodded.

"Less than half a face—a third, actually—was visible. And that for only the briefest of moments." I shook my head. "It doesn't tell us much."

Mick clutched her robe. "Could it be a vampire?"

"Vampire?"

"I saw a face near the victim's throat. I saw no second body so it had to be lying down with the victim so her body was blocking our view."

"Then why the beheading?" I asked. "Why the evisceration? So much blood was splashed about and wasted. That is not vampiric behavior."

"I—I don't know. I guess I'm not thinking clearly."

The Zombie Mistress got up. "You poor ting, you are exhausted! In fact, you are all too weary to tink clearly. I will have your beds prepared."

Daggoth got up. "I guess it's too late to work out travel arrangements back to the tower tonight. May I use your crystal ball to call home?"

I looked at him. "I thought you always carried a piece of magic mirror with you."

"Yeah, but clair/ular is so expensive these days I only use it for emergencies."

We bid one another good night and I followed after Lucretia as she led me up the stairs to my guest chamber. I thought about asking her about her stroll around the grounds with Captain Jenks but finally decided that I had enough worries on my plate at the present. What I really needed was a little time alone and a good night's sleep.

Once inside, I closed the door, stripped off my clothing and contemplated the all-too-familiar female form I now inhabited. During my last trip into the Program Matrix my dreambody had been afflicted with a strange form of metamorphy: every day, at sunrise and sunset, I had metamorphosed in form, switching back and forth between my Halfelven avatar, Riplakish of Dyrinwall, and my original Human form. If this was a variation on the same malady, I could expect a return to normal come sunrise.

Sighing, I slid between the sheets, figuring the wait would be a short one in conscious terms: I was exhausted. I slipped into black unconsciousness like a diver entering dark water.

#

I awoke to a gentle weight settling down across my hips. "Riplakish…" sighed a breathy voice. A hand reached down and probed the blankets between my legs. "…Riplakish of Dyrinwall…I am for thee…" Moonlight from the unshuttered window illumined a feminine form crouched over me on the bed. She was naked and very up-front about it.

"Excuse me," I murmured, "but do I know you, madam?"

Quiet laughter that was all too smug for my tastes was my only answer. That and a hand tracing a pattern up the bedclothes that covered my torso.

"I'd like to know what you think you're doing," I insisted.

"Know…know…*know me,* Riplakish of Dyrinwall!" She leaned over me, a three-dimensional erotic dream suspended before my face. "I know the thoughts that make you burn in the night…I know your secret desires," she whispered. "I am the woman of your dreams—"

"You're a Succubus, right?"

She faltered. "I—command me—taste—"

"Look," I said, "only Succubae and really bad erotica use dialogue like this, and I'm trying to give you the benefit of the doubt, here."

"I am for you, Riplaki—"

I sighed. "Who sent you and what do they want?"

"What—what *you* want. I am your fantasy! I am—"

"You're rather new at this, aren't you? I know most of Lilith's sisters and you don't look familiar at all."

She grasped the top of the blanket and flung it aside.

"Besides which," I continued as she stared at my unmasculine form, "you didn't reconnoiter the room and check your subject before waking him." I *tch-tch'ed* her. "Definitely an amateur."

"I have the wrong room!" she gasped. And fairly leapt from the bed.

"Hold on, Sweetheart," I said as she moved toward the door. "You've got the right room: I am Riplakish of Dyrinwall." She hesitated and I rolled over to light a candle on the nightstand. "Right room, right guy, wrong body."

"You—you're a Metamorph?"

"In a manner of speaking." The wick caught and a soft glow highlighted my nocturnal visitor.

Her skin was dusky with a ruddy glow to it. While the candlelight may have limited my full range of vision, her skin was all she wore and that provided me with ample opportunity to make judgment. And speaking of amplitude, she was all curves and rounded bounty, fleshily ripe, an obvious temptation to men of obvious tastes.

Her eyes gleamed redly, reflecting tiny pinpoints of flame and, as she licked her lips, I could see pointed teeth behind that striptease tongue. "Shapeshifter or no," she purred, "I am still for thee, Riplakish of Dyrinwall." She began to saunter back toward the bed. As she did, her form flowed into new configurations.

Masculine ones. Someone was still excited.

And it still wasn't me. "Look, ah—?"

"Janus."

"Of course," I sighed. "Well, Succubus or Incubus, this just isn't going to work."

"It could if you would try being cooperative," he growled.

"But that's just the point: I have no intention of being cooperative." I folded my arms—somewhat awkwardly due to my own reconfigured anatomy—across my chest. "Now unless you start explaining who sent you and the real purpose of your visit, I'm going to have to treat you as a hostile transplanar materialization."

"Meaning what?" he huffed.

"The Twelve Words of Power, for starters."

That rocked him. Already he was deflating to 'half-mast.' "You wouldn't," he whimpered.

"Try me, Buttercup. I might even hum 'Jesus Loves Me'."

"Okay, *okay!*" S/he sat on the foot of my bed and stared at the floor.

"Suppose you tell me just what in hell is going on," I coached.

"In Hell?" Janus shifted uneasily. "Civil war."

"*Civil* war?"

"Well, as civil as anything gets in Bureaucracy's Ultimate Pit. There's a power struggle going on between the various Powers and Principalities. My people want you in our corner."

Me? Why me? I repeated my questions out loud.

S/he shrugged. "Beats the heaven out of me. Rumor has it that you're the Demiurge incarnated. Though I was expecting someone a little more imposing."

"I'm not at my best until after my morning coffee. Now, just who are *your* people?"

Before the suc/incubus could answer, there was a creaking sound from the doorway and Janus disappeared in a puff of smoke.

A tremulous voice whispered: "Nicole…" And the door to my bedchamber stuttered open. It was Dr. Westbrook all dressed up in her Angel McRae avatar and not much else.

"Dagny," I sighed, "you should be in bed."

"I'm frightened," she whimpered, hands clutching the gauzy wisps of her nebulous nightie.

I would have been more pissed off, but it was no act. As she came closer I could see that there was no artifice in her disarrayed hair and terrified expression. The color had drained from her face and the hand that she placed in mine was as clammy as that of a day-old corpse.

"This is all very real, isn't it?" She made a timid, hunched gesture. "This mausoleum, those walking dead things—those horrible, nasty creatures in the woods that were going to—to eat us—" She stifled a sob. "This isn't just a dream, is it?"

My over-educated, oh-so-professional jailer appeared to be in the throes of a mild psychotic break of her own. I patted her hand trying to think of something comforting to say. "It's like a dream, kiddo. And, yes, it is dangerous. But it isn't really real, you know, and we are going to get out of here soon."

But not real *soon.*

Sitting on the bed now, she snuggled against me. "You're not going to let them get me," she pleaded. "You won't let them hurt me?"

Oboy.

I did *not* need hysteria or a complete mental breakdown further complicating matters at this point. In fact, I was hard pressed to think of *any* point at which these things might be convenient. "No, Dagny. I won't let them hurt you."

"I feel so foolish. I've always been the competent professional, full of contempt for the silly, emotional twits who gave my gender a bad name. But this—this is all too much! Monsters, in my profession, are Archetypes of the Unconscious. Psychological allegories to be expressed as abstract symbols. I don't know what's wrong with me—"

"A lot of people find their first experience with Hypnogogic Programming overwhelming."

"Can I sleep here tonight?" she asked, picking nervously at the coverlet.

Westbrook was obviously too distraught to return to her own, room much less spend the rest of the night alone. I nodded: "*Sleep*, Dagny. Nothing else."

"I'll be good," she said in a little girl's voice.

"No handsies," I reminded as she slid under the covers, beside me.

"Promise…" she murmured. And amazingly was asleep before I had finished extinguishing the candle. I sighed, plumped my pillow, and lay back down to ponder Janus' enigmatic revelation. It seemed to fit with our Demonic rescue at the Goblin's camp. The next questions were: which factions were involved and how did the exploding crystal ball in Daggoth's study tie in?

The door creaked again and the android replicant of Natasha Skovoroda glided into the room. *"My lord?"* she inquired in Misty Dawn's voice.

I reached over and relit the candle. "It's late, M.D. What are you doing up?"

"Ghosts have no need of sleep, milord. Nor doth this clockwork body I now inhabit. Furthermore, my sensors have registered an alien life-form in the vicinity and I am now functioning in Patrol Mode." She moved toward the bed. *"But I would speak with thee, as well, my—"* She stopped and cocked her head to the side. *"Inquiry: do I continue to address thee as 'my lord'? Or doth circumstances prescribe 'my lady' as being more appropriate?"*

I grimaced. "Ripley' will do nicely."

The haunted simulacrum turned her attention to the form beside me. *"I am not yet fully acclimated to this body, my love, but when I scan that one, I experience feedback that can only be defined as jealousy."* A series of *clicks* emanated from her torso and arms. *"Her proximity to you is causing my weapon systems to come online."* A subsonic hum was starting to vibrate the bed.

"Now, Misty—" *How does one deal with a possessive robot?* "—it's not her fault. She's not in love with me. Dr. Westbrook is in love with Nicole Doucet and is very confused right now. That's no reason to harm her, so control yourself."

"I cannot help it: it is a matter of programming."

Programming? "Then try something. Override. Escape sequence: control-alt-delete. Stand down all offensive systems."

"Weapon systems off-line," she acknowledged. *"Yellow alert status maintained."*

I fell back against my pillow.

"What ails thee, my love?"

I moaned. "It's late, M.D. And I am very tired." Though I doubted a good night's sleep would be sufficient to sort things out in the morning.

"Then I shall let thee sleep whilst I stand guard. Thou mayest—warning, warning: disturbance in proximity fields." Her head swiveled to face the door. *"Life-form approaching chamber entrance. Weapon systems coming back online."*

"Whoa, there," I sat back up. "Let's not get itchy trigger-fingers, yet."

The door squeaked open a little wider and Mick entered the bedchamber. In contrast to the rest of us, she wore a white linen nightgown that mercifully covered her from neck to ankles and carried a single, lit taper ensconced in a brass candleholder.

"Ripley?" she whispered.

"How now, spirit; whither wander you?"

"I couldn't sleep," she said, turning toward the sound of my voice. "I thought we might talk." As she caught sight of my android visitor, Janus reappeared in goatish, male mode, squatting on the end of the bed.

"My, my, my," he murmured, taking us all in. "A triumvirate of temptation!"

Mick did a silent count of the room's inhabitants and looked at the Incubus.

He shrugged and grinned roguishly. "Three out of four..."

The color in Mick's cheeks was unmistakable even in the flickering wash of candlelight. "I'm sorry," she responded coolly, "I didn't realize that you were occupied." She backed toward the door.

"Um," I said, "this isn't what it seems."

"Nicole, my love..." I glanced down at Westbrook who had already moved into her own dream state. "...kiss me again..." she sighed.

Misty Dawn's android form swiveled its attention back to the bed. Mick bolted out the door.

"Perhaps I had the right form the first time," Janus mused, transforming back to feminine configurations. After a moment's consideration, her features flowed again, and she became a dead ringer for Dagny Westbrook's avatar.

"Kiss me again," sighed the Angel McRae Succubus.

Misty Dawn turned to regard this new incursion into her territory.

"Out!" I growled.

"I have a mission to fulfill," Janus breathed.

"Yeah? Well, go on back to your masters and tell them that you're pissing me off!"

There was a sound not unlike the popping of a champagne cork and another form materialized. She was nearly a dead ringer for Janus' original manifestation, and I might have been fooled had s/he not already reappeared.

"Riplakish of Dyrinwall," the new Succubus breathed, "I am for thee." Then she paused as she realized there were no "hes" in the room.

Misty Dawn was turning about, trying to figure out the best position for covering all three intruders simultaneously.

"Oh, leave off, Bobbie," Janus groused. "The chap's not buyin' tonight."

The new arrival blinked twice. "Janus?"

The other remetamorphosed into its male aspect and jerked a thumb at me. "That's him. Or her, for the moment." (S)he shook his/her head. "Gave this one my best shots coming and going—both ways, if you know what I mean. Not interested, and knows about the recruitment angle." (S)he leaned forward conspiratorially and lowered his/her voice. "I think we're dealing with a triple-seven here."

The other's eyes widened. "No!" She turned and gave me a look usually reserved for lepers and science-fiction writers.

"Go ahead if you think you can do any better," Janus concluded, starting to fade to transparency. "Me, I got reports to file."

I smiled at Bobbie, executed a crude genuflection, and started humming "Nearer My God To Thee".

Bobbie squeaked and was completely dematerialized before Janus had finished fading from view.

That left Misty Dawn.

"Out," I said.

"I shall stand watch while you sleep."

"Outside my door. In the hall."

"But, my lord—lady—my—Ripley—"

"Out! That's an order!"

She went.

"And close the door!" I roared.

It was closed.

As I snuggled back down under the blankets, Westbrook turned over and sighed, "Kiss me, Nicole..."

"Put a sock in it, Dagny," I muttered as I reached out and extinguished the candle.

#

The remainder of the night was spent in restless, half-remembered tossings and turnings.

When I awoke again, I was beside myself.

The sun was just peeking over yon hill, outside the bedchamber window. The early morning light revealed a Zombie servant collecting the chamberpot from underneath the foot of our bed.

"Morning, Fitch," I mumbled as he shambled to the window. "How'd you get past my guardian Golem?" As I wiped sleep and hair from my bleary eyes, he dumped the pot's contents out the portal and onto the grounds below. "Hey, aren't you supposed to yell 'Gardyloo' or something, first?"

"Fitch fetch," my verbose valet answered.

"Up at the first flush of dawn," I yawned, sitting up in bed and stretching. Beside me, Dr. Westbrook stirred a bit in Angel McRae's body as prelude to her own awakening. On her other side, Riplakish of Dyrinwall was still sawing logs.

I stopped in mid-yawn and very slowly and deliberately looked down. I was still a female. It was technically past sunrise, and I hadn't changed back.

I looked over at the Half-Elven avatar I normally inhabited in the Fantasyworld Program. It—he—was starting to stir now.

As I reached across Westbrook to touch "Riplakish's" shoulder, a bright spark arced from his shoulder to my finger—or maybe it was vice-versa—and the shock knocked me right out of the bed. A yelp from the other side of the mattress told me that the shock had gone both ways.

Westbrook sat straight up in bed. "Oh, Nicole," she said, "I had the strangest dream!"

"Nicole?" rumbled an eerily familiar voice. "What's this about Nicole?" The head of my other avatar popped up on the other side of the bed. "Nicole!" he bellowed, catching sight of me.

It was too much on too little sleep. I screamed, and Fitch dropped our porcelain precursor to a bedpan.

Figuratively speaking, its former contents were about to hit the fan.

PART III

YIN, YANG, JUNG

Every man carries within him the eternal image of the woman...fundamentally unconscious, an hereditary factor of primordial origin engraved in the living organic system of the man, an imprint or archetype of all the ancestral experiences of the female, a deposit, as it were, of all the impressions ever made by woman.

—Carl G. Jung,
Collected Works: Vol. 17,
The Development of Personality—

ONE

—From the Pen of Daggoth the Dark—

Dearest Vashti,

I am taking pen in hand, eschewing other means of communication which might permit eavesdropping.

Much has happened since we spoke last night via crystal ball.

As I explained, Bob's had a relapse of his peculiar lycanthropy—or perhaps metamorphosis is a more correct term—only this time his avatar changed into Nicole Doucet! Furthermore, instead of the cycle running true to form, he did not revert back to normal come sunrise. Instead, another Riplakish of Dyrinwall *showed up sometime last night.*

Yes, there are two *Robert Ripleys in-program now!*

While multiple avatars wouldn't seem unusual given his last trip into the Matrix, the circumstances are radically different this time. This gets a little complicated so try to bear with me...

The last time, the computer split Ripley's psyche-file into multiple avatars—each self-aware but essentially a copy of the original *mind-set at the moment of program-entry. This time we seem to have two* different *Ripleys prior to Matrix insertion.*

When he previously withdrew from the Matrix, we assumed that Bob's consciousness returned to his own body in the outer reality. Apparently this was not the case.

We now believe that Bob woke up in a different body in a parallel dimension, so the memory upload never reached his body back in what is our "Universe Prime." That would mean the original Robert *Ripley came out of taction with no memories of anything that had happened to his avatar. For him it's as if his last excursion into the Programworld never happened. So he—Ripley Alpha, if you follow my channeling here—has now returned to sort things out.*

Lacking actual memories of Program events over the past month or so, Ripley Alpha *only knows what Borys Dankevych, Dr. Cooper, and the others on the Outside were able to tell him after the fact. So he's a little confused and skeptical about the other Ripley who looks like Nicole Doucet.*

Which brings us to Ripley Beta *(the one who downloaded from Nicole Doucet's body in the Parallel Universe and popped into his avatar back at our tower yesterday). He was most unhappy to wake up this morning and find himself still stranded in Doucet's body. He was even more unhappy to find the dreambody he had expected to wake up in already occupied by another version of himself.*

Anyway, as if all of this wasn't complicated enough, neither one of them is fully convinced that the other is who he—or she—says he/she is. Ripley Alpha *alludes to the uncertainty of the real Nicole's death and her penchant for deception. Ripley* Beta *claims visits from shape-changing Demons are his reason for questioning Ripley Alpha's identity. And both insist there's no way to prove either's legitimacy since The Machine itself has access to all of Ripley's memory-files. That means the Computer could create a duplicate that would be more convincing than the original.*

Even to his own self!

One corroborating witness for Ripley Beta's *story is a Dreamwalker who appears to be a psychiatrist from that parallel timeline where Nicole Doucet survived the aircar crash unscathed. But this Dr. Westbrook seems a little too unstable to be a totally reliable witness. In fact, she also seems to think that Ripley Beta really* is *Nicole Doucet. Or actually Nicole Doucet masquerading as Robert Ripley, masquerading as Nicole Doucet. (I told you this gets a bit complicated.)*

She also seems to be "smitten" with "her patient"—which seems to me to be a serious breach of ethics. So I have even less faith in any corroborating testimony that she might offer...

No one is really sure why the split is polarized along gender lines. This Dr. Westbrook nattered on about Carl Jung's theories on personality regarding the anima *and the* animus*—the* anima *being the personification of all feminine psychological tendencies in the male psyche and the* animus *as the male personification of the unconscious in woman—but it's all so much psychobabble to me.*

All that aside, we have several problems. First and foremost, there is some kind of imbalanced field-effect that is generated when the two Ripleys are in close proximity. While it isn't as extreme a dichotomy as matter and antimatter, there is definitely a positive and negative charge aspect. Until we know more, we've deemed it wise to keep the two Ripleys separated. For psychological as well as physical considerations.

Which brings me to the next problem.

Natasha Skovoroda's "shade" must still be retrieved from the Underworld. And the Calabastor City Watch has pressed me into a murder investigation.

So here is what we have agreed to do: Ripley Alpha *will undertake the mission to Abydos.*

I've asked Ripley Beta *to stay behind and help me with this inquiry. While he's technically* persona non grata *in Calabastor, the city watch will be looking for a Halfelven Bard, not a human woman. This investigation shouldn't take more than a few days—a week, at most—and will enable me to keep an eye on his condition in the meantime.*

I know you were concerned about my going to fetch Natasha's psyche file and now I think you should be relieved at the way things have worked out. I will see you as soon as things work out at this end.Til then,

All my love,
Richard

♂

Vashti set the letter aside and stared at me. "Let me get this straight. You are *the* Robert Remington Ripley—the Third—the one who reentered the Program at the Zombie Mistress' estate. *Not* the one who showed up here in Daggoth's tower a couple of days before, drunk as a skunk."

"The real Robert Ripley," I agreed.

She scowled. "Let's not go there just yet." She looked over the mechanical maid and the supermodel. "What about them?"

"Natasha's android goes with me," I said. "I'd like you to look after Dr. Westbrook while I'm gone."

"Wait a minute!" Angel McRae's look-a-like came up off the Naugahide sofa. "I'm still not convinced I did the right thing in leaving Nicole back at that Zombie-ridden mausoleum. The only reason I've tagged along this far is because this is the chance of a lifetime!"

Vashti refolded the letter and looked at me. "What is she talking about?"

"Going to Hell!" Westbrook enthused. "What wouldn't a psychiatrist give to actually travel through the depths of Human kind's religious subconscious? Satanic symbology, manifested metaphors, religious guilt distilled down to its most primitive and basic allegory!" She stabbed a finger at me. "It's this opportunity and this alone that got me to agree to this temporary separation!"

She didn't have to explain whom the separation was from, that was painfully obvious even though I seemed to have arrived late in the story. She was convinced that the Nicole who claimed to be me was the Nicole Doucet from a parallel universe—hers, in fact.

Maybe so.

Westbrook's explanation of her Nicole's issues of 'transference' would explain that one's insistence that she was really me, trapped in a Nicole avatar.

Maybe so…

If, however, we were dealing with the Nicole from my universe, it was the others who were in real danger, now. Our little trip to Hell would likely be a picnic in the park by comparison.

Yet, from the stories that Borys and Dorothy told me, it was highly unlikely that either could have survived their plunge deep in the underground chasms of Ortygia.

I raised my hands, shrugging off the thought. "Okay, okay!" According to Daggoth and my so-called "other self," anything was better than letting the psychiatrist in the supermodel avatar tag along to Calabastor with them. Their perception of what constituted an actual problem eluded me: Angel McRae's clone certainly wasn't hard on the eyes. And it certainly couldn't hurt to have a psychiatric specialist along, considering the circumstances.

"I'm going, too," Vashti said suddenly.

"What? Why?"

"I have my reasons." Her eyes drifted away. "I'm bored."

"This isn't going to be fun," I pointed out.

"You'll need help. I'm experienced," she nodded toward Westbrook, "she's not."

I grimaced: I couldn't very well argue the "danger aspect" as long as I was willing to take an inexperienced Dreamwalker along. "I still don't like it."

"And why not?" she asked archly. "Don't want a chaperon along for your little 'party'?"

I hadn't thought of it from that perspective. I grinned. "And welcome you are!" I said, giving her my hand. "Now let's get started!"

♂

We spent the next two hours going through the armory and Vashti's closets. Above the latter was a hand-lettered sign in AOL™ calligraphy declaring: **YOU'VE GOT CHAINMAIL!**

I didn't take any time at all. I wore what Riplakish of Dyrinwall always wore: a tunic or *gambeson* and girdle of light doeskin, over which I wore a shirt of Gnomish chainmail, over which I wore a jerkin and trousers of green and dun-colored dragonskin. High-top moccasin boots, double swordbelts with scabbards, bow case with quiver, and a leather headband completed my ensemble.

The Golem was the next easiest to outfit. Since her armor and weaponry were already resident as a self-contained system, we dressed her in a white, ankle-length, muslin chemise with a red cotton bodice that matched the color of Natasha Skovoroda's hair and a wide stomacher-belt of black cowhide. She looked deceptively demure.

Not so my ex-wife: Vashti had donned a sky-blue kirtle that matched her eyes, but overlaid it with a bishop's mantle of fine bronze chainmail and a stomacher of studded brass scales, both of which brought out the reddish highlights of her honey-blonde hair. Capping that hair was a copper and bronze helm—a *celata*. Completing her outfit was a *sipar*—a Persian bronze shield, nearly eighteen inches in diameter and covered with runes and mystic symbols—and, slipped through a belted loop on her hip, a mace that looked like it had been designed by H.R. Giger, a mutant crossbreed that claimed morning stars, *morgensterns*, and holy-water sprinklers in its formidable ancestry.

Dr. Westbrook—"Angel"—had apparently decided to live her newfound fantasy to the hilt. By the time I could catch up to her at the back of the armory, she was already modeling a chainmail bikini before one of the polished steel mirrors.

"Absolutely not!" I roared.

She struck a defensive pose, feet spread, hands on her very visible hips. "And why not? I think I happen to look just great!"

There was no debating that particular point and Vashti chimed in to her defense: "It's what most of the Amazon warrior-maids wear into battle."

I sighed and pulled a dagger from one of the weapons racks. "Here," I said, offering it to Angel hilt-first, "stab me."

Her mouth fell open. "What?"

I pulled open my jerkin exposing the mithril links of my chainmail shirt. "Heart or gut: take your pick."

Vashti's nod helped Westbrook past her hesitancy. She brought the blade slowly down until the tip scraped along the silvery links.

"Harder."

She frowned and started jabbing the blade in short, little staccato thrusts that would have scarcely skewered a mouse.

"Harder!"

She finally drew her arm back far enough to put a little force into it. There was a "chik" sound and the tip of the dagger's blade broke off.

I took the poniard from her and walked away, saying: "Now, it's my turn."

I turned when there was a twenty-foot distance between us and hurled the dagger so that it flew hilt-first. The pommel caught her halfway between breastbone and umbilicus, just far enough off the solar plexus to keep her from losing her lunch. Her hands flew to her stomach and she hurriedly sat down as her legs turned to jelly.

"That was cold!" Vashti snapped.

"Shut up," I said to her. I walked back to "Angel" and leaned over. "Listen to me and listen very carefully. You can't let the Fantasy seduce you here because the dangers are no longer make-believe! What you are wearing is not armor, it's window-dressing!"

If she had anything to retort, it would be another five minutes before she'd have the wind to voice it.

"If the Fantasyworld Program makes it standard issue for Amazon warrior-maids, that's fine, because most of them aren't real people," I continued. "They're sub-programs, artificial constructs of The Machine. They're just so much window-dressing, too." While I didn't buy into the AIs being nothing more than cardboard props, this was hardly the time to get sidetracked on that particular argument. "The Machine is programmed to warp its parameters of 'reality' to conform to people's dimwitted expectations of myth and fantasy, ignoring history and logic in the process.

"But don't let the picturebook effect lull you into a false sense of security: this is a very dangerous place. You can't have a good story without conflict and you can't have a good adventure without danger, and the Matrix serves up both with a vengeance. But *you're* not a recyclable sub-program; you're a human being, even though your psyche inhabits a computer-generated body. And because there's a glitch in the biofeedback routines, you *can* die! You can't be stood up again like a knocked-down bowling pin!"

"I think she gets the point," Vashti coached.

"Yeah?" I rounded on her. "Well, I guess *I* don't! I still don't know why I'm taking either of you along on this particular ride. It's a damn-fool thing to do myself, but to take anyone *else* who's a True Spirit is both stupid and criminal to my way of thinking!"

"I don't need your permission," Angel Westbrook croaked, as she wobbled back up and on her feet. "I'm an adult who has made my own choice in this. While I—'appreciate'—your input on this matter, I don't need your consent. Now, suppose you help me pick out something a little more practical."

A half-hour later I stepped back to admire my handiwork. "Now," I announced (to Vashti as much as to Angel), "do you feel protected or what?"

The suit of field plate just stood there like a museum exhibit but a voice echoed from behind the fully visored, bascinet helm: "Very protected. The only problem is I can't move."

I frowned. "I'll admit that it may be a little heavier than you're used to but I'll bet the real problem is that some of the joints have seized up. Here..." I reached down to help move her left leg.

The next thing I knew I was on the floor with two hundred pounds of maiden and metal on top of me. *"Et 'er of'!"* I wheezed.

The Golem lifted Angel, armor and all, off of me with one hand while Vashti helped me to my feet.

"We'll take it from here," my ex-wife said. "In the meantime, I've put together the items that Richard requested and put them at the center of the teleportation glyphs. Why don't you go see that they get sent properly."

That last sentence was neither a question nor a request. I went to do as I was told.

♀

Mick helped me lift the pile of clothing and carry it to the table, while Daggoth explained the mechanics of pentagram-to-pentagram teleportation to the Zombie Mistress.

I sorted through everything. Twice.

Daggoth wandered over as I was conducting my third search and dividing the big pile into lots of little piles. "They're not there," he said amiably.

"What's not here?" I asked, somewhat less amiably.

"Your campaign clothing: mithril shirt, dragonskin pants and vest, boots, katana and wakizashi—"

I quickly had his collar in my fist and was experimenting with the tourniquet effect by twisting the material tighter. "Where are they?" I hissed.

"No doubt being worn by Riplakish of Dyrinwall," he whispered in a strangled undertone. To his credit he made no attempt to free himself. Even after I released his collar and grabbed the front of his robe with both hands.

"*I'm* Riplakish of Dyrinwall," I said in a somewhat strangled tone of my own.

"Not at the moment you aren't," he observed mildly. "At the moment you bear an uncanny resemblance to Nicole Doucet, and we have no reason to suspect that's going to change anytime soon."

"So what am I going to wear?" I asked, still trying to avoid the inevitable certainties that the newly arrive pile of clothing had suggested.

"Well," continued Daggoth, "I have this little plan—"

"Yeah, I know you and your little plans! Like the time you talked me into judging that little beauty contest. 'It'll be easy,' you said. 'Just three contestants,' you said. 'What's so hard about looking at gorgeous women,' you said. 'I'm sure there'll be a nice reward for it,' you said. 'Just pick one and give her this golden apple as first prize,' you said."

"Hey," he protested, "we might've headed off the Trojan War if you'd made the right choice. How was I to know you had the hots for Athena?" A look of surprise ricocheted through his eyes. "Say, you don't suppose your present condition could have anything to do with sour grapes on Aphrodite's or Hera's part, do you?"

I tightened my grip oh his robe and pulled his face right up to mine. "*What. Plan.*"

"Look," he said, peeling my fingers off of his robe without as great an effort as I might have hoped. "The City Watch have turned Calabastor upside down and come up with zip. They sent for a guy named Garrett down in TunFaire, but he's tied up with another case, so we're it."

"It," I said.

"This is a case that needs finesse."

"Finesse," I said.

"Sometimes you need a little finesse."

"Sometimes you need a—" I caught myself.

"We'll need to be discrete. Go incognito. Sleuth around."

"In disguise," I said.

"Precisely!" Daggoth concluded, as if no further explanation were necessary.

I picked up a wad of clothing and threw it at him. "So, what am I going to wear?"

He retrieved a sequined halter-top festooned with baubles, bangles, and bright, shiny beads. "This," he said, holding it up by the shoulder straps.

"No," I said.

"This serial killer has been preying on prostitutes," he explained, holding it up against me to gauge the fit. "What better cover than you as a streetwalker and me as your pimp?"

"Give a few minutes, I'll think of something."

"What about me?" Mick wanted to know.

We both looked at her.

"Um, another pimp?" Daggoth ventured.

"I hate you," she answered with a touch of good humor.

"I hate him more," I said. With greater sincerity.

TWO

♀

There is this quaint little folk legend *cum* urban myth that has been popularized in entertainment fiction for centuries where the heroine (or occasionally the hero) kicks the bad guy between the legs, seriously taking the wind out of his sails.

This time it didn't work.

Not that it works a lot of the time, you understand: that's the problem with these little *faux* fables. Oh, a well-placed kick to the whirligigs will incapacitate if not outright kill a man. But, most of the time, a foot on the upswing isn't going to go under and come up behind the you-know-what and arrive on target with sufficient force. There's no need to go into graphic detail here or draw schematics to prove that the male anatomy somewhat shields itself—you can either figure it out on your own or have somebody else explain it to you later. Just take my word for it: if you're looking to take the fight out of a guy, a kick to the groin—nine times out of ten—will miss the precise spot.

It *will* hurt him.

But it *won't* incapacitate him.

In fact, it will just make him mad: I leaned to the right and the chair flew past my head, only to ricochet off the wall and slam into my hip. A moment ago he was trying to tear my clothes off. Now he was more interested in tearing my arms and legs off.

Hindsight is a relatively useless thing but I couldn't help wondering if there had been any way to avoid this little tête-à-tête…

♀

Frankly, I had expected trouble a lot sooner. You don't pull a twelve-hour pub-crawl through the seediest parts of Calabastor's waterfront without running into some kind of grief—especially when you're undressed and looking for it.

Although the label identified the seamstress as Holly of Frederick's Wood, my outfit bore little resemblance to medieval period costuming. Fantasy is the operative word here, and costumes often had more than one function to fulfill. Mine was tailored to display my "wares," exposing generous expanses of leg, midriff, and décolleté—not to mention gooseflesh. The night was warm and muggy though there was an intermittent cool wind skipping across the harbor and through the half-doors of this quaint little tavern known as *The_Hard Roc* cafe. But it wasn't the temperature fluctuations that had given rise to most of my goosebumps

"Hey, Alphonse," a rat-faced little man had asked, "how much for Miss Merry Legs, here?"

"Beat it, peewee!" I snapped. "I'm off duty!"

Daggoth's reflexes were a bit off. "Hey," he murmured as the little jerk retreated back into the morass of the barroom crowd, "oughta ask some questions, first..." The lateness of the hour coupled with a pitcher of ale was having a definite effect on my phony pimp.

"Daggoth—"

"Supposed to ask questions...get leads..." he mumbled.

My patience had just disappeared along with the little man in the crowd. "Listen, Bucko; I'm tired. It's been a long night and I'm still black and blue from this afternoon's little sojourn through that scummy little gin joint—what was it called?"

"The Hook & Tail," he belched.

"Yeah, that's the one. Well, when Mick gets here, we're going home."

"Home?" he asked blearily.

"Back to the inn," I amended. I was as irritated by his uncharacteristic drinking binge as I was by the events of the last twelve hours. "I'm going to bed. Alone. I've had it up to here," and remembering the little rat-faced man, "and down to there! I'm calling it a night!"

"Doesn't look like a knight..." Daggoth muttered as trouble picked that moment to walk through the swinging doors.

Trouble looked like a sailor. Correction: he looked like a big, ugly, mean-minded brute who had spent some time at sea.

Since we couldn't leave until Mick showed up I decided to continue my attack on Daggoth's decoy strategy. "This isn't working," I started.

"So many men, so little time," he agreed, studying his reflection near the bottom of his stein.

I glanced at the big, burly seaman as he shoved his way through the crowd and then I looked toward the doors for Mick. She was supposed to meet us here after checking with some of her contacts down by the wharves. I was looking for a homely woman disguised as a homely man in sailor's garb and my eyes came back to the tavern's new arrival. He was homely as well and he was dressed like a seaman but there was no mistaking him for our friend. He bellied up to the bar, announcing to the entire room that he was Barnacle Bill the Sailor and bellowed to the barkeep for whiskey and women, and not necessarily in that particular order.

Daggoth leaned over and murmured: "A typical prospect, wouldn't you say?"

The trouble was my ersatz procurer thought every man within a three-block proximity was a likely suspect. "No, I wouldn't say." And I didn't like how the term "suspect" was evolving into the word "prospect."

"Dr. Westbrook suggested the killer might be a sea-faring man." It was a tenuous theory but the ocean was a convenient disposal unit for those three missing heads.

I shook my head. "Dagny suggested a number of professions that would allow for the perp's coming and going at night."

He spread his hands. "We've got to start somewhere."

"We?" I glared at him. *"Start? I've* been working the waterfront for the better part of a day while *you* chat up the barkeeps!"

"I'm trying to pull down some more leads—"

"*Leads?* I'll give you a *lead*—"

At the bar, now, Crustaceous William was demanding to see someone named Eskimo Nell and claiming to be a good friend of Deadeye Dick and Mexico Pete.

"Our slasher," I continued, "is not picking up his victims in taverns and roadhouses. He's getting the streetwalkers, the ones who are already alone out there and in the dark. That's why there's no witnesses."

"If you've got any better ideas—" he began.

"Now there's a likely looking coffee grinder!" bellowed our new arrival. I looked up to see Barnacle Bill regarding me with an expression that left Salacious in the dust and was well across the county

line into Predatory. "Shag yer bubbles over here, Nockstress, so's I can give 'em a squeeze!"

Startled, I stared back at him. "Bubbles?" I looked at Daggoth. *"Bubbles?"*

"C'mon, Jane Shore," the sailor hollered, "hoist it over here! Tell yer jack-gagger I've got yer price!" There was some laughter but most of the bar's patrons had heard it all before.

"Jane," I said, "Shore."

"Go on," Daggoth coached. "This could be our man."

I looked at him ready to blister his ears for all his seeming concern for my health and welfare but all that came out was: "Bubbles?"

The big, redheaded mariner started to shove through the crowd toward our table. "Hey soss-brangle—I'm talkin' to you!"

"Why don't you go over there and see what he wants?" Daggoth whispered.

"Because I know what he wants!" I hissed back. "What every man who's spoken to me since we hit town wants!"

"The point is to get information out of him."

"The point is, I can't keep posing as lift-skirt when I don't deliver. And horny Neanderthals like Billy the Squid, here, are going to be short on information and long on giving out grief when I don't come across." I saw the thought flicker at the back of his eyes. "And *don't* you even *think* about it!"

"Yo, Prosser; tell yer piece-of-trade to show a little more respect!" As Barnacle Bill had grown louder, the room had grown quieter: more people were taking an interest in the proceedings now.

I looked at my partner in deception. "Are you going to tell him to shove off? Or is it my turn to be the man, here?"

Daggoth scowled drunkenly.

"Hey," I said, "you're the pimp. It's your job to look after your girls. So look after me."

"What do you suggest?"

I spread my hands. "Hey, as long as I'm in female form I seem to have lost all my spellcasting abilities. You want me to kibitz for you?"

Daggoth shook his head and, after a moment's hesitation, began a somatic gesture. I felt the tingle of gathering forces…

And then it happened.

Vashti had warned me but it wasn't the same as actually seeing it happen. Daggoth the Dark stopped moving. At first it looked as if he had suffered a *petit mal* seizure. But a few moments more and the effect was more like a hologram stopped in "freeze-frame" mode. Then he flickered like an old kinescope image and, for a moment, I could actually see right through him.

That's when a large meaty hand fell on my shoulder.

"C'mon, Notch-girl, let's go upstairs and dance the mattress jig."

I tried to pull my shoulder away. "Haul anchor, cabin boy; this harbor is closed for the evening."

His hand not only stayed on my shoulder; it squeezed and lifted me right out of my chair. "You forget yerself, green-goods: I'll do me business with the stablemaster." He gave Daggoth a brief glance. "Well, whadaya say, belswagger? Any objections to me taking the wren upstairs and threading the needle?"

Daggoth sat there, frozen, and continued to flicker.

"No objections, croshabelle; let's go."

The Nicole form I currently inhabited was actually a bit taller than my Halfelven avatar but her musculature was less dense and lacked the upper body strength I needed to pry myself loose from this goon.

So I stomped on his foot.

That loosened his grip enough for me to twist free but his fingernails raked my shoulder and he kept a portion of my halter-top in his fist. I tried to re-stretch the remaining material as I backed away but the mooring strap was gone and my left breast bobbled free, waving like a matador's cape before the bull. The crowd whistled approvingly but my assailant scowled at my public display of resistance. "You like it rough, bawdy-basket? That's just fine with me." His hands made grasping motions and his knuckles whitened. "I like my meat tenderized…" He lowered his head and rushed at me.

My choices were simple: fight or flight. And while my current form made the latter choice eminently more logical, my former instincts took over: I kicked our sailor boy right in the barnacles.

As I was saying: it only made him mad.

♀

There was a table between us now. When he dodged left, I dodged left—my left to his left, of course. And my right to his right. We had a momentary stalemate: he had run out of chairs, and my reflexes were better than his. I glanced over at Daggoth who had stopped flickering but was still transfixed in some unknown paralytic state. I could expect no help there.

Bill dove under the table, his fingers brushing my ankles as I leapt up on the tabletop. Like most bar-room tables, one leg was shorter than the others, and it tilted like one of the pinball machines in *Sal & Tony's Arcade Emporium.* I staggered over the edge and grabbed for a dangling chandelier. Caught it with one hand. My luck with barroom chandeliers was consistent: its anchor chain broke with a loud *chak* and we both landed on an adjacent table, smashing it to the floor, scattering cards, poker chips, drinks, and patrons. My outfit made an attempt to scatter with them. I might have been even more mindful of the cool breeze coming in off the harbor but for the multitude of hot, sweaty hands that helped me up, providing generous support to my bosom and backside. Those same solicitous hands then propelled me forward, into the arms of Barnacle Bill.

"Gotcha, girlie!" he snarled. A fine mist of fish and garlic washed over my face like sea spray and his fingers tightened like painful tourniquets around my arms, forcing them down and pinning them against my sides. "What say we finish this down here and treat everyone to the full measure of your charms." It wasn't even remotely a question, and he leaned in close to sandpaper the tops of my breasts with the coppery three-day stubble on his face and neck.

I couldn't move. I could barely squirm. Which only seemed to inflame him further. "Bill," I sighed deeply, "your lips…"

He raised his face from my cleavage. "What about my lips?" he leered.

"They're just below your *nose*," I said, leaning down and sinking my teeth into that bulbous appendage.

He screeched like a spanked monkey and brought his hands up to my throat. No good: I wasn't letting go. He loosed his grip, and I wasn't sure where his hands had gone until they smashed against the back of my head. You could call it a meeting of the minds—only the bone density of our respective foreheads kept our brains from mingling like a couple of scrambled eggs. Unfortunately, his skull seemed thicker than mine: I was still trying to figure out how there could be fog and stars at the same time when I felt his hands grasp the front of my clothing. A moment later I was on my way to the floor again. My garments didn't go with me.

I shouldn't have been afraid.

True, I was losing this fight and my assailant must have outweighed me by a hundred pounds. But I'd lost bigger fights against tougher foes and had the excrement pounded out of me by opponents bent on doing me a lot more harm than Barnacle Billy here. And my temper, which had redlined before this fracas had even started, was usually proof against any lack of confidence.

The madder I get, the more fearless I become and, by those standards, I should have reached an emotional zone of total invulnerability by now.

But I was suddenly afraid.

Which *really* made me mad!

And, curiously, that much more fearful and tearful.

It wasn't fair! And that made my eyes water in strange and unnerving ways because "fairness" was an expectation I had rid myself of many years before.

Bad enough that my arms and legs were suddenly useless but, even more worrisome, the paralysis was creeping into my brain, dissolving my last inclinations of resistance. Greater than the fear that I wouldn't be able to offer even a token struggle or act of defiance, was the growing horror that I was probably going to cry while he had his way with me.

It was like a war was going on inside my brain and body, with the tide of battle surging in one direction and then in the other.

Now I was back to being mad. And while he still had me effectively pinned, he was going to have to free one of his hands in a moment to unbutton his fly. If my corresponding hand could reach the four-inch, inlaid wooden hair-stick at the nape of my neck, I was going to treat these fifteenth-century barflies to a preview of the twentieth-century corndog.

But before we could find out who would ultimately "pin" whom, Barnacle Bill threw himself on top of me. That should have crushed what was left of my wind, my strength, my consciousness…

Except he never landed.

He hovered, arms and legs spread, just a scant six inches above my own prone form. His face conveyed a depth of surprise surpassing even my own. The room was suddenly quiet.

"I think you owe this lady an apology, sirrah," a quiet voice said. It was soft but deep and oh-so-rife with controlled menace.

"What—" choked Bill, trying to twist in order to look behind and above him. I could see now that my levitating lothario was suspended by his belt and that was making serious inroads on his comfort and his air supply.

"An *apology*, dolt. To the *lady*."

The sailor flung his arms about, trying to grasp the owner of the voice, who held him a couple of feet off of the floor. As he flailed like a frenzied sand crab, he opined on what would happen once he regained his feet.

"The *lady* is wanting an apology. If *I* want anything out of you, I'll read your entrails," the voice rumbled. B.B. suddenly flew sideways, taking out two tables and an assortment of chairs that were blocking his path to the bar. The mugs, candles, and bowls on top of the bar jumped a good six inches upon Bill's arrival.

I looked up and caught a glimpse of dark, chiseled features as my rescuer unfastened the clasp at his throat and, turning like a matador, swirled his cloak down and over me, affording some warmth and modesty. He stalked to the bar and grasped the back of Bill's belt and lifted him, one-handed, from his nest of shattered lumber. A moment later Bill was back, hovering at my side, and contemplating the sawdust patterns on the barroom floor.

"Now, *varlet*, one last time: an apology to the lady. Loud enough for everyone to hear. I'll not ask again."

Bill muttered something under his breath but it didn't sound anything like an apology.

The stranger's free hand sought the area between the sailor's legs, closed into a fist and tightened.

"Urp!" said Bill. "Sorry. Sorry! Sorrysorrysor*rysorrysorry!*"

The stranger's knuckles turned white, so did Bill's face. "*SorryohgodsIamSOSORRY!*" he finished, two octaves higher.

Tall, dark and handsome turned his face to address me. "How says my lady? Shall I dismiss this ruffian? Or chastise him further?"

"Let us be done," I wheezed, propping myself up to a sitting position.

"Barkeep!" my rescuer called. "How much for yon window?"

"T-two gold," came the stuttering reply.

"I'll go you five," he concluded, releasing Bill's barnacles and fished through his purse with his free hand. "For your trouble as well as the materials." A platinum disc went sailing across the room. So did Bill.

The bartender caught the first. The wall intercepted the second.

"Oops. Missed." The handsome stranger sounded only vaguely disappointed. He took three steps toward Bill before his hapless quarry got up and threw himself, headfirst, through the window. It was probably the smartest move Bill had made all night.

I turned to check on Daggoth before thanking my mysterious rescuer. He wasn't flickering but he still wasn't moving. He'd keep for another few minutes, I decided as I turned back to address my hero of the hour. Maybe I was still shaky from my near-rape experience but I decided that if Tall, Dark, and Handsome wanted a kiss for his efforts, it was the least I could do. Actually, the most I *would* do—and no tongues—but I certainly wasn't going to get involved in a long, drawn-out, discussion of gender transmogrification and how I was actually an example of cross-dressing taken to the penultimate level.

I turned back and found myself face-to-face with familiar features. "What happened to you?" Mick asked.

The handsome stranger was gone.

♂

"This traveling down to The Underworld…what are the odds on round-trip tickets?" Angel asked as she swung up and into the saddle of a chestnut bay.

"It can't be all that hard," My ex-wife mused as her palomino danced in anticipation. "After all, Robert visited The Infernal City before and came back. So how hard can it be?"

"About as hard as burglarizing the same house twice." I kicked the door to the stall open. "When they know you're coming back for a second try."

"But you are the Demiurge incarnate, right? I mean you're practically one of the gods when you invoke your Programmer status." Vashti's confidence was starting to destabilize.

"Pick any cultural mythology." I double-checked the girth straps on Ghost's flight-saddle and led him out of his stall. "You'll find at least one good story about a god or hero travelling to the Underworld to perform some quest or mission, usually more. The Greeks had a hat full of 'em." I mounted up as Vashti triggered the counterweight to the stable doors. Beyond them stretched an underground passage leading out and up to a concealed exit in the nearby forest. "Just about every one ends with the protagonist signed up for an extended visit."

As we started riding up the gradual incline, proximity spells triggered small witchlights that extinguished again once we had passed them by.

"I don't like this," she muttered.

"I thought you were bored."

"So how do we get there?" Angel seemed anxious to change the subject.

"Good question."

My ex scowled. "Bad answer."

"Depends on which Hell we want to go to," I continued, trying to ignore her. "If we want to enter Hades, there's the caverns of Acherusia in Epirus, or Heraclea Pontica, or an entrance gate near Cape Taenarum and another at Colonus, dedicated to the Eumenides..."

"It's all Greek to me," Vashti murmured.

I fought back a smile: clearly I was out of practice on the ignoring stuff. "The Egyptian Underworld lies to the West where the sun sets. The Assyro-Babylonian Underworld lies beneath the earth, beyond the abyss of the Apsu, inside the Seven-fold Walls. The Underworld of the Phoenicians, Canaanites, and Hittites lies under The Mountain of the North. Niflheim or Niflhel, the Norse Mist-world, is located between the roots of Yggdrasil, to the north of the immense abyss, and is guarded by the monstrous Garm. If we head for the Finno-Ugric Underworld, Tuonela, we'll have a three-week march ahead of us: a week through thickets, a week through woods, then a week through deep forests."

Angel made a face.

"Easier than the Abode of the Dead for India's mythos," I said.

Vashti nodded. "The moon, right?"

"Very good, Grasshopper. And unless you're prepared to turn the travelling arrangements over to Cyrano de Bergerac, I suggest we cross that one off our itinerary. Likewise the Chinese Underworld."

"Hard to reach?" Angel asked as we approached the vine-curtained mouth of the passage. No witchlights glimmered these last thirty yards lest they betray our exit point to outsiders.

"Initially, no. It lies beyond the Gate of Demons—Kuei-men-kuan—at the town of Feng-tu on the river How Nai-ho, crossed by three bridges. But there are eighteen hells distributed among ten law-courts to which they are attached. I figure there's easier ways of getting into Hell than going through the legal system."

We ducked and the leafy shroud of greenery seemed to part a little to permit us exit. The darkness of the final stretch of passageway helped in adjusting to the glimmer of moonlight outside. I didn't have to look behind me to know that the cave was once again invisible behind a wall of ivy. Of course, secret exits with concealed lighting and camouflage vines aren't very effective when you're jabbering away while you're slipping out.

"What about the Japanese mythologies?"

Vashti jumped in: "Two routes. We can either take a sloping and very winding road which begins in Izumo province or a bottomless abyss situated on the seashore." She grinned at me (although it looked more like a nervous grimace than anything else). "And for two hundred bonus points can you tell me the delightful name of Japanese Hell?"

"Which would you prefer?" I grumped. *"Yomi-tsu-kuni,* the Land of Darkness, *Ne no Kuni,* the Land of Roots, or *Soko no Kuni*, the Deep Land?" Apparently my nerves were starting to show, as well.

Angel furrowed her brow. "Aren't there any back doors into Hell?"

"Of course," said a new voice. "Thousands, in fact. More people end up in Hell via the back doors than the obvious entrances."

"Who goes there!" Vashti demanded sharply. I just tugged Ghost to a stop and leaned upon the saddlehorn as a nightmare creature moved out of the shadows.

Actually, two nightmare creatures. One *was* an actual Nightmare: a Hellmount that looked like a horse until you noticed its fiery red eyes, hooves of iron, and the shadow patterns that rippled across its inky hide. The steam venting from its flared nostrils was also a dead giveaway.

The rider removed all doubt of her quadruped's taxonomy. A Demoness sat astride the hellmount wearing form-fitting black, scaled leather that contrasted nicely with her pearlescent skin. Small, vestigial horns peeked through her mist of bonewhite hair and leathery batwings fanned back from her shoulders.

She looked vaguely familiar.

"Well met, Riplakish," the Demoness said, reining in her Nightmare steed. "I see thou'rt more prepared this time."

"Prepared?" Vashti wanted to know.

"Three human sacrifices to propitiate the Elder gods of the Abyss," she answered with a razor-toothed smile.

THREE

♂

"Madam, do I know you?"

The Demoness smoothed back a startled expression. "You were not so discomforted to be seen with me while I was made Human."

Human? *Ah!* "Lilith?"

"Have you consorted with so many Succubae that I am easily forgotten?"

Vashti cleared her throat. "Succubae?"

"You look different."

"A little eyeliner…" she preened, "…some blush…"

"No, I mean, you look like you got a promotion."

"Nay. I am still an Archdemoness."

Hmmm. The last I had heard, Orcus had threatened to do this. "I think I preferred the Lily Munster look."

"Liked her better as a Succubus, did you?" Vashti muttered.

"You said that before," Lilith pouted.

"What? When?"

"The last time you were a True Spirit." Hmm. *I* hadn't been present during Natasha Skovoroda's last incursion into the Matrix so I wouldn't have been a "True Spirit" then. Maybe there was something to this Nicole/Alternate Me story after all.

"What's this about three sacrifices?" Angel/Westbrook wanted to know.

"She was just kidding." I turned to the Archdemoness. "Tell her you were just kidding."

Lilith sighed. "I know this fool too well to think he would contemplate such actions so, yea, I made a jest of sorts." Her face grew grim. "E'en though it be, in truth, a wise stratagem."

"Meaning what?" Angel still wanted to know. Vashti was uncharacteristically quiet.

"Meaning ye two be his vulnerabilities as allies. The golem, I wot, can take care of itself. But ye would serve his purpose best as gifts to the Dark Powers that shall encompass thee soon."

Vashti finally jumped in. "Who invited her along?"

"Thou needst all the help thee can get," Lilith answered.

"Agreed. But why should we invite *you* along?"

"Ladies—" I tried.

"So you're a Demon?" Angel asked, taking in the batwings, fangs, and peekaboo horns with wide-eyed enthusiasm.

"Archdemon," Vashti corrected.

"-Ness," Lilith tacked on.

"Oh, come now." In spite of her smile, Vashti's claws were definitely out now. "Not still beholden to ancient gender modifiers, are we? Actor/actress, hunter/huntress, author/authoress—that all went by the board in the late twentieth century."

The Archdemoness smiled just enough to show the tip of one elongated tooth. "Remember where you be, dearie: 'twill be hundreds of years before the twentieth, much less the twenty-*first*, century shows its face around here."

Angel turned to me. "Is she going to take us to Hell?"

Lilith chuckled. "Mayhap, Gretchen. Though *that* tart-tongued Amazon," she nodded at Vashti, "may prove sufficient for your leader. The word Below is that she hath given Riplakish more than a few tours of Hell during their past incarnations."

The golem had the self-contained weaponry but it was my ex-wife's eyes shooting twin lasers at the moment. "Rob! Have you been discussing our personal business?"

This definitely wasn't helping.

♀

A night wind was bringing moisture in off the choppy waters of Terhan Bay making the air heavy with humidity. The scream that came from the alley across the street would have awakened the dead in most villages, but Calabastor's turgid mists were as effective in muffling their urgency as a pillow placed over the face of the victim. Mick and I looked up and down the street; no one ventured out of any of the nearby taverns. We looked at each other: two unarmed women alone in the dark. Without speaking a word we dropped the stoned sorcerer we were supporting between us and ran for toward alleyway where the cry had originated.

In my Halfelven avatar I would have had the advantage of infravision in negotiating the darkness. Nicole's human eyes gave no such advantage and neither of us was equipped with lantern or torch. Careful consideration would rule against such a response but then careful consideration would have never found me in any of my Matrix-related predicaments of the past year.

All that mattered was someone was in trouble and be damned if we would stand across the street and wait for more convenient circumstances.

I pushed ahead of Mick as we entered the narrow confines of the darkened alley. Whoever was hidden in the deeper darkness of the unlit passageway would have the advantage in being able to see us while we were effectively blind. While I figured I was better equipped—or at least more experienced—to deal with a hidden assailant, I hadn't counted on him having a cannon. There was no concussive roar, no muzzle flash, but the cannonball was still most effective: it smashed into me, smashing me into Mick.

The dim confines of the alley turned to boundless darkness.

♂

"You!" Angel suddenly exclaimed. She pointed a lacquered nail at Lilith. "You're an archetype!"

"Archdemoness. We've already covered this point, honey."

"No. I mean an arche*type!*"

In her pique, Lilith was losing the archaic phraseology from her speech patterns. "Who're you calling a 'type'?"

Angel turned to me. "She's an archetype, right?"

I shrugged. "Anytime you approach the metaphysical, you deal with allegory and symbolism. So, yeah, I guess a Demon—"

"Archdemoness."

"—would qualify as an archetype of sorts."

Angel shook her head and her ponytail waved languorously. "Not Freudian, Campbellian."

"Campbellian?"

"Joseph Campbell. 'The Hero With A Thousand Faces.' Surely you've read him?"

"Surely I have. He's *de rigeur* for anyone taking mythological studies."

"Then you know what I mean."

"Well, I don't," Vashti groused. "Who's Joe Campbell?"

I looked at Angel who looked back at me.

"Author," she said, "academic."

"Anthropologist, mythologist," I added.

"He took Carl Jung's concepts of archetypes and mythic content to new levels and in new directions."

"And that's where Lily comes in, right?"

The archdemoness glared at my ex. "Lilith!"

Angel nodded. "The question is: which one?"

"Which archetype?"

"I am not a 'witch' or a 'type!' I am an Archdemon!"

"Ess," Vashti reminded.

"Yes!"

"So what type archetype are we talking here?"

Angel looked at me. "I may need a little help here."

I sighed. "Well, the specialized list is somewhat long but the basic components break down to the Hero, the Mentor, the Threshold Guardian, Herald, Shapeshifter, Shadow, and Trickster. Every myth or legend can be diagrammed in regard to the archetypes and the roles they play, as well as the three stages of action in each quest or story."

Vashti brightened. "So, there's like a mythical blueprint? We can do this by the numbers?"

"You may not like the numbers before we're finished."

"But we can start by identifying Miss Forked-tongue, right?"

"Hey!"

"It's not that simple," Westbrook mused. "An archetype can change categories as the story progresses, or fall into more than one category at the same time." "Doesn't sound like a very well organized system, if you ask me."

I was about to point out that no one had asked her when she leaned forward in her saddle and considered Lilith with a cocked eyebrow. "So what kind of archetype would fit Evil-Demon-bitch-from-Hell?"

I was afraid that Lilith would go ballistic, but she merely smiled in return. "I believe we were discussing *me,* Dearie. It can't always be about you."

"Let's run down the list," I suggested, hoping a little mental exercise would prove distracting.

Westbrook picked up the cue. "Well, at the top of the list is the Hero."

"'Tis thee, milord." It was the first time Misty Dawn had spoken all morning and everyone turned to look at her. *"'Tis true!"* she insisted. *"Milord Riplakish hath always championed the cause of the good, the weak, and the lowly."*

Vashti smirked. "A nice excuse for the crowd you hang out with, dear."

"Present company..." I rejoined.

"Since you are leading this expedition into Hell, I think your identity is a given," Angel continued, "so let's move on down the list."

"Mentor."

We all turned to stare at the android.

"I am learning to access the Matrix databases. Mythology, religion, philosophy, science...so much is beyond my ken. But simple referents—I can scan articles and retrieve specific abstracts."

"*Specific* abstracts?" Vashti mused. "Isn't that an oxymoron?"

"Oxymoron." Misty Dawn's artificial brow furrowed: *"Accessing..."*

"Never mind. Let's get back to Mentor."

"The wise old man or old woman," Angel added.

"Don't look at me." Lilith was clearly displeased. "Do I look like an old woman to you?"

"Mentor was a male. All translations of The Odyssey confirm this. Although Homer's works would appear to be more fiction than reliable history, it can be assumed that the consistency of gender in the various versions—"

I interrupted. "It's not an issue of gender..."

"You're a fine one to talk." My ex, of course.

"...we're speaking of Mentor in the abstract."

"Ah. I see. Then: 'mentor,' noun; a trusted counselor or guide, a tutor—"

"We're speaking of archetypes, M.D., not dictionary definitions."

"Though it's pretty close for our purposes," Angel amended. "The Mentor archetype is a character who serves the role of counselor, guide, or tutor. This archetype usually takes the form of an old man or woman as age is symbolic of experience and wisdom."

Lilith smiled. "Skip the 'old' part and that will probably mean me."

"Guide, maybe." Vashti smiled in turn and, for a moment, her teeth seemed more pointed than Lilith's. "But trusted counselor? I don't think so."

Angel shook her head and contemplated the Archdemoness. "Since we are going to Hell, I figure you more for the role of 'Herald' or 'Threshold Guardian'."

I saw the look on Vashti's face. "Maybe it would be easier to place this in a more complete context."

"Please."

"Most myths break down into a three-part structure. There are further stages under each segment, but the primary structure can be defined as Departure, Descent, and Return."

"In our case," Angel added, "we are departing the world we know, planning to descend into Hell, and return to this world with Natasha Skovoroda's psyche-file when we are done."

"It's that Return-structure part that has me the most concerned," Vashti muttered.

"In another sense," I continued, "we depart the real world when we climb into a Cephtronics Cradle and undergo psyche-extraction, descend into the Matrix where we experience otherworldly adventures, and then return to the real world when we are done."

"Assuming we don't die in the process," Vashti added under her breath.

"So, already we can see that three-part structure is adaptable on more than one level. It's the same with archetypes." I gestured around our circle. "Each of us here is the Hero within the context of our own experience. And sometimes we may act as Mentor for one another."

"And sometimes a Mentor can be a Herald, as well," Angel added. She turned to the Archdemoness. "The Mentor issue is debatable at this point, but you could still be a Herald."

"My name is *not* Harold! My name is *Lilith!*"

"It's the archetype for a messenger who issues the 'call to adventure.'"

Vashti was skeptical. "But we were already on our way to Hell before Miss Pointy-teeth showed up."

I shrugged. "So...you think Threshold Guardian?"

"That depends," Angel replied, giving Lilith an appraising look. "Will she attempt to hinder or aid us in our underworld travels."

The Archdemoness sniffed. "I owe the Bard, here, much and I hope to owe him more ere his business below is done. The rest of you I could give two hoots in Hell about." She examined a razor-sharp talon. "And I mean that in the most literal sense."

Angel pondered. "But if all goes according to mythic form, there will be at least one Threshold Guardian—likely more—and they will complicate our quest to reach Dyantha's shade in the underworld."

"That would be us," said the old, one-eyed man sitting astride the eight-legged horse. On either side were two large men wearing breastplates and bearskins, mounted on large horses that made Clydesdales look absolutely petite. Two other riders were riding flank, behind them.

The road ahead was effectively closed.

♀

Sergeant Smedley was one hundred per cent Vampire-proofed. In fact, the garlic on his breath would drive off most humans, as well. Were it not for the fact that I was trying to shake off a concussion and incapable of rising unassisted, I would have fled the vicinity.

"'Ere now, Miss Doosay. Cap'n Jenks'll be right back. You just rest gentle fer now."

"My friend?" I croaked. The cannonball had hit me square in the breadbasket and I still had trouble getting my breath.

"She'll be fine," said a familiar voice. "She took quite a spill with you on top of her. But you took the brunt of the blow."

I eased myself up on my elbows and saw my handsome stranger tending to Mick. His cloak was slashed and dark with blood.

"You're hurt!"

"I was stupid. I heard the scream, saw you run into the alley, and followed as fast as I could. Finding you down and injured, I was momentarily distracted and turned my back to the darkness." He bared his teeth. They were white and even. "I allowed the villain that one opportunity…no more. He was the one fortunate to escape with his life."

"It would seem that you are my guardian angel, this night, good sir."

He executed a sweeping bow while still on his knees and propping up Mick with one, well-muscled arm. "At your service, milady."

"Milady!" It was Jenks. "Sink me, madam! I cannot believe my good fortune conjoined with your ill luck!"

I turned reluctantly. "Captain. Has there been another murder?"

"Dem me, yes!" He was huffing and puffing as he toddled toward us from the back street that was now half-illuminated with flickering torches. His eyes were wide and bright and his lips twitched as if he tightly wound and awaiting unnatural release. "I know you will gainsay me, Mistress, but I tell you that you really should not look."

I was less inclined to argue with him this time, but, of course, I needed to anyway. I turned to ask my handsome stranger for assistance in getting to my feet, but he was gone again.

♂

"Riplakish of Dyrinwall," the old, one-eyed man bellowed, "I would speak with thee!"

I took in the eyepatch, the eight-legged horse, and then the two big guys flanking him on either side. As imposing as this triumvirate was, it was the woman and the little guy on smaller mounts farther back on the trail who might bear the most watching.

Vashti cleared her throat. "You know these guys?"

I nodded and slowly drew my katana-longsword. "Woden," I said, saluting the old man on his octoped.

"Woden: principal god of Teutonic mythology, called 'Odin' by the northern tribes, also called Othin," Misty Dawn elaborated. *"Head of the Aesir pantheon, the all-father, god of victory and battle, father of the slain, god of the dead, law-giver, the one-eyed, god of the hanged—"*

"Enough," I murmured.

"So much for hanging out with the good, the meek, and the lowly," Vashti whispered.

I saluted the burly, redheaded giant to his left. "Donar. Long time no see."

"Donar: ancient Germanic storm god; identified by early Romans with Jupiter but better known as Thor among the Icelandic cultures, particularly Norway. Also known as Horagales in Lappish and Thunor in Anglo-Saxon. War deity, also closely associated with the skies, storms, and sea travel. Viking god of justice—"

"You're being rude, M.D."

Teeth glimmered in his bushy, red beard and muscles bunched in a massive, freckled arm as he raised Mjollnir above his head. "To-ho, Bard! When our business is done, I ask a boon!"

I shook my head. "Alas, I travel without my harp."

"Thou never should'st have taught him that song, milord."

"What song?" Vashti wanted to know. Donar's scowl of disappointment was more than a little unnerving.

"It's title be 'If I Had A Hammer.'"

"Which he always wants me to sing over and over and over," I muttered. "And then only the first verse."

"'Tis most fitting, though. He doth hammer in both the morning and the evening."

"All over this land," I agreed.

"Ho, young godling," rumbled the third, raising an arm that ended as a handless stump, "hast thou forgotten me so soon?"

"Forgotten you? Nay," I said. "Whenever I hear the wolves howl at first frost, it always brings a Tyr to mine eye."

The god slapped his thigh with his remaining hand and roared with laughter. "An excellent jest! Though I prefer Tiwaz to any other name in my travels."

The android turned toward me. *"Thou makest a pun, milord: Tiwaz, Tiw, Teiwa, Ziu—Tyr."*

"Let's not—"

"Germanic sky god, god of war."

Vashti rolled her eyes: "Aren't they all?"

"—give any more theo-mythic dissertations, right now, huh, M.D.?" I resheathed my sword and moved my horse a little toward Woden. As I passed by Angel, I leaned over and spoke very softly. "See those two in the back? The smallish fellow is Loki, and while he fits the archetypal definition of Shapeshifter, he's always operating in full-blown Trickster mode."

"And the other," she asked, "the woman?"

"Hel: 'Shadow.' Without a doubt." I rode forward, to a point halfway between my party and theirs.

"Speak, All-father; Riplakish of Dyrinwall attends to thy words."

The old man smiled and I remembered that Woden was hardly any trustworthier than Loki was. And Loki's reputation for deceit rivaled Coyote's and beat every other deity in every other pantheon, hands down. "We would ride with thee on thy quest and offer our swords—"

Donar cleared his throat.

"—and hammer—in thy service."

Oh dear.

My first rule of thumb in dealing with deities is never owe them anything. Offers of divine aid always come with hidden price tags. And even when they don't have hidden motives they tend to muck things up with a volatile mix of careless enthusiasm and a total disregard for the laws of physics.

"A generous offer, milord," I answered slowly, "but unnecessary, to be sure. We anticipate no difficulties on our journey..." This was quickly turning hopeless—as the bards say, "Never lie to a liar or attempt to deceive a deceiver." I smiled wanly.

"But we ride to the same destination," Woden purred. "Surely there is mutual advantage to our traveling together?"

I turned and looked back at Lilith. "Does *everyone* know our itinerary?"

The Archdemoness seemed to be occupied with something on the shoulder of her cloak and didn't immediately answer.

"Oh, for Hilde's sake!" Loki kicked his mount forward and closed the distance between us. "The others may act like thou'rt *Gotterdammerung* personified, but the fact remains that thou'rt riding into the jaws of death. Never mind the legions of the Underworld that would harrow up thy blood and freeze thy marrow, thy puny swords have not sufficient power to gainsay a frost giant, much less the pride of the Aesir before thee."

I smiled. "Don't think we're up to the task?"

He smiled back. "'Tis said thy bark is worse than thy bite."

I made my smile grow and gestured back toward the rest of my party. "Pick my weakest companion."

Loki's grey blue eyes narrowed. I knew he was considering the frightful, archdemoness astride her nightmare mount, Vashti and Angel, decked out in chainmail with mace and maul. Then he smiled and I knew he had settled on Misty Dawn in her cotton and muslin gown. "The unarmed wench, of course."

I nodded. "Thou'rt correct. She is the weakest among our most puissant band." I motioned for the android to ride forward.

As she reigned in alongside me, I pointed at a lone pine tree, some seventy feet tall, on the hill a hundred yards or so away.

"M.D., pretend that tree is a frost giant and he just said something rude about my mother."

The android considered and extended a slim white arm. A moment later a particle beam emerged from her palm and disintegrated the top of the hill and the tree in a blue-white flash that momentarily blinded us. There was a small clap of thunder as air rushed in to fill the space that was previously occupied by wood, needles, and several tons of earth and stone.

I blinked away the afterimage of the flash and took in the expressions of the Norse pantheon. Loki and Tiwaz were still in shock. Donar was staring at Misty Dawn like moon-struck adolescent in love. But Woden's expression unnerved me. His eyes filled with naked pleading, he repeated his offer to accompany us into the Underworld.

And then he spoke the forbidden word, a word that no god dare speak lest Ragnarok be invoked before its time.

"Please?"

Now I was scared.

FOUR

♀

Daggoth the Dark pulled himself up and sat on a trunk directly behind the driver's bench seat on the wagon. "This is ridiculous," he fumed.

"This is a lot of things," I agreed, trying to keep the spokeless, iron-girt wheels in the shallower ruts of the road. "And though 'ridiculous' ranks high on the list, there are a few choice adjectives that I would invoke first."

"We aren't going to solve this Calabastor ripper case by running off on extraneous research trips."

"Bugger the investigation," I snapped, snapping the reins for good measure. "We're not going back until we come up with a cure for your condition!"

"It's nothing—"

"Nothing?" I looked at Mick. "Did he say 'nothing'?"

She nodded.

"Did it look like nothing to you?"

She shook her head. "Seemed like something to me."

"You keep out of this," he said. "I understand that you weren't even there when it happened."

"She was there in time for the reboot sequence," I said. "She helped me carry you back to the inn."

"I walked—"

"Your feet dragged the ground while we shouldered you between us."

"You know, as a woman, you've got some mouth on you."

I looked at Mick. "Was that a sexist remark?"

She nodded. "Sounded like a sexist remark to me."

"Look, this is no big deal—" The wagon bounced over a half-buried stone and he suddenly leaned over the side and regurgitated what looked like three tankards' worth of ale.

"Great," Mick observed. "We get knocked down, run over, and then get to tour another crime scene that would give a splatterpunk nightmares, then stay up all night waiting for the livery stables to open—and he's the one barfing!"

"That's my guy; a real Duke Pukem."

"Yeah," he retorted, wiping his mouth with the hem of his sleeve, "and you're a regular Norma Bates."

"Okay," I sighed. "Let's pretend that you're not my friend. That I don't give a damn about whether your existence is eventually reduced to a continuous, background-looped subroutine on the Avatar Array."

"Fine." I'll swear he was actually pouting.

"Fine. Except it's still not fine. I no longer have spell casting abilities, someone else has possession of my armor and weapons, *and* I'm supposed to be the bait for a demented killer in the seediest, nastiest, dirtiest—" I eyed Mick, "—help me out here."

"What Dr. Ripley is trying to say is that his life is turning out to be a real drag."

I looked for her to crack a smile. She didn't.

I sighed. "Look, it's hard enough trying to figure out how to look after myself, without having to look after the two of you, as well." I waved away both protestations of their being able to take care of themselves. "Yeah, whatever. Anyway, Yudu the Necromancer is the closest spellcaster I trust and I'd like to consult with her, first. If we can come up with a cure, we'll be back on the Calabastor waterfront before you can say Mr. Mxyzptlk backwards. Whadaya say?"

"Trouble," Mick said.

"Trouble?"

She nodded and pointed down the road. "Trouble."

Trouble was a very large barbarian warrior in a very small loincloth, standing in the middle of the road and leaning on a huge, unsheathed sword like it was a fancy walking stick.

"Well, well. Looky here," he said, tipping his horned helm back on his head. "My favorite lockdown lover. How's tricks, Nicky?"

It was "Lech" Luther.

♂

"I don't like it." I didn't mean to speak out loud. We had been riding all night with few breaks and I was tired.

Angel, riding on my right, looked over at me in surprise. "I can understand your reluctance to ride into the jaws of Hell with minimal support. But I'd think having a quintet of Norse gods at your side has now improved the odds considerably."

"You'd think so, wouldn't you?" Vashti chimed in to my left. "But with him there's always something. Always the attitude. You should try living with him."

"I'm not Dr. Westbrook's type, Dear."

"See what I mean?"

I sighed. I seemed to be doing that more often of late. "I used to be sweet and charming. I wonder what sort of influences could precipitate such a personality shift?"

"What are you suggesting? That I—*don't* turn away when I'm talking to you! What are you looking at back there?"

"Hel," I murmured.

"Methinks hell rides to your left, Bard," Lilith chortled.

Angel leaned over and whispered, "I think she picks on you when she gets nervous."

"She's always nervous," I answered.

"What?" Vashti was distracted from her retort to the Archdemoness. "What did you say?"

I leaned the opposite direction to confab with my ex-wife. "Look, it's bad enough that Woden or Odin—all the serious Norse gods—are practically begging us to let them come along. Something is seriously wrong here." I glanced over my shoulder. "Worse, to have Loki along and riding at my back. But what really peels my myelin is the lady back there," I said, trying to make my nod barely noticeable.

"You mean the one with the domino make-up on?"

"Um," I said, "it's not make-up."

"What? You're telling me her face is really half-black and half-white? And that the black half…" she snuck another look, "…isn't really a face?"

The left side of Hel's face was featureless. Not just in the sense that it was devoid of eye, half nose, and half mouth, but in the manner in which it absorbed all light. As if it were an infinite emptiness that tunneled through space and time to the very end of the universe. Where bared by her garments, her left arm and leg were also blacker than black, a total absence of color that suggested limb-shaped rents in the fabric of reality.

"The Norse goddess of the underworld is the ancient precursor of proto-Christian damnation," I whispered.

"Hmmm. Just add fire and brimstone—and an extra 'l.'" She frowned. "So, isn't she a little out of her element?"

"My point precisely."

"So why don't you ask her what she's doing out of the pit?"

"Are you serious?"

"Men! Is this some kind of missing gene thing? Can't stop and ask for directions when you're lost. Can't just come out and just ask the gods, 'What's up, guys? I can't help noticing that you're more than a little somewhere-over-the-rainbow…"

"Will you stop—"

"'…What's the point-spread on Minnesota? Is Yggdrasil another species of Yggplant? Can I get a bumper sticker that says, 'Balder Is Beautiful?' If someone tells Odin to go Frig himself…"

"Vashti—"

"…does he run back to Valhalla to visit the queen? Whoa, is that a drinking horn in your girdle or are you just happy to see me?'"

"Don't kibitz," I murmured through clenched teeth.

"Perimeter alert!" All heads snapped up at the sound of the android's voice and it took just seconds to locate the trigger for her warning.

There was a small army of gods running toward us with weapons drawn and the unholy gleam of battle-fever in their eyes.

♀

"If you're supposed to be a woman, how come you're so ugly?"

Mick smiled sweetly. "Ugly is as ugly does."

The barbarian blinked. Not only did he not have any kind of a comeback; he probably didn't even know that he had just been verbally body-slammed.

"I mean, Nicky here," he finally continued, "has always claimed to be a man but here she is, just as feminine inside this computer headgame as she is in the real world."

Daggoth cleared his throat. "Actually she really is who she says she is. A man, I mean. Robert R—"

"Shaddup, you old coot! I got eyes in my head—" Limbach had rounded on the befuddled sorcerer with a sudden viciousness that only a select few of the sanitarium's clientele had been privileged to witness.

Mick muttered something that sounded like "And that's about it."

"—and I don't need no friends of hers tryin' to interfere with me in the performance of my duties."

Warning bells went off in my head. "Um, 'duties?'"

The barbarian reached into his haversack and rummaged around. "Miss Doucet, here, is a patient of Wallbank Sanitarium and is subject to all rules and regulations while outside the confines of secured quarters. That includes her being under the supervision of a senior member of the sanitarium staff. As Dr. Westbrook is currently not present, all discretionary authority rests with me…" He pulled out a pair of iron manacles.

I started backing away. "Uh-uh."

"Standard operating procedures include body restraints when the patient evidences delusional episodes." He twirled a heavy metal cuff at the end of its chain. "Guess your 'I'm-a-man' thing would qualify, wouldn't it?"

"Here now—" Daggoth began. That's as far as he got. Limbach released another foot of chain and swung it in a half circle, smashing Daggoth down on the wagon bed and knocking Mick clean out of her seat.

I turned and ran.

Limbach wanted me, not them. I couldn't help them by staying but I could draw him away before anything worse happened—and there was no way that I was going to let him put me in any kind of restraints. I ran as if my very life depended on it.

Knowing Limbach, it very well might.

Broken down to basics, the Dreamlands world programs were structured as RPGs—games taken to the ultimate level of virtual realism. And, as such, advantage accrued to the more experienced players. The longer your avatar stayed alive and completed various tasks and adventures, the more powerful your avatar became. There were other modifiers, of course, but the bottom line: a strong, smart, and agile third-level avatar has its work cut out for it if it tries to take on a weak, slow, and stupid but forty-seventh level avatar.

As Riplakish of Dyrinwall, I could handle Limbach's barbarian with one hand tied behind my back. As Nicole Doucet, however, I was at some disadvantage: I had no idea as to how The Machine classified my current avatar. In the real world, Nicole Doucet had been an expert fencer, a champion equestrienne, and an Olympic-class archer. Inside the Matrix she had retained those skills, perhaps added new ones.

But did her native abilities become mine now that I wore her avatar? It might be that I just looked like her without actually inhabiting the same avatar.

But even if I didn't actually acquire her proficiencies, I was still smarter than Limbach, knew more about The Matrix than even the most experienced Dreamwalker, and—judging from the growing distance between us—I was more fleet of limb, as well. I smirked as I glanced back over my shoulder a third time. Not only faster and more agile, but possessed of better stamina and endurance: the barbarian looked winded and we had barely gone a mile from the wagon.

But, in looking back to gauge my advantage, I lost it. I tripped over something—a root, most likely—and went sprawling.

I scrambled to my feet as quickly as I could—not as quickly as I might, as I was still dressed in one of the costumes Daggoth had selected to lure Calabastor's slut-slayer. But I still might have evaded the barbarian's grasping fingers were it not for my lengthy tresses. Back in Wallbank Sanitarium I had short-cropped Nicole's hair; here I had not yet gotten around to rustling up a pair of shears. I suddenly found myself jerked backwards, the follicles at the back of my head exploding in fiery protest. I was slammed down to the ground on my back and Limbach stepped forward to straddle me.

Big mistake.

I tried the same maneuver I'd attempted on Barnacle Bill the night before. Kicking "under and up" is not the same as "being under" and "kicking up." I had better aim and better leverage. The trick was to wriggle out of the way before he collapsed on top of me.

The next trick was to figure out what to do about all of those spears pointed at me from just a few feet away…

♂

The "army" was approaching in two parts.

To the rear rode an assortment of animal-headed humanoids. Although there were several human faces, a variety of cat, bull, jackal, bird, crocodile, snake, and cow heads resided above human shoulders.

The Egyptians were in town.

Running before them, in the vanguard, was a squad of pale-skinned, blond-on-blonde deities wearing leather, furs, and wool.

"Methinks the desertlords will have them in another moment," Tyr observed quietly.

"It is shameful how they flee!" Thor was clearly disgusted. "They should stand their ground and fight!"

"Fight?" Vashti was clearly taken aback. "They're outnumbered three to one!"

"More than even odds for any god of the North," Thor insisted. "Ukko and his brood would make as if to stand against us for authority in the Northern Realms, yet they would be gainsaid by sandscum. Ptah!" He spat to the side and made a moue of distaste.

"No matter the victor, here," Loki said, riding up from behind us, "the conflict will weaken the survivors and that can only strengthen us in making our claims."

Tyr shook his head and turned to Odin. "I like it not, milord. It is true that the Finns trespass upon our territory and can be unpleasant neighbors. But as Northmen, they be like distant kin, while the 'Gyptians are an alien foe. Methinks we need embrace them as allies for now."

"What?" wondered Thor aloud, "Is not the Demiurge here ally enough?"

I gave the redheaded thundergod a look. "You talking about me, Chuckles? 'Cause at the moment we're just two guys riding in the same direction."

Odin nodded absently. "I can keep Ukko in his place. But I like not the mien of the one called Ra. And Set reminds me overmuch of Loki."

"Hey!"

Tyr grinned. "Which is worse? The jackal who acts like a god? Or the god who acts like a jackal?"

"Don't talk about me like I'm not sitting right here."

Two ravens fluttered down and landed upon Odin's shoulders. Each sidled up near his head and inclined their beaks towards an ear.

"One at a time, damn you! I am the All-father, not the All-listener! Hugin, you go first."

"It's my turn! Hugin went first last time!"

"Did not!" squawked the other black bird.

"Did too!"

"Did not!"

"Did too!"

Hugin turned to Odin. "Who are you going to believe? Me? Or some old bag of feathers?"

Odin smiled with his teeth. "Hugin, you are Thought. But Munin, here, is Memory and I think it be her turn."

Munin opened her beak and silently waggled her tongue.

"Be gracious, old crow, and make your report."

"I have much to tell—"

"Cut to the chase, Muni; tell him about the Bab-asses!"

Munin ruffled her feathers and muttered something unintelligible.

"The gods of the Babylonians and Assyrians? What about them?" Odin demanded.

"Nergal," I muttered, remembering a barroom encounter, "Ereshkigal…."

"An alliance," Hugin hissed, "with the Egyptians!"

"I'm telling this!" Munin squawked.

"Not quickly enough!"

"Donar!" Woden was suddenly decisive, "show the desert-dwellers how their pretty staffs and scepters make efficient lightning rods."

"Aw, Pa! I want to see 'em fight!"

"Maybe we'll get lucky, boy" Tyr offered, "and we'll all get to fight."

Loki scowled. "If the gods of the east unite, it would be prudent for the gods in the north to stand, shoulder to shoulder…"

"And if we do," said an unpleasant and raspy voice behind us, "will that not give Kalma greater claim to that which is mine?"

I felt a cold shiver reverberate between my shoulderblades. Bad enough to have a whole passel of deities running at us with weapons drawn, but the idea that something had drawn Hel up and into the world was monumentally disquieting.

Odin shook his head. "I will deal with Ukko and Tuoni…"

"How, All-father?"

He puffed out his cheeks. "I will make them an offer they cannot refuse." He nodded to the burly redhead. "Donar, remind Ukko that there is more to being a thundergod than making a lot of noise."

"Huh?"

"It's Hammer-time," I coached.

"Oh." A light finally switched on upstairs. "Yeah!" Apparently being able to throw lightning didn't make you as *fast* as lightning.

"Ukko is the Finnish-Ugric god of thunder," I explained to Vashti as Thor lifted Mjollnir from its leather holster.

"Of course."

Grasping the thong on the handle's pommel, Thor began to whirl the great hammer above his head. "I do not care for Tuoni nor his accursed offspring," he grumbled, "but I like the beast-heads even less!" Fingers of electricity crawled about the leather-wrapped handle and iron-girt stone head, and a cloudy vortex began to form in the great hammer's wake. Thunder rumbled in the distance, beyond the approaching mass of divinities. The air around us seemed to thicken, and there was a brilliant flash as lightning suddenly arced between Mjollnir and the staves and wands carried by Egyptian gods.

The desert divinities staggered to a halt and were momentarily occupied with extinguishing the newly found torches in their hands.

"Hah!" roared the Norse thundergod as he resheathed his hammer. His expression of triumph was slightly marred by the nimbus of frizzed hair that stuck out in all directions as a result of the static buildup.

Loki smirked. "Nice 'fro, bro."

A war chariot rumbled toward us, bearing a slightly younger and prettier version of Odin, sans eyepatch: Ukko. At his side was a lovely, white-haired matron: Rauni. Their comeliness made the contrast all the greater with the creatures who ran beside and behind.

There were Tuoni and Tuonetar who ruled over the land of death in Tuonela. Close at hand was their son who had no name but was commonly referred to as "the crooked-fingered" or "the bloodstained." He had the look of a young giant who had died a few weeks past and was too stupid or too mean to acknowledge the fact.

His sisters were worse.

Here was Kipu-Tyttö, the goddess of illness, and Kivutar and Vammatar. Given the choice of a forced marriage, I'd put my own eyes out and go with the Gorgons. And they weren't the worst. Loviatar, the "source of all evil," the "origin of a thousand scourges," was bringing up the rear. At least her children weren't tagging along. Eight of them had names: Pleurisy, Colic, Gout, Phthisis, Ulcers, Scabies, Canker, and Plague. The ninth, a "fatal spirit, a creature eaten up with envy," was not given a name but the description had circulated widely.

I forced a smile and was thankful that we were upwind from Tuoni's baleful brood. "So, where's Kalma? Someone have to stay home and keep the dead in line?"

Tuonetar nodded—well—gravely. "We could not risk usurpers staking a claim whilst we fight for what is ours. Surma is adequate to the task but none too bright. He needs his mistress close to hand."

"Mmmm," I said, nodding sagely. At least I hoped I looked sagelike. "Excuse me a moment." I rode over to Lilith and jerked my head toward the rear of the party. She followed me to a small copse of trees some twenty yards away. I rested my forearms on the pommel of my saddle and leaned forward. "Lilith, what in Hell is going on?"

"It would appear that the Egyptian gods were pursuing the Finno-Ugric gods until the Norse gods intervened."

I shook my head. "No. I mean what down *in* Hell is going on?"

She stared at me, trying for a puzzled expression. I hoped my earlier attempt at sagacity was more convincing.

"Look, the last time we met, you hinted at some kind of power struggle going on down below. People—I use the term loosely—were taking sides, and somehow I was peripherally involved. Or perhaps it was my doppelganger—*don't* give me that innocent look! I don't know if you could have pulled it off while you were alive but you're a few hundred years past that possibility now."

She was spared having to answer by a cry from Vashti: "They're reforming their ranks!"

The Egyptian gods were getting ready to attack.

FIVE

♀

Imagine the Swimsuit Competition in the Ms. World Beauty Pageant.

Now imagine that the contestants all wear teensy little outfits of leather and chainmail instead of Lycra and smart-fabrics. Never mind history or taste or just plain common sense, it's Dreamland's program version of Fantasyworld Amazons.

Before you get caught up in the vision, let me add that while Cephtronics was responsible for re-compiling the sex-appeal portion of my original program, they had apparently left the baseline of the original parameters intact. So imagine beauty pageant contestants with the speed of Bruce Lee, the strength of Arnold Schwartzenagger, and the attitude of Steven Segall. I smiled, thinking how Lech Luthor was about to wake up to his biggest nightmare.

Princess Aeriel Morivalynd, beauteous daughter of Queen Hippolyta, next in line for the Amazon throne, and my adoring and occasional fiancée, stepped to the fore of the forest of spears and stood over me, arms akimbo and fists on lovely hips.

I grinned. "Hi Aeri."

She didn't grin back. And her voice was decidedly unadoring when she finally spoke through clenched teeth.

"*Bitch!* I have you now!"

I looked down at the remnants of my streetwalker costume and my peekaboo bosom. Hmmm.

"You may hope for a quick death," she continued, "but I intend for you to suffer!"

"Suffer?"

"Greatly!"

"Greatly?"

"You shall pay the fullest measure for murdering my beloved!"

Oboy.

♂

My options, at this point, were simple. I could wait for the Egyptian gods to close the distance and engage in battle—with me ostensibly on the side of the Norse gods by default. I could retreat like a bat out of Hell—only I hadn't made it to Hell, yet, and running away wasn't going to help me retrieve Natasha Skovoroda's digital shade. Or I could try and negotiate a truce before we achieved Ragnarok on the Nile.

I kicked Ghost into a galloping charge and urged him skyward. Everyone hesitated as the *glamour* dissolved and great, snowy-pinioned wings unfolded from my mount's shoulders. In the twinkling of an eye, my "horse" was revealed as one of the Pegasi, and I soared on toward the suddenly hesitant ranks of Egyptian deities.

As I leveled off some thirty feet up, I glanced back and saw Misty Dawn following me on the ground. Then Lilith and Vashti urged their mounts forward, either shamed by the fembot's fearless loyalty or entirely too trusting of my ability to handle the situation.

The Northern gods held back, waiting to see what damages the Demiurge would inflict on "the enemy."

I hoped the Egyptians knew their Norse/Germanic aerial profiles. Although my clothing and hair were distinctive enough up close, at a distance a Half Elf astride a winged horse might look a little too much like a Valkyrie.

Ahead and below the hawkheaded Ra raised his charred staff. In a moment I would find out whether he was signaling a halt to the other gods in his army. Or a barrage of thaumaturgic ack-ack on the odd-looking "Air Maiden" headed his way.

♀

"No, really, Aeri, it's me! I just look like the woman who killed me. I mean, of course I'm not dead anymore, even though I was at the time. More than once, actually."

Bound at the wrists and ankles and suspended upside-down from a pole, it was hard to get a good look at Aeriel's face as I was carried along. I could only glean hope in the fact that she hadn't killed me yet.

"We are almost to the Pit of Judgement," she announced curtly.

But not a lot of hope.

"How can I prove I am who I say I am?" I could hardly think straight. Swaying back and forth while turning my head to address my would-be executioner left me dizzy and disoriented. "How about something only Riplakish would know? Like that tiny mole under—"

"You are a witch!" she snapped. "And could easily scry such hidden intimacies by divination!"

"I'm no witch," I protested, "but I do admit that the process of finding that particular little landmark was 'divine.'"

I think she colored at my remark. It was hard to tell from my location.

"The gods will decide your guilt or innocence," she continued in a decidedly strangled tone. "They will chose between you and yon rapist. The one bearing the greatest guilt will die at the hands of the other."

I parted my thighs and raised my head to look back between them. There, similarly trussed and suspended from a two-pole frame, swayed Luthor Limbach's barbarian avatar, borne on the shoulders of four hefty Amazon warrior maids. The picture was suddenly clear: trial by combat. With the Amazons helping Lech get his hands on me, after all.

"How can this be fair? He's more than twice my size and three times as strong!" I almost pointed out that I was a "mere woman" before remembering that such sentiments would not play well in present company.

"If you really are who *you* claim to be, this muscle-bound oaf will not last thirty seconds. If you are whom *I* believe you to be, it is my hope that he will take his time and be open to suggestions."

I showed my disdain for her plan by turning my head and indecorously spewing my breakfast.

So much for stoicism.

♂

A humanoid with the head of an Egyptian ibis stood at Ra's side and they consulted beak to beak as I eased my winged mount to a gentle landing before them. The Egyptians gripped the remains of their staves and wands tightly, watching warily, but made no more threatening moves for the moment.

"Demiurge..." Ra said.

"Ra. Thoth," I nodded to each in turn.

"Do you side with the Frost Trolls, then?" the sungod asked.

"I side with no one at the moment. I was riding in this direction when the Frost...er...folk...decided to travel the same direction."

"Then you do not champion their cause?"

I looked over the assortment of animal-headed demigods. The course of our conversation would either trigger a divine bloodbath or postpone hostilities until I could sort things out. If I was the prime creator that everyone seemed to think I was, it behooved me to do better by my creation than let them tear each other apart.

"I have not decided, yet." I heard some murmuring in the ranks. "Come," I continued, riding into their midst, hoping to turn them away from the pending collision with the Northern deities, "tell me of your grievances and perhaps I shall champion your cause..."

♀

There's an old saying—something along the lines of your whole life passing before your eyes when you're about to die. If true, the only hopeful thing about Aeriel's threats was that I had yet to run through the cineoptic experience of all things I had ever done.

Instead, I was running through the mental list of all things I had yet to do. Particularly in regard to the Fantasyworld Program.

Popping up in my long list of unfinished business was a vow I had made—not so terribly long ago—to return to the Matrix and do something about the slave pens in Calabastor.

I had never gotten so far as to decide whether I was going to lead an actual insurrection or just reprogram the manumission codes in the civilization presets. Now, stripped of any spellcasting abilities and bound by strong cords and weak flesh, I was unable to do anything for those unfortunate souls traded daily upon the auction blocks. Indeed, their pitiable state was more hopeful than mine: gladiator candidates could expect better treatment from their masters while they yet lived.

I doubted the average Dreamwalker had given much thought to the truly brutal quality of life endured by the NPCs, AIs, and computer constructs that inhabited this milieu. Cephtronics had certainly rejected my arguments on the moral issues. The gladiators, orphans, widows, slaves, serfs, soldiers, prisoners, pickpockets, prostitutes—Human and Demihuman—were so much window dressing, bits and bytes assembled for the entertainment of the Dreamwalkers who paid their money and played the "game." They couldn't imagine that each creature had it's own hopes and dreams, felt pain and loss, came with a personal history and aspired to a nobler legacy. A True Spirit shouldn't, wouldn't, couldn't imagine that anything else inside the Matrix had its own soul, digital or otherwise.

And Mike Straeker and I, with the extra advantage of programmer status, had been further distanced from the unpleasantness of daily medieval life and death. Our godslike status had insulated us from consequence and we had forgotten that great ability should be wed to matched responsibility.

So far, our responses had not matched our abilities.

In my own vanity and pride I had thought to someday free hundreds, perhaps thousands, of unfortunate wretches. Instead, I had returned to the Matrix to reclaim my own life and rescue just one friend from a permanent psychefile crash. And I couldn't even manage to pull off even one of those simple, little tasks.

If Robert R. Ripley was, indeed, the Demiurge incarnate for Fantasyworld, no wonder so many of its inhabitants were the heirs of suffering and hopelessness.

♂

By the time the Egyptians had finished telling their side of the story, my suspicions were confirmed.

I knew what the problem was.

But I didn't know what had caused it.

And, more importantly, I didn't know how to fix it.

"Then you will champion our cause and banish these trespassers?" Ra demanded.

"I will think upon it," I said. "I shall make camp here, between you and the Frost Folk, and I will consider your petition until tomorrow. Come morning, I shall render judgment."

I couldn't be sure that the Egyptians were scowling. Animal features are hard to read but I got the definite impression that they weren't making happy faces.

Ra raised his staff—somewhat reluctantly, I thought—and nodded his assent. "When the sun rises again we shall have our answer. By that time our cousins from Babylon and Assyria shall have arrived."

Slowly, grudgingly, the Egyptians turned and retired from the field.

I had just succeeded in postponing a bloodbath. But the delay only ensured a bigger disaster on the morrow if I didn't come up with a more peaceable solution before dawn.

I hoped the sungod wouldn't pull a premature sunrise: it was going to be a short enough night as was.

♀

The best parts about the long and vertiginous journey to the Pit of Judgement were the loss of circulation in my hands and feet, the nausea and dry heaves, and the neck and back spasms: I not only forgot about how badly I needed to go to the bathroom, but I was no longer afraid to die. In truth, I was getting a little overeager when we finally arrived. There are some things worse than death. Like another mile being lashed upside down to a tote pole.

Once we arrived it took awhile to get the feeling back in my hands and feet. Judging from the barbarian's steady stream of profanity, he was having similar problems.

The Pit of Judgement was some nine feet deep and roughly diamond-shaped, approximately sixteen feet to a side. Smooth, packed earth formed the slightly sloping sides and floor. Dark splashes of blood and ichor discolored the dirt and odd bits that might once have been parts of something organic were wedged in the crevices.

Aeriel's voice spoke behind me. "You dwell upon your fate."

"Actually," I swallowed a spoonful of bile that kept fighting to crawl up my throat, "I'm just reflecting upon how hard it must be to keep the corners swept out."

"I want you to suffer for what you have done!"

"Gee, Aeri, I'm not used to hearing that until after the honeymoon. And speaking of honeymoons, the last I heard you were getting hitched to a frog."

"My mother stopped the wedding ere—" She shook her head. *"Don't* you mock his memory!" she hissed. "Don't compound your crimes by pretending to be him!"

We were saved further repartee by the arrival of a shaman.

I'd never seen an elderly Amazon. Cephtronics used femme fatales to juice the hormones of the male (or similarly inclined) Dreamwalkers, so the median age appeared to be twenty-two with a four-year range in either direction. So in designing a tribal elder, some programming drone decided that the appropriate ancient crone would be about 40-something who might pass as thirty were it not for the long, grey hair, braided with bits of rawhide, feathers, and fine silver chain, into a thick braid. The wise-woman greeted Aeriel while the others gathered around, herding Limbach to the edge of the pit at spear-point, and then considered me with a grave expression.

"You have a familiar appearance," she said finally.

"Yeah, you too. Ever sing with Dolly Parton and Linda Ronstadt?"

"Ignore her senseless babbling," the Amazon princess advised. "This one is not right in the head."

"If so," the shaman answered, "trial by combat would be negated and all challenges be considered void."

"She is evil and must pay!"

"Perhaps," was the calm reply, "but what of the life that grows within her now? Must two die for the crimes of one?"

"She's pregnant?" Aeriel screeched.

I think I fainted.

♂

Odin and company were no more pleased by my temporary truce than the Egyptians. Not only was I postponing "the fun" but they were expecting the Demiurge to kick some serious Babylonian butt.

The only butt I was interested in kicking at the moment, however, belonged to a certain close-mouthed Archdemoness who'd been holding out on me. Strangely, she was suddenly nowhere to be found.

I conjured a campaign tent between the two hostile camps and then laid a thaumaturgic minefield across no-man's land, a series of guards-and-wards that would provide a wakeup call should anyone go sleepwalking during the night.

I laid out my bedroll and tried to make myself comfortable. I hadn't slept last night and I figured there wasn't much chance of getting any shuteye after the sun went down tonight. Right now it was broad daylight and my tent was the center of attention for both the—ahem—"Sandscum" and the "Frost Trolls." Since I had failed to come up with a really good plan in the past twenty minutes, I figured a nap was top priority. Besides, I've found that there's a definite link between my subconscious and my Devious quotient. Maybe tapping into my Alpha state would help me figure out my next move.

The first stage of my plan became immediately apparent: getting rid of my tent-mates if I wanted any quality snooze time.

The psychiatrist in the supermodel avatar sat cross-legged across from me.

I smiled at her.

She smiled at me.

"Good night," I said.

"Why would she lie to us?" my ex wanted to know, pacing back and forth like a nervous parrot.

"Technically, she hasn't told an untruth," Westbrook observed. "She's been less than forthcoming…obviously knows more than she's volunteered."

"I thought she was supposed to be your friend," Stephanie fumed, glaring at me.

"I tend to think of her as more of an ally than an actual friend," I said, yawning.

"Hell of an ally."

"Precisely my point."

"But why would she want to keep us in the dark?" Westbrook asked.

"I don't know," I mumbled and rolled over.

"Well, what *do* you know?" Stephanie grumbled.

"Aside from hearsay," I murmured, "not bloody much."

"Robert…?"

Gods help me; I knew that tone all too well. And I didn't relish a rehash of certain marital dynamics that would follow if I didn't take this conversation seriously. I sat up and clasped my hands in front of my knees. "The avatar of Nicole Doucet who claims to be an alternate memory download of myself..." I hesitated: this was just too weird even before we got to the explanation. "...claims that there may be some sort of insurrection going on down in the nether regions. She...he...oh hell, whoever this character is—"

"She is thee, my lord. You may trust me in this wise."

Vashti chimed in. "It'll go a whole lot easier if you just go along with the most popular premise."

I gave my ex the raised eyebrow: she knew better than to expect me to "go along" without sufficient documentation and six months of clinical trials. "Anyway, the *other* me says that *another* me—"

"The one from a parallel universe," Vashti coached.

I hesitated: another raised eyebrow would be too much, too soon. Stephanie liked taking subcutaneous excursions whenever I was around, and once she knew she was under your skin she took her time in returning to the surface. "—yeah, *that* me—"

"The evil you. Although that sounds suspiciously like an oxymoron."

"Up periscope, dearest."

"Up..." she blinked and put a hand to her mouth to stifle a yawn, "...what?"

Westbrook giggled. She was enjoying the show, subtext and all.

"The alternate universe me," I continued, while Stephanie ran submarine analogies through her head for referents, "supposedly led a hoard of demons and devils in an attack on the surface world. Against my other *other*self, apparently."

"What doth it mean, my lord?"

"It means he can't get along with anyone," Vashti answered. "I don't get the periscope bit, though."

"Rig for silent running," I snapped. "My other self claimed that Lilith had made some allusions to a power struggle going on below with Powers and Principalities taking sides. Daggoth says that recent attempts to contact Orcus have been rebuffed in some very unpleasant ways."

"Now we've got different cultural pantheons going up against each other on the surface world," Westbrook mused, "and the issue at hand would seem to be 'turf.'"

I grimaced, remembering an early glitch in the programming that had the Greek and the Roman gods duking it out over the real estate on Mount Olympus. Prying Zeus and Jupiter apart had been a nightmare. Think Godzilla versus King Kong using the Dresden chinaworks as their arena. We'd been very careful to program powerful buffers into The Matrix, rendering the deities of differing cultures and milieus invisible and undetectable to one another. It was one thing to have Mars and Vulcan quarrel over Venus—gods will be gods, doncha know. It was quite another to have Mars and Ares line up their troops to decide, once and for all, just who was really the one and only god of war.

"According to Dante," Westbrook mused, "Lucifer claimed that it was better to reign in hell than serve in heaven."

Vashti snorted. "I wonder what advice he would offer under the present circumstances."

"It is not the poetry of Dante Aligeri that begs the question," Misty Dawn said, *"so much as the lyrical stylings of John Fogarty."*

"John Fogarty?" I asked, knowing I shouldn't.

She nodded. *"Who will stop the reign?"*

There was a distant sound of thunder and we stared at the android, open-mouthed.

♀

My wrists were bound behind me when I came to. Fortunately I was sitting on the ground with my back against a tree and that position versus my previous predicament brought an involuntary sigh of luxury.

Aeriel must have been hovering nearby because she was suddenly in my face. "Who is he?" she demanded harshly. "Who's the father?"

Good question. "I have no idea."

"No idea? Not even a guess?"

"None."

Her eyes grew wide. "You…*slut!*"

Maybe. I knew that *I* hadn't had sex with anyone while wearing this body. Had Nicole been intimate with someone while in the Matrix and before she died? Had she come into the possession of a digital fetus that The Machine passed along to me when it assigned me her avatar?

Unpleasant memories began to stir, slithering up from the back of my consciousness. I remembered that one of the two Nicole's—the one from the alternate reality—had been the lover and protector of my "alternate world" self. Surely they had availed themselves of their reconstructed bodies at the first opportunity…

Then I remembered my own lusty reunion with the Nicole restored from my own reality. "One way or another," I finally said, "I think I know who the father might be…"

"Tell me!"

I almost said "me" but I was wise enough to know how that would play. "Riplakish of Dyrinwall," I answered, knowing that that answer wouldn't play much better.

It didn't.

"You lie!"

"Why would I lie?"

"You gamble that I will not kill you while you carry his child!"

I was too tired to argue persuasively. "Well, do I win?"

"Hillary," Aeriel called over her shoulder.

The wisewoman reappeared. "Yes, Highness?"

"I need to know if my beloved, the royal consort, is the father of this sl—woman's child. Can you make an augury?"

She nodded. "If you can bring me something that was his."

"What sort of thing?"

"The more personal the better."

The Amazon princess reached into the depths of her marvelous cleavage and produced a copper locket. It was a cunning piece of metalwork involving two large copper coins that had been hammered out into a pair of concave disks and then hinged together so that there was a space at the center. From this compartment she drew a lock of hair. "This was his." She offered it reluctantly. "Do you need it all?"

"Half should be sufficient, dear." She took the portion that Aeriel reluctantly offered and left to scry the DNA *dweomer*.

Aeriel turned back to me but seemed at a loss for words. My stomach was still queasy from the vertigo of travel, my newfound morning sickness, and the shock of this past hour's revelations, but I forced a smile. "I'm hoping it's a girl. How about you?"

She opened her mouth. Closed it. Opened it again. Finally spoke in carefully controlled tones. "It matters not for you whether it be a man-child or another daughter for our tribe. You will be permitted to carry either to term, and if the child be male it will be left in a village for adoption." Her lips curled into a pale smile to match mine and she bent down to retrieve the barbarian's greataxe. "You think I must delay my revenge for nine months." She ran her thumb along the edge of the curved blade. "Consider, however, that you do not need arms or legs to keep a child in your womb." She let the axe fall at my feet, turned on her heel, and stalked off.

I felt like crying.

Was I afraid? No. I had been in much tougher situations. Was I upset about being pregnant? Strangely, no. I felt an unaccustomed sense of satisfaction—almost a "glow."

But as I watched the setting sun lengthen the shadows across the ground, I felt shadows lengthen across my heart as well. Despite Aeriel's crude assurances, I was afraid for my child.

♂

"Suppose you could use your access codes and programmer status to reinstall the Matrix buffers?" Vashti pondered. "Would that put all the gods back into their own program sectors?"

"Maybe," I said. "But, assuming I could manage that level of access, it would be like repartitioning a hard drive without reformatting the whole magilla."

"'Tis pos—"

"I know it's possible on one level," I said, "but restoring the buffers probably won't be enough. It was one thing to keep them all ignorant of one another and happy in their own little slices of heaven and hell while the buffers were originally in place. Now that they're aware of the existence of other divinities it may well be impossible to put all of the worms back into the can."

"You think they'll go looking for one another?"

"If their programming runs true to form…"

"You're saying that because they're gods," a recumbent Westbrook mused, "absolute power and an eternity of willful behavior would drive them to establish dominance over any perceived challenge to their status quo."

"Bingo."

Her eyelids drooped and there was another peal of thunder from without the tent.

"Now what?"

"Do you think one of the thundergods—" Vashti's question was cut short by wide-mouthed yawn. Her hand wasn't quite quick enough to hide her uvula.

"I don't know," I said, buckling on my swordbelts, "but if Odin's boys are breaking the truce I'll kick their heads so far up their Asgard, they'll be using Bifröst for toe-floss."

"Oooo, mighty tough talk for—" Vashti yawned again.

"Hey, I may not know how to fix the entire Matrix, and taking on two complete pantheons at the same time may be a bit daunting, but I can still show a handful of Aesir who's Demiurge around here." I stalked out of the tent without waiting for a reply.

SIX

♀

"Lemme get this straight," Luthor was saying. "These broads hate men, right?"

I'd tried ignoring him. It didn't work. The deepening twilight did a more than adequate job of blending him into the shadows, but he wouldn't shut up. In fact, telling him to shut up only encouraged him. The trees to which we were tied to were too far apart for anything beyond kicking a little dirt in his direction.

"'Hate' is a little strong," I said. "Let's just say they don't have a lot of use for the male gender."

"So they're lezbos, right?"

"Lesbians?" I don't know why I even tried.

"Yeah, queer for each other. You hear the one about the Dutch boy who stuck his finger in the dyke?"

"You're disgusting. And they're not gay, Lech," I growled, "they're just Amazons."

"I don't get it, Nicky. What're you sayin'?"

"I'm not—" This was hopeless. "Look, we programmed them to be like the mythical Amazons. They're tough, fierce, warrior women who think they're better than men."

"Hey, all the women I know think they're better than men. That doesn't mean they won't screw around."

"Amazons don't 'screw around.' If they have sex—which they rarely do—it is only to preserve their bloodlines for progeny."

The barbarian let out a low whistle. "So you're tellin' me that you created these human-like women and programmed 'em not to like men but also fixed it so's they're not turned on to women, either. No wonder they're so pissed off alla time!"

I stopped listening. Fortunately Limbach's contentment with that last zinger gave me ample time to meditate upon its inherent truth. So, trying not to listen, I assumed the hissing sound was the last vestiges of my deflating ego. Lech Luther, of all people, had just called my sexual ethics into question and I had no adequate come back.

Then I realized that the sound was coming from overhead.

"Pssssst."

I looked up. The face peering down at me, haloed by a particularly fat cluster of leaves and vines, was hard to make out in the deepening twilight. "Nicole?" it stage-whispered.

I nodded: this wasn't the time or place for long, drawn-out explanations.

A boy of perhaps fifteen suddenly fell out of the tree in slow motion. As he dropped toward me I could see he hung from a rope, wound through a series of metal loops in his belt. He wore brown leather-strapped leggings and a vest over a grey tunic, and a knife was clenched between his teeth. Dozens of leafy boughs were thrust through the rings and straps on his outer vestments but the camouflage effect was lost as he left the concealment of the crown: he looked like a large, leafy spider descending on a thick strand of webbing.

I glanced over at Limbach. He was all eyes but holding his tongue for the moment.

The kid dropped down behind me and I felt a brief pressure as the ropes pressed about my wrists a little tighter. Suddenly they were free and he pressed the knife's hilt into my hands. "Your ankles. Hurry," he hissed.

Clumsy from lack of circulation, I fumbled with the knife as he ascended back into the branches above me. "Hey," Limbach hissed as I sawed at the ropes about my lower legs, "what about me?"

Like I was going to cut him loose to come after me again?

But unless I wanted him to sound the alarm, I'd do best to jolly him along. "Keep your loincloth on, Lech; we've still got to figure out an escape route."

"Well, hurry up! We ain't got much time!"

Actually, we were all out of time. As I cut through the last strand hobbling my feet, I looked up and saw Aeriel and two of her warrior maidens walking toward us. The intervening trees and the dusk-strained darkness that pooled beneath their branches would only give us a fleeting moment's advantage. I looked up and saw the kid coming back down, feet first this time. "Grab hold," he said as he bounced a couple of inches above the ground.

He looped a leather strap about my waist as I threw my arms around his neck. Before I could take a deep breath we moved up and sideways—a good thing as the rate of our ascent would have had some unpleasant consequences had we hit the tangle of branches directly above us.

Mixed invectives rose with us as we cleared the treetops: the shrill profanity of a thwarted Amazon princess and the basso counterpoint of barbarian oaths at being abandoned. Some days you can't please anyone.

♂

Exiting the tent was like entering a cave.

The storm had appeared as if by magic: the sky was already drowned in a boil of inky clouds, ushering in a premature night. The preternatural darkness, devoid of moon and stars, seemed to oppress the campfires that glimmered throughout the camps on either side of "nogod's land" and I had to conjure a tagalong witchlight just to keep from stumbling over my own feet.

Except for the static crackle of distant thunder, all was quiet. The intermittent strobes of heat lightning gave snapshot impressions that both camps were deserted. I felt the hair on the back of my neck stand to attention as my floating orb of witchlight stuttered and went out.

I stood stock-still, eyes and ears straining.

Something was out there.

I could feel it coming toward me in the darkness. The lightning gave no proof and I could hear nothing between the vague mutterings of thunder, still I knew that something stalked in the darkness between the dying cookfires. Now the hairs on my forearms were stirring, lifting: it was coming closer.

I laid my right hand on the pommel of Caladbolg, crossed my left arm over and grasped the hilt of Balmung. "By the pricking of my thumbs..." I murmured.

"Something wicked this way comes," said the voice behind me.

I leapt and whirled, both swords clearing their scabbards before my feet touched the ground.

The eldritch blue glow of the Elven longsword and the baleful red glare of the Dwarven shortsword glimmered across the still, dead features of Natasha Skovoroda. "Tasha..."

"Nay, milord. Technically I am—"

"Misty Dawn," I breathed.

"Dost thou mind if I accompany thee? The others are aslumber and I have naught to do."

"Frankly, M.D., I'd be glad for the company." I sheathed Balmung but kept the Elven longsword drawn, telling myself it was only for the additional illumination and almost believing it.

"Shouldist thou not be sleeping, milord? Everyone else is."

"Everyone?"

"I have done a complete scan of both camps. All entities within perimeters exhibit suppressed Alpha rhythms and decreased rates of respiration consistent with states of unconsciousness."

Had we programmed the gods to require sleep? I couldn't recall those specific parameters. Surely it wasn't natural on the eve of a potential battle for both sides to retire before sundown or at the outbreak of an unexpected storm. At the very least I expected the posting of sentries and the holding of late-night councils of war. "What about the horses? Have you scanned for animal life?"

She nodded. *"Not a creature is stirring, not even a mouse."*

I checked: not even the hint of an artificial smile on that artificial mouth.

The wind suddenly picked up, roaring like an express train from Aeolus. I started to hunch against the force of the storm and then realized that there was no force. Not even a breeze. The sound of a full-blown gale continued to grow even though the air about me was hauntingly still. I cast about, trying to discern the source of the sound.

"Milord! Look!"

Her white arm was a dim extension in Caladbolg's blue glow. I followed its trajectory beyond her pointing finger to the crest of the nearest hill. There, atop the crest, I could make out two dancing figures. I use the term "dancing" advisedly: they capered, they leapt, they whirled, they flung their appendages about with wild abandon. In the darkness, from this distance, with only the inconsistent backdrop of heat lightning, I could only guess that they were humanoid.

"M.D., can you scan and identify those things?"

She dropped her arm but continued to stare at the dancing figures. *"Imaging. Constructing three-dimensional template."*

Lightning suddenly forked down in the form of a bolt, linking earth and sky in a harsh umbilical cord of acintic brightness. It struck the top of the hill between the two capering creatures. They continued to frolic, seemingly unabashed by the near miss.

"Accessing Matrix database."

"I think you can limit your search to the supernormal index."

"I have a possible match. Data is incomplete, however, and there is a twenty percent chance of error."

"Give me your best guess."

"The closest match would appear to be in the Australasian Deities and Demigods Index. Specifically the Lightning Brothers chronicled by the Wardaman people of Delamere in Australia's Northern Territory. The Warlpiri and Mudbura also make mention of them. The larger one may be Yabiringi, the younger brother. I believe Yagjabula, the older brother, is the smaller one, as he wields Djugalutba, the enchanted stone axe that—warning! Warning! Perimeter alert! Sentient life-forms approaching!"

The roaring was growing in intensity and volume; it was coming our way.

Before redrawing Balmung I cast another "light" spell. This time I opted for several globes of ball lightning in lieu of the witchlight. Ball lightning is generally less stable than sorcerous swamp gas but the night air was charged from the nearby strikes on the hilltop and the globes seemed to glow brighter than usual.

Two figures materialized at the edge of my expanded perimeter of light.

"M.D., can you analyze new incursions?"

She made no answer and I turned to face her. "M.D.?"

"...yes...milord...?" her voice seemed drowsy.

"What do you see?"

"...sheep..." she mumbled, *"...electric sheep...."* Her eyelids clicked shut and she lost all semblance of life, artificial or otherwise.

"Misty?" I grabbed her arm and tried to shake it. It was like trying to shake a statue. I reached into a beltpouch and fished out the android's remote. The display blinked the words **SLEEP MODE** on and off in yellow letters. I tried the reboot sequence. There was no response.

*Dick*ed.

♀

The other end of the rope was wrapped, in tandem, around the waists of Mick and Daggoth. They were kneeling upon a flying carpet—although "floundering" carpet was probably more apropos at the moment.

The rug was another two-passenger model. Carrying three would strain its aerodynamic design. Hauling four with half the load dangling over the side was begging more miracle than magic. We barely cleared the next copse of trees.

The kid had me pressed tightly against him and it didn't feel like safety was his only concern. "Nicole, are you all right?" he asked over the rush of the wind and the rustle of branches about our ankles. The kid had nice eyes. Familiar eyes.

True Spirit eyes.

"Bernie, is that you?"

"You—you know me?"

"It's Ripley, Mr. Mudge."

His grip never wavered but I saw the flash of surprise in his eyes followed by disappointment. Then, finally, an infinite sorrow settled in.

"I'm sorry, Bernie. Nicole Doucet really is dead."

His grip never wavered but he held me closer. "I guess I have to believe you now," he whispered in my ear. A moment later I felt warm tears against my cheek.

♂

Two figures entered my field of illumination. Their skin was blacker than the darkness that encompassed us. I couldn't make out gender at this distance.

I *could* tell that they were aboriginal and radiated age and power like two great bonfires giving off heat and light. Perhaps they were the Ungambikula or the Bagadjimbiri or maybe even the Wawilak Sisters. If a third personage appeared it might mean they were the Djanggawuls. For now I could just make out two forms as they did a slow, crouching, turning dance as they progressed through the camps. One hand each grasped a cord that was being whirled above their heads and produced the eerie sounds of unearthly winds: bullroarers.

The term "organized religion" is an oxymoron.

Take Christianity. The number of separate denominations, sects, cults, conferences, and creeds number in quadruple digits now. Put any five believers in a room and try to get three of them to agree on any four points of doctrine.

See what I mean?

And here we're talking about stuff written down a couple of thousand years ago that has remained essentially unchanged since.

The Australasian aboriginal mythos is nowhere near an "organized" theology. It's a lot older and has been maintained by different indigenous peoples and tribes isolated on different parts of the continent utilizing rock paintings and oral traditions. So a clear-cut identification process was hampered by an unfamiliar mythos lacking a central theocratic authority and the loss of my cyberlink to the Matrix database.

I could only surmise that the beings I observed were either some variant of the first-ancestors or the original creators—whatever the names and backstories the various peoples may have assigned to them. Literally and figuratively, I was pretty much in the dark here.

I had little difficulty identifying the three giant beings that followed them, however.

Wandjina.

Three times as large as a human, they drifted, ghostlike, their white faces contrasted by the red halo that radiated out from their heads. The rest of their bodies were marked by contrasting swirls of white and ochre, symbolizing the essence of water and blood.

The myths regarding the Wandjina are more universal and numerous. They were said to have come from the skies and some *Chariots of the Gods* enthusiasts believe that they may have actually been prehistoric alien astronauts.

If they were from outer space, they had some major mojo. The Wandjina were supposed to bring the monsoon rains that bestowed life on the barren lands. Legend held that they also were the divine lawgivers, establishing religion, customs, and rites and teaching the peoples their dances and songs. The latter was a neat trick as the Wandjina have no mouths.

They glided silently in the wake of the First Ancestors. At least I assumed they were silent: I couldn't hear anything over the unearthly moaning of the bullroarers.

One of them stopped and stared at me. The gods of mythology are often too much like us to deserve their omnipotence. But there was nothing human in these dark, alien eyes. I felt a chill as they swept over me like black searchlights and came to rest on my android companion. The god moved toward us, gliding like an implacable juggernaut. What to do? Run? Attack? Taken dispassionately, the creature had done nothing I could label as hostile, yet its unhuman nature unnerved me in ways that creatures both monstrous and evil had never been able to influence. Indecision froze me in the midst of my fight-or-flight reflex, and the Wandjina slid past me in a half-dozen strides.

Natasha Skovoroda's robotic double was picked up like a doll and the Wandjina began to pluck at her torso. "Hey!" I yelled, moving toward it in what I hoped was a menacing manner. "Put her down!"

The Wandjina did, although I doubted it was much impressed by my pointy little light show. I ran to the android as the giant creature turned and rejoined Aussies On Parade. Although a cursory glance indicated no damage to the rest of her appearance, her belly hung open and Natasha Skovoroda's soul jar was missing.

Refereeing two armies of gods waging bloody battle over property rights in Hell suddenly seemed small potatoes as I considered the retreating backs of the Wandjina moving off toward the hills and fading into the outer darkness. Not only did they have my means of recovering Natasha's soulfile and any possibility of reviving her in the real world, they probably had Misty Dawn's spirit trapped within, as well.

The question was, what could I do about it? I had serious questions about my ability to tangle with one Wandjina, never mind three. But what else could I do? Pack up and go home?

I patted the fembot on the shoulder and reclosed her abdominal compartment. "No guts, no glory," I groused.

And started after the eerie retinue.

INTERLUDE

(ROADS NOT TAKEN)

...And that has made all the difference.

—Robert Frost,
The Road Not Taken—

I dreamt the past was never past redeeming:
But whether this was false or honest dreaming
I beg death's pardon now.

—Richard Purdy Wilbur,
The Pardon—

θ

Something tugged at my sleepy right foot.

The rest of sleepy me rolled over and came up against warm softness. The urge to snuggle was overwhelming.

"What happened to your toes?" chirped a perky little voice.

"Uumhuhmmm?" I responded, making a vague attempt to swim out of a frothy tangle of blankets.

"Ron," my wife stage-whispered, "Daddy's trying to sleep."

"But he hasn't got any toes," my youngest son insisted pleasantly. His tone made it clear that he was neither grossed out nor even particularly concerned—but that such a fascinating oddity did overrule all other issues and begged for immediate discussion. Such are the social priorities of three-year-olds.

"Daddy had an accident a long time ago," Mommy explained, moving her warm, snuggly softness so that she could better discuss the matter with my amateur podiatrist. "He hurt his foot and the doctors weren't able to put his toes back on."

"Is that why Daddy looks like a pirate?"

I grinned. The eyepatch had long been Ronnie's favorite evidence that his dad was more interesting than anyone else's was.

"Yes," Stephanie said, "it was the same accident that made daddy look like a pirate."

She poked me under the blankets. "Arrrr," I growled softly into the pillow.

"Did it hurt real bad?"

Stephanie hesitated. When your children are very young the lies come easily: you want to assure them that the world is not a mean and scary place and that the good guys really did live happily ever after.

Rolling over, I answered for her: "Yes it did. It hurt quite a lot. Like the time your sister tripped you and you skinned your knees on the driveway. But mommy kissed my foot and made all the hurt go away." I didn't explain that mommy came along a few years after the aircar crash, when I had added "frequent drunk" to the list of my infirmities. She leaned over and kissed the side of my forehead.

Maybe the good guys did live happily ever after, after all.

"*Mo-om!*" Ron's sibling nemesis appeared in the doorway.

"Hermione, your father's trying to sleep."

"No rest for the wicked," I murmured.

Out of the corner of my eye I saw her cross her six-year-old arms and lock her stance. "The Brat's already woke him up."

"Don't call your younger brother a brat, dear."

"I'm *not* a brat! *You're* the brat!" came the gleeful rejoinder.

"What is it, honey?" I sighed. This would go a lot faster and easier if we kept the conversation on track.

"The *other* Brat is hacking my Barbieworld!"

"Don't call either of your brothers brats, dear."

I sighed, turned, and wriggled toward the edge of the bed. Hermione had precipitated the situation a couple of months back by creating a backdoor into the boys' Hasbro program so that Barbie could date G.I. Joe. *Ken is such a wuss,* was her all-encompassing explanation. Eight-year-old Harry's response had been to give the virtual fashion mannequin a hairy chest and a bass voice. It took me three hours to restore the software presets. "Why is your brother hacking into Virtual Barbieworld?" I mumbled.

"Cause he's mean!"

"Has Barbie been bothering G.I Joe again?"

"He should be so lucky," my wife whispered.

"Midge and Skipper kidnapped him!" Ron announced.

"Shut up, Brat!"

"Hermione!"

"Made him put on a dress and makeup!" the Brat sing-songed with unbridled glee. His older sister glared at him but Ron was safely ensconced between us and he grinned back at her in triumph.

"Who says the Battle of the Sexes takes no prisoners?" I rolled up and sat on the edge of the bed. "Ronnie, go tell your brother I want to see him in here right now."

He monkeyed down the sheets and hit the floor running: this was way better than missing toes.

I looked down at the remnants of my left foot and considered the aircar crash that taken the life of Nicole Doucet and left me permanently scarred. The memory had been the most terrible wound of all.

But like the physical wounds, the memory had closed up and the scars had gone from angry red to bruised blue and finally achieved a pale, near invisibility. More numb than painful after all these years, the body compensates for loss. Life, it would seem, was no different.

Except, whatever passions were lost in the skies over Paris were replaced fourfold in my sunny bedroom this morning.

I slid my feet into waiting slippers and tried not to smile as Harry entered, with Ron practically dancing in his wake.

My eldest son was struggling to find an expression that said he had done nothing to apologize for without being openly defiant. Hermione was having less luck keeping "smug" in check. And Ronnie's face made no secret of the fact that he was pleased to see either of his older siblings called on the carpet as long as daddy and mommy weren't too mad.

"What are you doing, son?"

"Hermione—" he began.

I held up a hand to stop him. "I didn't ask what your sister had done. I asked what you are doing."

He frowned and brushed his dark hair out of his eyes. "I was resetting the bio—"

I held up my hand again. "I don't want the details. Just tell me what you are trying to accomplish. What do you hope the outcome will be?" In other words, what's the plan?

He gave Hermione a dirty look. "I want to make her sorry for messing around with my AIs. I want her to be afraid to trespass in my programs again."

"Ah." I turned to my daughter. "Herms, tell your brother what you'll do after he makes you sorry. Be honest, now."

A ghost of a smile tugged at the corner of her mouth but she wouldn't give in to it under parental scrutiny. "I'll reset—" She saw my hand come up. "I'll get even. And then some."

Ronnie danced and clapped his hands and laughed. I almost hated to quash his delight.

I turned to my wife. "Hmmm," I said, "seems like we've got a problem here."

She nodded gravely, the dancing delight even more prominent in her eyes than the three-year-old's. "It looks like they'll never stop trying to get even with each other."

I raised my eyebrows. "You mean as soon as one of them thinks they've 'gotten even,' the other will do something back so they'll never both be satisfied?

"That's right. They'll just keep going on and on and on."

"And on and on and on and on and on—" Ronnie chimed in, thoroughly captivated by the homegrown concept of the Five-Hundred-Year War.

"So, what do we do?" she pondered in a serious voice.

"Maybe I can help." I crooked my finger at the two combatants. All three stepped forward, Ronnie crowding from the rear so as not to miss any juicy parts of the judicial process. "I think you two can work out a truce without my help. Especially since it should be obvious that getting even isn't going to work for either of you."

"Well, she started it."

"Did not!"

My hand shot up and after a moment's silence I curled three fingers and pointed at them with my index finger. "You will make peace before the hour's up. It will be a mutual agreement that you both are satisfied with. You *can* do this. And do you know why?"

They shook their heads sullenly.

"Because if you don't, here is what I will do to fix the problem for you."

Ronnie leaned in, eyes as wide as saucers.

"I will reprogram the passwords and lockouts on all of your programs for a whole month." I pointed to Harry. "I will give Hermione full access to your virtual worlds and I shudder to think what sorts of indignities will be visited upon the space marines with your sister in charge."

Hermione's smile was short-lived as I turned my finger in her direction. "And do you think you're going to want Barbie's Dreamworld back once Harry and Ronnie have spent even a couple of weeks there? It might be good for Ken but I'll bet Midge and Skipper's fashion sense will be permanently damaged."

Hermione's face went white. Harry was visibly trembling. Ron was edging from puzzlement to disappointment: this wasn't working out as entertainment at all.

"Better get started on the Peace Accord," I said. "The clock says there's just fourteen minutes until the deadline."

They exited. Ron kept looking back at us as he followed, as if asking how something so potentially right could have suddenly gone so disappointingly wrong.

My wife tugged me back onto the bed. "You are as wise as Solomon, my king."

"Indeed," I murmured as she straddled me, bending down and affording me a generous view down the top of her pajamas. "The Bible says that Solomon had many wives and concubines."

"He must have been one heck of a farmer."

"What?"

"Concubines. Aren't those wheat harvesters?"

"You!" I pulled her down and rolled over so that I was on top. "Combines are wheat harvesters."

"Corn harvesters?" she asked innocently, batting her eyes.

"I'll show you harvesters," I growled, bending down to nuzzle her neck.

"Ooooh," she squealed, "I'm being reaped!"

"Maybe I'd better shut the bedroom door."

"Maybe you'd better lock it," she agreed.

ϕ

"I can't have children."

I stared down at her, disconcerted as much by her ability to converse in *non-sequitars* during sex as by the topic itself. Her face was still flushed, framed with tendrils of jet and sable hair. Her eyes wide and dilated with pleasure, yet her mind dwelled on an impossible aftermath. "How many times have we had this conversation?"

"It is always going to be an issue," Nicole gasped, clinging to me fiercely. "How can you not be a father?"

"I can be a father."

"But I can't be a mother."

We'd been over this countless times, before and during the two years following our wedding. It wasn't just a problem with the plumbing; she couldn't contribute to a surrogate pregnancy. And despite my protestations that adoption was fine—and, in some ways, a superior option—she continued to grieve over her inability to mix her genetic material with mine.

"Can't we just be happy to be alive? And to have each other?"

She half smiled and half frowned, a Mona Lisa smirk no one else could duplicate. "Alive." She brushed my own damp hair away from my face. "Will there ever come a time when you can go forty-eight hours without thinking about the crash? It's been two-and-a-half years: it's *morbid!"*

I rolled off of her and landed off of the towel. Sand was immediately drawn to my most intimate surfaces like iron filings to a magnet. "Aargh! Now I gotta rinse!"

She stretched up her hand as I stood. "Me too."

Hand in hand we ran down the beach and into the warm, frothy surf. The water was unseasonably warm, even calculating the season and the Global Warming Indices. It barely cooled our flesh of the aftereffects of rutting in the afternoon sun.

As we splashed back toward our towels and picnic hamper, the apologetic tide surging around our ankles, I said, "I don't think it's morbid to think about our good fortune and be grateful."

"The insurance settlement was very generous."

"We didn't need the money."

"True." She picked up her towel and hammocked her derriere. "Between our endorsement deals for taking the gold at the Paris Olympics and the Master Classes we both teach, we would live comfortably without it." She began to rumba with the terrycloth that effectively dried her backside while applying centrifugal force to other portions of her anatomy sending drops of moisture in all directions. The overall effect was mesmerizing. "But we couldn't afford to live like a king and queen in a tropical paradise with seven miles of our own private beach."

My own towel technique consisted of dabbing at myself, here and there. I knew from long experience that I'd completely air-dry halfway up the ten minute walk back to the house.

"That's not what I'm grateful for and you know it." I scuffed gritty feet into thonged sandals and was momentarily distracted by the sight of my toes. Why ten wriggling toes would seem suddenly unusual, I had no idea. I turned my attention back to the more satisfying distraction of my wife's nakedness. "It was a one out of a hundred chance that I was able to ditch the aircar in the middle of the Seine. A hundred feet either way and we would have ended up dead or crippled for life."

"I'd prefer dead." She picked up the black thong and considered stepping back into it.

"Either way, we were extremely lucky that we were able to walk away—"

"Swim away."

"—without a scratch. Even minor injuries might have kept either of us from gold medals—or even competing—in the Olympics that month."

"Or our wedding the week after." She decided against reapplying wet butt-floss and slung it over her shoulder where it made a wet smacking sound against her scapula.

"Which is what I am most grateful for. I don't think you would have ever married me if a close brush with mortality hadn't put you in a different frame of mind."

She sighed as I hefted the food basket and gave the area one last look for litter. "You make it sound like I wouldn't commit to you because I don't love you. That you had to trick me to get me to the altar." She walked up to me, curling her toes over mine, pressing her breasts into my solar plexus. "I love you madly. Desperately. Deeply!" She laid her head against my chest. "But I don't feel like I have a right to bind you to me for life when I cannot be a mother to your children."

"Semantics," I murmured into her hair.

"Biology," she whispered. "Flesh of your flesh."

"I can't imagine my life without you."

"I would rather have died in the skies above Paris than grow old with you and see you regret lost opportunities." She turned her face up to mine. "I love you, my Robert—more than life itself!"

Her kiss was like the wine of life itself. The sound of the surf and the beating of our hearts like the throb of the universe, breathing in and out. A little faster now.

ψ

As our lips parted, she sighed. "Sam was wrong. A kiss is not just a kiss."

"Sam?" I asked. The setting sun bathed Natasha's face with a rosy blush that softened the lines of age and blotting the grey streaks so that her red hair had the luster of spun wine. For a moment she was as young and fresh as the day she had walked into my fencing class, twenty-four years earlier, looking to seduce a crippled ex-hacker. For a moment I felt a fiercer passion, the joy of youth and the unseen roads ahead versus the fields of bliss and contentment we feel lucky to find in our later years. For a moment I was lucky to have it both ways.

"Casablanca, Darling. The Bogart classic. Dooley Wilson played the part of Sam, the piano player at Rick's. Remember the song?"

"Where Bogie says 'Play it again, Sam?'"

"Humphrey Bogart never said 'Play it again, Sam.'"

"Sure he did. It's the best-known line from 'Casablanca'."

"A cultural myth. It was Ilsa who said 'Play it, Sam. Play *As Time Goes By.'* Later on, Rick tells Sam, 'If she can stand it, I can: play it.'" She shook her head. "How sad that a Russian knows early American cinema better than a native."

"How sad," I said, "that my wife is smarter than me."

"Smart enough to marry you."

"Not that smart. I saw how Dankevych was making eyes at you. Before and after we escaped the Matrix. If you had played your cards right, you could have become the First Lady of Russia."

"And how would that have served either of our homelands? Borys was a great leader but without your diplomacy, there might have come a war that laid waste to the earth."

"Ah, so you married me for pragmatic reasons."

She reached into the hood of my parka and caressed my cheek with a mittened hand. "Why would I desire to be First Lady for a few short years when I am much happier being the second wife of Ambassador Ripley for the rest of my life?"

"We might have avoided all those years of shuttle diplomacy, splitting our home between Washington and Moscow and living out of suitcases. If we had just gone back into the Matrix and gotten the real Walter Hanson back in his own body—"

She laid a finger over my lips. At least I think it was a finger: the mitten made it difficult to tell. "I am so glad Colonel Kerensky talked you out of it. You might have ended up trapped or killed and the rest of the world would have had no hope—no idea." She shook her head. "Instead you are a well-beloved statesman of two great nations. Not to mention the most wonderful lover and best friend in two different universes."

"You're making me blush."

"It is just the setting of the sun."

She turned and laid her head on my shoulder. We both looked out at the wild beauty of the Ural Mountains as the maroon orb melted down into purple shadowed peaks. A few flakes of snow swirled down to chase the fading of the light.

"Clouds are moving in," I observed. "Think we'll get a storm?"

"A blizzard? No. There will be snow. A great deal of snow over the next seventy-two hours. But it will fall thick and soft and gently and be wonderful to watch from inside a warm chalet."

"Lucky for us we have such a chalet. Warm and all."

"And private," she agreed, slipping an unmittened hand inside my parka. "Not a soul around for miles."

"And for at least three d-days." Her hand was cool against my sweaty chest. "M-maybe more depending on skiing conditions. My editor will be happy."

Her hand had started to tweak my nipple. It stopped. "Your editor?"

"I've put my writing career on hold for twenty-five years to play political pattycake, my dear. It's time to get back in the saddle."

"Whose saddle?" she pouted.

"It's going to be good writing weather: sixty pages, maybe more; trapped inside with no distractions."

Another tweak became a pinch. "*No* distractions?" She withdrew her hand and zipped me to my chin. "It is getting colder."

"That's one way of putting it."

"I am going inside now. Bring more logs when you come."

"Tasha, we have plenty of firewood inside already. We don't even need the fireplace."

"I need the fireplace. There is a great bearskin rug before it and I will be naked upon it before the sun is below Cossack's Ridge."

I felt a silly grin coming on. "We made love on that rug this morning. We made love for almost two hours."

"Only two hours," she said, backing from the balcony with a come hither smile. We have three days of snowy solitude to do better."

"Better? I'm not young anymore!"

She paused before the glass doors leading to the second story of our mountaintop honeymoon cottage. "Bushka, you are a former Olympian. What are records but something to always be broken?"

"I never got to compete. The accident—"

"All long past. A chance to go for the gold awaits you within."

"I was a fencer, not a pole-vaulter."

"You bring the pole. I'll do the vaulting." She voice-coded the glass door for a partial aperture and slid through the narrow opening so as to minimize any heat loss. Immediately she began shedding clothing, leaving a trail of garments across the floor as she made her way toward the great stone fireplace. The years had been kinder to her than to me. And in that twilight zone twixt the setting sun and the flickering fire she seemed as newborn as the goddess Venus first emerging. Then, as she sat upon the great bearskin rug and leaned back, her body a dark silhouette against the red and golden flames of the hearth, the image of Botticelli merged with dim memories of antique trucks and ancient mudflaps.

"Hot dog!" I said, suddenly feeling younger myself. I spun on my heel and headed for the woodpile.

It took some extra effort to pry the frozen logs apart. I could have invoked my dignitary status to have staff assigned to our dacha during our little getaway, but that would have violated the core principles of having a secluded hideaway in the first place. It certainly would have curtailed our experimentation with the homonyms "bearskin" and "bare skin." So I worked a half dozen logs loose with numb hands, hefted them in my aching arms, and counted the price of admission cheap.

And it wasn't great sex. Or, rather, the sex *was* great—but it wasn't primarily that that had me grinning like a loon. It was finding love after losing Nicole and a short, disastrous marriage to Stephanie. I couldn't have imagined that I'd ever find love again—much less that it would last these many years and that I would find it with a woman sent to drug and seduce me into participating in industrial and political espionage. Life was funny.

Maybe that explained the big, goofy grin on my face right now.

As I voice-coded the door and slipped back inside the chalet, I felt the grin fade.

Natasha S. Ripley, my wife of twenty-three years, reclined upon the flat furry hide, her upper back and shoulders propped up by the bear's great head, her own thrown back so that it's snout nestled the base of her skull. The arc of her body lifted her breasts like a young maiden's and her belly seemed as taut and concave as during our first honeymoon more than two decades ago.

"Take me, Bushka," she growled; "take me like the Tartars took Kraków!" She frowned as she realized my attention was directed to the corner by the fireplace instead of her pagan offering.

I don't know which was more unsettling about our unannounced visitor: the face that was hauntingly familiar or the fact that his head was protruding through the wall.

"Who—?" I started but my wife remembered first.

"Riplakish!" she said as my old Fantasyworld avatar stepped through the cabin wall as if it were a clever hologram. "Robert, it is your old Dreambody!"

No wonder I hadn't placed it more quickly: we are less cognizant of our own appearance than those around us, and it had been more than twenty years since I had last entered the Dreamlands' Matrix. Still—the mottled dun and green dragonskin pants and vest over the mithril shirt, the twin swords slung across the hips, the plaited leather headband, as well as the HalfElven features—were as fresh a match for my memory as if the intervening years were but a brief dream.

I nodded. "Riplakish of Dyrinwall. My Dreamlands' avatar."

My old avatar set down a large, twin-handled vase that he had carried through the wall and into the room. "I'm afraid the metaphysical shoe is on the other foot, Bobby." He straightened and gave Natasha a brief glance.

He had better control than I had. I kept glancing down at my lovely wife, torn between desire, curiosity, and the need for some kind of decorum. "What do you want?"

"I've come for Natasha's psyche-file."

"Her what?"

"Natasha Skovoroda—"

"Natasha *Ripley.*"

"Of course," he said soothingly. "I don't want to upset you." He looked around, his eyes hesitating in Natasha's direction more than once. Maybe his control wasn't that much better. "I doubt, though," he continued, "that the subroutines here will permit you to get too upset. It would run counter to the shell context."

"What are you talking about? And how can you be here when you're nothing but a computer program?"

"I've come for Natasha's True Spirit. Her body is on life-support and will soon die if I can't upload her psyche-file to restore her higher brain functions." He turned to my wife who was slowing rising as if awakening from a dream. "Are you ready to abandon your avatar and come with me?"

"Stay away from her." He was right about one thing: although I was very confused, I didn't feel particularly upset.

He picked the vase up and uncapped it.

"What are you doing," I demanded.

"Return with me, Tasha. Use this vessel as your temporary transport. Trust me to see you home."

She swayed slightly, her eyes fluttering, and I stepped in quickly to catch her as her body began to sag. "What have you done?" I asked over my shoulder.

"Don't worry," he replied as he recapped the vase. It seemed to glow now and gave an impression of subtle shifts of color. "Her pseudo-routine should reset in a moment and you can continue in your little fantasy. In time you'll forget I was ever here and never be troubled by the knowledge that you are trapped in Hell."

"What are you talking about?" I was prevented from doing anything to stop him with Natasha's dead weight crumpled in my arms.

"Don't fret too much, Bob; leave all that angst-work to me." He tied a pair of leather straps to each of the vase's handles. "After all, I'm the real Robert Remington Ripley the Third." He slipped his arms through the leather straps and shrugged the vase onto his shoulders as if it were a knapsack. "You are the computer simulation."

And with a little wave, he stepped through the cabin wall as if it were an empty illusion.

"Darling. Bushka." Natasha looked up at me. "Are you going to ravish me?" She squirmed in my arms. "Or stand there with your mouth open?"

I looked at the wall. It seemed very solid. I looked at my wife. She seemed irresistible.

She was right: there were better things to do than stand there with my mouth open.

PART IV

THE HIDDEN DOOR

The dream is the small hidden door in the deepest and most intimate sanctum of the soul, which opens into that primeval cosmic night that was soul long before there was a conscious ego and will be soul far beyond what a conscious ego could ever reach.

—Carl Gustav Jung,
The Meaning of Psychology for Modern Man—

Heav'n but the Vision of fulfill'd Desire,
And Hell the Shadow from a Soul on fire,
Cast on the Darkness into which Ourselves,
So late emerged from, shall so soon expire.

—The Rubáiyát of Omar Khayyám: Stanza LXVII
(5th Translation by Edward Fitzgerald)—

Sleep is the twin of death.

—Homer

ONE

The absence of moons or stars made the darkness outside more profound though not absolute.

A gridwork of roadways stretched in all directions, each lined with buildings that glowed like rows of Chinese paper lanterns. Most were houses of varying sizes, shapes, and architectural styles. Here and there were more anomalous structures: a yacht floating in a pond-sized fragment of ocean, a penthouse suite minus the hundred stories that should have been stacked underneath, a habitat section from the Alpha 3 space station, and…

"Oh great. An elm on Nightmare Street."

I resettled the weight of Natasha Skovoroda's souljar on my back and trotted down the lane toward what looked like a glowing section from the trunk of a giant sequoia tree.

As I drew close, the outer bark changed, the golden, glowing exterior growing more translucent like a thinly stretched amber membrane. It was nearly transparent as I finally came close enough to touch. I stopped and considered the two familiar figures inside. I could hear their conversation.

§

"I thought I had lost you for sure," I said, bending down to kiss her forehead.

Misty Dawn would have none of that. Her arm came up and hooked behind my neck. She guided my mouth down to hers. I came up for air feeling as if I was the one suffering significant blood loss.

"Wilt thou lose me now?" she gasped, her bandaged chest laboring with pain and desire.

"Of course not."

"Then marry me," she insisted fiercely. "The healing draught hath saved my life. It be for naught lest thou heal my heart!"

"But thou—you—are not a True Spirit—" I stammered. Before I could say more a head poked through the wall of the Hamadryad's great, mystic tree.

Bad enough having a head intrude upon a private moment in one's boudoir. Worse when the head appears to be your own and it isn't on your shoulders.

"Go on," it said in my own voice. "Marry the girl. You're not a True Spirit either. And it's best to have someone in your arms when Hell surrounds you."

§

I pulled my head back from the tree and patted Tasha's receptacle. "If Misty Dawn had lived and that scene had played out in her actual tree, we would have been a good sixty feet off the ground.' I rehoisted sistah souljar and, turning, found myself face to face with Lilith.

"How did you get here?"

"I might ask you the same thing."

"This is my turf, buddy-boy; you don't belong here!"

"Yeah? Then how come I'm in every house, apartment, cabin, internal and external place all up and down this road?"

She hesitated. "That might be a bit hard to explain."

"No, it isn't. This is Hell. Or one of its suburbs, anyway. And this is my street." I started walking on toward the next intersection. "The question is, how far does my street go? And, I'm wondering, if this is Robert Ripley Street, is there also a Robert Ripley Boulevard? A Robert Ripley Lane? Maybe a cul de sac with a Robert Ripley Circle?" I managed a weary smile. "Now I truly know how Mephistopheles felt in Chris Marlowe's *Faustus* when he uttered his famous line."

"Better to reign in Hell than serve in Heaven?"

"That's Milton's *Paradise Lost.* Totally different context."

There was an expression of amazement on her shadowed features. "Then you understand?"

"Hell, yes. Lakes of Fire may work for the kids and rolling big rocks up steep hills may frighten the sissies. But anyone who's lived long enough to experience that life and pain go hand in hand knows that Hell has little to do with the issues of the flesh.

"Hell, my dear, is very simple. Fundamental, actually. Hell—distilled to its very essence and broken down to basics—is Regret. Capital R. Anything else is just window-dressing." I looked around. "And I see that my eternal torment is to be the doomed and lonely wanderer, adrift in darkness with tableaus of what might have been content and happy lives if I had but chosen or acted differently."

"You seem to have risen above your suffering most admirably," she said, amazement giving way to archness.

I shrugged. "Been there, done that. *Still* do that, for that matter. Hell doesn't wait for us to die. And, for some of us, regret begins remarkably early, spattering our souls with acid memories and anticipatory wounds. We see the roads not taken and we can imagine the destinations not reached. Forget the verses of Kipling's poem and tack on the word 'only' as a modifier. The soulless coupling of those two words point to every private purgatory. 'If only;' the pregnancy of our discontent."

Lilith seemed surprised. "How do you bear it? I cannot experience such, as I am not a True Spirit, but I can imagine enough to wonder how you can know what you might have had—how you can feel the loss, it's irrevocability, and—"

"And still keep on a-keepin' on?"

She nodded solemnly.

"Something as harsh and cruel as Regret itself," I said. "Hope."

"Hope? Hope is cruel?" She was struggling to keep up.

"Don't they teach you youngsters anything at Demon U.? As long as we have hope we can continue to be hurt, to bleed afresh in our yearning. Once hope dies, the body becomes the soul's own catacomb. You can't hurt the emotionally dead." I stopped and considered a cottage that glowed like a votive candle, one lot down on a side street. Through the translucent walls I could see a pair of young lovers and I used the descriptive noun in the active rather than the passive context. He was a Halfelven bard, she, a Demoness made human. I turned to Lilith. "My regret or yours?"

Her face was like stone. Firelit stone. "We are all in Hell while we stand in this place."

"Well," I said, turning away, "I wish I had some time. I'll bet I could see some real interesting sights."

She cleared her throat. "Define 'interesting.'"

"Betcha got a lot of interesting people down here."

"We cater to all the sins."

"And do you cater to all of the sinners?"

"Who are you looking for? We've got heroes in Hell, rebels in Hell, crusaders in Hell, angels in Hell, masters in Hell, prophets in Hell, kings in Hell—"

"With such legions of Hell, I'm surprised there's not all out war in Hell."

"Oh, we've got that; war is Hell. But the main problem is the writers in Hell."

I decided to let that one slide. "Any tourist spots I should visit before I take my leave?"

"You're so sure you *can* leave?" She folded her arms across her chest. "How did you get down here, anyway? The Powers and Principalities have every gate and portal on White Alert. There are demon hit-squads out looking for you."

"Really? Who wants me so badly?"

"Everybody! Do you have any idea as to what's going on down here?"

"Some, no thanks to you. There's some kind of power struggle going on between the gods and The Underworld seems to be the focal point."

She nodded. "It started here. If it's not resolved soon, the Conflict may spread all the way to the Top. Every faction—each pantheon—figures that they can't win without either recruiting you to their cause or preventing you from helping one of the other sides." She looked around. "We'd better keep moving. There are patrols in the area in case you do make it this far. I'm only one of them."

I reached out and chucked her under the chin. "You, Lily? Hell's belles, we never did decide whether you were a Herald or a Threshold Guardian."

"Maybe you should run down the rest of the list of Archetypes," said another voice. The same voice as Lilith's, but coming from another Lilith who was standing just across the street. "How about 'Shapeshifter'?" she called. "Or maybe 'Shadow'. Definitely 'Trickster' I think."

I looked from one to the other. "I'll be damned!"

"That's the plan," answered the Lilith next to me, executing a little shimmy like an exotic dancer. I stepped back and put a hand to the hilt of Caladbolg as she began to convulse and change form.

"'Ware, Riplakish; 'tis a Demon Lord!"

Worse than that, it seemed. The creature was scabbing over with plate armor and a visored helm. The other Ripley had mentioned something about an editing Dæmon fitting this description but he/she/it hadn't said anything about the size of the battleaxe that suddenly materialized in this one's hands.

"Strike quickly, Demiurge! A Knight of the Living Dead is most vulnerable whilst it still retains some semblance of another's form!"

I pulled the Elven longsword and brought the blade around in a smooth, sweeping arc that sent the creature's head tumbling across the street, through the lawn, and bumping up against the door of the nearest "house."

The door opened and Bob Ripley peered out, clad only in a pair of boxer shorts.

"Who is it, darling?" called a voice from the interior of the faux dwelling.

He peered up and down the street, his gaze passing through us as if we were more unsubstantial than he.

"No one, I guess," the faux me answered. "It's broad daylight and I don't see a single soul."

I thought his choice of words was chilling enough but then Sondra Quebedeaux appeared behind him with even less on. "Come back inside then, you great big hunk of man!" She dragged him back inside like a predatory trapdoor spider.

I murmured, "Why this is Hell, nor am I out of it…" And started on down the street with a measured tread.

"Riplakish! Wait!" The Archdemoness ran after me. "What will you do?"

"My first priority is to get Natasha's psychefile uploaded to her True Form outside the Matrix. So the first order of business is to make like Meat Loaf and leave."

"How will a mundane food dish enable your escape?" she pondered.

I shook my head. "Probably should have gone with a Led Zeppelin reference."

"I tracked you on the surface world. I saw the Skygods create the portal that brought you here."

I nodded. "The Wandijas exist in the Dreamtime. By following in their wake I was able to catch a slipstream into Abydos."

"Lucky for you they were going where you needed to go."

"Luck? In the Matrix?" I rubbed my chin. "No, I don't think so. But I'm not about to look a gift horse in the mouth, Trojan or otherwise."

"But these Wandija have passed beyond the Necropolis. How will you get through the sentry points?"

"I've been thinking about that. Tell me, does The Wild Hunt still pass through Hades domain?"

"Aye. Even now the Master of the Hunt is gathering damned souls from the Fields of Asphodel for the next excursion."

"How soon will they depart?"

She shrugged. "I know not, save that they will regroup in the Stygian Marsh."

I grasped her shoulders. "Where? Precisely. I can't be stopping to ask for directions."

"Near Charon's landing, where the rivers Styx, Cocytus, Pyriphlegethon, and Acheron conjoin. There the Hunt's Master gives the hellhounds their final orders ere they depart for above."

"Ah." I ran through everything I could remember about The Hunt's variables. "Then I do have a plan of sorts."

"That's good."

"But I need your help."

"Not so good."

"It's a chance to upgrade from Herald to Sidekick."

"Campbell never mentioned such an archetype."

"Been reading have you?"

"What mythos hath spawned such creature?"

"American West, circa nineteenth century. When you get some vacation time go visit Frontierworld. In the meantime, I need a favor."

"As I said, not so good. What is the favor?"

"I need to borrow your horse."

"This just gets worse and worse."

"And a hat."

"A hat?"

"Do you have a suburb down here for radio personalities?"

"Right next door to the writers, borough. I know Howard Stern personally."

"I'll just bet you do. But I'm more interested in Don Imus…"

§

It was well known that Hephestus had his workshops spread throughout the volcanic Isle of Lemnos. What wasn't so well known was the fact that gimpy Greek also provided stable space for the rest of the Olympians. Deep within the catacombs that opened above and below, were the stalls that housed the various steeds of legend, as well as the chariots of Helios, Apollo, and other dieties. Even Hades' wheels—generally referred to as "Pluto's Four-Horse Open-Slay" by the rest of the Ambrosia-and-Nectar set—was kept within.

Heph didn't actually stoop to performing any stable duties himself. In fact, "stoop" was one of those words I dropped from my vocabulary whenever the god of the forge was around: ole Hopalong Crutchady was a might bit sensitive, and guess who taught Thor how to throw a big heavy hammer with deadly accuracy? The dwarfish Cedalion, Heph's number one assistant, oversaw the actual running of the stables and it was the genie-like Cabeiri who did most of the day-to-day taskwork. I did not want to run into either, so I waited behind one of the great bronze doors outside the underground entrance.

When Lilith finally appeared, she was leading her Nightmare mount with a sack slung across the razored saddle. The jet-black steed danced, striking sparks from the rocky ground as she handed me the reins. "B," she said, addressing the horse-shaped darkness, "this is Riplakish. He is my…friend. You shall carry him through the Wild Hunt today. Do not lose him or allow any harm to come to him, or Mommy will be very angry." Her mount shook his head and snorted, venting twin jets of blistering steam.

"Riplakish," she continued, taking my hand and placing it upon the creature's sizzling forehead, "this is Beuntoyou. Be nice to him."

"Nice," I said as the Nightmare rolled his glowing red eyes and clicked his teeth. His teeth included double sets of fangs. I gave her the look. "Beuntoyou?"

She nodded as she opened the bag and sorted through its contents. "Named after the Prophet Jeremiah's horse. Don't worry, you'll get it…" She handed me a battered Stetson, similar to the headgear that The Duke used to fancy.

"Awww, now why do they do this?" I pulled the sunburst of feathers that were tucked into the hatband in the front and tossed them back to her. "If I wanted to look like a dude I'd get me a shirt with some rhinestones. You can tuck that back in when I send the hat back."

She tossed the feathers aside. "You can keep the hat. I told him that it was a Rush order and he didn't want it back." She handed me a black silk kerchief folded into a triangle.

I put the hat on my head, tied the kerchief across my face so that only my eyes were showing, and then enlisted her aid in securing the souljar just behind the saddle.

"Hurry," she said, the Master of the Hunt is gathering the next train of lost souls now.

I stepped to the Nightmare's side and tried to get my foot in the stirrup. He danced a little and I had to waltz along like some kind of two-bit tenderfoot. "Whoa! Whoa Beuntoyou!" I put my foot back down and turned to the Archdemoness. "Oh. Funnee. Very."

She waggled a finger at the beast. "Beuntoyou! Obey!" She almost looked stern. "Or Mommy won't let you have any creatures for dessert tonight."

Beuntoyou stopped doing the cha-cha and stood with his head down while I mounted. "That's better," I said, sounding much more confident than I felt. "I owe you one, Lily."

"Indeed. And how shall thou repay me?" She smiled, showing pointed teeth. "Perhaps you will grant me a boon?"

"Um," I said. "A boon?"

She laughed. A little sadly, I thought. "Fear not. I would not ask thee aught but what you would willingly give." She grasped her mount's face and spoke to his ear. "Go now. Join the Master's hunt and carry him safely until he is ready to dismount." Her Nightmare's launch was all out of proportion to the gentle smack she administered to his hindquarters.

The blurred landscape gradually resolved into a sharpened clarity as I found my rhythm in the saddle. I cast about for landmarks in case I had to fall back on Plan B. Actually, there was no Plan B yet, but there *were* landmarks, and I might need to figure an alternate escape route if this didn't work.

Off to my right was the river Pyriphlegethon, its fiery chop of lava waves lending a baleful orange glow to the great fence of bronze marking the boundaries of Tartarus. In the distance, rising out of its dark depths, was the Tower of Iron where sat bloody-robed Tisiphone, keeping an eternal, sleepless watch. I turned Beuntoyou in the opposite direction, hoping the guardian Erinye had not taken notice of me and sounded some silent alarm.

We approached the river Eridanus that bordered the Fields of Elysium behind Hades' palace. I turned the Nightmare so that we gave it wide berth. Beuntoyou didn't have wings like Ghost, but that didn't keep him from leaving the ground. In moments we were galloping more than a foot in the air, skipping across the dark waters toward a spit of dead ground that bordered the hindquarters of the river Lethe. I held my breath, trying to avoid the ingestion of any airborne droplets of Lethe's amnesia-inducing waters.

Down that dark and misty flood bobbed a ship of Egyptian design.

Recalling that Ra, the Egyptian sungod, sailed underground rivers during the night, I turned my mount to cut well behind the strange craft's stern. As we skipped across the second tributary, I scanned the boat for any sign of life or light. I saw none.

Again we gained dry, dusty land and I turned Beuntoyou to follow Lethe's outer bank. As we turned back toward the more populous part of Hades' kingdom, I could make out the couching figures of the not-so-damned souls who were stooping to drink from the river's waters of forgetfulness. There is a flinty mercy in that baptism that washes all memory away.

I urged the demon mount to greater speed and clutched at my hat as we charged back across Lethe and headed for the river Styx.

The problem with Hell is that I didn't actually design it.

Michael Straeker had been the Chief of Programming for the finished Fantasyworld program and had subcontracted a lot of program sectors out to other scholars and programmers. While I had done the lion's share of setting up the program baseline, Straeker had been in charge of the final product and that was before the Matrix had been corrupted by the Anomaly and begun recreating itself into new realities. With other mythologies vying for the real estate of the damned, I could only guess at the current geography of Hades.

The Greeks themselves, had been a little inconsistent. According to legend, the kingdom of the dead was encircled by four major "waterways:" Cocytus, the river of lamentation; Pyriphlegethon, the river of fire; Styx, the river of the unbreakable oath by which the gods swear; and, um, oh yeah, Lethe, the river of forgetfulness.

While the Styx gets all the PR hustle for having Charon as crossing guard and turning Achilles' epidermis into kevlar, it would have been insufficient to keep the dead corralled for all eternity without the additional challenges of the other three. The problem was in charting their actual courses and making sure I was headed in the right direction.

The general idea was that all of these creepy canals came together at the Acherusian Lake and encompassed the Stygian Marsh, just "north" of Charon's Landing and "south" of the Meadows of Asphodel, where the dead are sorted and pallid white flowers glimmer like eyes in the darkness.

I was hoping that the landscaping hadn't changed too much.

Across Styx was another, larger patch of desolate ground that was banded on the far side by the murky waters of Acheron, River of Woe, as the two rivers flowed toward their convergence with Cocytus and fiery Pyriphlegethon. My best guess was that I was on the right course. I made landfall and tugged the reins hard to the right.

Whether The Hunt might serve as needed was a greater guess on my part.

The mythic tradition of The Wild Hunt was even more diverse than the Greco-Roman accounts of the land of the dead. While the popular accounts hold that the Master of the Hunt, the hellish hounds with eyes of flame, and the cadre of dead attendants are of Celtic origins, the actual antecedents are spread throughout the European continent. In Norway the dark hoard is the Oskorei; in Sweden and Denmark they are known as the Odensjakt. The French believe the family of Harlequin is the source of this Mardi Gras of mayhem, while the Germans name it Wutan's or Wuet's Army depending on which province you find people willing to talk about it. Descriptions of The Hunt vary slightly, but they all come down to Hell's chatteldrive of the damned.

I adjusted the kerchief over my face and pulled the hat down so that the brim shadowed my eyes as I approached the "X" where the waters of the Acheron and the Styx came together to mingle with Cocytus and Pyriphlegethon. As we splashed over the roiling surface of the rivers' convergence, I saw the hooded figure of Charon seeming to stand on the water off to my left, his boat and seated passengers hidden by low-lying mist. I tried to make out the three-headed form of Cerberus, but Hades' ultimate junkyard dog was nowhere to be seen. Maybe Heracles had taken him for another walk.

Chaos reigned as I arrived at the Stygian Marsh.

The Wild Hunt has little to do with Greek Mythology, though the acolytes of Bacchus and Artemis have borrowed liberally form its example. Rather, the horned one schedules stops in the various Hells to gather the damned for his mad chase through the desolate, twilight places. Awhile back, while scrying for Nicole's body through my crystal ball, I had discovered that one of the Anomaly-created convergences between the Fantasyworld and Frontierworld programs was located right here in Hades' underworld kingdom. The wild huntsman not only organized the Wild Hunt in Fantasyworld but also trail-bossed the Ghost Riders in the sky on their aerial cattle drives in Frontierworld.

Yippie ki-yay, Yippie ki-yo...

Adding to the usual bedlam that accompanied the gathering of the damned for the hunt was a new sound this time around: the caterwauling of hundreds of cats.

Tabbies and calicos and Siamese and Burmese and tortoiseshells and every hue and pattern imaginable, longhairs and short, the fractious felines were everywhere. Chasing skeletal mice, stalking wraiths, nibbling the decaying fingers of corpses that stooped to pet them, they milled about the dead like a bubbling carpet of fur. I almost swore that I'd be damned before deciding I'd best watch my tongue.

In spite of the confusion of kitties it wasn't hard to find my quarry: off to my right I saw five mounted cowboys, off to my left rode a dozen and more. All I needed now was Rosa's Cantina.

Riders! crackled a dark voice in my head. *You have a herd to deliver to El Diablo before sunrise. A thousand head of cats! And not one may be lost during the drive or you will all roast in Hell for the next thousand years—*

There were some rude noises from the dark riders.

—or be reincarnated as singing cowboys at fat-farm dude ranches for the next ninety days!

Amid gasps and groans, everyone sat a little stiffer in the saddle.

The Master of the Hunt rose into the air above us, utterly dark and featureless, the antlers of a great stag sprouting from the sides of his head like some kind of hellish radar array. He raised a gnarled, twisted staff, and the wind about us rose with it, swirling in the crooked screw-like pattern of the enchanted stave. *The rest of you, come with me and hunt the newly damned!*

The wind rose and spun with cyclonic force, lifting us all into the air and rushing us toward the surface of the earth. Higher and higher we rose, tumbling like thistledown caught in a Texas dust devil. A crack of thunder and the earth was rent above our heads, the exit from Death's dark womb.

As we spilled out into the night air, I twisted and unfastened the souljar, pulling it to my chest. This time I was smart and took the extra time to cast a Flying spell before diving out of the saddle. Beuntoyou hesitated and then turned and leapt into the sky to follow the Ghost Riders as I swooped behind a boulder and waited for The Wild Hunt to pass out of sight.

It wouldn't take long. The hounds moved with supernatural speed, their huge, coal-dark paws churning a good foot above the ground. The souls of the damned paced them, some appearing to stride as if shod with seven-league boots while others made no pretense of running but glided like the jet stream was their tail wind. In no time at all, they were a mile down the road, and I was starting to relax.

That's when a heavy hand fell on my shoulder from behind.

This is bad, I thought. And I turned.

It was bad. It was *very* bad.

The horned Master of the Hunt glared down at me with eyes of flame. *"Riplakish,"* he said. *"I have you at last!"*

And then he took off his antlered helm, and I saw that it was even worse than I had imagined.

TWO

♀

I settled down into my bedroll and thanked the darkness for being merciful.

The flickering reflection of the campfire did more to conceal the anguish on the young Rogue's face than reveal it. It also made it easier to remember that this slender, young avatar held the mind and personality of an adult lawyer, who actually looked like a well-dressed sumo wrestler, when he finally spoke.

"She used to sing me this song," he said, staring into white-hot core of the fire. "'My Attorney Bernie,' I think it was called."

I nodded, refolding a spare blanket into a makeshift pillow. "Dave Frishberg. Old song. Obscure."

"Nicole loved old, obscure things. It was just one facet of her charm."

"Not many people knew that," I said.

"Most people who loved her—and there were a lot of them," Daggoth mused quietly from his tangle of blankets in the wagon bed, "—didn't know her at all."

Mick sat, leaning back against a wagon wheel. "I watched her win the Olympic gold when I was young. I thought then that she was a pretty lady. As a grown up, I'm stunned even now when I look over at Ripley and see her in the flesh—so to speak. It would be hard not to love her."

She had to be kidding. With my hair all dirty and tangled and what was left of my clothes in torn disarray?

"Love..." I heard the distaste in Mudge's voice. "What a travesty of semantics. 'Love' is a gutter word, trucked out upon every occasion of hormonal surges and lustful imaginings. Is there any word used more selfishly? More fraught with illusion and deception?" He shook his head. "If I would express the breath and depth of my feelings for her, my willingness to sacrifice everything for nothing more than just her smile and gentle regard—I must use the same word that others would mouth with no more thought than to just possess her body."

I wanted to remark that possessing her body wasn't all it was cracked up to be, but this didn't seem to be the time. I said that I understood, instead. Mick echoed my sentiments.

Mudge turned to her; his face half-eclipsed in the penumbra of darkness beyond the fire. "Forgive me, madam; I do not mean to be snide or insulting when I say that you most likely would not understand. First of all, you did not know her. Had you experienced the palpable force of her personality, the quickness of her wit, the kindness and generosity of her spirit, you might understand how unimportant the outward packaging might be. Secondly, as a woman, you have been oriented for the entirety of your life by the shallow dictates of culture and society that sets undue emphasis on appearance over substance. If you have not been subsumed, yourself, by these twisted mores, you have had ample opportunities to observe and experience these prejudices in others. Particularly men."

She nodded. "The beautiful and the ugly are equally afflicted," she said. "It is the misfortune of most beautiful woman to be unaware of their own oppression."

Mudge gave her a searching look. "Then perhaps you do understand. Perhaps you would believe me if I said that I loved her irrespective of her physical appearance. Had accident or disease robbed her of her superlative beauty, I would have loved her regardless. Perhaps better: an exquisite face and form is often more hindrance than asset in forging bonds of trust and intimacy."

She looked back just as searchingly. "Perhaps I would believe you." Several seconds passed before she broke eye contact and turned to Daggoth. "How about you, Sorcerer?"

Behind the sideboard of the wagon Daggoth sounded befuddled. "How about me?"

"You seemed to be quite taken with that supermodel when we arrived. What was her name? Amy—?"

"Angie. Angel McRae."

"Right. You find her to be beautiful, right?"

"Beautiful? She'd make a bishop kick a hole in a stained-glass window!"

"And you're certainly no bishop." I clucked my tongue at him. "But don't you have enough distractions between Stephanie and

Queen Hippolyta?" Secretly I was relieved to have the focus off Nicole and on to anyone else.

He rose up and gave me a look. "The Amazon queen isn't my fault. It's the Matrix acting out. You should know how that sort of thing gets out of hand better than anybody. Besides, she's not real." He gave me another look. "And I know *you* won't say anything to Stephanie. You understand. It's a guy thing."

"Not to mention tattling to my ex might be interpreted as prejudicial on my part."

"Well—yeah. But. Having Angel McRae in close proximity is one of those male fantasy things. It's not really being unfaithful."

I thought I saw Mick cock an eyebrow in the shadows.

"You haven't forgotten that, here, 'Angel' is actually Dagny Westbrook," I reminded him. "You're wasting your time fantasizing over a woman who not only *isn't* the true object of your lustful imaginings, but is incapable of feeling reciprocal passion for you—or any other member of your gender, for that matter." That sounded wrong somehow. I probably should have said *our* gender. I hoped Bernard Mudge was getting some subtext out of this turn in the discussion. It was awful uncomfortable to act as surrogate confessor for his grief and loss while I was the spitting image of the *object* of his grief and loss.

Daggoth waved his hand. "Details."

"So it really is about the outer packaging," Mick said. "You probably don't even know anything about the real Angela McRae beyond her holo-ads and net-spreads."

Daggoth frowned. "I know more than you might think."

"Like what?"

"Like she has an IQ of two hundred and seventeen. Like the fact that she has a master's degree in History and a minor in Archeology. That she has used her own money to finance digs on three different continents. That she paints and sculpts and holds a silver *monkron* in *Muay Thai* kickboxing."

I let out a low whistle.

"What?" Mudge wanted to know.

"Defining *Muay Thai* practitioner as a kickboxer is somewhat akin to describing a Karate black belt as someone who's pretty fair scrapper." I looked at Daggoth. "Did you say '*silver* monkron?'

That means she's a national finalist in the Amateur Division. That quite possibly makes her deadlier than anyone else you're likely to meet in The Game. Lucky for you she isn't actually here."

"Why?" He looked vaguely surprised. "I think she'd like me."

"Why?" Mick shot back, then smiled sheepishly. "I mean she's probably very snooty—being a supermodel and all."

"Oh, I don't know," Mudge said. "Sounds like the lady may have a surprisingly intact value system."

"Maybe, but I wouldn't put all my eggs in that basket." Daggoth leaned forward. "The way I figure it, a woman like that has all the boytoys she could ever want. What I figure, is a woman like that is going to be ultimately drawn to power."

"Maybe you should define what you mean when you say 'a woman like that.'" There was a flinty edge in Mick's voice. "A woman like what?" Heavy emphasis on the "what."

Mudge reached over and patted our homely compatriot on the knee. "Please, let him speak. It is said that when the student is ready, the master will appear." He managed a wry smile. "I'm ready for a change in my luck, and yon Wizard's counsel sounds as if it might be very interesting." Heavy emphasis on the "very."

She nodded and suddenly they were sharing a smile that looked very conspiratorial.

"Now I am not young and handsome," Daggoth continued, "but that is not a problem because I am powerful."

"Powerful silly," I murmured and Mick and Mudge's grins grew broader.

"I mean, I am the Chief of Programming and a twenty-third level Wizard—a triple threat in terms of The Matrix."

I redid the math and only came up with double-threat. Daggoth had imbibed a fair amount of wine to lessen the headache that Luthor the Barbarian had dished out earlier. Apparently the wine was dulling more than just the pain.

"I *could* reprogram my appearance so that I was young, virile, and handsome. Since I would be actually altering my avatar the change would be more than merely cosmetic, I really would be young and virile, as well as handsome."

"Not to mention modest and a silver-tongued charmer," I said, and giggled. Maybe Daggoth wasn't the only one affected by the wine.

"Ah, you are correct, sir! I could practice being charming in ways that would work specifically on her."

"And how would you do that?" Mick asked.

"I would construct a replica of Angela McRae and try a variety of approaches until I found the most effective ones."

I was suddenly very sober. "You would?"

"And, after I'd perfected my technique, I would offer to put my powers at her service."

"I'll just bet you would," Mick chuckled.

"Nay, madam. Not in the crass and crude contexts that you allude to. At least, not at first." He stood. "Instead I would offer to make her victorious in the next DreamQuest Tournament."

"And how would you do that?" I asked. "There are no more DreamQuest tourneys now that the Programworlds are closed to the public."

"First of all, I would do what Natasha Skovoroda once wanted you to do. What hundreds of Gamer groupies have asked Dreammasters to do since the year Dreamlands opened to the public. Give specialized training—"

"Divulge Programworld secrets? Artificially boost skills and abilities?" There was no trace of a smile on Mick's face now.

"As I recall you specifically and illegally entered The Matrix to get special training from our resident Demiurge in drag."

"It's not the same thing."

"It isn't? Are you going to tell me that you don't know anything about the underground tourneys?"

"Underground tournaments?" I asked.

Mick was silent.

"What? Did you think that Sculthorpe boy, his froggy friend, and Ms. I-Want-To-Be-A-Bard over there are the only illegal program incursions since Dreamlands was closed to the public? A hundred hackers breach the firewalls every day using their own homegrown brain-basters and neuralrigs. Most REMrunners are caught or choose to duck back out again within a few hours to a few days. There are some, however, who have made extended visits and there are rumors that the most experienced hackers are planning their own little clandestine contest within the next few months." He looked back at Mick. "Right, my dear?"

"Your tone," she said, "sounds a tad condescending."

"Does it?" he asked mildly.

"All I asked for was training in a different class. I only asked once. I have come along with all of you, placing myself in danger and offering whatever assistance I can give with no further expectations than to be treated with a little respect and dignity. By and large you have all been polite. I'm aware that I don't live up to your standards of attractiveness and I can handle that embarrassing little pause, that hesitation as you glance away or consider the proper phrase for a sentence in my presence.

"What I do *not* want right now is to be lectured by a drunken chauvinist who thinks he can get his jollies dressing up some mannequin to look like his favorite pinup girl and pitching woo."

Daggoth snorted while Mudge and I looked at each other for an emergency escape hatch. "Woo?" The sauced Sorcerer shook his head. "Pitching woo? You misunderstand on two fronts. First, the replica I would construct would be no mannequin. It would, for all intents and purposes, *be* Angel McRae. Look like her, talk like her, move like her. But more than some animated homunculus, it—her—*she*—would *think* like her."

"What would you know about how the real Angela McRae thinks?"

"That's the point I was trying to make a few minutes ago, my lady. I don't. That's why I would need to practice with the next best thing—the all-but-the-real-thing, to see what works and what doesn't."

Mudge appeared to be baffled but Mick proved a quicker study. Dawning horror replaced the look of stupefaction on her face. "You're saying you could create a duplicate avatar of McRae and then download a copy of her psychefile? To practice putting the moves on the real thing?"

Daggoth nodded and, for a moment, I thought his head would fall off. "Crudely but succinctly put." Maybe it already had for all intents and purposes.

♂

The horned Master of the Hunt was an imposter.

Towering over me, his great, iron-gloved hand clamped to my shoulder, was the chief god and King of the Greco-Roman

Underworld. The Greeks worshipped him as Hades, hence the name of his kingdom. The Romans knew him as Pluto, but he was no Mickey-mouse deity. His name was often translated as "Dis," the Latin word for rich, as he was also known as the God of Wealth. He got that moniker from all of the precious metals hidden in the earth. Make no mistake, however: when you were "dissed" by Jupiter's Low-Down brother, there was no profit to be found in your amortization column.

What a lot of people don't know is that Hades is the King of the Dead—but not Death, him- or "it"-self. The immortal personification of the Big Sleep was another deity whom the Greeks called Thanatos and the Romans named Mors.

Or Orcus.

Which, Hades was explaining, was his problem.

And apparently now was mine.

"Okay," I said, as we sat on a couple of boulders, "let me see if I've got this straight. My old buddy Orcus has usurped the throne to your kingdom and driven you into exile—"

Hades' expression changed from distress to shock. "Orcus is your *ally*?"

"Sarcasm, D. Jeez, you gods are so literal-minded, it's a wonder the Greeks ever invented the oracle."

"Then you are not the ally of Death?"

"Listen, Chuckles; I didn't just break into Hell, steal a friend's soul, and hotfoot it back out again because I'm graveyard groupie. If I could write a Hollywood screenplay it would be 'Death Takes A *Permanent* Holiday' or *'Beat* Joe Black and Blue.'"

The former King of the Underworld looked hopeful. "Then thou wilt help me?"

"Whoa! Hold on there, D. While I'll admit that I owe Fat Boy more than one comeuppance, I've got other fish to fry. Besides, why should I help you? Wouldn't I and the rest of the living be better served by letting all the gods of the dead duke it out for supremacy and then take on the vastly weakened victor?"

"I saved you from the Goblins."

"What Goblins?"

"When you and Daggoth—oh. I see. It was the other you. It's been hard to keep track of all of you, lately."

"No joke."

"I did not make a jest. I merely—"

"Don't worry about it, D. I take it that the other me owes you her life."

He straightened himself in an attempt to regain a little dignity. "Actually, in the end, every living being owes me their life."

"Yeah, well, we can engage in metaphysical thumb-wrestling later. Right now I've got an overdue soul to deliver and you've got a usurper to unsurp. Maybe we can do a deal."

"A deal?"

"You want me to help you out of the goodness of my heart?"

He considered. "You do have a reputation for that."

"Yeah. Well. Reputations aren't all that they seem." Actually, I probably would help him out just to restore balance to the Matrix. But it couldn't hurt to get a little help with my other projects. "I have needs, too, you know."

"I can make you wealthy beyond your wildest dreams."

"Why is it you guys with *all* the money always think it's *only* about money?"

"Women, then. I can offer you your heart's desire. The damned not only offer a selection of the most beautiful, but also the most skilled, the most experienced—"

"No."

"And the Succubae—"

"Dammit, *no*. Have you forgotten whom you're talking to? Why would I want something off the rack when I can design and program to my own tastes?"

He shrugged. "The rumor is that you're not into that, either."

"True."

"You're not human."

It was my turn to shrug. "You've been talking to my ex-wife. Speaking of talking, have you had a chat with Tartarus?"

"What? All of them?"

I looked down at the ground and scuffed at the ground with my boot, presumably looking for my patience. The all-powerful are so used to having everything their way that their higher brain functions often atrophy. "Not Tartarus the *place,*" I explained with better humor than I felt, "Tartarus the *Titan*. Remember? Father of monsters. The guy Echidna, Typhon, and Thanatos call Daddy? Maybe he'd—"

"No." He gave me that look that suggested the higher brain functions of Programmers and Demiurges could atrophy, as well. "The sire of Orcus—whom I've kept in exile for the better part of eternity—has just seen his son make it to the top of his profession. Now why would he want to help me bring him back down?"

"Better chance for a plea bargain when we win?" I suggested.

"You sound very confident."

"Surely you have loyal troops you can count on."

"Loyalty? In Hell? You're as naïve as the rumors say you are."

Clearly I needed to work on this rep thing.

"The Manes will follow whomever's in charge at any given moment. Orcus has made a lot of promises to a lot of Demons, offering them Devil status. He's told the Devils that Michael has gotten old and careless, and that it's time to make another run at Heaven—get their wings back and such. You can tell these ninnies have never read Tom Wolfe."

"*Thomas* Wolfe," I corrected absently. "Any other power blocs down below that you can rally to your side?"

"None that I can think of. He's bribed all the Powers and Principalities."

"Well, if it's really all that hopeless then what do you expect me to do? Challenge Death Incarnate to a personal duel?" I saw the look in his eyes. "No! Absolutely not! If there's anything that I am sure about when it comes to my rep, it's that I built it on being a consultant, not a combatant."

"Then tell me how to win back my throne."

"Give me a minute, will ya? Taking on the hordes of Hell needs a bit more thought. Besides, you haven't heard my terms, yet…."

♀

"It's not possible!"

Surprisingly, Mick appeared to be more agitated over the idea that Daggoth could clone Angel McRae than Mudge over the possibility of using the same process to resurrect Nicole Doucet.

But then Mudge still seemed to be in the process of mentally connecting all of the dots.

"It shouldn't be," I said quietly, "but my other self has gone off to Hell to retrieve Natasha Skovoroda's psychefile to attempt the reverse."

"But—but—Angel McRae's avatar hasn't been killed…so her psychefile wouldn't be in Hell. Or Heaven, for that matter."

"But all psychefiles are stored in backup copy formats when they're not actually in use. In fact, they're even backed up during use in the event of accidents." I turned to Daggoth. "Messing with one of *your* backed-up psychefiles is what got us into this whole mess in the first place."

"I'm not so sure—"

"You won't do it!" Trembling, the slender youth in strapped leather was on his feet, a white knuckled hand on the hilt of his dagger.

"I won't? And why is that?" the Wizard asked mildly. "Who's going to stop me?"

Mick rose behind him but Mudge waved her back. "You won't do it because it's *wrong*. You're drunk and tired and, judging from your bruises, you're in more than a little pain. You won't do it because you're a decent man and we all have the right to spout off a little about hypotheticals when our desires are seemingly out of reach."

"But that's just the point, boy. Our desires don't have to be out of reach."

Don't do this, Mike, I thought as hard as I could at him. But I doubt he would have heard me if I had shouted.

"What?" Mudge sputtered. "You're talking about bringing back Nicole from the dead?"

"Why not?" He nodded at me. "The other Bob Ripley is currently running around Hell to do that very same thing for Natasha Skovoroda. No one has voiced any objections to that little quest before now."

"That's different," I said.

"How is it different?"

I opened my mouth but he cut me off.

"Before you answer, decide which Nicole you're denying resurrection to. Yours?" He pointed at Mudge who trembled as Mick's arms encircled him from behind. "Or his?"

"I know it should matter," Nicole's family solicitor said in an uneven voice. "But either one alive is better than both dead."

"Things are not always equal, Mr. Mudge. Ask Nicole's ex-fiancé about the difference between the woman he was to marry and the woman you worshipped from afar. Both tried to kill him.

Both fell into the same chasm. Yet they were *both* different individuals. One is not the other."

The fire burned low while I recounted the final moments of the two Nicole Doucets in the caverns beneath the Isle of Ortygia. I hoped no one could see my face now as we sat in silence.

"I can only imagine your grief," Mudge finally said from somewhere across the stain of dying embers. "If Nicole had hated me so—had tried to kill me—well, I don't know how I could go on living."

Daggoth cleared his throat. "Well, Ripley didn't. He died. She actually killed one of his avatars. It's possible that she killed others that he doesn't consciously know of. That may be one of the reasons that he can't accept the possibility of her resurrection in any form."

I stared down at the angry red heart of the fire's remains. "My Nicole is—was—mad. It would be pointless to even try and bring her back under the circumstances. Given her state of mind and the suffering she endured for all those years, it would be inhumane."

"But *my* Nicole was not," Mudge argued. "She was trying to protect the Robert Ripley she knew and loved in our universe. Surely you can respect that?"

"I don't know. The woman I knew and loved wouldn't have accepted that kind of solution. She would have tried to find another way. I think there was a touch of madness in her, too. Perhaps the seeds of instability were always there, dormant and buried too deep when we were young and our lives were largely untroubled."

"But you don't know. And you have no right to play God!"

"Bernie…" Mick's voice was soothing and sorrowful. "This is their universe. In the Matrix, they both *are* gods. No one's talking about a death sentence for Nicole. She's already gone."

"But they could bring her back," he said. "The sorcerer has already said as much."

"We were never able to find either of their bodies," I said.

"But Daggoth has said that he can create a new avatar! And he wouldn't even have to do that! You could upload her psychefile to her body back in my world! If she is mad, she's already in the custody of the Wallbank Sanatorium! They could help her! And she'd be in a place where she couldn't harm anyone even if your worst fears were true!"

"What about it, Roberta?" Daggoth asked. "The boy has a very good point."

"Don't call me Roberta," I said.

"Don't call me a boy," Mudge echoed.

"Where's the hole in his logic?" Daggoth continued. "Or are you afraid of surrendering your only escape from the Matrix?"

"What?"

"The way you got back in may be your only way back out."

Before I could even consider the issue in any context, Mudge freaked out.

"Damn you!" he shrieked, wrenching himself out of Mick's embrace. "Don't do this!"

"Calm yourself, boy. We're merely having a theoretical discussion."

But Mudge didn't calm himself. Instead, he hurled his dagger into the sideboard just inches below Daggoth's face and launched into a litany of profanity that would've made Barnacle Bill blush. Mick joined in a moment later. When I saw what they saw I almost opted for three-part harmony. Instead, I got a death-grip on my sanity before it could turn heels and run.

"Stand down!" I yelled. "He's not doing it! Though I wish to gods he was."

Daggoth turned to follow our gaze.

He grew pale.

Froze.

Flickered around the edges.

At the very edge of the firelight, bobbing and floating several feet above the ground was a head.

Without a body.

Bad enough to see a disembodied head, trailing intestines and giblets like a Portuguese Man-o-war.

Worse to see it mimic a semblance of life through grotesqueries of expressions and a grinning mouth filled with razored teeth.

But what put sanity on the back burner and opened the pits of madness at our very feet was one unmistakable fact.

It was Nicole Doucet's head.

♂

"That's three tasks for which you are asking my aid," Hades shouted over the rumble of the chariot wheels. "I have set only one task before you."

"It's not the number of favors," I shouted back, "but the size of job that counts. You want me to help you get Hell back? That's a pretty tall order. We're not just talking about a scepter-waving contest with Orcus. I'm supposed to take on the gods and demigods of all the major—not to mention a number of the minor—pantheons just so you can be King of the Dead People! Have you ever thought of retiring and taking up a hobby? Something more exciting than ruling over the deceased? Like watching paint dry, or writing closed captions for late-night infomercials—"

"Enough!" Hades thundered. "I need not bargain with you! You will set things right because you cannot choose to do otherwise."

Oops, busted.

"It matters not what I promise. I might set myself against thee and thou wouldst still move heaven and earth to restore The Balance."

"Yeah? You think you've got me all figured out?"

He glared into the darkness. Fortunately the god of the Underworld and his four black steeds operated safely in the dark; you can take the god out of the grave but you can't take the grave out of the god.

"Thou'rt the Demiurge," he rumbled.

"Meaning what?"

"Meaning thou'rt The Archon," called a familiar voice to my right. "You are the creator of the material world."

Beuntoyou paced us, running at a full gallop as Hades' chariot tore through the night, Lilith sitting serenely in the saddle as if riding a carousel at the county fair. While there was more than enough room in the great dark chariot, even with Cedalion at the reins, she had chosen to regain her mount and ride alongside.

I turned back to Hades. "Don't tell me that Plato is required reading for your minions."

"Nay," she called, "'tis but for mine own need to know."

"Need to know what?"

"Need to know of thee. Though mine interests be anything but Platonic."

"I do not understand," Hades groused.

"'Tis said that Riplakish is the Demiurge incarnate. 'Twas easy enough to visit the philosopher's shade in the fields of Elysium and inquire after such matters."

I cleared my throat. "We've never actually met, you know."

"He named the Creator God the Demiurge in the *Timaeus.*"

"Yeah? Well he was just using a little poetic license. The word originally meant 'public worker.' *Demioergós, demiourgós*—any artisan plying his trade for the public."

"Once upon a time," she said. "But even before Plato words like *technítes* and others were used for craftsmen while words like demiurge and *toû kósmou* were as set aside for the Great Artificer or Fabricator, the Architect of the universe."

"Yeah, yeah, I know. But while *demiourgós* was eventually adopted as a synonym for the Creator, it wasn't synonymous with the Supreme Being."

"Because the Greeks presupposed the existence of matter," she argued. "When they spoke of one who produces out of nothing they used the term *ktístes.* But let's leave the Hellenes out of this; Gnosticism perceived a much more interesting relationship between God the Creator and Demiurge the world-shaper."

I groaned. "Oh, well; if you're gonna bring the Gnostics into this..."

Hades fumed. "What are you two talking about?"

"The Gnostics," I explained, "not only held that the Demiurge was inferior to the supreme spirit or *Propatôr,* they also qualified the relationship as 'antagonistic,' with the world-shaper possibly being the personification of The Carnal—if not outright Evil."

"Who are these Nosties?" Hades asked.

"Never mind." Lilith smothered a smile. "The bottom line is that this particular sect sort of pegged him like the Mazdeans with Ahriman."

Hades' countenance brightened. "Ah! The evil counter-creator of Ormuzd!"

"Very much like," she agreed.

I didn't. "The wonderful wizard of Ormuzd: that's very much of a stretch," I argued. "The Gnostics had a tough time totally agreeing on anything. The majority view—"

"—had the Demiurge as the counterbalance to Jehovah. The Gnostic Satan."

I scowled at her. "First, an expert on Plato and Greek philosophy and now a New Testament scholar. What happened to your characterization of the Archon?"

She dimpled. "Antinomian Gnosticism is so much more fun. And it gives a girl hope that you might actually turn out to be evil."

I turned to Hades. "Ignore her. The only relevant part of the Gnostic view was that the Demiurge was the creator of the material world, to which I might—*might*, mind you—plead 'guilty.' Also that the Demiurge was not God but the Archon, or chief of the lowest order of spirits or aeons: also maybe guilty. They believed that the Demiurge was able to endow man only with the *psyche*—or sensuous soul. The *pneuma,* or rational soul, had to be bestowed by God. True Spirits are way beyond my purview."

The god of the Underworld shook his head. "I understand little of this conversation save that thou art the one who brought form and order out of chaos."

"Chaos?" I sighed. "Just call me Maxwell Smart."

Lilith simpered. "Oh Max…"

♀

It was like looking into a haunted mirror.

The face floating in the darkness at the edge of the firelight was a demonic caricature of my own. Or Nicole's own, to be technically correct.

Its eyes glowed like green foxfire, unholy portals of baleful light that appeared to be soulless, yet cunning. Its mouth was a twisted travesty: lips that had whispered words of love a lifetime ago now pursed around a tangle of barbed teeth, a pointed purple tongue sliding along the sharpened edges in obscene anticipation.

"Come away!" commanded another voice, back in the blackest depths of the darkness.

"I want what is mine," hissed the head, bobbing like the tattered remains of a marionette suspended on a rubber string.

"Not until we know about the child!"

While Mudge and I could hardly tear our eyes away from the floating abomination wearing Nicole's shattered features; Mick cast about, trying to locate the source of the second voice.

"The child is here!" the head rasped.

"Are you sure?" The voice in the darkness moved. Circled to the left. "Where?"

"It is yet unborn!"

"You are sure?"

"I can smell *it inside her!"*

That did it.

The thrall had definitely gone out of this encounter for me. I jumped to my feet and snatched a firebrand from the campfire. "Yeah? Well, fe fi fo this, you ugly headcase!"

The head snarled and bobbed a little closer. *"Valentine, does Orcus want the child alive?"*

"No. Just evidence of its demise."

"Then I want what is mine now!"

"The Wizard is neutralized but we no longer have the element of surprise."

Planting my feet in an imaginary "batter's box" I cocked the torch back in my right hand and curled the fingers of my left hand in a come hither gesture. "You wanna play Marie Antoinette? Come on, bitch; I got you and your friend front row tickets for Less Miserables. Which is what we'll all be if you just come a little bit closer."

She accepted my invitation. With an inhuman shriek, the head flew straight at me, moving at a speed that mocked my leaden reflexes. I swung the torch already knowing that I was going to miss by a mile. That razored maw filled my vision as the creature rushed toward my face.

At the last instant it turned, torn from its deadly trajectory by an arrow that suddenly appeared to pin its long, ropy intestine to a nearby tree. The creature's shriek of pain and rage was cut short as her momentum caused it to smack face-first into the trunk as it wrapped around the tree like a grotesque tetherball.

I turned, trying to sight where the arrow had come from while mindful of the second voice that might suddenly attack as well.

I did not have long to wait. My handsome stranger from the waterfront bar rode into the dim circle of firelight. His bow was half-drawn with another arrow nocked and he guided his horse with his knees.

"Well met, handsome stranger," I said graciously.

"Would that we were better met, beauteous lady," he answered, his eyes only momentarily resting on me as they searched the darkness for further threat. "It would be best if someone could build up that fire and do it soonest." We were operating in near darkness and needed more light right away.

I started to look for more wood to toss on the embers but stepped back as I heard Mick chant: "Luminous voluminous… numerous!"

The glow from the embers increased, coalesced into a brightly glowing sphere, then shattered into a dozen glowing orbs the size of my fist that floated about, above our heads. The campsite was now as illuminated as a well-lit room with track lighting.

Almost immediately there was a great storm-like sound: the rumble of a heavy chariot preceded by the thundering hooves of four great dark horses and an iron-footed Nightmare. I spared a brief glance for Pluto, Lilith, and my Halfelven avatar before turning back to the tree where Nicole's demon head was now pinioned.

Except now it wasn't.

The head was gone.

THREE

♀

"A what?" Mudge was still trembling: aftershocks from seeing the distorted visage of his beloved in such a horrifying context.

Come to think about it, I wasn't so calm, myself.

"A Penangglan," I repeated. It's one of the Malaysian vampire species."

"It was just her head!" he choked. "And…and…"

"Her guts," I finished bluntly. "I know. That's how you can tell. The Penangglan is always female. At sundown its head separates from its body and flies about trailing its innards. It usually seeks women in labor or children for its meals."

"Didn't look like any vampire I've ever heard of," Mick said.

"You're confining the vampire MO to the European variety," my male alter ego clarified. "Bram Stoker popularized the Eastern European breed in the novel Dracula, but there are close to a hundred different kinds or species—each with its own set of rules and behaviors—spread throughout every continent in the world."

"Except Antarctica," I said.

"And we're just not sure about that," he said.

"Hey," I reminded, "we're talking about mythology here."

"No," Riplakish said, "we're talking about mythology *there. Here*, mythology *is* reality."

I shrugged. When I'm right, I'm right.

"You said she was a Malaysian vampire?" Mudge was tracking well enough to ask the next logical question.

"You may have noticed," my other self answered, "that the Fantasyworld program blurs the lines between different cultures, mythologies, and historical periods."

"There are three or four different species of bloodsuckers in the Malaysian mythos," I continued, "but the Penangglan is the only vampire in the known lore that plays hide-and-go-seek with its own head. It also explains the gap in Smedley's memory."

"What? How?"

"Well, legend holds that the shock of seeing the Penangglan's disembodied head often afflicts victims and witnesses with hysterical amnesia. That's why so little is known about them. We saw a pair of eyes looking back at us—or, rather, at Smedley—from across the victim's throat. When the Penangglan rose into the air, the shock caused Smedley to blank out. Between that instant and the moment that Jenks arrived with reinforcements, this 'Valentine' must have entered the alley and done the dismembering as Penangglans lack the advantage of hands." I snapped my fingers. "Vinegar!"

The others stared at me. "Vinegar?" Mudge asked.

"Back at the Zombie Mistress' palace, when we went into Sergeant Smedley's memoryfile, Mick noticed there was a slight scent of vinegar present at the crime scene."

She nodded. "Along with drops of blood and ick."

"Drops of blood and bile and such as would drip from the entrails that trail from a Penangglan's head," Daggoth mused.

"And vinegar?" Mudge was clearly puzzled.

"When a Penangglan feeds," I explained, "its appended organs tend to swell. Not much, but enough so that when it returns to its body, it is unable to—um—dock—until the intestines and such are shrunk down a bit. According to folklore, it must immerse its entrails in vinegar before such conjoining is possible."

"You're taking this pretty calmly," Mudge said, "considering it was Nicole's head and she not only seemed to want your body from the shoulders down, she wanted your child, as well."

"Child?" Riplakish wanted to know. "What child?"

"Her unborn child," Mick clarified.

My other self stared at me. "You're pregnant?"

I shrugged. "That's the rumor."

"Who's the father?" He looked over at my handsome stranger who was still mounted, watching the proceedings with amused interest. "Him?"

I shrugged again. "To answer your questions in sequential order: 'I don't know' and 'no.' I think." I saw the thought pass behind his eyes. "Hey, don't even go there! If this avatar actually did the deed to begin with, it was before I set up housekeeping. It's just as likely that some supernatural process is involved."

"Oh? Like what? You're the Virgin Mary, now?"

Why is it that men always lapse into sarcasm when they're emotionally challenged? "*Think*, Bob..." I ran my hands down my sides and over my hips. "If this is Nicole's analog then maybe *you're* the father—"

"*What? I* wasn't in the program when that happened! *You* were!"

"Maybe so. But it was *your* avatar that was intimate with *this* avatar."

"So what are you saying? That I'm...I mean *you're* the father *and* the mother?"

"There is always the possibility," the handsome stranger suddenly said, "that the Matrix itself has impregnated you."

"I'm sorry," Riplakish said, not sounding very, "but who are you, again?"

"Call me Enki." Perfect white teeth flashed in a smile and piercing blue eyes crinkled at the corners.

"Enki?" Mudge pondered, "What kind of name is Enki?"

The god of the Underworld produced a cigar and a match. "Sumerian."

"Sumerian?" Riplakish echoed. I really had to stop doing that.

"As in the Sumerian god of Wisdom?" I asked.

Hades struck the match on a chariot wheel spoke. "Nah. The real Enki is short and bald and much older."

"Could be a disguise."

He bit one end off of the cigar and lit the other. "With a really big nose."

"An illusion?"

Hades and Enki gave each other a long, measured look. "This," he finally said, "ain't," between puffs, "the same guy."

Lilith cleared her throat. "I hate to interrupt our little game of 'What's In A Name" but the clock is ticking, gentlemen."

Mick had sidled over and now leaned in close. "Given our current milieu, shouldn't that be more along the lines of 'the hourglass is filling' or something?"

"Demons," I murmured back, "operate on the transplanar strata which tends to be transspatial, as well. She could have just as easily said 'the cesium atoms are vibrating.' And, by the way, since the subject of illusions was just raised; that little light spell you cast back there wasn't a standard mage spell."

She put a hand to her chest and batted her eyes at me. "It wasn't?" All innocence.

"Why didn't you tell me that you're an Illusionist?"

She gave me the look that such a question deserved. "What's the point in being an Illusionist if you go around announcing it to everybody?"

Riplakish clapped his hands to get our attention. "Ladies? We've got a lot to do and not much time to do it in."

"Please don't do that," I said.

"Do what? Clap my hands?"

"Hand clapping is merely symptomatic."

"Symptomatic?" It was obvious that he didn't have the slightest clue.

I walked over to him and lowered my voice. "You're being a jerk."

"What? Because we've got serious business to take care of and I need your help?"

"So, if Hades and Zeus were exchanging a couple of sentences off to the side, you'd clap your hands and say, 'oh boys…'?"

"That's different."

"Why? Because they're gods? Or because they're guys?"

"I wouldn't clap my hands at a couple of gods—unless I was seriously annoyed with them."

"Oh, so you're seriously annoyed with me?"

"Not yet, but I think I'm getting closer as this conversation progresses."

"Well, give this a little thought, Mister Oink-oink: the gods aren't real. Mick and I are. She's more than she seems and *I* am the Demiurge incarnate. That should buy us a little more respect than any duo of counterfeit deities."

"*You* are not the Demiurge incarnate; *I* am. You can't even cast a spell or access our programmer codes. For all intents and purposes, you might as well *be* Nicole Doucet." He gave me another look. "Mister Oink-oink?"

"So you're not so much disrespecting me as 'you' transmogrified into the 'weaker sex'…" I paused to let him catch up, "…as you're dissing 'me' as Nicole? Man, whatever did she *ever* see in us?"

"You think I'm trying to *dis* you?"

Hades head came up. "Hey!"

Riplakish raised his hands. "Look, I'm sorry for whatever I've said or done to make you feel disrespected. And if you want to go into extra innings on this, I'll show up for the extended beating. But the sun is coming up in a few hours, and I have to come up with a way of keeping half the gods of the Fantasyworld from putting on the ultimate WW Four Smackdown before then. If I can't, then I have to get Natasha Skovoroda's psychefile uploaded to her real body and the rest of us out of the program before the Matrix is destabilized beyond recovery. And you should be particularly interested in speeding the process along as getting you out will be problematic, to say the least."

I folded my arms in front of my chest. "Say *more* than the least. Why am I going to be problematic?"

"Becuzz…." Daggoth's voice was slurred but comprehensible as he began to emerge from his system-crash state. "Yoo hev no bod dee to up lod to."

♂

I could see by the look at the back of her eyes that her true dilemma was starting to sink in now.

Despite the differences in our respective timelines over the past few weeks, there was still enough of a whole common lifetime to enable me to know my mind. Even though it was standing across from me and looking through Nicole Doucet's eyes. Still, as I tried to imagine how I would take the news if I were in her shoes, the idea was too uncomfortable to hold on to for more than the briefest of moments.

"But…but…it's my body, too! Just as much as it is yours."

"Maybe. Maybe not." I raised my hands. "Look, I'm not trying to challenge your identity. Except that it's a simple fact that every time we download into our avatars, we are subtly different by the time we return to the real world. Cause and effect, decisions and consequences, we are involved in the process of change every minute that we live our lives and sometimes that process complicates the reacquisition process when we exit the Fantasyworld program.

"You've told me how, during your last sojourn in the Matrix, a virus split Robert Ripley into multiple avatars. Each one, while he—you—lived, began to build a separate cluster of memories while undergoing those transformative changes that are part and parcel of progressive personality development. How could all of those separate aspects of yourself be reintegrated into one body, one brain, without suffering a total mental and emotional melt-down?"

"But there's only two of us now," she said. "And it's only been a few days."

"No. It's been more like a few weeks if not months. During your previous program incursion you experienced progressive memory and personality development and then you uploaded to Nicole Doucet's body in a parallel universe. As a result, I have no memory of that last adventure. It's as if it never happened.

"In the meantime, you've spent a considerable amount of time in another universe, in another body. A body that isn't even your—*my*—own gender much, less identity. Appropriately enough, you were incarcerated in a mental hospital—"

"Gee, thanks."

"—where you were largely unsuccessful in convincing the mental health professionals that you were sane." I shrugged. "Sorry."

"And now that you're back, the experience would appear to be so pervasive that you can no longer manifest in your own avatar. Never mind the fact that *you* uploading to our body back in the Cradle would essentially murder *me.* Even if I were out of the picture, your own ability to reintegrate into the organic receptacle for Robert Remmington Ripley the Third is extremely suspect."

"Why? Because I've spent a little time wearing a female avatar? I had no idea how sexist I used to be!"

"There's an example right there," I said. "You already think of me as being very different from you."

"Why? Because I have a woman's perspective, now?" I stopped. "Uh..."

"'Uh' is right. The gap between us is more than just a matter of time and experience."

She shook her head. "Other Dreamwalkers have utilized cross-gender avatars."

"Yeah. But the data you're drawing on is pre-Anomaly. We both know that the presets and program lockouts have mutated and that there are no safeties on the psychefile folders. We don't know what effects that may have, other than that the old limitations have been done away with. But, on top of that, you resided in Nicole Doucet's organic receptacle for a significant period of time outside of the Matrix. You thought with her brain, steeped your electrochemical processes in her hormonal and genetic soup. We're not talking cross-dressing at the skin-deep level. This goes to the bone and beyond."

"Wait. I need to think…"

"One other thing," I said, feeling really crappy about what I was about to say. "As soon as you abandon this avatar, it will abort the baby."

"No. No!" She folded her arms about her middle. "I won't let that happen! Why would it happen?"

"I don't really know that it would," I said, the taste of ashes in my mouth. "I lied just now. At least I think I did. I really don't know what would happen to the baby."

"What?" She glared at me fiercely. "Why?"

"To convince you with your own reaction that this is no longer a matter of computerized costuming. You're already forming a bond with the life inside you. It's becoming part of your identity."
"It's not real," she said.

"Then let's make arrangements with an apothecary and abort it. As soon as possible since it's only a hindrance to the tasks we must accomplish."

"It's not alive in the sense that I'm alive. But it still deserves a chance to live in the sense that all AIs exist."

"Does your argument proceed from a logical premise? Or an emotional one?"

"Does it matter?" she asked defiantly.

"Only in the sense of convincing you that you're no longer *Robert* Ripley."

"Well, I'm not Nicole Doucet!"

"Of course not."

"Then *who* am I?"

"Gods help me," I said, "I really don't know."

♀

I couldn't think. And we were running out of time.

The clock on Natasha Skovoroda was running down. Dawn would signal the beginning of an Apocalypse that could well destroy the very Matrix itself.

And I couldn't think!

I looked up at the me I could no longer be. "What do we do?"

He shook his head. "I don't have all the answers yet. But here's what I do know. First"—he began ticking each point off on the fingers of his left hand—"I've got to get Natasha's soulfile back to the Zombie Mistress ASAP. Second, we all need to be ready to exit the Program on a moment's notice. If this all blows up in our faces, we may have just moments to extract or die. Third, we need to find a way to stop this unholy war before sunrise."

"Not just stop," Hades interjected, "but send everyone home. For good. That's the deal: I get my kingdom back."

"Deal?" I said. "What deal?"

The god of the Underworld started to answer, but Riplakish held up his hand. "The 'deal' is we get to kick Orcus's pointy-tailed ass out of Hell permanently."

I grinned. "Okay, I'm in."

Mudge stepped in between us. "What about Nicole?"

Everyone looked at me.

"No. Not him, Nicole. The real Nicole," Mudge insisted.

Everyone looked at him.

"The dead Nicole," Mick clarified.

"The one from his universe," I expanded.

"The Wizard here," Mudge explained, "said he could import her psychefile into another avatar. If you can use Natasha Skovoroda's file to resurrect her actual body in your universe, you should be able to get Nicole's psychefile and upload it to her body back in mine."

"Thot yu dident lyk thee idea a liddle while ago," Daggoth buzzed from the back of the wagon.

"You were talking about something totally different then."

"Divverent? How?"

"We don't have time to debate this, right now," Riplakish said. He turned to me. "It's a moot point anyway since it's your only way back out."

"Maybe," I said. This particular discussion wasn't finished yet, but we needed to get started on the problem-solving stage of the first three problems on the list. As well as one other. "As long as some of us are going to the Zombie Mistress's palace, we need to add Daggoth to the scavenger-hunt list."

"I'mm okayy."

"You're not okay. We were headed there anyway. And since Natasha's souljar is headed that way, too, there's no wasted motion. The next question is, what about gathering reinforcements?"

"Recruiting other gods to help put down an insurrection of these gods?" Riplakish was incredulous. "You might as well try to put out the campfire by tossing coal oil on it!" Humans were out of their league, of course, and he went on to explain that Hell's minions weren't likely to be of any help either.

"Maybe," I said, getting a glimmer of an idea. "Maybe not." I turned to Mudge. "I need you, Bernie. I need your help if we're going to save this world. It's a long shot, and we don't have much time. It's dangerous, but I can not only promise you the adventure of a lifetime, but the chance to see how good you really are!"

"How good I really am?"

"As a lawyer."

He gave me a long, searching look. "We're going to Hell, aren't we?"

I nodded. "I have no right to ask you to do this. For your own sake you should skedaddle back to your suspension tank right now."

He nodded thoughtfully. "If I leave now, I can't save Nicole."

I laid my hand against his cheek. "Bernie, honey, I don't know that we could save her even if we had all the time in the world."

"I know." His voice was strained. "But I have to try. Even if it is hopeless." He brushed at a tear. "Especially if my Nicole is that poor, damned, undead thing." And he could say no more.

Mick stepped up. "What about me?"

"Like I said before, get out. Now. As fast as you can."

She shook her head. "If he can go, so can I. Don't tell me that a good Illusionist wouldn't come in handy."

Hades spoke up. "In the Land of the Dead there are no illusions permitted. You would be unarmed in hostile territory."

"I'll take my chances," she said.

"I can't let you go," I answered.

She looked at me sadly. "Chivalry or a little residual chauvinism? Trust me, I won't be totally defenseless: illusions take many forms."

I growled. Using Nicole's vocal chords the effect was less than I hoped. "Okay. I don't like it, but we'll be taking Pluto along for extra muscle, so we won't be totally defenseless."

"Who? Me?"

"Anyone else here named Pluto? Or should I call you Goofy?" I didn't give him a chance to respond. I turned to Riplakish. "Give me Balmung. I need a weapon and this avatar should be able to handle a shortsword without difficulty. You take the wagon, the souljar, and Daggoth to Yudu and see what she can do about his condition after you've restored Natasha. Take Lilith along for additional protection but I don't think the Pennangglan will bother you. I'm what she wants and, once we're in Hell, she'll be the least of my worries."

"If time is of the essence, you may be wasting some of yours." Hades dropped the stub of his cigar and ground it out with a sandaled foot. "Yon Wizard shall shortly be under my authority. Mayhap you will postpone the hour. But no efforts shall gainsay the process more than a few days."

"Oh yeah?" Riplakish unbuckled the belt and scabbard bearing the enchanted Dwarven blade. "Says who?"

"I am the Overlord of Death," the god replied, climbing up into his chariot. "I know my subjects. And he shall soon be one of them. No man, Wizard or Programmer, may cheat Death forever."

"Wee don hev time for thiz," Daggoth buzzed. "Led's ged goingg."

"He's right," I said, taking the swordbelt and strapping it across my hip. "Lets move out, people. Assigned tasks by the numbers and we meet on the battlefield before sunrise." I walked over to Hades' chariot and climbed on, Mick and Mudge getting up behind me.

Riplakish nodded and moved toward the wagon. "We're not shooting for eternity, D," he called over his shoulder, "just another two score and ten. I think getting your kingdom back buys us a little cooperation."

Hades sighed. "Even a god has limitations." He turned to me. "Where shall I take thee?"

"Hell, of course."

"Of course. But my kingdom is vast and time is short."

"Well," I tugged at the rags that were barely keeping me modest, "anywhere along the way that I can pick up some more clothing..." And then I told him who we were looking for.

His face grew grave. "I can get you close. But not even a god would go there willingly. I fear you may lose everything; your soul just the half of it!"

"Desperate times call for desperate measures."

Hades lips were a thin, tight line as he nodded to Cedalion. The whip cracked once and we were off like a runaway rocket.

In my haste, I had forgotten all about my handsome stranger.

FOUR

♀

The black-scaled bodysuit was comfortable and heat-repellent, plus it looked good on me. In fact I was pretty sure that I looked better in it than Lilith, who, if masculine memory sufficed, looked pretty damn good in it herself. I refastened Balmung's scabbard and belt so that the sword graced my hip for a quick right-hand draw. Then ran a quick brush through my sable hair: live fast, die young, and leave a good-looking corpse. One last check ("dramatic winter" I decided) and I turned reluctantly from the mirror. The sand in the hourglass was running short, and I hoped I'd have the opportunity to thank Lilith for the use of her place after this was all over. Maybe we could discuss how to accessorize black dragonskin…

Dressed in similar black attire, the others waited in the chariot: Hades, Mudge, and…

"Dagny! What the Hell are you doing here?"

The gorgeous blonde in skin-tight leather smiled. "I'm not Dagny Westbrook, Ripley. I'm Mick."

"Mick?" It suddenly came together—what had been in front of me all along. "Mick Rae." Though I might still want to ask our Illusionist why she chose such an ugly exterior for her avatar. "Angel *Mick* Rae."

"Call me Angie." She extended her hand to help me up into the chariot. "The god of the Underworld was right. Illusions are not allowed in Hell."

I looked down at my feminine curves and shivered.

♂

Lilith nudged her Nightmare in close enough to speak softly. "I could let you take Beuntoyou and ride ahead with the souljar. You would get there faster."

"I won't leave him." It was hard to concentrate on keeping the witchlights just ahead of the horses where they could provide maximum light for the trail and not spook the horses.

"Then what about me riding ahead with the souljar?"

"No."

I couldn't take my eyes off of the road but I heard the pain in her voice. "You don't trust me, then."

Egad, where was Dagny Westbrook when I needed her? "I trust you, Lil. But the fates of two True Spirits lie in my hands and I can't turn loose of either one."

"Because I'm not a True Spirit," she said sadly.

"Lil, there are over fourteen billion True Souls outside The Matrix and I don't know more than one or two I would turn either task over to, either. If I had no choice, I would trust you more than the rest. But as long as I have a grip on each, I ain't letting go of either."

"That's the nicest thing you've ever said to me."

I growled, remembering our little exchange down in Abydos. "Well, I figure since the end of the world may be just around the corner I might as well be nice to everybody."

She giggled—a truly scary sound when made by an Archdemoness. "I know thee too well to believe such gammon. Besides, I prefer thee grumpy: 'tis thy natural estate."

I was saved the necessity of further banter as we crested a hill and spied the yard torches of the Zombie Mistress's estate.

♀

Hades' chariot swept down into the Underworld like a golden thunderbolt scattering Demons and Devils like leaves and thistledown in the engine backwash of a 787.

"Daggoth is going to be so disappointed that he missed you," I said, clutching the edge of the driving box and trying desperately to keep tossing my digital cookies.

"But he didn't 'miss' me," Angel said. "We spent quite a bit of time together."

"Yeah. Well. What I probably should say is Daggoth will be so embarrassed."

A quirky, Mona Lisa smile slipped across her perfect lips. "Embarrassed by which? The way he talked about Angel McRae in

Mick's presence? Or the way he treated Mick while Angel was watching?"

I shook my head. "I gotta say, this is a side of Mike Straeker that I never noticed before."

"Maybe because you're finally experiencing him and all the other men in your life as a woman now."

"Hey now," Mudge said from the back of the chariot.

She turned to him and her smile was sincere now. "Present company excepted." Leaning back toward me, she confided, "So many men, so little respect."

"They couldn't get past your looks," I said.

"We fly to beauty as an asylum from the terrors of finite nature."

"Emerson," Mudge said. "I prefer Goethe. 'Visible in a thousand different utterances of the creative mind.'"

"'And is as various as nature herself,'" she finished.

"What are they nattering on about?" Hades wanted to know.

"Beauty," I said. "How we all tend to judge a book by its cover."

"Book?"

"We assign value to people according to their outward appearances. It's like judging the worth of a scroll on the value of its sheepskin rather than the quality of its contents."

"You people..." He shook his head. "The conversations..." He scowled as a flock of Erinyes scattered before his straining destrieres. "There is a special place in Hell for those who squandered their years *talking* about life instead of living it. Women who are beautiful should embrace their gifts from the gods. A woman who bemoans her comeliness is an unnatural creature. She twice scorns her blessings by disdaining what she is given and thus dismisses what others lack.

"You're a guy, D; I doubt that you'll get it. But let me put it this way: nobody is gonna remember you for the way you look in a toga."

"What's wrong with the way I look in a toga?"

Just because you were god of the Dead didn't mean your ego was equally deceased. "What I'm saying is you're known for your accomplishments more than you're known for your appearance."

"So?"

"It's not the same with women. Particularly, *beautiful* women. We are known and judged by how we look, not who we are."

"So?"

The old so-and-so. I sighed. "Never mind. It's pointless when even the gods have hormones."

That set him off. "Oh yeah! Hormones! You women!"

Angie joined in. "We women?"

"Yeah, even Persephone is always going on about male hormones! You women are all alike: when it's *our* hormones, we're filthy, disgusting, out of control animals. But! When it's *your* hormones, we're supposed to be sensitive, tolerant, patient, and understanding. We—we are supposed to *respect your* hormones! But *you!* You denounce us for ours! How about a little hormonal equality, huh? Huh?"

Before either of us could think of an adequate rebuttal, the chariot touched down, and Hades hauled back on the reins. We came to an abrupt stop. Well, most of us, anyway; the contents of my stomach promised to keep moving for some time to come. I eased the buckle on Balmung's sheath belt another notch, as it seemed to have grown snugger during our flight.

"We're here," Hades announced.

I looked around. A great cliff face reared upwards to our right; a vast, cracked and scorched plain stretched off in the other three directions. In the distance I could make out the silhouette of Tartarus by the dim flare of the girdling Pyriphlegethon.

"Where are they?" I asked. "I don't see anyone else."

"Oh, my dear!" Hades tried for a laugh but looked more constipated than jovial. "They are not kept in my domain! We must go deep for that kind!" He gestured to the cliff face and an iron door suddenly appeared, set into stone.

♂

A raised dais dominated the great circular room. Two tables were arranged side-by-side, connected at the midpoint by a credenza that turned the grouping into a giant "H" on its back. Dyantha—Natasha Skovoroda's avatar—lay upon one of the tables, cocooned in an ovoid of pearly light. A dead ringer for the robo-golem that the spirit of Misty Dawn currently haunted, it looked as dead as anything you would ever want to see. The profound stillness of her form defied anyone to believe that she might ever draw breath again. The only movement came from the pale nimbus of light that encompassed her corpse. It slowly dimmed and contracted—once—before returning to a state of foggy stasis, surrounding her pearlescent flesh.

The Necromancer carried the souljar to the crossbar that connected Natasha's table to the empty one. Setting it down in the center, she stepped back and clapped her hands. Above us, the domed ceiling became transparent. A triad of moons shone down into the room adding silver highlights to the milky nimbus that surrounded Natasha's body.

Supported between Fitch and Abercrombie, Daggoth brandished a wand and nodded to the Necromancer.

"You are sure you are up to dis?"

"I have to be." The Sorcerer's speech had lost its monotone buzzing but he looked pale and shocky, his skin nearly transparent at times. If he flickered again, I wasn't sure that he would come back.

The Zombie Mistress flourished her wand and chanted. Daggoth incanted in counterpoint.

Slowly, Dyantha's body rose into the air until she floated nearly a foot above the surface of the stone table. Then, as a shadow passed over the faces of the three moons, the urn glowed with an inner light. That light intensified, pulsed. Then a pseudopod of glowing force snaked from the mystic jar to the motionless form. As it made contact with the cloud of light around Dyantha's body both amphora and female began to glow and pulse in rhythm.

A minute went by.

Before another could elapse, Daggoth dropped his wand and collapsed in the grasp of the two Zombie servants.

"Was it enough?" I asked as they carried him to a couch against the wall, near the door.

"De spell, for all intents and purposes, was complete," she said. She looked from the couch to the dais where Natasha's avatar was slowly settling back down onto the table. Then she looked back to the couch. "I must see what I can do for dis one, now. As for de Amazon, we must wait and see."

I looked at Lilith who had retired to the corner shortly after we had arrived. Her presence made the Zombies nervous and she was doing her best to keep a low profile. "We can't wait. We have one other task to attempt before sunrise. Maybe it will help, maybe it won't."

"Do you need anyting from me?"

"I'll need something to carry two more psychefiles in. Maybe three."

Yudu shook her head. "I only have one dat is ready. Two, if you can wait for me to reformat de one we just used for Dyantha."

"How long?"

"For a full formatting spell? About an hour."

"How about a simple erase and clean?"

"Ten minutes. But—"

"It'll have to do." I spoke to Lilith. "Can your Nightmare carry us both?"

She nodded. "We will have to ride—snug."

I smiled. "Just as long as it isn't side-saddle."

♀

There were letters chiseled into the rock around the door. To the left it read:

Per me si va nella città dolente,
Per me si va nell' eterno dolore,
Per me si va tra la perduta gente.

"It's Italian," I said. "And that's about all that I can make of it."

Angel McRae worked her way up beside me. "Let me give it a shot." She peered at the stone flanged verse and began to hesitantly recite: "Through me the way into the…woeful city. Maybe…'city of desolation'." She moved to the second line. "Through me the way to…sorrows diuturnal."

"Diuturnal?" I asked.

"Eternal Pain," Mudge offered.

"Lovely."

"Through me the way," McRae continued, "among the lost…people? Creation?" She turned her attention to the other side of the door.

"Don't bother," Mudge said. "I'll make it simple: 'Justice Moved My Maker on High/ Divine Power Made Me and Supreme Wisdom and Primal Love/ Before Me Nothing Was Created But Eternal Things and I Endure Eternally'." He pointed to the script above the door. "I may not know as much Italian as Ms. McRae but I have a more than passing acquaintance with Dante Alighieri's *Divina Commedia.*"

Above the door was a single line in Italian but repeated in a variety of languages. The language immediately below it read: Abandon Every Hope, Ye That Enter.

"Yeah," I groused, "me too. But I find very little divinity and even less comedy in Dante calling the shots from here on out."

"Going downa," said a voice.

The iron door had slid aside and a small man wearing a dark cassock and wide-brimmed hat gazed out at us. I assume he gazed at us: the sunglasses he wore obscured his eyes and a dark moustache provided equal concealment for his mouth. He looked us over while we returned the favor and contemplated the small iron chamber that he occupied. "Hey," he finally said, "you folksa inna or are you outa?"

"In," said Hades. "They're in. I'm not. But take them with my authority."

The moustache turned up on the ends. "Hey, Mister P! Beena longa time! You don-a ever come to see us no more!"

"Too much red tape, Guido. Besides, it's just too dangerous, even if I do claim diplomatic immunity." Then he told the little man who we were here to see.

The ends of the moustache turned back down and he let out a low whistle. "Shoulda be an interestin' trip. Don-a usually get to go that-a far. This gonna be a one a-way?"

I shook my head. "That's not the plan."

"Hey," he said, nodding upwards, "you reada that inscriptione one-a more time-a. It say: Abandon alla plansa ye who enter."

I shrugged trying desperately for nonchalant. "Hey, that's not Hell, that's life in general."

"Okay by me." He nodded pleasantly. "All aboard-a."

As we moved to enter the small chamber McRae whispered to Hades: "That's the worst accent I've ever heard in my life."

Hades shook his head. "He's not really Italian." He turned to leave but hesitated. Looking back over his shoulder, he added: "And he's not really a priest."

With that the iron door slid shut, blocking our view of the outer planes of the Greek underworld. The little man grasped a lever set into the wall and pushed it gently forward. The small, iron walled chamber shook slightly and then we felt a smooth acceleration as the room began to descend.

"Circle-a One: Limbo," he announced as the first of nine circles lit up on the panel beside the door. "The virtuous unbaptized-a"

The second circle lit. "Seconda level. The Lustful. Also Minos's courtroom-a."

Then: "Circle-a Three: The Gluttonous. Other points of interest: Cerberus's kennels."

Followed by: "Numbera Four: the Avaricious and the Prodigal. We got your Hoarders, Spendthrifts, and the Miserly."

The fifth circle lit. "The fifth-a ring—also known as the 'filth-a' ring: Stygian mud, all properly landscaped-a for the Wrathful and-a the Sullen.

"Number-a six-a. We gotta you Heretics. Also concourse levels to the City of Dis. Parking tickets are not-a validated, no way, no how."

We were getting close to the bottom of the panel: the seventh circle lit up. "And here we keepa da Violent-a. The Management assumes-a no responsibility for your safety at dis-a level. Of course, the Management takes-a no responsibility for your safety at-a any level.

"I shoulda also mentioned we offer unguided tours of the Minotaur's Labyrinth at this-a level," he added as the eighth circle illuminated. "Number-a eight—Malebolge: the Fraudulent. We gotta them all-a: the Panderers and Seducers, the Flatterers, the Simoniacs, the Fortunetellers, the Barrators—how you say?"

Angel leaned over and whispered: "Sounds like a bunch of grifters if you ask me."

"Griafters! Si! We gotta your Hypocrites, your Thieves, your Evil Counselors, Sowers of Discord, and Falsifiers."

Surprisingly, the elevator didn't stop and the final circle came on. "Circle-a Nine: the Treacherous. The Traitors to Kindred, Country, Guests, and Masters. And-a lasta but not leasta, the Lair of the Great Three-Headed-a Worm."

The elevator came to a stop but the door did not open. The little man produced a key and inserted it at the bottom of the panel of lit circles. As he turned it, the room gave a little lurch and began to descent again.

"Um, I thought there were only nine circles of Hell," I said nervously.

The little man shook his head. "You think we would-a put them where they would-a have access to other-a people down-a here? It's-a good-a thing you're not-a in charge of anything-a!"

Finally, after another five minutes of non-narrative descent, the elevator came to a quivering stop. At least I think it was the elevator; it may have been my knees.

The door slid open. "Been-a nice-a knowin' you-a."

I grasped the hilt of the Dwarven shortsword. "Courage," I said to my companions as I stepped through the door. "If we fail here, it matters naught for us: there will be nothing to return to by midday."

"Easy for you to say," Mudge muttered. "If things go badly, all you'll probably do is die. I doubt they'll let me off so easy..."

♂

The journey from the Zombie Mistress's Palace to Daggoth's Tower was two days' ride on horse-back or ninety minutes by flying carpet, if you were going full tilt. Lilith's Hell-mount got us there in half an hour.

Daggoth gave me all the passwords before we left, so we were able to pass through all of the guards and wards instead of taking the extra hour or so I'd need to use the neutralizing counterspells. Lilith and I threw open the door to the Sorcerer's library three minutes after dismounting.

It was impossible to tell the color of the walls, or even their original composition. There were bookshelves everywhere you looked. From floor to ceiling there was nothing to be seen but book spines: a veritable riot of colors in all manner of widths and heights and bindings. The only portions of wall space not groaning under a fully loaded shelf of books, tomes, grimoires, and ledgers were faced with file drawers and cases stacked high and deep with scrolls and codices of parchment, vellum, papyrus, pergamum, and hide.

And a door.

It was nondescript except for a pair of moons above the lintel. At that moment they were showing gibbous and three-quarter phases respectively. I reached up and dialed each disk to the full-moon position. The door slid open and we stepped through.

An ancient city gleamed whitely in the moonlight.

On the other side of the door we stood on a hill and looked down on the incredible marble sprawl that was the megalopolis of

Alexandria in olden times. To the north lay twin bays that opened out to the Mediterranean Sea. The dark waters danced and sparkled with the reflected light from the three full moons overhead and the fiery beacon from the great lighthouse on the island between the two harbors.

"Well?" Lilith asked impatiently.

"I'm getting my bearings. I've never actually been here."

"Um, where actually is here?"

"Alexandria, the crown jewel of the ancient, civilized world."

"Why is there a dimensional portal from your friend's library to Alexandria?"

"Well, for starters," I said, starting down the hill, "Alexandria had a better library. Of course, the lighthouse got all the press for being one of the seven wonders of the Ancient World, but the city boasts a number of architectural wonders, any one of which would make it noteworthy. You've got the Ptolemaic Palace system that covers a lot of real estate from the promontory of Silsila, stretching to the south and west." I pointed to various landmarks, adding: "There's the Temple of Serapis, the last stronghold of Paganism against Christianity; the Heptastadion Dike that runs out to sea for a full mile, connecting the Isle of Pharos to the mainland; and the Caesarion, which makes the Trump Tower look like an Anasazi high-rise.

"The substructure of the city is this amazing labyrinth of cisterns, some of which are four or five stories deep and supported by a subterranean forest of columns and chambers carrying water from the Nile and from Lake Mareotis…"

"And you say that you've never actually been here," Lilith challenged.

"Not personally. But you can't be a student of ancient history and not know about Alexandria. This is where Archimedes invented the famous pump that bears his name. Euclid developed his theories and wrote his comprehensive analyses of geometry, proportions, number theories, even a treatise on optics while residing here. The Alexandrine astronomer Eratosthenes correctly measured the Earth's diameter more than fifteen centuries before Copernicus and Galileo were born, and Aristarchus of Samos, another prominent Alexandrine, suggested the heliocentric hypothesis—that the Earth revolved around the sun and not vice-versa—back in the third century, BCE! The level of culture and knowledge was simply astonishing for any group of people in Western civilization before—or possibly since."

"So you're saying that your friend had this portal ensorcelled for weekend getaways?"

I shook my head. "Actually he did it for the library card." We reached the bottom of the hill and started for the nearest city gate. "The lighthouse," I pointed at the fifty-story tower still visible on the far side of the city, "is what pulls in all of the tourists, it being one of the Seven Wonders of the World. But for the serious academicians, it's the Mouseion and Library that makes Alexandria the number one hot spot on the Mediterranean."

"Must be some library."

"Oh yeah. It was *the* Library. You might call it the precursor of the Internet. Kallimachos is said to have cataloged four hundred thousand mixed scrolls and ninety thousand unmixed scrolls, with an additional forty-two thousand in the Serapeum. The Ptolomies were obsessive about collecting books and such. The Septuagint translation of the Old Testament into Greek was produced there. The Library at Alexandria should have been on the Wonders of the World tour. I guess phallic structures doing tricks with fire and mirrors was a little sexier for the average ancient."

"Well, I guess even that isn't enough to keep the locals partying until dawn," Lilith said as we reached the gate. "Looks like everyone's in bed."

I looked for guards at the gate. There were none. I looked for traffic on the street leading into the city: even in the wee hours, a city half the size of Alexandria would have had a degree of hustle and bustle. But nada here: all of the visible thoroughfares were empty. I felt the short hairs on the back of my neck start to rise. "This isn't right," I said, drawing Caldabolg from its sheath.

The city was a wonder in white marble. By day the glare of sunlight on the myriad of white stone surfaces was said to be enough to blind most people, requiring panoplies of green silk to cut the glare. Certainly the moonlight reflected from the marble provided more than enough illumination to travel the streets at night without the necessity of a torch or a lamp. It also made it quite obvious that the southern section of the city was deserted.

"I don't like it," I growled, "but we don't have time to wait for sunrise." I started up the thoroughfare at a light jog.

"Okay," the Archdemoness said as she tried to match my pace, "you haven't exactly connected the dots for me, but I'm guessing that these backup files you're looking for are in this library/museum."

"Correct." We passed the boulevard that ran from the Sun Gate in the east to the Moon Gate in the west. "I didn't design the Backup System but if one were to look for an appropriate analog for the storage vault, I doubt you could come up with something better."

"How about Atlantis?" she puffed.

"Atlantis? Why?"

"Bubble memory."

I let that one ride while we jogged another ten blocks or so.

She finally broke the silence. "A copper piece for your thoughts…"

"I'm trying to remember."

"Remember what?"

"Why I brought you along with me."

I could feel her grin at my shoulder. "In case you got into trouble."

"I'm always in trouble."

"Then maybe you should marry me."

"I don't believe in mixed marriages."

"Robert, any marriage you enter into is going to be a mixed one."

"Don't flirt with me." I was suddenly grumpy.

"Why not?"

"Because it isn't real."

"What's not real?" I could feel her smile disappearing. "Me? Am I not real?"

"Your feelings. How you feel toward me; that's not real."

"Cogito eggo sum," she snapped.

"I think, therefore I waffle?"

"Ego! *Ego* sum. I think, therefore I am."

"Descartes. Mind/body dualism."

"Duelists?"

"No. Dualism. Descartes developed the concept of interactionism, holding that the body and the mind mutually affect each other. This in spite of the fact that he defined the body as extended physical material while the mind—*res cogitans*—was unextended."

"Unextended?"

"'Extended,' as applied to the physical body, means taking up space or having physical volume. Consciousness, which he lumped in with mind and soul, takes up no space and has no physical volume, therefore it is 'unextended' by definition. Yet, Descartes held that the spiritual side of the mind/body equation was just as real." I realized that I was babbling on in my unease at finding the city streets deserted.

"The defense rests."

"Huh?"

"Never mind."

We continued on in silence for a dozen and more blocks. Though I looked everywhere as we traveled through the city, I saw no lights in the darkened recesses of the colonnaded courtyards or buildings: not a lamp nor a torch nor a glimmering candle.

"How much farther?" Lilith wheezed.

"I don't know. As I said, I've never been here before."

"Well, what about monads?"

"What?"

"Monads? Gottfried Wilhelm Leibnitz, co-inventor of calculus?"

"Calculus isn't my strong suit." I didn't like where this conversation seemed to be going.

"Leibnitz believed that all matter is alive and animated throughout with monads."

"Monads," I said.

"Monads are evolving units of consciousness. They're the most fundamental metaphysical points, which have always existed and can never be destroyed. The monad is the principle of continuity between the physical and the psychological realms, present in both rational creatures and inanimate matter."

"Oh. *Those* monads."

"Leibnitz postulated that monads vary in the amount of consciousness or clarity of their perceptions. He believed that every monad has the power to represent the entire universe within itself. That each is a world in miniature, a microcosm, a 'living mirror of the universe.' Yet each monad has its own unique point of view, with its own characteristic degree of clarity."

"Been taking night classes?"

"It's just that you're the Demiurge, and some of us were hoping—"

"We're here!" I said.

We stopped and stared.

"Why," Lilith finally asked, "is there a giant horse's rear protruding from the library entrance?"

It was a large, wooden horse, set on a wooden platform with wheels. Whoever had tried to maneuver it into the museum entrance had looped ropes around the base of the neck and tilted it forward to get its equine head under the lintel of the entryway. As that would seem the most difficult part of gaining egress, it seemed odd that the process had been halted with the great beast half in and half out.

There was no way to squeeze around it: its wooden flanks filled the postern with scant inches to spare on either side. We had to duck under its belly and pass between its legs to enter the building.

I thumped my head as I passed into the darkness of the museum's interior. I cast a witchlight and considered the dangling hatch that hung from the chest of the wooden structure. The interior was hollow.

"Uh-oh."

I tossed out a handful of glowing globes and directed them around the antechamber. I saw only disarray.

"What happened here?" Lilith whispered.

I didn't know, but I had a sinking feeling in the pit of my stomach. "Come on."

The building was an architectural spiral, like a conch shell set with the narrow tip pointed skyward. Here and there were doors providing direct egress to the next inner spiral, and each one opened into another room or corridor of chaos and destruction. The vandalism of statues, models, displays, and *objets d'art*, along with torn tomes and scorched scrolls, seemed both deliberate and random.

Anger and horror and sorrow were gradually replaced by grim resolve. I pulled out my mental list of responsibilities engendered by Cephtronics and added one more cleanup task to the inventory.

Or, rather, two: restoring the library and museum was one task. Finding the entities responsible was entirely another. But unless I accomplished the second, addressing the first would be an act of futility.

"I don't like the looks of this," Lilith whispered.

I tried to find some positive aspect to the situation: "At least there's no sign of blood, no evidence of bodies."

At least there weren't until we reached an inner room with a large, brass-bound, oaken door set in the far wall. A great marble bench was set up against the door. A familiar figure sat on the bench, a brightly-lit lantern by his side.

"Enki…isn't it?"

He smiled. For all its friendliness, the smile, seemed rather sad. "You're finally here. There isn't much time."

"What are you doing here?"

"Trying to help." He stood up. "I could have given you the bad news and saved you this trip but I knew that you would have to see for yourself. So I waited for you here."

"Funny," I said, "but I figured you'd be more likely to chase off to Hell after the other me."

He shrugged. "Are the two of you really so different?"

"You mean aside from the obvious gender issues?"

He shrugged again. "Maybe not so obvious, my love." He wavered—not unlike Daggoth during one of his seizures at the first. Then he metamorphosed. Shape and size and features flowed, ran together, reconfigured.

Masculine became feminine.

Enki disappeared.

Pallas took his place.

"What's in a name?" she asked. "Should we judge a book by its cover? A love by its gender?"

"Yowza!" said Lilith.

FIVE

♂

One of the attractions of Dreamwalking was the opportunity to wear a computer-generated body that approached physical perfection. And, since Cephtronics catered to the full range of fantasies available in their Programworlds, there was always a glut of feminine pulchritude at every turn. Exotic beauty was commonplace. Those inhabitants who weren't penultimate on the Richter scale of Beauty were merely attractive or comely. It was nearly impossible to stand out against that sort of canvas unless you took the opposite approach, as Angie had in her "Mick" persona.

Pallas, however, managed the impossible. And surpassed it. In fact, she left "near perfection" so far back in the dust that she changed the whole standard of measurement.

She still dressed in the leather jerkin and pants she'd worn when we first met on the morning after Misty Dawn's death. As before, the tailoring seemed more appropriate for a woman of—ahem—lesser proportional diversity: the *cuir-bouilli* jerkin was more vest than split breastplate, and the crisscrossed leather thongs that held her outfit together here and there were almost as strained as my sense of propriety. It was doubly embarrassing since Pallas was the Ego-manifestation of the sentient supercomputer that ran The Matrix, and she manifested this way for my benefit.

Although there was no doubt in my mind that Enki *was* Pallas as he/she transformed, I could see differences in her appearance now. Oh, she still had the coffee-and-cream skin, the unearthly, elemental beauty. Now, as before, she seemed to embody the physical concept of the perfect woman that nested somewhere down in my subconscious libido. But her wild cascade of smoke-brown hair had more red tones now and fewer sable highlights. Her eyes were much more like Nicole's, her nose not unlike Misty Dawn's, and her generous mouth and full lips like Stephanie's, Lilith's, and Euryale's respectively. Was she intentionally changing the bait? Or was this an unconscious manifestation to my feelings toward those involved?

"So," I said, "what's with this Enki thing?"

"Beloved," she answered, "if you cannot fathom my motives even now, then we have not time sufficient while on these premises."

"What does she mean by that?" Lilith wanted to know.

"That we don't have time to get into—"

"No," she cut me off, "I mean what is this 'beloved' stuff?"

"Ladies," I said with some degree of uncertainty, "let's just keep moving for now."

Pallas smiled that same sad smile, turned, and picked up the marble bench that was blocking the door. It had to weigh near a half a ton and she hefted it like a piece of patio furniture.

"Jeez—" Lilith clapped her hands to her mouth. "I can't believe I almost said—"

The door swung open, revealing the room beyond.

"Holy—" I breathed.

"Crap!" the Archdemoness exclaimed.

♀

I don't know what I expected below the ninth level of Dante's Hell; the mausoleum motif certainly wasn't out of place. But the effect was greatly distorted by the miles of gray marble corridors with vaulted ceilings rising to three-story heights and hundreds of polished oaken doors embellished with heavy brass fixtures.

"Where do we go?" I whispered.

"I'll know it when I see it," Mudge answered.

"What about that?" Angie pointed at the largest set of oaken doors we had yet seen.

The brass plates gleamed, the inset cut-crystal roundels glowed like baleful eyes, and great cables of maroon velvet draped in bloody grins between bronze pillars. A fearful power seemed to emanate from the threshold, causing us to stop in our tracks.

I turned to Mudge. "Is this it?"

His eyes narrowed. "No." He squared his shoulders and stepped forward. "But it will get us closer..."

♂

Pallas raised the lantern and beckoned. "As you have said, Beloved: time is short. Sooner in is soonest out."

We edged into the next chamber. The room was large but the hundreds of ovoids that crowded the floor compromised its spaciousness. Imagine a prolific, glow-in-the-dark watermelon patch with all the melons standing on end in orderly rows.

A little under a meter in height, each ovoid glowed in the darkness with a bioluminescent pulse, giving the darkened chamber a greenish blue heartbeat effect. The ovoids were arranged in staggered queues with portions of some rows pulsing in counter-cadence to the majority. It made the overall effect simultaneously mechanical and biological.

"What are these things?" I whispered. "Pods? Eggs?" They brought to mind some old, twentieth-century entertainment vids that had tied such items to unpleasant dénouements.

Lilith bent over one at the end of a nearby row. "They're very pretty. But I think they bear more of a resemblance to Buckminsterfullerene."

I stared at her. "What?"

"You know: buckyballs. Do you suppose they're very heavy?" She reached out her hand.

"Don't touch that, Lilith; you don't know where it's been!"

Pallas swung the lantern, gesturing to a columned arch set into the far wall of the room. We picked our way around the profusion of pods and followed her to stand between the twin columns.

"You'll need your Program Access Code," she said.

"Why?" But even as I asked the question the code came forward from the back of my memory and I invoked it without even thinking about it.

The wall between the columns slid back and offered access to the building's inner core. Inside was a different kind of architecture—an anachronism, a design that would be unknown for more than twenty-five hundred years following the fall of ancient Alexandria. The core had been designed with "filing cabinets" three stories high and a robot retrieval system that could search and select individual backup files and folders in a matter of microseconds. I say "had been designed" because the filing system was no longer operational.

The cabinets had been torn apart, the folders flung about, and the content files, each about the size of a note card and covered with nanoscript, were shredded past the point of recovery.

I was trying to imagine what could have accomplished such grand yet systematic destruction when the realization arrived like a brick through a plate glass window: *the backup psyche-files for Nicole and Daggoth were gone!*

And not just *their* files, but *everyone's* backups were now irretrievable! Whatever happened now—to them, to us, to anyone in the Matrix—was permanent!

And that's when I noticed the Wurm.

It was nesting near the ceiling where a few of the cabinet tops remained bolted to the wall. Perhaps it was asleep: it had no discernable eyes and was more wormlike than dragonian in form and feature. I motioned to the others and attempted by elegant sign language that it was "time to get the mother-loving-hell out of here."

They nodded agreeably, even enthusiastically, and we quietly exited to the adjacent chamber.

"What—" Lilith began as we passed under the columned arch.

I shushed her. "No talking," I whispered, slipping between two rows of pulsing pods.

"Yess, come to uss," sighed a feminine voice.

"Dammit!" I stage-whispered, "I said no talking!" Then I realized the voice was coming from the other side of the room.

From one of the Vampires.

♀

The waiting room was nicely appointed in Second Empire style, down to the faux mantelpiece, couch, and two chairs. There were no windows, the door behind us might as well have been painted on the wall and, where a mirror would have been commonplace, a massive bronze ornament stood in its stead. The Louis-Philippe end table with a stack of scrolls a millennium or so out of date was jarringly out of place and yet so obviously apropos that I almost laughed out loud.

Angela was examining the bronze monstrosity on the mantle. "A Barbedienne, if I'm not mistaken," she said.

"You are mistaken," I said. "It's Sartre."

"Sartre? Jean Paul Sartre?"

"The entire room is existentially Sartre." I nodded back at the one-way door. "No exit."

"Ah," said Mudge, "but is the riddle Sartre?"

We looked back at the far wall where the young Rogue was standing. The wall looked bare and blank at first glance but, after a moment's concentration, finely scripted letters resolved themselves in nearly invisible lines of text.

"Latin. *Great,*" I said sarcastically.

Angela smiled at my tone. "Carborundum illegitimi est," she admonished.

Mudge shrugged. "I found a ready grasp of Latin immensely helpful during my studies in legal tort reform. I think I can work out the gist, here." He took a step back and slowly worked through five of the six lines:

"'I cut through evil like a double-edged sword…and chaos flees at my approach. Balance I single-handedly upraise…through battles fought with heart and mind…instead of with my gaze.' The last line isn't Latin."

"It's Greek," said Angela. "Basic translation: 'Who am I?' How nice, a riddle to pass the time while we wait."

"Um, guys." I sat on the couch and propped my aching gams on one of the chairs. "I've got this really bad feeling that we're stuck here until we solve the riddle."

"And what if we can't solve it?" Angel wanted to know.

Mudge and I just stared at the wall.

"Oh."

♂

According to the standard eastern-European mythos, decapitation is one of the surefire methods of Vampire extermination. Of course the Malaysian variety had their own set of rules, which explained why a couple of the women were holding their heads under their arms.

There were four of them. They had crossed the threshold and started across the carpet of pods.

"Oh man," I said, "this *isn't* real!"

"That's what Berkeley claimed."

I looked at Lilith. "Who?"

"Bishop George Berkeley. Born 1685. Died 1753. Berkeley, California is one of his namesakes."

"Hon, we're in Alexandria, Egypt. Berkeley, California is more than a thousand years in the future and *right now* we've got some issues to deal with."

"I'd say the question of reality is a fairly serious issue," Pallas chimed in. "Berkeley believed that only things we ever experience are the perceptions, thoughts and feelings within our own minds. That the material realm is potentially nothing more than an illusion."

"Why are we talking about this right now?" I asked. Maybe the girls had too much faith in my presumed status as the local Demiurge.

The four undead streetwalkers had waded through the pods to the midpoint of the chamber. A fifth, shadowy figure was lurking in the passage just beyond the doorway in the opposite wall.

Lilith sniffed. "You brought it up."

Pallas nodded. "You've always waffled when it comes to dealing with this particular issue. Even now you're trying to change the subject."

"We've got Vampires coming toward us!"

"Ah," Lilith held up a finger, "but are they real Vampires?"

I drew my sword and said something to the effect of: gee whiz, they surely did *look* like real Vampires.

Pallas took that opportunity to point out that if these Vamps were real then everything else related to The Matrix was real, including themselves.

To which I pointed out—gesturing with the point of Caladbolg's glimmering blade—that "real" within the context of The Matrix was not the same as "real" pertaining to the "real world" outside of the Matrix.

Pallas and Lilith had reiterated the Western idealist philosophy as posited by Berkeley and Hegel and had just begun to add the Hindu and Buddhist tenets when the fanged female closest to us tripped and fell against one of the pods.

"You don't have to explain the Hindu concept of Shiva's dream," I was saying as the pod flickered erratically. "Most religions contain some version of the 'we only exist within the Mind of God' axiom, even if it isn't an established orthodoxy."

The pod burst open and that effectively tabled the discussion.

The thing that emerged had the appearance of a diatom. An incredibly magnified diatom: what hovered in mid air was about the size of a regulation basketball. Translucent and luminescent, it floated and glimmered like a miniature ghost moon. Instead of lunar mountains and craters, its teal surface was covered with a fuzzy carpeting of cilia, broken here and there by stalks of capsomers and what looked like a portaled epivalve and hypovalve.

The Vampire that had stumbled against the pod regained her feet and reached out a tentative hand to touch the luminous orb. The outer skin of the orb dimpled, then enveloped her fingers, flowing over her hand so that it was encapsulated within the gelatinous core. She tried to shake it off but the ball elongated, flattening into an ellipse and engulfing her arm up to the elbow. As it did so, small threads of crimson snaked through the pale green-blue interior. In moments the interior opaqued and color-shifted from blue to purple to maroon. The vampire shrieked and thrashed about, clawing at the rubbery cocoon with her free hand. Then she stumbled into several adjacent pods.

"Oh Crom!" I said as they repeated the birthing process, spewing forth additional spheres. "*Viroids!*"

Three more orbs attached themselves to the closest Vampire. Then two others found nearby targets. As those Vampires reacted, a chain-reaction ensued. Suddenly the center of the room was in motion—Vampires thrashing and shrieking, pods erupting, Viroids swooping and attaching to the writhing bodies. I backed towards the entry to the inner core, Pallas and Lilith flanking my movement. The first Vampire was completely engulfed by Viroids now, her form undergoing a degradation of contour and configuration.

"I think I know," said Lilith, "why there aren't any bodies lying around."

♀

"Actually, this is an easy one." Mudge grinned and faced the wall. "The answer is: 'Justice.'"

"Justice," I said.

He nodded.

"You're sure?"

"I'm a lawyer. Every courthouse I've ever entered, every courtroom I've ever worked, has at least one statue of Justice."

Angela nodded thoughtfully. "Woman in flowing robes, brandishing a sword and holding a set of balance scales."

"Wearing a blindfold," he finished. "I even heard this riddle back in my freshman days in law school."

"Maybe you heard it wrong," I said. "Nothing's happening."

He cleared his throat. "Justice," he announced loudly. "The answer is *Justice.*"

Again nothing happened.

"Maybe you mis-translated?"

He scanned the Latin text and shook his head. "Any variants still require the same, final answer."

I turned to Angel. "Are you sure about your Greek?"

She spread her hands. "It's a very simple sentence: 'What is my name?'"

I sat up. "What?"

"I said 'what is my name?'"

"No you didn't."

"Yes I did."

"She's right," Mudge said. "That's exactly what she said."

"No." I nodded back to Angela. "You may have a better acquaintance with Greek and you, counselor, may know the law, but I am a writer and I know the rules of language usage. The first time she translated the last line she said: 'Who am I?' That is a more generalized question, which may be satisfied by the answer 'Justice.' But now you are saying the question is *'what* is my *name,'* a more specific query which begs a more specific answer."

"And while Justice will serve to identify the statue of the blindfolded goddess bearing sword and scales," Angel mused, "it's not her actual name."

"So, now what?" Mudge walked back to the other chair and sat down. "Do we start throwing out names until we get the right one?"

"Probably not," I said, getting up and stretching. The riddle is in Latin and the question is in Greek. I'm the resident expert in Greek and Roman mythology—or what passes for it inside the Matrix. The answer has to be either Justitia, Dike, or Themis. My money is on the last."

The far wall began to slide open with an ominous rumble.

A single shaft of light appeared in the darkness beyond, illuminating a giant stone figure. It was an immense statue of Themis, holding aloft the twin scales of the law and hefting the terrible sword of retribution.

Then it moved.

The statue was actually a stone Golem.

And as it advanced on us, the scales came down and the sword came up.

♂

We stopped just short of the arch. I could hear the rumble of smashed cabinetry shifting inside: the Wurm was no longer dormant. Pallas turned to me. "Got any ideas?"

I nodded and stepped sideways, pressing my back to the wall. The first spell took a minute to cast, and, when it was done, each of us wore a golden medallion hanging from a chain about our necks.

"Jewelry?" Lilith fingered the ornate emblem that dangled from her chain. "I mean, necklaces are always nice, but—"

"It looks like a protective talisman," Pallas explained, examining her own. "Ah, the mystic seal of Doctor Solomon." She looked up. "But is it enough to ward off the Viroids *and* the Wurm?"

I couldn't answer as I'd already begun the second spell. This one took a lot longer to boot up and the creature in the core poked its head through the archway just as a golden utility belt materialized around each of our waists.

"Run!" I yelled.

We ran, plowing through pods, flying Viroids, and dissolving Vampires, the Wurm following after a moment's hesitation. I barely had time to slam the door behind us as we skidded into the next chamber. Pallas picked up the marble bench and slammed it across the lower portion of the door and I cast a Wizardbar spell across the whole thing.

"Think that'll hold it?" I asked Pallas.

"No." She nodded at the retreating figure running down the far corridor. "I don't think he does, either."

I took a step and then decided we didn't have time. "Fastest way out?" I asked.

"Same way you came in," Pallas answered. "Got any other appropriate spells handy?"

I shook my head. "I was going to conjure protective shield bearing the escutcheon of the clan McAfee but we can't play defense forever. Unfortunately, it's going to take more than a little sword-work to stop a thing that big and powerful, and I'm out of my depth, offensively, when it comes to viral manifestations."

Lilith was looking at the buckle of her utility belt. "Who's Norton?" she wanted to know.

The door began to splinter.

We ran some more.

We threaded the doors, rooms, and corridors in record time, hearing the brassbound and bench-reinforced door shatter as we came to the wooden horse blocking the outer entryway. "I don't like the guy who sent this," I growled as we clambered between its fetlocks, "and I like his sense of humor even less."

"Assuming it is a 'guy,'" Lilith said as Pallas tossed her lantern up against the horse's rear.

"You think it might be a woman?" I asked as the hemp tail caught fire and the lamp oil spread rivulets of flame across the wooden buttocks.

"Not necessarily. I just don't flip to the male default every time."

"What? And I do?"

"That's not the question to ask right now." Pallas pointed up at the hills rising above the southern gate. "The question is: Can we make it back up to Daggoth's portal before the Wurm catches us?"

I looked up at the hills and was disturbed to see that two of the moons had set and the night sky was noticeably lighter. I shook my head. "It doesn't matter. Even if we could make it, we can't leave this thing running around loose in the Program. Come on." I started up the road toward the twin harbors.

The great lighthouse of Alexandria stood between the eastern and western estuaries and rose to the height of a fifty-story building—which I had to keep remembering as we kept running and never seemed to get any closer.

"Got any other spells up your sleeve?" Lilith puffed from somewhere behind me.

"Such as?"

"Maybe a teleportation spell?"

I shook my head. "I'm a little low on reserve manna points now. I thought you were the one who had the teleportation routine down to a fine art."

"Yeah. Well. I can 'port back down to Hell and return. In fact I could take both of you with me. But I got the distinct impression…that you're not leaving until…the mess is cleaned up here."

"Right." An idea occurred. "Can you port us both back down to Hell and then return us to a different location?"

"No. I can take you down with me. And *I* can return to a different location. But I can't bring either of *you* back from Hell. There are safeties on the transplanar teleportation…hierarchies to prevent unauthorized escapes. You'd have to get yourself back…just like the last time."

"Then get out and save yourself," I said.

"Surely you know me better than that!"

"How about you tell us the plan," Pallas suggested, "so she can 'port out and then 'port up to our destination. That way one of us won't be puking his or her guts out when we arrive."

"Not much of a plan," I wheezed. "I figure our best bet is to get to the lighthouse. If we can lure it to the top and then push it off, the fall might well kill it."

"That's your plan?"

"I didn't say it was a good plan."

"It hardly qualifies as any kind of plan at all!"

"You got a better one?"

"I'll meet you there." I heard a popping sound behind me and now only two sets of running footsteps echoed against the marble walls.

Three more blocks and we came to the northernmost city limits. The lighthouse was still more than a mile away on the Isle of Pharos.

"Every time I think I should be angry with you," Pallas said, "you do something like this."

"Like what?" We had stopped and I was leaning over, trying to decide whether to heave now or save it for a more propitious moment. "Come up with some hare-brained scheme that is likely to fail and screw everything up past redemption?"

"No. I should be angry that you created this Programworld and then abandoned us to Cephtronics Board of Directors who are even worse than the shallow, coarse, and corrupt gods who purport to control things here. We are left to the mercies of inconsistent programming, venal corporate policies, and sociopath hackers who do not recognize that we have consciousness, life, and therefore rights alongside the rest of all creation."

She reached out and caressed the side of my face with her hand. "Then you come back and time and again, risk your own life to make things right. And you don't risk your existence for all of your creation. Rather you do it for this part or for that: as if a smaller portion of your handiwork was more precious that the entirety of him who created it.

"Why do you risk yourself piecemeal? Why do you not redeem the whole?"

"I don't know," I said. "I don't know how! I don't have sufficient power, sufficient authority, to accomplish what you say. I can only act as opportunity and strength permit. And neither seem to come around very often."

The ground rumbled behind us.

"Rest period over?"

"Oh yes."

We started across the Heptastadion Dike. If there had been two extra slots on the Wonders of the World roster, the Dike would have made the list along with the Library. It was seven stades long—a mile, in modern terms—and not only divided the two harbors but provided access to the Isle of Pharos and the lighthouse proper.

Behind us, the Wurm sounded. The tiles cracked down the center of the street and then exploded upwards. The beast shot out of the ground like a fabric-covered spring from a can of fake peanut brittle.

Pallas grabbed my arm and suddenly we were at the far end of the Dike, stepping onto the island while the creature landed in the bay just a thousand yards behind us. She grabbed me while I was off balance and kissed me as the backwash slopped up and over our feet. "The fact that you care and the fact that you try makes me love you all the more." I could make out her features now in the dim light that fanned across the waters of the eastern harbor. Sunrise was coming! If it was imminent here, how soon would it rise where the gods prepared for their epic battle?

An hour?

A half-hour?

Less?

"We're out of time," I said, pulling her toward the base of the lighthouse. We rushed through the nearest door and circled the interior, searching for access to the fuel supply for the flame at the top. All we found were a pair of spiral staircases and a rudimentary elevator system for transporting gear aloft.

The lift was a simple windlass-and-pulley mechanism. Judging from the harness traces and thresh-covered ramp, mules or oxen had been utilized for lifting the cage from the ground floor. A small counter-shaft ran adjacent to the main shaft for the return line and counter-weight platform. I saw nothing fancy and was vaguely disappointed that the Alexandrines hadn't come up with something more innovative.

I felt somewhat more disappointed to find that someone had left the lift up above instead of returning it to the ground floor.

"Can you get me up those stairs as fast as you got me to the other end of the breakwater?"

She considered the stepped spirals and shook her head. "Too confined and convoluted. I can carry you faster than you can climb, but it will still take us several minutes to reach the top."

The tower suddenly shook from a heavy blow, and a faint scream echoed down from above. "Okay. That tears it." I stepped onto the counterweight platform and grabbed the rope.

Pallas looked at the square return shaft above my head that barely measured two feet to a side. "You're not—"

"Race you," I said, cutting the rope just below my grip. And I shot up the shaft like a runaway rocket. I counted on the openings on each floor to provide breaks in the shaft's interior darkness to enable me to keep track. Unfortunately, the intermittent flash of lamplight indicated that all floors were not currently illuminated so an accurate count was out. I switched over to a "one-one-thousand, two-one-thousand count" while trying to calculate my speed times the apparent distance between stories. Trying to do both while approaching both terminal velocity and a termination point at the top of the shaft made it impossible to do either reasonably well.

So I fell back to Plan C.

I guessed.

Or, rather, I panicked. I grabbed at the next opening that was flashing by and let go of the rope. I crawled through the opening and tumbled out onto the floor of a corridor. At the far end, where it cornered, I saw a spiral staircase. I ran down the hall and started up the staircase. Pallas was two floors below me.

"Showoff," she called.

The tower suddenly shook again and cracks appeared in the masonry of the outer wall. Then she was behind me, pushing. "Come on, you're holding up the show."

"Hey, watch those hands." My legs felt leaden, my lungs burned like fire. I stumbled to the next level and moved aside for Pallas to pass. She grabbed my arm, tossed me across her shoulder, and ran up the next round of steps while I contemplated her derriere close-up and upside-down. Another man might have been embarrassed. But Pallas was more than human and, besides, the view was mesmerizing.

The tower rocked again and she almost dropped me.

"Hey," said a voice up above. "This is part of the plan?"

"I thought I heard you scream," I said.

"What?"

"He said he thought he heard you scream," answered Pallas.

"Oh. Well. There's a giant Wurm trying to pound its way into the tower."

"It was a most undemonlike shriek."

"What?"

"He said it was a most undemonlike scream," Pallas answered.

"I didn't say 'scream,' I said 'shriek.'"

"If you're going to talk to my buttocks, don't expect a literal translation."

The tower shook again.

Pallas stumbled against the balustrade. I looked out over the edge and reached for the railing. "You grab that banister, and I'm going to go over backward right on top of you!"

I pulled my hand back. "You must have eyes in the back of your head."

"Or some other part of her anatomy," said the voice overhead.

"Don't mind her," I said as Pallas growled. "She's just trying to change the subject from her sissygirl squealing."

"Squealing?" There was nothing remotely "sissygirl" in Lilith's tone now. "Maybe the bard should favor us with a song."

"A song?" Pallas simultaneously translated right down to the same question mark: "A song?"

"Yeah. That English backside song." She started humming an old folk tune.

"What? Why is she humming 'Danny Boy'?"

"It's not 'Danny Boy'," I said. "It's Londonderry Air."

"London—"

"Derry Air," I repeated, running the two words into one pronunciation.

Her back clenched along with her—well, she got the pun. "Cheeky," I said.

The tower shuddered twice and bricks fell out of the arched dome overhead. We topped the staircase and Pallas set me down. Either the floor continued to shake or my legs were still wobbly.

We were on the top of the third stage of the tower now, the pinnacle that provided the beacon for all ships within fifty kilometers. Overhead was a cupola roof supported by six pillars which left the sides were open for visibility. Fed by the well at the tower's core, flames at the platform's center shot twenty feet into the air. A circular track surrounded the core, which enabled a great parabolic mirror to be moved about, amplifying the light from the sun by day or the fire by night.

I leapt across the track and considered the structure of the flame pit. On the other side of the platform was a set of levers and a hand pump. "Let me guess," Pallas said as she joined me. "Someone forgot to leave the directions out in plain sight."

"Well, I don't think it's very complicated." I pointed at the largest lever. "My guess is that one engages the main pump. Ancient texts suggest that the fuel was raised by a series of Archimedean screws to the top reservoir, which would be under our feet here. That dual-action handle should be a secondary pump for priming the wick. I would imagine the other controls are for adjusting the fuel flow, adjusting the wick, maybe controlling the mirror."

The mirror was surprisingly complex. It appeared that the ancients had hammered hundreds of thin sheets of silver, which had been highly polished and affixed to a flexible canvass, in a moveable frame. Thousands of glass beads were strung directly in front of the apparatus, forming what looked like a crude fresnel lens arrangement. As I marveled at the complexity of the whole apparatus, the sun broke the horizon behind me; its image turned upside-down and multiplied thousands of times in the curtain of glass. A moment later it was too bright to even glance at.

"Uh, guys?" Lilith called. "The Wurm has turned!"

I ran to the controls and pulled on the lever that looked like it would control the wicking mechanism. Guessed right, pulled wrong. The flames shot up thirty feet and licked at the tiled ceiling. I pushed instead of pulled and the flames damped down. Flickered. Died.

I moved to a wheel and considered the options. Pallas joined me. "Clockwise to increase the flow? Counterclockwise to decrease the fuel?"

"Maybe." I hurried to the firepit, stepping gingerly over the hot bricks and tiles. The nozzle was a slotted ceramic wedge attached to a woven cable that served as a wick. I pulled on it and managed to expose a meter and a half of cable. I pulled harder.

Nothing budged.

The tower shuddered.

"It's coming!" Lilith called.

"Turn the wheel!" I yelled.

"Which way?"

"Clockwise—I think!"

"No!" Lilith called. "It's plumbing!"

I stared at her.

"Righty-tighty, lefty-loosey."

I stared at her.

Pallas called: "Turning to the left!"

A viscous fluid dribbled from the slot in the ceramic wedge. It also oozed from the cable's weave, soaking my hands and sleeves. "More!" I yelled. "Which side is it on?"

"Uh!" said Lilith. "This one!" She started backing between the pillars, toward the interior.

"I want this thing wide open!" I shouted.

"It is!" Pallas shouted.

The petroleum smell was stronger, but the fuel only dribbled onto the floor a foot or so in front of me. It was time for a backup plan.

The Wurm's head appeared over the edge of the platform.

"Back up!" I yelled.

♀

The battle went on endlessly. Angela and I kept circling, waiting for an opening to wade into the fray, but it looked hopeless. The contest was between Mudge and the Golem; and Mudge was starting to look a little ragged around the edges.

Finally, he raised a hand: "Hold!"

The Golem leaned on her sword, looking as though she could go another three weeks without breaking a sweat.

"Do you resign?"

"Resign?" Mudge drew himself up and regained a portion of his formerly crisp composure. "Resign! Madam, I have answered over fifty questions of legal jurisprudence flawlessly! Your queries have covered points in Constitutional Law, Criminal Law, Business and Corporate Law, International Law, Military, Real Estate, Health—even Tax Law! How many more questions must I correctly answer before you are satisfied and allow us to pass?"

"Counselor," she said severely, "I would caution you to mind your tone lest I find you in contempt."

I cleared my throat. "Point of order?"

The Golem turned her stony head and regarded me with an unencouraging expression. "Approach."

"May it please the court, this hardly seems just…"

"And who are you?" She turned back to Mudge. "Is this your co-counsel?"

"Well," Mudge looked a little worried, "in a manner of speaking."

"Then you may retire while I cross-examine your co-chair."

"Like bloody hell," I said. "If you are the goddess of justice, we've got grounds for a hell of a malpractice suit!"

"I beg your pardon?"

"You'll do more than beg for a pardon if we don't get a little tort reform right now! We are not in a court of law and this is not an issue of legalities!"

The Golem cocked her head and gave my words a moment's consideration. "Go on," she said finally.

"Maybe you've been down here too long—Hell is bureaucracy taken to its ultimate corruption, after all. And considering the duties that have been laid upon you, I don't wonder that you find yourself acting uncharacteristically."

"Your point?" she rumbled, fixing her eyes on the sharpened end of her sword.

"That if you are, indeed, the embodiment of Justice, you will practice justice rather than legal jurisprudence. In other words, you will be *fair.*"

"Fair," she said.

"That means you don't get to go on endlessly asking questions until he fails. That means," I put my hands on my hips and stamped my foot, "we take turns!"

"Take turns?"

"It's only fair. It's only just."

She nodded slowly. "That is fair. That is just."

"And the first side that cannot answer correctly, retires."

She considered that one a little longer. "Objection sustained. Go ahead, Counselor; pose your question. Anything pertaining to the law or the legal system."

"Um," I said, "give me a moment."

"You realize, of course, that I am conversant with all written legal codes from the tablets of Hammarabi to the third Geneva Convention."

Mudge looked at me like a drowning man who has just been thrown a life preserver and discovered that it's made of lead.

"Okay," I said. "Here's your question: what is the difference between an ideal legal system and a glacier?"

The Golem straightened up and then leaned forward to peer at me more closely. "What?"

I repeated the question.

"There is no codified statute in any databased legal system pertaining to such a relationship!"

"In other words, you don't know the answer."

"There is no answer because...because such a relationship falls outside the parameters of recorded law. There is no correlation—"

"You don't know the answer."

"The question isn't fair; it doesn't address actual—"

Mudge interrupted with a wagging finger: "You did say 'any question pertaining to the law or the legal system.'"

"But it's—it's a *riddle!*" she sputtered.

"So, go on; take a stab at it. Or do *you* resign?"

Her brow furrowed (which made a sort of cracking sound). "How is the legal system like a glacier?"

"No. What is the *difference* between an *ideal* legal system and a glacier?"

She pondered for several minutes.

"Um, you may have eternity but we're on a tight schedule, here."

She glared at me and then relaxed. "The answer is…both grind slowly…?"

I shook my head. "The difference, Themis. Not what they have in common."

"But a riddle must invoke some rule of commonality to be fair. And don't invoke Lewis Carroll on me."

I held up my hands. "No ravens and writing desks here. Last call."

She stared off into space. Finally a sigh and: "All right! What *is* the difference between an ideal legal system and a glacier?"

"One is justice," I smiled, "and the other is just ice."

The Golem stared at me. "You may pass." A smile slipped out, but she added, "And may God have mercy on your soul."

The lights came up and the darkness evaporated to reveal a balustrade beyond. As we walked toward it, the space beyond dropped away to reveal a vast chamber below. Stepping to the edge of the parapet we looked down on our quarry.

"My God!" I said as the roaring rose to an unholy din.

"There are so many!" Angela exclaimed. "There must be thousands!"

"Hundreds of thousands!" Mudge breathed.

"More," I corrected. "And I gotta wonder about turning them loose. The cure may well be worse than the disease…"

♂

The foreparts of the Wurm came crashing onto the platform, smashing one of the support columns. The ladies scattered. I hoisted the cable and dribbled more fuel onto my boots.

The creature turned its blind face toward me and undulated forward. I stumbled back and tripped over the edge of the firepit.

The Wurm reared up and then plunged toward me. I rolled aside at the last moment and the bullet-shaped snout went crashing through the floor of the pit. Half of its body length followed along with the wick and ceramic head.

With the plan derailed, it seemed prudent to relocate. I looked around: the ladies had already departed. I got up and observed that the thrashing hind parts of the creature were pounding away at the column next to the stairs. There were no stairs on the opposite side of the platform, but then there was no five hundred pounds of thrashing tail, either. I ran to the edge and looked down. While I didn't have enough juice left for a flying spell, I could probably manage a Featherfall that would let me survive a fifty-story drop.

Probably…

"Robert!"

I looked up and the sunrise momentarily dazzled me. When my vision cleared, I could see Pallas hanging over the edge of the roof, seven meters above my head. She stretched her hand toward me. "Come up here!"

I gave her my dubious expression: who did she think I was? Plasticman?

She cupped her hand and turned her palm toward me. I rose into the air and was gently levitated to a spot on the roof beside her. There was something to be said for having a girlfriend with superhuman abilities—as long as you didn't tick her off.

Lilith had scrambled up the side of the dome and was holding on to the statue of Poseidon. A good decision as the tower was starting to shudder again.

The Wurm exploded out of the side of the fuel reservoir and fell to the ground below. The forty-five-story drop didn't kill the beast, but it certainly hurt it. The thing slowly undulated back toward the city.

Lilith was exasperated. "Great! It's between us and the exit again."

"We still have to kill it," Pallas observed.

"And we don't have much time," I grunted as I swung back over the edge and dropped down on to the platform. The glare of the rising sun bouncing off the mirror momentarily blinded me, and I had to wait for purplish afterimages to fade before attempting to navigate. I stood still, giving my discomfort some serious thought.

By the time I moved to the mirror, the Wurm was halfway across the Heptastadion Dyke. I pushed the apparatus around the track to triangulate the mirror with the sun and the city. The track had blocks placed to prevent such positioning but the damage from the Wurm's impact in the pit made the obstacles easy to kick out of the way.

"What are you doing?" Pallas moved to help me.

"Indulging myself in a little quiet reflection." I experimented with a series of handles on the frame that altered the curve of the silvered canvas. A bright patch of sunlight suddenly appeared on one of the buildings near the north shore.

Then it dimmed noticeably.

"Lilith! You're blocking the sun!"

"Well, excuse me!" She moved to the other side of the mirror. "What are you doing?"

I tried another pair of handles. "Legend had it that the mirror in Alexandria's lighthouse did more than amplify the firelight at night." I tried raising one while lowering the other. "Some accounts claimed it could be used to set fire to enemy ships that approached the harbor during the day."

"Aahh!" they said.

I finally found the focus combination and pulled the bright patch into a tight, white oval. "Help me swing this a little more to the right." The apparatus grumbled another foot along the track and I found my target as the Wurm moved off of the Dyke and started back into the city.

The white oval crossed its flank and the creature squirmed like a scalded slug. A moment later the remaining fuel on its hide erupted into flames.

"Think that'll kill it?" Pallas asked as we headed for the stairs.

"I hope so. We may already be too late in getting back."

Lilith brought up the rear. "Just goes to show you…"

"What?" I asked, knowing I'd be sorry that I did.

"The early nerd gets the Wurm."

PART V

BEAUTY'S DUTY

I slept and dreamed that life was beauty.
I woke—and found that life was duty.
—Sturgis Hooper,
Beauty and Duty—

What we dream up must be lived down, I think.
—James Ingram Merrill,
The Book of Ephraim—

Torn by dreams,
By the terrible incantations of defeats
And by the fear that defeats and dreams are one.
—Wallace Stevens,
Men Made Out of Words—

ONE

♂

Other gods had arrived during our absence. The number of tents on both sides had doubled, while separate camps sprung up off to the sides, suggesting that this would be more than a two-sided contest. Forget chess analogies; battle strategies here would be more like three-dimensional Chinese checkers.

Lilith hauled back on the reins as soon as we sighted the camp, but her Hellmount was doing better than Mach 2 and it took us more than three miles to slow to maneuvering speed and turn around.

The sky was gray, promising imminent dawn as we galloped up to my tent at the center of nogods' land. Six people stood beside a dwindling campfire, waiting for us.

Vashti and Dr. Westbrook were miffed that they had been left behind during our excursion into Hell. They were ready to bust my balls about letting them sleep in until Lilith offered to take them there, herself, and give them a personal tour.

Seeing two Natasha Skovorodas unnerved me. The android version, possessed by the spirit of Misty Dawn, looked none the worse for the wear. She, like the others, had apparently exited her "sleep mode" once the Wandija had passed into the mountain. The other Natasha, dressed in twin scraps of Amazon battle armor, embraced me and kissed me slowly and passionately. For a moment I flashed back to a snowbound chalet in one of Hell's suburbs. Then I heard the clicking of Misty Dawn's android armaments coming on-line and I stepped back.

"Thank you, Robert, for saving my life," the real Natasha said.

I smiled. "Consider it my wedding present. But if you really want to thank me, get out of here right now! Invoke your exit codes and bail out of the Matrix. It's about to get real ugly."

She shook her head somberly. "That is precisely why I must stay. You would not abandon me in death. How can I abandon you in life? From what they say, you will need every ally you can muster."

I gazed at the vast panoply of tents and campfires. "Four more or forty won't make much of a difference in trying to separate an army of gods. As Demiurge, even I don't have the power to put a stop to this without shattering the Matrix."

"Still," said Daggoth walking up to me, "between the two of us programmer-types, we should be able to make a serious dent in the festivities this morning."

Mike Straeker's avatar looked wan and pale, almost to the point of transparency. We clasped each other's forearms. His felt less than substantial. "Mike," I said, "the file archives have been destroyed. We weren't able to recover yours. I'm sorry."

Vashti looked stricken and took his arm as if to keep him from fading away. He smiled. "You mean I'll only be able to cheat Death once?" He shook his head gently. "Somehow that seems…more than a little fair."

The Zombie Mistress joined us. "He would not stay and rest. So I came wit' him. I have summoned de dead. Dey are coming. But I do not think dey will fight against those specific gods who rule over their souls." She spread her hands. "It is de best I can do."

I nodded. "Has there been any word from the others?" Their faces said that there had not. "Then all I can say is what will be, will be."

Vashti muttered: "Thank you, Doris Day."

"This is Cephtronics' day of reckoning. Too bad the Board of Directors isn't here to reap the dividends of their irresponsible policies," I said bitterly. "They turned a bunch of programmers loose to create the ultimate tourist trap. They directed them to create complex life forms and societies for the sole purpose of satisfying the baser urges of their paying customers. Bad enough they turn Dreamwalkers loose whose primary interests boil down to the urge to steal something, slay something, or screw something.

"But, even with the majority of Dreamwalkers locked out of the system, their creation still isn't safe or sane. The creatures they've given life to, given consciousness with all the attendant emotions, desires, hopes, and dreams—they're locked into an oppressive, primitive hierarchy whose masters," I gestured at the camps of the gods who surrounded us, "are as venal and corrupt as anything the dregs of human society can offer. And, God forgive me, I participated in the process."

"Well," said Daggoth, "I don't know that they're all that bad..."

"It's still wrong," I insisted. "It's a form of bondage that they have no hope of breaking."

"Hey, Honest Abe," my ex called, "someone's coming this way."

The horizon blushed pink, now, and the camps around stirred. A column of mounted riders moved between the groupings of canvas and silk, riding toward us.

The Amazons had arrived.

The lead rider leapt from the saddle and ran toward us. *"Beloved!"* Princess Aeriel flung herself at me. "You're *alive!"* She sobbed and laughed and kissed my face, my hands. Over the commotion I heard hear Misty Dawn's weapon systems coming back online.

After things settled down some abbreviated explanations brought everyone up to speed. The word had gone out, and the Amazons had pledged to stand with us. Others were coming as well, but I doubted that they would get here in time.

As we spoke, another Amazon dismounted and ran toward us. As he approached I realized the gender was wrong and that this would be one of their male captives. The big, burly Barbarian threw himself at my feet where he groveled and begged for mercy.

I looked at Aeriel. "What's the story on this one?"

"Typical male," she sniffed. "Abuser, bully, and rapist. We removed him from general circulation and redirected his stamina and genetic potential to some constructive use. Next Spring should see a brood of healthy girl babies for our tribe."

"He doesn't seem very enthusiastic about his newfound largess of feminine propinquity."

"Oh, he was at first. Complained about not being on top, that sort of thing, but basically enjoyed it the first few times."

"Um, Aeri; haven't I talked to you about this stamina issue before?"

"Yea, though I believe it is merely an issue of attitude. Once the potion is administered, he male body is capable of fresh ejaculate every fifteen minutes for up to thirty-six hours."

"It's cruel."

"It is justice and kinder. We even administer a salve to reduce blistering."

Dagny Westbrook stepped forward. "Luther? Is that you?"

The barbarian shrieked then threw himself prostates at her feet. "Oh, Dr. Westbrook! Take me back! I wanna go back to the sanitarium! I'll be good! I promise! You can lock me up! Please! I won't be no trouble! I'll be nice! Plee-ee-eese!" The last word dissolved into a fresh round of sobbing.

Westbrook looked at me. "What do you think?"

I nodded. "There are still some things that a Demiurge can do." I pointed at the blubbering Barbarian. "Twizzle, twazzle, twozzle, twome; time for this one to go home."

Luthor Limbach's muscle-bound avatar sparkled around the edges, spun in a circle, and then completely disappeared.

"What happened to his avatar?" Vashti asked.

Natasha nodded. "When the Dreamwalker exits the program, the avatar remains behind under the computer's control."

"Maybe it has something to do with his avatar being generated in a parallel universe, in a different system interface." I turned to Dagny. "I'd keep an eye on him. You know the old saying about atheists in foxholes."

She nodded.

"And now it's time for you to go back as well."

"No." She stepped back. "I want to help, too. It's taken me a couple of days to get my mental legs under me. Seeing all of this had given me a fresh perspective on…so many things. And I still need to look after Nicole."

I looked at the pinpoint of dazzling gold cresting the eastern mountains. "I'm not sure that will be possible. Our time is just about up, and if the others aren't back from Hell now it means they're probably not coming."

She opened her mouth but the sound of trumpets and battle horns drowned her reply. Riders from each of the camps approached us.

Anu of Mesopotamia, who had won his kingdom through a dice game, and Marduk from Babaylon, slayer of Tiamat, led the horde. Teshub of the Hittites followed with Angra Mainyu of the Persians and Mot of the Canaanites. The Egyptians, the Greeks, the Roman, the Norse, and the Finns were coming, as well, along with Vishnu, Indra on his sacred Elephant and wrathful Kali from India. Raven and Coyote approached as delegates from the northern tribes of the Native Americans while Huitzilopochtli and Mictlantecuhtli represented Central America's deities. From the east came Yu Huang Shang-ti and the Monkey King, Sun Wu-k'ung of the Chinese delegation, Izanagi and Amaterasu Omikami from the Isle of Nippon. Svarog rode alone from the camp of the Slavs, as did the horned Cernunnos of the Celts, Nana Buluku of the African Fon and Shango of the Yoruba. In the distance I saw Pele and Rangi of the Pacific Islands running afoot. There were others I didn't recognize, but it didn't matter. Once they determined whose side I was on, I would become the immediate target for all of the rest of the gods in the Matrix. My life expectancy would be measured in seconds, rather than minutes.

I hurriedly saddled and mounted Ghost so that I could meet the vanguard away from the tent and my companions. I saw no point in including my friends in the final palaver at ground zero. I rode out to a gentle rise in the field and waited as the emissaries closed around me.

Odin maneuvered Sleipnir and Ra his chariot so as to address me from opposite sides. No one spoke for a moment. I waited. I wasn't the one who was in a hurry to get this fracas off and running. Finally the "Allfather" grunted: "Well?"

"Demiurge," asked the Egyptian sungod, "with whom do you stand?"

Everyone leaned forward. I fancied that I could see knuckles tightening around staves and pommels.

"Myself," I said quietly.

"What? What did he say?" The question echoed through the ranks. Coyote laughed. He nudged Raven and they backed away.

"You said you would choose come sunrise," Ra reminded.

"I did choose, Hawkeye." I looked out over the assemblage. "What are we doing here? Fighting over turf? This started out over who should rule in Hell. Now it seems to have spread to which pantheon will rule the whole magilla. Isn't it enough to be a god? To have powers and abilities far beyond those of mortal men? Why must you fight for more? More what? Territory? Acolytes?"

Vishnu spoke up. "There are far too many gods for the world beneath us."

"Oh, yeah; you're a fine one to talk!" Cernunnos groused, shaking his antlers. "Not only do you Brahmans have more deities than you know what to do with, you have ten avatars for yourself alone!"

"I've only used nine, so far."

"It's not how many gods there are," interrupted the Monkey King, "so much as the problem of overlaps."

"Overlaps?" I asked.

"There's only one sun," Apollo called out. "How can Ra claim to be sungod without disenfranchising me?"

Amaterasu the Japanese sungoddess bristled. "You Greeks ought to clean up your own back yard before you start complaining about the bigger picture."

"What does that mean?"

"Hello? Helios?" the Peruvian sungod taunted. "And don't give us that Roman doubling crap!"

"Hey, Apu-Punchau," Apollo shot back, grabbing his toga in an insulting location, "I got your sunbeams right here!"

The Incan deity colored. "Come over here, Goldilocks, and I'll put that lyre of yours where the sun *don't* shine!"

"Ooooh! Well, Inca-*dinka*-do!"

That did it. They all started yelling and pushing and brandishing their weapons. In another minute, the battle would be fully underway.

"Hold! Hold!" Odin bellowed. "I want to know what the Demiurge will do when Ragnarök begins!"

The mob roared in agreement then gradually fell silent as they waited for my answer. Beyond them, their respective armies shifted restlessly.

"What is your intent?" Marduk asked quietly as the silence grew.

I looked around, thinking that I might as well go down fighting. "You are gods."

"Well, duh," someone said softly from the back.

"For whatever reasons you have been granted the privilege of the elevated positions you hold in this universe. But, you are right: there are too many of you." I paused. I heard no murmuring now. "Whosoever is given great power also acquires great responsibility. Until this day, you have each ruled over a specific geography and a particular people. I now ask you a question. Have you ruled well?

"Have you administered justice? Do you answer the prayers of those who worship you? Are you worthy of their adoration? Do their children go to bed hungry? And do your acolytes love you? Or fear you?"

I leaned forward in the saddle. "If there is one, just one of your adherents who has been neglected, mishandled, abused, or abandoned—then I say shame! *Shame!* Get you back into your mountain aeries, your fountainheads, your cavernous depths! Work to earn your glories and sacrifices! Work to be worthy of the worship.

"Because if you are still here wanting to squabble over new territory in five minutes, I will unmake you! I will blot you out of existence, out of history, out of all memory! And I will piss on your ashes." I glared at the lot of them. "Now *go home!*"

Some of them backed up. For a moment it looked as if it would actually work.

But others held their ground and the moment passed.

"So," growled Odin, "for the first part of the battle, it is all of us against you."

"Guess so, Popeye," I growled back.

A roar went up from the forces grouped in the south. A moment later the divine troops parted to reveal a chariot speeding toward us like a golden bullet. As it drew near, I could make out Cedalion at the reins, with Hades and my alternate self wearing Nicole Doucet's face and form, standing to either side. The absence of Mick and Mudge didn't worry me so much as the absence of any other form of backup. The chariot drew near, forcing a path through the inner circle, until it skidded to a stop across from me.

"Well, well, well," sneered Hel, "look who finally decided to show up for the party. Hades, I heard that you had Dis-appeared!"

"I should expect a half-assed remark from a goddess with half an ass," he replied as Ripley/Nicole stepped down from the box. "I'm not staying." He looked around at his fellow deities. "If you have any sense, you'll leave too." He nodded to Cedalion who snapped the reins.

Huitzilopochtli jeered: "Running away, Greek?"

"Not from you, Polysyllable," Hades called as his chariot rolled south. He pointed to the north. "From them!"

As everyone turned to look, my feminine alter-ego shouted, "The Army of the Demiurge approaches! If you surrender now, we will offer you reasonable terms!"

Everyone stared at her, mouths agape. Me included.

♀

Nobody was buying.

I looked up at Riplakish and smiled. "I take it you're not having any luck with them, either."

"If there's one trait common to divine beings," he answered, "it's that very few of them suffer a lack of confidence."

While that was true, no one seemed willing to start the hostilities until they got a better look at the new troops.

They didn't have long to wait.

They formed an indistinct line at first. As they drew closer, the line resolved into separate figures, advancing shoulder to shoulder. Behind them stretched a column of reinforcements extending as far back as far as the eye could see. The column filled the width of the valley.

Now the gods about us shifted uneasily in their saddles and chariots. A few developed nervous tics.

"Where didst thou find so many warriors, Demiurge?" Zeus asked.

"From Hell," I answered pleasantly.

A chorus of whispers arose, each invoking the name of their own Underworld. Lilith worked her way through the crowd on her Hellmount and offered her hand to me. As I swung up into the saddle behind her, Kali grinned bloodily. "What sort of Demons or Devils do you command, wench?"

I grinned back at her. "Neither Demon nor Devil, Cruella."

"They look human," called Teshub from his slightly better vantage point.

"They are," I said. Everyone stared as the Demiurge's army advanced.

Details emerged as they grew closer. Some were arrayed in black, others in brown; most wore gray. All carried brown, black, or beige rectangles like shields in one hand. As they drew nearer, they each produced small pointed devices in their other hand and began to beat upon the rectangles, making an unnerving, hollow, thumping noise.

"What are those things?" Anu wondered. "Weapons?"

"No...." Nana Buluku peered at the pointed instruments. "They look like styli or...*fountain pens!*"

"Oh man!" Shango exclaimed. "And…and…those things they're carrying…they're not shields! They're *briefcases!*"

"Holy Shiva!" Indra yelled.

"Mother of Gog and Magog!" cried Angra Mainyu.

Pele screamed. "They're lawyers!"

The gods all shrieked like chorus girls. Pandemonium ensued. They turned as one to flee to the north and staggered to a stop: a second wave of lawyers advanced from that direction, tapping their pens against their briefcases. The armies that were poised to rain down death and destruction upon one another now rushed together, mingling in the camaraderie that comes when familiar enemies are threatened by the common foe.

In the midst of the bedlam, Riplakish nudged his Pegasus close to us. Lilith nudged her Nightmare over next to him. "I don't believe this," he said. "They're immortals! Why don't they attack?"

"Attack lawyers?" I shook my head. "They wouldn't dare. For every ten they destroyed, a hundred would take their place. For every hundred, a thousand!"

Lilith grinned. "Right now it's business. If any god attacks, it becomes *personal.*"

"Not even a god would want to go there," I added.

We looked out over the "battlefield" as the masses came together. Someone was yelling, "All your base are belong to us!" as the gods whirled into a more tightly compacted mass with no avenue of escape. At first each pantheon was surrounded by a platoon of lawyers. Which quickly became a company. Finally, the individual deities were separated out and given over to a squad of attorneys.

"Now what happens?" Riplakish wondered.

"It's over," I answered as Mudge made his way though the crowd to us.

He nodded in weary agreement. "For all intents and purposes, it is over. Oh, there'll be weeks of depositions, then months of filing motions, at least a year of pre-trial discovery…"

"And then the trial?" Riplakish asked.

"Maybe."

My Halfelven avatar looked at me.

"They're gods," I explained. "Petty, vainglorious, impetuous, impatient, little tinpot dictators who won't have the stamina to see the legal process through to the bitter end. Especially since claims to one another's territory are weak and suspect at best, and are actually moot, as the court has already ruled in favor of a higher authority."

"A higher authority?"

"The Creator Prime. The Master Programmer. The one being who brought them into existence." He/I still looked confused so I elaborated. "The Demiurge."

Riplakish frowned. "But more than one person was responsible: Straeker, the programming staff..."

I shrugged. "Showing up is nine-tenths of the law in this case. The point is this: as corrupted as the Anomaly may have rendered it, and as much as it may rebel against its artificial status, the Matrix still recognizes that everyone and everything owes its existence to the Programmers. Just being a True Spirit and coming from outside of the system gives you special status inside any Programworld. The fact that you're a Programmer gives you authority. And because we're Robert Remmington Ripley, author of the Kishkumen Chronicles, the base for a major portion of Fantasyworld, we have greater jurisdiction than any artificially created god subroutine. In Fantasyworld we *are* the Creators Prime."

"So, other than getting the lawyers to go back to Hell after this gets settled out," Riplakish mused, "we're done here."

"Not quite," I said. "There's still the little matter of fixing what's wrong with Daggoth's avatar, my pregnancy and exit strategy, Nicole's undead relationship with the Calabastor slasher, and some unfinished business with a certain demigod who skipped today's party."

The Halfelven Bard looked around. "Orcus."

I nodded. "He wanted Hell. I say we give him some."

♂

We held a council of war that evening at Daggoth's Tower.

Getting there was no picnic. First, hundreds of thousands of dead people showed up, and the Zombie Mistress had to get them all turned around and sent back to their graves before they started asking the lawyers complicated probate questions.

Daggoth looked not only weak but transparently fragile and had to travel slowly. Mick showed up and tried to help Vashti with him but the stubborn sorcerer clearly wanted Dr. Westbrook's supermodel avatar to lean on rather than the homely REMrunner. For some reason that made my other self chuckle and shake her head as if Daggoth was making a major mistake. I guess women look at things differently than men.

Pallas showed up in her Enki form, shushed me when I started to say something to my feminine alter-ego, and offered to visit the chasm where both Nicoles had fallen to their deaths in the Corpus Callosum to see if there were any clues pertaining to one of them manifesting as a Pennanglan.

Likewise, Lilith volunteered to do a little espionage work back in Hades and track Orcus' movements for us.

By the time we got things sorted out and returned to Daggoth's Tower, midnight had arrived.

♀

"I'm not real keen on this," I said as Vashti pulled the cover off of Daggoth's brand new crystal ball. "The last time we tried to scry Hell, we got some really bad vibes."

Riplakish snorted. "Bad vibes?"

Vashti pointed to where sawdust had been swept into several small piles. "See that? That used to be the furniture."

"Oh."

Dr. Westbrook entered the room.

"How's he doing?" I asked.

"Resting. Though under protest. I left Mick to keep an eye on him."

"No wonder he's protesting," my dumber self smirked. I gave him "the eye" and the smirk was replaced by a look of befuddlement.

"He doesn't feel that resting is going to make any difference," Westbrook continued. "Quite frankly it's not exactly a bio-medical condition so I'm at a loss to know how to proceed."

Vashti looked at the two different avatars for Bob Ripley. "Well? You're the ones who have had practical experience in Matrix manipulation."

We shrugged helplessly.

"Most of the original program creation was achieved through direct psi-linkage," Riplakish said.

"My best guess," I added, "is that if resting doesn't help, at least it won't hurt."

"Sort of along Einstein's conservation of energy rule," he added.

"Though neither of us qualifies as a quantum mechanic," I finished.

The crystal orb suddenly lit up of its own accord. A moment later blurred features resolved themselves into the face of Enki, my handsome stranger.

"I've found something," he announced into one of the pieces of magic mirror we had loaned to him and Lilith before their departures.

What he had found were the remains of two avatars: Riplakish of Dyrinwall and Nicole Doucet. By all rights there should have been three bodies. One Riplakish and two Nicoles—one from my universe and the one whose body I had inhabited for a month in the parallel universe.

The question was: which one had survived the fall? Assuming that becoming an undead, bloodsucking Pennanglan could be considered as "surviving."

"Where are you?" I asked.

"About seven miles down into the abyss, where they landed."

"How did you reach the bottom?"

"It's not the bottom," he answered, "I found them on a ledge about seven miles down. The rift is bottomless."

"So the other body could well be much farther down," Riplakish mused over steepled fingers.

"Wait a minute," I said. "How could you rappel down seven miles of cliff face?"

"I didn't rappel—" he started to say.

♂

"Breaker-one-nine," a familiar voice interrupted, "break nineteen!"

"I hate it when you people use that archaic CB lingo," Vashti groused.

I looked over at my other self. "Did you hear that? 'You people'…"

She was nodding but saying, "I don't understand how he could get down that far. Is he a Magic User?"

But Enki was gone, replaced by the image of our favorite Archdemoness. "Hello? Can you hear me?"

"Come on back, mojo mama."

"Oh!" Vashti stalked out of the room.

Lilith peered back at us through her scrap of magic mirror. "Okay, I see you now. Orcus has apparently barricaded himself inside Hades' palace and no one seems to know what his plans are next."

"What seems to be the mood of the other denizens of Hell?" I asked.

"When word got out about the army of attorneys routing the rest of the gods, all the Demons and Devils came slinking back to their posts with their tails between their legs and their pitchforks dragging in the ash. Frankly? I think the Damned are damned glad to know that things should be getting back to normal soon."

"Define normal," my other self muttered.

"So when are the lawyers coming to serve the eviction papers?"

"I'll contact Mudge," I said. "There was still a fair amount of bedlam when we left and he said that some of the paperwork would need to be drafted before—"

A scream echoed down the stairwell from the floor above and we both exploded out of our chairs. As we ran from the room and tore up the staircase, a succession of crashes from the next level were made more ominous by the absence of any other vocal outcry.

As we topped the stairs, I saw Mick through the open door to Daggoth's bedchamber. She hurtled across the room, foot and fist first in a classic flying kick. A tremendous smacking sound of flesh striking flesh was followed by her flying back through the doorway, posterior first. We dodged as she sailed past and impacted against the wall of the corridor.

Ripley/Nicole rushed to her aid while I ran to the door.

Orcus filled a third of the bedchamber. Broken furniture littered the remaining two-thirds. Daggoth rose from the floor amidst the wreckage of his bed while Vashti stood off to his side, working on a battle-spell.

She was too slow: Orcus pointed a taloned claw and a jet of flame crawled through the air, toward her.

She stepped to the right, concentrating on weaving the proper somatic gestures.

The stream of fire curved to follow her.

No time to cast a countermeasure! I threw myself toward my ex-wife, hoping my enchanted chain mail would take the brunt of the netherfire.

Daggoth beat me to it. He leapt in front of Vashti just as the flames arrived and lit up like a Roman candle. He flickered erratically, flashed…

…and was gone!

"No!" she screamed, reaching out to empty air where her protector had stood just a moment before.

I turned to confront the demigod but only saw his forearm as it crashed into my face.

I lost a moment.

The next thing that I knew, I was crumpled against the far wall, staring blearily at Orcus as he grabbed Vashti and opened a dimensional portal.

"Now, I think you will come to me," the Deathgod said, "and come soon."

A wisp of smoke marked his departure.

TWO

♀

Mudge found us down in the armory.

"We seem to have hit a snag," he said. "I've got two companies of attorneys and a platoon of law clerks stationed around the Infernal Palace. But we can't serve paper on Orcus until he comes out or invites us in."

"Not a problem," I said, trying to fit Vashti's *stomacher* of studded brass scales across my slightly expanded midsection.

"Oh? You've got new information? Because the word on the street is that this Orcus has no intention of coming out anytime soon."

"Doesn't matter," Riplakish answered as he slid a pair of throwing knives into his boots. The blades gave off a blue, shimmery aura and made a faint buzzing sound. "We're going in."

Mudge shook his head. "Maybe you don't understand. You can't legally serve him if you make a forcible entry."

"They know." Seated in the corner and jacked into conduit leading down to the nuclear reactor in the sub-sub-sub-basement, Misty Dawn announced, *"They are going in to assassinate the deathgod."*

The lawyer/rogue's mouth dropped open. "Assassinate?"

"Perhaps my interpretation is incorrect. Ripley Number One made references to Orcus regarding the fact that he had carnal relations with pregnant women and proposed the removal of his cranium for the purpose of excreting down his esophagus. Ripley Number Two made mention of the subject's parentage which apparently involved a female canine and an unknown male progenitor. He then went on to suggest the creation of an additional anus for the deathgod approximating the dimensions of the Black Hole of Calcutta. My interpretation of the terminology was that they intend to bring about the death of Orcus—though, at one point, Ripley Number One said that she wanted to fornicate with him upwards in a most unpleasant way. So I calculate the probability of their wanting to do him terminal harm at ninety-one point seven percent with only an eight point three percentile chance that kinky sex is involved."

Mudge stared at us. "You're going to kill Orcus?"

"I prefer to think of it as Ethical Cleansing," I said, adjusting Vashti's bishop's mantle of bronze chain mail across my chest and shoulders. Unfortunately her *stomacher* wouldn't fit. I went to work on adapting one of Daggoth's belts with scraps of Elvish chain.

He looked over at Riplakish. "When did the plan change?"

"When he showed up an hour ago, killed Daggoth, and abducted Vashti," answered one of the two Angel MacRaes coming down the stairs and into the armory.

Mudge did a triple-take. "Mick? Dagny?"

"They're not coming," Riplakish growled.

"Like Hell," said the real supermodel. It wasn't hard to tell them apart though their avatars were superficially identical: Mick was still limping from the vicious backhand Orcus had dealt her upstairs.

"Well, I'm not staying behind," Dagny said. "I was promised a trip to Hell and I'll be damned if I'm staying behind!"

I stepped to the mirror and tried on one of my ex's celatas. "Dagny, you have no combat experience. Your avatar is the equivalent of a level-one character." The copper and bronze helm kept slipping down rakishly above one eye. Was Vashti's head bigger than mine? Er, bigger than Nicole's? "We're not taking the tour this time, we're going in fast, hitting hard and, if we survive, we should be back out before you can explain the difference between cognitive dissonance and dissociative fugue states."

"I'm going," Angel McRae announced. The intensity of her words was undermined by the chainmail bikini she had found where Dagny had last discarded it.

"Absolutely not!" roared Riplakish.

"And certainly not wearing that," added Mudge.

"You seem to forget," she said, "that I went one-on-one with your demon bogeyman while you were downstairs making vid-calls."

"You seem to forget that he mopped the floor with you," I countered, trying to bend the helmet between my thighs to make a better fit.

"Lived to tell the tale," she shot back.

"What's this?" Dagny asked, hefting an ovoid that had the appearance of a baroque pineapple.

"It's the Holy Hand Grenade of Antioch," Riplakish said. "Put it back in the box."

"Bet I wouldn't be helpless if I took this along." She noticed the glass case Daggoth had removed from Misty Dawn's tree. "Wand of Xagyg," she read, "In Case of Armageddon, break glass."

"Don't even think about it," I said, trying the *celata* on again. It fit…after a fashion.

"Well, before you go trying any Son of Rambo stuff," Mudge said, "how about letting my people serve a writ of habeas corpus?"

"Habeas corpus," the fembot intoned. *"Latin. Legal term. Literally: 'you must have the body'."*

"I'll habeas his corpus," my other self muttered as I buckled the belt under my bosom so that the Elvish chain fell across my stomach.

"Shouldn't you wait?" Mick asked. "Or rest or meditate? If you're going to use any major spells—"

"It's covered," he said and chugged down a whole flask of Manna-carb™. He disconnected the energy plugs from the fembot. "We don't have any time to waste. Every minute that goes by is another minute that he has Stephanie in his clutches." "Vashti," I corrected. I didn't want to consider the very real possibility of Stephanie's demise. *Clutches? Hoo boy.*

Lilith appeared. "Is everybody ready?"

"We are," I buckled Balmung's scabbard across my hip. "They're not."

"Hey!" Mudge stepped forward. "What about me?"

"You want to do something useful?" Riplakish asked as he, Misty Dawn, and I stepped close to the Archdemoness. "Get your legal beagles to track down this Valentine person and see if you can serve a subpoena on him. My guess is: you find him, you find Nicole. What's left of her, anyway."

"Hey!" Mick tried one last time, turning to Riplakish and pointing at me. "If you won't take us, how come you're taking her?"

He glanced over at me. "Because she's not a she. She's a he even if she sometimes acts or talks like a she."

"Prove that I'm not," I said perversely.

"Great. I'm going back to Hell and my backup is She-man of Castle Numbskull!"

"Going down," Lilith announced.

I blinked and we were in Hell.

♂

The Infernal Palace was over a mile away, flickering dimly in the subterranean gloom.

"Couldn't you have gotten us any closer?" I asked.

Lilith appeared to be confused. "I—I seem to have been diverted."

"Aye," said a familiar voice. "You have—and for good reason." Hades appeared out of the darkness.

"My lord," the Archdemoness said as she bowed. She started to straighten and then bowed again. "My lady!"

A pale, solemn woman appeared at Hades' side. "Persephone," he purred, "allow me to present to you the Demiurge, Riplakish of Dyrinwall, and his companions…"

I bowed.

The robot curtsied. "*I am Misty Dawn, your ladyship.*"

My other self grimaced as she bowed and, after a moment's hesitation, growled: "Roberta."

The Queen of the Underworld looked us over. "They seem very…mortal…to accomplish what a god, himself, seems unable to do." I couldn't tell in the stygian darkness but I think Hades actually colored. "In any event, I have been approached by those who would aid you and, thusly, aid us. I bring them to you now."

Two specters stepped from behind her: Daggoth the Dark and Nicole Doucet.

♀

Nicole came to me first. She took my hands in her cold grasp. "You wear my flesh well, better than I if you are, indeed, with child."

"Which Nicole are you?" I asked.

"The one who lost her way trying to save the Robert Ripley she loved and adored. The one who was murdered by her own self."

"And that other self?" I felt a catch in my voice. "The Nicole from my universe? What became of her?"

"There isn't time," answered Daggoth, laying a hand on her shoulder, "to tell the tale twice. And I must give you something that you're going to need very badly to survive…"

♂

As Daggoth and my female doppelgänger put their heads together, the shade of Nicole Doucet drew me aside. "Daggoth has asked me to fill you in on…the circumstances of our deaths."

"Your deaths," I said.

"Mine and…the other me. The one from your space/time continuum."

"I wasn't there," I said, "but I've heard the details."

She looked down. "I owe a greater apology to your other self," she said quietly, "but even though you were not consciously present, it was a wrong against you, as well." She sighed. "Ah, my Robert! Even if my death is a partial atonement, I am eternally tormented by the knowledge that I very nearly destroyed the love that I was not worthy of in exchange for a love that was not worthy of me." She looked up and her eyes were moist and filled with pain. "But enough of my selfish regret. Time is short and I must tell you of our deaths and what came after."

Then she told me of her death in mid-fall, of how the arrows had ended her life well before her shattering impact on rocks far below; of waking up in an isolated portion of the Underworld next to her other, ghastly self and under the cruel, pitiless gaze of Orcus, Roman god of Death; of how he offered them both a grand scheme of revenge and a second chance—a way to return to the land of the living.

This Nicole refused. She wanted atonement, not retribution. The other, denied the resolution of her madness that she had sought in death, accepted. But Orcus could not grant what was not his to give. Instead of life, he gave the other Nicole a form of unlife. She became undead. A Pennanglan. And he compounded his lies with the assurance that if she could find a body like her own, she need only replace its head with her own to be fully restored and achieve some sort of twisted victory over those who had abandoned her in her crippled flesh so many years before.

As bad as all of that was, the worst was yet to come. She told me who "Valentine" was.

By the time she finished her face was wet from a deluge of sorrow. I took her cold hands in mine. "What can I do?" I asked.

"Stop them," she whispered. "Make an end to it. A *final* ending."

"I mean for you. What can I do for you?"

She put a hand to my cheek. "You can't do anything for me," she said. "Don't you understand? You are powerful in a god-like way. But you are not God. You are still a man, and I am a woman, and we each must bear the responsibility for ourselves—as everyone else must answer for their own lives, their own choices. You cannot shoulder anyone else's burdens. You have your own to bear."

"Bob," my other self called, "we've got to go. Now."

"There must be something…"

"What?" she asked softly. "What could you do for me here in Pluto's dusty realm? My life is done. The only mercy I can know is to drink from the River Lethe—but not yet. No, not yet. I feel I must know my pain a while longer before I can let it go. And I hope to know an end to the suffering of my other self."

I looked over at Roberta. "I think I know what you mean."

"If I could hope for one other thing…"

"Yes," I said, "tell me."

Her eyes filled with infinite tenderness. "Je voudrais voir des yeux sombres d'amour et des prunelles brillantes d' joie…" She turned and disappeared into the darkness while I stood frozen in time, remembering the hills of Avignon.

I should like to see eyes dark with love and pupils shining with joy.

♀

On the way to the Infernal Palace we passed a football stadium with a halftime show eternally in progress, an outdoor recital featuring a succession of eleven year-olds working their way though a four-octave arrangement of Heart and Soul, and a nondescript building where, through a succession of windows, we saw a faculty meeting, a community awards dinner, a doctor's waiting room, and a public television pledge drive.

I glanced at Lilith as we jogged. "Dr. Westbrook would be disappointed."

The Archdemoness nodded. When you have an eternity to torment the damned, pitchforks, fire, and brimstone are so passé.

"So," Riplakish said as he dropped back to match my pace. "What did Daggoth want? Did he have some sort of plan for a Resurrection spell?"

I shook my head, half-distracted by the worry that all this jiggling up and down was unhealthy for the child that I was carrying. "He wanted me to give Stephanie a message."

"A message?"

"It's personal."

His eyebrows shot up. "Hey, if he told you it's practically the same as telling me."

"It's a woman thing."

I didn't think his eyebrows could go any higher. I was wrong. "A *woman* thing?"

"I rest my case." I observed furtive movement in the gloom ahead of us. "He also had a present for me." Signaling that we had company, I slowed my pace and said to the android, "I need a scan. Do a sweep, fifty yards to either side of our current path toward the Infernal Palace."

"What present?" Riplakish asked, his eyes locked on the darkness ahead.

"Six Humans, one Elf, all female. Minimal chainmail. Armament consists of nine daggers, three longbows, two shortbows, five longswords, two shortswords, one whip. Gender, accoutrements, and sigils match corresponding Amazon profiles. One avatar scans as being in taction with an outside consciousness, the rest are NPC/AIs."

"One of them is a True Spirit?"

"A Dreamwalker. Yes."

"Shit!"

"I cannot perform that function. As a ghost I can no longer perform eliminatory functions and this clockwork shell will not exude its nuclear core for another five thousand years."

"What is it?" Riplakish asked.

"Amazons ahead," I said. "Sounds like Aeriel's band. And I think Faun and Natasha are with her."

"You mean Dyantha. After Natasha exited the program her avatar would still perform according to her psyche profiles."

"M.D. says somebody in the group is still in taction."

"Down here? Shit!"

"I cannot perform that function."

"So how did they get down here?"

"Why don't we ask them?"

♂

"How did you get down here?" I asked after peeling Aeriel's lips from mine.

"We followed the skull into the Tartarean Caverns. We lost the creature in the dark, but following the Trail of Orpheus brought us down here."

"The skull?" I asked.

"The Pennanglan," Dyantha answered. "I explained to Princess Aeriel that capturing the Vampire would be of great import to her consort."

The princess had folded her arms and was tapping her foot. "She did not explain that we would go to the Kingdom of Hades for it."

"We would have snared it before it entered the caverns," she retorted, "but you let it get ahead of us."

Aeriel frowned. "Is that a joke?"

I tried to hide my own smile.

"Are you making mock of me?"

I turned my embryonic grin into a grimace. Roberta snorted quietly.

But not quietly enough: my Amazon betrothed whirled around and noticed my doppelganger in drag for the first time. "You!" She turned back to me. "It is the murderous bitch who tried to kill you! Fear not, Beloved; for I shall end this threat here and now!"

I put a hand on her arm as she pulled her sword from her sheath. "Hold, Aeri. She's not who you think."

"What say you?"

"You've got the wrong girl. The one who looks like her and tried to kill her—er—me, is dead. In fact, the one you really seek is the Vampire."

"The disembodied one?"

"Aye. This one here is mine ally." Funny how the old archaic forms slip back into your speech when you have an appropriate conversant to work with. "In fact, we're very close." Roberta was waving and making slashing gestures in front of her throat while the Amazon princess was turned toward me.

Aeriel looked doubtful. "If she is not truly evil then she be a most intemperate and saucy bi—wench. She even implied that the babe she carries is of your issue."

Hmmm. If I were to be truthful in the most literal sense…

"What? Your face—your silence—" She looked back at Roberta who had stopped making hushing signals and now stared at the ground with a hand to her forehead. "You trollop! You strumpet!" She turned back to me. "And you! You…you…" Her face went from scarlet to white and I know that she was way beyond "creep" and somewhat past "bastard" now, searching for the penultimate approbation. "You…*man!*"

Ouch!

"You…you…wait! I'm going…I'm going to…" She burst into tears. "…tell my mother!" she wailed. She turned and ran off into the darkness.

"Well, that went badly," Lilith observed as the other Amazons followed their leader to offer solace and companionship. Dyantha remained but watched the retinue of sisterhood fade into the gloom.

"Looks like the wedding is off," I agreed.

"Yeah," said my female self, "laugh it off, you half-Elfed moron. She may not be a twenty-first century Rhodes Scholar, but she's in the upper one-percentile of this world's inhabitants and the computer's fixed it so she's crazy in love with you. She'd kill for you and, probably against all tribal codes, die for you. Even if it's impossible for you to contemplate a real relationship with her, she deserves better from you than flippancy. I think she's earned some respect here."

"Sorry," I said. "I didn't mean to dis her."

A voice in the darkness behind us said: "Hey!"

"Maybe I should go after her."

"Are you kidding?" She shook her head. "The Pennanglan is somewhere loose down here and we've still got to rescue Stephanie and kill a minor god—"

"By most mythological indices, a god of Death is not defined as 'minor.'"

"—so running off after Queen Hippolyta's favorite daughter and making up isn't the best plan of action right now. Maybe never. Better if that girl gets her head on straight and dumps you for someone who isn't so afraid of emotional commitment."

I felt my face grow hot. "What are you saying? That I'm some sort of emotional cripple?"

"More gimp than cripple," she countered.

"Oh yeah? Well, it takes one to know one!"

"Proximity scanners activated: incoming."

Pallas appeared with Mudge, Mick, and Westbrook in tow.

Westbrook took in our expressions and asked: "Are we interrupting anything?"

"The Demiurge was getting in touch with his feminine side."

We turned and stared at the fembot with open mouths.

"Well, we have news," Mudge prompted. "Pallas showed us how to use Daggoth's magic mirror to run a database check on all program inhabitants corresponding in any variation to the name 'Valentine.' Dr. Westbrook helped cull the short list by determining what characteristics would make him a likely partner for our undead quarry."

"I've got one name that stands head-and-shoulders above the rest," Dagny said. "What?" she asked, taking in our expressions. "Oh. Sorry. Anyway, we've got a very sick boy on our hands. And he'd be dangerous enough without an undead accomplice."

I gave them The Look. "And after we told you to stay put, you've come all the way to Hell to tell us because…?"

"We pinged him through the Matrix database and got a return near the Infernal Palace," Mick answered. "We figured that you ought to know ASAP and, despite your mutual protestations of being the only boys bad enough, we thought we ought to lend a hand."

Riplakish turned to me. "You hear that? She thinks you're still a boy."

I shrugged. "Acceptance is a long time coming."

Pallas stepped between us. "It's no longer an issue of firepower or who outclasses what. Your Valentine is a REMrunner."

Up until now it had been a simple mission of utterly destroying a god.

Suddenly it had gotten very complicated.

THREE

♀

The ring of creatures around the Infernal Palace looked like a gathering of the Hieronymus Bosch fan club. "Now see? Here's the problem," I told Mudge as we squeezed through a throng of bird-headed humanoids with arms where their legs should be. "Once 'The Underworld' became synonymous with 'Hell' every mythological kingdom of the dead started cross-referencing each other with christopopcultural imagery and data files as their nexus."

"So we've got to do more than just send all the gods back to their own turf and make them agree to stay there," Riplakish added. "We've got to close the programmatic loopholes and establish a central, governing authority."

I groaned. "What? An elected, governing board comprised of representatives from each pantheon with rotating terms?"

My other self bared his teeth in a parody of a grin. "You know my favorite scripture." It wasn't a question.

"Yeah, Bob three-sixteen: For God so loved the world that He didn't send a committee."

He nodded. "Besides the problems inherent in accomplishing anything by council, there's the basic problem of recognized authority."

"Recognized authority?" Angel queried. It was still easy to tell them apart: Dagny was too busy rubbernecking at all the Demons and Devils to follow our conversation. She could barely follow us in the physical sense with all the allegorical goodies going on around her.

"It's a religious thing," I explained. "The Jews don't recognize Jesus as the Messiah, the Protestants don't recognize the Pope as the head of the Christian Church, and the Baptists don't recognize each other in Hooters or the liquor store."

"Religious groups tend to recognize their own authority," Riplakish elaborated, "and no one else's in matters spiritual and philosophical. It's more of a toss-up in matters physical and legal but compromise and submission are hard to find in the lexicon except where they apply to everyone else."

"What about 'render unto Caesar?'" she asked.

"That's the problem here," I said as we emerged from the crowd and stood before the palace doors. "There is no Caesar. No central authority to maintain order out of chaos and keep everyone else at least moderately in line."

Riplakish nodded. "When Daggoth summoned the Machine to appear inside of its own Program, he inverted the access process and overwrote the safeties and lockouts. The Anomaly wrested control of the Matrix from Cephtronics and loosed the hounds of chaos."

"And, effectively, everything has been going to Hell ever since," Angel observed.

"Things fall apart; the center cannot hold / Mere anarchy is loosed upon the world…" We turned to stare at the fembot. We seemed to be doing that a lot as of late. *"Yeats,"* she explained, *"William Butler. I accessed his written visions a while back. This particular prophecy seemed relevant."*

"It's not—" Riplakish began.

"Maybe it is," I countered. Then I gestured, concentrating on Michael Straeker's legacy. A burst of light and heat struck the massive palace doors which, though locked, barred, and fused with protection spells, collapsed into a smoldering pile of rubble.

"Wha—"

"You asked me what Daggoth's gift was a while back," I said. "He gave me his Programmer codes. Since I can't access my own codes while another me is in the system and he can't utilize his now that he's been Archived, he thought I ought to have my Programmer status back." I dropped my hand to my belly. "Especially since I'm spellcasting for two, now." I stepped over the debris and strode into the palace

After a moment, the others hurried to catch up.

"'The blood-dimmed tide is loosed,'" Misty Dawn observed from the rear, *"'and everywhere / The ceremony of innocence is drowned.'"*

"'The best lack all conviction,'" I murmured, "'while the worst / Are full of passionate intensity…'"

♂

First we encountered the trapdoor that opened into a pit filled with spikes.

Then we avoided the tripwires that fired crossbow bolts from three directions.

By the time we had passed through the collapsing stone archway and dodged the giant scythe that swung out of a hidden alcove, I was seriously ticked off. And I wasn't the only one.

"What is he doing?" my other self fumed. "He knows we're not going to fall for any traps under twelfth level and the best of this lot barely rates as a 'six!'"

I nodded in agreement. "Not to mention the fact that no one else is coming in here until we walk out again."

"So," said Angel, "if Orcus doesn't expect to stop you, maybe he just expects these traps to slow you down."

"Or," posed Mudge, "maybe he's trying to make you overconfident before springing something far more challenging."

"What other motivation could he have?" Dyantha asked.

"He could be doing it to make you angry."

We stopped and looked back at the other Angel, Dr. Westbrook.

"He could be doing it to make you angry," she repeated.

"Why would he want to do that?" my other self wondered aloud. "I would think he'd be wanting to make nice with us instead of antagonizing us further."

"This is Hell," Lilith reminded us. "We don't know how to 'make nice' down here. 'Antagonizing' is what we do best."

"Databased articles on tactics and strategy suggest that anger clouds judgment. Perhaps the Deathgod's purpose is to anger us so that we make tactical errors at critical moments."

"I have found, in my profession," Dagny continued, "that sometimes people are simply motivated by their own anger—a desire to make their adversaries experience anger or impotence, even though it is counter-productive to their own cause."

The debate was put on hold as we approached another door.

"Shall I blow it?" Roberta asked me. Her index finger was still smoking from the last gated portal she'd zapped.

"I've heard that power is an aphrodisiac," I replied, "but I think you should consider a little abstinence now and then."

She rolled her eyes. "Oh yeah. It never changes. A man with power is admirable while a woman with power is a bitch."

"Um," I said, "it's hard to think of you as a bitch. A bastard, maybe, but never a—"

"Proximity alert! Multiple lifeforms registering in the chamber beyond. Alert. Alert. Repeat, multi—"

"Identify," I snapped. "What are they?"

"Unable to specify. The wall is diffusing my readings."

"Generalize then. Are they human or Demon?"

"Humanoid...Demihuman. Non-specific to Hell."

Roberta looked at me. "Prisoners? Hostages?"

"We pull the others back and go in quietly," I decided. "The element of surprise should give us time to evaluate the situation and still have time to act before losing the advantage."

We crept to the door. Listening to the indistinct murmur of voices on the other side, I turned the handle carefully.

There are days when nothing happens the way it should. Under the circumstances, the door should have been locked—even bolted from the inside. The latch should have rattled and released with an unmistakably loud click. The hinges should have squealed and groaned like the souls of the damned as I pushed it open an inch, then two. Instead, it opened silently and effortlessly and the babble beyond became intelligible.

"How much longer?"

"That thing said sometime today."

"I don't like it."

"Aw, you never like anything."

"He's got a point. Remember where we are."

"It's not so much *where* we are. We all said we were willing to go to Hell for the girl. It's who we're dealing with that makes me nervous."

"It's *what* we're dealing with that makes me nervous."

"Who, what: I don't like it any better than you but this may be our last, best chance for justice."

"Yeah, but even if we get the drop on him, who's to say we can find our way back up and out?"

"Would've been simpler if we'd brought the girl along; got it done here."

"Are you nuts? Why would you want to bring her here? Besides, did you see the way that thing kept looking at her?"

"Like it was hungry..."

"Gave me the creeps!"

"Got any threes?"

"Go fish!"

Roberta put her mouth close to my ear and whispered, "I count six different voices."

I nodded and signaled that I would enter first. I eased the door open and stepped into the room.

Instead of six, there were seven. As there were no books in the room to put on the chairs, they had chopped a foot or so off of each table leg, causing it to cant drunkenly and imperil the stacks of poker chips. Cards fell from stubby little hands as they looked up from their play.

"No," I said.

"He's here!" they chorused. And reached for their weapons.

♀

I was lucky. Had I taken two more steps to move into backup position, he would have trampled me as he exited—no, *shot* from the room. His retreat was punctuated by a series of crashes and, seconds later, the doorway vomited Dwarves. Seven, in fact. Very familiar-looking Dwarves.

"Come back here!" they yelled. "You cad!" And: "You masher!" Not to mention: "You'll do the right thing by that girl!" Snow White's diminutive guardians were still fierce in their determination to get Riplakish and their young female ward to the altar.

Misty Dawn moved up beside me. *"The traps would appear to have grown more sophisticated."*

"At least more complicated," Dyantha amended.

As my male version fled down the corridor, a familiar squad of Amazons entered from the far end.

"Uh-oh," I said.

"Beloved!" Princess Aeriel cried.

"Houston, we have a problem."

"Forgive me for doubting you!" our betrothed wailed.

Riplakish couldn't slow down in time. He ran into Aeriel's arms and, together, they whirled in a mad embrace. "I should know that thou wouldst not consort with other women in unseemly ways!"

The Dwarves arrived and, trying just as unsuccessfully to block their forward momentum, plowed into the Amazon squad. It didn't help that one of the Amazons was an Elf.

"Unhand him, strumpet!" the grumpy one yelled. This did not go over well with the Amazons who were already shoving back. What really set things off was the next Dwarf's demand: "You're coming back with us and marrying the fair Lady White or ah-ah-Ah-CHOO!"

While a skirmish unfolded around them, Aeriel grabbed Riplakish's shirtfront. "Marry *who?"* she yelled.

"Snow White!" he yelled back over the shrieking and screaming. The Amazons were even noisier. "Except I'm not marrying her!"

The happiest Dwarf now looked decidedly unhappy. "Thou churl! You think you can steal the virtue of our stepdaughter and abandon her?"

Aeriel twisted the shirt material tightly. "You got that slut Roberta with child and now you're stealing another maiden's virtue?" That hysterical tone was back in her voice again.

The Amazons looked back up the hall at me. The Dwarves followed their gaze. "Hey," I said, raising my hands, "it wasn't my idea."

The Dwarves all looked back at Riplakish. "Rapist!" they screamed in unison. The battle circle imploded.

"M.D., I need an area stun, the far end of the hall. Now!"

The fembot raised her hands and a momentary, pale blue pulse filled the end of the corridor. All the combatants collapsed, unconscious.

"How much time?" I asked the android.

"Due to the wide variety in size and physiology the period of unconsciousness will vary among individuals. I calculate a minimum of twenty minutes before the earliest return to consciousness; a full hour to bring the last awake."

"We'll have to separate them before that," I said. "And carry Riplakish with us."

"What? Forward?" Mudge was incredulous. "What if we run into this Orca?"

"Databases reference orca as killer whales."

"Okay. Orcus, killer god. The point is we could be looking for Nicole and this Valentine back outside while everyone recovers. Then we can come back later when things settle down and have the big showdown."

"This is not just a personal vendetta," I said. "Time is of the essence if we're going to rescue Stephanie. Nicole can wait a little longer."

His face grew stony. "Maybe I look at Nicole's situation as a rescue mission, as well."

"Another hour or two isn't going to make much difference in her case."

Mudge started to respond but Angel McRae reached out and touched his cheek. "Bernard," she said gently, "saving your Nicole may well prove more difficult than killing a god. One is simply a matter of concentrated firepower while the other may involve a great deal of time and all of our talents in a carefully coordinated effort. Wouldn't it be better to get this over quickly so we can all focus on what's best for Nicole?"

His mouth was a tight line but he nodded after a moment and we all set to work peeling the Dwarves and the Amazons apart.

"Lilith," I said as Misty Dawn hoisted an unconscious Riplakish over one shoulder, "someone needs to stay behind and watch over our sleeping beauties until they awaken. I wouldn't want any of them to come to harm."

The Archdemoness frowned. "Are you ditching me? We archetypes have feelings, too, you know."

"Nobody wants to ditch you. But I need someone to stay behind who is powerful enough to protect them and smart enough to send them off in the wrong direction when they wake up. And there's another reason."

"What?" she asked, sulking.

"Even if we win this encounter, you could lose. What will your status be, down here, if we kill your lord and master and word gets out that you went up against one of your own?"

She frowned. And then slowly tried a tremulous smile. "You just want me out of the line of fire. Just like him, you worry about me."

I smiled back. "You know us too well."

"Not in the Biblical sense," she said saucily.

I waggled a finger at her. "Don't make this more complicated than it already is."

A groan from one of the Dwarves got things moving. A moment later we were hurrying past the truncated poker table and starting down the next corridor.

♂

When I first edged into consciousness, I found myself bent over some sort of lopsided rail and bounced gently along. There was something oddly familiar about all this. But, while it didn't exactly hurt, it wasn't doing wonders for the contents of my stomach, either. Opening my eyes didn't help at all so I kept them closed. Ditto, my mouth: the first things likely to emerge there would not be words.

"That doesn't look very comfortable." The voice belonged to Riplakish.

"My internal sensors register no discomfort."

"I mean for him."

"His comfort is not germane so long as he remains unconscious."

"Still, it would seem that there are better ways to carry him."

"This is known as a 'fireman's carry.' Not only is it more efficient in terms of my stress load, it enables me to keep my arms and hands unencumbered for offensive and defensive situations as they develop."

"Well, let's see what develops here. Put him down."

We stopped moving and I was lowered onto my back. A hand reached inside my vest and groped around. I reached up blindly, in turn, and felt my fingers close around a female breast.

"Hey!" It was Roberta's voice.

I opened my hand and my eyes. "Sorry," I slurred. "But if you're going to cop a feel then it's only fair—"

"I need the spectacles," she snapped.

"Spectacles?" I was still a little fuzzy.

"The optics of Haroun al-Rashid."

Ah. I sat up. The room swam and I closed my eyes again. Doing my own groping, I produced the spectacle case from an inner vest pocket. They were taken from my hand and I lay back down. "Wha' happened?"

"Dwarves? Amazons? Snow White? Aeriel Morivalynde? Riot? Hello?"

"A lot of fuss over one lousy kiss," I groused.

"Well, not to pat ourselves too much on the back but *lousy* kisses rarely get anybody stirred up. Besides, Aeri's worked up over more than just a kiss. She thinks you're my baby's father."

I sighed. "Don't you?"

"More likely that *I'm* the baby's father. And mother." I shrugged. "Or maybe The Machine done the dirty deed. Maybe we'll have a better idea once it's born."

"So you're having it?"

"How can you even ask such a thing?"

"Well, it's not exactly a planned pregnancy."

"Maybe that's the point. I couldn't have imagined this happening, much less planned it. I have to believe this is happening for a reason."

"And what possible reason could that be?"

"I'm at a total loss. And I have other things on my mind. Ask me again after we've eliminated Orcus and taken out this Valentine and the Pennanglan."

I opened my eyes and tried sitting up again: better. I looked around: not so good. "Where is everyone?"

"Sleeping." Even if I hadn't noticed the frustration in her expression, it was plainly evident in her voice. "We tried a detour around the main corridor, thinking we might circle the throne room and flank Ol' Hornhead. We ended up cutting through the greenhouse."

*"Green*house?" I tried to picture a greenhouse in subterranean depths of Hades' kingdom. "What does the god of the Underworld grow down here?"

"Poppies," Misty Dawn answered.

"Poppies," Roberta echoed.

"Poppies would make them sleep," I agreed.

"Especially the ones that Hades cultivates. Only Angel, Misty Dawn, and I were able to make it to the far end. I sent M.D. back in to drag the others out but they're still snoozing quite soundly in one of the antechambers. Ms. McRae stayed behind to keep an eye on them."

"The robot would have been better protection."

"I considered it but Angie insisted and I needed someone with me who could carry you and atomize the palace if Orcus prevails."

I gingerly worked my way to my feet. "Have you noticed how protective she's been toward our rogue barrister?"

"Yes. Though I'm surprised that you have."

"What? Noticed?" I was a bit miffed with her attitude. "Why wouldn't I have noticed? We're the same person, after all."

She shook her head. "We're not. Not anymore."

"What are you saying? That you're really a woman now?"

She looked down and contemplated her feminine form. "Define 'woman.' For that matter, define 'really.' If you mean, am I now a woman in the mental and emotional sense, the answer is: I don't know. I think of myself as 'Ripley.' Just as you think of yourself as 'Ripley.' And, although neither of us is the Ripley that existed six months ago, we're still Ripley in spite of the changes and experiences that have come our way since then.

"If we were the same Ripley up until six months ago, you know that we never particularly took our gender as our primary source of identity. We were male, yes, and liked the ladies, and did our share of the macho bullshit that goes with being male in our society. But it wasn't high on our list of defining qualities."

This was starting to creep me out a little. "Are you suggesting that we were in the closet?"

"What?" She stared at me and laughed suddenly. "Oh! No. I am not saying that we were gay." She stopped laughing. "At least I don't think so. No. What I am saying is that genderfication is not just chromosomes and genetic hard-wiring. Gender roles are more a matter of societal orientation and parenting than individual choices during the formative years. I'm just saying that we played along like everyone else until one of us suddenly found herself on the other side of the divide.

"Now I'm in unknown territory and I'm not sure what my emotional landmarks are. You are, as far as I can analyze my own memories, a confirmed heterosexual. But as for me? I don't know what I am or what I really feel. If I develop an attraction for men, does that mean I'm a gay man in digital drag? A computerized transsexual? Or have I become a heterosexual woman in the complete sense of Matrix nomenclature?"

"Well," I asked, irritated at my own squeamishness. "What do you feel?"

She hugged herself and smiled. "I feel like a mother."

"Well," I said, stepping toward her and giving ourselves a hug. "It wouldn't be the first time we've been called that."

♀

"My sensors are not calibrated to register magical dweomers."

"Just scan for mechanical traps," I said, hooking the stems behind my ears and settling the lenses before my eyes, "The optics will reveal any spell residue."

Initially everything looked the same—a bit blurry at first while the lenses adjusted to my vision, but the room hadn't changed. The carpeting was the color of arterial blood, while the walls and ceiling were as black as the pit. The dark outline of a pentagram was scorched into the carpet at the center of the room and a faint haze of smoke still hung in the air suggesting recent combustion.

I thumbed the nosepiece on the spectacles and shifted the optics' enchanted filters. The room looked much the same, only a little dimmer, and the haze now had a greenish hue with bits of sparkles here and there. The pentagram, however, had morphed into a set of glowing, golden lines. The area inside the star shimmered like heatwaves above hot pavement, though I could discern no change in temperature.

"I detect no mechanical traps nor do I scan any chemical or biological threat. I am, however, reading a carrier wave."

"A what?" Riplakish asked. "Define."

I focused on the shimmer and thumbed the bridgepiece for extreme definition and magnification. The area now glistened with tiny motes in barely perceptible strands and chains. I stared at the sparkly bits and tried to fathom their familiar appearance. It didn't help—the optics had reached their limits of magnification.

"Unknown. Carrier wave appears to be an information transmission conduit of unknown type and origin."

"Numbers!" I said. "Digital code packets!"

"Can you trace the signal?" Riplakish asked.

"Negative. Carrier is degrading, signal is being terminated."

I jumped across the lines and into the center of the pentagram. The room turned inside out and became a squalid, unkempt studio apartment. Plates of half-eaten food littered the floor amid drifts of unlaundered clothes, scraps of paper, and unidentifiable bits of detritus. A rat scurried toward a pile of refuse overflowing from a waste receptacle in the corner. I saw a makeshift REMrunner terminal and a black market cephalic harness rig that crept across the end of a magna-futon as connectors of fiber-op were dislodged by my/his hands. As our taloned hand reached between our legs to dislodge the catheter I saw a monstrous, jutting phallus, unhuman in size and configuration. I gasped and became aware of myself within myself. Our taloned fingers came up, sliding over our skull and riding past the smooth dark horns to the final connectors and—

The universe exploded in searing flames!

I dodged, leapt, and—

The room snapped back in place with the black walls and red floor. I had landed outside of the pentagram that was now filled with a star-shaped column of fire that extended a good six feet into the air. "Damn!" I said. "He's utilizing a firewall to block our access!" I looked over at the android and, for a moment, could see the ghostly Wood Nymph flicker amidst the circuitry of Natasha Skovoroda's form.

"What did you see?"

I looked at Riplakish. Only he wasn't Riplakish in the enchanted gaze of the optics: Robert Remington Ripley the Third, stood there staring at me with concern, his Halfelven avatar only a vague, smaller shadow about his True Form.

I looked down at my belly, a little more convex than it should have been this early in the game.

"What is it?" Ripley asked again.

"I think it's going to be a girl," I said.

"I mean, what about the pentagram?"

I took off the spectacles and handed them to Ripley—who was Riplakish once more. "I want you to look at me."

"What?"

"Put the optics on, adjust for True Sight, and look at me. Tell me what you see."

He took the spectacles and fitted the enchanted eyewear to his face. Before he could focus we heard a heavy thump followed by a scream from the room beyond.

"That sounded like Stephanie!" he said and ran to the door.

♂

The door was locked.

I stared at the lock in X-ray mode and saw that the device was relatively simple. I saw a second latching mechanism that seemed out of place and *that* gave me pause. I stepped back and reached for the lock picks in my beltpouch.

"That's gonna take too long," Roberta said. "Misty, kick the door in!"

As the android moved past me I dropped one of the picks. "Hold on! There's some kind of extra latch—" The door shattered under the application of the fembot's dainty foot. "—and it may be booby-trapped," I finished lamely

There was another heavy "thump" and then the sound of grinding gears. "What part of 'hold on' were you unclear on?" I asked between clenched teeth.

"Hold on: to get a grip. Ostensibly to brace for impact or leverage while kicking the door in."

"How about 'wait a minute'?"

"Possible but unlikely interpretation. More properly tied to the phrase 'hold up.' *If your intention was to request a delay of action—"*

Leaving the dithering dumbot behind, I dodged through the doorway and entered a large chamber. An iron cage at the far end of the room held my ex-wife. As Stephanie's True Appearance was so close to her avatar's, I forgot for a moment that I was looking at Vashti.

The Pennanglan was another matter.

One glimpse of the demented soul behind that disembodied head and I ripped the spectacles from my face. Better and worse: the Vampire form *was* easier to look at but it was also headed right toward me. "Misty Dawn!" I barked, "don't let that creature leave the room!" Her weapon systems clicked as they came online.

"Take your weapons offline," Roberta commanded, behind me. "The object is containment and capture."

"Acknowledged. What stratagem do you suggest?"

"Just play goalie for now," I said. "Don't let her past the door."

"Goalie?"

"Access database," Roberta suggested. "Reference Mia Hamm."

"Accessing," she replied as I ran toward the iron cage. *"Ah. Downloading video."* As the head flew past in the opposite direction, I had the insane urge to say 'bread and butter.' But I didn't. *"Interpreting data. Processing."* There was a 'thud,' and the head passed me again, going in the same direction now.

"Ripley!" my other self screamed. "To your right!"

I was almost to the cage. I glanced to my right. Looked again. A section of the wall had opened to reveal a recessed alcove. A hulking, shadowy figure stood inside.

Orcus!

♀

Even before he left his hiding place the scepter gave him away. The ornamental rod of carved obsidian was topped by a skull of ivory and set with rubies and garnets that glowed like baleful demonic eyes. It was a dangerous weapon in anyone's hands—this I learned when I had appropriated it a few years back, then had a most instructive lesson in how absolutely devastating it could be when wielded by the Deathgod, himself.

When I saw the deathwand emerge from the hidden chamber, I knew that we had only moments to press our advantage before this battle turned very one-sided. I pointed my left hand at the place where he would emerge and braced it with my right while settling into a standard shooter's stance. Summoning Daggoth's Program Codes to the forefront of my memory, I focused on channeling as much destructive power as possible into a force projectile and waited, the energy continuing to rise like floodwaters piling up against a dam.

The wand came up and out. The Deathgod's grip looked odd, however, and it took another couple of seconds to realize why. Instead of grasping the rod in his taloned grip, the wand appeared to emerge from his palm, as though the lower end of the artifact was buried within the demigod's wrist.

I couldn't wait any longer. Another moment and he would bring the wand to bear on Riplakish. I fired my sorcerous salvo, hitting the wand itself.

The deathwand flared red and purple and was knocked aside. Orcus stumbled out of his hideyhole shrieking and waving it about. A stream of profanity followed. My next blast went wild as parts of the ceiling began to fall.

♂

The mere sight of the god of Death was enough to turn most legs to jelly. The sight of Orcus capering, shrieking, and waving his deathwand would unhinge most folk not already in the first category. I managed to keep my feet. But the impact of a five hundred-pound ceiling stone crashing into the floor just a few feet away completed the cumulative effect and I went sprawling. Seconds later Nicole's disembodied head swooped through the space I had just vacated.

The sound of ratcheting gears was louder, now, coming from the opening in the ceiling. Even louder was the rattle of iron bars as Stephanie shook her cage. "Get up!" she yelled. "Get me out of here!"

"Yes…Dearest…" I fumbled to my knees.

"Hurry!"

"Coming…Dearest…" I lurched toward the cage. So did Orcus. I pulled my katana longsword from its scabbard. "Back off, hornboy! Get your own ex-wife!"

The deathwand came up.

I dove for the floor and rolled.

The flying head just missed me again.

"I could use a little help here!" I yelled.

♀

"Should I assist the Archdruid?"

"Negative. Keep that doorway buttoned up. Try to hit that head with a stun beam." I moved farther into the room so that I could get a better bead on the Deathgod.

Another stone dropped from the ceiling, sending tremors through the floor and dropping me to my knees and Orcus on his keister. Riplakish was crawling toward Vashti's cell, which left our mutual adversary up to me.

Orcus stumbled forward as if he was drunk, his movements strangely off for his larger frame. But then, I was no paradigm of grace myself under the current circumstances. And he hadn't lost his grip on the deathwand—as strange as that grip appeared—and that spelled serious problems for us if I couldn't bring him down in the next few moments.

As I cranked up another load of arcane energy, a third stone fell from the ceiling and a crack appeared in the floor at its impact site. A blue stun beam sizzled past my shoulder as the

Pennanglan swooped back in my direction: trouble above, below, betwixt and between.

"I want my body back!" it screeched, tumbling through the air and taking refuge behind one of the great fallen stone blocks.

"Ditto, Cabbagehead," I muttered as I swung my hand to re-aim at Orcus.

KerBLAM!

A section of the far wall disappeared in a flash of coruscating light, and the resulting concussion jolted the room again. Three more stone blocks crashed down from the ceiling and a network of cracks zigzagged across the floor. Nicole's fearsome head shot out from behind the previous block and rocketed up into the gaping hole its departure had left in the ceiling.

I looked back over my shoulder and saw Angel McRae standing behind the fembot, pointing a smoking wand into the room. "What are you doing?" I yelled.

"Helping!"

"Not with that, you won't!" I stumbled back toward her. Another face appeared beside her: Angel McRae. "Dagny?"

The one holding the wand said: "Yes?"

"Hand it here!"

"Why? I can help!"

"The Wand of Xagyg is a potent artifact," I said, gingerly taking it out of her hand. "It can make or unmake entire worlds! You cannot properly wield it without dispensation from the Coastal Wizards Union."

"Look out!"

At Angel's warning, I ducked instinctively. There was the sound of a thudding impact just above and to the right of me followed by a spattering of gore. "What was that?" I asked, looking up.

"I'd call it a foul-tip, pop-up," Angel said, looking higher.

The android raised her arm and fired off another stun beam.

I whipped off my celata and ran backward about ten feet. I threw out my arm and caught the undead head in the bronze cap. "And she's *ooouuuutttt!"* I announced as I trotted back over and handed the cap and decapitated to the Angel that was Dagny Westbrook. "You want to help? Go grab a tapestry or a tablecloth or something and wrap this thing up before it comes to!"

Mudge was standing behind Angel, rubbing his eyes and yawning. "I'll help," he said.

♂

I decided I wouldn't ask for help again.

My eyes were slowly recovering from the blast that took out the back wall. An actinic afterimage filled my vision and I had to watch for Orcus out of the corner of my eye as I clambered toward the sound of Stephanie's voice.

Parts of the floor were canting at a slight downward angle where the impacts from the ceiling stones had opened large cracks and smashed the undergirding supports. I wasn't sure what lay below but I thought I saw a reddish-orange flicker through the larger gaps and I smelled the distinct odor of brimstone.

This was taking way too long.

And not in the manner that my ex kept carrying on about, but in that we should have been dead by now. Never mind the falling ceiling blocks or the necrotic noggin of Nicole; the only hope we originally had of surviving a head-on collision with the god of the Dead was to hit him first, hit him hard, and then pile on with everything that we had. It hadn't worked out that way, and so there was that nagging question of why we were still alive.

Not that I was inclined to sit around and give it my undivided attention. I saw movement at the edge of my peripheral vision and threw myself back from my apparent trajectory. It was impossible to tell if the dodge had enabled me to escape a blast from the deathwand: most deathspells are silent and invisible.

"Hey, Orc, ol' buddy," I called. "Finding somebody to take your place in the Deathgod department is going to be a real pain in the ass! So, how's about we sit down and cut a deal that will make everybody happy?"

"You're negotiating with him?" my ex screeched. "You're the Demiurge, fer Cromssake! Kick his Demon ass!"

"Shut up, Stephanie!" I yelled.

♀

"Shut up, Stephanie!" I yelled.

Riplakish seemed a little dazed, and getting Orcus' attention was the last thing he needed.

"Hey, Hornhead!" I shouted, moving away from the doorway where we were all bunched up and presenting a tempting target. "None of the gods are coming out of this with any advantage. Ain't no way you're gonna get any extra mileage, either. In fact, you're in deeper doody than the rest. You killed Daggoth and kidnapped Vashti. So here's the best deal you're going to get and it's only on the table for thirty seconds."

Orcus stood half-crouched, holding the deathwand at a peculiar angle, and looked from Riplakish to me—and back again. The Halfelf was fumbling with the optics of al-Rashid, trying to get the stems rehooked behind his ears.

"Give us Vashti back—now and unharmed. And give us the one called Valentine—"

"No!" the Deathgod cried.

And raised the deathwand.

FOUR

♂

As I fumbled with the optics, I added up all the things that were bothering me. First, it was taking Orcus far too long to do us any damage, much less dole out individual deathspells. Second, while our current shake-and-bake environment would mess with anyone's equilibrium, Ol' Hornhead seemed clumsier than usual. He even held his own deathwand with uncharacteristic awkwardness.

Third, was the matter of his voice…

As I put the lenses in position, the after-image faded and my vision cleared.

"Hey now," I said. Then I yelled: "Hey! It's not—"

And the room exploded.

♀

As the deathwand came up, I ordered: "Misty Dawn! Particle beams! Now!"_and discharged the Wand of Xagyg. For a full two seconds enough destructive force unleashed itself in the room to sink an armored aircraft carrier—and all of it directed into the five by eight-foot space occupied by the Deathgod.

Was it possible to kill Death personified?

Whatever the answer might be to that abstract question, Orcus was gone. In fact, nothing remained in, or *of*, approximately one-third of the chamber. Walls, floor, ceiling, and everything in-between—all evaporated.

Disintegrated.

Vanished.

Unmade.

I stood there, shocked by the sudden stillness—the sudden nothingness.

But while the nothingness remained, the stillness didn't.

"Rob! *Rob!*" Stephanie's voice sounded high and thin and vibrated with barely repressed hysteria. "Are you all right?"

Riplakish crouched near the edge of the missing floor, his hair singed, his clothing tattered and smoking. He turned toward me and pulled the shattered optics away from his face. "We've made a terrible mistake."

♂

"Are you sure?" Roberta grabbed my arm to steady me as I limped toward the doorway.

"That it was Valentine?" I shook my head. "Hell, I don't know what this guy really looks like. But it all fits."

"You're sure it wasn't Orcus?" Stephanie asked.

Another ceiling stone fell behind us as we exited the room and we all jumped a little. The sound of ratcheting gears grumbled into silence.

"I was half-convinced *before* I got the optics on."

"He didn't act like Orcus," Roberta said. "Didn't move like him, didn't sound like him…and he held the deathwand funny."

"It was strapped to this kid's hand. It was tied on so he couldn't let go."

"With the layered-on Glamour, it appeared as if the wand emerged from the Deathgod's arm," Roberta elaborated.

I nodded.

"But why?" Stephanie asked.

"It was a diversion," Lilith said.

"A deadly one," I agreed.

"He knew he was in trouble," Roberta added. "Even if the lawyers let him off lightly, the other Underworld gods would remember who started this little power play. Especially Hades."

"But why kidnap me?" Stephanie asked. "And why kill Daggoth?"

"Daggoth may have been an accident," I said. "His recent condition made him more vulnerable than usual. But it worked for him. Dagny was right: he wanted us to come after him and he wanted us to come fighting mad."

"But why?"

"He was planning on getting out," Roberta reasoned. "But he needed to cover his tracks. He needed a body on the Outside that wasn't closely monitored. That meant using a REMrunner. Valentine would have provided the perfect profile: antisocial, a loner—no one would notice a change in personality once Orcus took over his body and disconnected from the Game."

"The Game," Lilith muttered.

"Maybe he had a deal with Valentine," I continued. "But if he was to be sure that this guy wouldn't change his mind, wouldn't blow the whistle, he had to kill him—destroy his psychefile and any back-ups—after he had taken control of his body in the Outer World. The backups—everyone's—were destroyed recently. All that remained was to arrange for Valentine's murder shortly after his own escape."

"That's where we came in," observed Angel.

"Right. And here's the beauty of this plot. By getting us all revved up and creating the illusion that Valentine was Orcus, not only do we remove the evidence of Orcus' escape route, but we believe that Orcus is dead and gone so there's no further need to go looking for him."

Mudge seemed unsatisfied. "He presumed a lot. How did he know you wouldn't examine the body and discover the enchantment?"

"Orcus is a god. A minor one, I grant you, but still a god and specifically the god of Death. He knew that we knew that capture was too dangerous and that the only way to take him down was to go in with full spells blazing. The question of killing "Death" made it certain that we would choose Unmaking and Disintegration spells. To further the odds that we would cast first and ask questions later, he both pared the party down and antagonized the remainder with a series of traps. Then put us in a room with a whacked-out flying head and falling ceiling stones that endangered Stephanie and anyone else who entered. It was not an environment conducive to hesitation or second-guessing."

"If Valentine had zigged instead of zagged after being released into the room, one of those five-hundred pound boulders might have pancaked him. Voila: case closed. It wasn't a perfect plan, but it was pretty damn good."

I stepped into the center of the charred pentagram and looked up at the scorched ceiling. "It's already gone cold," I observed.

"I scan no signal, no carrier, no static: there is no evidence of relay access or status."

"He's gone," Lilith said, "and he's not coming back."

Dagny shook her head but did not take her eyes off of the squirming bundle that she and Mudge guarded so carefully. "It all seems so incredible."

The Archdemoness looked surprised. "That he would want out? Even if his plot to rule Hell had succeeded, he still would have been tempted by the Outer World. Even as we all have since learning that such a thing is, indeed, possible. But knowing that he had failed, that the gods themselves had been put to rout, that it was just a matter of time before he would be judged by Hades and the Demiurge him—*er*—self, he knew he had best depart now."

"Got out while the getting was good," I muttered.

"And burned his bridges behind him," Lilith finished.

"Burned more than that," Roberta said, looking back toward the room she had effectively destroyed just ten minutes earlier.

I looked at her. I could guess what I was thinking. "Hold that thought," I said. "We were set up. If everything had gone according to his plans, we still wouldn't know."

"But we should have known," she/I insisted. "And we do know!"

"And just what exactly *do* we know?" I challenged.

"That we're complicit. That we—that *I'm* the one who blew away that kid!"

Lilith stared at us as if we'd lost our minds. "Wait a minute. I understand that you're unhappy that Orcus has escaped to your Outer World. But are you upset that you killed a sick, sadistic pervert who was doing things that made some of Hell's own minions squeamish?"

"He was a True Spirit," Roberta said. "I had no right."

"No *right?"*

"He was obviously sick," Dagny said. "He should have been treated, not punished."

I pointed out: "But we had no way of knowing that. We thought we were facing Orcus."

"So let me get this straight..." The Archdemoness looked from Roberta to me, and then back, again. "It was all right for you to come charging down here with plans to knowingly murder a god. But you're suddenly all contrite and regretful when you accidentally kill a murderous True Spirit?"

"It's not the same thing," Mudge said. "Vigilantism—"

"It *started out* as vigilantism! What are you saying, Counselor? That it's not the same thing? Killing a god or killing a True Spirit?"

Mudge frowned uncertainly. "Well, it's not…"

"Damn straight! Orcus was the way he was because someone made him that way. Right, Demiurge?"

I nodded after a moment's pause.

"But you get all weepy over this sick bastard who comes to our world and uses it as his private game reserve?"

"It certainly wasn't right," Angel said, "but I think we're concerned over the fact that this Valentine was a True Spirit."

"Well, Hell, yes." Lilith's voice dripped sarcasm. "We can kill Orcus because he's not one of 'us' but the pervert and murderer who is a True Spirit gets special consideration even though nobody preprogrammed him to do what he did!"

"That's a bit specious," Dagny retorted. "We're all 'preprogrammed' to a certain degree."

"Well then, if I accept that, then the only real difference is that you 'True Spirits' base your 'life worthiness' on your Outsider status! The only difference between you and this Valentine is not attitude but a matter of degree!"

"Nobody's suggesting this Valentine shouldn't have been brought to justice," I soothed.

"Just a different standard of justice," Lilith shot back.

I opened my mouth to disagree but Roberta spoke first.

"She's right."

PART VI

SLEEPERS AWAKE

We are near awakening when we dream that we dream.

—Baron Friedrich von Hardenberg,

Pollen—

Hope is a waking dream.

—Aristotle,

Diogenes Laertius, Lives of Eminent Philosophers, bk. V—

ONE

♂

Twenty-four hours later I knew that the biggest challenge of the whole adventure was almost over: I was having a civil conversation with my ex-wife.

"He would have wanted you to have it," I said.

"But what would I do with a Wizard's tower?" she asked.

"Live in it."

She shook her head. "I'm leaving the Fantasyworld program, remember?"

"You'll need a place to stay when you visit."

"I'm not coming back. There's nothing for me here, now."

A dozen snappy comebacks fought to get to the front of my mouth but I swallowed them before saying, "Your avatar will need a place to live even when you're not in taction. Or are you planning on sending Vashti back to live with the Amazons?"

She shivered. "Actually, it gives me the creeps to think of the Computer animating this body when I'm not in the Game. Since I'm not coming back, I've decided to delete it along with my backup files once I'm back out." She put her hand on my arm. "I think the best thing is to pass the tower along to you—the other you—which would be the closest thing to keeping it in the family. Especially since it looked like there's going to be a family." She suddenly looked sad.

"What?" I asked softly. "What's wrong."

Smiling weakly, she said, "Nothing, really."

"It didn't look like nothing."

"Oh…" She sighed. "I always wondered what would have happened if we'd had children. Would it have been the glue that held us together through the tough times?"

"Hey." I touched her gently on the chin. "Aren't you the one who's always telling me to never look back?"

Her smile firmed up. "Yeah. It's just that whenever I see children, there's always this little pang..." The smile slipped a bit, caught, and returned. "...A little sense of 'what if' mixed with regret."

"Hell," I explained, "*is* regret. Hell is 'what if'."

"You speak very knowingly."

"Who else knows how to give you hell like I do?"

Without warning, she hugged me fiercely. "Please, Robbie! Let's leave right now! We'll never come back here, either of us! This place will only bring us sorrow!"

"'Like a land of dreams, so various, so beautiful, so new,'" I murmured into her hair. "'Hath really neither joy, nor love, nor light, /nor certitude, nor peace, nor help for pain...."

"'...And we are here as on a darkling plain'," she added, pushing away from me. "I should have known you'd have some sort of quip up your sleeve."

"Uh," I said, regarding my suddenly empty arms, "I've never thought of Matthew Arnold's *Dover Beach* as a 'quip.' A quote, probably. But a quip?"

She brushed at her eyes. "Never mind. You don't—you wouldn't understand. Your other self might have a clue, but..."

She stepped forward and hugged me again but the embrace was perfunctory, her manner businesslike now. Linking her arm in mine, she tugged. "Let's go find the others. It's about time for the last train to Parallelville."

I let her lead me along to Daggoth's library where Angel, Dagny, Dyantha, and Mudge were drinking tea and sharing a final confab before their Program withdrawals.

Mudge and Dagny stood. "Is Nicole all right?" her legal guardian asked.

"Secured, sedated, and sleeping like a baby," I said. "When she wakes up she should find herself back in the body that she's wanted so desperately."

"Under *competent* psychiatric care," Dagny added. "I'll make my recommendations as soon as we get back, Mr. Mudge, and you can choose her psychiatrist from a list of the best."

"I hope that won't be necessary, Doctor," he replied. "Given the unique circumstances of this patient's history—not to mention the nature of parallel realities—I can't think of anyone better briefed and more—sensitive—to the nuances of this particular case."

Dagny nodded and then looked at me. "Don't worry, Dr. Ripley. And you can tell the other Dr. Ripley not to worry either. I won't excuse myself by invoking the midlife crises defense. But things are different, now. The patient returning to the Wallbank Sanitarium is a different Nicole Doucet. And so, I daresay, is the doctor in charge."

Mudge nodded. "We've had some long talks about this. Between the two of us, I believe we can do more for Nicole than a whole battery of shrinks." He turned to Angel McRae. "Angie, it's been more than a pleasure knowing you. If the Angel McRae in my universe is half as bright and half as nice as you, she's one hell of a woman!"

Angel jumped up and, ignoring his outstretched hand, pulled him against her in an impassioned hug. "The feeling's mutual, big guy. If Nicole wasn't in the picture I'd make you promise to look the other me up."

"Oh. Well," he stammered, turning a little pink, "I don't think—"

"Shhh!" She silenced him with a finger to his lips. "I know you're a one-woman man. Just think nice thoughts about me. now and then." Then she kissed him—and he went from pink to scarlet.

Mick was liberal with her kisses. I got one as Mudge and Westbrook left for the spell chamber. Stephanie went with them.

"How come a nice girl from the Midwest can't meet any nice guys until she skips the coast and sneaks into an illegal computer program?"

I didn't have an answer for that one and she kissed me again. "That's for the other you," she said. "Be sure and pass it along." She turned and clasped hands with Dyantha. "I'll remember what you said."

"Ditto," replied the redheaded Amazon.

Angel followed after Dagny and Mudge: her departure was scheduled first.

"Well," Dyantha said, "so many kisses, so little time."

"What?" I said.

And then *she* kissed me—and a bit more intensity than Angel's double farewell buss. Looking into her eyes I was reminded that Natasha Skovoroda still inhabited her avatar.

"Tasha," I said, when I finally came up for air. "Why are you still here? Borys has to be going out of his mind!"

She smiled. A little like Stephanie, I thought. "Borys Dankevych will have me for the rest of his life. Unless…" The word lay there between us, taking a long time to fade away. "You saved my life," she finally offered.

Damn. What are you supposed to say when someone says something like that? "Aw shucks, ma'am, twarn't nothin'."

She reached out and knuckle-popped me on the arm. "Ow." Why were women always doing stuff like that to me? I'd have to ask Roberta when I got the chance.

Natasha stared down at the ground as if she was suddenly shy. "I was hoping for a chance to properly thank you before we left the Program."

"Natasha, there's no need to thank me. It was the least I could do—"

"Do not!" she snapped. "Do *not* belittle what you did for me. You did not save my life only: I was dead. You went to Hell for me. I cannot imagine the horrors you must have experienced—the awful visions that will haunt you to the end of your days. You went there for me and brought me back out! Do not dishonor either of us by saying it was unimportant!"

I thought of the "horrors" I had witnessed in retrieving Natasha's psychefiles and wondered what sorts of fearsome tableaus she would find if she sought out her own road of regret in Hell. I didn't have much time for reflection as she grabbed my shirtfront and pulled her face up to mine. "I want to *thank* you," she said, spacing each word for emphasis.

"You don't need—"

"I *want* to do this. *Understand?"* I was definitely going to have to iron this shirt when we were done.

"What about your fiancé?

She sighed. "I love Borys, I know I will have a good life with him and I can be happy. If you cared for me in such a way, I could be happy, also. It would be different. But good. Even more intense. But more difficult, I think, too."

"Tasha—"

"Hush." Again, she laid a finger to my lips. "It is all right that you do not want me in that way. Still, I am not a married woman, yet, and while we are still in the Program it is not for real, anyway. We could make a nice memory for both of us. Yes?"

I smiled but shook my head slowly. "It would be a very nice memory, I'm sure. But you are wrong about one thing." I took her hands in mine so they were no longer stressing my shirt. "It's just as real in here as it is Outside. Maybe more so."

She stared up at me and after a long moment nodded once. "You are most probably right."

Putting my arm around her shoulders, I steered her toward the doorway. "You're just getting cold feet. Everybody gets the pre-nuptial jitters."

She leaned her head on my shoulder as we headed for the stairs. "You are a good friend."

That's me, everybody's buddy. "Let me tell you something that I learned recently. There can be more than one great love in your life…"

"Where did you learn that?"

"Um, in Hell, actually…"

♀

I pushed back from the crystal ball with a sigh. "Well, it's settled. The Coastal Wizards Union will work the Trans-relocation spell in exchange for the Wand of Xagyg."

Riplakish came into the study and pulled a chair back from the scrying table. Dyantha waved briefly from the doorway and continued down the hall as he sat across from me. "You're sure you want to give it up?"

"It's a good deal. The wand is pretty well used up, and the Wizards basically want to archive it for historical purposes." I shrugged. "By law of succession, it really belongs to them, anyway. And getting a flock of Wizards to move Daggoth's tower—lock, stock, and nuclear reactor—next to Misty Dawn's enchanted tree is no small bargain."

"You're sure you want to do this?" He wasn't talking about the Trans-location spell now.

"Where am I going to go?" I asked. "There ain't room enough in our body for the two of us, Podnuh."

"There's Nicole's body—the one you spent six months wearing in the parallel universe."

I shook my head. "It *is* Nicole's body. She should have it back."

"We're pretty sure it isn't the same Nicole."

"Does that matter? Perhaps this arrangement is more righteous. She gets back what she lost so many years ago and maybe Dr. Westbrook will find a way to give her back her sanity, as well."

"Seems like a long shot."

"Westbrook's not a bad shrink. She just fell in love with an illusion."

"She fell in love with *you.* Are you going to trust someone who prefers women and can't tell when she's attracted to a man?"

"Am I a man?" I sighed. "Even I don't know what I am, any more. The point is that we all get pretty stupid when we first fall in love. And we all spend most of our lives being confused by the packaging. As I recall, *we* don't have the best track record in the Romance Department, either."

"Ouch."

"More like sustained screaming," I said with a smile. "Dagny's had a good long look at things, now: at herself, at her real patient, at how things are never what they truly seem. I'm betting on her newfound perspectives and strong sense of commitment to help Nicole. Not to mention Bernard Mudge's devotion."

He held up a hand. "This is where we would discuss the power inherent in the love of a good man."

I grinned. "Don't be too sarcastic: a girl's gotta hope."

"I still don't like the idea of you being trapped here."

Taking a long, deep breath, I told him, "It's not just a matter of how many seats are available on the escape pod." I put a hand to my quickening belly. "There's another life to consider."

"And you don't trust the Machine."

I laughed. "Don't *trust* the Machine? We've *never* trusted the Machine. Ever since we were dragged back to Cephtronics, kicking and screaming, it's been all about trying to fix what is wrong with the Machine, Cephtronics, the Matrix…"

"Ourselves," he added quietly.

I nodded. "And this child may be part of the solution."

He started to roll his eyes, then stopped and looked down. "We always make a mess and then leave. Is that it?"

Again, I nodded. "Lilith was right. We try to have it both ways in the Matrix. We can't fix a world if we treat it like a thing. We can't step in and slip back out like we do in failed relationships. We have to commit. The Matrix needs a full-time Demiurge. Not an indifferent god who shows up from time to time for his or her own selfish reasons."

"And we couldn't create a supreme deity? Never mind the other gods; we could program him—or her—to be kind and just and perfect."

"Maybe we've started the process, already," I said, patting my stomach.

"Hmm. Maybe." He stood. "Remember the 'vision' of William Butler Yeats? The one Misty Dawn quoted on the way into the Infernal Palace?" He turned to the fembot who was assembling more furniture in the corner. "M.D., what are the last two lines of 'The Second Coming'?"

"'And what rough beast, its hour come round at last, / Slouches towards Bethlehem to be born?'"

I grinned. "No child of mine is going to slouch!"

I got up and together we walked toward the staircase.

"I don't like the idea of leaving you in-program, alone and unprotected," he said.

Shaking my head, I told him, "With the Chief of Programming's personal access codes, I'll continue to be one of the most power personages in the Matrix. And I don't think I'm going to be alone."

"Pallas?"

I nodded. "Or Enki. Male or female, the Machine's Ego hasn't seemed to lose interest."

He laughed, a bit ruefully, I thought. "Since we created portions of the Matrix out of our own minds, Dr. Westbrook could probably make the case for an Oedipal complex."

"And if the Machine is somehow responsible for this pregnancy—"

"Don't lets go there," he said. "It gets a bit too backwoods-Appalachian for my taste."

"Never underestimate the love of a good computer."

"Oh please."

"Hey, I have someone to look after me if I do need looking after. Two someones, counting Misty Dawn."

"Two some*ones?"* he asked, "Or some*things?"*

"It's you I worry about," I said quietly. "Who's going to look after you?"

♂

In the end, it wasn't as complicated as we feared.

Natasha Skovoroda invoked her withdrawal code and uploaded to her restored body in the "Real" world. After her avatar returned to computer control, we broke the "bad news" to "Dyantha." Within minutes she was running for the stables. Within hours she would bring the dire news to Princess Aeriel Morivalynde and the rest of the Amazon nation.

That didn't give us a lot of time.

The trickiest departure involved getting Westbrook, Mudge, and the Pennanglan back to the parallel universe. The first part was fairly simple, as the Zombie Mistress combined her spellcasting powers with ours to provide the raw power required to teleport them across the Corpus Callosum, into the region where our Programworlds intersected. The second part was trickier as we had to de-compile and reverse-engineer the sequence of cantrips that had landed me in Nicole's body in my previous upload. One wrong algorithm and Nicole would be singing "I ain't got no body," for the rest of eternity.

Everyone held his or her breath until a little long-distance crystal gazing indicated that everything had gone off without a hitch.

Stephanie's departure could have been difficult. Her withdrawal was normal but we had to override the computer to keep it from animating her avatar once she'd abandoned it. Looking down at Vashti's deathly stillness, I felt a disquieting finality to our relationship—a greater emptiness than the horrible loneliness that followed our actual divorce.

I looked up at Roberta who looked back with a haunted expression of her own. "Any last-minute business?" she asked.

I shook my head, feeling an unaccustomed surge of fear and uncertainty.

She pointed an ebony staff at me. Green fingers of flame danced at the black rod's tip. "Then it's time for you to die."

EPILOGUE

The sun had set but he made no effort to call up the lights in the room. A pair of comscreens provided the only illumination now, bathing his face in a cold, blue wash.

He had deleted the majority of the messages: dozens of congratulatory missives from people he hardly knew, hundreds more from absolute strangers. "To His Excellency, the Right, Honorable Robert R. Ripley III, U.S. Ambassador to the Russian Federated Republics," they all began.

Ambassador of what? he wondered, *for what?*

Kerensky was long gone, Hanson was back in his body and practically in the White House, the Russian president was on his honeymoon, and the world was safe. Even from the Roman god of Death.

One of the screens held the police report regarding the murder investigation of one Michael Valentine Smith, free-lance hacker, part-time drug addict, and convicted sex offender. Correction: former *everything* on the list. The report stated that Smith had dropped out of sight for a couple of months and, upon his return, was allegedly involved in a murderous altercation with his dealer over some unpaid accounts. The accused murderer was arrested while allegedly trying to fence the deceased's neuralrig and porn collections. The accused claimed "self-defense" while telling a story of extremely odd language and behavior on the deceased's part. "Dude didn't seem to know who and where he really was," he recounted. "Told me he was some sort of god—the god of Death. I sent him back to his rightful kingdom…"

It was a comforting thought that justice, denied in one world, could still be found in another.

Lots of comfort in the remaining messages.

Borys Dankevych on audio-scrambler, thanking Ripley for suggesting a certain dacha in the Ural mountains for Natasha's and his honeymoon, and please enjoy the magnum of vodka as the first of many gifts due to his Best Man and soon-to-be-officially-received diplomatic envoy. Just before the message terminated he could hear Natasha's voice saying, "Bushka, please! Come back to the fire—"

Synchronicity: the morning's news telex, on page three, insinuated that Walter Hanson and Stephanie Harrell had been spending an inordinate amount of time together in public and (it was rumored) in private.

Life goes on.

Also in the social news: The Beautiful People were all a-twitter over the news that supermodel Angel McRae had pursued and proposed to the man of her dreams—an overweight and only moderately successful attorney named Bernard Mudge. Mudge seemed as bewildered as the rest of the über-lovelies, but McRae would only comment: "I feel as though I knew him in another lifetime; I hope to be the one worthy of his regard this time around."

Yes, it was nice to believe in justice deferred and justice achieved.

On the second screen, a personal email from a Cephtronics server unknown to all but a handful of people—most of them not even "real" by the legal precedent set by Ripley vs. Cephtronics some years before—read as follows:

To: *RRR3@whitehouse.emmisary.gov*
From: *Lookedatlovefrombothsidesnow@enchantedforest.mtx*

Dear Me,

You were right. It was best to disconnect the Machine's backup profiles for your Riplakish avatar. We had a lovely service and the funeral pyre burned well into the second day.

Everyone came.

Just everyone! The Rabble, the Amazons, people and non-people I hadn't seen in years—from above and below, they all turned out.

You should have been there.

Of course *that* would have been a bit difficult, so just let me say on our behalf, it was very touching. I didn't know we were so well regarded. Well, except for the Calabastor crowd who attended that ball where, well, you know…

Father Thyme gave the eulogy and there wasn't a dry eye in the grove. I think Misty Dawn exhausted her supply of optical lubricant. And Lilith was inconsolable! She actually threw herself on the burning pyre—not that it scorched her or anything, given who and what she was and where she came from. Still, it was an impressive gesture.

And if she bought the story that you and Vashti succumbed to a delayed curse left behind by the god of Death, then you can be sure that *no one's* going to question your demise.

The Amazons held a sacred ceremony, designating you, in effect, a posthumous woman in spirit. Little do they know… :)

Now that you're gone, Aeriel has come around, hinting that "our" child is going to need a godmother. She hasn't even stipulated that it be a girl so the seeds of change may already be taking root.

Anyway, as planned, your sudden "death" seems to have settled all accounts. Prince Rudolph Charming married Snow White last week and the royal auguries have determined that the blessed couple will live "happily ever after." Six of the Dwarves have received appointments as overseers in the royal mines. The dopey one has been appointed assistant town crier. I suspect Rudy has never been fond of the local media for their treatment of this whole royal romance scandal, and this is his revenge.

Speaking of romance, Misty Dawn has been spending less and less time in the android body. She says she is helping Daggoth the Dark adjust to his afterlife existence on the ethereal plane. It seems like an odd pairing to me, but I guess they have a lot more in common these days.

Lilith has joined a convent. More on that in my next email.

The Zombie Mistress reports that Captain Jenks has become a regular visitor out to her estate. According to her abbreviated chats with our necrophilic nebbish, there have been no further occurences of Calabastor's slattern slasher. There's been some unexpected fallout from the case, though. It seems that the City Watch is now being plagued with a wave of Vampire hookers. Valentine's treatment of Nicole's victims may have covered up the initial evidence of vampiric feeding, but the aftereffects will out. "Getting some head" has taken on a whole new meaning with Calabastor's ladies of the evening.

On a more serious note, we once discussed the concept of the archetype, and I can't help but wonder about the role that my child and I will assume in time. No stables or stars for us, no skull-popping entrances, no white elephants bearing lotus blossums. We will have no she-wolves for wetnurses, no bottle formulas of ambrosia and nectar, no glass cradles awash on the flood.

Am I worthy to be a god? Am I worthy to raise one? The answers are easy: no and no. But in our arrogance and our ill-considered power, we created an entire world—multiple worlds, in fact. And while human nature makes us unfit and dangerous acolytes of Lord Acton's axiom, our humanity compels us to take responsibility.

I don't know how we can take responsibility for any other life when we can barely take responsibility for our own…yet I strongly believe that we cannot create life and then turn our back on it. Whatever the excuse. Perhaps in loving and parenting my child, I will finally learn how to love and parent an entire world.

This, then, is my archetype, my role, my destiny. Not god, not goddess nor demiurge. Just…Mother.

What will I teach this child? What will this child teach me? When I rock the cradle will I learn to rule a world?

These are fearsome, yet wonderful questions. I have never been so afraid in all my life! And I have never felt so alive or known such hope!

The time is drawing near and so much is yet to be done that I must close for now.

Joseph Conrad wrote in 'The Heart of Darkness' that 'we live as we dream—alone.' Well, Dreamland is behind you and, through me, you are absolved of any further responsibilities here. Because I have been you and you have been me, neither of us can truly be alone. So I pray that you may find the love and purpose in your life that I have finally found in mine.

Best,
Roberta Ripley (the First)

He sat for a long time, staring at the second monitor before switching both of them off. Then he sat for awhile longer in the darkness.

Finally, with dreamlike slowness, he reached for the magnum of vodka and broke the seal.

Was it a vision, or a waking dream?
Fled is that music—Do I wake or sleep?

—John Keats,
Ode to a Nightingale—

Those who have compared our life to a dream were right….
We sleeping wake, and waking sleep.

–Michel Eyquem de Montaign,
Essays, bk II—

Wm. Mark Simmons

William Mark Simmons spent his formative years in Independence, Missouri (Harry Truman's home town) and pursued a double major in Theatre and Mass communications, graduating from Central Missouri State University with a degree in the latter. He has taught Speech and Communications classes, Emergency First Aid certification cources, and Fencing. He has worked as an actor, director, musician, and entertainer, hosting his own shows in both Television and Radio while winning awards as a journalist and copywriter. Simmons currently manages a public radio station in Louisiana, hosts a classical music progam, and is an adjunct faculty member of the University of Louisiana at Monroe. He is the author of five novels; his first, *In The Net of Dreams,* was a finalist for the Compton Crook Award and made the *Locus* "Best" list in 1991.

He can be contacted through his website at:

www.sff.net/people/wm.mark.simmons

"After years of searching, I finally obtained a copy of *The Questing of Kedrigern* at a convention. Your Kedrigern stories are the kind I wish I had written."—L. Sprague de Camp

"A grand and silly adventure."—Craig Shaw Gardner

"Quite Funny"—*Starlog*

The Kedrigern Chronicles Volume One:
The Domesticated Wizard
by
John Morressy

A wizard's life is not an easy life. One never knows who, or what, one's next client will be, or what kind of unpleasantness he, or she, or it, is bringing. So when a young man of 160 or so—no age at all for a wizard—meets a beautiful enchanted princess and releases her from a cruel spell, it seems the perfect chance to settle down to a life of cozy domesticity. With a bit of magic here and there to take care of the housework and a loyal house-troll to do the heavy lifting, things ought to be idyllic.

And they would be, if it weren't for the unreasonable clients, the barbarian swordsmen, the home furnishings with minds of their own, the otherworldly intruders, and the rest of those annoying day-to-day problems of the profession.

The Selespridar have locked us, the planet Earth, part of our solar system, and our sun up in a force field because the rest of the Galaxy plain and simple does not want to associate with us.

Do we care? Not really. We have Mallworld, the shopping center almost the size of a planet.

So come along and play human pinball at the arcades, order your custom-designed baby at Storkways, Inc., experience your ultimate death at the Way Out Suicide Parlors—death by vampire is a special way to go, and just one of the three-hundred ways you can decide to end your life.

The Ultimate MallWorld
by
S. P. Somtow

Here collected together for the first time are all the short stories, ads, and illustrations for S. P. Somtow's *Mallworld.*

Included in *The Ultimate Mallworld* are all the original stories (one story was left out of the Starblaze trade edition), all the ads for the Mallworld products (left out in the TOR mass market re-printing), and all the original artwork by Karl Kofoed (the artwork was not included in the TOR edition).

This edition also contains two new Mallworld stories written by Somtow, along with their new interior illustrations by the original artist Karl Kofoed.

Come check out our web site for details on these Meisha Merlin authors!

Kevin J. Anderson

Robert Asprin

Robin Wayne Bailey

Edo van Belkom

Janet Berliner

Storm Constantine

John F. Conn

Diane Duane

Sylvia Engdahl

Rain Graves

Jim Grimsley

George Guthridge

Keith Hartman

Beth Hilgartner

P. C. Hodgell

Tanya Huff

Janet Kagan

Caitlin R. Kiernan

Lee Killough